Un

"*Until I Find You* tak̶̶̶̶̶̶̶̶̶̶̶̶̶̶est novel of recent years.̶
—*San Francisco Chronicle*

"Its artistry is so compelling . . . a wonderfully thought-provoking book."
—*Chicago Sun-Times*

"An often stunningly visual novel. . . . Irving is a compulsive, wildly inventive storyteller. . . . As always, his writing is enormously readable and accessible. His prose is determinedly straightforward and clear."
—*Los Angeles Times Book Review*

"As emotionally resonant and as intellectually stimulating as anything in *The Cider House Rules* or *A Widow for One Year*. . . . *Until I Find You* is a novel more eloquent and elegiac than *Garp*. . . . A worthy novel because it provides such a detailed map of human nature and because it is the most ambitious offering from a great storyteller. . . . Monumental."
—*The Kansas City Star*

"Despite its gargantuan heft, [*Until I Find You*] moves nimbly from a standing start to warp speed."
—*The New York Times Book Review*

"Is it well written? Of course. . . . Irving's remarkable style, which . . . has made its mark on American literature, shines. . . . In some exquisite passages, Irving captures the rare and dazzling love of young children."
—*The Philadelphia Inquirer*

"Throughout a nearly four-decade career . . . New Englander Irving has challenged our puritanical assumptions by treating sexual deviance as the norm. It is no small thing, then, to say that *Until I Find You* is his most erotically fraught work yet."
—*The Village Voice*

"For a novel that features child abuse, several tragic deaths and a genuine madman, this is—weird as it sounds—a very funny book. . . . *Until I Find You* has one of the most satisfying endings I've read in ages. . . . It's a great payoff."
—*Newsweek*

"With Jack Burns, Irving has created his most complex protagonist: a character that will charm, repel and eventually redeem himself in the eyes of most readers. . . . A real heart-stopper of a story—and one of his finest novels to date."
—*Milwaukee Journal Sentinel*

"*Until I Find You* is Irving's longest book, and it's also the most intimate story he's ever told. . . . Knowing that he's invested so much real-life drama into the story makes the bittersweet ending all the more moving."
—*People Magazine*

"Irving restores to the novel the good sense of predecessors like Cervantes, Fielding and Dickens."
—Baltimore *Sun*

"For critics who still hold fast to seeing Irving as the twentieth- and twenty-first-century incarnation of Dickens, *Until I Find You* may turn out to be Irving's *David Copperfield*. . . . [This book] is Irving at his operatic finest. There is plenty of over-the-top melodrama, twisted, out-of-left-field comedy, heartbreaking tragedy and a stouthearted, transcendent hero."
—*The Denver Post*

"Irving's strength has always been his characters, and this novel is rich with them. . . . Jack Burns is so strong, so perfectly realized, that he sets a new standard for the author. . . . The whole story will reverberate long after the cover is closed. . . . A rewarding and meaningful experience."
—*Library Journal*

Praise from Canada

"A marvel of craftsmanship. . . . It's audacious, to say the least, to expect a character with a hole in his heart to carry so hefty a novel. But so cathartic a book could easily have escaped Irving's control, and it never really does, a tribute to his artistry and his courage."
—*Maclean's*

"The novel is rich in character and bawdy in tone, with crackling dialogue and, as one should expect, healthy doses of the absurd and the arousing (no one writes about sex as insightfully—or as disturbingly—as Irving). . . . *Until I Find You* is well worth the significant investment of time it requires. Irving, however, raises the stakes significantly partway through the book. . . . [Jack's] discovery turns the novel's first half . . . on its head. It's a bold move, deconstructing both Jack's life and many of the key elements of Irving's body of work in a single stroke. It's also shocking and profoundly affecting, the sort of daring act only the best of writers can pull off. And Irving makes it seem effortless."
—*Georgia Straight* (Vancouver)

"The novel suggests that what matters most is not the story but the odd, concrete detail lodged in our memory, the detail that unlocks feeling when recalled. . . . Irving has tapped into an entire culture in which sex is used as an antidote to 'sorrow and boredom' and where the innocence of the young is almost methodically despoiled."

—*Toronto Star*

"*Until I Find You,* the long-awaited new novel from Irving, is perhaps his finest book. . . . Powerfully intimate, epic storytelling."

—*The Globe and Mail*

"Only John Irving . . . could think up such characters. . . . You can't help marveling at the wealth of his invention and the discipline it must take for him to spread it all at our feet."

—*The Vancouver Sun*

"One of the temptations with a new novel by John Irving is that the reader will become so involved in the story that he/she will zip through it just to see how it will work out. . . . Savour the book. . . . Irving is Irving, and he gives his loyal readers a particular type of pleasure in being caught up in and caring for Jack Burns. There is simply no one else who writes like he does."

—*The Edmonton Journal*

"As ever, Irving is at his best with the family relationships he creates. They are simultaneously touching and infuriating. It is with these relationships that Irving firmly grasps universal truths and puts a chokehold on his readers. . . . Irving's descriptions . . . force the reader to relate to the characters in a way they would not in most works of fiction."
—*Calgary Herald*

"A new John Irving novel is always a literary event, and this one, his 11th, is classic Irving, a story of betrayal, absent parents, wrestlers, sexual deviance and the thousands of small ways a family can inflict pain. . . . It's an amazing ride through the life of a damaged man. Irving, always a risk-taker, has created characters difficult to like, put them in revolting situations and dared his readers not to care. . . . Brilliant in so many ways."
—*Winnipeg Free Press*

"*Until I Find You* . . . cuts closer to the bone than any of [Irving's] previous works."
—*Ottawa Citizen*

Praise from
the United Kingdom

"A feast for his fans. . . . One of Irving's defining traits is his skill for mixing tragedy with comedy, the rough with the smooth, and in *Until I Find You* he shows no sign of losing that skill."
—*The Guardian* (London)

"Irving, at 63, is one of the great American novelists and unrivalled as a storyteller. *Until I Find You,* his 11th novel, is possibly his most powerful, indubitably his most personal. . . . Teeming with a cast as colourful as any Dickens ever contrived."
—*The Sunday Herald* (Scotland)

"It is Irving's ability to move effortlessly from observations of intuitive precision to scenes of farce that makes his world so distinctive. He runs the gamut of social opposites with uninhibited exuberance, while at the same time evoking scenes with a minimum of gestures, so that a single phrase leaps from the memory when recalled a hundred or so pages later. . . . Not since *A Prayer for Owen Meany* has he given his hero such a distinctive fate . . . or gathered a cast of such memorable characters."
—*The Herald* (Glasgow)

Also by John Irving

BOOKS

The Fourth Hand

My Movie Business

A Widow for One Year

Trying to Save Piggy Sneed

A Son of the Circus

A Prayer for Owen Meany

The Cider House Rules

The Hotel New Hampshire

The World According to Garp

The 158-Pound Marriage

The Water-Method Man

Setting Free the Bears

SCREENPLAYS

The Cider House Rules

Books published by The Random House Publishing Group are available at quantity discounts on bulk purchases for premium, educational, fund-raising, and special sales use. For details, please call 1-800-733-3000.

A Novel

JOHN
IRVING

BALLANTINE BOOKS • NEW YORK

Sale of this book without a front cover may be unauthorized. If this book is coverless, it may have been reported to the publisher as "unsold or destroyed" and neither the author nor the publisher may have received payment for it.

Any dialogue or behavior ascribed to the characters in this book—those who are real people as well as the characters who are imagined—is entirely fictitious. This is a novel.

2006 Ballantine Books Mass Market Edition

Copyright © 2005 by Garp Enterprises, Ltd.

All rights reserved.

Published in the United States by Ballantine Books, an imprint of The Random House Publishing Group, a division of Random House, Inc., New York.

BALLANTINE and colophon are registered trademarks of Random House, Inc.

Originally published in hardcover in the United States by Random House, an imprint of The Random House Publishing Group, a division of Random House, Inc., in 2005.

Permission acknowledgments appear on page 843.

ISBN 0-345-49230-7

Printed in the United States of America

www.ballantinebooks.com

OPM   10 9 8 7 6 5 4 3 2 1

*For my youngest son, Everett,
who made me feel young again.
With my fervent hope that when you're
old enough to read this story, you will
have had (or still be in the midst of)
an ideal childhood—as different from
the one described here as anyone
could imagine.*

What we, or at any rate what I, refer to confidently as memory—meaning a moment, a scene, a fact that has been subjected to a fixative and thereby rescued from oblivion—is really a form of storytelling that goes on continually in the mind and often changes with the telling. Too many conflicting emotional interests are involved for life ever to be wholly acceptable, and possibly it is the work of the storyteller to rearrange things so that they conform to this end. In any case, in talking about the past we lie with every breath we draw.

—WILLIAM MAXWELL,
So Long, See You Tomorrow

Contents

III
Lucky

IV
Sleeping in the Needles

V
Dr. García

I

The North Sea and the Baltic

I

In the Care of Churchgoers and Old Girls

According to his mother, Jack Burns was an actor before he was an actor, but Jack's most vivid memories of childhood were those moments when he felt compelled to hold his mother's hand. He wasn't acting then.

Of course we don't remember much until we're four or five years old—and what we remember at that early age is very selective or incomplete, or even false. What Jack *recalled* as the first time he felt the need to reach for his mom's hand was probably the hundredth or two hundredth time.

Preschool tests revealed that Jack Burns had a vocabulary beyond his years, which is not uncommon among only children accustomed to adult conversation—especially only children of single parents. But of greater significance, according to the tests, was Jack's capacity for consecutive memory, which, when he was three, was comparable to that of a nine-year-old. At four, his retention of detail and understanding of linear time were equal to an eleven-year-old's. (The details included, but were not limited to, such trivia as articles of clothing and the names of streets.)

These test results were bewildering to Jack's mother, Alice, who considered him to be an inattentive child; in her view, Jack's propensity for daydreaming made him immature for his age.

Nevertheless, in the fall of 1969, when Jack was four and had not yet started kindergarten, his mother walked with him to the corner of Pickthall and Hutchings Hill Road in Forest Hill, which was a nice neighborhood in Toronto. They were waiting for school to be let out, Alice explained, so that Jack could see the girls.

St. Hilda's was then called "a church school for girls," from kindergarten through grade thirteen—at that time still in existence, in Canada—and Jack's mother had decided that this was where Jack would begin his schooling, although he was a boy. She waited to tell him of her decision until the main doors of the school opened, as if to greet them, and the girls streamed through in varying degrees of sullenness and exultation and prettiness and slouching disarray.

"Next year," Alice announced, "St. Hilda's is going to admit boys. Only a very few boys, and only up to grade four."

Jack couldn't move; he could barely breathe. *Girls* were passing him on all sides, some of them big and noisy, all of them in uniforms in those colors Jack Burns later came to believe he would wear to his grave—gray and maroon. The girls wore gray sweaters or maroon blazers over their white middy blouses.

"They're going to admit *you*," Jack's mother told him. "I'm arranging it."

"How?" he asked.

"I'm still figuring that out," Alice replied.

The girls wore gray pleated skirts with gray kneesocks, which Canadians called "knee-highs." It was Jack's first look at all those bare legs. He didn't yet understand how the girls were driven by some interior unrest to push their socks down to their ankles, or at least below their calves—despite the school rule that knee-highs should be worn knee-high.

Jack Burns further observed that the girls didn't see him standing there, or they looked right through him. But there was one—an older girl with womanly hips and breasts, and lips as full as Alice's. She locked onto Jack's eyes, as if she were powerless to avert her gaze.

At the age of four, Jack wasn't sure if he was the one who couldn't look away from her, or if she was the one who was trapped and couldn't look away from him. Whichever the case, her expression was so knowing that she frightened him. Perhaps she had seen what Jack would look like as an older boy, or a grown man, and what she saw in him riveted her with longing and desperation. (Or with fear and degradation, Jack Burns would one day conclude, because this same older girl suddenly looked away.)

Jack and his mom went on standing in the sea of girls, until the girls' rides had come and gone, and those on foot had left not even the sound of their shoes behind, or their intimidating but stimulating laughter. However, there was still enough warmth in the early-fall air to hold their scent, which Jack reluctantly inhaled and confused with perfume. With most of the girls at St. Hilda's, it was not their perfume that lingered in the air; it was the smell of the girls themselves, which Jack Burns would never grow used to or take for granted. Not even by the time he left grade four.

"But why am I going to school *here*?" Jack asked his mother, when the girls had gone. Some fallen leaves were all that remained in motion on the quiet street corner.

"Because it's a good school," Alice answered. "And you'll be safe with the girls," she added.

Jack must not have thought so, because he instantly reached for his mom's hand.

In that fall of the year before Jack's admission to St. Hilda's, his mother was full of surprises. After showing him the uniformed girls, who would soon dominate his life, Alice announced that she would work her way through northern Europe in search of Jack's runaway dad. She knew the Baltic and North Sea cities where he was most likely to be hiding from them; together they would hunt him down and confront him with his abandoned responsibilities. Jack Burns had often heard his mother refer to the two of them as his father's "abandoned responsibilities." But even at the age of four, Jack had come to the conclusion that his dad had left them for good—in Jack's case, before he was born.

And when his mom said she would work her way through these foreign cities, Jack knew what her work was. Like her dad, Alice was a tattoo artist; tattooing was the only work she knew.

In the Baltic and North Sea cities on their itinerary, other tattooists would give Alice work. They knew she'd been apprenticed to her father, a well-known tattooer in Edinburgh—officially, in the Port of Leith—where Jack's mom had suffered the misfortune of meeting his dad. It was there he got her pregnant, and subsequently left her.

In Alice's account, Jack's father sailed on the *New Scotland*, which docked in Halifax. When he was gainfully employed, he would send for her—or so he had promised. But Alice said she never heard from him—only *of* him. Before moving on from Halifax, Jack's dad had cut quite a swath.

* * *

Born Callum Burns, Jack's father changed his first name to William when he was still in university. His father was named Alasdair, which William said was Scots enough for the whole family. In Edinburgh, at the time of his scandalous departure for Nova Scotia, William Burns had been an associate of the Royal College of Organists, which meant that he had a diploma in organ-playing in addition to his bachelor's in music. When he met Jack's mother, William was the organist at South Leith Parish Church; Alice was a choirgirl there.

For an Edinburgh boy with upper-class pretensions and a good education—William Burns had gone to Heriot's before studying music at the University of Edinburgh—a first job playing the organ in lower-class Leith might have struck him as slumming. But Jack's dad liked to joke that the Church of Scotland paid better than the Scottish Episcopal Church. While William was an Episcopalian, he liked it just fine at the South Leith Parish, where it was said that eleven thousand souls were buried in the graveyard, although there were not more than three hundred gravestones.

Gravestones for the poor were not permitted. But at night, Jack's mom told him, people brought the ashes of loved ones and scattered them through the fence of the graveyard. The thought of so many souls blowing around in the dark gave the boy nightmares, but that church—if only because of its graveyard—was a popular place, and Alice believed she had died and gone to Heaven when she started singing for William there.

In South Leith Parish Church, the choir and the organ were behind the congregation. There were not more than twenty seats for the choir—the women in front, the men in back. For the duration of the sermon, William made a point of asking Alice to lean forward in the front row, so that he could see all of her. She wore a blue robe—"blue-jay blue," she told Jack—and a white collar. Jack's mom fell in love with his dad that April of 1964, when he first came to play the organ.

"We were singing the hymns of the Resurrection," was how Alice put it, "and there were crocuses and daffodils in the grave-yard." (Doubtless all those ashes that were secretly scattered there benefited the flowers.)

Alice took the young organist, who was also her choirmaster, to meet her father. Her dad's tattoo parlor was called Persevere, which is the motto of the Port of Leith. It was William's first look at a tattoo shop, which was on either Manderston Street or Jane Street. In those days, Jack's mom explained, there was a rail bridge across Leith Walk, joining Manderston to Jane, but Jack could never remember on which street she said the tattoo parlor was. He just knew that they lived there, in the shop, under the rumble of the trains.

His mother called this "sleeping in the needles"—a phrase from between the wars. "Sleeping in the needles" meant that, when times were tough, you slept in the tattoo parlor—you had nowhere else to live. But it was also what was said, on occasion, when a tattoo artist died—as Alice's father had—in the shop. Thus, by both definitions of the phrase, her dad had always slept in the needles.

Alice's mother had died in childbirth, and her father—whom Jack never met—had raised her in the tattoo world. In Jack's eyes, his mom was unique among tattoo artists because she'd never been tattooed. Her dad had told her that she shouldn't get a tattoo until she was old enough to understand a few essential things about herself; he must have meant those things that would never change.

"Like when I'm in my sixties or seventies," Jack's mom used to say to him, when she was still in her twenties. "You should get *your* first tattoo after I'm dead," she told him, which was her way of saying that he shouldn't even *think* about getting tattooed.

Alice's dad took an instant dislike to William Burns, who got *his* first tattoo the day the two men met. The tattoo gripped his right thigh, where William could read it when he was sitting on the toilet—the opening notes to an Easter hymn he'd been rehearsing with Alice, the words to which began, *"Christ the Lord is risen today."* Without the words, you'd have to read music, and be sitting very close to Jack's father—perhaps on an adjacent toilet—to recognize the hymn.

But then and there, upon giving the talented young organist his first tattoo, Alice's dad told her that William would surely become an "ink addict," a "collector"—meaning he was one of those guys who would never stop with the first tattoo, or with the first *twenty* tattoos. He would go on getting tattooed, until his body was a sheet of music and every inch of his skin was covered by a note—a dire prediction but one that failed to warn Alice away. The tattoo-crazy organist had already stolen her heart.

* * *

But Jack Burns had heard most of this story by the time he was four. What came as a surprise, when his mother announced their upcoming European trip, was what she told him next: "If we don't find your father by this time next year, when you'll be starting school, we'll forget all about him and get on with our lives."

Why this was such a shock was that, from Jack's earliest awareness that his father was missing—worse, that he had "absconded"—Jack and his mother had done a fair amount of looking for William Burns, and Jack had assumed they always would. The idea that they *could* "forget all about him" was more foreign to the boy than the proposed journey to northern Europe; nor had Jack known that, in his mom's opinion, his starting school was of such importance.

She'd not finished school herself. Alice had long felt inferior to William's university education. William's parents were both elementary-school teachers who gave private piano lessons to children on the side, but they had a high regard for artistic tutelage of a more professional kind. In their estimation, it was beneath their son to play the organ at South Leith Parish Church—and not only because of the class friction that existed in those days between Edinburgh and Leith. (There were differences between the Scottish Episcopal Church and the Church of Scotland, too.)

Alice's father was not a churchgoer of any kind. He'd sent Alice to church and choir practice to give her a life outside the tattoo parlor, never imagining that she would meet her ruin *in* the church and *at* choir practice—or that she would bring her unscrupulous seducer to the shop to be tattooed!

It was William's parents who insisted that, although he was the principal organist for the South Leith Parish, he accept an offer to be the assistant organist at Old St. Paul's. What mattered to them was that Old St. Paul's was Scottish Episcopal—and it was in Edinburgh, not in Leith.

What captivated William was the organ. He'd started piano lessons at six and had not touched an organ before he was nine, but at seven or eight he began to stick bits of paper above the piano keys—imagining they were organ stops. He'd already begun to dream about playing the organ, and the organ he dreamed about was the Father Willis at Old St. Paul's.

If, in his parents' opinion, to be the assistant organist at Old

St. Paul's was more prestigious than being the principal organist at South Leith Parish Church, William just wanted to get his hands on the Father Willis. In Old St. Paul's, Jack's mother told him, the acoustics were a contributing factor to the organ's fame. The boy would later wonder if she meant that almost any organ would have sounded good there, because of the reverberation time—that is, the time it takes for a sound to diminish by sixty decibels—being better than the organ.

Alice remembered attending what she called "an organ marathon" at Old St. Paul's. Such an event must have been for fundraising purposes—a twenty-four-hour organ concert, with a different organist performing every hour or half hour. Who played when was, of course, a hierarchical arrangement; the best musicians performed when they were most likely to be heard, the others at the more unsociable hours. Young William Burns got to play before midnight—if only a half hour before.

The church was half empty, or emptier. Jack's mother was the most enthralled member of the audience. The slightly inferior organist whose turn was next would also have been in attendance—the player-in-waiting who had the midnight slot.

William didn't want to waste Old St. Paul's fabled reverberation time by selecting a *quiet* piece. To the degree that Jack could understand his mom's story, his father was playing to be *heard;* he'd chosen Boellmann's Toccata, which Alice called "rousing and noisy."

Outside the church, a narrow alley ran alongside Old St. Paul's. Huddled against the wall of the church, seeking shelter from the rain, was one of Edinburgh's down-and-outs—in all likelihood a local drunk. He had either passed out in the alley or intentionally bedded down there; he may have slept there most nights. But not even a drunk can sleep through Boellmann's Toccata—not even outside the church, apparently.

Alice enjoyed acting out how the drunken down-and-out had presented himself. "Would you stop that fucking racket? How the fuck can I be expected to get a good night's fucking sleep with that fucking bloody fuck of a fucking organ making a sound that would wake the fucking dead?"

It seemed to Alice that the drunk should have been struck dead for using such language in a church, but before God could take any action against the down-and-out, William resumed playing—with a vengeance. He played so loudly that everyone ran out of Old St. Paul's, including Alice. The organist with the midnight slot stood in the rain with her. Jack's mom told Jack that the foul-mouthed man was nowhere in sight. "He was probably searching for a resting place beyond the reach of Boellmann's Toccata!"

Despite such a reverberating performance, William Burns was disappointed by the organ. Built in 1888, the Father Willis would have been more highly valued if it were still in its original condition. Alas, in William's estimation, the organ had been "much fiddled with"; by the time he got to try it, it had been restored and electrified, a process typical of the anti-Victorianism of the 1960s.

Not that Alice could possibly have cared about the *organ*. More devastating to her: when William left his job as the organist at South Leith Parish Church to play the Father Willis at Old St. Paul's, there was no hope of her following him to be a choirgirl there. In those days, there was an all-male choir at Old St. Paul's—and from the congregation, Alice could see only William's back.

How she envied that choir! There was not only a procession, wherein the choir followed the cross, but the choir sat at the front of the church—in view of everyone—not at the back, unseen, as in Leith. Jack's mother was particularly miserable when she discovered that she wasn't the only choirgirl who'd fallen in love with Jack's father, but she was the only one who was pregnant.

As the new assistant organist at Old St. Paul's, William Burns was answerable to the senior organist and the priest; that William had knocked up a tattoo artist's daughter from Leith was a matter that his ambitious parents and the Scottish Episcopal Church didn't take lightly. Whose decision it was—"to whisk him away to Nova Scotia," as Jack's mom put it—would forever remain unclear to Jack, but both the church and William's parents probably had had a hand in it.

The counterpart of Old St. Paul's in Halifax, the Anglican Church of Canada, was simply called St. Paul's. They did not have a Father Willis. The church with the best organ in Halifax was the First Baptist Church on Oxford Street. William Burns must have been told to make up his mind in a hurry. There's no other explanation for why he chose the denomination over the organ—the music, not the church, was what mattered to him.

But the organist at St. Paul's in Halifax was retiring; the timing was providential.

The swath that William was alleged to have cut in Halifax in all likelihood included a choirgirl or two. (There was also talk of an older woman.) He wore out his welcome with the Anglicans in a hurry; according to Jack's mother, his father wouldn't have lasted a day longer with the Baptists.

William's parents reportedly told Alice that they never sent him money or hid his whereabouts from her. The first claim is conceivably true—William's parents had little money. But it was harder for Alice to believe that they didn't conspire to hide him from her. And when William was forced to flee Halifax—not long before Alice's arrival there—he must have needed money. He'd been tattooed again, as Alice discovered when she first went looking for him—at Charlie Snow's tattoo shop in Halifax, where the power for the electric machines was supplied by car batteries. And it would be a while before William found a job, and more quickly lost it, in Toronto.

Alice never blamed Old St. Paul's for whatever role the church may have played in arranging William's passage to Nova Scotia. It was the parishioners of Old St. Paul's—and surprisingly *not* her congregation in South Leith—who took up a collection to send Alice to Halifax to find him.

Furthermore, the Anglican Church of Canada looked after her in Halifax, and they did an honest job of it. But first they put her up in the St. Paul's Parish House, at the corner of Argyle and Prince streets, to await her delivery day. By this time, she was not only pregnant; she was "showing."

Jack Burns was alleged to have been a difficult birth. "A C-section," his mom told him around the time of their arrival in the first of those Baltic and North Sea ports. At four, the boy took this to mean that he was born in the C-section of a hospital in Halifax—a part of the hospital designated for difficult births. It was a little later—probably during, not after, their European travels—that Jack learned what a birth by Cesarean section meant. Only then was it explained to the boy that this was why it was not proper for him to take a bath with his mother, or to see her naked. Alice told Jack that she didn't want him to see the scar from her C-section.

Thus Jack Burns was born in Halifax, under the care of churchgoers at the *other* St. Paul's. As his mother remembered them—for the most part, fondly—they demonstrated considerable sympathy for a wayward choirgirl from the Church of Scotland, and they expressed the utmost contempt for the licentious organist who was one of their own. Scottish Episcopalians and Canadian Anglicans were cut from the same religious cloth. Apparently, it was because of those Anglicans at St. Paul's in Halifax that William did not long remain in hiding in Toronto.

"The church was onto him," as Alice put it.

In the meantime, after Jack was born in Nova Scotia, his mother went to work for Charlie Snow. Charlie was an Englishman who'd been a sailor in the British Merchant Navy in World War One; he was reputed to have jumped ship in Montreal, where Freddie Baldwin, who was also from England and had fought in the Boer War, taught him how to tattoo.

Both Freddie Baldwin and Charlie Snow had known the Great Omi. People paid to see the Great Omi's tattooed face; he used to come to Halifax with a circus. When he walked around town, he wore a ski mask. "No one got a free look," Jack's mom told him. (This amounted to more nightmare material for the boy; Jack couldn't stop himself from imagining the terrible tattoos on the Great Omi's face.)

From Charlie Snow, Alice learned to rinse the tattoo machines with ethyl alcohol; she cleaned the tubes with pipe cleaners, which she'd soaked in the alcohol, and every night she boiled the tubes and needles in a steamer. "The kind meant for cooking clams and lobsters," Alice said.

Charlie Snow made his own bandages out of linen. "There wasn't much hepatitis then," Alice explained.

She told Jack that Freddie Baldwin had given Charlie Snow his most impressive tattoo. Over Charlie's heart, Sitting Bull sat facing General Custer, who stared straight ahead, unseeing, on the far right of Charlie's chest. Dead-center on Charlie Snow's breastbone was a full-sailed ship; a banner, unfurled from Charlie's clavicle, said HOMEWARD BOUND.

Charlie Snow wouldn't get home to his final resting place until 1969, when he was eighty. (He died of a bleeding ulcer.) Alice learned a lot from Charlie Snow, but she learned how to do a Japanese carp from Jerry Swallow, whose tattoo name was Sailor Jerry; he'd become Charlie Snow's apprentice in 1962. Alice liked to say that she and Jerry Swallow "apprenticed together" with Charlie Snow, but of course she'd already been apprenticed to her father at Persevere in the Port of Leith.

Long before she'd docked in Halifax, Jack's mother knew how to tattoo.

Jack Burns had no memory of his birthplace; until he was four, Toronto was the only town he knew. He was still an infant when his mom caught wind of his father and what he was up to in Toronto, and they followed him there from Halifax. But Jack's dad had left town ahead of them, which was getting to be a familiar story. By the time the boy could comprehend his father's absence, William was rumored to be back in Europe, having crossed the Atlantic once again.

For much of his young life, Jack would wonder if the story of his dad's exploits in Toronto was what first led his mom to St. Hilda's. Unthinkably, the school had hired William Burns to train the senior choir, which was composed of girls in grades nine through thirteen. William also gave private lessons in piano and organ; these were almost exclusively for the older girls. One can only imagine what Jack, as a teenager, would think of his father's adventures at an all-girls' school! (William's noticeable contribution to the girls' musical education led St. Hilda's to make him the principal organist at the daily chapel services as well.)

Not surprisingly, William's success at St. Hilda's was short-lived. Although a girl in grade eleven—one of his piano students—was the first to succumb to his charms, it was a grade-thirteen girl whom he got pregnant. He later drove the girl to Buffalo for an illegal abortion. By the time Alice got to town with her illegitimate child in tow, William had fled, and Jack and his mother were once more welcomed by churchgoers.

St. Hilda's was an Anglican school; the school's chapel, where many of the St. Hilda's graduates were later married, was a Toronto bastion of the Anglican Church of Canada. The few scholarships to the school that existed in the 1960s were funded by the Old Girls' Association, a powerful alumnae organization. Children of the clergy were generally helped first; other decisions regarding who got financial aid were arbitrary. In addition to the Anglicans and the school faculty and administration, the Old Girls quickly heard of Alice and her condition. (Jack, of course, was the condition.) Thus, when Alice told Jack that she was arranging his admittance as one of the few new boys at St. Hilda's, he assumed that his mom had the Old Girls' help.

In fact, Alice and Jack had already been lucky; they'd found lodgings in the home of an Old Girl from St. Hilda's. Mrs. Wicksteed was a warhorse for the alumnae association. Inexplicably, upon her husband's death, she'd also become a champion of unwed mothers. She not only battled on their behalf—she even took them in.

Mrs. Wicksteed was a widow long past grieving; she lived virtually alone in a stately but not too imposing house at the corner of Spadina and Lowther, where Jack and his mom were given rooms. They were not big and there were only two of them, with a shared bath, but they were pretty and clean with high ceilings.

The Old Girl's housekeeper, whose name was Lottie, was a former Prince Edward Islander with a limp. Lottie became the boy's nanny while Alice sought the only work she knew.

In the 1960s, Toronto was hardly a tattoo mecca of North America. Alice's apprenticeship to her dad in Persevere—and her secondary education in Halifax, with Charlie Snow and Sailor Jerry—had overqualified her for Toronto's tattoo parlors. She was way better than Beachcomber Bill, who (for reasons unknown to Jack) didn't offer her a job, and she was also better than the man they called the Chinaman, who did. His real name was Paul Harper and he didn't look Chinese, but he knew that Alice was the best tattoo artist in Toronto in 1965; he hired her without a moment's hesitation.

The Chinaman's shop was on the northwest corner of Dundas and Jarvis. Near the old Warwick Hotel, there was a Victorian house with steps leading down to a basement door. The tattoo parlor was in the basement, and you entered it directly from the sidewalk on Dundas; the curtains on the basement windows were always drawn.

As a child, Jack Burns occasionally remembered to include Paul Harper in his prayers. The so-called Chinaman helped Alice launch her career in what would be the city of her choice, even if it would never be Jack's.

But it's no good being beholden to some people; indebtedness can come with a price. While the Chinaman never made Alice feel obligated to him, Mrs. Wicksteed was another matter. That she meant well was unquestioned, but to say, as her divorced daughter did, that Jack and Alice were her "rent-free boarders" would be a misuse of "rent-free."

Mrs. Wicksteed rashly decided that Alice's Scottish accent was a lowering mark upon her social station—more permanently damaging than her exotic, if unsavory, involvement with the tattoo arts. As Jack understood things, it was Mrs. Wicksteed's belief that his mom's burr was both a violation of English—that is, as Mrs. Wicksteed spoke it—and a curse that would condemn "poor Alice" to a station lower than Leith for all eternity.

As an Old Girl with deep pockets and an abiding devotion to St. Hilda's, Mrs. Wicksteed hired a young English teacher there, a Miss Caroline Wurtz, who was expected to change Alice's offensive accent. Miss Wurtz, in Mrs. Wicksteed's view, not only excelled in enunciation and diction; it seemed she also lacked an interfering imagination that might have found Alice's burr likable. Or possibly Miss Wurtz more deeply disapproved of Alice—the accent, in her view, being the *least* offensive thing about the young tattoo artist.

Caroline Wurtz was from Germany, via Edmonton; she was an excellent teacher. She could have cured anyone of a foreign accent—she attacked the very word *foreign* with a confident air. And whatever the source of her seeming disapproval of Alice, Miss Wurtz clearly doted on Jack. She could not take her eyes off the boy; sometimes, when she looked at him, she seemed to be reading his future in the contours of his face.

As for Alice, her attachment to Scotland had eluded her; she submitted to Caroline's enunciation and diction as if there were nothing in her own language she held dear. Her father's death—after her arrival in Halifax, but before Jack was born—and William's rejection had made Alice no match for Miss Wurtz.

Thus, in addition to losing her virtue on one side of the Atlantic, Alice lost her Scottish accent on the other.

"It was not a lot to lose," she would one day confide to Jack. (The boy assumed that his mother meant the accent.) Alice seemed to bear neither Miss Wurtz nor Mrs. Wicksteed a grudge. Jack's mom wasn't a well-educated woman, but she was nonetheless well spoken. Mrs. Wicksteed was most kind to her, and to Jack.

As for Lottie, with her limp, the boy loved her. She always held his hand, often taking it before he could reach for hers. And when Lottie hugged him, Jack felt it was as much for her own sake as it was to make him feel loved.

"Hold your breath and I'll hold mine," she would tell the boy. When they did so, they could feel their hearts beating chest-to-chest. "You must be alive," Lottie always said.

"You must be alive, too, Lottie," the boy replied, gasping for breath.

Jack would later learn that Lottie had left Prince Edward Island in much the same condition as his mother had been when she sailed for Halifax—only Lottie's child was stillborn upon her arrival in Toronto, where Mrs. Wicksteed and the network of St. Hilda's Old Girls had been most kind to her. Whether you called them Anglicans or Episcopalians, or worshipers in the Church of England, those Old Girls *were* a network. Considering that Jack and his mom were waifs in the New World, they were fortunate to be in the Old Girls' care.

2

Saved by the Littlest Soldier

Because Stronach is an Aberdeenshire name, Alice's dad, Bill Stronach, was known in the tattoo world as Aberdeen Bill—notwithstanding that he'd been born in Leith and had little to do with Aberdeen. According to Alice, who was his only child, Bill Stronach spent a drunken weekend in Aberdeen—one of those weekends when everything went wrong—and as a result, he was Aberdeen Bill for the rest of his life. As a younger man, before Alice was born, Aberdeen Bill had traveled with circuses. He'd tattooed the circus people in their tents at night, usually by the light of an oil lamp. He'd learned to make his best black ink from the soot on oil lamps, which he mixed with molasses.

In the fall of 1969, before Jack and his mom left for Europe, Alice wrote letters to the tattoo artists she had heard of in those cities she and her son would be visiting. She said she'd learned her trade at Persevere in the Port of Leith; that she was Aberdeen Bill's daughter would suffice. There wasn't a tattooer worth his needles in those Baltic and North Sea ports who hadn't heard of Aberdeen Bill.

Jack and Alice went to Copenhagen first. Ole Hansen was in the shop at Nyhavn 17; he'd received Alice's letter and had been expecting her. Like Aberdeen Bill, Tattoo Ole was a sailor's tattooer—a maritime man. (He would never have called himself a tattoo artist; he preferred to say he was a tattooist or a tattooer.) And like Aberdeen Bill, Tattoo Ole was a man of many hearts and mermaids, serpents and ships, flags and flowers, butterflies and naked ladies.

It was Tattoo Ole—then a young man, in his early forties—who gave Alice her tattoo name. She and Jack walked into Ole's shop on Nyhavn, with the boats slapping on the choppy water of the gray canal—a late-November wind was blowing off the

Baltic. Ole looked up from a tattoo-in-progress: a naked lady on the broad back of a half-naked man.

"You must be Daughter Alice," Tattoo Ole said. Thus Alice had a name for herself before she had her own tattoo parlor.

Tattoo Ole hired her on the spot. For the first week, Ole did all the outlining and assigned her the shading; by the second week, he was letting her do her own outlining.

All that seemed to matter at Tattoo Ole's was that Ole Hansen was a maritime man and Daughter Alice fit in. After all, she'd grown up practicing on her father; she'd poked her first tattoos by hand, before her dad had shown her how to use the electric machine.

From Persevere, her father's shop in Leith, Alice was familiar with the acetate stencils that Tattoo Ole used. She could do a broken heart or a heart torn in two, or a bleeding heart in thorns and roses. She did a scary skull and crossbones and a fire-breathing dragon; she could do a killer version of Christ on the Cross and an exquisite Virgin Mary, with a green tear on her cheek, and some sort of goddess who was captured in the act of decapitating a snake with a sword. She did ships at sea, anchors of all kinds, and a mermaid sitting sidesaddle on a dolphin. Alice also did her own naked ladies, refusing to copy any of Ole's stencils.

Tattoo Ole's naked ladies had an element that bothered her. The slim vestige of pubic hair on his women was arched like an upside-down eyebrow, like a smile with a vertical line slashed through it. There was often more evidence of hair in the ladies' armpits. But the only criticism Alice would make to Ole's face was that she preferred her naked ladies "from the back side."

Ole's other apprentice, Lars Madsen, who was called Ladies' Man Lars or Ladies' Man Madsen, was a semiconfident young man who told Alice he liked his naked ladies any way he could get them. "From the front side *and* the back side," he said.

Alice would generally respond, if at all, by saying: "Not around Jack."

The boy liked Ladies' Man Lars. Jack's mom had almost never taken him to the Chinaman's shop in Toronto. Although Jack knew a lot about her skills and training as a tattoo artist, his mother had never been keen for him to see her work. But there was no Lottie to look after the boy in Copenhagen, and until Tattoo Ole found them two rooms with a bath in the chambermaids' quarters of the Hotel D'Angleterre, Jack and his mom slept in the tattoo parlor at Nyhavn 17.

"I'm sleeping in the needles again," Daughter Alice would say, as if she had mixed feelings about it.

Despite reservations, she had let Jack play with the electric machine before. To the boy's eyes, it resembled a pistol, although its sound is more comparable to that made by a dentist's drill, and it is capable of making more than two thousand jabs a minute.

Until Jack and Alice went to Copenhagen, what little needle-work Jack had been allowed to do was practiced on an orange or a grapefruit—and only once, because his mom said fresh fish were expensive, on a flounder. (A fresh flounder, Aberdeen Bill had told Alice, was the closest approximation to human skin.) But Ladies' Man Lars let Jack practice on *him*.

Lars Madsen was a little younger than Jack's mother, but he was a whole lot greener as an apprentice; maybe that was why he was generous to the boy. After Tattoo Ole saw the needlework Alice could do, poor Lars was strictly limited to shading. With some exceptions, Ole and Alice let Lars color in their outlines, but Ladies' Man Madsen let Jack outline *him*.

This was a bold, even a reckless, thing for Lars to let a four-year-old do. Fortunately, Jack was restricted to the area of Madsen's ankles, where some "scratcher" (a bad tattooist) had etched the names of two former girlfriends, which were now an impediment to Lars's love life—or so he believed. The boy was given the task of covering up the old girlfriends' names.

Actually, twenty percent of all tattoos are cover-ups—and half the unwanted tattoos in the world incorporate someone's name. Ladies' Man Madsen, who was blond and blue-eyed with a gap-toothed smile and a crooked nose from a lost fight, had one ankle wreathed with small red hearts budding on a green thorny branch—as if an errant rosebush had grown hearts instead of flowers. The other ankle was encircled by black links of chain. The name entwined on and around the branch was *Kirsten;* linked to the chain was the name *Elise.*

With the tattoo machine vibrating in his small hand, and making his first penetrating contact with human skin, the boy must have borne down too hard. The client, unless drunk, is not supposed to bleed, and Madsen had been drinking nothing stronger

than coffee. The needles should not draw blood—provided they
puncture the skin no deeper than one sixty-fourth of an inch, or
even one thirty-second. Jack obviously went deeper than that
with poor Lars. The Ladies' Man was a good sport about it, but
with the thin sprinkling of the ink and the surprisingly more
vivid spatter of the blood, there was a lot to wipe away. Madsen
was not only bleeding; he was glistening with Vaseline.

That Lars didn't complain was more than a testimony to his
youth. He must have had a crush on Alice—possibly he was trying to win her affection by sacrificing his ankles to Jack.

While Alice was in her early twenties, and Lars in his late
teens, at their age, almost any difference takes on an unwar-
ranted magnitude. Moreover, Madsen's facial hair did little to
help his cause. He wore with a misplaced arrogance the merest
wisp of a goatee, which seemed not so much a beard as an over-
sight in shaving.

The Madsen family business was fish. (Selling them, not tattooing them.) The fish business was not one that Ladies' Man
Lars longed to join. His talent at tattooing may have been limited, but, in the tattoo world, Lars Madsen had found a measure
of independence from his family and the world of fish. He rinsed
his hair with fresh-squeezed lemon juice every time he shampooed. The problem was not unlike Kirsten and Elise, the former
girlfriends who clung to his ankles; Lars believed that the smell
of his family's business had permeated even the roots of his hair.

Tattoo Ole closely examined Jack's cover-up of Kirsten—the
one entwined with hearts and thorns—and announced that Herbert Hoffmann in Hamburg could not have done better. (Despite
this accolade, Lars Madsen kept bleeding.)

Alice's method of covering up letters consisted of leaves and
berries. Out of every letter, she told Jack, you could construct a
leaf or a berry—or an occasional flower petal. Some letters had
more round parts than others; you could make a berry out of
anything that was round. The letters with angles instead of round
parts made better leaves than berries. A flower petal could be either pointed or round.

Kirsten yielded more leaves than berries, and one unlikely
flower petal. Together with the untouched hearts and thorns, this
left Lars's left ankle wreathed with a confused bouquet; it looked
as if many small animals had been butchered, their hearts scattered in an unruly garden.

Jack had higher hopes for covering up Elise, but those black links of chain made a startling background to any combination of leaves and berries—besides, an *E* is not easily converted to anything remotely resembling vegetation.

The four-year-old had chosen a sprig of holly for his second effort on human skin. The sharp, pointed leaves and the bright-red berries struck him as ideal for a name as short as Elise; yet the result called to mind a destroyed Christmas decoration that someone had mockingly affixed to a chain-link fence.

Nevertheless, Tattoo Ole's only comment was that the legendary Les Skuse in Bristol would have been envious of Jack's needlework. This was high praise, indeed. Only Ole making some remark about Aberdeen Bill sitting up in his grave to take notice could have been more flattering, but Ole knew Alice was sensitive to references that placed her dad in his grave.

She'd not been there to scatter his ashes through the fence guarding the graveyard at South Leith Parish Church, although her father had arranged for a fisherman to scatter his ashes in the North Sea instead. And Ole only once mentioned the sad fact that Aberdeen Bill had drunk himself to death, which every tattoo artist in the North Sea and the Baltic knew.

Was it his daughter's disgrace—her running off to Halifax, to have her wee one out of wedlock—that drove him to drink? Or had Aberdeen Bill always been a drinker? Given the weekend when everything went wrong in Aberdeen, maybe his daughter's departure had merely exacerbated the problem.

Daughter Alice never spoke of it. Tattoo Ole never brought the subject up again, either. Jack Burns grew up with hearsay and gossip, and the boy got a good dose of both at Nyhavn 17.

In typical four-year-old fashion, Jack had left to his mother the cleaning up and bandaging of the Ladies' Man's ankles. A tattoo usually heals itself. You keep it covered for a few hours, then wash it with some nonperfumed soap. You never soak it; you should use a moisturizer. Ole told Jack that a new tattoo felt like a sunburn.

While the four-year-old's cover-ups may have failed in the aesthetic sense, the names of those two girlfriends were successfully concealed. That Ladies' Man Madsen had encircled his ankles with a shrub of what looked like body parts—worse, with what Tattoo Ole called "anti-Christmas propaganda"—was another matter.

Poor Lars. While Ole had nicknamed him "Ladies' Man," the opposite seemed true. Jack never saw him with a girl or heard him speak of one. Naturally, the boy never met Kirsten or Elise—only their names, which he covered in ink and blood.

Like any four-year-old, Jack Burns didn't pay close attention to adult conversations. The boy's understanding of linear time *might* have been on a level with an eleven-year-old's, but what he understood of his father's story came from those private little talks he'd had with his mother—not what he managed to overhear of Alice's dialogue with other grown-ups. In those conversations, Jack drifted in and out; he didn't *listen* like an eleven-year-old at all.

Even Ladies' Man Lars remembered meeting William Burns, although Tattoo Ole had done the needlework and there was no shading of the musical notes. William's tattoos were all in black; there was *only* outlining, apparently.

"Everything about him was all in black," as Ole put it.

What Jack might have made of this was that his father wore all-black *clothes*—that is, if the boy registered the remark at all. (Given Ole's fondness for Daughter Alice, the blackness might have been a reference to William's unfaithful *heart*.)

As for Ole's nickname for Jack's dad, the boy had correctly overheard the tattooer call him "The Music Man."

Ole had transferred some Christmas music by Bach to William's right shoulder, where the tattoo lay unfurled like a piece ripped from a flag. Either Bach's *Weihnachtsoratorium* or his *Kanonische Veränderungen über das Weihnachtslied,* Alice guessed; she knew many of the pieces the young organist liked to play. And in the area of William's kidneys, an especially painful place to be tattooed, Ole had reproduced a rather lengthy and complicated phrase by Handel.

"More Christmas music," Ole said dismissively. Alice wondered if it came from the Christmas section in the *Messiah*.

Tattoo Ole was critical of two of William's previous tattoos—not Aberdeen Bill's work, of course. (Ole much admired the Easter hymn on The Music Man's right thigh.) And there was what appeared to be a fragment of another hymn, which wrapped his left calf like a sock missing its foot. This one had words as well as music, and Ladies' Man Madsen had been so struck by the tattoo that he even remembered the words. They are sung throughout the Anglican Communion: *"Breathe on me, breath of God."*

Alice knew the rest. It sounded more like a chant than a hymn, but she called it a hymn, which she said was simply a prayer put to music. (She had sung it to Jack; she'd even practiced it with William.) By both Ole's and Lars's high esteem of the breath-of-God tattoo, Alice surmised this would have been Charlie Snow's or Sailor Jerry's work; her old friends had spared her the details of the tattoos they'd given William in Halifax.

Lars was less critical of The Music Man's two *bad* tattoos than Tattoo Ole was, but the Ladies' Man agreed that the needlework was not impressive. There was more music on William's left hip, but the tattooer had not anticipated how the bending of William's waist would scrunch some of the notes together.

On the slim evidence of this description, Alice decided he'd been to see Beachcomber Bill in Toronto—although she later admitted that the Chinaman was also capable of such a miscalculation. The second mistake, where some notes were lost from view because they curled around the underarm side of William's right biceps, could have been committed by either of those men.

From Tattoo Ole and Ladies' Man Madsen, Jack and his mom had a pretty good idea of The Music Man's body-in-progress. He was an ink addict, all right—a collector, as Aberdeen Bill had predicted.

"But what about *his* music?" Alice asked.

"What about it?" Tattoo Ole replied.

"He must be playing the organ somewhere," Alice said. "I assume he has a job."

Jack Burns remembered the silence with a fair amount of accuracy, if not the conversation that followed. For one thing, it was never what you would call *quiet* in Tattoo Ole's shop. The radio was always tuned to a popular-music station. And at the moment Jack's mom raised the issue of his dad's whereabouts, which (even at four) Jack recognized as the centermost issue of her life, there were three tattoo machines in operation.

Tattoo Ole was working on one of his naked ladies—a mermaid, without the inverted eyebrow that Alice disapproved of. The recipient, an old sailor, appeared to be asleep or dead; he lay unmoving while Ole outlined the scales on the mermaid's tail. (It was a fishtail with a woman's hips, which Alice also disapproved of.)

Ladies' Man Madsen was also hard at work, shading one of Ole's sea serpents on a Swedish man. It must have been a constrictor, because it was squeezing a bursting heart.

Alice was applying the finishing touches to her signature Rose of Jericho. This one was a beauty that half covered the heart side of a boy's rib cage. To Alice, he looked too young to know what a Rose of Jericho was. Jack was *much* too young to know what one was. The way it had been explained to him was that a Rose of Jericho was a rose with something hidden inside it.

"A rose with a mystery," his mother had told him.

Concealed in the petals of the rose are those of that *other* flower; you can discern a vagina in a Rose of Jericho, but only if you know what you are looking for. As Jack would one day learn, the harder to spot the vagina, the better the tattoo. (And in a good Rose of Jericho, when you *do* locate the vagina, it really pops out at you.)

Three tattoo machines make quite a racket, and the boy getting the Rose of Jericho had been audibly crying for some time. Alice had warned him that the pain of a tattoo on the rib cage radiates all the way to the shoulder.

But when Alice said, "I assume he has a job," Jack thought the electricity had failed; even the radio fell quiet.

How can three tattooers, without a word or signal to one another, take their feet off their respective foot switches simultaneously? Nevertheless, the three machines stopped; the flow of ink and pain was halted. The comatose sailor opened his eyes and looked at the unfinished mermaid on his reddening forearm. The Swede getting the color in his heart-squeezing serpent—over his heart, of all places—gave Lars a questioning look. The weeping boy held his breath. Was his Rose of Jericho, not to mention his agony, finally over?

Only the radio started up again. (Even in Danish, Jack recognized the particular Christmas carol.) Since no one had answered her, Alice repeated her inquiry. "He must be playing the organ somewhere," she said again. "I assume he has a job."

"He *had* one," Tattoo Ole said.

With that change of tense, Jack wondered if they had once more arrived too late to catch his dad, but the four-year-old might have misunderstood; he was surprised that his mother didn't betray her disappointment. Her foot was back on the switch and she went on about her business, hiding the rose-red labia among the flower petals. The Rose-of-Jericho boy commenced to moan; the old sailor, who was patient about acquiring his mermaid, closed his eyes; Lars, forever engaged in coloring-in, saw to it that the serpent's grip on the heart over the Swede's own heart appeared to tighten.

The walls of Tattoo Ole's shop were covered with stencils and hand-painted drawings. These possible tattoos were called "flash." Jack occupied himself by staring at a wall of flash while Ole elaborated on the absconding-father story. (This was one of those moments when the boy's attention wandered.)

"He was playing the organ at Kastelskirken," Ole said. "Mind you, he wasn't the head guy."

"The assistant organist, I suppose," Alice ventured.

"Like an apprentice," Lars offered.

"Yes, but he was good," Tattoo Ole said. "I admit I never heard him play, but I heard he was quite the player."

"Quite the ladies' man, too, we heard . . ." Lars began.

"Not around Jack," Alice told him.

The area of flash on the wall that had caught Jack's eye was what they called Man's Ruin. They were all tattoos on the theme of various self-destructions peculiar to men—gambling, drink, and women. The boy liked best the one of a martini glass with a woman's breast, just the nipple, protruding from the drink like an olive; or the one that similarly portrayed a woman's bare bum. In both cases, floating in the glass—like ice cubes—were a pair of dice.

Jack's mother did a swell Man's Ruin, a little different from these. In her version, a naked woman—seen, naturally, from the back side—is drinking from a half-full bottle of wine. The dice are in the palm of the woman's hand.

"So there was some *trouble* at Kastelskirken?" Alice asked.

Ladies' Man Madsen nodded enviously.

"Not around Jack," was Tattoo Ole's answer.

"I see," Alice said.

"Not a choirgirl," Ole offered. "She was one of the parish-ioners."

"A military man's young wife," said Ladies' Man Lars, but Jack must have misheard him; the boy was still staring, open-mouthed, at the woman's nipple in the martini glass, as dumbstruck as if he were watching television. He didn't see his mother give Lars a not-around-Jack look.

"So he's left town?" Alice asked.

"You should inquire at the church," Ole told her.

"I don't suppose you heard where he went," Alice said.

"I heard Stockholm, but I don't know," Ole answered.

Lars, who had finished with the Swede's sea serpent, said: "He won't get a decent tattoo in Stockholm. The Swedes come here to get tattooed." Lars looked quickly at the Swede. "Isn't that right?"

The Swede proceeded to pull up the left leg of his pants. "I got *this* in Stockholm," he said.

There on his calf was quite a good tattoo—good enough to have been one of Tattoo Ole's or Daughter Alice's. A dagger with an ornate green-and-gold handle had been thrust through a rose; both the petals of the rose and the hilt of the dagger were edged with orange, and twisted around the rose and the dagger was a green-and-red snake. (Evidently the Swede was fond of serpents.)

Jack could tell by his mom's expression that she admired the needlework; even Tattoo Ole agreed it was good. Ladies' Man Madsen was speechless with envy, or perhaps he was imagining his near-certain future in the family fish business.

"Doc Forest did it," the Swede said.

"What shop is he in?" Ole asked.

"I didn't know Stockholm *had* a shop!" said Lars.

"He works out of his home," the Swede reported.

Jack knew that Stockholm was not on their itinerary; it wasn't on his mom's list.

Alice was gingerly bandaging the boy with the sore ribs. He had wanted the Rose of Jericho on his rib cage so that the petals of the flower would move when he breathed.

"Promise me you won't show this to your mother," Alice said to the boy. "Or if you do, don't tell her what it is. Make sure she doesn't take a *long* look."

"I promise," the boy told her.

The old sailor was flexing his forearm, admiring how the contractions of his muscles moved the mermaid's tail, which still needed to be colored in.

It was almost Christmas; the tattoo business was good. But

the apparent news that William had escaped—to Stockholm, of all places—did little to lift Alice's holiday spirits, or Jack's.

And it was always dark when they left the shop on Nyhavn, even at four or five in the afternoon. Whatever time it was, the restaurants on Nyhavn were already cooking. By now Jack and Alice could distinguish the smells: the rabbit, the leg of deer, the wild duck, the roasted turbot, the grilled salmon, even the delicate veal. They could smell the stewed fruit in the sauces for the game, and many of those Danish cheeses were strong enough to smell from a winter street.

For good luck, they always counted the ships moored along the canal. Perhaps because it was almost Christmastime, the lighted arch that stood over the statue in the square by the D'Angleterre seemed to them an abiding kind of protection; the hotel itself was decorated with lighted Christmas wreaths.

On the way to their chambermaids' rooms, Jack and his mom often stopped for a Christmas beer. The beer was dark and sweet, but strong enough that Alice diluted Jack's with water.

One of Alice's clients at Tattoo Ole's—a banker who had different denominations of foreign currency tattooed on his back and chest—told her that Christmas beer was good for children because it prevented nightmares. The boy had to admit that, since he'd been drinking it, the banker's remedy for bad dreams seemed plausible: either he'd not had a nightmare in a while or he'd not had one he could remember.

In Jack's dreams, he missed Lottie—how she had hugged him, without reservation, how they'd held their breath and felt their hearts beating chest-to-chest. One night at the D'Angleterre, Jack had tried to hug his mom that way. Alice had been impatient about holding her breath. Feeling the thump of her heart, which seemed to beat at a slower, more measured pace than Lottie's, Jack said: "You must be alive, Mom."

"Well, of course I am," Alice replied, with more detectable impatience than she had demonstrated when he'd asked her to hold her breath. "You must be alive, too, Jackie—at least you were, the last time I looked."

Without his knowing exactly how or when, she had already managed to extricate herself from the boy's embrace.

The next day, before the sun was up—in Copenhagen, at that time of year, this could have been after eight o'clock in the morning—Jack's mother took him to the Frederikshavn Citadel. "Kastellet," the historic fortification was called. In addition to the soldiers' barracks, there was the commandant's house and the Citadel Church—the Kastelskirken, where William Burns had played.

Is there a boy who doesn't love a fort? How exciting for Jack that his mom had brought him to a *real* one! He was more than happy to amuse himself, as Alice asked him to do.

"I would like to have some privacy when I speak to the organist," was how she put it.

Jack was given the run of the place. His first discovery was the jail. It was behind the Citadel Church, where a prison aisle ran along the church wall; there were listening holes in the wall, to enable the prisoners to hear the church service without being seen. It was a disappointment to Jack that there were no prisoners—only empty cells.

The organist's name was Anker Rasmussen—a typical Danish name—and according to Alice, he was both respectful and forthcoming. Jack later found it odd that the organist was in uniform, but his mother would explain that a soldier-musician was what one might expect to find in a citadel church.

During William's brief apprenticeship to Rasmussen, the young man had mastered several Bach sonatas as well as Bach's Präludium und Fuge in B Moll and his *Klavierübung III.* (Jack was impressed that his mom could remember the German names of the pieces his dad had learned to play.) William was quite the hand at Couperin's *Messe pour les couvents,* too, and Alice had been right about the Christmas section from Handel's *Messiah.*

As for the seduced parishioner, the military man's young wife, Jack's mother told him little—only enough that the boy assumed his father hadn't been asked to leave Kastelskirken for flubbing a refrain.

When Jack tired of the jail, he walked outside. It was freezing cold; the medium-gray daylight merely darkened the sky. While the boy was thrilled to see the soldiers marching about, he kept his distance from them and went to have a look at the moat.

The water around Kastellet was called the Kastelsgraven; to a four-year-old's eyes, the moat was more of a pond or a small lake—and to Jack's great surprise, the water was frozen. He'd been told in Tattoo Ole's shop that the Nyhavn canal rarely froze, and that the Baltic Sea almost *never* froze; except in only the coldest weather, seawater didn't freeze. What, then, was in the moat? It had to be freshwater, but Jack knew only that the water in the moat was frozen.

There are few wonders to a child that equal black ice. And how did the four-year-old know the water was frozen? Because the gulls and ducks were walking on it, and he didn't think the birds were holy. Just to be sure, Jack found a small stone and threw it at them. The stone bounced across the ice. Only the gulls took flight. The ducks raced to the stone as if they thought it might be bread; then they waddled away from it. The gulls returned to the ice. Soon the ducks sat down, as if they were having a meeting, and the gulls walked disdainfully around them.

At times far away, at other times marching nearer, the soldiers tramped around and around. There was a wooden rampart near the frozen moat's edge; it was like a thin wooden road with sloped sides. Jack easily climbed down it. The round-eyed staring of the gulls taunted him; the ducks just plain ignored him. When the boy stepped onto that black ice, he felt he had found something more mysterious than his missing father. He was walking on water; even the ducks began to watch him.

When Jack reached the middle of the moat, he heard what he thought was the organ in the Citadel Church—just some low notes, not what he would have called music. Maybe the organist was calling upon the notes to enhance a story he was telling Alice. But Jack had never heard notes so low on the scale. It wasn't the organ. The Kastelsgraven itself was singing to the boy. The frozen pond was protesting his presence; the moat around the old fort had detected an intruder.

Before the ice cracked, it moaned—the cracks themselves were as loud as gunshots. A spiderweb blossomed at Jack's feet. He heard the soldiers yelling before he felt the frigid water.

The boy's head went under for only a second or two; his hands reached up and caught a shelf of ice above him. He rested his elbows on this shelf, but he hadn't the strength to pull himself out of the water—nor would the shelf of ice have held his weight. All Jack could do was stay exactly where he was, half in and half out of the freezing moat.

The gulls and ducks were put to flight by the racket of the soldiers' boots on the wooden rampart. The soldiers were shouting instructions in Danish; a bell in a barracks was ringing. The commotion had brought Alice and a man Jack assumed was the organist. *In a crisis of this kind, what good is an organist?* Jack was thinking. But Anker Rasmussen, if that's who he was, at least *looked* more like a military man than a musician.

Alice was screaming hysterically. Jack worried that she would think this was all his father's fault. In a way, it *was,* the boy considered. His own rescue struck him as uncertain. After all, if the ice hadn't held him, how would it hold one of the soldiers?

Then Jack saw him, the littlest soldier. He'd not been among the first of the soldiers to arrive; maybe Anker Rasmussen had fetched him from one of the barracks. He wasn't in uniform—only in his long underwear, as if he'd been asleep or was sick and had been convalescing. He was already shivering as he started out across the ice to Jack—inching his way, as Jack imagined all soldiers had been trained to do, on his elbows and his stomach. He dragged his rifle by its shoulder strap, which he clenched in his chattering teeth.

When the soldier had crawled to the hole Jack had made in the ice, he slid the rifle toward Jack—butt-end first. Jack was able to grasp the shoulder strap in both hands while the soldier took hold of the barrel at the bayonet-end and pulled the boy out of the water and across the ice to him.

Jack's eyebrows were already frozen and he could feel the ice forming in his hair. When he was on the surface again, he tried to get to all fours, but the littlest soldier yelled at him.

"Stay on your stomach!" he shouted. That he spoke English didn't surprise Jack; the surprise was that he didn't have a soldier's voice. To Jack, the soldier sounded like a fellow child—a boy, not yet a teenager.

As if Jack were a sled, he lay flat and let the littlest soldier pull him across the frozen moat to the rampart's edge, where Alice was waiting. His mom hugged and kissed him—then she suddenly slapped him. It was the only time Jack Burns remembered his mother striking him, and the second she did so, she burst into tears. Without hesitation, he reached for her hand.

Jack was wrapped in blankets and carried to the commandant's house, although he didn't remember meeting the commandant. The littlest soldier himself found clothes for Jack. They were too big for him, but Jack was more surprised that they were civilian clothes—not a soldier's uniform.

"Soldiers also have off-duty clothes, Jack," his mom explained—not an easy concept for a four-year-old.

When Jack and his mother were leaving Kastellet, Alice kissed the littlest soldier good-bye; she had to bend down to do it. Jack saw him standing on his toes to meet her kiss halfway.

That was when Jack got the idea that his mom should offer his rescuer a free tattoo—surely soldiers, like sailors, were fond of tattoos. Alice seemed amused at the notion. She approached the littlest soldier again, this time bending down to whisper in his ear instead of kissing him. He was certainly excited by what she said; her offer clearly appealed to him.

It turned out that Jack and Alice had more reason to go to Stockholm than to meet the talented Doc Forest. Anker Rasmussen told Alice that the organist at the Hedvig Eleonora Church in Stockholm, Erik Erling, had died three years ago. He'd been replaced by a brilliant twenty-four-year-old, Torvald Torén. Torén was rumored to be looking for an assistant.

Alice expressed surprise that William would seek a position as an assistant to an organist younger than he was. Anker Rasmussen took a different view: William was clever and talented enough to be a good organist; now was the time for him to travel, to play on different organs, to pick up what he could learn or steal from other organists. In Rasmussen's opinion, it was not just the trouble with women that kept motivating William to move on.

Jack's mother told him that she was disconcerted by Anker Rasmussen's theories; she had fallen in love with William Burns because of how he played the organ, yet she'd not considered that the instrument itself had seduced him. Did William restlessly need to be around a bigger and better organ, or at least a different one? Was it in the tradition of the way a young girl can love horses? (No doubt it further disconcerted Alice to realize that William might have liked trading mentors as much as he liked trading women.)

Jack assumed they would be leaving for Stockholm right away, but his mother had other ideas. Through the Christmas holiday, there was much money to be made at Tattoo Ole's. If a tattoo artist as good as Doc Forest was working out of his home in Stockholm, tattooing was barely legal there. Alice decided that it wouldn't be easy for her to make money in Stockholm; she thought she should take advantage of the holiday season at Tattoo Ole's before she and Jack continued their journey.

At Nyhavn 17, they said a prolonged good-bye. Jack didn't remember posing for a photograph there, on the street in front of Tattoo Ole's, but the sound of the camera shutter was over-familiar to him. Obviously someone was snapping pictures.

Alice was so popular with the clients, many of them sailors on Christmas leave, that she worked until late at night. Ladies' Man Madsen was less in demand. He often walked Jack to the D'Angleterre while Alice tattooed on.

Lars would sit on the bed in Jack's room while the boy brushed his teeth; then the Ladies' Man would tell Jack a story until Jack fell asleep. Madsen's stories never kept Jack awake for long. They were self-pitying tales of Lars himself as a child. (Mostly misadventures with fish, which struck Jack as easily avoidable; yet these catastrophes were of immeasurable importance to Lars.)

While the boy slept in the narrower of the chambermaids' rooms, which was divided from his mother's bedroom by a bathroom with two sliding doors, Ladies' Man Madsen read magazines on the toilet. Jack sometimes woke and saw Lars's silhouette through the frosted glass of the bathroom door. Often he fell asleep on the toilet with his head on his knees, and Alice would have to wake him up when she came home.

At his request, Alice gave Lars a tattoo. He wanted a broken heart above his own heart, which he claimed was broken, too. Alice gave him a blushing-red heart, torn in half horizontally; the jagged edges of the tear left a bare band of skin, wide enough for a name, but both Alice and Tattoo Ole urged Ladies' Man Madsen against a name. The ripped-apart heart, all by itself, was evidence enough of his pain.

Lars, however, wanted Alice's name. She refused. "Your heart's not broken because of *me*," she declared, but maybe it was.

"What I meant," said Ladies' Man Madsen, summoning an unexpected dignity, "was that I wanted your *tattoo* name."

"Ah—a *signature* tattoo!" cried Tattoo Ole.

"Well, okay—that's different," Alice told Lars.

On the very white skin between the pieces of his torn heart, she needled her name in cursive.

Daughter Alice

For his thoughtful care of Jack, Alice was grateful to the Ladies' Man. "There's no charge," she told him, as she bandaged his broken heart.

Jack didn't know what gift his mom might have made to Ole. Perhaps there was no gift for Ole—not even Alice's coveted Rose of Jericho, which Tattoo Ole much admired.

Their last night in Copenhagen, Ole closed the shop early and took them to dinner at a fancy restaurant on Nyhavn. There was an open fireplace and Jack had the rabbit.

"Jack, how can you eat Peter Cottontail?" his mom asked.

"Let him enjoy it," Lars told her.

"You know what, Jack?" Tattoo Ole said. "That can't be Peter Cottontail, because Danish rabbits don't wear clothes."

"They just get tattooed!" cried Ladies' Man Madsen.

When no one was looking, Jack scrutinized the rabbit for tattoos but didn't find any. The boy went on eating, but he must not have had enough Christmas beer.

That night, very late, he had a nightmare. He woke up naked and shivering. He had just fallen through the ice and drowned in the Kastelsgraven. More terrible, Jack was joined in death, at the bottom of the moat, by centuries of soldiers who had drowned there before him. The cold water had perfectly preserved them. Illogically, the littlest soldier was among the dead.

As always, the light in the bathroom had been left on—as a night-light for Jack. He slid open the two doors of frosted glass and entered his mother's bedroom. Whenever he had a bad dream, he was permitted to crawl into bed with her.

But someone had beaten him to it! At the foot of his mom's bed, which was as narrow as his own, he saw her upturned toes protruding from the bedcovers. Between her feet, Jack saw the soles of two more feet—these toes were pointed down.

At first, for no comprehensible reason, the boy believed it was Ladies' Man Madsen. But closer inspection of the stranger's bare feet revealed to Jack two *un*-tattooed ankles. Also, the feet between his mother's feet were too small to belong to Lars. They were even smaller than his mom's—they were almost as small as Jack's!

In the light from the bathroom, something else caught the boy's eye. On the chair, where his mother often put her clothes, was a soldier's uniform, which Jack thought was about his size.

However, when he put the uniform on, it was bigger than he'd estimated. He had to roll up the cuffs of the pants and cinch the belt in its last notch, and the shoulders of the shirt and jacket were much too broad. The epaulets touched his upper arms—the sleeves entirely covered his hands.

If he'd had to guess, Jack would have said that the littlest soldier's uniform was at least a size larger than his civilian clothes—the ones Jack had borrowed to wear following his misadventure in the moat. (The soldier's *off-duty* clothes, his mom had called them.)

Undaunted by this clothing mystery, which seemed of no consequence at the time, Jack was determined to stand at attention at his mother's bedside. When she and the littlest soldier woke up, Jack would salute them—as soldiers do. (Given the costume and the boy's intentions, his mom would later refer to this episode as Jack's first acting job.) But while he was standing there, at attention, he realized they were not asleep. The gentle movement of the bed had at first escaped his notice. Although his mother's eyes were closed, she was awake; her lips were parted, her breathing was rapid and shallow, and the muscles of her neck were straining.

All that could be seen of the littlest soldier was his feet. He must have been lying with his head between Alice's breasts, which were under the covers; he was probably recovering from a nightmare, or so Jack deduced. (That would explain the quivering of the bed.) Besides, Jack knew it was a night for bad dreams, having just had one himself; it seemed perfectly obvious to the boy that the soldier had suffered one, too, and had therefore climbed into bed with his mom. Jack no doubt still thought of the soldier as a fellow child.

Suddenly the littlest soldier's nightmare returned with a vengeance. He violently kicked the covers off—Jack saw his bare bum in the bathroom light—and Alice must have squeezed him too hard, because he whimpered and groaned. That was when her eyes opened and Jack's mom saw him standing there—another little soldier, this one at attention. Alice didn't recognize her son at first; it must have been the uniform.

Her scream was a shock to Jack, as it was to the littlest soldier. When he saw the four-year-old in uniform, he screamed, too. (He sounded like a little boy again!) And Jack was suddenly so afraid of the mutual nightmare they must have been having that he, too, began screaming. He also peed in his pants—actually, in the littlest soldier's pants.

"Jackie!" his mother cried, when she caught her breath.

"I dreamed I drowned in the moat," Jack began. "Dead soldiers, from the past, were with me. *You* were there, too," he told the littlest soldier.

The soldier didn't look so little now. Jack was astonished at the size of his penis; it was half as long as the bayonet on the rifle he'd used to rescue Jack, and it was thrust forward, at an upward angle, in the manner of a bayonet, too.

"You better go," Alice told the littlest soldier.

True to his calling, he took orders well; he marched straightaway into the bathroom, without a word of protest, and when he'd done his business there, he came back to Alice's bedroom to fetch his clothes. Jack had taken off the soldier's uniform, folded it neatly on the chair, and crawled into bed with his mom.

Together they watched the littlest soldier dress himself. Jack was embarrassed about pissing in his rescuer's pants, and he could tell the exact moment when the little hero discovered what had happened. An expression of uncertainty and distress was on his face—not unlike the anxiety and discomfort Jack had seen there when the brave lad was inching across the thinly frozen moat in his long underwear.

But after all, he was a soldier; he gave Jack a glance of vast understanding and grudging respect, as if the boy's peeing in his pants struck him as appropriate to the situation. And before he left, the littlest soldier gave Jack and his mother what Jack had intended to give them: a proper salute.

Despite having seen him stark naked, Jack hadn't noticed a tattoo—not even a bandage. The boy thought about it, in lieu of falling back to sleep—which would, in all probability, return him to his nightmare about drowning in the Kastelsgraven.

He asked his mom his troubling question. "Did you give him a free tattoo? I didn't see one."

"I . . . certainly *did* give him one," she replied, with some hesitation. "You just missed it."

"What was it?" Jack asked.

"It was . . . a little soldier," she answered, with more hesitation. "It was even littler than him."

Having seen his half-a-bayonet of a penis, Jack had revised

his impression of how *little* the soldier was, but all he said to his mother was: "Where did you put it?"

"On one of his ankles—the left one," she said.

The boy thought that the bathroom light must have been playing tricks on him, because he'd looked closely at the soldier's ankles and hadn't seen a tattoo there. He assumed that he'd just missed it, as his mom had said.

Jack fell asleep in her arms, as he often did after nightmares—and not at all in such an uncomfortable-looking position as the one the littlest soldier had taken up with her.

That was Copenhagen, which Jack Burns wouldn't visit again for almost thirty years. But he would never forget Tattoo Ole and Ladies' Man Madsen, and their kindness to his mom and him. Or the frozen moat—the Kastelsgraven, which almost claimed him. Or the littlest soldier, who saved him—and by so doing, saved his mother, too.

In reality, Jack understood little of what had happened there. Although he didn't know it, a pattern had begun. At the time, he had lots to learn, especially in those areas his mom kept largely to herself—not only the meaning of a free tattoo but all the other things as well.

And when he had that nightmare about drowning in the moat, it was always the same. He had already drowned. There was no more struggle, only a lasting cold. In eternity, Jack was joined by centuries of Europe's dead soldiers. The little hero who'd saved him stood out among them—not for the disproportionate size of his penis but for the stoic quality of his frozen salute.

3

Rescued by a Swedish Accountant

One day, when Jack was older, he would ask his mother why his father hadn't gone to England—why they'd not looked for him there. After all, England has its share of women and organs—and a long-established history of tattooing as well.

Alice simply said that William was Scots enough to hate the English. He would never have gone to England for a woman, let alone for an organ—not even for a tattoo. But William Burns wasn't quite Scots enough to have kept the Callum, was he?

From Copenhagen, Alice and Jack took the ferry across the sound to Malmö and then the train to Stockholm. In Sweden, in January, the hours of daylight are few. It was the New Year, 1970. It seemed that William had gone underground not long after his arrival, and Doc Forest wouldn't open his first tattoo parlor for two years. Doc was almost as hard to find as William Burns.

Alice and Jack went first to the Hedvig Eleonora Church. The building was a glowing dome of gold, surrounded by tombstones in the snow; the altar and the altar rail were also gold. The organ façade was a greenish gold, and the pews were painted a gray-green color—a faint, silvery tint, not as dark as moss. The glass in the paired, symmetrical windows of the rotunda was uncolored, as somber as the winter light.

The Hedvig Eleonora was the most beautiful church Jack had ever seen. It was Lutheran, with a fine choir tradition. This time, William had made the fond acquaintance of three choirgirls before the first learned of the third. Although it was the second choirgirl, Ulrika, who exposed him, surely the other two, Astrid and Vendela, were just as upset. Until then, William had been doing rather well—assisting Torvald Torén on the organ at the

Hedvig Eleonora, and studying composition at the Royal College of Music in Stockholm.

Poor Astrid, Ulrika, and Vendela—Jack later wished he could have met them. He remembered meeting Torvald Torén; even to Jack, Torén seemed young. Twenty-four *is* young, and Torén was a slight man with quick movements and lively eyes. Jack had the feeling that his mom was as utterly disarmed by Torén as she was by his devastating news of the three choirgirls. And unlike many organists Jack would meet, Torvald Torén was well dressed. The boy was struck by the businesslike efficiency of Torén's black briefcase, too.

Given his youth, his alert presence, his bright future—he was teaching the organ to a few carefully selected students—Alice may have seen in Torén all the promise that William had once embodied. Jack thought at the time that it might have been hard for his mom to say good-bye to Torvald Torén. As Jack and Alice were leaving the Hedvig Eleonora, the boy saw his mother turning to look at that golden altar—and out in the snow, in what struck them both as Stockholm's perpetual darkness, Alice kept glancing over her shoulder at the lighted dome of the church. But Jack had heard very little of Alice's conversation with Torén; the church itself and the young organist's appearance had completely captured the four-year-old's attention.

Here they had yet to find Doc Forest, and William was already underground! But Alice believed that William was incapable of passing through a port without being tattooed, and somewhere in Stockholm there was at least one good tattoo artist. Just possibly, Doc Forest might know where William had gone. If only to distract himself from the pain, a man getting a complicated tattoo is inclined to talk.

In the meantime, while they were trying to find Doc Forest, Alice was spending a fair amount of money. They were staying at the Grand, which was the best hotel in Stockholm. Their room faced the Old Town and the water, with a view of the wharf where the boats to and from the archipelago docked. Jack would remember posing with one of those ships as if he were the captain, just stepping ashore. He knew the hotel was expensive because his mom said so on a postcard she sent to Mrs. Wicksteed, which she read out loud to him. But Alice had a plan.

The Grand was near the opera and the theater—people met

there for drinks and dinner. Local businessmen had breakfast and lunch there, too. And the lobby of the Grand was both bigger and less gloomy than the lobby of the D'Angleterre. Jack lived in that lobby as if the hotel were his castle and he was the Grand's little prince.

Alice's plan was simple, but for a while it worked. Jack and Alice had few dressy clothes, and they wore them day and night; their laundry bill was expensive, too. Looking most unlike the solicitors they were, they ate a huge breakfast every morning. The buffet was included with the price of their room; it was their only complete meal of the day. While they gorged themselves, they would try to spot the tattoo-seekers among the well-heeled people eating breakfast.

They skipped lunch. Few people at the Grand ate lunch alone, and Alice knew that the decision to get a tattoo was a solitary one. (You didn't make a commitment to be marked for life in the company of colleagues or friends; in most cases, they tried to talk you out of it.)

In the early evening, Jack stayed alone in the hotel room, snacking on cold cuts and fruit, while his mom checked out the potential tattoo clients at the bar. Later at night, after Jack had gone to bed, Alice would order the least expensive appetizer in the dining room. At the Grand, apparently, many hotel guests ate their dinners alone—"traveling businessmen," in Alice's estimation.

Her approach to a potential client was always the same. "Do you have a tattoo?" (She'd even mastered this in Swedish: "*Har ni någon tatuering?*")

If the answer was yes, she would ask: "Is it a Doc Forest?" But no one had heard of him, and the answer to the first question was usually no.

When a potential client said he or she *didn't* have a tattoo, Alice asked the next question—in English first, in Swedish if she had to. "Would you like one?" ("*Skulle ni vilja ha en?*")

Most people said no, but some would say maybe. *Maybe* was good enough for Alice—all she ever needed was her pretty foot in the door.

When Jack couldn't sleep, he recited this dialogue; it worked better for him than thinking about Lottie or counting sheep. Maybe what made Jack Burns an actor was that he never forgot these lines.

"I have the room and the equipment, if you have the time."
(*"Jag har rum och utrustning, om ni har tid."*)

"How long does it take?" (*"Hur lång tid tar det?"*)

"That depends." (*"Det beror på."*)

"How much does it cost?" (*"Vad kostar det?"*)

"That depends, too." (*"Det beror också på."*)

Jack would wonder one day at the line "I have the room and the equipment, if you have the time." Were those traveling businessmen, whom Alice solicited alone, ever confused by her intentions? The one lady who said she wanted a tattoo wanted nothing of the kind. Not only was she surprised to find a four-year-old in Alice's hotel room; she wanted him to leave.

Alice refused to send Jack away. The lady, who was neither young nor pretty, seemed greatly offended. She spoke English very well—in fact, she may have been English—and she was the likeliest source of the hotel manager discovering that Alice was giving tattoos in her hotel room.

The tattoo machines, the pigments, the power pack, the foot switch, the little paper cups, the alcohol and witch hazel and glycerine, the Vaseline and paper towels—there was such a lot of stuff! Yet everything was put away, completely out of sight, when the maid came. As underground as tattooing was in Stockholm, Alice knew that the Grand would not have been happy to discover she was earning an income at that enterprise there.

Though he later suspected that the trouble with the hotel manager probably came from the English-speaking lesbian, at the time, Jack wasn't aware of the negotiations that transpired between his mother and the manager. He simply observed that his mom's attitude toward the Grand abruptly changed. She began to say things like, "If I don't get a lead on Doc Forest today, we're out of here tomorrow"—although they continued to stay. And Jack often woke at night to find her absent. He was too young to tell the time, but it seemed to him that it was very late at night for anyone to be having dinner in the dining room. So where was Alice on those nights? Was she giving a free tattoo to the hotel manager?

They were lucky to meet the accountant. Jack would soon wonder if, in every town, his mother needed to meet someone in order for them to be saved. It was a little anticlimactic to be rescued by an *accountant,* especially after encountering such a hero as the littlest soldier. Naturally, not knowing he was an accountant, Jack and his mom spotted him in the Grand at breakfast.

Torsten Lindberg was his name, and he was so thin that he seemed in need of more than a meal. But breakfast was a huge event for him, as it was for Jack and Alice. They'd noticed him *not* because he looked like a potential tattoo client, but because he had heaped on his plate a platter-size serving of herring— Jack and Alice hated herring—and Lindberg was making his way through the fishy mound with remarkable relish. With no thought of asking this tall, lugubrious-looking man if he had a tattoo or wanted one, Jack and his mother watched him eat, spellbound by his appetite. They couldn't help but wonder if the breakfast buffet at the Grand was *his* only complete meal of the day, too. At least in his appetite, if not in his taste for herring, he seemed a kindred soul.

Probably they were staring; that would explain why Torsten Lindberg began to stare at them. He said later that he couldn't help but notice how much *they* were eating—just not the herring. As a shrewd accountant, he might have guessed that they were trying to keep their expenses down.

Jack had carefully removed the mushrooms from his three-egg omelet; he'd saved them for his mom. She'd finished her crêpes and had saved her melon balls for him. Lindberg plowed on, devouring his archipelago of herring.

Whoever thinks accountants are penny-pinchers and emotional misers, not to mention joyless in the presence of children, never met Torsten Lindberg. When his great meal was finished— before Jack and Alice were through with their breakfast, because they were still scouting the café for potential tattoo clients— Lindberg paused at their table and smiled benevolently at Jack. He said something in Swedish, and the boy looked to his mom for help.

"I'm sorry—he speaks only English," Alice said.

"Excellent!" Lindberg cried, as if English-speaking children were in special need of cheering up. "Have you ever seen a fish swim without water?" he asked Jack.

"No," the boy replied.

While his dress was formal—a dark-blue suit and necktie— his manner was that of a clown. Lindberg may have looked like a man attending a funeral—worse, like a skeleton dressed for an overlong coffin—but in presenting himself to a child, he took on the magical promise of a circus performer.

Mr. Lindberg removed his suit jacket, which he handed to Alice—both politely and presumptuously, as if she were his wife. He ceremoniously unbuttoned one sleeve of his white dress shirt and rolled it up above his elbow. On his forearm was the aforementioned fish without water; actually, it was an excellent tattoo, and the fish looked very much as if it belonged there. The fish's head curled around Lindberg's wrist, the tail extending to the bend at his elbow; the tattoo covered most of his forearm. It was almost certainly of Japanese origin, though not a carp. The colors alternated between an iridescent blue and a vibrant yellow, blending to an iridescent green, which turned to midnight black and Shanghai red. As Torsten Lindberg tightened the muscles of his forearm, and slightly rotated his wrist and lower arm, the fish began to swim—undulating in a downward spiral, like a fantail diving for the palm of Lindberg's hand.

"Well, now you have," Mr. Lindberg said to Jack, who looked at his mother.

"That's a pretty good tattoo," she told Lindberg, "but I'll bet it's no Doc Forest."

He replied calmly, but without hesitation: "It would be awkward to show you my Doc Forest in a public place."

"You know Doc Forest!" Alice said.

"Of course. I thought *you* did!"

"I only know his work," Alice answered.

"You obviously know something about tattoos!" Lindberg said, with mounting excitement.

"Put your fish away," Alice told him. "I have the room and the equipment, if you have the time." (In retrospect, it disappointed Jack that he and his mom never learned the Swedish for "Put your fish away.")

They took Torsten Lindberg to their hotel room, where Alice showed him her flash and set up her outlining machine. The latter action was premature, as it turned out. Torsten Lindberg was a connoisseur; he wouldn't get any tattoo on the spot.

First of all, he insisted on showing Alice his other tattoos—including the ones on his bum. "Not around Jack," Alice said, but he assured her that the tattoos were safe for children to see.

It was no doubt the crack in Lindberg's ass that Jack's mom hadn't wanted him to see. But a thin man's bum is only a mild shock, and Lindberg had nothing more offensive than an eyeball on the left-side cheek and a pair of pursed lips on the right. The eye appeared to be glancing sideways at the crack in his scrawny ass, and the lips looked like a kiss that had been newly planted there—when the lipstick was still wet.

"Very nice," Alice said, in a way that let Mr. Lindberg know she disapproved of his display. He quickly pulled up his pants.

But he had other tattoos—in fact, many. The public life of an accountant is generally conducted in clothes. Possibly none of Mr. Lindberg's business associates knew that he was tattooed— certainly not that he had an eyeball on his ass! He also had a Tattoo Ole, which Alice recognized right away; it was Ole's naked lady with her oddly upturned eyebrow of pubic hair. There was something a little different about this naked lady, however. (Jack couldn't tell what was different about it, because his mother wouldn't let him have a closer look.) And Torsten Lindberg had a Tattoo Peter from Amsterdam and a Herbert Hoffmann from Hamburg as well. But even among this august company, it was the Doc Forest that most impressed Alice.

On Mr. Lindberg's narrow, sunken chest was a tall clipper ship in full sail—a three-masted type with a fast hull and a lofty rig. Under its bow, a sea monster was cresting. The serpent's head was as big as the ship's mainsail; the beast rose out of the sea on the port side of the bow, but the tip of its tail broke water off the starboard side of the stern. The doomed ship was clearly no match for this monster.

Alice announced that Doc Forest had to have been a sailor. In her view, the sailing ship on Torsten Lindberg's chest was better than that HOMEWARD BOUND vessel on the breastbone of the late Charlie Snow. Torsten Lindberg knew where Doc Forest lived— he promised to take Jack and Alice to meet him. And the following day Lindberg would make up his mind about what kind of tattoo to get from Alice.

"I am inclining toward a *personalized* version of your Rose of Jericho," he confessed.

"Every tattooed man should have one," Alice told him.

Mr. Lindberg didn't seem convinced. He was a worrier; it was the worrying, more than his metabolism, that kept him thin. He was worried about Alice's situation at the Grand, and about Jack's well-being in particular.

"Even in the Swedish winter, a boy must have exercise!" Did Jack know how to skate? Lindberg asked Alice.

Learning to skate had not been part of Jack's Canadian experience, Alice informed him.

Torsten Lindberg knew the remedy for that. His wife skated every morning on Lake Mälaren. She would teach Jack!

If Alice was at all alarmed at how readily Mr. Lindberg offered his wife's skating services, she didn't say—not that Jack would have heard what his mother said. The boy was in the bathroom. He had a stomachache, having eaten too much for breakfast. He missed the entire skating conversation. By the time Jack came out of the bathroom, his winter exercise had been arranged for him.

And it didn't strike the four-year-old as odd that his mother spoke of Lindberg's wife as if she'd already met the woman. "She's as robust as Lindberg is lean," Jack's mom told him. "She could keep a beer hall singing with her relentless good cheer."

Alice further explained to Jack that Mrs. Lindberg had no desire to be tattooed herself, although she liked them well enough on Lindberg. A big, broad-shouldered woman who wore a sweater capable of containing two women the size of Alice, Mrs. Lindberg took Jack skating on Lake Mälaren as her husband had promised. Jack noted that Agneta Lindberg seemed to prefer her maiden name, which was Nilsson.

"Who wouldn't agree that Agneta goes better with Nilsson than it does with Lindberg?" Alice said to her son, putting an end to that conversation.

What most impressed Jack was how well the large woman could skate, but that Agneta became so quickly out of breath bothered him. For someone who skated every morning, she got winded in a hurry.

The personalized Rose of Jericho that Torsten Lindberg had selected might be a three-day job—given his limited availability. The outlining would take nearly four hours; perhaps the shading of the cleverly concealed labia would require a fourth day.

It was unfortunate that Jack's mother didn't let him take a close look at the finished tattoo, for had the boy seen what Lindberg meant by a *personalized* version of Alice's Rose of Jericho, he might have realized that there were other things that were not as they seemed.

* * *

Lake Mälaren is a large freshwater lake that discharges itself into the Baltic Sea right next to the Old Town at a place called Slussen. When it doesn't snow too much, the lake is perfect for skating. Despite his experience with the thin ice on the Kastelsgraven, Jack had no fear of falling into Lake Mälaren. He knew that if the ice could support Agneta, it could easily hold him. And when they skated, she often took his hand in hers—as assertively as Lottie had. While Jack learned how to stop and to turn, and even how to skate backward, Alice completed the Rose of Jericho on Torsten Lindberg's right shoulder blade. It was the shoulder that he turned toward his wife when they were sleeping, Jack's mom told him. When Agneta opened her eyes upon her husband in the morning, there would be a vagina hiding in a flower. When he was older, Jack would wonder why a woman would want to wake up to that—but tattoos were not for everybody. Without the Torsten Lindbergs of this world, Jack's mother wouldn't have become such a successful Daughter Alice.

When Mr. Lindberg's Rose of Jericho was finished, he took Jack and Alice to meet Doc Forest. Where Doc lived was no place special, but for the walls of flash in the small room where he'd set up his tattoo practice. Alice much admired Doc. He was a compact man with forearms like Popeye's, a neatly trimmed mustache, and long sideburns. He was sandy-haired with bright, twinkling eyes, and he had indeed been a sailor. He'd gotten his first tattoo in Amsterdam from Tattoo Peter.

Doc regretted that he couldn't hire Alice as his apprentice, but it wasn't easy for him to find enough work to support himself; in fact, he was looking for a benefactor, someone to help him finance a first shop.

As for The Music Man—because, of course, William Burns had found Doc Forest—this time it had been either an aria quarta or a toccata by Pachelbel, Jack's mom told him. She mentioned a Swedish movie that had made some piece by Pachelbel famous. "Or maybe that was Mozart," Alice added. Jack wasn't sure if she meant the music in the Swedish movie or his dad's tattoo. But the boy was badly distracted by a snake. (An entire wall of flash was devoted to snakes and sea serpents, and other monsters of the deep.)

"I don't suppose you have any idea where William might have gone," Alice said to Doc Forest. She'd outworn her welcome at the Grand, or maybe the manager of the Grand had outworn his welcome with her.

"He's in Oslo, I think," Doc Forest said.

"Oslo!" Alice cried. There was more despair in her voice than before. "There can't be anyone tattooing in Oslo."

"If there is, he's doing it out of his home, like me," Doc replied.

"Oslo," Jack's mom said, more quietly this time. Like Stockholm, Oslo wasn't on their itinerary.

"There's an organ there," Doc added. "An old one—that's what he said."

Of *course* there was an organ in Oslo! And if there was anyone, good or bad, tattooing there—even if only in his home—William would find him.

"Did he mention which church?" Alice asked.

"Just the organ—he said it had a hundred and two stops," Doc Forest told her.

"Well, that shouldn't be too hard to find," Alice said, more to herself than to Doc or Jack.

A theme was emerging from the wall of flash, and the boy had almost grasped it—something having to do with snakes wrapped around swords.

"You should stay at the Bristol, Alice," Torsten Lindberg was saying. "You won't get as many clients as you got at the Grand, but at least the manager isn't onto you."

Years later, Jack would consider all that Lindberg might have meant by "onto you." But Alice made no response, other than to thank the accountant; naturally, she thanked Doc Forest, too.

Doc picked Jack up in his strong arms and whispered, "Come back and see me when you're older. Maybe then you'll want a tattoo."

Jack had loved the lobby of the Grand, and waking in the morning to the ships' horns—the commuter traffic from the archipelago. He'd enjoyed skating on Lake Mälaren with Agneta Nilsson, the formidable *Mrs.* Lindberg. Aside from the darkness, he would have been content to stay in Stockholm, but he and his mom were on the move again.

They traveled by train to Göteborg, then by ship to Oslo. Much of this journey must have been beautiful, but all the boy would remember was how dark it was—and how he felt cold. After all, it was still January and they were way up north.

* * *

Given all their tattoo paraphernalia, they had a lot of luggage. Upon their arrival anywhere, they never looked as if they were visiting for a short time. At the Hotel Bristol, the front-desk clerk must have thought they'd come for an extended stay.

"Not your most expensive room," Alice informed the clerk, "but something nice—not too claustrophobic."

They would be needing a hand with their bags, the clerk was smart enough to observe; he called for a bellboy and gave Jack a friendly handshake, but the handshake hurt the boy's fingers. Jack had never met a Norwegian before.

The Bristol's lobby was not so grand as the Grand's. Jack hoped he wouldn't have to get used to it. It didn't matter to him that the organ was an old one; for all he cared, the stupid organ could have had *two* hundred and two stops.

So far, Jack and his mom were indebted to three tattooers, two organists, a small soldier, and a tattooed accountant. In whose debt would they be *next*? the boy wondered, as they followed the bellboy and their luggage down a dark, carpeted hall.

Their hotel room at the Bristol was small and airless. When they checked in, it was already dark outside—it almost always was—and the view from their room was of another building. (There were some dimly lit rooms with their curtains closed, which spoke to Alice of dull, silent lives—not the life she had once imagined with William, anyway.)

They'd not eaten since their last breakfast at the Grand. The bellboy told them that the Bristol's restaurant was still serving, but he urged them not to dally. Jack's mother had forewarned her son that the restaurant was no doubt expensive and they should order sparingly.

Jack didn't much care for the bellboy's suggestions. "You must try the cloudberries," he said, "and of course the reindeer tongue."

"Have the salmon, Jack," his mom said, after the bellboy had gone. "I'll split it with you."

That was when the boy began to cry—not because his fingers still throbbed from the front-desk clerk's handshake, or because he was hungry and tired and sick of hotel rooms. It wasn't even because of that winter darkness special to Scandinavia—the absence of light, which must compel more than a few Swedes and Norwegians to jump into a fjord, if it's possible to find one that's not frozen. No, it was not the trip but the *reason* for the trip that made him cry.

"I don't *care* if we find him!" he cried to his mother. "I hope we *don't* find him!"

"If we find him, you'll care—it'll mean something," she said.

But if they were his father's *abandoned responsibilities,* didn't that mean that his dad had already expressed his disappointment with them both? Hadn't William rejected Alice *and* Jack, and wouldn't finding him mean that he might reject them *again*? (Not that the boy, at four, could ever have expressed these thoughts, but this was what he was feeling—this was what he was crying about.)

At his mother's insistence, Jack stopped crying so that they could go down to dinner.

"We'll share the salmon," Alice told the waiter.

"No reindeer tongue," Jack said, "no cloudberries."

Virtually no one else was eating in the restaurant. An elderly couple sat in silence; that they had nothing to say to each other did not necessarily predispose them to wanting a tattoo. A man was alone at a corner table. He looked depressed beyond desperation, a candidate for a fjord.

"A tattoo can't save him," Alice said.

Then a young couple came into the restaurant. It was the first time Jack saw how his mom was affected by a couple in love; she looked like a surefire fjord-jumper, one who wouldn't even hesitate.

He was thin and athletic-looking, with long hair to his shoulders—like a rock star, only better dressed—and his wife or girlfriend couldn't take her eyes or her hands off him. She was a tall, lanky young woman with a wide smile and beautiful breasts. (Even at four, Jack Burns had an eye for breasts.) Whether they were guests at the hotel or Oslo natives, they were as cool as any young couple who'd ever walked into Tattoo Ole's. Probably they'd already been tattooed.

"*Ask* them," Jack said to his mom, but she couldn't bear to look at them.

"No," she whispered, "not them. I can't."

Jack didn't understand what was the matter with her. They were a couple in love. Wasn't being in love a pilgrim experience, like getting your first tattoo? Jack had heard his mom and Ole talk about those turning points in people's lives that inspire a tattoo—almost any pilgrim experience will do. Obviously this young couple was having one. And if they were guests at the hotel, they'd probably already had sex that evening—not that Jack knew. (In all likelihood, they couldn't wait to eat their dinner so they could have sex *again*!)

Not even the presence of the waiter, who stood ready to tell them the specials, could keep them from fondling each other. After the waiter had left with their order, Jack nudged his mom and said: "Do you want *me* to ask them? I know how to do it."

"No, please—just eat your salmon," she said, still whispering.

Even in that brutal weather, the young woman wore a skimpy dress and her legs were bare. Jack thought that they *must* have been staying in the hotel, because no one would have gone out in such a dress—not in that weather. He also thought that he spotted a tattoo—it might have been a birthmark—on the inside of one of her bare knees. It turned out to be a bruise, but that was what propelled the boy out of his chair and gave him the courage to approach the couple's table. His mother didn't come with him.

Jack walked right up to that beautiful girl and said the lines he still said in his bed to help him sleep.

"Do you have a tattoo?" (In English first. But if he'd spoken in Swedish, most Norwegians would have understood him.)

The girl seemed to think Jack was telling her a joke. The guy looked all around, as if he'd misunderstood what sort of place he was in. Was the boy what amounted to live entertainment? Jack couldn't tell if he'd embarrassed the young man, or what else was the matter with him; it was almost as if it pained him to look at Jack.

"No," the young woman answered, also in English. The guy shook his head; maybe he didn't have a tattoo, either.

"Would you like one?" Jack asked the girl—*just* the girl.

The guy shook his head again. He regarded Jack strangely, as if he'd never seen a child before. But whenever Jack looked at him, he looked away.

"Maybe," his beautiful wife or girlfriend said.

"I have the room and the equipment, if you have the time," Jack told her, but something had distracted her. Neither she nor the man was looking at Jack; instead they were staring at his mom. She'd not left her table but she was crying. Jack didn't know what to do.

The girl, seemingly more concerned for Jack than for his

mother, leaned so far forward that the boy could smell her perfume. "How long does it take?" she asked him.

"That depends," Jack managed to say, only because he knew the lines by heart. He was frightened that his mom was crying; in lieu of looking at his mother, Jack stared at the girl's breasts. He became even more alarmed when he could no longer hear his mom crying.

"How much does it cost?" the guy asked, but not as if he were serious about getting a tattoo—more like he was trying not to hurt Jack's feelings.

"That depends, too," Alice said. She had not only stopped crying; she was standing right behind her son.

"Maybe some other time," the guy said; a certain bitterness in his voice made Jack look at him again. His wife or girlfriend only nodded, as if something had frightened her.

"Come with me, my little actor," Jack's mom whispered in his ear. The guy, for some reason, had closed his eyes; it was as if he didn't want to see Jack go.

Without turning around, the boy reached behind him. His hand, the one the clerk had hurt, instinctively found hers. When Jack Burns needed to hold his mother's hand, his fingers could see in the dark.

4

No Luck in Norway

Alice found few clients for tattoos in Oslo. Among the foreign guests and restaurant-goers at the Bristol, those intrepid souls who accepted her offer had been tattooed before.

Because their breakfasts at the Bristol were included in the price of their room, Jack and his mom continued their habit of overindulging in that meal. During one such exercise in overeating, they met a German businessman who was traveling with his wife. The German had a Sailor's Grave on his chest (a sinking ship, still flying the German flag) and a St. Pauli lighthouse on his right forearm—the solid maritime tattooing of Herbert Hoffmann, whose shop in Hamburg was just off the Reeperbahn.

The German wanted Alice to tattoo his wife, who already had an eighteen-inch lizard tattooed on her back. After breakfast, the businessman's wife selected an iridescent-green spider from Alice's flash. Alice tattooed an all-black spiral on the German woman's earlobe; the spider, suspended from a red thread, hung out in that hollow between her collarbone and her throat.

"Ambitious work, for Oslo," Alice told the German couple.

Alice was looking forward to meeting Herbert Hoffmann; she'd always wanted to visit St. Pauli. Hoffmann, like Tattoo Ole and Tattoo Peter, represented those Baltic and North Sea tattoos she'd first seen in her dad's shop. She knew that Tattoo Ole had given Herbert Hoffmann his first tattoo machine, and that Hoffmann had been tattooed by Ole and Tattoo Peter.

Jack's eagerness to get a look at Herbert Hoffmann was less professional. Ole had told the boy that Hoffmann had a big bird tattooed on his ass—the entire left cheek of his bum was a peacock with its fan in full-feather display! And Jack's curiosity about Tattoo Peter had less to do with his reputation as a tattoo artist than the tantalizing fact that he had one leg.

But if seeing the German's Herbert Hoffmanns made Alice wish she were in Hamburg, she was further disappointed that she was a whole week in Oslo before she got to tattoo a first-timer—"virgins," Alice called them. Perhaps no one in Norway was seeking a pilgrim experience—at least not of that kind, or not at the Bristol.

In their continuing gluttony at breakfast, which stood in fla-grant contrast to their near-starvation tactics at lunch and dinner, Jack learned to prefer gravlaks to smoked salmon. The cloud-berries, which were offered with repeated zeal to children at every meal, turned out to be quite good; and while it was impos-sible to avoid the reindeer in one form or another, Jack managed to resist eating the poor creature's tongue. But despite limiting their lunches and dinners to appetizers and desserts, the cost of their food was greater than the amount Alice was earning. And no one in Oslo wanted to talk to them about William. In Norway, the alleged object of William's desire (and his subsequent ruin) was a girl too young to be comfortably discussed—even among adults.

From the front entrance of the Bristol, the view of the Oslo Cathedral is slightly uphill. From that perspective, the first dark morning they saw it, the Domkirke appeared to rise out of the middle of the road at the end of the long street marked by trolley tracks. But they never took the streetcar; the cathedral was within easy walking distance.

"I'll bet that's the one," Alice said.

"Why?" Jack asked.

"I just bet it is."

The Domkirke looked important enough to have an old organ with one hundred and two stops. A German-made Walcker, the organ had been rebuilt in 1883 and again in 1930. The exterior dated back to 1720. It had been painted gray in 1950—the origi-nal was green—and its grayness enhanced what was monumen-tal and somber about the Walcker's old baroque façade.

The Oslo Cathedral was brick, the dome that greenish color of turned copper, and the tower clock was large and imposing. The clock's face suggested an elevated self-seriousness, beyond Lutheran, as if the building's purpose lay more in the enshrinement of sacred relics than in the usual business of a house of worship.

Consistent with this impression was Jack and Alice's first encounter with the church's interior. There were no candles; the cathedral was illuminated by electric lights. Huge chandeliers were hung from the ceilings; old-fashioned bracket lamps cast a fake candlelight on the walls. The altar, which unmiraculously combined the Lord's Last Supper with His Crucifixion, was as festooned with bric-a-brac as an antiques shop. The short, squat staircase leading to the pulpit was ornate, with wooden wreaths painted gold. Overhanging the pulpit, as if the firmament itself were about to fall down, was a floating island of angels—some of them playing harps.

No one was playing the organ; not a soul was praying in a pew, either. Leaning on her mop as if it were a cane, only a cleaning woman was there to greet them—and she did so warily. As Alice would later explain to Jack, no one even marginally associated with the Domkirke wished to be reminded of William. Jack was a reminder.

When the cleaning woman saw the boy, she froze. She drew in her breath and stiffened her arms, the mop held in both hands in front of her; it was as if her mop were the Holy Cross, and, clinging to it for protection, she hoped to fend Jack off.

"Is the organist here?" Alice asked.

"*Which* organist?" the cleaning woman cried.

"How many are there?" Alice replied.

Scarcely daring to take her eyes off Jack, the cleaning woman told Alice that a Mr. Rolf Karlsen was the organist in the Domkirke. He was "away." The word *away* caused Jack to lose his concentration; the church suddenly seemed haunted.

"Mr. Karlsen is a big man," the cleaning woman was saying, although it wasn't clear if *big* referred to his physical size or his importance—or both.

No minister of the church was present, either, the cleaning woman went on. By now she was waving her mop like a magic wand, though such was her transfixed gaping at Jack that she was unaware of her efforts. Jack was looking everywhere for her pail, which he couldn't find. (*How can you work a mop without a pail?* the boy was wondering.)

"Actually," Alice began again, "I was looking for a *young* organist, a foreigner named William Burns."

The cleaning woman closed her eyes as if in prayer, or with the hopeless conviction that her mop might turn into an actual crucifix and save her. She solemnly raised the mop and pointed it at Jack.

"That's his son!" the cleaning woman cried. "You'd have to be blind not to recognize those eyelashes."

It was the first time anyone had said Jack looked like his father. Jack's mother stared at him as if she were aware of the resemblance for the first time; she seemed suddenly no less alarmed than the cleaning woman.

"And you, poor wretch, must be his wife!" the cleaning woman told Alice.

"I once wanted to be," Alice answered. She held out her hand to the cleaning woman and said: "I'm Alice Stronach and this is my son, Jack."

The cleaning woman first wiped her hand on her hip, then gave Alice a firm handshake. Jack knew how firm it was because he saw his mom wince.

"I'm Else-Marie Lothe," the woman said. "God bless you, Jack," she said to the boy. Remembering the clerk at the front desk of the Bristol, Jack didn't shake her outstretched hand.

Else-Marie would not discuss the details of what had happened, except to say that the entire congregation couldn't put "the episode" behind them. Alice and her son should just go home, the cleaning woman told them.

"Who was the girl this time?" Alice asked.

"Ingrid Moe is not a girl—she's just a *child*!" Else-Marie cried.

"Not around Jack," Alice said.

The cleaning woman cupped Jack's ears in her dry, strong hands and said something he couldn't hear; nor could he hear his mother's response, but there was no "poor wretch" in Else-Marie's final remark to Alice. "No one will talk to you!" Else-Marie called after them, as they were leaving the Domkirke, her words echoing in the empty cathedral.

"The girl will—I mean the *child*," Alice said. "I'll talk to Ingrid Moe!"

But it was Jack's impression that, when they came a second time to the Oslo Cathedral, they were shunned. The cleaning woman wasn't there. A man on a stepladder was replacing burned-out lightbulbs in the bracket lamps mounted on the walls. He was too well dressed to be a janitor. (An especially conscientious parishioner, perhaps—the church's self-appointed fussbudget.) And whoever he was, it was clear that he knew who Jack and Alice were—he wasn't talking.

"Do you know William Burns, the Scotsman?" Alice asked, but the man just walked away. "Ingrid Moe! Do you know *her*?" Alice called after him. Although the lightbulb man kept walking, Jack had seen him flinch. (And there was that overfamiliar sound of the camera shutter again—when Jack was holding his mother's hand in front of the Domkirke. Someone took their picture as they were about to return to the Bristol.)

Finally, on a Saturday morning, an unseen organist was playing. Jack reached for his mother's hand, and she led the boy to the organ. He would wonder, only later, how she knew the way.

The organist sat one floor above the nave; to reach the organ, you needed to climb a set of stairs in the back of the cathedral. The organist was so intent on his playing that he didn't see Jack and Alice until they were standing right beside him.

"Mr. Rolf Karlsen?" Alice's voice doubted itself. The young man on the organ bench was a teenager—in no way could he have been Rolf Karlsen.

"No," the teenager said. He'd instantly stopped playing. "I'm just a student."

"You play very well," Alice told him. She let go of Jack's hand and sat down on the bench beside the student.

He looked a little like Ladies' Man Lars—blond and blue-eyed and delicate, but younger and untattooed. No one had broken his nose, which was as small as a girl's, and he was without Lars's misbegotten goatee. His hands had frozen on the organ stops; Alice reached for his nearer hand and pulled it into her lap.

"Look at me," she whispered. (He couldn't.) "Then listen," she said, and began her story. "I used to know a young man like you; his name was William Burns. This is his son," she said, with a nod in Jack's direction. "Look at him." (He wouldn't.)

"I'm not supposed to talk to you!" the student blurted out.

With her free hand, Alice touched his face, and he turned to her. A son sees his mother in a certain way; especially when he was a child, Jack Burns thought his mom was so beautiful that she was hard to look at when she put her face close to his. Jack understood why the young organist shut his eyes.

"If you won't talk to me, I'll talk to Ingrid Moe," Alice told him, but Jack had shut his eyes—in sympathy with the student, perhaps—and whenever the boy's eyes were closed, he didn't hear very well. There were too many distracting things happening in the dark.

"Ingrid has a speech impediment," the student was saying. "She doesn't like to talk."

"Not a choirgirl, I guess," Alice said. Both Jack and the young man opened their eyes.

"No, certainly not," the teenager answered. "She's an organ student, like me."

"What's your name?" Alice asked.

"Andreas Breivik," the young man said.

"Do you have a tattoo, Andreas?" He appeared too stunned by the question to answer her; it was not a question he'd expected. "Do you want one?" Alice whispered to him. "It doesn't hurt, and—if you talk to me—I'll give you one for free."

One Sunday morning, before church, Jack sat in the breakfast room at the Bristol, stuffing his face even more than usual. His mom had told him that if he stayed in the breakfast room while she gave Andreas his free tattoo, Jack could eat as much as he wanted. (She wouldn't be there to stop him.) He'd been back to the buffet table twice before he began to doubt the wisdom of his second serving of sausages, and by then it was too late; the sausages were running right through him.

Although his mother had instructed him to wait for her in the breakfast room—she would join him for breakfast when she had finished with Andreas, she'd said—it was clear to Jack that he was in immediate need of a toilet. There must have been a men's room on the ground floor of the Bristol, but the boy didn't know where it was; rather than risk not finding it in time, he ran upstairs and along the carpeted hall to their hotel room, where he pounded on the door for his mother to let him in.

"Just a minute!" she kept calling.

"It's the *sausages*!" Jack cried. He was bent over double when Alice finally opened the door.

Jack raced into the bathroom and closed the door behind him, so quickly that he hardly noticed the unmade bed or his mom's bare feet—or that Andreas Breivik was zipping up his jeans. The student's shirt was untucked and unbuttoned, but Jack hadn't spotted the tattoo. Andreas's face looked puffy, as if he'd been rubbing it—especially in the area of his lips.

Maybe he'd been crying, Jack thought. "It doesn't hurt," Alice had promised, but Jack knew it did. (Some tattoos more than others, depending on where you were tattooed and the pigments that were used—certain colors were more toxic to the skin.)

When Jack came out of the bathroom, both his mother and Andreas were fully dressed and the bed was made. The tattoo machines, the paper towels, the Vaseline, the pigments, the alcohol, the witch hazel, the glycerine, the power pack, the foot switch—even the little paper cups—had all been put away. In fact, Jack didn't remember seeing any of that stuff when he raced through the bedroom on his way to the bathroom.

"Did it hurt?" Jack asked Andreas.

Either the young organ student hadn't heard the boy or he was in a state of shock, recovering from the pain of his first tattoo; he stared at Jack, dumbfounded. Alice smiled at her son and rumpled his hair. "It didn't hurt, did it?" she asked Andreas.

"No!" he cried, too loudly. Probably he was in denial. Not another Rose of Jericho on the rib cage, Jack guessed; there hadn't been time. Something small in the kidney area, maybe.

"Where did you tattoo him?" Jack asked his mom.

"Where he'll never forget it," she whispered, smiling at Andreas. Possibly the sternum, Jack imagined; that would explain why the teenager trembled at Alice's touch. She was pushing him, albeit gently, toward the door; it looked as though it hurt him to walk.

"Just keep it covered for a day," Jack told Andreas. "It will feel like a sunburn. Better put some moisturizer on it."

Andreas Breivik stood stupefied in the hall, as if even these simple instructions were bewildering. Alice waved good-bye to him as she closed the door.

By the way Jack's mother sat down on the bed, Jack knew she was tired. She lay back, with her hands behind her head, and began to laugh in a way her son recognized; it was the kind of laughter that quickly turned to tears, for no apparent reason. When she started to cry, Jack asked her—as he often did—what was the matter.

"Andreas didn't know anything," Alice sobbed. When she got

control of herself, she added: "If he'd known anything, he would have told me."

They would be late for church if Alice paused now for breakfast; besides, she said, Jack had eaten enough breakfast for both of them.

Whenever they had their laundry done at the Bristol, it was returned with shirt cardboards; their clothes were folded among the shirt cardboards like sandwiches. Jack watched his mom take one of these stiff white pieces of cardboard and write on it in capital letters with the kind of felt-tipped pen she used to mark her tubes of pigment. The black lettering read: INGRID MOE.

Alice put the shirt cardboard under her coat and they walked uphill to the Domkirke. The Sunday service had already begun when they arrived. The organ was playing; the choir was singing the opening hymn. If there'd been a procession, they'd missed it. Jack was thinking that the great (or at least *big*) Rolf Karlsen must have been playing the organ, because the organ sounded especially good.

The church was nearly full; they sat in the back pew on the center aisle. The minister who gave the sermon was the lightbulb man. He must have said something about Jack and Alice, because in the middle of his sermon a few anxious faces turned their way with expressions that were both pained and kind.

There was nothing for Jack to do but stare at the ceiling of the cathedral, where he saw a painting that frightened him. A dead man was stepping out of a grave. Jack was sure that Jesus was holding the dead man's hand, but that made the boy no less afraid of the walking corpse.

Suddenly the minister pointed to the ceiling and read aloud from the Bible in Norwegian. It was strangely comforting to Jack that the parishioners were all staring at the frightening painting with him. (It would be years before Jack understood the illustration or saw the English translation, which was of that moment in John 11, verses 43 and 44, when Jesus brings Lazarus back to life.)

Now when He said these things, He cried with a loud voice, "Lazarus, come forth!"

And he who had died came out bound hand and foot with graveclothes, and his face was wrapped with a cloth. Jesus said to them, "Loose him, and let him go."

When the minister cried, "Lazarus," Jack jumped. Lazarus and Jesus were the only words he'd understood, but at least he knew the dead man's name; this was strangely comforting, too.

When the service was over, Alice stood in the center aisle beside their pew with the shirt cardboard held to her chest. Upon leaving the church, everyone had to walk by her and the sign saying INGRID MOE. A boy about Jack's age was the acolyte; he led the congregation out, carrying the cross. He passed Alice in the aisle, his eyes cast down. The minister, whom Jack thought of as the lightbulb man, was the last to come up the aisle; normally, he was the first to follow the acolyte, but he had purposely lingered behind.

He stopped beside Alice with a sigh. The lightbulb man's voice was gentle when he spoke. "Please go home, Mrs. Burns," the minister said.

If she'd noticed the *Mrs. Burns,* Alice made no attempt to correct him; maybe, on his part, it was not a misunderstanding but another kindness.

The minister put his hand on her wrist, and, shaking his head, said: "God bless you and your son." Then he left.

Jack concluded that, since even the cleaning lady had blessed him, they were big on God-bless-yous in Norway. Certainly Lazarus, leaving his grave, seemed predisposed to offer a blessing.

Back at the Bristol, Alice sipped her soup. (That was their lunch—just the soup.) But if Alice had lost her enthusiasm for spotting future tattoo clients, Jack thought he saw one. A young girl stared at them from the entrance to the dining room; she had a child's face on an overlong body, and she refused to let the maître d' show her to a table. Jack doubted that his mother would tattoo her. Alice had her rules. You had to be a certain age, and this baby-faced girl looked too young to be tattooed.

The instant Alice saw her, she knew it was Ingrid Moe. Alice told the waiter to bring another chair to the table, where the tall, awkward-looking girl reluctantly joined them. She sat on the edge of her chair with her hands on the table, as if the silverware were organ stops and she were preparing to play; her arms and fingers were absurdly long for her age.

"I'm sorry he hurt you. I'm sorry for you that you ever met

him," Alice told the young girl. (Jack assumed his mom meant his dad. Who else could she have meant?)

Ingrid Moe bit her lip and stared at her long fingers. A thick blond braid hung down her perfectly straight back, reaching almost to the base of her spine. When she spoke, her exquisite prettiness was marred by what an obvious strain it was for her to speak; she clenched her teeth together when she talked, as if she were afraid or unable to show her tongue.

Jack thought with a shiver of what an agony it might be for her to kiss someone, or to kiss her. Years later, he imagined his father thinking this upon first meeting her—and Jack felt ashamed.

"I want a tattoo," Ingrid Moe told Alice. "He said you knew how to do it." Her speech impediment made her almost impossible to understand, at least in English.

"You're too young to get a tattoo," Alice said.

"I wasn't too young for *him*," Ingrid replied.

When she said the *him*, she curled back her lips and bared her clenched teeth; the muscles of her neck were tensed, thrusting her lower jaw forward as if she were about to spit. It was tragic that such a beautiful girl could be so instantly transformed; the not-so-simple act of speaking made her ugly.

"I would advise you not to get one," Alice said.

"If you won't do it, Trond Halvorsen will," Ingrid struggled to say. "He's not very good—he gave William an infection. He gives everyone an infection, I think."

Perhaps hearing the girl say *William* made Alice flinch—more than the news that he'd been infected by dirty needles or a bad tattooist. But Ingrid Moe misunderstood Alice's reaction.

"He got over it," the girl blurted out. "He just needed an antibiotic."

"I don't want to tattoo you," Alice told her.

"I know what I want and where I want it," Ingrid answered. "It's on a part of me I don't want Trond Halvorsen seeing," she added. The way she contorted her mouth to say the name *Trond Halvorsen* made him sound like a kind of inedible fish. Ingrid spread the long fingers of her right hand on the side of her left breast, near her heart. "Here," she said. Her hand cupped her small breast, her fingertips reaching to her ribs.

"It will hurt there," Alice informed her.

"I want it to hurt," Ingrid replied.

"I suppose it's a heart you want," Alice said.

Maybe a broken one, Jack was thinking. He was playing with his silverware—his attention had wandered off again.

Alice shrugged. A broken heart was such a common sailor tattoo that she could have done one with her eyes closed. "I won't do his name," she said to Ingrid.

"I don't want his name," the girl answered. Just a heart, ripped in two, Jack was thinking. (It was something Ladies' Man Madsen used to say.)

"One day you'll meet someone and have to explain everything," Alice warned Ingrid.

"If I meet someone, he'll have to know everything about me eventually," the girl responded.

"How will you pay for it?" Alice asked.

"I'll tell you where to find him," the girl said. But Jack wasn't listening; Ingrid's speech impediment disturbed the boy. The girl might have said, "I'll tell you where he wants to go."

So much for rules. Ingrid Moe was not too young to be tattooed after all. She was no child; she just looked like one. Despite her baby face, even Jack knew that. If he'd had to guess, Jack would have said she was sixteen going on thirty. He didn't know that a world of older women awaited him.

At midday, the amber light that suffused the hotel room made Ingrid Moe's pale skin seem more golden than it was. She sat stripped to her waist on one of the twin beds, Alice beside her. Jack sat on the other twin bed, staring at the tall girl's breasts.

"He's just a child—I don't mind if he watches," was how Ingrid had put it.

"Maybe *I* mind," Alice said.

"Please, I'd like to have Jack here while you do it," Ingrid told her. "He's going to look just like William. You know that, don't you?"

"Yes, I know," Alice answered.

Possibly Ingrid didn't mind the boy seeing her because she had no breasts to speak of; even so, Jack couldn't take his eyes off her. She sat very straight with her long fingers gripping her knees. The blue veins in her forearms stood out against the gold of her skin. Another blue vein, which began at her throat, ran down between her small breasts; that vein seemed to have a pulse in it, as if an animal lived under her skin.

Alice had outlined the whole heart, which touched both the

side of Ingrid Moe's left breast and her rib cage, before Jack got the idea that it was *not* a broken heart—not a heart ripped in two, as he'd thought Ingrid had requested—but an *un*broken one. (Without a mirror, Ingrid couldn't see the tattoo-in-progress; besides, she kept staring straight at Jack, who was paying more attention to her breasts than to the tattoo.)

Even when Alice did the outlining on Ingrid's rib cage, the girl sat completely still and didn't make a sound, although tears flowed freely down her cheeks. Alice ignored Ingrid's tears, except when they fell on the girl's left breast; these errant tears she wiped away, as perfunctorily (with a dab of Vaseline on a paper towel) as she wiped away the fine spatter of black ink from the outlining.

It wasn't until Alice began to shade the heart red that the strangeness of it became apparent. Given the slight contour of Ingrid's breast, the plump little heart seemed capable of beating. The rise and fall of Ingrid's breathing gave the tattoo a visible pulse; it looked real enough to bleed. Jack had seen his mother tattoo a heart in a bed of flowers, or frame one with roses, but this heart stood alone. It was smaller than her other hearts, and something else was different about it. The tattoo held the side of Ingrid Moe's left breast and touched her heart—the way, one day, an infant's hand would touch her there.

When Alice was finished, she went into the bathroom to wash her hands. Ingrid leaned forward and put her long hands on Jack's thighs.

"You have your father's eyes, his mouth," she whispered, but her speech impediment made a mess of her whisper. (She said "mouth" in such a way that the mangled word rhymed with "roof.") And while Alice was still in the bathroom, Ingrid leaned farther forward and kissed Jack on the mouth. The boy shivered as though he might faint. Her lips had opened so that her teeth clicked against his. Naturally, he wondered if her speech impediment was contagious.

When Alice came back from the bathroom, she brought her hand mirror with her. She sat beside Jack on the twin bed while they watched Ingrid Moe have her first look at her finished heart. Ingrid took a good, long look at it before she said anything. Jack didn't really hear what she said, anyway. He'd gone into the bathroom, where he put a gob of toothpaste in his mouth and rinsed it out in the sink.

Maybe Ingrid was saying, "It's not broken—I said a heart ripped in two."

"There's nothing the matter with your heart," Alice might have said.

"It's ripped in two!" Ingrid declared. Jack heard that and came out of the bathroom.

"You only think it is," his mom was saying.

"You didn't give me what I wanted!" Ingrid blurted out.

"I gave you what you *have,* an actual heart—a small one," Alice added.

"Fuck you!" Ingrid Moe shouted.

"Not around Jack," Alice told her.

"I'm not telling you anything," the girl said. She held the hand mirror close to her tattooed breast. It might not have been the heart she wanted, but she couldn't stop looking at the tattoo.

Alice got up from the twin bed and went into the bathroom. Before she closed the door, she said: "When you meet someone, Ingrid—and you will—you'll have a heart he'll want to put his hand on. Your children will want to touch it, too."

Alice turned on the water in the sink; she didn't want Ingrid and Jack to hear her crying. "You didn't bandage her," Jack said—to the closed bathroom door.

"*You* bandage her, Jackie," his mother said over the running water. "I don't want to touch her."

Jack put some Vaseline on a piece of gauze about as big as Ingrid Moe's hand; it completely covered the heart on the side of her breast. He taped the gauze to her skin, being careful not to touch her nipple. Ingrid was sweating slightly and he had a little trouble making the tape stick.

"Have you done this before?" the girl asked.

"Sure," Jack said.

"No, you haven't," she said. "Not on a breast."

Jack repeated the usual instructions; after all, he was pretty familiar with the routine.

"Just keep it covered for a day," the boy told Ingrid. She was buttoning up her shirt—she didn't bother with her skimpy bra. "It will feel like a sunburn."

"How do you know what it feels like?" the girl asked. When she stood up, she was so tall that Jack barely came to her waist.

"Better put a little moisturizer on it," he told her.

She bent over him, as if she were going to kiss him again. Jack clamped his lips tight together and held his breath. He must have been trembling, because Ingrid put her big hands on his shoulders and said: "Don't be afraid—I'm not going to hurt you." Then, instead of kissing him, she whispered in his ear: "Sibelius."

"What?"

"Tell your mom he said, 'Sibelius.' It's all he thinks about. I mean going there," she added.

She opened the door to the hall, just a crack. She peered out as if she had a recent history of being careful about how she left hotel rooms.

"Sibelius?" Jack said, testing the word. (He thought it must be Norwegian.)

"I'm only telling you because of *you,* not her," Ingrid Moe said. "Tell your mom."

Jack watched her walk down the hall. From behind, she didn't look like a child; she walked like a woman.

Back in the hotel room, the boy cleaned up the little paper cups of pigment. He made sure the caps on the glycerine and alcohol and witch hazel were tight. He put away the bandages. On a paper towel, Jack laid out the needles from the two tattoo machines—what his mom called the "Jonesy roundback," which she used for outlining, and the Rodgers, which she used for shading. Jack knew his mother would want to clean the needles.

When Alice finally came out of the bathroom, she couldn't hide the fact that she'd been crying. While Jack had always thought of his mother as a beautiful woman—and the way most men looked at her did nothing to discourage his prejudice—she was perhaps undone to have tattooed the breast and golden skin of a baby-faced girl as young and pretty as Ingrid Moe.

"That girl is a heart-stopper, Jack," was all she said.

"She said, 'Sibelius,' " Jack told his mom.

"What?"

"Sibelius."

At first the word was as puzzling to Alice as it had been to Jack, but she kept thinking about it. "Maybe it's where he's gone," the boy guessed. "Where we can find him."

Alice shook her head. Jack took this to mean that Sibelius was another city not on their itinerary; he didn't even know what country it was in.

"Where is it?" Jack asked his mother.

She shook her head again. "It's a *he*, not an *it*," she told him. "Sibelius is a composer—he's Finnish."

Jack thought she'd said, "He's finished"—meaning that the composer was dead.

"He's from Finland," Alice explained. "That means your father has gone to Helsinki, Jack."

Helsinki was definitely not on their itinerary. Jack didn't like the sound of it one bit. Not a city with *Hell* in it!

Before leaving for Finland, Alice wanted to have a word with Trond Halvorsen, the bad tattooer who'd given William an infection. Halvorsen was what Tattoo Ole would have called a "scratcher." He worked out of a ground-floor apartment in Gamlebyen, in the eastern part of Oslo; what passed for a tattoo shop was his kitchen.

Trond Halvorsen was an old sailor. He'd been tattooed "by hand" in Borneo, and—again without the benefit of a tattoo machine—in Japan. He had a Tattoo Jack (Tattoo Ole's teacher) on his right forearm and one of Ole's naked ladies on his left. He had some simply awful tattoos, mostly on his thighs and stomach; he'd done them on himself. "When I was learning," he said, showing Alice and Jack his myriad mistakes.

"Tell me about The Music Man," Alice began.

"I just gave him some notes he asked for," Halvorsen said. "I don't know what the music sounds like."

"I understand you gave him an infection, too," Alice said.

Trond Halvorsen smiled; he was missing both an upper and a lower canine. "Infections happen."

"Do you clean your needles?" Alice asked.

"Who has the time?" Halvorsen replied.

A pot was bubbling on the stove, something with a fish head in it. The kitchen smelled of fish and tobacco in more or less equal parts.

Alice couldn't hide her disgust; even Halvorsen's flash was dirty, his stencils smudged with cooking grease and smoke. Some pigments had hardened in the open paper cups on the kitchen table; you couldn't tell what their true colors had been.

"I'm Aberdeen Bill's daughter, Alice." She suddenly seemed uninterested in her own story. "I once worked with Tattoo Ole." Her voice trailed away.

"I've heard of your dad, and everyone knows Ole," Halvorsen said; he seemed unembarrassed by her evident disapproval.

Jack was wondering why they'd come.

"The Music Man," Alice said, for the second time. "I don't suppose he told you where he was going."

"He was angry about the infection," Trond Halvorsen admitted. "When he came back, he wasn't in a mood to talk about his travels."

"He's gone to Helsinki," Alice said. Halvorsen just listened. If she already knew where William had gone, why was she bothering Halvorsen? "Do you know any tattoo artists in Helsinki?" Alice asked.

"There's nobody good there," he answered.

"There's nobody good *here*," Alice said.

Trond Halvorsen winked at Jack, as if acknowledging that the boy's mother must be hard to live with. He stirred the pot on the stove, briefly holding up the fish head for Jack to see. "In Helsinki," Halvorsen said, as if he were talking to the fish, "you can get a tattoo from an old sailor like me."

"A scratcher, you mean?" Alice asked.

"Someone working at home, like me," Halvorsen told her; he was sounding a little defensive now, even irritated.

"And would you know such a person as that in Finland, good or not?" Alice asked.

"There's a restaurant in Helsinki where the sailors go," Trond Halvorsen said. "You get yourself to the harbor, you look for a restaurant called Salve. Someone will know it—it's very popular."

"Then what?" Alice said.

"Ask one of the waitresses where you can get a tattoo," Halvorsen told her. "One of the older ones will know."

"Thank you very much, Mr. Halvorsen," Alice said. She held out her hand to him, but he didn't shake it. Even scratchers have their pride.

"You got a boyfriend?" Halvorsen asked her; he smiled, showing his missing teeth again.

Jack's mother rumpled the boy's hair and pulled him against her hip. "What do you think Jack here is?" she said to Halvorsen.

Trond Halvorsen never did shake Alice's hand. "I think Jack here looks just like him," the scratcher said.

* * *

Back at the Bristol, they packed in silence. The clerk at the front desk was happy they were checking out. The lobby was overcrowded with foreign sportswriters and skating fans. The world championships in speed skating were due to take place at Bislett Stadium in the center of Oslo in mid-February, but the journalists and fans had arrived early. Jack was sorry they were leaving; he'd been hoping to see the skaters.

That February, the temperature in Oslo was eight degrees below average. The cold weather meant fast ice, the front-desk clerk said. Jack asked his mom if speed skaters skated in the dark, or were there lights at Bislett Stadium? She didn't know.

He didn't ask his mother what Helsinki would be like, because he was afraid she might say, "Darker." In the pale midday light, their hotel room again had an amber hue, but without the golden glow of Ingrid Moe's skin, Oslo seemed plunged in an eternal darkness.

In his dreams, Jack still saw that girl's inflamed ribs and the throbbing heart on the side of her breast. When he'd held the gauze against her skin, he could feel the heat of her tattoo; her hot heart had burned his hand through the bandage.

When Jack and Alice made their way down the carpeted hall where he'd watched Ingrid Moe walk away—like a woman—the boy was thinking that their search for his father was also a dream, only it was never-ending.

One day or night, they would walk into a restaurant—a popular place called Salve, where the sailors in Helsinki went—and they would meet a waitress who'd already met William Burns. She would tell them what she'd told him—namely, where to go to be tattooed—but by the time they went there, William would have acquired another piece of music on his skin. According to Jack's mother, his father also would have seduced some woman or girl he'd first met in a church—and no amount of sacred music could persuade a single member of that church's congregation to help Jack and Alice find him.

Once again William would have vanished, the way the greatest music from the best organ in the most magnificent cathedral can drown out any choir and displace all other human sounds—even laughter, even grief, even sorrow of the kind Jack heard his mother give in to when she believed he was fast asleep.

"Good-bye, Oslo," Jack whispered in the hall, where he believed that Ingrid Moe had walked away with a whole heart—not one ripped in two.

His mom bent down and kissed the back of his neck. "Hello, Helsinki!" she whispered in his ear.

Once again, Jack reached for her hand. It was the one thing he knew how to do. As it would turn out, it was about the only thing he really knew.

5

Failure in Finland

They took the long trip back to Stockholm, the way they had come—then sailed from Stockholm to Helsinki, an overnight voyage through the Gulf of Finland. It was so cold that the salt spray froze on Jack's face if he stood outside for more than a minute. Undaunted by the weather, some Finns and Swedes were drinking and singing songs on the icy deck until midnight. Alice observed that they were also throwing up—with best results to the leeward side of the ship. In the morning, Jack saw some Finns and Swedes who had suffered the misfortune of throwing up to the windward side of the vessel.

Alice found out from the drunks, many of them young people, that the hotel in Helsinki best suited to a tattoo artist's circumstances was the Hotel Torni, where the so-called American Bar was a hangout for well-off students. One of the Finns or Swedes on deck referred to it as the place where you went to meet brave girls. "Brave girls" were right up Daughter Alice's alley, since she took "brave" to mean that the girls (and the boys who wanted to meet them) would be open to being tattooed.

The hotel itself had seen better days. Because the old iron-grate elevator was "temporarily" out of service and they were on the fourth floor, Jack and Alice became well acquainted with the stairs, which they climbed holding hands. They had a room without a bath or a toilet. There was a sink, although they were advised not to drink the water, and a view of what appeared to be a secondary school. Jack sat on the window seat and looked with longing at the pupils; they seemed to have many friends.

The bath and the WC, which Jack and his mother shared with some other guests on the floor, were a fair hike down the twisting hall. The hotel had a hundred rooms; one day, when Jack was bored, he made his mom count them with him. Fewer than half had their own bathrooms.

Yet Alice had been right to choose the Torni. From the beginning of their stay, she did a brisk business among the clientele at the American Bar. While only a few of the girls Jack saw were beautiful—and he had no experience with whether or not they were brave—many of them, as well as even more of the boys, were courageous about being tattooed. But in the tattoo business, drunks are bleeders; in Helsinki, Jack saw his mother go through a lot of paper towels.

In a week's time, Alice was earning almost as much money as she'd made at Tattoo Ole's in the Christmas season. Jack often fell asleep to the sound of the tattoo machine. Once again you could say they were sleeping in the needles.

At the restaurant called Salve, Jack and Alice took an opinionated waitress's advice—they ordered the poached Arctic char instead of the fried whitefish or the freshwater pike-perch. For a first course, they politely tried the reindeer tongue, largely because it was an increasing burden to avoid it; to Jack's surprise, the tongue was not rubbery and tasted good. And for dessert, he had the cloudberries. They were a dark-gold color, and the slight sourness of the fruit contrasted nicely with vanilla ice cream.

Jack's mom waited until he'd finished his dessert before she asked the waitress if she knew where to get a tattoo. It was not the answer Alice expected.

"I hear there's a woman at the Hotel Torni," the waitress began. "She's a guest at the hotel, a foreigner—a good-looking woman, but a sad one."

"Sad?" Alice asked. She seemed surprised. Jack couldn't look at her; even he knew she was sad.

"That's what I hear," the waitress replied. "She's got a little boy with her, just like you," she added, looking at Jack.

"I see," Alice said.

"She hangs out at the American Bar, but she does the tattooing in her hotel room—sometimes while the kid's asleep," the waitress went on.

"That's very interesting," Alice said. "But I was looking for someone else, another tattoo artist—probably a man."

"Well, there's Sami Salo, but the woman at the Torni is better."

"Tell me about Sami Salo," Alice said.

The waitress sighed. She was a short, stout woman whose clothes were too tight; her feet appeared to hurt her. She squinted whenever she took a step, and her fat arms jiggled, but she wasn't much older than Jack's mother. Under her apron, she kept a dish towel with which she commenced to wipe the table down.

"Listen, dearie," the waitress told Alice in a low voice. "You don't want to bother Sami. He already knows where to find you."

Alice seemed surprised again; maybe she hadn't realized that the waitress knew *she* was the tattoo artist at the Hotel Torni. But they hadn't been hard to figure out. In Helsinki, who else fit the description of a young woman and a little kid who spoke American-sounding English?

"I want to meet Sami Salo," Alice said to the waitress. "I want to ask him if he's tattooed someone I know."

"Sami Salo doesn't want to meet you," the waitress told her. "You're putting him out of business, and he's not happy about it. That's what I hear."

"I'm impressed by all you manage to hear," Alice said.

The waitress turned her gruff attention to Jack. "You look tired," she told him. "Are you getting enough sleep? Is all the tattooing keeping you awake?"

Jack's mom stood up from the table and held out her hand to her son. The restaurant was noisy and crowded; Finns can be loud when they eat and drink. The boy didn't quite catch what his mother told the waitress. He could only guess it was something along the lines of "Thank you for your concern"; or more likely, "If you want to stop by the Torni some evening, I'll be happy to tattoo you where it really hurts." Alice might also have given the waitress a message for Sami Salo; that the waitress and Sami were friends was pretty obvious, even to Jack.

They didn't go to Salve again. They ate at the Torni and called the American Bar their home.

But what about the church? Jack would wonder, as he was falling asleep. Why weren't they asking someone about the particular organ his father might be playing in Helsinki? Where were the destroyed young women who'd had the bad luck to meet William here? And what about Sibelius?

Jack wondered if his mom was growing tired of looking for his dad—or, worse, if she was suddenly afraid of finding him.

Maybe it had occurred to her how awful it would be to finally confront William, only to have him walk away with a shrug. Surely William must have known they were looking for him. Church music and tattooing were both small worlds. What if William decided to confront them? What would they have to say for themselves? Did they actually *want* him to stop running and live with them? Live with them *where*?

Helsinki is a hard place to be afflicted with self-doubts. Alice appeared to be unsure of herself. She would not get up at night to go to the bathroom without waking Jack and forcing him to walk down the hall with her; she wouldn't let him leave the hotel room by himself, either. (Some nights Jack peed in the sink.) And those evenings when she roamed the American Bar, so-liciting clients, Jack often watched her from the crow's-nest perspective of the iron-grate elevator, which was frozen in seem-ingly permanent disrepair on the floor above the bar.

Whenever a prospective client decided to get a tattoo, Alice would look up at the out-of-service elevator and nod her head to Jack, who was suspended in it like a boy in a birdcage.

Jack would watch Alice lead the client to the stairs. Then he exited the elevator and ran up the stairs to the fourth floor ahead of them. He was usually waiting by the door to their room when his mother brought the tattoo customer down the hall.

"Why—fancy seeing you, Jack!" his mom would always say. "Is it a tattoo you've come for?"

"No, thank you," Jack would always reply. "I'm too young to be tattooed. I'm just an observer."

It may have been a silly ritual, but it was their routine and they stuck to it. The client recognized that they were a team.

By their third week in Helsinki, Jack had forgotten all about Sibelius. Two young women (brave-looking girls) approached Alice in the American Bar. They asked her about a tattoo—one they wanted to share. In the elevator, one floor above them, Jack couldn't really hear what they were saying.

"You can't share a tattoo," he thought his mother said.

"Sure we can," the tall one replied.

Maybe the short one said, "We shared you-know-what to-gether. Sharing a tattoo can't be that bad."

From the broken elevator, Jack saw his mom shake her head—not her usual signal. He'd seen her say no to young men who were too drunk to be tattooed, or to two or more men; she wouldn't take more than one man at a time to their room. These two women, Tall and Short, were different; they made Alice seem awkward. Jack thought that his mother might already know them.

Alice abruptly turned and walked away. But the brave girls followed her; they kept talking to her, too. Jack got out of the elevator when he saw his mom start up the stairs. Tall and Short came up the stairs behind her.

"We're not too young, are we?" the tall one was asking.

Alice shook her head again; she just kept walking up the stairs with the two young women following her.

"You must be Jack," the short one said, looking up the stairs at the boy. It seemed to Jack that she even knew where to look for him. "We're both music students," the short one told him. "I'm studying church music, both choral and the organ."

Alice stopped on the staircase as if she were out of breath. The two girls caught up to her on the half-landing between the first and second floors. Jack stood waiting for his mom on the second-floor landing, looking down at the three of them.

"Hello, Jack," the tall girl said to the boy. "I play the cello."

She wasn't as tall as Ingrid Moe—nor as breathtakingly beautiful—but she had the same long hands. Her curly blond hair was cut as short as a boy's, and over a cotton turtleneck she wore a grungy ski sweater with a small herd of faded reindeer on it.

The other girl, the short one, was plump with a pretty face and long, dark hair that fell to her breasts. She wore a short black skirt with black tights, knee-high black boots, and a black V-neck sweater that was too big for her. The sweater was very soft-looking and had no reindeer on it.

"Music students," Alice repeated.

"At Sibelius Academy, Jack," the tall young woman said. "Did you ever hear of it?" The boy didn't answer her; he kept looking at his mother.

"Sibelius . . ." Alice said—in a way that implied the name hurt her throat.

The short, plump girl with the pretty face looked up the stairs and smiled at Jack. "You're definitely Jack," she said.

The tall one came up the stairs two at a time. She knelt at Jack's feet and framed his face in her long hands, which were slightly sticky. "Look at you, Jack," she said; her breath smelled like chewing gum, a fruit flavor. "You're a dead ringer for your dad."

Jack's mother came up the stairs with the short girl beside her. "Take your hands off him," Alice told the tall girl, who stood up and backed away from the boy.

"Sorry, Jack," the tall girl said.

"What do you want?" Alice asked the music students.

"We told you—a tattoo," the short girl answered.

"We also wanted to see what Jack looked like," the tall young woman confessed.

"I hope you don't mind, Jack," the short one said.

But Jack was *four.* How is it possible that he remembered, with any accuracy, what Tall and Short truly said? Isn't it more likely that, for days—for weeks, even *months*—after he met these girls, he would ask his mother the meaning of that conversation on the stairs in the Hotel Torni, and his mom would tell him what she wanted him to hear? It might not be Tall's and Short's actual words that he "remembered," but Alice's unalterable interpretation of William abandoning them.

There would be times when Jack Burns felt he was still on those stairs—not only because the elevator was more than *temporarily* out of service, but also because Jack would spend years trying to discern the difference between his mother's version of his father and who his father really was.

Jack did remember this: when his mom started up the stairs again, he had not let go of her hand. The music students kept pace with them, all the way to their floor. Jack could tell that his mother was agitated because she stopped at the door to their room and fumbled around in her purse for the key. She'd forgotten that Jack had it—that was part of their routine.

"Here," he said, handing the key to her.

"You could have lost it," she told him. Jack didn't know what to say; he'd not seen her so distracted.

"Look, we just wanted to meet Jack," the tall young woman went on.

"The idea for the tattoo came later," the short one said.

Alice let them into the room. Again it seemed to Jack that his mom already knew them. Inside the room, Alice turned on all the lights. The tall girl knelt at Jack's feet once more. She might have wanted to take his face in her hands again, but she restrained herself—she just looked at him.

"When you get older, Jack," she said, "you're going to know a lot of girls."

"Why?" the boy asked.

"Be careful what you tell him," Alice said.

The short girl with the pretty face and long hair knelt at Jack's feet, too.

"We're sorry," the two girls said, in chorus. Jack couldn't tell if they were speaking to him or to his mom.

Alice sat down on the bed and sighed. "Tell me about this tattoo you want to share," she said, staring at a neutral zone between the two young women—purposely not looking at either one of them. Alice must have sensed an aura of wantonness about these brave girls, and she knew Jack was affected by them.

The tattoo Tall and Short wanted to share was another variation of a broken heart—this one torn apart vertically. The left side would be tattooed on the heart-side breast of the tall young woman; the right side would go on the heart-side breast of the short one. Not a very original idea, but even Jack was learning that there was little originality in the instinct to be tattooed. Not only were broken hearts fairly common; the ways to depict them were limited, and the part of the body where a depiction of a broken heart belonged was self-evident.

In those days, a tattoo was still a souvenir—a keepsake to mark a journey, the love of your life, a heartbreak, a port of call. The body was like a photo album; the tattoos themselves didn't have to be good photographs. Indeed, they may not have been very artistic or aesthetically pleasing, but they weren't ugly—not intentionally. And the old tattoos were always sentimental; you didn't mark yourself for life if you weren't sentimental.

How could tattoos be original, when what they signified was something ordinary? Your feelings for your mother; the lover who left you; the first time you went to sea. But these were mostly maritime tattoos—clearly sailors were sentimental souls.

So were these music students, Tall and Short. They may have been vulgar, but Alice didn't seem to hate them—and they were old enough to be tattooed. Even to Jack, they were noticeably older than Ingrid Moe.

* * *

The tall one's name was Hannele; under her faded-reindeer sweater and the cotton turtleneck, she wasn't wearing a bra. Despite Jack's precocious interest in breasts, what struck him most about Hannele was that her armpits were unshaven. She was a broad-shouldered young woman with breasts not much bigger than Ingrid Moe's, and the astonishing hair in her armpits was a darker blond than the hair on her head. Over her navel, like a crumpled top hat the color of a wine stain, was a birthmark the shape of Florida.

When Alice began with the Jonesy roundback, Hannele pursed her lips and whistled. Jack had trouble following the tune over the sound of the tattoo machine. Hannele had placed herself on the window seat, with her legs spread wide apart. It was a most unladylike position, but Hannele was wearing blue jeans and she was, after all, a cellist; no doubt she sat that way when she played.

Years later, when a naked woman played the cello for Jack, he would remember Hannele and wonder if she'd ever performed naked for William. Jack would again feel ashamed that he might have such a moment in common with his dad. He would understand what must have attracted William to Hannele. She was a brave girl, without question; she went right on whistling, even when Alice's outline of her half-a-heart touched her rib cage.

While Alice was shading Hannele's broken heart with the Rodgers, Jack sat on the big bed with the short, plump girl. Her name was Ritva; she had bigger breasts than Hannele, and Jack was trying to stay awake until it was Ritva's turn to get her half-a-heart.

He must have looked sleepy because his mom said: "Why don't you brush your teeth, Jack, and get into your pajamas."

The boy got up and brushed his teeth in the sink, where he was repeatedly told not to drink the water. Alice kept a pitcher of drinking water on the washstand, and Jack was instructed to rinse his mouth out with the drinking water after he brushed his teeth.

He put on his pajamas while hiding behind the open door to the wardrobe closet, so that neither Ritva nor Hannele would see him naked. Then he got back on the bed beside Ritva, who pulled the bedcovers down. Jack lay still, with his head on the pillow, while Ritva tucked him in. There was only the sound of the tattoo machine and Hannele's faint but brave whistling.

"Sweet dreams, Jack," Ritva said; she kissed him good night. "Isn't that what you say in English?" she asked Alice. " 'Sweet dreams'?"

"Sometimes," Alice said. Jack noticed the truculence in her voice; it seemed unfamiliar to him.

Maybe "sweet dreams" was a phrase William used. It could have been something he'd said to Alice and Ritva *and* Hannele— because Hannele's brave whistling stopped for a second, as if the pain of the shading needles on her left breast and that side of her rib cage had suddenly become unbearable. Jack guessed it was the "sweet dreams" that had hurt her, not the tattoo.

The boy was fighting sleep; involuntarily, his eyes would close and he would reach out his hand and feel Ritva's soft sweater and the fingers of her warm hand closing around his smaller fingers.

Jack might have heard his mother say, "I don't suppose you know where he's gone."

"He didn't tell us," Hannele may have answered, between whistles.

"He's got you and Jack hounding him," Jack distinctly heard Ritva tell his mom. "I guess that's enough."

"He said 'hounding,' did he?" Alice asked.

"*I* said it," Ritva told her.

"We say it all the time," Hannele said.

"Wouldn't you agree that Jack is his responsibility?" Alice asked them.

They both agreed that Jack was his father's responsibility, but this was one of those Helsinki conversations that the boy at best half heard in his sleep. Jack woke once and saw Ritva's pretty face smiling down at him; from her expression, he knew she must have been imagining his dad in the unformed features of Jack's face. (Even today, Jack occasionally saw that pretty face in his dreams—or when he was falling asleep.)

He never did get to see Ritva's plump breasts—or learn if her armpits were unshaven, like Hannele's. When he woke again, Hannele's sleeping face was on the pillow beside him; she was wearing the cotton turtleneck but not the ski sweater. She must have fallen asleep while she was waiting for Alice to be finished with Ritva's half-a-heart tattoo. Jack could hear the tattoo machine, but his mother blocked the boy's view of Ritva's breasts and armpits. Over his mom's shoulder, Jack could see only Ritva's face; her eyes were tightly closed and she was grimacing in pain.

Hannele's sleeping face was very close to Jack's. Her lips were parted; her breath, which had lost the fruity scent of her chewing gum, was faintly bad. Her hair gave off a sweet-and-sour smell—like hot chocolate when it's stood around too long and turned bitter in the cup. Jack still wanted to kiss her. He inched his face nearer hers, holding his breath.

"Go to sleep, Jack," his mom said. Her back was to him; he had no idea how she knew he was awake.

Hannele's eyes opened wide; she stared at Jack. "You have eyelashes to die for," she said. "Isn't that what you say in English?" Hannele asked Alice. " 'To die for'?"

"Sometimes," Alice said.

Ritva choked back a sob.

Under the covers, Hannele's long fingers lifted Jack's pajama top and tickled his stomach. (Even today, he sometimes felt those fingers in his dreams—or when he was falling asleep.)

The knock on the hotel-room door was abrupt and loud; it woke Jack from a dream. The room was dark. His mother, snoring beside him, hadn't stirred. The boy recognized her snore. He knew it was her hand, not Hannele's, on his hip.

"Someone's at the door, Mom," Jack whispered, but she didn't hear him.

The knock came again, louder than before.

Occasionally the clientele at the American Bar got restless, waiting for Alice to return to the bar. Some drunk who wanted a tattoo would come to the room and pound on the door. Alice always sent the drunks away.

Jack sat up in bed and said in a shrill voice: "Too late for a tattoo!"

"I don't want a tattoo!" a man's angry voice shouted from the hall.

Jack had not seen his mother so startled since the night of the littlest soldier. She sat bolt-upright in bed and clutched Jack to her. "What do you want?" she cried.

"You want to know about The Music Man, don't you?" the man's voice answered. "Well, I tattooed him. I know all about him."

"Sami Salo?" Alice asked.

"Let's make a deal," Salo said. "First you open the door."

"Just a minute, Mr. Salo."

Alice got out of bed and covered her nightgown with a robe. She took out her flash, her best work, and spread it over the bed. Jack, in his pajamas, lay adrift in the maritime world—a child on a bed of hearts and flowers, ships in full sail, and half-naked girls in grass skirts. The four-year-old lay amid snakes and anchors, among Sailor's Graves and Roses of Jericho, and his mom's version of Man's Ruin. There was her Key to My Heart and her Naked Lady (from the back side) with Butterfly Wings—the latter emerging from a tulip.

· The boy lay among her flash as if he'd just awakened from a tattoo dream. When Alice opened the door to Sami Salo, she stepped aside and let him walk past her into her world. He was a scratcher, as Alice had guessed; she knew he could never avert his eyes from her superior work.

"The deal is . . ." Salo started to say; then he stopped. He scarcely glanced at Jack—the flash had seized his attention completely.

Sami Salo was a haggard-looking older man with a gaunt, soul-searching expression; he wore a navy-blue watch cap pulled down over his ears and a peacoat of the same color. He was sweating from wearing his winter clothes on his walk up four flights of stairs, and his breathing was ragged. He didn't speak; he simply stared at Alice's best work.

Salo's favorite might have been a toss-up between Alice's Rose of Jericho and her Key to My Heart—the key held horizontally against the naked lady's breasts, the keyhole you-know-where. (The tattoo was unique among Alice's naked ladies in that the lady was *not* seen from the back side.)

To judge him by his defeated expression, Sami Salo was his own version of Man's Ruin. "The deal is . . ." Alice prompted him.

Salo removed his watch cap as if he were about to bow his head in prayer. He unbuttoned his peacoat, too, but he just stood there. He wore a dirty-white sweater under the peacoat; the faded-gray fingers of a skeleton's hand reached above the crew neck of the sweater, as if holding Salo by the throat. It was as bad an idea as any tattoo Alice had ever seen—or so Jack concluded from his mother's expression. It was a blessing that the rest of the skeleton was covered by the sweater.

Jack and Alice didn't see any of Sami Salo's other tattoos—nor was Salo in a mood to converse.

"The deal is," he began again, "I tell you about The Music Man and you leave town. I don't care where you go."

"I'm sorry your business is suffering," Alice told him.

He accepted her apology with a nod. Jack was embarrassed for the poor man; the boy buried his head under the pillows. "I'm sorry if my wife spoke rudely to you at the restaurant," Salo may have said. "She doesn't much like having to work nights."

His wife would have been the opinionated waitress at Salve, Jack guessed. With his head under the pillows, the four-year-old found that the adult world seemed a nicer place. Even Jack could tell that Mr. Salo was a lot older than his overworked wife, who looked young enough to be his daughter.

Their apologies stated, there was little more that Alice and Sami Salo needed to say to each other.

"Amsterdam," the scratcher said. "When I inked a bit of Bach on his backside, he said he was going to Amsterdam."

"Jack and I will leave Helsinki as soon as we can arrange our travel," Alice told him.

"You're a talented lady," Jack heard Salo say; he sounded as if he was already in the hall.

"Thank you, Mr. Salo," Alice replied, closing the door.

At least Amsterdam was a town on their itinerary. Jack couldn't wait to see Tattoo Peter, and his one leg.

"We mustn't forget St. John's Church, Jack," his mother said. Jack had thought they were on their way to the shipping office, but he was wrong. "That was where your father played. We should at least see it."

They were close to the sea. It had snowed overnight; the branches of the trees drooped with the heavy seaside snow.

"Johanneksen kirkko," Alice told the taxi driver. (She even knew how to pronounce the name of the church in Finnish!)

St. John's was huge—a red-brick Gothic edifice with two towers, the twin spires shining a pale green in the sunlight. The wooden pews were a dark blond that reminded Jack of the hair in Hannele's armpits. The church bells heralded their arrival. According to Alice, the three bells played the first three notes of Handel's *Te Deum*.

"C sharp, E, F sharp," the former choirgirl whispered.

The round altarpiece featured a tall, thin painting—the conversion of Paul on his way to Damascus. The organ was a Walcker from Württemberg, built in 1891. It had been restored in 1956 and had seventy-four registers. Jack knew that registers were the same as stops; he didn't know if the number of registers made a difference in how loud an organ was, or how rich it sounded. (Since William Burns had been demonized in Jack's eyes, the boy didn't have a consuming interest in his father's instrument.)

In Helsinki, on such a sunny day, the light through the stained glass sparkled on the pipes, as if the organ—even without an organist—was about to burst into sound all by itself. But the organist was there to greet them. Alice must have made an appointment to see him. His name was Kari Vaara, and he was a hearty man with wild-looking hair; he appeared to have, seconds ago, stuck his head out the window of a speeding train. His actions were marked by the nervous habit of clasping his hands together, as if he were about to make a life-altering confession or fall to his knees—the suddenly shattered witness to a miracle.

"Your father is a very talented musician," Vaara said almost worshipfully to Jack, who was speechless; the boy wasn't used to hearing his dad *praised.* "But talent must be nurtured, or it withers." His voice sounded like the lower registers of an organ.

"We know about Amsterdam," Alice interjected. She appeared fearful that Kari Vaara was about to reveal a terrible truth—something in the not-around-Jack category.

"Not just Amsterdam," the organist intoned. Jack looked at the Walcker organ, half expecting it to issue a refrain. "He's going to play in the Oude Kerk."

The reverence with which Vaara spoke was wasted on Jack, but his mom was glad to know the church's name.

"The organ there is special, I suppose," Alice said.

Kari Vaara took a deep breath, as if he were once more preparing to stick his head out the window of that speeding train. "The organ in the Oude Kerk is *vast,*" he said.

Jack must have scuffed his feet or cleared his throat, because Vaara again turned his attention to him. "I told your father that *big* is not necessarily *best,* but he is a young man who must see for himself."

"Yes, he has always had to see everything for himself," Alice chimed in.

"Not always a bad thing," Vaara offered.

"Not always a *good* thing," Alice countered.

Kari Vaara leaned over Jack. The boy could smell the soap on the organist's clasped hands. "Perhaps *you* have talent for the organ," Vaara said. He unclasped his hands and spread his arms wide, as if to embrace the Walcker. "Would you like to play?"

"Over my dead body," Alice said, taking Jack's hand.

They went up the aisle and out of the Johanneksen kirkko. The sunlight was shimmering on the newfallen snow. "Mrs. Burns!" Vaara called after them. (Had she told him she was Mrs. Burns?) "They say that in the Oude Kerk, one plays to both tourists and prostitutes!"

"Not around Jack," Alice said, over her shoulder. Their taxi driver was waiting; the shipping office was their next stop.

"I mean only that the church is in the red-light district," Vaara explained.

Alice stumbled slightly, but she regained her balance and squeezed Jack's hand.

There was mention of traveling by ship from Helsinki to Hamburg, and then taking the train from Hamburg to Amsterdam. But that was the long way to go, and perhaps Alice was afraid she might *stay* in Hamburg; her desire to meet and work with Herbert Hoffmann was that strong. (Maybe they wouldn't have gone back to Canada; Jack might never have attended St. Hilda's, and all the rest.) She'd sent Hoffmann so many postcards that Jack had memorized the address—8 Hamburger Berg. If they had sailed to Hamburg—if they'd seen St. Pauli and the Reeperbahn, and Herbert Hoffmann's Tätowierstube at 8 Hamburger Berg—they might have stayed.

But they found passage on a freighter from Helsinki to Rotterdam. (In those days, freighters frequently had passenger accommodations.) Then they took the train from Rotterdam to Amsterdam, a short trip. Jack remembered that train ride. It was raining; some of the fields were flooded. It was still winter, but there wasn't any snow. Out the window of the train, it looked as if spring would never come. Alice rested her forehead against the pane.

"Isn't the glass cold?" Jack asked.

"It feels good," she replied. "Maybe I have a fever."

Jack felt her forehead—she didn't feel too warm to him. She shut her eyes and nodded off. Across the aisle, a businessman-type kept glancing at Alice. Jack stared at the man until he looked away. Even at four, the boy could stare anybody down.

Jack was excited about Tattoo Peter's one leg, and he must have been trying to imagine the size of the *vast* organ in the Oude Kerk. But a question of a different kind popped into his head.

"Mom?" he whispered. He had to speak a little louder to wake her from her sleep. *"Mom?"*

"Yes, my little actor," she whispered back; she hadn't opened her eyes.

"What is the red-light district?"

Alice gazed without seeing out the window of the rushing train. When she shut her eyes again, the businessman across the aisle sneaked another look at her. "Well," Alice said, with her eyes still closed, "I guess we're going to find out."

6

God's Holy Noise

After Amsterdam, Alice was a different woman—one whose small measure of self-confidence and sense of moral worth had been all but obliterated. Jack must have noticed that his mother had changed—not that he would have known why.

On the Zeedijk, the northeastern-most street of the red-light district, there was a tattoo parlor called De Rode Draak—The Red Dragon. The tattoo artist in that shop, Theo Rademaker, was called Tattoo Theo. The nickname mocked Rademaker because, in Amsterdam, he was forever in the shadow of Tattoo *Peter*.

Rademaker's second-rate reputation didn't discourage William Burns, who'd had Tattoo Theo etch a cramped fragment from Samuel Scheidt, "We All Believe in One God," in a crescent shape on his coccyx. The music was partially obscured by the words, *"Wir glauben all' an einen Gott"*—it was William's first tattoo in Amsterdam.

He was later tattooed by Tattoo Peter, who told him Tattoo Theo's work was amateurish and gave The Music Man a Bach tattoo—"Jesu, meine Freude" ("Jesus, My Joy"). Tattoo Peter wouldn't say where—only that the music and the words were, in this case, not at war with each other.

His real name was Peter de Haan, and he was arguably the most famous tattoo artist of his day. Tattoo Peter's lost leg was one of the more tantalizing mysteries of Jack's childhood; it was a gift to the boy's imagination that his mom refused to tell him how it happened. What chiefly impressed Alice was that Peter de Haan had tattooed Herbert Hoffmann, and the two men were friends.

Tattoo Peter's shop was in the basement of a house on the St. Olofssteeg—thus William was tattooed twice in the red-light district. William Burns was a man who was meant to be musically marked for life, Tattoo Peter said, but Alice would be marked for life because of him.

The basement shop on the St. Olofssteeg was very warm. Peter frequently took off his shirt when he tattooed a client; he told Alice that it gave the customer confidence in him as a tattoo artist. Jack understood this to mean that the client couldn't help but admire Tattoo Peter's own tattoos.

"In that case," Alice told Peter, "I'll keep my shirt on." What Jack made of this was perfectly logical: since his mom didn't have any tattoos of her own, the customer might lose confidence in her altogether.

Peter de Haan was a fair-skinned, bell-shaped man with a pleasant, clean-shaven face and lustrous, slicked-back hair. He usually wore dark trousers and sat with his one leg facing the entrance to the tattoo parlor—the stump of his missing leg half hidden on a wooden bench or stool. He sat with his back very straight; he maintained excellent posture sitting down. But Jack never saw him stand.

Did he use crutches or two canes; or, like a pirate, did he strap on a peg leg? Did he come and go in a wheelchair? Jack didn't know—he never saw Peter come or go.

Jack would one day hear that Peter's son was his apprentice, but Jack remembered seeing only one other apprentice at Tattoo Peter's besides his mom. He was a scary man named Jacob Bril. (Possibly Bril made such an impression on Jack that he simply forgot Peter's son.)

Jacob Bril had his own tattoo parlor in Rotterdam; he closed it on the weekends and came to Amsterdam, where he worked at Tattoo Peter's from noon to midnight every Saturday. His faithful clientele would line up to see him; every fan of Bril's was a dedicated Christian.

Jacob Bril was small and wiry—an austere skeleton of a man—and he gave only religious tattoos, of which his favorite was the Ascension. On Bril's bony back was a depiction of Christ departing this world in the company of angels. In Bril's version, Heaven was a dark and cloudy place, but his angels had splendid wings.

For the chest, Jacob Bril recommended Christ's Agony—Our Savior's head bleeding in His crown of thorns. Christ's hands and feet and side were also bleeding; according to Bril, the blood was essential. On his own chest, in addition to Our Savior's bloody head, Jacob Bril had a sacred text—the Lord's Prayer. On his upper arms and forearms were a Virgin Mary, a Christ Child, and two Mary Magdalenes—one with a halo, one without. He'd saved his stomach for that most frightening figure of Lazarus leaving the grave. (Alice liked to say that the Lazarus tattoo was responsible for Bril's indigestion.)

It was reasonable to hope that the two Mary Magdalenes might predispose Bril to forgiveness—especially in regard to those working women in their windows and doorways in the red-light district. But Bril made his disapproval of the prostitutes plain. From where he got off the train, at the Central Station, Jacob Bril could have walked to Tattoo Peter's on the St. Olofssteeg without once passing a prostitute; in fact, the most direct route from the train station to the tattoo parlor did not go through the district. But Bril stayed in a hotel on the Dam Square, the Krasnapolsky. (In those days, the Krasnapolsky was considered quite a fancy hotel; it was certainly too fancy for Bril.) And whether leaving or returning to the Krasnapolsky, Bril made a point of walking every street of the red-light district—both to and from Tattoo Peter's.

When he walked, Jacob Bril's pace was as quick as his rush to judgment. Two canals divided the district; Bril patrolled both banks of the two, as well as the side streets. In the narrowest alleys, where the women in their doorways were close enough to touch, Bril hurried by at a frenzied pace. The women who saw him coming withdrew as he passed. (Jack used to think it was because Bril caused a draft.) One day, Jack and his mom followed Bril from the Krasnapolsky. They couldn't match the little man's speed; Jack would have had to run just to keep Bril in sight.

The Krasnapolsky was an overfancy hotel for Jack and Alice—not just for Jacob Bril—but they'd had a bad experience in a cheaper place. De Roode Leeuw (The Red Lion) was on the Damrak, just opposite a department store where Jack once became separated from his mother and managed to get lost for five or ten minutes.

At The Red Lion, Jack was fascinated by a rat he found in the hotel's poolroom, behind the rack for the pool cues. Jack discovered that by inserting a cue in one end of the rack and wiggling it, he could make the rat run out the other side.

The Red Lion was a hotel favored by sales reps. A previous guest had left a sizable stash of marijuana in one of Jack's bureau drawers. Jack discovered it while looking for his underwear, and used it to replace the bedraggled hay in a crèche his mom had given him at Christmastime in Copenhagen. Thus Jack's Little Lord Jesus lay in a bed of pot, and Mary and Joseph and various kings and shepherds (together with an assortment of other crèche figures) were knee-deep in hemp, not hay, when Alice discovered them. She was led to the crèche by the smell.

De Roode Leeuw was not the hotel for them, Alice said, but Jack never saw her throw the marijuana away. They moved to the Krasnapolsky. Staying in a hotel above their means was becoming old hat for Jack and Alice, although being in the same hotel with Jacob Bril would never have been their first choice. The rat at The Red Lion was friendlier than Bril was.

As for trying to follow Jacob Bril through the red-light district, Jack and Alice tried it only that once. Not only was Bril too fast—he didn't appreciate their company. Usually, when Jack and his mother walked through the district to and from Tattoo Peter's, they liked to play a game. They tried to take a slightly different route each time; that way, they got to know all the prostitutes. Most of them were friendly. In a short while, they knew Jack's name; they called his mom by her tattoo name, Daughter Alice.

The few women in their doorways and windows who were unfriendly to Jack and Alice were conspicuously so. Most of them were older women—to Jack, some of them looked old enough to be his mother's mother—but a few of the younger women were unfriendly as well.

One of the younger ones was bold enough to speak to Alice. "This is no place to be with a child," she said.

"I have to work, too," Alice told her.

In those days, most of the women in the red-light district were Dutch—many of them not from Amsterdam. If a woman from Amsterdam wanted to be a prostitute, she might go to The Hague; women from The Hague, or from other Dutch cities, or the country girls, came to Amsterdam. (Less of a scandal for the family; not so much shame.)

This was around the time families came to Holland from their native Suriname. To see a brown-skinned woman in the red-light district in 1970 was increasingly common. And before the Surinamese, there were the brown-skinned girls of a lighter hue from Indonesia—a former Dutch colony.

It was one of the darker-brown women from Suriname who gave Jack a present. What surprised him was that he'd never seen her before, but she knew his name.

She was in a window, not in the red-light district but on either the Korsjespoortsteeg or the Bergstraat, where Jack and his mom went to make some inquiries about his dad. Jack thought the Surinamese woman was a mannequin—she was sitting so still, and she was so statuesque—but she suddenly came out on the street and gave him a chocolate the color of her skin.

"I've been saving this for you, Jack," she said. The boy was too surprised to speak. His mother reproved him for not thanking the woman properly.

Most weekday mornings, when Jack and his mom walked through the red-light district on their way to Tattoo Peter's, not many women were working—they went to work earlier on the weekends. At night, of course, every red light was on and the district was teeming; sometimes the prostitutes who knew and liked Jack and Alice were too busy to say their names, or so much as nod in their direction.

Even before the spring came, when the weather was still cool, the women were more often in their doorways than their windows; they liked to talk to one another. They wore high heels and short skirts, and blouses or sweaters with low necklines, but at least they wore clothes. And their friendliness—to Jack, if not always to his mother—enabled Alice to mislead her son about the nature of prostitution.

In those days, one saw only men visiting the prostitutes; Jack observed that the men looked most unhappy to be seen doing so. And when the men left, they were always in a hurry, which stood in sharp contrast to how slowly they had walked in the district (and how many times they'd passed a particular prostitute's doorway or window) before they *finally* made up their minds about which woman to visit.

Alice explained that this was because they were unhappy and indecisive men to begin with. A prostitute, Jack's mom told him, was a woman who gave advice to men who had difficulty understanding women in general—or one woman, such as a wife, in particular. The reason the men looked ashamed of themselves was that they knew they should really be having such an important and personal conversation with their wives or girlfriends, but they were inexplicably unable or unwilling to do so. They were "blocked," Alice said. Women were a mystery to them; they could pour out their hearts only to strangers, for a price.

Jack didn't know who paid whom, until his mom explained that the men did the paying. It was an awful job to have to listen to these miserable men, his mother said. She clearly took pity on the prostitutes, so Jack did, too; she had contempt for the men, so he also had contempt for them.

But Jack and Alice's contempt could never measure up to that of Jacob Bril. Bril had a palpable scorn for the prostitutes *and* their customers. He was full of contempt for Jack and his mom, too. It was because she was an unwed mother and Jack was an illegitimate child, Alice told her son.

Bril also disapproved of Alice because she was a tattoo artist; he said that it was not a decent woman's business to touch half-naked men. Bril himself would not tattoo a woman—except on her hand or forearm, or on her foot or ankle. Any higher up her leg was "too high," he said; any other part of a woman's body was "too intimate."

Women seeking religious tattoos on either too high or too intimate a part of their bodies were told to see Daughter Alice, although Bril disapproved of her giving religious tattoos. She was not religious enough to do them sincerely, he said.

Alice did a small, pretty cross with roses, which young women liked to tuck in their cleavage—as if the cross were an overlong necklace with an invisible chain. She did a Christ on the Cross that was shoulder-blade-size. (It lacked some of the agony and much of the blood of Bril's dying Jesus.) And she did Our Savior's head in His crown of thorns, usually on an upper arm or thigh, which Bril criticized because he found her Christ's expression "too ecstatic."

"Maybe my Jesus is already entering Heaven," Alice explained.

Jacob Bril dismissed this with a violent gesture. He drew his forearm across his chest, as if he were about to give Alice a whack with the back of his bony hand.

"Not in my shop, Bril," Tattoo Peter told him.

"Not around Jack." (Alice's usual refrain.)

Bril looked at the two of them with a venom he normally reserved for the prostitutes.

Jack and Alice never saw Jacob Bril leave Tattoo Peter's, which he did every Saturday at midnight, when the red-light district was overflowing in the relentless pursuit of its principal enterprise—every girl was working. Jack would wonder later how long it took Bril to get back to the Krasnapolsky, passing every prostitute in every window and doorway.

Did his pace never slow? Was there ever a woman who made him stop walking? Did the fire and brimstone only leave his eyes when Bril was asleep, or did Hell burn even more brightly in his dreams?

Many Saturdays, because Alice disliked sharing Tattoo Peter's otherwise warm shop with Jacob Bril, Peter would propose that she take her talents over to the Zeedijk and see if she could teach a thing or two to Theo Rademaker at The Red Dragon.

"Poor Tattoo Theo," Peter would say. "I'll bet he could use a break today. Or a lesson from Daughter Alice."

The much-maligned Tattoo Theo was not in the category of a scratcher; he simply had the misfortune to share the red-light district with a tattoo artist as good as Tattoo Peter. Rademaker was by no means as bad as Sami Salo or Trond Halvorsen—it was judgment that he lacked, Alice said, not ability. And Alice liked Tattoo Theo's young apprentice, Robbie de Wit. It was well known in the neighborhood that Robbie doted on her.

Jack and Alice skipped Jacob Bril's company whenever they could. (Bril hardly missed them; he wanted them gone.) De Rode Draak was a welcome change of scenery for Jack and his mom—lots of tourists went there, especially on a Saturday. Some of those Saturdays, if Tattoo Peter had more clients than he and Jacob Bril could handle, Peter was generous enough to send his customers to The Red Dragon—cautioning them to ask for Daughter Alice.

Rademaker must have been grateful for the extra business, though it may have caused him some inner pain to hear a new client request Alice. Tattoo Theo liked Alice, and she liked him. For Jack and his mother, their life had a pattern again; their first weeks in the red-light district were not unlike their happiest days in Copenhagen with Tattoo Ole and Ladies' Man Madsen.

Like Lars, Robbie de Wit made an effort to win Alice's affection by being nice to Jack. While Alice liked Robbie, that was as far as it went. She shared Robbie's fondness for Bob Dylan; they both sang along with the Dylan songs that drowned out the sound of the tattoo machines in De Rode Draak. Rademaker liked Dylan, too. He called Dylan by his real name, which he always said in the German way—as it would turn out, incorrectly.

"Shall we listen again to der Zimmerman?" Tattoo Theo would say, winking at Jack, who was in charge of playing the old albums. (In German, one listens to *den* Zimmerman.)

Jack liked the wisp of whiskers on Robbie de Wit's chin, which reminded him of Ladies' Man Madsen's efforts to grow a beard in the same place. Because Jack's crèche figures, including the Baby Jesus, still smelled like pot, he recognized the sweet scent of marijuana in Robbie's hand-rolled cigarettes, but the boy didn't keep count of how many times his mother might have taken a toke. She said it helped her to follow the tune when she sang along with Bob.

Rademaker had worked on a fishing boat one summer off the coast of Alaska; an "Eskimo tattooer" had given him the tattoo of the seal on his chest and the one of the Kodiak bear on his back.

Relatively speaking, Jack and his mother were happy—or so it seemed to Jack.

His mom sent another postcard to Mrs. Wicksteed. At the time, Jack didn't know that Mrs. Wicksteed had sent them money; that they continued to stay in hotels above their means was, in part, Mrs. Wicksteed's idea. She was a good Old Girl, all right. (Maybe Mrs. Wicksteed believed that a good hotel was as much a safeguard of Alice's future as losing her Scottish accent.)

The postcard was of one of Amsterdam's narrow canals; of course you couldn't see the prostitutes in their windows or doorways in the picture. "*Jack sends his love to Lottie,*" Alice wrote. Jack wouldn't remember if there was more to the message. He drew a smiling face next to Lottie's name; there was just enough room beside the face for him to write the initial *J.*

"Lottie will know who it is," his mom assured him.

Off to Toronto went the postcard with Jack's happy face.

· But what about that little boy whose capacity for consecutive memory, when he was three, was comparable to that of a nine-year-old? What had happened to Jack's retention of detail and understanding of linear time, which, when he was four, were equal to an eleven-year-old's?

Not in Amsterdam, where Jack imagined he had lived with his mother for a couple of months before they ever set foot in the Oude Kerk and heard that *vast* organ. In reality, of course, Alice wouldn't have waited a week to go there.

The Oude Kerk, the Old Church in the center of the red-light district, was probably consecrated in 1306 by the Bishop of Utrecht and is the oldest building in Amsterdam. The church survived two great fires—the first in 1421, the second in 1452—and the altars were badly damaged in the iconoclastic fury of 1566. In 1578, when Amsterdam officially became a Protestant city, the Oude Kerk was stripped of its Roman Catholic decoration and renovated to suit the Protestant religious service. The pulpit dates from 1643, the choir screen from 1681. Rembrandt's first wife is buried in the Old Church, and there are five tombs in commemoration of seventeenth-century Dutch sea heroes.

The organ, which Kari Vaara correctly called *vast,* is also old. It was built by Christian Vater of Hamburg, Germany, in 1726. It took Vater two years to build the huge and beautiful instrument of forty-three stops, which went immediately out of tune the moment more than one register was pulled. The organ's failure was also vast—for eleven years, it was out of tune. Finally, a man named Müller was assigned the task of dismantling the Vater organ to investigate the problem. It took him five years to fix it.

Even so, the organ in the Oude Kerk continued to be out of tune most of the time; it is tuned before every concert because of the temperature in the old building—the Oude Kerk cannot be heated properly.

It was cold in the Old Church that day, and Jack and his mom sat on the organ bench with the *junior* organist—a dough-faced kid who was too young to shave. He was a child prodigy, apparently. Alice said she was told all about the youngster's talent by the *senior* organist, Jacob Venderbos, who'd been too busy to see her. (Venderbos also played the organ at the Westerkerk in Amsterdam, and at churches in Haarlem and Delft.) Alice got to talk to his fifteen-year-old apprentice instead.

The young genius's name was Frans Donker, and he was as afraid of Alice as any boy that age could be. Like Andreas Breivik, he couldn't look at her when he talked. As near as Jack could tell, what his mother learned from the frightened child prodigy was that Kari Vaara had been wrong to think that his father had been hired to play the organ in the Oude Kerk—he'd been hired only to keep it in tune. For this ongoing and demanding service, William was permitted to practice on the vast instrument. It was indeed a special organ, Frans Donker told Jack and Alice—"both great and difficult"—and William not only kept it in better tune than anyone could remember; his practice sessions were both famous and infamous. (By now Jack was distracted by the smell of baby powder and thoroughly confused.)

"I have the greatest respect for William—as an organist," young Donker was saying.

"I thought he was just an organ-*tuner* now," Alice replied.

Frans Donker let her remark pass. He solemnly explained that, from early morning through the evening, the Oude Kerk was a most active church. In addition to the religious services and choir rehearsals, various cultural events, which were open to the public, were scheduled at night—not only concerts and recitals, but also lectures and poetry readings. It simply wouldn't do to have someone tuning an organ during the Old Church's lengthy working hours.

"So when did he do it?" Alice asked.

"Well . . ." Young Donker hesitated. Maybe he said, "William wouldn't start the tuning until after midnight. Most nights, he wouldn't begin his practice sessions until two or three in the morning."

"So he was playing to an empty church?" Alice asked.

"Well . . ." Frans Donker hesitated again. Jack was completely bored, his mind elsewhere, but he thought he heard Donker say: "The Oude Kerk is a very big church, a very *reverberant* building. The reverberation time is five seconds." The child prodigy glanced at Jack and explained: "That's the time it takes for the echo of what you play to come back to you."

"Oh," the boy said; he was falling asleep.

Young Donker couldn't stop explaining. "Your father's favorite Bach toccatas were written with the effect of a big space in mind. Space enlarges music—"

"Forget the music," Alice interrupted him. "Was he playing to an empty church?"

"Well . . ."

If what followed was hard for Alice to understand, it was way over a four-year-old's head. If the reverberation time *within* the Oude Kerk was five seconds, how long did it take for the echo of the organ in Bach's most dramatic works—his D Minor Toccata, for example—to reach the prostitutes in their rooms on the Oudekerksplein, the horseshoe-shaped street that surrounded the Old Church? (Six or seven seconds, maybe? Or did the whores hear it in five seconds, too?)

Outside the church, the organ would have been muted, but at two or three in the morning, when the action in the red-light district was winding down, the cold winter air would have carried the sound well beyond the Oudekerksplein. The women working in the narrowest, nastiest alley—in the nearby Trompettersteeg— would have had no trouble hearing William Burns playing his beloved Handel or his favorite Bach. Even across the canal, on the far side of the Oudezijds Voorburgwal, the prostitutes still standing in their doorways would have heard him.

"At that time of night, many of the older prostitutes are ready to go home—they stop working," Frans Donker managed to say, with trepidation—as if this part of his story might be in not-around-Jack territory. (Donker didn't know that Jack believed prostitutes were simply tireless advice-givers, trying to teach the most pathetic of men what they needed to learn about women.)

There were many older prostitutes working in the red-light district in those days—some in their sixties—and a lot of them worked in the ground-floor rooms surrounding the Old Church. The older women in the district might have been more easily moved by church music than their younger counterparts, although Donker admitted that a few of the younger prostitutes became overnight fans of Bach and Handel.

"You mean the prostitutes came to hear him play?" Alice asked.

Frans fidgeted on the organ bench; he slid to one side, then the other, on the smooth leather seat. (*There's that baby-powder smell again,* Jack was thinking.)

Years later, the smell of baby powder would remind Jack of the prostitutes; he could almost see the tired women taking their makeup off and hanging the costumes of their profession in their small closets. They didn't wear high heels or short skirts when they went home—or when they came to work in the morning or afternoon. Their street clothes were blue jeans or old slacks; their boots or heavy shoes had no heels to speak of, and they usually wore an unflattering but warm-looking coat and a wool hat. They didn't look like prostitutes, except that it was two or three in the morning and what other sort of woman would be out at that time by herself?

What was it about the organ music that arrested them and held them captive in the red-light district for an hour or two longer? Frans Donker explained that there would usually be a dozen or more women in the Old Church, and that many of them stayed until William stopped playing; this was often as late as four or five in the morning, when the Oude Kerk was very cold.

William Burns had found his audience—he was playing to prostitutes!

"They certainly appreciated him," the boy genius continued—with the authority that only a child prodigy, or a lunatic, possesses. "I occasionally got up at that time to hear him play myself. Each time I came, more women were here. He's very good—William knows his Bach and Handel cold."

"Forget the music," Alice said again. "Just tell me what happened."

"It seems that one of the women took him home with her—actually, more than one of them did."

But that wasn't what happened, or all that happened. (This time, blame the baby powder for Jack's loss of concentration.)

The administration of the Oude Kerk probably believed it was unsavory—that William should be playing to prostitutes, not to mention consorting with them. After all, it was a church. They must have fired him, or something like that. And the prostitutes—a few of the older ones, anyway—made a fuss. There was a protest. Amsterdam was always having demonstrations. From the Krasnapolsky, Jack and Alice had seen their share of demonstrations in the Dam Square. It was the time of the hippies. Alice was tattooing a lot of peace symbols, and (often in the genital area of both boys and girls) that insipid slogan of the times *Make love, not war.* Surely one or more of the protests they witnessed were anti–Vietnam War demonstrations.

Maybe the prostitutes in the red-light district took William's side *and* they took him in. "They saw him as a persecuted artist," Frans Donker said. "Some of them see themselves that way."

As for where William was now, the boy genius looked at Jack, not at Alice, when he spoke: "You'd have to ask the prostitutes. I'd start with the older ones."

Alice knew which prostitutes to ask. They were mostly, but not all, the older ones; they were the women in the district who'd been conspicuously unfriendly.

"Thank you for your time," Alice told the junior organist. She got up from the bench and held out her hand to Jack.

"Don't you want me to play something for you?" Frans Donker asked. Jack's mother was already pulling her son to the narrow stairs. They were in a kind of loft at the rear of the Old Church's great hall, above and hidden from the congregation; the towering organ pipes rose for twenty feet or more above them.

"Play something William plays, if you want to," Alice told the young organist. She had no intention of staying to listen.

As they were leaving, Jack saw Donker sprinkle the leather bench with baby powder. It *was* baby powder! The seat of the prodigy's pants was covered with it. The powder helped him slide sideways along the bench. He couldn't reach from one end of the three-tiered keyboard to the other without sliding left to right, and back again, on the slippery leather.

A wooden pediment rose over the keyboard; the wood was riddled with screw holes where the old brass fittings had fallen or been stripped away. The organist's only view, beyond his music, was confined to a panel of stained glass. Everything surrounding Donker was old and worn, but none of this mattered when he began to play.

Alice could not escape the Oude Kerk in time. The deep sonority, the perfect tone placement, the responding antiphony, and the resounding echo—Bach's Toccata and Fugue in D Minor—hit them hard as they were going down the stairs. Jack would long remember the wooden handrail on one side of their winding descent. What served as a handrail on the other side was a waxed rope the color of burned caramel; the rope was as thick as a man's wrist.

They staggered out of the stairway as if the great sound had made them drunk. Alice was seeking a hasty exit from the church, but she made a wrong turn. They found themselves in the center aisle, facing the altars; now they were surrounded by the enormous noise.

In the middle of where the congregation normally sat was a bewildered gathering of tourists. A tour guide appeared to have been struck mute in midsentence—his mouth open, as if the

Bach were coming from him. Whatever lecture he'd been delivering would have to wait for the toccata and fugue to be finished.

Outside on the Oudekerksplein, in the failing early-evening light, the prostitutes in their windows and doorways could hear the music, too. It was evident that they knew the piece Donker was playing; doubtless they'd listened to Bach's Toccata and Fugue in D Minor many times in the early-morning hours. By the prostitutes' critical expressions, Jack and his mother knew that William played this piece better than young Frans.

Jack and Alice hurried away. It was no time to make inquiries of the unfriendly women—not while the music was playing. The great sound followed them to the Warmoesstraat; God's holy noise pursued them past the police station. They were more than halfway to Tattoo Peter's on the St. Olofssteeg before the vast organ was out of earshot.

Was William's career as an organist in decline? Was he merely *tuning* organs, practicing but not performing—or performing only at unsociable hours to an unrefined audience? Or was it actually a privilege just to *hear* that vast organ in the Oude Kerk?

It was a sound both huge and holy. It compelled even prostitutes, who are disinclined to do anything without being paid, to give themselves over to it absolutely—to just *listen*.

7

Also Not on Their Itinerary

On November 9, 1939, Leith suffered its first German air raid. No damage was done to the port, but Alice's mother miscarried in an overcrowded air-raid shelter. "It was back then that I should have been born," Alice always said.

If Alice had been born "back then," her mother might not have died in childbirth and Alice might never have met William Burns—or if she met him, she would have been as old as he was. "In which case," she claimed, "I would have been impervious to his charms." (Jack somehow doubted this, even as a child.)

If the boy couldn't remember the name of the Surinamese prostitute who gave him a chocolate the color of her skin on either the Korsjespoortsteeg or the Bergstraat, he did remember that those two small streets, between the Singel and the Herengracht, were some distance from the red-light district—about a ten- or fifteen-minute walk—and the area was more residential and less seedy.

As to what rumor of William led Alice to make inquiries there, it was either Blond Nel or Black Lola who told her to consult The Bicycle Man, Uncle Gerrit. Black Lola was an older white woman whose hair was dyed jet-black, and Uncle Gerrit was a grouchy old man who did the prostitutes' shopping on his bicycle. He carried a notebook in which the women wrote down what they wanted for lunch or a snack. He objected to the girls who gave him too extensive a shopping list, and he refused to shop for tampons or condoms. (If there were a Tampon or Condom Man who did errands for the prostitutes, Jack and his mom never met him.)

The women teased Uncle Gerrit incessantly. He would stop shopping for a particular prostitute, just to punish her for teasing him—usually for only a couple of days. A rake-thin prostitute named Saskia was in the habit of asking Alice and Jack to buy her a sandwich. Saskia was a ceaselessly ravenous young woman, and Uncle Gerrit was always mad at her. She gave Jack or his mom the money for a ham-and-cheese croissant almost every time she saw them. When Jack and Alice passed by again, they would give Saskia the sandwich—provided she wasn't with a customer.

Because Saskia was a popular prostitute, Jack got to eat a lot of ham-and-cheese croissants. Alice didn't mind buying a sandwich for Saskia with her own money. Like many women in the red-light district, Saskia had a story to tell, and Alice was a good listener—that is, if you were a woman. (Women with sad stories seemed to know this about Alice, probably because they could see she was a sad story herself.)

Saskia had a two-man story. The first man to hurt her was a client who set fire to the poor girl in her room on the Bloedstraat. He tried to squirt her in the face with lighter fluid, but Saskia was able to shield her eyes and nose with her right forearm; she was badly burned, but only from her wrist to her elbow. When the wound healed, Saskia adorned her burn-scarred arm with bracelets. In the doorway of her room on the Bloedstraat, Saskia would extend the arm into the street and jingle her bracelets. It got your attention—you had to look at her. Saskia attracted a lot of customers that way.

She was too thin to be pretty—and she never opened her mouth when she smiled at a potential client, because her teeth were bad. "It's a good thing prostitutes aren't expected to kiss their customers," she told Jack, "because no one would want to kiss me." Then she grinned at the boy, showing him her broken and missing teeth.

"Maybe not around Jack," Alice cautioned her.

There was something wildly alluring about Saskia, with those jingling bracelets all on one arm—her left arm, the unburned one, was bare. Maybe men thought she was a woman who would lose control of herself; possibly her aura of a damage more internal than her burned arm attracted them. You could see, like a flame, the hurt in her eyes.

The second man in Saskia's two-man story was a client who beat her up because she wouldn't take her bracelets off. He'd heard about her burn and wanted to see the scar. (At the time,

Jack assumed this was a man in even more need of advice than the prostitutes' usual customers.)

Saskia made such a wail that four other women on the Bloedstraat and three girls who worked around the corner on the Oudezijds Achterburgwal heard her and came to her rescue. They dragged the man in acute need of advice out on the Bloedstraat, where they whipped and gouged him with coat hangers and hit him with a plumber's helper—all this before one of the women got a clean·shot at his head with the metal drain plug of a bidet, with which she beat him bloody. He was senseless and raving, and no doubt still in need of advice, when the police came and took him away.

"That was what happened to your teeth?" Jack asked Saskia.

"That's right, Jack," she said. "I show my burn scar only to people I like. Would you and your mom like to see it?"

"Of course," the boy replied.

"Only if we're not imposing," Alice answered.

"You're not imposing at all," Saskia said.

She took them into her small room, closing the door and the curtains as if Jack and his mother were her customers. Jack was astonished by how little furniture there was in the room—just a single bed and a night table. The lighting was low—only one lamp, with a red glass shade. The wardrobe closet was without a door; mostly underwear hung there, and a whip like a lion tamer would use.

There was a sink, and the kind of white enamel table you might expect to see in a hospital or a doctor's office. The table was piled high with towels, one of which was spread out on the bed—in case the men in need of advice were wearing wet clothes, Jack imagined. There was no place to sit except on the bed, which was an odd place to give or get advice, Jack thought, but it seemed natural enough to Saskia, who sat down on the bed and invited Jack and Alice to sit down beside her.

One by one, she took her bracelets off and handed them to Jack. In the red glow from the lamp with the glass shade, the boy and his mom examined the wrinkled, raw-looking surface of Saskia's scar, which resembled a scalded chicken neck. "Go on, Jack—you can touch it," she said. He did so reluctantly.

"Does it hurt?" he asked.

"Not anymore," Saskia replied.

"Do your teeth hurt?" the boy inquired.

"Not the missing ones, Jack." One by one, she let him put her bracelets back on; he was careful to do it in the right order, biggest to smallest.

Who could refuse to bring that thin, hungry girl a sandwich? Jack despised Uncle Gerrit, The Bicycle Man, for being so mad at Saskia that he refused to shop for her. But the cranky old prostitute-shopper had his reasons. He'd often parked his bicycle outside the Oude Kerk in the early-morning hours; he had more than once slipped into a pew in the Old Church and listened to the elevating music. Uncle Gerrit was a William Burns fan. Maybe Saskia wasn't.

"You should talk to Femke," The Bicycle Man said to Alice. "*I* was the one who told William to see her! Femke knows what's best for the boy!"

While this made no sense to Jack, he could tell that Uncle Gerrit was mad at his mother, too. Jack and his mom were standing on the Stoofsteeg as The Bicycle Man pedaled away. He turned the corner and pedaled past the Casa Rosso, where they showed porn films and had live-sex shows—not that Jack had a clue what they were. (More advice-giving, for all he knew.)

The prostitute in the doorway at the end of the Stoofsteeg was named Els. Jack thought she was about his mother's age, or only a little older. She had always been friendly. She'd grown up on a farm. Els told Jack and his mom that she expected she would one day see her father or her brothers in the red-light district. And wouldn't they be surprised to see her in a window or a doorway? She would not ask them in, she said. (They were somehow beyond advising, Jack assumed.)

"Who's Femke?" Jack asked his mom.

Els said: "I'll tell you Femke's story."

"Maybe not around Jack," Alice said.

"Come in and we'll see if I can tell it in a way that won't offend Jack," Els said. As it turned out, either Els or Alice would tell Femke's story in a way that totally confused the boy.

Els always wore a platinum-blond wig. Jack had never seen her real hair. When she put her big arm around Jack's shoulders and pulled his face against her hip, he could feel how strong she was—like you'd expect a former farm girl to be. And Els had the bust and the announcing décolletage of an opera singer; her bosom preceded her with the authority of a great ship's prow. When a woman like that says she'll tell you a story, you better pay attention.

But Jack was instantly distracted; to his surprise, Els's room was very much like Saskia's. Once again, there was no place to sit except on the bed, on which there was a towel spread out, and so the three of them sat there. Alice needn't have been concerned that Femke's story was not-around-Jack material. The boy was mesmerized by the prostitute's room and her gigantic breasts. Jack couldn't comprehend what Els had to say about Femke, who he thought was a relative newcomer to the advice-giving business. Confusingly, Femke was also the well-heeled ex-wife of an Amsterdam lawyer. Maybe they'd been partners in the same law firm—all Jack heard was something about a family law practice. And then the plot thickened: Femke had discovered that her husband made frequent visits to the more upscale prostitutes on the Korsjespoortsteeg and the Bergstraat. She'd been a faithful wife, but she made Dutch divorce history in more than the alimony department.

Femke bought a prominent room on the Bergstraat, on the corner of the Herengracht; it was unusual for a prostitute's room in that it had a basement window and the door was at the bottom of a small flight of stairs. Both the doorway and the window were below sidewalk level, so that pedestrians looked down at the prostitute, who was also visible from a passing car.

Was Femke so enraged that she would actually *buy* a room for prostitution and rent the space to a working prostitute—thus, eventually, making a profit from the sordid enterprise that had wrecked her marriage? Or did she have something more mischievous in mind? That Femke herself appeared in the basement window or the doorway on the Bergstraat, and that a few of her first clients were business associates of her former husband— including some gentlemen who had known the couple socially— was certainly a shock. (Apparently not to Femke—she was aware that she was attractive to most men, if not to her ex-husband.)

She was met with mixed reviews from her fellow prostitutes on the Korsjespoortsteeg and the Bergstraat. Her very public triumph over her former husband was much admired, and while it was appreciated that Femke had become an activist for prostitutes' rights—after all, she was a woman whose convictions, which were so bravely on display, had to be respected—she was herself not a *real* prostitute, or so some prostitutes (Els among them) believed.

Femke certainly didn't need the money; she could afford to be choosy, and she was. She turned many clients down—a luxury unknown to those women working in the red-light district *and* the prostitutes in their windows or doorways on the Korsjespoortsteeg and the Bergstraat. Furthermore, the customers Femke turned down were humiliated. The first-timers might have thought that *all* the prostitutes were as likely to reject them. A few of Femke's fellow sex workers on the Bergstraat claimed that she hurt their business more directly. Not only was Femke the most sought-after of the prostitutes on the street, but when she spurned a client—in full view of her near neighbors in their doorways and windows on the Bergstraat—the ashamed man was sure to take his business to another street. (He didn't want to be in the company of a woman who'd seen Femke turn him down.)

Yet she had her allies—among the older prostitutes, especially. And when she discovered those other music lovers assembled in the Old Church in the wee hours of the morning, Femke established some fierce friendships. (Was Jack wrong to imagine that it might have been an easy transition for both choirgirls and prostitutes to make—namely, to love the organist as a natural result of loving his music?)

To judge Femke by her revenge against her ex-husband, one might have thought she would have been more possessive in her attachment to William Burns. But Femke had rejoiced in his music, and in his company. In her liberation from her former husband, she'd discovered another kind of love—a kinship with women who sold sex for money and *gave* it away selectively. If more than one of the music lovers in William's audience at the Oude Kerk had taken him "home," how many of them had given him their advice for free?

Jack would wonder, much later, if those red-light women were his father's greatest conquest. Or were women who gave advice to men for money inclined to be stingy advice-givers to those rare men they *didn't* charge?

To a four-year-old, it was a very confusing story. Then again, maybe you had to be a four-year-old to believe it.

* * *

Confusing or not, that was Femke's story, more or less as Els told it—altered (as everything is) by time, and by Alice's retelling of the story to Jack over the ensuing years. When the boy and his mother went to see Femke in her room on the Bergstraat, it was clear she'd been expecting them.

Femke didn't dress like a prostitute. Her clothes were more appropriate for a hostess at an elegant dinner party. Her skin was as golden and flawless as her hair; her bosom swelled softly, and her hips had a commanding jut. She was in every respect a knockout—like no one Jack had seen in a window or a doorway in Amsterdam before—and there emanated from her such a universal disdain that it was easier to believe how many men she turned away than to imagine her *ever* accepting a customer.

What a sizable contempt Femke must have felt for Alice, who had ceaselessly chased after a man who'd so long ago rejected her. Femke's evident contempt for children struck Jack as immeasurable. (The boy may have misinterpreted Femke's feelings for his mother; Jack probably thought that Femke disliked *him*.) He instantly wanted to leave her room, which, compared to the other two prostitutes' rooms he'd seen, was almost as pretty as Femke—it was also lavishly furnished.

There was no bed, just a large leather couch, and there were no towels. There was even a desk. A comfortable-looking leather armchair was in the window corner, under a reading lamp and next to a bookcase. Perhaps Femke sat reading in her window, not bothering to look at the potential clients passing by; to get her attention, the men must have had to come down the short flight of stairs and knock on her door or on the window. Would she then look up from her book, annoyed to have had her reading interrupted?

There were paintings on the walls—landscapes, one with a cow—and the rug was an Oriental, as expensive-looking as she was. In fact, Femke was Jack's first encounter with the unassailable power of money—its blind-to-everything-else arrogance.

"What took you so long?" she said to Alice.

"Can we go?" Jack asked his mom. He held out his hand to her, but she wouldn't take it.

"I know you're in touch with him," Alice told the prostitute.

" '. . . in touch with him,' " Femke repeated. She moved her hips; she wet her lips with her tongue. Her gestures were as ripe with self-indulgence as a woman stretching in bed in the morning after a good night's sleep; her clothes looked as welcoming to her body as a warm bath. Even standing, or sitting in a straight-backed chair, her body appeared to loll. Even sound asleep, Femke would look like a cat waiting to be stroked.

Hadn't someone said that Femke chiefly, and safely, chose virgins? She picked young boys. The police insisted that Femke require them to show her proof of their age. Jack would never forget her, or how afraid she made him feel.

Virgins, Alice had explained to Jack, were inexperienced young men—no woman had ever given them advice before. That late afternoon in Femke's room on the Bergstraat was the first time Jack felt in need of some advice regarding women, but he was too afraid to ask.

"*If* you're still in touch with him, perhaps you'll be so kind as to give him a message," Alice continued.

"Do I look *kind*?" Femke asked.

"Can we go?" Jack asked again; his mom still wouldn't take his hand. Jack looked out the window at a passing car. There were no potential clients looking in.

Alice was saying something; she sounded upset. "A father should at least know what his son *looks* like!"

"William certainly knows what the boy looks like," Femke replied. It was as if she were saying, "I think William has seen enough of Jack already." That's the kind of information (or misinformation) that can change your life. It certainly changed Jack's. From that day forth, he'd tried to imagine his father stealing a look at him.

Did William see Jack fall through the ice and into the Kastelsgraven? Would The Music Man have rescued his son if the littlest soldier hadn't come along? Was William watching Jack eat breakfast at the Grand Hotel in Stockholm? Did his dad see him stuffing his face at that Sunday-morning buffet at the Hotel Bristol in Oslo, or suspended in the derelict elevator above the American Bar at the Hotel Torni in Helsinki?

And on those Saturdays in Amsterdam when Jack often sat in the window or stood in the doorway of The Red Dragon on the Zeedijk, just watching the busy weekend street—the countless men who roamed the red-light district—was his father once or twice passing by with the crowd? If William knew what his son looked like, as Femke had said, how many times might Jack have seen him and not known who he was?

But how could he *not* have recognized William Burns? Not that William would have been so bold as to take off his shirt and show Jack the music inscribed on his skin, but wouldn't there have been sŏmething familiar about his father? (Maybe the eyelashes, as a few women had pointed out while peering into Jack's face.)

That day in Femke's room on the Bergstraat, Jack started looking for William Burns. In a way, Jack had looked for him ever since—and on such slim evidence! That a woman he thought was a prostitute, whǫ may have been lying—who was unquestionably cruel—told him that his dad had seen him.

Alice had contradicted Femke on the spot: "She's lying, Jack."

"You're the one who's lying, to yourself," Femke replied. "It's a lie to think that William still loves you—it's a joke to assume that he ever did!"

"I know he loved me once," Alice said.

"If William *ever* loved you, he couldn't bear to see you prostitute yourself," Femke said. "It would kill him to see you in a window or a doorway, wouldn't it? That is, *if* he cared about you."

"Of course he cares about me!" Alice cried.

Imagine that you are four, and your mother is in a shouting match with a stranger. Do you really hear the argument? Aren't you trying so hard to understand the *last* thing that was said—to interpret it—that you miss the *next* thing that is said, and the thing after that? Isn't that how a four-year-old hears, or doesn't hear, an adult argument?

"Just think of William seeing you in a doorway, singing that little hymn or prayer I'm sure you know," Femke was saying. "How does it go? '*Breathe on me, breath of God*'—have I got it right?" Femke also knew the tune, which she hummed. "It's Scottish, isn't it?" she asked.

"Anglican, actually," Alice said. "He taught it to *you*?"

Femke shrugged. "He taught it to all the whores in the Oude Kerk. He played it, they sang it. I'm sure he played it for you and you sang it, too."

"I don't need to prove that William loved me—not to *you*," Alice said.

"To *me*? What do *I* care?" Femke asked. "You need to prove it to *yourself*! Wouldn't it bother William—if you accepted a customer or two, or three or four? That is, *if* he ever cared about you."

"Not around Jack," Alice said.

"Get a *babysitter* for Jack," Femke told her. "You've got a *few* friends in the red-light district, haven't you?"

"Thank you for your time," Alice said; only then did she take Jack's hand.

Walking from the Bergstraat, they reentered the red-light district on the Oudekerksplein. It was early evening, just growing dark. The organ in the Oude Kerk wasn't playing, but the women were all in their doorways—as if they knew Jack and Alice were coming. Anja was one of the older ones; she was on and off in the friendliness department. It must have been one of Anja's *off* nights, because she was humming the tune to "Breathe on Me, Breath of God," which seemed a little cruel.

It's not much of a tune. As a communion prayer, sung instead of spoken, the words matter more than the tune. Like many simple things, Jack thought it was beautiful; it was one of his mom's favorites.

They next passed Margriet, one of the younger girls, who always called Jack "Jackie"; this time she said nothing. Then came Annelies, Naughty Nanda, Katja, Angry Anouk, Mistress Mies, and Roos the Redhead; they were humming the tune of the hymn, which Alice ignored. Only Old Jolanda knew the words.

"Breathe on me, breath of God . . ." she was singing.

"You're not going to do it, are you?" Jack asked his mother. "I don't care if I ever see him," the boy lied.

Maybe Alice said, *"I'm* the one who wants to see him, Jack." Or she might have said, *"He's* the one who wants to see *you,* Jackie."

When Alice told Tattoo Peter about Femke's idea, the one-legged man tried to talk her out of it. Peter had Woody Woodpecker tattooed on his right biceps. Jack got the impression that even the woodpecker was opposed to the idea of his mom singing a hymn in a prostitute's window or doorway.

Years later, he would ask his mother what ever happened to the picture she took of him with Tattoo Peter's Woody Woodpecker. "Maybe the photograph didn't turn out," was all she said.

After posing with the woodpecker, Jack and his mom walked down to The Red Dragon, where Robbie de Wit rolled Alice some joints, which she put in her purse. Perhaps Robbie took their picture with Tattoo Theo. (Jack used to think: *Maybe that photo didn't turn out, either.*)

They bought a ham-and-cheese croissant for Saskia, who was busy with a customer on the Bloedstraat, so Jack ate the sandwich while they walked over to the corner of the Stoofsteeg, where Jack drifted in and out of his mom's conversation with Els. "I don't recommend it," Els was saying to Alice. "But of course you can use my room, and I'll look after Jack."

From the doorway of Els's room, Jack and his mom couldn't see Saskia's window or doorway on the Bloedstraat; they had to cross the canal in order to see if Saskia was still busy with her client. She was. By the time they walked back to Els's room, Els was with a customer of her own. Jack and Alice went back to the Bloedstraat and chatted with Janneke, the prostitute who was Saskia's nearest neighbor.

"What's with the hymn?" Janneke asked Alice. "Or is it some kind of prayer?" Alice just shook her head. The three of them stood out on the street, waiting for Saskia's client to slink out the door, which he did a few minutes later. "If he had a tail like a dog, it would be between his legs," Janneke observed.

"I suppose so," Alice said.

Finally Saskia opened her curtains and saw them on the street. She waved, smiling with her mouth open, which was never the way she would smile at a potential customer. Saskia told Alice she could use her room, too, and that—between her and Els—Jack would be properly looked after.

"I really appreciate it," Alice told the burned and beaten girl. "If you ever want a tattoo . . ." Her voice trailed away. Saskia couldn't look at her.

"It's not the worst thing," Saskia said, to no one in particular. Alice shook her head again. "You know what, Jack?" Saskia asked; she seemed eager to change the subject. "You look like a kid who just ate a ham-and-cheese croissant, you lucky bugger!"

In Amsterdam, all the prostitutes were registered with the police. The women were photographed, and the police kept a record of their most personal details; some of these were probably irrelevant. But if the prostitute had a boyfriend, that was relevant, because if she was murdered or beaten up, it was often the boyfriend who did it—usually not a customer. There were no minors among the prostitutes in those days, and the police were on the friendliest possible terms with the women in the red-light district; the police knew almost everything that went on there.

One morning, which felt almost like spring, Jack and Alice went to the Warmoesstraat police station with Els and Saskia. A nice policeman named Nico Oudejans interviewed Alice. Saskia had requested Nico; both when she'd been burned and when she'd been beaten up, he had been the first street cop to arrive at the scene on the Bloedstraat. Jack may have been disappointed that Nico was wearing plainclothes, not a uniform, but Nico was the red-light district's favorite officer—not just a familiar cop on the beat but the policeman the prostitutes most trusted. He was in his late twenties or early thirties.

To the boyfriend question, Alice said no—she didn't have one—but Nico was suspicious of her answer. "Then who's the guy you're singing for, Alice?"

"He's a *former* boyfriend," Alice said; she put her hand on the back of Jack's neck. "He's Jack's father."

"We would consider him a boyfriend," the policeman politely told her.

Possibly it was Els who said: "It's just for an afternoon and part of one night, Nico."

"I'm not going to admit any customers," Alice might have told the nice cop. "I'm just going to sit in the window or stand in the doorway, and sing."

"If you turn everyone down, you're going to make some men angry at you, Alice," Nico said.

It must have been Saskia who said: "One of us will always be nearby. When she's using my room, I'll be watching out for her; when she's using Els's room, Els will be hanging around."

"And where will you be, Jack?" Nico asked.

"He's going to be with me or Els!" Saskia replied.

Nico Oudejans shook his head. "I don't like the sound of it, Alice—this isn't your job."

"I used to sing in a choir," Alice told him. "I know how to sing."

"It's no place to sing a hymn or say a prayer," the policeman said.

"Maybe you could come by from time to time," Saskia suggested to him. "Just in case she draws a crowd."

"She'll draw one, all right," Nico said.

"So what?" Els asked. "A new girl always draws a crowd."

"When a new girl takes a customer inside and closes the curtains, the crowd usually goes away," Nico Oudejans said.

"I'm not going to admit any customers," Alice might have repeated.

"Sometimes it's easier than saying no," Saskia said. "Virgins, for example—they can be nice."

"They're quick, too," Els told Alice.

"Not around Jack."

"Just not too young a virgin, Alice," Nico Oudejans said.

"I really appreciate it," Alice told him. "If you ever want a tattoo—" She stopped; maybe she thought that if she offered him a free tattoo, the policeman would construe this as a bribe. He was a nice guy, Nico Oudejans. His eyes were a robin's-egg blue, and high on one cheekbone he had a small scar shaped like the letter *L*.

Out on the Warmoesstraat, Alice thanked Els and Saskia for helping her get permission from the police to be a prostitute for an afternoon and part of one night. "I figured it would be easier to talk Nico into it than to talk you out of it," Saskia said.

"Saskia always does what's easier," Els explained. The three women laughed. They were walking the way Dutch girls sometimes do, side by side with their arms linked together. Alice was in the middle; Els was holding Jack's hand.

The Warmoesstraat ran the length of one edge of the red-light district. Jack and Alice were on their way back to the Krasnapolsky. Els and Saskia were going to help Alice pick out what to wear—she wanted to wear her own clothes, she said. Alice didn't own a skirt as short as the ones Saskia wore in her window or doorway on the Bloedstraat, or a blouse with a neckline as revealing as the ones Els wore when she was giving advice on the Stoofsteeg.

It must have been about eleven in the morning when they came to the corner of the Sint Annenstraat. Only one prostitute was working, way at the end of the street, but even at that distance, she recognized them. The prostitute waved and they waved back. Because they were looking down the Sint Annenstraat, into the district, they didn't see Jacob Bril coming toward them on the Warmoesstraat. They were still walking four abreast; there was no way Bril could get around them. He said something sharply in Dutch—a curse, or some form of condemnation. Saskia snapped back at him. Even though Els and Saskia were not dressed for their doorways, Bril surely recognized them; after all, he'd made quite a comprehensive study of the prostitutes in the neighborhood.

The three women had to unlink their arms for Jacob Bril to pass by them; it might have been the first time Bril had been forced to stop walking in the red-light district. Of course Bril knew Alice—she was standing between the two prostitutes. As for the boy, Bril always appeared to look right through him; it was as if he never saw Jack.

"In the Lord's eyes, you are the company you keep!" Jacob Bril told Alice.

"I like the company I keep just fine," Alice replied.

"What would you know about the Lord's eyes?" Els asked Bril.

"Nobody knows what God sees," Saskia said.

"He sees even the smallest sin!" Bril shouted. "He remembers every act of fornication!"

"Most men do," Els told him.

Saskia shrugged. "I find I forget it, most of the time," she said.

They watched Jacob Bril scurry down the Sint Annenstraat, as purposefully as a rat. The lone prostitute at the far end of the street was no longer in her doorway; she must have seen Bril coming.

"Jacob Bril is a good reason for me to be off the street before midnight," Alice said. "I can't imagine what he'd say if he saw me sitting in a window or heard me singing in a doorway." She laughed in that brittle way, the kind of laughter Jack recognized as a precursor to her tears.

It was Els or Saskia who said: "There are better reasons than Bril to be off the street before midnight."

They came out of the Warmoesstraat in the Dam Square and walked into the Krasnapolsky. "What's fornication?" Jack asked.

"Giving advice," Alice answered.

"Good advice, mostly," Saskia said.

"Necessary advice, anyway," Els added.

"What's sin?" Jack asked.

"Just about everything," Alice answered.

"There's good sin and bad sin," Els told Jack.

"There *is*?" Saskia said; she looked as confused as Jack was.

"I mean good advice and bad advice," Els explained. It seemed to Jack that sin was more complicated than fornication.

Entering the hotel room, Alice said: "The thing about sin,

Jack, is that some people think it's very important and other people don't even believe it exists."

"What do *you* think about it?" the boy asked. Alice appeared to trip, although Jack saw nothing that she could have tripped on; she just started to fall, but Els caught her.

"Damn heels," Alice said, but she wasn't wearing heels.

"Now listen, Jack," Saskia spoke up. "We've got a job to do— making sure your mom wears the right clothes is important. We can't be distracted by a conversation about something as difficult as sin."

"We'll have that conversation later," Els assured the boy.

"Have it once the singing starts—have it without me," Alice said, but Els just steered her to the closet.

Saskia was already looking through Alice's dresser drawers. She held up a bra that would have been much too big for her but not nearly big enough for Els. Saskia said something in Dutch, which made Els laugh. "You're going to be disappointed in my clothes," Alice told the prostitutes.

The way Jack remembered it, his mom tried on every article of clothing in her closet. Alice was always very modest around Jack. He never saw his mother naked or half naked, and for an hour or more in the Krasnapolsky was the first time he saw so much of her in a bra and panties; even then, Alice clasped the sides of her breasts with her upper arms and elbows, and crossed her hands on her chest to cover herself. Jack actually saw more of Saskia and Els than he did of his mother, because the two women surrounded her as they dressed and undressed her—they were full of advice.

Finally a dress was chosen; it struck Jack as pretty but plain. The dress was like his mom—*she* was pretty but plain, at least in comparison to how the women looked and dressed in the red-light district. It was a sleeveless black dress with a high neckline; it fit her closely, but it wasn't too tight.

Alice didn't own a pair of genuine high heels, but the heels she chose for the occasion were medium-high—or they were high for her—and she put on her pearl necklace. It had belonged to her mother; her father gave it to her on the day she left Scotland for Nova Scotia. Alice thought they were cultured pearls, but she didn't really know. The necklace meant a lot to her, no matter what kind of pearls they were.

"Won't I be cold in a sleeveless dress?" Alice asked Saskia and Els. The women found a fitted black cardigan in the closet.

"That sweater is too small for me," Alice complained. "I can't button it up."

"You don't need to button it," Els told her. "It's just to keep your arms warm."

"You should leave the sweater open and hug your arms around yourself," Saskia said, showing her how to do it. "If you look like you're a little cold, that's sexy."

"I don't want to look sexy," Alice replied.

"What's sexy?" Jack asked.

"If you look sexy, the men think you can give them good advice," Els explained. The two prostitutes were fussing over Alice's hair, and there was still the matter of lipstick to resolve— and makeup.

"I don't want lipstick, I don't want makeup," Alice told them, but they wouldn't listen to her.

"Believe me, you want lipstick," Els told her.

"Something dark," Saskia said. "And eye shadow."

"I *hate* eye shadow!" Alice cried.

"You don't want William looking in your eyes and really seeing you, do you?" Els asked her. "I mean, supposing for a moment that he actually shows up." That quieted Alice; she let the women make her up.

Jack just watched the transformation. His mother's face looked more chiseled, her mouth bolder; most foreign of all was the darkness shrouding her eyes, which made her look as if someone close to her had died and she was keeping the death from Jack. Overall, his mom looked a lot older.

"How do I look?" Alice asked.

"You look smashing!" Saskia said. (There were always a lot of Englishmen in the red-light district. Saskia probably thought that "smashing" sounded good in English.)

"Forget a crowd—you're going to draw a *mob,*" Els told Alice, but Alice didn't necessarily like the sound of that.

"How do *you* think I look, Jackie?" she asked.

"You look very beautiful," he told her, "but not really like my mom." This seemed to alarm her.

"You look like Alice to me," Saskia said reassuringly.

"Sure you do," Els told her. "All we did to her, Jack, was make her more of a secret."

"What's the secret?" Alice asked.

"Els means we had to hide you a little," Saskia said.

"What we hid was the *mom* in her, Jack," Els added.

"Because that's just for *you* to see," Saskia said, rumpling the boy's hair.

"I'll be fine," Alice announced. She turned away from the mirror and didn't look back.

The red-light district in Amsterdam is smaller than many tourists realize. It is such a warren of tiny streets—at peak hours, densely populated—that first-time visitors get lost in the maze and imagine that the prostitutes in their windows and doorways go on forever. In truth, you could stroll from one end of the district to the other—from the Damstraat to the Zeedijk—in under ten minutes. From the area of the Old Church to Saskia's room on the Bloedstraat, or Els's room on the Stoofsteeg, was less than a five-minute walk.

On a Saturday afternoon, word of a new girl in a window or a doorway spread quickly. A woman who didn't look like a prostitute, singing what sounded like a hymn, was dividing her time between a doorway on the Stoofsteeg and one on the Bloedstraat. The story raced through the red-light district like a fire. Before nightfall, the older women working on the Oudekerksplein had linked arms and come to hear for themselves how Daughter Alice could sing. Anja came with Annelies and Naughty Nanda; Katja came with Angry Anouk and Mistress Mies. Around suppertime, Roos the Redhead showed up with Old Jolanda. The aging prostitutes said nothing and didn't stay long. They had expected Alice to make a fool of herself, but when a pretty woman has a pretty voice, she rarely looks or sounds like a fool.

To those men prowling the streets, Alice's singing might have seemed as beguiling a come-on as the jingling bracelets on Saskia's burned arm; yet Alice rejected all comers. She was a woman occupying a prostitute's doorway, or sitting in a prostitute's window, but she just shook her head to every potential client who expressed an interest in her; she occasionally needed to interrupt her hymn and more firmly say no. Once, when she was using Els's room, Alice had to tell a particularly persistent gentleman that she was waiting for her boyfriend and did not want to miss him by being busy with a customer when he showed up. (Saskia supplied a Dutch translation and the man finally went away.) And when she was using Saskia's room, Alice was heckled by a bunch of young men. She must have turned down one of the boys, or all of them, and in response to being spurned, they had gathered around her doorway and were loudly singing a song of their own.

Alice went inside Saskia's room and closed the door; she sat in the window, still singing the words to "Breathe on Me, Breath of God," although no one could hear her. Els told the boys to move on; all but one of them were still arguing with her when Nico Oudejans suddenly appeared in the Bloedstraat. When the boys didn't walk away fast enough, Nico shouted at them and they began to run. The one boy who hadn't argued with Els was running backward—he simply couldn't take his eyes off Alice.

Nico smiled at Jack, who waved to his mom in the window. She just went on singing. "I'll keep checking on her, Jack—and on you, too," the policeman said.

It would have been easier to invite the men inside the room; their disappointment in being denied advice ran the gamut from utter incomprehension to anger. Some would simply look embarrassed and skulk away—others were baffled or belligerent. Alice just kept singing; she wouldn't even stop long enough to eat a ham-and-cheese croissant, which Saskia and Jack brought her. And not long after dark, Tattoo Theo paid her a visit. He had stuffed a basket with a bottle of wine and some fruit and cheese, but Alice wouldn't accept it. She gave Rademaker a hug and a kiss; then she waved Els and Jack over to her doorway and gave them the basket. Naturally, they took the food and wine to Saskia, who was always starving.

Robbie de Wit showed up, too. He looked heartbroken at the sight of Alice singing soundlessly in Saskia's window. Robbie had brought her a couple of marijuana cigarettes, which Alice accepted; when she left the window for the doorway, she would light one of the joints and take a hit from it while she went on singing.

It would be years before Jack made the connection—namely, that it was one of those nights Bob Dylan could have written a terrific song about.

Around ten o'clock that night, when the red-light district was very crowded, Els and Saskia and Jack accompanied Alice on the short walk from Saskia's room on the Bloedstraat to Els's room on the Stoofsteeg. Els was carrying Jack. The boy was half asleep, with his head on her shoulder. Alice didn't sing when she was changing rooms. "Do you think William's ever going to show up?" she asked.

"I *never* thought he was going to show up," Saskia said.

"You should call it a night, Alice," Els told her. She unlocked the door to her room, and Alice took up her usual position in the doorway. She was about to start the hymn again when she saw Femke coming toward her on the Stoofsteeg.

"You're not singing," Femke said.

"He's not coming, is he?" Alice asked her.

Both Saskia and Els started in on Femke—they were furious and let her know it. Jack woke up, but he had no idea what they were saying. It was all in Dutch. Femke didn't back down to them, not a bit. Els and Saskia kept after her. Jack thought Els was going to throw Femke down on the cobblestone street, but they stopped shouting when Alice began to sing. Jack had never heard her do "Breathe on Me, Breath of God" any better. Femke looked undone by her voice. Possibly Femke said, "I didn't think you'd actually *do* it." Alice just kept singing—if anything, a little louder. But Jack was so out of it, for all he knew, Femke might have said, "I didn't think he'd actually *accept* it."

As Jack understood things, his father was playing a piano on a cruise ship—or *someone* was. The piano seemed to surprise Alice, but most organists learn how to play piano first—certainly William had. Maybe the surprise was that William wanted to sail to Australia and get tattooed by Cindy Ray.

Alice had switched hymns, but she was nonetheless continuing to sing—heedless of such a small thing as punctuation, or the fact that William might already have been on his way to Australia. "*The King of love my Shepherd is,*" she sang. (She just kept repeating that line.)

Did William hope that Australia would be too far away for Alice and Jack to follow him there? Jack was falling asleep on Els's big, soft bosom. Alice had switched hymns again and showed no sign of stopping. "*Sweet Sacrament divine,*" she sang repeatedly. The purity of Alice's voice followed Femke down the street. By the time Femke left the Stoofsteeg, Alice had switched back to "Breathe on Me, Breath of God" and Jack woke up.

"You can stop now, Alice," Saskia said, but Alice wouldn't stop.

"Where's Australia?" Jack asked Els. (He just knew that Australia wasn't on their itinerary.)

"Don't worry, Jack—you're not going anywhere near Australia," Saskia said.

"It's on the other side of the *world*," Els told him. The boy felt better thinking that his dad might be on the other side of the world; yet this wouldn't prevent Jack from imagining that his father was somehow watching him from a crowd.

"Come on, Alice—it's time to stop," Saskia said.

"*The King of love my Shepherd is*," Alice started up again, a little tonelessly.

They'd been so interested in watching Femke's departure that they hadn't noticed Jacob Bril's arrival. It wasn't even midnight, but there was Bril on the Stoofsteeg, and he wasn't walking. He stood paralyzed in a religious rage. "That's a hymn you're singing—that's a *prayer*!" Bril yelled at Alice.

She looked right at him and went ahead with "Sweet Sacrament Divine." (In her state of mind, maybe three hymns—or just their titles—were all she could remember.)

"Blasphemy!" Bril shouted. "Sacrilege!"

Saskia said something in Dutch to him; it didn't sound especially religious. Els stepped up to Bril and shoved him; he dropped to one knee but kept himself from falling with the heel of one hand on the cobblestones. When he straightened up, Els shoved him again. He managed to stay on his feet, but he bounced off the side of the building. "Not around Jack," Els told him calmly. She stepped forward to shove him again, but Bril backed away from her.

"Where's Nico when you need him?" Saskia said facetiously— Els didn't appear to need Nico's help.

Alice began again with "Breathe on Me, Breath of God." That was when they all saw him—the boy who had not argued with Els, the one who'd run backward out of the Bloedstraat. He was there because he needed another look at Alice. This time, he was alone. Els spoke to him in Dutch; she looked as if she intended to shove him, now that Bril was retreating.

"Leave him alone. He was the only nice one," Alice told Els; she had finally stopped singing. She smiled at the boy, who stood helplessly in front of her. "He looks like he needs advice, doesn't he?" Alice asked.

"Alice, you don't have to," Saskia said.

"But he looks like he needs advice," Alice said.

"Saskia or I can give it to him," Els told her.

"I think it's *my* advice he wants," Alice said.

"You should call it a night, Alice," Els repeated.

"Would you like to come inside?" Alice asked the boy. He didn't look as if he understood English. Els translated for him and he nodded.

"Come on, Jack," Saskia said; she took his hand. "I could use a ham-and-cheese croissant. Couldn't you?"

The boy in need of advice had an olive complexion and very dark hair, cut short; he was small-boned with wide, staring eyes and features as fine as a girl's. He had not moved since he'd been invited inside the prostitute's room—he just stood there. He'd wanted to have another look at Alice, never imagining that he would get up the nerve to ask her again, or even have the opportunity to do so—that is, if he'd asked her the first time. (From the look of him, he'd been too scared; probably one or more of his friends, the hecklers, had asked her.)

Els stepped up behind him and pushed him toward Alice, who took his hand and pulled him inside the room; the top of his head barely came to her chin. When Alice had closed the door and the curtains, Els joined Saskia and Jack. "Is he a virgin?" Jack asked them.

"Definitely," Els said.

Remembering what Nico Oudejans had said to his mom at the police station, Jack asked: "Is he too young a virgin?"

"Nobody's too young at this time of night," Saskia said.

Jack had been napping half the afternoon and night—first for an hour or so in Els's room, and then in Saskia's, and of course in Els's arms when she carried him here and there—but now he was exhausted. When they got back to Saskia's room, Saskia closed her curtains so Jack could go to sleep. She stood in her doorway, guarding him, while—every fifteen or twenty minutes—Els would walk back to her room on the Stoofsteeg to see if Alice was still advising the virgin.

Jack managed to stay awake for the first two trips Els took. "I thought Els said virgins were quick," the boy remarked.

"Go to sleep, Jack," Saskia said. "It's taking a long time because the virgin's English isn't very good. Your mom probably has to speak very slowly to him."

"Oh."

"Go to sleep, Jack."

Much later, the sound of whispering woke Jack. The three women sat on the edge of Saskia's bed in the glow from the lamp with the red glass shade; there was hardly any room on the bed for Jack, who didn't let them know he was awake. His mom's string of pearls was broken. Els and Saskia were trying to help Alice put her necklace back together. "The clumsy oaf," Saskia said. "That's the trouble with virgins."

"He didn't mean to—he'd just never taken off a necklace before," Alice whispered. "I think they're cultured pearls. Is that good or bad?"

"You should have kept the necklace on, Alice," Els told her.

"He was really very sweet—he'd just never done *anything* before," Alice whispered.

"He must have had a lot of money, for all that time," Saskia said.

"Oh, I didn't charge him—that would have made me a *prostitute*!" The three women laughed. "Shhh! We'll wake up Jack," Alice whispered.

"I'm awake," he told them. "Did you give that boy some good advice?" he asked his mom. She gave Jack a hug and a kiss while Saskia and Els went on trying to reassemble her broken necklace.

"Yes, it was pretty good advice, I think," Alice replied.

"The best advice he'll ever get," Saskia said.

"At least for *free*," Els added. The three women laughed again.

"You'll have to take this damn thing to a jeweler," Saskia said, handing Alice the damaged necklace and a bunch of unstrung pearls. Alice put the loose pearls and the necklace in her purse.

Saskia and Els volunteered to walk them back to the Krasnapolsky, but Alice proposed a slight detour. She wanted to walk by the Oudekerksplein, just to show those old prostitutes she was still standing. "It's too late—most of them will have stopped working," Els told her.

"It's worth doing," Saskia said. "Even if only one woman is working, the others will hear about it."

It must have been two or three in the morning. They had just come off the Oudekennissteeg when the music hit them; it was even louder on the bridge across the old canal. That organ in the Oude Kerk was a holy monster. "Bach?" Jack asked his mother.

"It's Bach, all right," Alice said, "but it's not your father."

"How do you know?" Els asked. "Femke is such a bitch. You should at least have a look and see."

"It's Bach's Fantasy in G Major," Alice said. "It's popular at weddings." Weddings were not exactly William's cup of tea, apparently, but Saskia and Els insisted on having a look at the organist.

Alice wanted to walk around the Oudekerksplein before going inside the Old Church, so they did. Only one prostitute was standing in her doorway, listening to the music. She was one of the younger ones—Margriet. "You're up late, Jackie," Margriet said.

"We're *all* up late," Els told her.

They went into the Oude Kerk. Two of the older prostitutes were sitting in a pew, and one of them, Naughty Nanda, appeared to be asleep; the other one, Angry Anouk, wouldn't look at Alice.

They went to the staircase at the back of the great congregation hall, but only Saskia and Els and Jack started up the narrow stairs. Alice waited for them at the bottom of the staircase. "He's in Australia, or sailing to it," she said stubbornly. "Just imagine all the ladies he'll get to meet on a cruise ship!"

The faint, innocent smell of baby powder preceded their view of Frans Donker, the junior organist. The sudden appearance of Saskia and Els startled the boy genius—he stopped playing. Then Donker saw Jack standing between the two prostitutes.

"Oh, I suppose you thought it was your father," Frans said to Jack.

"Not really," Saskia said.

"Don't talk—just keep playing," Els told him. The child prodigy had returned to the Bach before they reached the bottom of the stairs.

"It's that Donker kid, right?" Alice asked. They all nodded. "He *plays* like an organ-tuner," Alice said.

Bach's Fantasy in G Major followed them past the Trompettersteeg, where several of the younger prostitutes were still selling themselves. They were nearly to the end of the Sint Annenstraat when they finally outdistanced the music.

"You're not going to Australia, are you?" Els may have asked Alice.

"No. Australia is too long and hard a trip for Jack," Alice might have answered.

"It's too long and hard a trip for anybody, Alice," Saskia said.

"I suppose so," was all Alice said. Her speech was uncharacteristically slurred, and her expression—from the moment Jack had awakened to the women's whispers on the Bloedstraat—was unfamiliarly dreamy and carefree. Jack would later assume that this had to do with how many joints she'd smoked, because—until Amsterdam—his mother and marijuana were not on close terms. But they were on close terms that Saturday night and Sunday morning.

Saskia and Els walked them back to their hotel—not because the two prostitutes thought the red-light district was unsafe, even at that hour, but because they didn't want Alice to run into Jacob Bril. They knew Bril was also staying at the Krasnapolsky.

After the women hugged and kissed Jack and Alice good night, Jack and his mom got ready for bed. It was the first time Jack remembered her using the bathroom ahead of him. Something amused her in there, because she started laughing.

"What's so funny?"

"I think I left my underwear in Els's room!"

The advice-giving business had clearly distracted her—and by the time Jack finished brushing his teeth, Alice had fallen asleep. Jack turned out the lights in the bedroom and left the bathroom light on, with the door ajar—their version of a nightlight. He thought it was the first time his mother had fallen asleep before him. He got into bed beside her, but even asleep, his mom was still singing. Jack was thankful it wasn't a hymn. And maybe the marijuana had resurrected Alice's Scottish accent, which, in the future, Jack could detect only when she was drunk or stoned.

As for the song, Jack had no way of knowing if it was an authentic folk ballad—something his mother had remembered from her girlhood—or, more likely, a ditty of her own imagination that, in her sleep, she'd put to music. (Why not? She'd been singing for half a day and night.)

Here is the song Alice sang in her sleep.

Oh, I'll never be a kittie
or a cookie
or a tail.
The one place worse than
Dock Place
is the Port o' Leith jail.
No, I'll never be a kittie,
of one true thing I'm sure—
I won't end up on Dock Place
and I'll never be a hure.

Hure rhymed with *sure,* of course. Jack thought it might be a nursery song, which—even in her sleep—his mother meant to sing for him.

Jack said their nightly prayer—as he always did, with his eyes closed. He spoke a little louder than usual, because his mother was asleep and he had to pray for both of them. "The day Thou gavest, Lord, is ended. Thank You for it."

They slept until noon Sunday, when he asked her: "What's a hure?"

"Was it something I said in my sleep?" she said.

"Yes. You were singing."

"A hure is like a prostitute—an advice-giver, Jackie."

"How can a person be a kittie or a cookie or a tail?" Jack asked.

"They're all words for an advice-giver, Jack."

"Oh."

They were walking hand-in-hand through the red-light district to Tattoo Peter's when the boy asked: "Where's Dock Place?"

"Dock Place is nowhere I'll ever be," was all she would tell him.

"How did Tattoo Peter lose his leg?" Jack asked for the hundredth time.

"I told you—you'll have to ask him."

"Maybe on a bicycle," the boy said.

It was midafternoon in the district; most of the women were already offering advice. All of them greeted Jack and Alice by name—even those older prostitutes in the area of the Old Church. Alice made a point of walking around the Oudekerksplein; they passed every window and doorway, at a pace half the speed of

Jacob Bril's. Not a soul hummed "Breathe on Me, Breath of God" to them.

They went to the St. Olofssteeg to say good-bye to Tattoo Peter. "Alice, you're welcome to come work with me anytime," the one-legged man told her. "Keep both your legs, Jack," Peter said. "You'll find it easier to get around that way."

Then they walked up the Zeedijk to say good-bye to Tattoo Theo and Robbie de Wit. Robbie wanted Alice to tattoo him. "Not another broken heart," she said. "I've had enough of hearts, torn in two or otherwise." Robbie settled for her signature on his right upper arm.

Daughter Alice

Rademaker was so impressed by her letter-perfect script that he requested one, too. Tattoo Theo got his tattoo on his left forearm, which he said he'd kept bare for something special. The lettering ran from the bend at Rademaker's elbow to the face of his wristwatch, so that every time he looked to see what time it was, he would be reminded of Daughter Alice.

"What do you say, Jack?" Tattoo Theo asked. "Shall we listen again to der Zimmerman?" (He wasn't German; he didn't know *der* from *den*. Not that Jack knew German, either—not yet.)

Jack picked out a Bob Dylan album and put it on. Robbie de Wit was soon singing along, but it wasn't Alice's favorite song. She just went on tattooing, leaving the singing to Robbie and Bob.

"When your rooster crows at the break of dawn," Bob and Robbie sang. *"Look out your window and I'll be gone."* At this point, Alice was starting the *A* in *Alice*. *"You're the reason I'm trav'lin' on,"* Bob and Robbie crooned. *"Don't think twice, it's all right."*

Well, it wasn't all right—not by a long shot—but Alice just kept tattooing.

Els took them to the shipping office, which was a confusing place—they needed Els's help in arranging their passage. They would take the train to Rotterdam and sail from there to Montreal, and then make their way back to Toronto.

"Why Toronto?" Saskia asked Alice. "Canada isn't your country."

"It is now," Alice said. "I'll never go back to sunny Leith—not for all the whisky in Scotland." She wouldn't say why. (Too many ghosts, maybe.) "Besides, I know just the school for Jack. It's a good school," Jack heard her tell Saskia and Els. His mom leaned over him and whispered in his ear: "And you'll be safe with the girls."

The idea of himself with the St. Hilda's girls—the older ones, especially—gave Jack the shivers. Once again, and for the last time in Europe, he reached for his mother's hand.

II

The Sea of Girls

8

Safe Among the Girls

It was Jack's impression that the older girls at St. Hilda's never liked having boys in their school. Although the boys couldn't stay past grade four, their presence—even the presence of *little* boys—was seen as a bad influence. According to Emma Oastler: "Especially on the *older* girls."

Emma was a menacing girl, and an older one. The grade-six girls were the oldest students in the junior school; they opened and closed the car doors for the little kids at the Rosseter Road entrance. When Jack started kindergarten in the fall of 1970— the first year St. Hilda's admitted boys—Emma was in grade six. He was five; she was twelve. (Some problem at home had caused her to miss a year of school.) On Jack's first day, Emma opened the car door for him—a formative experience.

Jack was already self-conscious about the car—a black Lincoln Town Car from a limousine service, which Mrs. Wicksteed used for all her driving needs. (Neither Mrs. Wicksteed nor Lottie drove, and Alice never got her driver's license.) The limo driver was a friendly Jamaican—a big man named Peewee, who was nearly as black as the Town Car. He was Mrs. Wicksteed's favorite driver.

What kid wants to show up for his first day of school in a chauffeured limousine? But Alice had not done badly by yielding to Mrs. Wicksteed's way of doing things. It seemed that the Old Girl was not only paying Jack's tuition at St. Hilda's; she was paying for the limo.

Because Alice often worked at the Chinaman's tattoo parlor until late at night, Lottie got Jack up for school and gave him breakfast. Mrs. Wicksteed had sufficiently roused herself in time to do the boy's necktie, albeit a little absentmindedly. Lottie laid out his other clothes at bedtime—on school mornings, she also helped him get dressed.

On those mornings, Jack would go into his mom's semidark room and kiss her good-bye; then Lottie would cross the sidewalk with him to the corner of Spadina and Lowther, where Peewee would be waiting in the Town Car. To her credit, Alice had offered to accompany her son on his first day.

"Alice," Mrs. Wicksteed said, "if you take Jack to school, you'll make it an occasion for him to cry."

Mrs. Wicksteed was firmly opposed to creating occasions for Jack to cry. While doing his necktie one morning, she told him: "You will be teased, Jack. Don't make it an occasion to cry. Cry only when you're physically hurt—and in that case, cry as loudly as you can."

"But what do I do when I get teased?" Jack asked her.

Mrs. Wicksteed wore a plum-colored dressing gown over a pair of her late husband's barber-pole pajamas. She always did the boy's tie while sitting at the kitchen table, warming her stiff fingers over her first cup of tea. Her white hair was in curlers and her face glistened with avocado oil.

"Be creative," she advised him.

"When I get teased?"

"Be nice," Lottie suggested.

"Be nice *twice*," Mrs. Wicksteed said.

"And the third time?" Jack asked her.

"Be creative," she said again.

When the necktie was done, Mrs. Wicksteed kissed him on his forehead and on the bridge of his nose; then Lottie wiped the avocado oil off his face. Lottie would kiss Jack, too—usually in the front hall, before she opened the outside door and led him by the hand to Peewee.

Lottie's limp, which was almost as disturbingly provocative to Jack as Tattoo Peter's missing leg, was a frequent topic of conversation between Jack and his mother. "Why does Lottie limp?" he must have asked his mom a hundred times.

"Ask Lottie."

But when he left for his first day of school, Jack still hadn't summoned the courage to ask his nanny why she limped.

"What's with the lady's limp, mon?" Peewee asked him in the limo.

"I don't know. Why don't you ask her, Peewee?"

"*You* ask her, mon —you're the gentleman of the house. I'm just the *driver*."

Jack Burns later thought he'd be able to see the intersection of Pickthall and Hutchings Hill Road from his grave—the way Peewee slowed the Town Car to a crawl, the way the older girls skeptically took for granted the arrival of another rich kid in another limo. It was a warm September morning; Jack was again aware of the girls' untucked middy blouses, loosely gathered at their throats by those gray-and-maroon regimental-striped ties. (In two years, they would all be wearing button-down collars with the top button unbuttoned.) But he would remember best the rebellious posture of their hips.

The girls never stood still—sometimes with their arms around another girl, sometimes with all their weight on one foot while they tapped the other. Sitting down, they bounced one leg on one knee—the crossed leg constantly in motion. The extreme shortness of their gray pleated skirts drew Jack's attention to their legs and the surprising heaviness of their upper thighs. The girls picked at their fingers, at their nails, at their rings; they scratched their eyebrows and their hair. They looked *under* their nails, as if for secrets—they seemed to have many secrets. Among friends, there were hand signals and subtle evidence of other sign language.

At the Rosseter Road entrance, where Peewee stopped the Town Car, the grade-six girls struck Jack as particularly secretive yet unrestrained. At eleven or twelve, girls think they look awful. They have ceased being children, at least in their estimation, but they have not yet developed into the young women they will become. At that age, there are great differences among them: some have begun to look and move like young women, others have boys' bodies and move as if they were shy young men.

Not Emma Oastler, who was twelve going on eighteen. When she opened the car door for Jack, he mistook the faintest trace of a mustache on her upper lip for perspiration. The hair on her strong, tanned arms had turned blond in the summer sun, and her thick, dark-brown braid fell over her shoulder and framed one side of her almost-pretty face. The weight of her braid, which reached to her navel, served to separate and define her budding breasts. Maybe a quarter of the grade-six girls had noticeable breasts.

When Jack got out of the limo and stood next to Emma, he came up to her waist. "Don't trip on your necktie, honey pie," Emma said. The boy's tie hung down to his knees, but until Emma warned him, he hadn't considered the danger of tripping on it. And Jack's gray Bermuda shorts, which he'd outgrown, were too short to be "proper"—or so Mrs. Wicksteed had observed. (Unlike the girls, the boys wore short socks.)

Emma roughly lifted Jack's chin in her hand. "Let's have a look at those eyelashes, baby cakes—oh, my God!" she exclaimed.

"What?"

"I see trouble ahead," Emma Oastler said. Searching her face, Jack saw trouble ahead, too. He also realized his earlier mistake—the mustache. Up close, there was no way you could confuse the soft-looking fuzz on Emma's upper lip with beads of perspiration. At five, Jack didn't know that young women were sensitive about having mustaches. It looked like a neat thing to have; naturally, he wanted to touch it.

If your first day of school, like your first tattoo, is a pilgrim experience—well, here was Jack's. And touching Emma Oastler's mustache would certainly prove to be character-forming. "What's your name?" Emma asked, bending closer.

"Jack."

"Jack what?"

For an agonizing moment, her furbearing lip made him forget his last name. But more than her mustache made him hesitate. He had been christened Jack Stronach. His father had abandoned him, without marrying his mother; Alice saw no reason for either of them to bear William's name. But Mrs. Wicksteed disagreed. While Alice made a point of *not* being Mrs. Burns, Mrs. Wicksteed believed that no child should suffer from illegitimacy; at her instigation, Jack's name was legally changed, making him "legitimate" in name only. Furthermore, Mrs. Wicksteed was an assimilationist; in the Old Girl's view, a Jack Burns would be more easily assimilated into Canadian culture than a Jack Stronach. No doubt she thought she was doing the boy a favor.

But Jack's hesitation to tell Emma Oastler his last name had attracted the attention of a teacher—the one they called The Gray Ghost. Mrs. McQuat was a spectral presence. She'd mastered the art of the sudden appearance; no one ever saw her coming. In her previous life, she may have been a dead person. What else could explain the chill that accompanied her? Even her breath was cold.

"What have we here?" Mrs. McQuat asked.

"Jack *somebody*," Emma Oastler replied. "He forgot the rest of his name."

"I'm sure you can inspire him to remember it, Emma," Mrs. McQuat said.

Although The Gray Ghost was not Asian, her eyes were forcibly slanted by how tightly her hair had been pulled back and knotted into a steel-gray bun. Her thin lips looked sealed in contrast to Emma's, which were usually parted. Emma's mouth was as open as a flower, and on her upper lip, her mustache was as fine as powder—like a dusting of pollen on a petal.

Jack tried to hold back his hand, his right index finger in particular. As quickly as Mrs. McQuat had appeared, she'd disappeared—or else Jack had closed his eyes, in an effort to stop himself from touching Emma's mustache, and he'd missed The Gray Ghost's departure.

"*Think*, Jack." Emma Oastler's breath was as warm as Mrs. McQuat's was cold. "Your full name—you can do it."

"Jack Burns," the boy managed to whisper.

Was it his name or his finger that surprised her? Maybe both. The simultaneity of saying his name at the exact same moment he ran his index finger over her downy upper lip was completely unplanned. The incredible softness of her lip made him whisper: "What's *your* name?"

She seized his index finger and bent it backward. He fell to his knees and cried out in pain. The Gray Ghost made another of her signature sudden appearances. "I said *inspire* him, Emma—not *hurt* him," Mrs. McQuat admonished.

"Emma what?" Jack asked the big girl, who was breaking his finger.

"Emma Oastler," she said, giving his finger an extra twist before she let it go. "And don't you forget it."

Forgetting Emma or her name would be impossible. Even the pain she caused him seemed natural—as if Jack had been born to serve her, or she'd been born to lead him. Mrs. McQuat may have recognized this in Jack's pained expression. He would realize only later that The Gray Ghost had undoubtedly been at St. Hilda's when Jack's father was sleeping with a girl in grade eleven and impregnating a girl in grade thirteen. Why else would she have asked, "Aren't you William Burns's boy?"

That rekindled Emma Oastler's interest in Jack's eyelashes, in a hurry. "Then *you're* the tattoo lady's kid!" Emma exclaimed.

"Yes," Jack said. (And to think he had worried that no one would know him!)

Another teacher was closely observing the new arrivals, and Jack recognized her perfect voice as if he'd heard it every night in his dreams—Miss Caroline Wurtz, who had cured his mother of her Scottish accent. Not only did she excel in enunciation and diction, but the pitch of her voice would have been recognizable anywhere—especially in Jack's dreams. In Edmonton, where she was from, Miss Wurtz would have been considered beautiful—without qualification. In a more international city, like Toronto, her fragile prettiness was the perishable kind. (More likely, she may have suffered some disappointment in her personal life—an illusory love, or an encounter that had passed too quickly.)

"Please give my regards to your mom, Jack," Miss Wurtz said.

"Yes, thank you—I will," the boy replied.

"The tattoo lady has a *limo*?" Emma asked.

"That is Mrs. Wicksteed's car and driver, Emma," Miss Wurtz said.

Once again, The Gray Ghost was gone—Mrs. McQuat had simply disappeared. Jack was aware of Emma's guiding hand on his shoulder, and of his jaw brushing her hip. She bent over him and whispered in his ear; what she said was not for Miss Wurtz to hear: "It must be nice for your mom and you, baby cakes." Jack thought she meant the Lincoln Town Car or Peewee, but Mrs. Wicksteed's patronage of "the tattoo lady" and her bastard son was a story that had gained admittance to St. Hilda's before Jack entered kindergarten. Emma Oastler was referring to Mrs. Wicksteed's broader role as their patroness. The boy also misunderstood what Emma said next: "Way to go, Jack. Not everyone is lucky enough to be a rent-free boarder."

"Thank you," Jack replied, reaching for her hand. He was happy to have made a friend on his first day of school. Since Mrs. Wicksteed's divorced daughter had also referred to Jack and his mom as rent-free boarders, Jack wondered if Emma's mom might be divorced. Maybe women in that situation were particularly sympathetic to a good Old Girl like Mrs. Wicksteed taking Jack and Alice under her wing.

"Is your mother divorced?" Jack asked Emma Oastler. Unfortunately, Emma's mother had been bitterly divorced for several years, and at least one consequence of her divorce had been so spectacularly ugly that she would permanently think of herself as *Mrs.* Oastler. For Emma, the subject was still as sore as a boil.

In what Jack misinterpreted as a gesture of intimacy and unspoken understanding, Emma squeezed his hand. He was sure she didn't mean to hurt him, although her grip was as fierce as the handshake of the front-desk clerk at the Hotel Bristol in Oslo. "Are you Norwegian?" he asked her, but Emma was breathing too hard to hear him. Either in her concerted effort to crush his hand or because she was struggling to control her loathing of what a man-hating monster her mother had become in the aftermath of her divorce, Emma's newly acquired chest was heaving. A tear, which Jack first mistook for a rivulet of sweat, had run down her cheek and now clung to her mustache— like a droplet of dew on new moss. Jack's misgivings about attending St. Hilda's momentarily evaporated. What a splendid idea it was to have the grade-six girls serve as guides to the younger children in the junior school!

On the stone stairs leading to the basement entrance, he stumbled, but Emma not only held him up; she hoisted him to her hip and carried him into his first day of school. Jack threw his arms around her in a flood of gratitude and affection; she returned his embrace so ferociously that he feared he might suffocate against her warm throat. They say that apparitions appear to those who are near fainting, which would explain why Jack first mistook The Gray Ghost for an apparition. There was Mrs. McQuat again—just as Emma Oastler was about to break his back or asphyxiate him with her twelve-year-old bosom.

"Let him go, Emma," The Gray Ghost said. Jack's shirt was untucked and hung almost to his bare knees, though it didn't dangle as low as his tie. He was slightly dizzy and gasping for breath. "Help him tuck in his shirt, Emma," The Gray Ghost said. As soon as she spoke, she was gone—returned to her world of the spirits.

Kneeling, Emma was Jack's height. His gray Bermuda shorts were not only too short; they were too tight. Emma had to undo the top button and unzip the boy's fly in order to tuck in his shirt. Under his shorts, her hands cupped and squeezed his buttocks as she whispered in his ear: "Nice *tushy,* Jack."

Jack had caught his breath sufficiently to pay her a compliment in kind. "Nice *mustache,*" he said—thus cementing their friendship for his remaining years at St. Hilda's, and beyond. Jack thought it must be a good school, as his mom had said, and here—in his first, exciting meeting with Emma Oastler—was probable evidence (at least to Jack) that he would be safe with the girls.

"Oh, Jack," Emma whispered in his ear—her incredibly soft upper lip brushing his neck. "We're gonna have such a good time together."

The arched doorways in the junior-school corridor made Jack Burns think of Heaven. (If there were a passageway to Heaven, Jack used to think, surely it would have arches like that.) And the black-and-gray triangles on the linoleum floors made him feel that school and the grown-up life after it was a game to be played—maybe a game he hadn't yet been exposed to, but a game nonetheless.

Another game was the miniature, broken-window view of the playground from the second-floor washroom—it was the only boys' washroom at St. Hilda's. The frosted-glass windowpanes were small and framed in black-iron squares. One of the panes was broken; it remained unrepaired through Jack's fourth-grade year. And the low urinals in the boys' washroom were not quite low enough when he was in kindergarten. He needed to stand on tiptoe and aim high.

There were the infrequent but intimidating appearances in that second-floor hallway of those older girls who were boarders; one could gain access to their residence through the junior school. Only girls in grade seven and up were admitted to residency, and there were no more than one hundred boarders out of the five hundred girls in the middle and senior school. (St. Hilda's was a city school—most of the students lived at home.)

The older girls who were boarders struck Jack as *much* older. Their detectable sullenness wasn't limited to the daughters of diplomats or the other foreign students, nor was their gloom regional in nature—the cousins who were called "the Nova Scotia sluts" were as depressed as the girl from British Columbia whom Emma Oastler called "the B.C. bitch." The boarders had about them a noticeable air of being banished. The boarders' choir made the most mournful music in the school.

Sightings of the girls in residency were unusual in the junior school, but once, in his grade-three year, Jack was emerging from the boys' washroom (still zipping up his fly), when he saw a couple of grade-thirteen girls striding toward him—a flash of nail polish, kneesocks rolled down to their ankles, shapely legs, wide hips, full breasts. Jack panicked. In his haste, his penis got snagged in his zipper. Naturally, he screamed.

"Sweet Jesus, it's a *boy*!" one of the big girls said.

"I'll say it is, and he's caught his miserable thing in his zipper," the other replied.

"When do they start playing with their things?" the first girl asked. "Stop screaming!" she said sharply to Jack. "You haven't cut it off, have you?"

"Let me do that," the second girl said, kneeling beside Jack. "I have a little brother—I know how to handle this."

"You have to *handle* it?" the first girl asked. She knelt beside Jack, too.

"Let me see it—get your hands off the thing!" the girl with the little brother told Jack.

"It *hurts*!" Jack cried.

"You've just pinched some skin—it's not even bleeding." The girl was at least seventeen or eighteen—maybe nineteen.

"When does it get big?" the first girl asked.

"It doesn't feel like getting big when it's stuck in a zipper, Meredith."

"It gets big when it *feels* like it?" Meredith asked.

The grade-thirteen girl held Jack's penis in her hand; with the thumb and index finger of her other hand, she gently tugged at his zipper.

"Ow!"

"Well, what do you want me to do?" the girl who'd come to his assistance asked. "Wait for you to grow up?"

"You've got lady-killer eyelashes," Meredith told Jack. "When you're old enough, you're going to get your penis stuck in all kinds of places."

"Ow!"

"Now it's bleeding," the second girl said. Jack was unstuck, but she went on holding his penis in her hand.

"What are you *doing,* Amanda?" Meredith asked.

"Just watch," Amanda said. She didn't mean for Jack to watch. Without looking, he could feel his penis getting big—or at least a little bigger.

"What's your name?" Meredith asked him.

"Jack."

"Feeling better, eh, Jack?" Amanda asked.

"Sweet Jesus, *look* at that thing!" Meredith said.

"That's nothing," Amanda said. "You can get bigger than that, can't you, Jack?" He was as big as he'd ever been before. He was afraid that if he got any bigger, he would burst.

"It's beginning to hurt again," he said.

"That's a different kind of pain, Jack." Amanda gave him a friendly squeeze before she let him go.

"Better not catch that whopper in your zipper, Jack," Meredith warned him. She stood up and ruffled his hair.

"Maybe you'll dream about us, Jack," Amanda said.

The cut on Jack's penis healed in a couple of days, but those dreams didn't go away.

Miss Sinclair, Jack's kindergarten teacher, echoed Alice's conviction that Jack would be safe with the girls. This illusion was further advanced by the participation of the grade-six girls in the kindergartners' nap time. Emma Oastler was a volunteer, along with two other grade-six girls—Emma's good friends Charlotte Barford and Wendy Holton. They were Miss Sinclair's nap-time helpers. These older girls were supposed to assist five-year-olds in falling asleep; that they kept the kindergartners awake was closer to the truth.

Miss Sinclair was distinguished in Jack's memory for her habit of condemning him to *nap* with three grade-six girls. What he remembered best about Miss Sinclair was her absence.

The naps began with what Emma Oastler called "a sleepy-time story." Emma was always the storyteller, an early indication of her future calling. While Wendy and Charlotte circulated among the children, making sure that their rubber mats were comfortably rolled out, their blankets snugly wrapped around them, and their shoes off, Emma began her story in the semidark room.

"You've had a bad day, and you're very tired," Emma's stories always began. For stories intended to induce sleep, they had the opposite effect—the kindergartners were too terrified to nap. In an oft-repeated classic among Emma Oastler's nap-time tales, Miss Sinclair lost the entire kindergarten class in the bat-cave exhibit at the Royal Ontario Museum. In reality, Jack's first school trip to the Royal Ontario Museum was led by his grade-*three* teacher, Miss Caroline Wurtz.

Miss Wurtz was the teacher Jack would remember most fondly, and not only for her fragile beauty; she was an important mentor for him in his early mastery of stage presence, another area in which she excelled. Miss Wurtz was a maven in the dramatic arts; in the innumerable school plays in which Jack performed at St. Hilda's, she was usually his director. However, her talents as a classroom teacher were lacking in comparison to her theatrical gifts; control of the grade-three class eluded her. Offstage, out of the fixed glare of the footlights—either in her undisciplined classroom or in the marginally more lawless outside world—Miss Caroline Wurtz was an easily confused creature, bereft of confidence and without an iota of managerial skill.

On school trips, Miss Wurtz could have been a star in one of Emma Oastler's sleepy-time stories—she was that inept. When she lost control of herself in the bat-cave exhibit at the Royal Ontario Museum, most of the grade-three kids were already suffering from total recall of Emma's classic horror tale. (That they were then eight-year-olds, not five-year-olds, hardly mattered; the real-life circumstances were frighteningly familiar to the *former* kindergartners who'd first heard of the bat cave from Emma's fiction.)

When the announcement on the museum loudspeaker informed them that some of the mammal displays were experiencing a temporary loss of electrical power, the children knew this was only the first chapter. "Don't panic," the voice on the loudspeaker said, while Miss Wurtz dissolved into sobs. "The power will be restored in no time." The ultraviolet lights in the bat habitat were still on; in fact, they were the *only* lights that were on, which was exactly the case in Emma's story.

138 | The Sea of Girls

In Emma's version, inexplicably, the defenseless children had no recourse but to crawl *into* the bat cave and sleep with the bats. Emma advised them to be aware of a crucial difference between the alleged "sucking habits" of the vampire bat and those of the giant fruit bat. The kids had to keep their eyes tightly closed at all times, or the ultraviolet light would somehow blind them; and while they slept, or only pretended to sleep, the children were told to pay close attention to the exact location of the hot, moist breath they would certainly feel before long.

If they felt the breath against their throats, that indicated the vampire; the kids were instructed to swat the bat away and protect their throats with both hands. (In Emma's own words: "Just go nuts.") If, however, the aforementioned hot, moist breath was detected in the area of their *navels*—well, that was the area of interest of the despicable giant fruit bat. It would heat the children's stomachs with its breath before licking the salt out of their belly buttons with its raspy tongue; while this sensation might be unpleasant, the children's injuries would be slight. In the case of a fruit bat, the kids were to lie still. In the first place, the giant fruit bat was too big to swat away—and, according to Emma, fruit bats only became truly dangerous when they were startled.

"But what would a startled fruit bat *do*?" Jack remembered Jimmy Bacon asking.

"Better not tell him, Emma," Charlotte Barford said.

The conclusion to Emma's tale of the kindergartners' abandonment in the bat habitat was nerve-wracking. When you consider that most of the children were too frightened to fall asleep, they surely knew that Emma Oastler and Wendy Holton and Charlotte Barford were breathing on them—not the bats. Nevertheless, the kids responded as instructed. The kindergartners having their navels breathed on kept still. In the many retellings of the tale, Jack learned to distinguish the not-so-subtle differences between Charlotte's and Wendy's and Emma's tongues. Their tongues were *not* raspy; indeed, discounting future nightmares, the children's injuries were slight. And they responded with appropriate zeal to the neck-breathing tactics of the vampire bat—in short, the kids went nuts, covering their throats and screaming while they swatted away.

"Time to wake up, Jack," Emma (or Charlotte or Wendy) always said. But he never went to sleep.

* * *

Charlotte Barford was a big girl, a grade-six virtual woman in the mold of Emma Oastler. Wendy Holton, on the other hand, was a feral-looking waif. If you overlooked the evidence of puberty-related troubles in the dark circles under Wendy's eyes—and her swollen, bitten lips—she could have passed for nine. Her smaller size and childlike physique didn't diminish Wendy's navel-licking capacity; her fruit-bat imitation was more aggressive than Emma's, more invasive than Charlotte's. (In keeping with her melon-size knees, Charlotte Barford's tongue was too broad and thick to fit in Jack's navel—even the tip.)

Did Miss Sinclair ever return to her kindergarten class and find the children refreshed from their naps? Did she mistake how alert they looked for their being well rested? The kids were relieved, of course, and no doubt looked it; that they'd survived another of Emma Oastler's sleepy-time tales, both the *not*-falling-asleep part and the always creative manner in which they were woken up, gave them thankful expressions.

Another classic among Emma's nap-time stories, and a close rival to her tale of the kindergartners' abandonment in the bat-cave exhibit at the Royal Ontario Museum, was her saga of the squeezed child. It was a tale with three different endings, but it began, as Emma's stories always did: "You've had a bad day, and you're very tired."

Jack napped between Gordon and Caroline French, brother-and-sister twins who had to be separated because they despised each other. Another set of twins in Miss Sinclair's kindergarten class, Heather and Patsy Booth, were identical girls who couldn't bear to be separated. When one of them was sick, the other one stayed home to grieve—or perhaps to wait her turn to be sick as well. When the Booth twins napped, they overlapped their rubber mats and wrapped themselves in the same blanket—possibly to simulate their former occupancy of the same uterus.

Both sets of twins became agitated, but in different ways, during the telling of the squeezed-child tale. The identical Booth girls sucked their shared blanket; they emitted a wet humming sound, which in turn upset Jimmy Bacon, who commenced to moan. The agitation of Gordon and Caroline French, the boy-girl twins on either side of Jack, was more physical in nature and came in unexpected bursts of frenzied, seemingly pointless activity. Under their separate blankets, the French twins thumped their heels on their rubber mats, their stiff legs drumming out of sync; as startling as this was, it was more disturbing when they stopped. The French twins stopped kicking so abruptly, it was as if they'd died of a shared disease—in spite of their enforced separation from each other.

The three possible conclusions to Emma Oastler's squeezed-child story had the kindergartners enthralled. "For three of you," Emma always said, "your bad day just got worse." Sudden heel-thumping from the French twins, which was quickly followed by their as-sudden deaths; identical blanket-sucking sounds intermingled with humming from the Booth twins; dire moaning from Jimmy Bacon. "One of you is spending the night with your divorced dad," Emma went on. "He has just passed out from too much sex." (Jack *hated* this part.)

Maureen Yap, a nervous girl whose father was Chinese, once interrupted Emma by asking: "What is too much sex?"

"Nothing you'll ever have," Emma answered dismissively.

Another time, when Jack asked Emma the same question, Emma said: "You'll know soon enough, Jack."

Jack shuddered under his blanket. He was relying on his flawed understanding of his mom's conversation in Amsterdam with Saskia and Els. If you looked sexy, Els had said, men thought you could give them good advice. Sex, therefore, was related to advice-giving; like advice, Jack guessed, sex could be good or bad. If the divorced dad in Emma Oastler's story had passed out from too much sex, Jack suspected this was the worst kind.

"Your dad has had bad girlfriends before," Emma continued, "but this one is just a kid. A skinny, tough kid," Emma added. "She's as tough as a stick, her fists are as hard as stones, and she hates you. You get in her way. She could have even more sex with your dad if you weren't around. After your dad passes out, she grinds her fists against your temples—you think she's going to crush your head!"

The French twins were flutter-kicking, as if on cue; more blanket-sucking, humming, and moaning. "Meanwhile," Emma always said, "one of you has a single mother who's passed out, too." (Jack *really* hated this part.)

"Too much sex *again*!" Maureen Yap usually cried.

"*Bad* sex?" Jack sometimes asked.

"A bad *boyfriend*," Emma informed the kindergartners. "One of the *biggest* bad boyfriends in the world. When your mother passes out, he comes and lies on top of you—he covers your face with his bare stomach."

"How do you breathe?" Grant Porter, a moron, always asked.

"That's the problem," Emma usually answered. "Maybe you can't." Unprecedented, out-of-sync heel-drumming from the French twins; soggy-blanket noises from the Booth twins; moans, approximating suffocation, from Jimmy Bacon.

"But what about your mother who has a *girlfriend*?" Emma asked. (Jack hated this part most of all.) "She has bigger breasts than all your mothers. She has *harder* breasts than all your dads' youngest girlfriends. She has *bionic* breasts," Emma said. "Like they have *bones* inside them—they're that big and hard." The very idea of breasts with *bones* inside them would, years later, still wake Jack Burns from a sound sleep—not that any of the kindergartners slept a wink during the squeezed-child saga. "Which of these poor kids are *you*?" Emma asked every time.

"I don't wanna be *anybody*!" Maureen Yap predictably cried.

"I especially don't want to be trying to breathe with the bad boyfriend's big belly on my face," Grant Porter usually made a point of saying.

"Not the breasts with *bones*!" James Turner, another moron, always yelled.

Sometimes Jack mustered the courage to say: "I think I like the tough, skinny girlfriend's fists of stone the *least*." But Emma Oastler and Wendy Holton and Charlotte Barford had already made their selections. With his eyes tightly closed, Jack could nonetheless sense them moving into their chosen positions.

The divorced dad's skinny, tough girlfriend with the fists of stone—well, that was Wendy Holton. She squeezed your temples between her knees. Her knees were as small and hard as baseballs. She could give Jack a headache in less than a minute—and the view up her skirt, when he dared to look, was disappointingly dark and unclear.

The unthinkable mother's girlfriend with the bionic breasts, the breasts with *bones* inside them—that was Charlotte Barford with her melon-size knees. No breasts ever felt like *knees*—not before there were implants, anyway. As for the view up Charlotte's skirt, Jack never looked; the imagined consequences of her catching him looking were too intense.

And the mom's bad boyfriend, the one who spread his bare belly on your face and made you fight for your last breath—that was Emma Oastler, of course. Jack first located her belly button with his nose; he found a little room to breathe there. Once, when he explored her navel with his tongue, Emma said: "Boy, do you ever *not* know what you're doing."

It was only slightly less scary at the *actual* bat-cave exhibit. While Miss Caroline Wurtz was losing her mind, the grade-three children could at least rest assured that only vampire bats and giant fruit bats might approach them. No divorced dads' bad girlfriends—no single moms' bad boyfriends *or* girlfriends— were hanging out in the bat habitat! Compared to these sexual predators of the recently divorced, what did the kids have to fear from mere *bats*?

As for those grade-three children who'd not attended kindergarten at St. Hilda's, they were initially unfrightened by the power failure in some of the mammal displays at the Royal Ontario Museum; they'd had no previous experience in the bat-cave exhibit to be frightened of. But the former kindergartners among them were frightened enough that their terror was infectious.

That Miss Wurtz was also afraid was at first unsurprising— she had a history of coming unglued in the grade-three classroom. However, in the bat-cave exhibit, Miss Wurtz could not call upon The Gray Ghost for help. In the environs of the junior school, Miss Wurtz was routinely rescued by the supernaturally sudden appearances of Mrs. McQuat. Not in the Royal Ontario Museum with Jack and his fellow third graders wailing around her; that they'd instantly closed their eyes further disconcerted Miss Wurtz.

"Open your *eyes,* children! Don't go to *sleep*! Not in *here*!" Miss Wurtz cried.

Caroline French, with her eyes firmly closed, offered the hysterical teacher some excellent advice: "Don't startle the fruit bats, Miss Wurtz—they're only dangerous if they're startled."

"Open your *eyes,* Caroline!" Miss Wurtz shrieked.

"If the hot, moist breath is at your throat, that's another matter," Caroline French went on.

"The *what* at my throat?" Miss Wurtz asked, her hands on her neck.

Jack's feelings for Miss Wurtz were deeply conflicted. He was embarrassed for her that she had no mastery of stage presence in a real-life crisis, but he believed she was beautiful. He secretly loved her. "She means a vampire bat," Jack tried to explain to Miss Wurtz, although Caroline French detested being interrupted. (Her brother interrupted her frequently.)

"You'll just frighten Miss Wurtz, Jack," Caroline said crossly. "Miss Wurtz—if the hot, moist breathing is at your *throat*, go nuts. Just swat it away."

"Swat *what* away?" Miss Wurtz wailed.

"But if you feel the breaths on your belly button, remain calm," Gordon French said, in seeming contradiction of his hostile twin sister.

"Just don't move," Jack added.

"*Nothing's* breathing on my belly button!" Miss Wurtz screamed.

"You see, Jack?" Caroline French said. "You've made it worse, haven't you?"

"Don't panic," the voice on the loudspeaker repeated. "The power will be restored in no time."

"I forget why we have to crawl *inside* the bat cave," Jimmy Bacon said. (None of them could remember that part of Emma Oastler's story.)

"Nobody's crawling *inside* the bat cave!" Miss Wurtz raved. "All of you open your *eyes*!" Jack thought of telling her that the ultraviolet lights would blind them somehow, but she seemed too upset for more bad news.

"I feel a fruit bat," Jack whispered, without moving, but it was Maureen Yap; she had dropped to her knees and was hyperventilating in close proximity to his navel.

"Stop that!" Miss Wurtz shouted. Jimmy Bacon was moaning while he rubbed his head against her hip. Miss Wurtz may not have meant to grab Jimmy by the throat, but Jimmy reacted in the vampire-bat fashion; he went nuts, screaming and swatting away. Miss Caroline Wurtz screamed, too. (And to think she believed so adamantly in "measured restraint" onstage!)

That was Jack's first school trip at St. Hilda's. Like much of his junior-school experience, it would have seemed slight without the necessary preparations for the journey ahead, which had been provided for him in kindergarten by Emma Oastler—the nap-time storyteller who had appointed herself his personal girl guide.

Oh, what a lucky boy Jack was! Safe among the girls, without a doubt.

9
Not Old Enough

When Jack started grade one, Emma Oastler and her companions had moved on to the middle school—they were in grade seven. Less fearsome girls became the grade-six guides of the junior school; Jack wouldn't remember them. Sometimes a whole school day, but rarely two in a row, would pass without his seeing Emma, who fiercely promised him that she would always keep in touch. And Jack's occasional sightings of Wendy Holton and Charlotte Barford were usually from a safe distance. (Fists-of-Stone Holton, as he still thought of Wendy. Breasts-with-*Bones*-in-Them Barford, as he would forever remember Charlotte and her melon-size knees.)

Miss Wong, Jack's grade-one teacher, had been born in the Bahamas during a hurricane. Nothing noticeably like a tropical storm had remained alive in her, although her habit of apologizing for everything might have begun with the hurricane. She would never acknowledge by name the particular storm she had been born in, which might have led the grade-one children to suspect that the hurricane still flickered somewhere in her subconscious. No trace of a storm animated her listless body or gave the slightest urgency to her voice. "I am sorry to inform you, children, that the foremost difference between kindergarten and grade one is that we don't nap," Miss Wong announced on opening day.

Naturally, her apology was greeted by collective sighs of relief, and some spontaneous expressions of gratitude— heel-thumping from the French twins, identical blanket-sucking sounds from the Booth girls, heartfelt moaning from Jimmy Bacon. That the grade-one response to her no-nap announcement did not inspire a storm of curiosity from "Miss Bahamas," as the children called Miss Wong behind her back, was further indication of the lifelessness of their new teacher.

During junior-school chapel service, which was held once a week in lieu of the daily assembly in the Great Hall, Maureen Yap whispered to Jack: "Don't you kind of *miss* Emma Oastler and her sleepy-time stories?" There was an instant lump in Jack's throat; he could neither sing nor make conversation with The Yap, as the kids called Maureen. "I know how you feel," The Yap went on. "But what was the *worst* of it? What do you miss *most*?"

"*All* of it," Jack managed to reply.

"We *all* miss it, Jack," Caroline French said.

"We all miss *all* of it," her irritating twin, Gordon, corrected her.

"Shove it, Gordon," Caroline said.

"I kind of miss the moaning," Jimmy Bacon admitted. The Booth girls, though blanketless, made their identical blanket-sucking sounds.

Did the grade-one children crave stories of divorced dads, passed out from too much sex? Did they long to be defenseless, yet again, in the bat-cave exhibit at the Royal Ontario Museum? Did they miss the single-mom stories, or the overlarge and oversexed boyfriends and girlfriends? Or was it Emma Oastler they missed? Emma and her friends on the verge of puberty, or in puberty's throes—Wendy Fists-of-Stone Holton and Charlotte Breasts-with-*Bones*-in-Them Barford.

There was a new girl in grade one, Lucinda Fleming. She was afflicted with what Miss Wong called "silent rage," which took the form of the girl physically hurting herself. When Miss Wong introduced Lucinda's affliction to the class, she spoke of her as if she weren't there.

"We must keep an eye on Lucinda," Miss Wong told the class. Lucinda calmly received their stares. "If you see her with a sharp or dangerous-looking object, you should not hesitate to speak to me. If she looks as if she is trying to go off by herself somewhere—well, that could be dangerous for her, too. Forgive me if I'm wrong, but isn't that what we should do, Lucinda?" Miss Wong asked the silent girl.

"It's okay with me," Lucinda said, smiling serenely. She was tall and thin with pale-blue eyes and a habit of rubbing a strand of her ghostly, white-blond hair against her teeth—as if her hair were dental floss. She wore it in a massive ponytail.

Caroline French inquired if this habit was harmful to Lucinda's hair or teeth. Caroline's point was that teeth-and-hair rubbing was probably an early indication of the silent rage, a precursor to more troubling behavior.

"I'm sorry to disagree, but I don't think so, Caroline," Miss Wong replied. "You're not trying to hurt yourself with your hair or your teeth, are you, Lucinda?" Miss Wong asked.

"Not now," Lucinda mumbled. She had a strand of hair in her mouth when she spoke.

"It doesn't look dangerous to me," Maureen Yap said. (The Yap occasionally sucked her hair.)

"Yeah, but it's *gross,*" said Heather Booth.

Patsy, Heather's identical twin, said, "Yeah."

Jack thought it was probably a good thing that Lucinda Fleming was a new girl and had not attended kindergarten at St. Hilda's. Who knows how Emma Oastler might have affected Lucinda's proclivity to silent rage? Between mouthfuls of hair, Lucinda told Jack that her mother had been impregnated by an alien; she said her father was from outer space. Although he was only six, Jack surmised that Lucinda's mom was divorced. Emma Oastler's saga of the squeezed child, no matter which ending, would have given Lucinda Fleming a rage to top all her rages.

Jack Burns avoided what was called "the quad," even in the spring, when the cherry trees were in bloom. The ground-floor rooms for music practice faced the courtyard; you could overhear the piano lessons from the quad. Jack occasionally imagined that his dad was still teaching someone in one of those rooms. He hated to hear that music.

And the white, round chandeliers in the dining room reminded him of blank globes—of the earth strangely countryless, without discernible borders, not even indications of land and sea. Like the world where his father had gone missing; William Burns might as well have come from outer space.

Jack looked carefully for evidence of Lucinda Fleming's silent rage for the longest time, never seeing it. He wondered if he would recognize the symptoms—if he'd had a rage of his own here or there, but had somehow not known what it was. Who were the authorities on rage? (Not Miss Wong, who'd clearly managed to lose contact with the hurricane inside her.)

Jack wasn't used to seeing so little of his mother; he left for school before she got up and was asleep before she came home. As for rage, what Alice had of it might have been expressed in the pain-inflicting needles with which she marked for life so many people—mainly men.

Mrs. Wicksteed, who did Jack's necktie so patiently but absentmindedly, stuck to her be-nice-twice philosophy without ever imparting to the boy what he should do if he were pressed to be nice a third time. That he was instructed to *be creative* struck Jack as a nonspecific form of advice; no silent rage, or rage of any kind, was in evidence there. And Lottie, despite having lost a child, had left what amounted to her rage on Prince Edward Island—or so she implied to Jack.

"I'm not an angry person anymore, Jack," Lottie said, when he asked her what she knew about rage in general—and the silent kind, in particular. "The best thing I can tell you is not to give in to it," Lottie said.

Jack would later imagine that Lottie was one of those women, neither young nor old, whose sexuality had been fleeting; only small traces of her remaining desire were visible, in the way you might catch her looking at herself in profile in a mirror. Glimpses of Lottie's former attractiveness were apparent to Jack only in her most unguarded moments—when he had a nightmare and roused her from a sound sleep, or when she woke him up for school in the morning before she'd taken the time to attend to herself.

Short of asking Lucinda Fleming to talk to him about her silent rage, which would have been far too simple and straightforward a solution for any six-year-old boy to conceive of, Jack worked up his courage and asked Emma Oastler instead. (If Emma wasn't an authority on rage, who was?) But Jack was afraid of Emma; her cohorts struck him as somewhat safer places to start. That was why he worked up his courage to ask Emma by asking Wendy Holton and Charlotte Barford first. He began with Wendy, only because she was the smaller of the two.

The junior school got a half-hour head start for lunch. How

fitting that it was under the blank globes of the dining-hall chandeliers, those unmarked worlds, where Jack spoke to Wendy. How well (and for how long!) he would remember her haunted eyes, her chewed lips, her unbrushed, dirty-blond hair—not forgetting her scraped knees, as hard as fists of stone.

"*What* rage was that, Jack?"

"Silent."

"What about it, you little creep?"

"Well, what *is* it, exactly—what is silent rage?" he asked.

"You're not eating the mystery meat, are you?" Wendy asked, viewing his plate with disapproval.

"No, I would never eat that," Jack answered. He separated the gray meat from the beige potatoes with his fork.

"You wanna see a little *rage,* Jack?"

"Yes, I guess so," he replied cautiously—never taking his eyes off her. Wendy had an unsettling habit of cracking her knuckles by pressing them into her underdeveloped breasts.

"You wanna meet me in the washroom?" Wendy asked.

"The *girls'* washroom?"

"I'm not getting caught with you in the *boys'* washroom, you dork." Jack wanted to think it over, but it was hard to think clearly with Wendy standing over him at his table. The word *dork* itself unsettled him; it seemed so out of place at a mostly all-girls' school.

"Forgive me for intruding, but aren't you having any lunch, Wendy?" Miss Wong asked.

"I'd rather die," Wendy told her.

"Well, I'm certainly sorry to hear that!" Miss Wong said.

"You wanna follow me, or are you *chicken*?" Wendy whispered in Jack's ear. He could feel one of her hard, bruised knees against his ribs.

"Okay," he answered.

Officially, Jack needed Miss Wong's permission to leave the dining hall, but Miss Wong was typically in an overapologetic mood (having blamed herself for attempting to force lunch on Wendy Holton, when Wendy would *rather die*). "Miss Wong—" he started to say.

"Yes, of *course,* Jack," she blurted out. "I'm *so sorry* if I've made you feel self-conscious, or that I may have delayed your leaving the table for whatever obvious good reason you have for leaving. *Heavens!* Don't let me hold you up another *second*!"

"I'll be right back," was all he managed to say.

"I'm sure you will be, Jack," Miss Wong said. Perhaps the faint hurricane inside her had been overcome by her contrition.

In the girls' washroom nearest the dining hall, Wendy Holton took Jack into a stall and stood him on the toilet seat. She just grabbed him in the armpits and lifted him up. Standing on the toilet seat, he was eye-to-eye with her; so he wouldn't slip, Wendy held him by the hips.

"You want to feel rage, *inner* rage, Jack?"

"I said *silent,* silent rage."

"Same difference, penis breath," Wendy said.

Now there was a concept that would stay with Jack Burns for many years—*penis breath*! What a deeply disturbing concept it was.

"Feel *this,*" Wendy said. She took his hands and placed them on her breasts—on her *no* breasts, to be more precise.

"Feel *what*?" he asked.

"Don't be a dork, Jack—you know what they are."

"This is *rage*?" the boy asked. By no stretch of his imagination could he have called what his small hands held *breasts*.

"I'm the only girl in grade seven who *doesn't* have them!" Wendy exclaimed, in a smoldering fury. Well, this was rage without a doubt.

"Oh."

"That's all you can say?" she asked.

"I'm sorry," Jack quickly said. (How to apologize was all he had learned from Miss Wong.)

"Jack, you're just not *old enough,*" Wendy declared. She left him standing precariously on the toilet seat. "When I knock on the door from the hall three times, you'll know it's safe to come out," she told him. "*Rage,*" Wendy said, almost as an afterthought.

"*Silent* rage," Jack repeated, for clarity's sake. He saw that he should approach Charlotte Barford a little differently on this subject. But *how*?

When Wendy knocked on the washroom door three times, Jack exited into the hall. Miss Caroline Wurtz looked surprised to see him; there was no one else in the corridor. "Jack Burns," Miss Wurtz said perfectly, as always. "It disappoints me to see you using the girls' washroom." Jack was disappointed, too, and said so, which seemed to instill in Miss Wurtz the spirit of for-giveness; she liked it when you said you understood how she felt, but her recovery from being *disappointed* was not always so swift.

Jack had higher expectations for what he might learn from Charlotte Barford. Charlotte at least *had* breasts, he'd observed. Whatever the source of *her* rage, it was not an underdeveloped bosom. Unfortunately, he hadn't fully prepared how he wanted to approach Charlotte Barford before Charlotte approached *him*.

Once a week, after lunch, Jack sang in the primary choir. They performed mostly in those special services—Canadian Thanksgiving, Christmas, Remembrance Day. They did a bang-up *Gaudeamus* at Easter.

> *Come, ye faithful, raise the strain*
> *Of triumphant gladness!*

Jack avoided all eye contact with the organist. He'd already met a lifetime of organists; even though the organist at St. Hilda's was a woman, she still reminded him of his talented dad.

The day Jack ran into Charlotte Barford in the corridor, he was humming either "Fairest Lord Jesus" or "Joyful, Joyful, We Adore Thee"—similar adorations. Jack was passing the same girls' washroom where Wendy Holton had forced him to feel her *no* breasts while imagining her rage—he would remember that washroom to his dying day—when Charlotte Barford opened the washroom door. With her hands still wet and smelling of dis-infectant from that awful liquid soap, Charlotte pulled him back into the washroom.

"*What* rage, Jack?" she asked, pinning him to a sink with one of her big, bare knees. There it was, in the pit of his stomach—a so-called breast with *bones* in it!

"The silent, inner kind—rage that doesn't go away," Jack guessed.

"It's what you don't know, what people won't tell you, what you have to wait to find out for yourself," Charlotte said, driving her knee a little deeper. "All the stuff that makes you angry, Jack."

"But I don't know if I *am* angry," the boy said.

"Sure you are," Charlotte said. "Your dad is a total *doink.* He's made you and your mom virtual *charity cases*. Everyone's betting on you, Jack."

"On *me*? What's the bet?"

"That you're gonna be a *womanizer*, like your father."

"What's a *womanizer*?" Jack asked.

"You'll know soon enough, squirrel dink," she said. "By the way, you're not touching *my* breasts," Charlotte whispered. Biting his earlobe, she added: "Not yet."

Jack knew the exit routine. He waited in the washroom until Charlotte knocked three times on the door from the hall. He was surprised, this time, that Miss Wurtz wasn't passing by in the corridor at that very moment—there was only Charlotte Barford, walking away. Her hips had the same involuntary roll to them that he remembered of Ingrid Moe's full-stride departure from the Hotel Bristol, although Charlotte's skirt was much too short for Oslo in the winter.

There was a lot he didn't know—not just what a *womanizer* was, but what were *charity cases*? And now, in addition to *penis breath* and *doink*, there was *squirrel dink* to ponder.

Jack could not imagine that this was "proper" material for his next necktie-tying conversation with Mrs. Wicksteed—not in her early-morning curlers and avocado oil, fortified only by her first cup of tea—nor did these issues strike the boy as suitable to raise with Lottie. Her earlier hardships, her undiscussed limp and the life she'd left behind on Prince Edward Island, did not predispose Lottie to stressful dialogue of any kind. And of course he knew what his mother's response would be. "We'll discuss this when you're old enough," his mom was fond of saying. Certain subjects were in the same category as getting your first tattoo, for which (according to Alice) you also had to be *old enough*.

Well, Jack knew someone who was old enough. When he was adrift in grade one, under the apologetic supervision of the weatherless Miss Wong, Emma Oastler was in grade seven, thirteen going on twenty-one. No topics were off-limits for conversation with Emma. There was only the problem of how pissed-off she was. (Jack knew Emma would be furious with him for speaking to Wendy and Charlotte first.)

Don't misunderstand the outlaw corridors and washroom thuggery—namely, the older girls' behavior *outside* the classroom. St. Hilda's was a good school, and an especially rigorous one—academically. Perhaps the demands of the classroom created an urgency to act up among the older girls; they needed to express themselves in opposition to the correct diction and letter-perfect enunciation, of which Miss Wurtz was not the only champion among the generally excellent faculty at the school. The girls needed a language of their own—corridor-speak, or washroom grammar. That was why there was a lot of "Lemme-see" stuff—all the "I'm gonna, dontcha-wanna, gimme-that-thing-*now*" crap—which was the way the older girls talked among themselves, or to Jack. If they ever spoke in this fashion in their respective classrooms, the faculty—not only Miss Wurtz—would have instantly reprimanded them.

Not so Peewee, Mrs. Wicksteed's Jamaican driver. Peewee was in no position to criticize how Emma Oastler spoke to Jack in the backseat of the Lincoln Town Car. To begin with, both Peewee and Jack were surprised the first time Emma slid into the backseat. It was a cold, rainy afternoon. Emma lived in Forest Hill; she usually walked to and from school. After school—in both her middle- and her senior-school years—Emma normally hung out in a restaurant and coffee shop at the corner of Spadina and Lonsdale with a bunch of her older-girl friends. Not this day, and it wasn't the cold or the rain.

"You need help with your homework, Jack," Emma announced. (The boy was in grade one. He wouldn't have much homework before grade two, and he wouldn't really need help with it before grades three and four.)

"Where are we taking the girl, mon?" Peewee asked Jack.

"Take me home with him," Emma told the driver. "We've got a *shitload* of work to do—haven't we, Jack?"

"She sounds like she's the boss, mon," Peewee said. Jack couldn't argue with that. Emma had slumped down in the backseat, pulling him down beside her.

"I'm gonna give you a valuable tip, Jack," she whispered. "I'm sure there will come a day when you'll find it useful to remember this."

"Remember *what*?" he whispered back.

"If you can't see the driver's eyes in the rearview mirror," Emma whispered, "that means the driver can't see you."

"Oh." At that moment, Jack couldn't see Peewee's eyes.

"We have such a lot of ground to cover," Emma went on. "What's important for you to remember is this: if there's anything you don't understand, you ask *me*. Wendy Holton is a twisted little bitch—never ask Wendy! Charlotte Barford is a one-speed blow job waiting to happen. You're putting your life *and* your doink in her hands every time you talk to Charlotte! Remember: if there's anything *new* that occurs to you, tell me first."

"Like *what*?" the boy asked.

"You'll know," she told him. "Like when you first feel that you want to touch a girl. When the feeling is un-fucking-stoppable, tell me."

"Touch a girl *where*?"

"You'll know," Emma repeated.

"Oh." Jack wondered if his wanting to touch Emma's mustache was necessary to confess, since he'd already done it.

"Do you feel like touching *me*, Jack?" Emma asked. "Go on—you can tell me."

His head didn't come up to her shoulder, not even slumped down in the backseat; there was the suddenly strong attraction to lay his head on her chest, exactly between her throat and her emerging breasts. But her mustache was still the most appealing thing about her, and he knew she was sensitive to his touching it.

"Okay, so that's established," Emma said. "So you *don't* feel like touching me, not yet." Jack was sad the opportunity had been missed, and he must have looked it. "Don't be sad, Jack," Emma whispered. "It's gonna happen."

"*What's* going to happen?"

"You're gonna be like your *dad*—we're all counting on it. You're gonna open your share of doors, Jack."

"*What* doors?" When Emma didn't answer him, the boy assumed that he had hit upon another item in the not-old-enough category. "What's a *womanizer*?" he asked, imagining he had changed the subject.

"Someone who can't ever have enough women, honey pie—someone who wants one woman after another, with no rest in between."

Well, that wouldn't be me, Jack thought. In the sea of girls in which he found himself, he couldn't imagine wanting *more*. In the St. Hilda's chapel, in the stained glass behind the altar, four women—saints, Jack assumed—were attending to Jesus. At St. Hilda's, even *Jesus* was surrounded by women. There were women everywhere!

"What are *charity cases*?" he asked Emma.

"At the moment, that would be you and your mom, Jack."

"But what does it *mean*?"

"You're dependent on Mrs. Wicksteed's money, Jack. No tattoo artist makes enough money to send a kid to St. Hilda's."

"Here we are, miss," Peewee said, as if Emma were the sole passenger in the limo. Peewee pulled the Town Car to the curb at the corner of Spadina and Lowther, where Lottie was standing with most of her weight on one foot.

"Looks like The Limp is waiting for you, baby cakes," Emma whispered in Jack's ear.

"Why, hello, Emma—*my,* how you've grown!" Lottie managed to say.

"We've got no time to chat, Lottie," Emma said. "Jack is having trouble understanding a few important things. I'm here to help him."

"My goodness," Lottie said, limping after them. Emma, with her long strides, led Jack to the door.

"I trust The Wickweed is napping, Jack," Emma whispered. "We'll have to be quiet—there's no need to wake her up."

Jack had not heard Mrs. Wicksteed called The Wickweed before, but Emma Oastler's authority was unquestionable. She even knew the back staircase from the kitchen, leading to Jack's and Alice's rooms.

Later it was easy enough to understand: Emma Oastler's man-hating monster of a divorced mother was a friend of Mrs. Wicksteed's divorced daughter—hence their shared perception of Jack and his mom as Mrs. Wicksteed's rent-free boarders. Emma's mom and Mrs. Wicksteed's daughter were Old Girls, too; they had graduated from St. Hilda's in the same class. (They were not much older than Alice.)

Calling downstairs to Lottie, who was aimlessly limping around in the kitchen, Emma said: "If we need anything, like tea or something, we'll come get it. Don't trouble yourself to climb the stairs, Lottie. Try giving your limp a *rest*!"

In Jack's room, Emma began by pulling back his bedcovers

and examining his sheets. Seemingly disappointed, she put the covers loosely back in place. "Listen to me, Jack—here's what'll happen, but not for a while. One morning, you're gonna wake up and find a mess in your sheets."

"*What* mess?"

"You'll know."

"Oh."

Emma had moved on—through the bathroom, to his mother's room—leaving him to reflect upon the mystery mess.

Alice's room smelled like pot, although Jack never saw her smoke a joint in there; in all likelihood, the marijuana clung to her clothes. He knew she took a toke or two at the Chinaman's, because he could occasionally smell it in her hair.

Emma Oastler inhaled appreciatively, giving Jack a secretive look. She seemed to be conducting a survey of the clothes in his mom's closet. She held up a sweater and examined herself in the closet-door mirror, imagining how the sweater might fit her; she held one of Alice's skirts at her hips.

"She's kind of a *hippie,* your mom—isn't she, Jack?"

Jack had not thought of his mom as a hippie before, but she *was* kind of a hippie. At that time, especially to the uniformed girls at St. Hilda's and the ever-increasing legion of their divorced mothers, Alice was most certainly a hippie. (A hippie was probably the *best* you could say about an unwed mother who was also a tattoo artist.)

Jack Burns would learn later that it was no big deal—how a woman could look at an unfamiliar chest of drawers and know, at a glance, which drawer another woman would use for her underwear. Emma was only thirteen, but she knew. She opened Alice's underwear drawer on her first try. Emma held up a bra to her developing breasts; the bra was too big, but even Jack could tell that one day it wouldn't be. For no reason that he could discern, his penis was as stiff as a pencil—but it was only about the size of his mother's pinkie, and his mom had small hands.

"Show me your hard-on, honey pie," Emma said; she was still holding up Alice's bra.

"My *what*?"

"You've got a *boner,* Jack—for Christ's sake, lemme see it."

He knew what a *boner* was. His mom, that old hippie, called

it a *woody.* Whatever you called it, Jack showed Emma Oastler his penis in his mother's bedroom. What probably made it
worse was that Lottie was limping around in the kitchen below
them, just as old Mrs. Wicksteed was waking up from her afternoon nap, and Emma gave his hard-on a close but disappointed
look. "Jeez, Jack—I don't think you'll be ready for quite a
while."

"Ready for *what*?"

"You'll know," she said again.

"The kettle's boiling!" Lottie cried from the kitchen.

"Then shut it off!" Emma hollered downstairs. "Jeez," Emma
said again, to Jack, "you better keep an eye on that thing, and tell
me when it squirts."

"When I *pee*?"

"You're gonna know when it's *not* pee, Jack."

"Oh."

"The point is, tell me *everything*," Emma said. She took his
penis in her hand. He was anxious, remembering how she'd bent
his index finger. "Don't tell your mom—you'll just freak her out.
And don't tell Lottie—you'll make her limp worse."

"Why does Lottie limp?" Jack asked. Emma Oastler was such
an authority, he assumed she would know. Alas, she *did*.

"She had an epidural go haywire," Emma explained. "The
baby died anyway. It was a real bad deal."

So you could get a limp from a childbirth that went awry! Naturally, Jack thought an epidural was a part of the body, a *female*
part. In the manner in which he'd assumed his mom's C-section
referred to an area of the hospital in Halifax where Jack was
born, so he believed that Lottie had *lost* her epidural in childbirth. Jack must have imagined that an epidural was somehow
crucial to the female anatomy; possibly it prevented limps. Years
later, when he couldn't find *epidural* in the index of *Gray's
Anatomy,* Jack would be reminded of his C-section mistake.
(That his mother had never had a Cesarean would be an even
bigger discovery.)

"Tea's brewing!" Lottie called to Jack and Emma from the
kitchen. Only when he was older would it occur to him that Lottie knew Emma was a menacing girl.

"Have a wet dream for me, little guy," Emma said to Jack's penis. She was such a good friend; she gently helped his penis find

its proper place, back inside his pants, and she was especially careful how she zipped up his fly.

"Do penises have dreams?" Jack asked.

"Just remember to tell me when *your* little guy has one," Emma said.

10

His Audience of One

Jack's grade-two teacher, Mr. Malcolm—at that time, one of only two male teachers at St. Hilda's—was inseparable from his wife, whom he daily brought to school for dire reasons. She was blind and wheelchair-bound, and it seemed to soothe her to hear Mr. Malcolm speak. He was an excellent teacher, patient and kind. Everyone liked Mr. Malcolm, but the entire grade-two class felt sorry for him; his blind and wheelchair-bound wife was a horror. In a school where so many of the older girls were outwardly cruel and inwardly self-destructive, which was not infrequently blamed on their parents' tumultuous divorces, the grade-two kids prayed, every day, that Mr. Malcolm would divorce his wife. Had he murdered her, the class would have forgiven him; if he'd killed her in front of them, they might have applauded.

But Mr. Malcolm was ever the peacemaker, and his shaving choices were ahead of their time. Growing bald, he had shaved his head—not all that common in the early 1970s—and, even less common, he preferred varying lengths of stubble to an actual beard or to being clean-shaven. Back then it was a credit to St. Hilda's that they accepted Mr. Malcolm's shaved head and his stubbled face; not unlike the grade-two children, the administrators of the school had decided not to cause Mr. Malcolm any further harm. The blind wife in the wheelchair made everyone take pity on him.

In the grade-two classroom, the children worked diligently to please him. Mr. Malcolm never had to discipline them; they disciplined themselves. They would do nothing to upset him. Life had already been unfair enough to Mr. Malcolm.

Emma Oastler's assessment of the tragedy was colored by her

own intimacy with human cruelty, but in her view of the Malcolms as a couple, Emma was probably not wrong. Mrs. Malcolm, whose name was Jane, fell off a roof at a church picnic. She was high school age at the time, a pretty and popular girl—suddenly paralyzed from the waist down. According to Emma, Mr. Malcolm had been a somewhat younger admirer of Jane's. He fell in love with her when she was paralyzed, chiefly because she was more available.

"He must have been the kind of uncool guy she would never have dated before the accident," Emma said. "But after she fell off the roof, Wheelchair Jane didn't have a lotta choices." Yet if Mr. Malcolm was her choice, even if he was her *only* choice, Jane Malcolm couldn't have been luckier.

The blindness was another story; that happened to her later, when she'd been married for many years. Jane Malcolm suffered from early-onset macular degeneration. As Mr. Malcolm explained to the grade-two class, his wife had lost her central vision. She could see light, she could make out movement, and she still had some peripheral vision. At the extreme periphery, however, Mrs. Malcolm experienced a loss of color, too.

The loss of her mind was another matter; there was nothing Mr. Malcolm could say to protect the kids, or himself, from that. Thus *periphery* and *peripheral* were the so-called vocabulary challenges for opening day in grade two—every day, there would be two more. As for *crazed* or *delusional* or *paranoid,* they were never words on the grade-two vocabulary list. But Wheelchair Jane was all those things; she'd been pushed past the edge of reason.

When Mrs. Malcolm would grind her teeth, or suddenly crash her wheelchair into Patsy Booth's desk, head-on, Jack often looked at Lucinda Fleming—half expecting that Jane Malcolm's visible rage might trigger a *silent*-rage episode in Lucinda. It was insanity to assault the Booth twins separately. Whenever Mrs. Malcolm attacked Patsy's desk in her wheelchair, Patsy's twin, Heather, also screamed.

On occasion, Mrs. Malcolm would snap her head from side to side as if to rid herself of her peripheral vision. Maybe she thought total blindness would be preferable. And when one of the second graders would raise a hand in response to one of Mr. Malcolm's questions, blind Jane would assume a head-on-her-knees position in her wheelchair—as if a man wielding a knife had appeared in front of her and she'd ducked to prevent him from slashing her throat. These dramatic moments of Mrs. Malcolm becoming unhinged made grade two a most attentive class; while the children listened carefully to Mr. Malcolm's every word, they kept their eyes firmly fixed on *her.*

For not more than three or four seconds, not more than twice a week, the tired-looking Mr. Malcolm would be at a loss for words; thereupon, Wheelchair Jane would start her journey of repeated collisions. She sailed forth up an aisle—the wheelchair glancing off the kids' desks as she rushed past, skinning her knuckles.

While Mr. Malcolm ran to the nurse's office, to fetch either the nurse or (for more minor injuries) a first-aid kit, Mrs. Malcolm would be left in the kids' tentative care. Someone held the wheelchair from behind so she couldn't careen out of control; the rest of the class stood petrified around her, just out of her reach. They were instructed to not let her get out of the wheelchair, although it's doubtful that seven-year-olds could have stopped her. Fortunately, she never tried to escape; she flailed about, crying out the children's names, which she'd memorized in the first week of school.

"Maureen Yap!" Mrs. Malcolm would holler.

"Here, ma'am!" Maureen would holler back, and Mrs. Malcolm would turn her blind eyes in The Yap's direction.

"Jimmy Bacon!" Mrs. Malcolm would scream.

Jimmy would moan. There was nothing wrong with Wheelchair Jane's hearing; she looked without seeing in Jimmy's direction upon hearing him moan.

"Jack Burns!" she shouted one day.

"I'm right here, Mrs. Malcolm," Jack said. Even in grade two, his diction and enunciation were far in advance of his years.

"Your father was well spoken, too," Mrs. Malcolm announced. "Your father is evil," she added. "Don't let Satan put a curse on you to be like him."

"No, Mrs. Malcolm, I won't." Jack may have answered her with the utmost confidence, but within the mostly all-girls' world of St. Hilda's, it was clear to him that he was fighting overwhelming odds. The Big Bet, which Emma Oastler spoke of with a reverence usually reserved for her favorite novels and movies, heavily favored the suspected potency of William's genes. If womanizing could be passed from father to son, it most certainly would be passed to Jack. In the eyes of almost everyone at St. Hilda's, even in what amounted to the severely *limited* peripheral vision of Mrs. Malcolm, Jack Burns was his father's son—or about to be.

"You can't blame anyone for being interested, Jack," Emma said philosophically. "It's exciting stuff—to see how you'll turn out." Clearly Mrs. Malcolm had taken a genetic interest in how Jack would turn out, too.

But the worst thing about Jane Malcolm was how she behaved when her husband returned to the grade-two classroom—with either the school nurse or the first-aid kit. "Here I am—I'm back, Jane!" he always announced.

"Did you hear that, children?" Mrs. Malcolm would begin. "He's come back! He's never gone for long and he always comes back!"

"Please, Jane," Mr. Malcolm would say.

"Mr. Malcolm *likes* taking care of me," Wheelchair Jane told the class. "He does *everything* for me—all the things I can't do myself."

"Now, now, Jane, please," Mr. Malcolm would say, but she wouldn't let him take her skinned knuckles in his hands. Slowly, at first, but with ever-quickening strikes, she slapped his face.

"Mr. Malcolm *loves* doing everything for me!" she cried. "He feeds me, he dresses me, he *washes* me—"

"Jane, darling—" Mr. Malcolm tried to say.

"He *wipes* me!" Mrs. Malcolm screamed; that was always the end of it, before she resorted to whimpers and moans.

Jimmy Bacon would commence to moan with her, which was soon followed by the remarkable blanket-sucking sounds that the Booth twins were capable of making—even without blankets. Heel-thumping from the French twins never lagged far behind. And Jack would steal a look at Lucinda Fleming, who was usually looking at him. Her serene smile betrayed nothing of the mysterious rage inside her. *Do you wanna see it?* her smile seemed to say. *Well, I'm gonna show you,* her smile promised— *but not yet.*

It was a not-yet world Jack lived in, from kindergarten through grade two. Pitying Mr. Malcolm was an education in itself. But more memorably, and more lastingly, Jack's education was as much in Emma Oastler's hands as it was in Mr. Malcolm's.

On rainy days, or whenever it was snowing, Emma slid into the backseat of the Lincoln Town Car and instructed Peewee as follows: "Just drive us around, Peewee. No peeking in the backseat. Keep your eyes on the road."

"That okay with you, mon?" Peewee always asked Jack.

"Yes, that would be fine, Peewee. Thank you for asking," the boy replied.

"You're the boss, miss," Peewee would say.

Scrunched down low in the backseat, Jack and Emma chewed gum nonstop—their breath minty or fruity, depending on the flavor. Emma would let Jack undo her braid, but she would never let him weave it back together. With her braid undone, Emma had enough hair for both of them to hide their faces under its spell. "If you get your gum stuck in my hair, honey pie, I'm gonna kill you," she often said—but once, when Jack was laughing about something, Emma suddenly sounded like his mother. "Don't laugh when you're chewing gum—you could choke."

There was the puzzling moment when they checked on her *training* bra, as Emma disparagingly called it. From what Jack could tell, the instructions the bra had given to her breasts were already working. At least her breasts were getting bigger. Wasn't that the point?

Speaking of growing, his penis had made no discernible progress. "How's the little guy?" Emma would invariably ask, and Jack would dutifully show her. "What are you thinking about, little guy?" Emma asked his penis once.

If penises could dream, Jack didn't know why he was surprised to hear that they could think as well, but the little guy had demonstrated no trace of a thought process—*not yet.*

After grade two, Jack's sightings of Mr. Malcolm were limited mainly to the boys' washroom, where the teacher occasionally went to weep. But Jack most frequently caught Mr. Malcolm in the act of examining his facial stubble—as if the shadow of his beard-in-progress or his mustache-in-the-making were his principal (maybe his only) vanity.

Sightings of Mrs. Malcolm were also rare. Usually not more

than twice a day, one of the girls' washrooms would be posted with an OUT OF ORDER sign, which meant that Mr. Malcolm was attending to Wheelchair Jane. The girls were instructed to respect their privacy.

Once Jack heard the unmistakable sound of Mrs. Malcolm slapping her husband in the washroom. The boy tried to hurry in the hall, to outrun the sound, but he could never outdistance Mr. Malcolm's pathetic "Now, now, Jane," which was quickly followed by his "Jane, darling—" upon which some commonplace clamor in the corridor drowned out the repeated melodrama. (Several grade-six girls were passing; naturally, they sounded like several *dozen*.)

In Jack's remaining two years at St. Hilda's, there were many times when he missed Mr. Malcolm, but he did not miss being a witness to the grade-two teacher's perpetual abuse. From then on, when Jack saw people in wheelchairs, he felt no less pity for them—no less than before he met Mrs. Malcolm. Jack just felt *more* pity for the people attending to them.

The little guy and Jack were eight years old when they started grade three. Even before his penis demonstrated its capacity for having dreams and ideas entirely of its own devising, the little guy and Jack had begun to live parallel (if not altogether separate) lives.

That Miss Caroline Wurtz had a "perishable" beauty was enhanced by her being petite. Certainly she was smaller than any of the grade-three mothers. And Miss Wurtz wore a perfume that encouraged the grade-three boys to invent problems with their math. Miss Wurtz would correct a boy's math by leaning over his desk, where he could inhale her perfume while taking a closer and most desirable look at the fetching birthmark on her right collarbone and the small, fishhook-shaped scar on the same side of her throat.

Both the birthmark and the scar seemed to inflame themselves whenever Miss Wurtz was upset. In the ultraviolet light of the bat-cave exhibit, Jack vividly remembered her scar; it was pulsating like a neon strobe. How she got it was in the category of Jack's imagination close to Tattoo Peter's missing leg and Lottie's limp, although the latter subject was further complicated by the boy's mistaken assumption that an epidural was a vital part of the female anatomy.

That Charlotte Brontë was Miss Wurtz's favorite writer, and *Jane Eyre* her bible, was known to everyone in the junior school; an annual dramatization of the novel was their principal cultural contribution to the middle and senior grades. The older girls might have been more capable of acting out such ambitious material—not only Jane's indomitable spirit but also Rochester's blindness and religious transformation—yet Miss Wurtz had claimed *Jane Eyre* as junior-school property, and in both grades three and four, Jack was awarded the role of Rochester.

What other boy in the junior school could have memorized the lines? "Dread remorse when you are tempted to err, Miss Eyre: remorse is the poison of life." Jack delivered that line as if he knew what it meant.

In grade three, the first year Jack played Rochester, the grade-*six* girl who played Jane was Connie Turnbull. Her brooding, rejected presence made her a good choice for an orphan. When she said, " 'It is in vain to say human beings ought to be satisfied with tranquillity,' " you believed her. (Connie Turnbull would never be a tranquil soul.)

Of course it was ludicrous when it was necessary for Jack-as-Rochester to take Connie-as-Jane in his arms and cry: " 'Never, never was anything at once so frail and so indomitable.' " He only came up to her, and everyone else's, breasts. " 'I could bend her with my finger and thumb!' " Jack cried, to the accompanying laughter and disbelief of the audience.

Connie Turnbull looked at him, as if to say: "Just try it, penis breath!" But it wasn't only his memorization skills and his diction and enunciation that made Jack so captivating as an actor. Miss Wurtz had taught him to take command of the stage.

"*How?*" he asked her.

"You have an audience of one, Jack," Miss Wurtz told the boy. "Your job is to touch one heart."

"Whose?"

"Whose heart do you want it to be?" Miss Wurtz asked.

"My mom's?"

"I think you can touch her heart anytime, Jack."

Whose heart could old Rochester touch, anyway? Wasn't it *Jane* who touched one's heart? But that wasn't what Miss Wurtz meant. She meant who would want to watch Jack but remain unseen; who was the likeliest stranger in the audience, whose interest was *only* in Jack? Who wanted to be impressed by Jack while sparing himself the boy's scrutiny?

Jack's audience of one was his *father*, of course. From the moment he imagined William, Jack could command every inch of the stage; he was on-camera for the rest of his life. Jack would learn later that an actor's job was not complicated, but it had two parts. Whoever you were, you made the audience love you; then you broke their hearts.

Once Jack could imagine his father in the shadows of every audience, he could perform anything. "Think about it, Jack," Miss Wurtz urged him. "Just one heart. Whose is it?"

"My dad's?"

"What a good place to begin!" she told the boy, both her birthmark and her scar *inflaming* themselves. "Let's see how that works." It worked, all right—even in the case of Jack's miniature Rochester to Connie Turnbull's bigger, stronger Jane. It worked from the start.

When Rochester says, "Jane! You think me, I daresay, an irreligious dog—" well, Jack had them all. It was ridiculous, but he had Connie Turnbull, too. When she took his hand and kissed it, her lips were parted; she made contact with her teeth and her tongue.

"Nice job, Jack," she whispered in his ear. Connie continued to hold his hand for the duration of the applause. He could feel Emma Oastler hating Connie Turnbull; from the unseen audience, Emma's jealousy swept onstage like a draft.

But what Jack liked best about the Rochester role was the opportunity to be blind. Doubtless he was drawing on the collision-course lunacy of Mrs. Malcolm, but playing blind afforded Jack another opportunity. When he tripped and fell in rehearsals, it was Miss Wurtz who rushed to his aid. (Her ministrations to his injuries, which were entirely feigned, were *why* he tripped and fell.)

His penis's first *thoughtful* reaction was not to Connie Turnbull French-kissing his hand—God, no. The little guy's first idea of his own was clearly in response to Miss Caroline Wurtz. The older-woman thing, which had begun in Oslo with Ingrid Moe, would haunt Jack Burns all his life.

Miss Wurtz's hands were not much bigger than a grade-three girl's, and when she comforted a child—sometimes, when she just spoke to him or her—she would rest one of her hands on the child's shoulder, where he or she could feel her fingers tremble as lightly as the movements of a small, agitated bird. It was as if her hand, or all of Miss Wurtz, were about to take flight. Not one of the grade-three children would have been surprised if, one day, Miss Wurtz had simply flown away. She was that delicate; she was as fragile as a woman made of *feathers*. (Hence "perishable," in another sense.)

But Miss Wurtz could not manage the grade-three classroom. The kids were no more badly behaved than other third graders, although Roland Simpson would later, as a teenager, spend time in a reform school and ultimately wind up in jail. And Jimmy Bacon's penchant for moaning was only a small part of his wretchedness—Jimmy was no joy to be with on a regular basis. He once dressed as a ghost for the grade-three Halloween party and wore *nothing,* not even underwear, under a bedsheet with holes cut out of it for his eyes. Jimmy was so badly frightened by one of The Gray Ghost's sudden appearances—Mrs. McQuat was the grade-four teacher—that he *pooed* in his sheet.

But Miss Wurtz was so delicate that she might not have been able to manage a kindergarten, or her own children. Did her strength emerge only onstage? Alice's theory about Miss Wurtz was intuitive but unkind. "Caroline looks like she never got over somebody. Poor thing."

Jack Burns took from Miss Wurtz a lifelong lesson: life was *not* a stage; life was *improv.* Miss Wurtz had no tolerance for improvisation; the children learned their lines, speaking them exactly as they were written. That Jack was born with superior memorization skills was a considerable advantage in the theater; that Miss Wurtz encouraged Jack to imagine his audience of one was a gift both she and his missing father gave him. But Jack was as attentive a student of Miss Wurtz's failure in the classroom as he was of her instructions for success onstage. It was evident to him that one could not succeed as a player in *life* without developing improvisational skills. Yes, you needed to know your lines. But on some occasions, you also had to be able to make your lines up. For what she could teach him, but primarily for what she had failed to master herself, Miss Wurtz captured Jack's attention; not surprisingly, she would live in his memory (and remain a part of his life) longer than any of the third-grade girls.

Jack often dreamed of kissing Caroline Wurtz, at which moments she was never dressed as a schoolteacher. In his dreams, Miss Wurtz wore the kind of old-fashioned underwear Jack had first seen in Lottie's mail-order catalogs. For reasons that were disturbingly unclear to him, this type of underwear was advertised for teens and unmarried women. (Why women wore a *different* kind of underwear after they were married was, and would remain, a mystery to Jack.)

As for Miss Wurtz's real attire, in the classroom, she occasionally wore a cream-colored blouse you could almost see through, but—because it was cold in the grade-three room—she more often dressed in sweaters, which fit her well. Jack's mother said they were cashmere sweaters, which meant that Miss Wurtz was buying her clothes with something more than a St. Hilda's faculty salary.

"The Wurtz has *gotta* have a boyfriend," Emma said. "A *rich* one, or at least one with good taste—that would be my guess."

Jack had repeatedly denied Emma's accusation that Connie Turnbull gave him a boner every time she French-kissed his hand—or that when he-as-Rochester took Connie-as-Jane in his arms, with his head buried in her breasts, there was any response from the little guy. It hadn't yet occurred to Emma that Jack had a hard-on every minute he spent in close proximity to Caroline Wurtz, whether or not he was in her *actual* company or she were in various stages of undress in his dreams.

As for The Wurtz, as Emma called her, having a rich boyfriend *or* one with good taste—or even an *ex*-boyfriend—Jack didn't want such a character to exist, lest he invade the boy's dreams of Miss Wurtz in her mail-order corsets and girdles and bras.

Jack didn't dream about the grade-three girls at all, not even Lucinda Fleming, who'd managed—for more than two years—to keep her silent rage well hidden. And if, in his dreams, Miss Wurtz had the faintest trace of a mustache on her extremely narrow upper lip—well, that was Emma Oastler's doing. He couldn't control his attraction to Emma's upper lip, especially in his dreams. More and more, when the little guy came alive, he did so not at Jack's bidding but independently.

"Any news, Jack?" Emma would whisper in the backseat of the limo, as Peewee drove them around and around Forest Hill.

"Not yet," Jack answered. (He had guessed, *correctly,* that this was the safest thing to say.)

At night, after Lottie had put him to bed, Jack often went into his mother's room and climbed into her bed and fell asleep there. Given their different schedules, his mom was almost never there. She would come home and crawl into bed long after he'd fallen asleep. Sometimes, in her half-sleep, she would throw one of her legs over Jack, which always woke him up. There was the smell of cigarette smoke and pot in her hair, and the gasoline-like tang of white wine on her breath. Occasionally they would both be awake and lie whispering in the semidarkness. Jack didn't know why they whispered; it wasn't because Lottie or Mrs. Wicksteed could hear them.

"How are you, Jack?"

"I'm fine. How are *you*?"

"We're becoming like strangers," Alice whispered one time. Jack was disappointed that his mother hadn't seen him act, and he said so. "Oh, I've seen you act!" Alice said.

Jack meant in *Jane Eyre,* or in Miss Wurtz's other exercises in dramatization. While The Wurtz loved the stage, she preferred adapting novels. It would occur to Jack only later that, by choosing to dramatize novels, Miss Wurtz controlled every aspect of every performance. There was no playwright to give the children the wrong directions. Miss Wurtz adapted her favorite novels for the theater *her* way. If, as actors, they were instructed to take command of the stage, The Wurtz was absolutely in charge of every action they undertook—of every word they uttered.

Later Jack would realize what wonderful things Miss Wurtz left *out* of her adaptations. She was in charge of censorship as well. When The Wurtz adapted *Tess of the d'Urbervilles,* she made much more of the "Maiden" chapter than she made of "Maiden No More." More disturbing, she cast Jack as Tess.

"Nobody blamed Tess as she blamed herself," the dramatization began. (Miss Wurtz, with her perfect diction and enunciation, was a big fan of voice-over.) Jack was, without a doubt, a good choice to play "a mere vessel of emotion untinctured by experience."

But even in a dress—a white gown, no less—and even as a milkmaid, the boy could take command of the stage. " 'Phases of her childhood lurked in her aspect still,' " Miss Wurtz read to the audience, while Angel Clare failed to ask Jack-as-Tess to dance. What a wimp Angel was! Jimmy Bacon, that miserable moaner who pooed in a sheet, was the perfect choice to play him.

" '. . . for all her bouncing handsome womanliness,' " Miss Wurtz fatalistically intoned, " 'you could sometimes see her twelfth year in her cheeks, or her ninth sparkle from her eyes; and even her fifth would flit over the curves of her mouth now and then.' "

All the while, Jack-as-Tess had nothing to do. He stood on-stage, radiating sexless innocence. He was prouder of his role as Rochester, but even as Tess, he had his moments—sexless innocence not least, if not best, among them. What Tess says to d'Urberville, for example (d'Urberville, that pig, was played by the thuggish Charlotte Barford, whom The Wurtz wisely borrowed from the middle school): " 'Did it never strike your mind that what every woman says some women may feel?' " (Charlotte Barford looked as if she-as-he had thoroughly enjoyed seducing him-as-her.)

When Jack buried his dead baby in the churchyard, he could hear the older girls in the audience—they were already crying. And the tale of Tess's undoing had only begun! Jack spoke Hardy's narration as if it were dialogue over the baby's grave. " '. . . in that shabby corner of God's allotment where He lets the nettles grow,' " Jack began, while the older girls in the audience imagined that this could be *their* predicament, which Miss Wurtz, if not Thomas Hardy, had cleverly intended, " '. . . and where all unbaptized infants, notorious drunkards, suicides, and others of the conjecturally damned are laid,' " Jack-as-Tess carried on, stimulated by the weeping older girls. (No fan of improvisation, Miss Wurtz had not permitted Jack to skip the "conjecturally," though he'd repeatedly flubbed the word in rehearsals.)

When Jack said, " 'But you would not dance with me,' " to that wimp Jimmy-Bacon-as-Angel-Clare, the hearts of the older girls in the audience were wrenched anew. " 'O, I hope that is of no ill-omen for us now!' " Jack-as-Tess told Jimmy-as-Angel, while the girls wept afresh—because, with Hardy, what *wasn't* an ill omen? The girls knew Tess was doomed, as unalterably as Miss Wurtz wanted them to know it.

That was The Wurtz's message to the girls. Be careful! Anyone can get pregnant! Every man who isn't a wimp, like

Jimmy-Bacon-as-Angel, is a pig, like Charlotte-Barford-as-d'Urberville. And Jack-Burns-as-Tess got Miss Wurtz's message across. Caroline Wurtz's junior-school dramatizations amounted to moral instructions to the middle- and senior-school girls.

Jack was in grade *three*. A dramatization of *Tess of the d'Urbervilles* was incomprehensible to him. But the message of the story wasn't for Jack. At St. Hilda's, the most important messages were delivered to the older girls. Jack was just an actor. Miss Wurtz knew he could handle the lines, even if he didn't understand them. And in case a total idiot (among the older girls) might have missed the point, *all* the dramatizations were of novels wherein women were put to the test.

When Jack played Hester Prynne in The Wurtz's adaptation of *The Scarlet Letter,* he couldn't persuade his mom to come see him as an eight-year-old adulteress with the letter *A* on his-as-her chest. "I hate that story," Alice whispered to her son in the semidarkness of her bedroom. "It's so unfair. I'll ask Caroline to take some pictures. I'll look at photographs, Jack, but I don't want to see that story *dramatized*."

Miss Wurtz shrewdly recognized in Wendy Holton's preternaturally thin, cruel body—in her unyielding knees, her fists-of-stone hardness—a perfect likeness to the obsessed and vengeful Roger Chillingworth. Once again, in casting, The Wurtz robbed the middle school of one of Jack's former tormentors.

The Reverend Dimmesdale was lamentably miscast, although in choosing Lucinda Fleming, who was a head taller than Jack was in grade three, Miss Wurtz might have been hoping that Lucinda's silent rage would select a pivotal moment of Dimmesdale's guilt in which to erupt onstage and frighten the bejesus out of them all. Perhaps when Dimmesdale cries to Hester: "May God forgive us both! We are not, Hester, the worst sinners in the world. There is one worse than even the polluted priest!" That might have worked, had Lucinda Fleming simply lost it at that moment—had she begun to bash her head against the footlights or made some woeful, demented effort to strangle herself in the stage curtains.

But Lucinda kept her rage to herself. She may have been as tortured as the Reverend Dimmesdale, but she seemed to be saving her long-anticipated explosion for an offstage moment. Jack was convinced it was something she was saving just for him. But being onstage with Lucinda-as-Dimmesdale was better than being backstage with Wendy-as-Chillingworth, because—once she was out of Miss Wurtz's sight—Wendy held Jack personally responsible for her being cast as Chillingworth in the first place. (Admittedly, it was a thankless part.) Therefore, *The Scarlet Letter* was a bruising production for Jack. Wendy punched him or kneed him in the ribs whenever she could get away with it.

"My goodness," Alice whispered to her son in the semidarkness. (She could tell he was sore just by touching him.) When she turned on the light, she said: "What are those Puritans doing to you, Jack? Are you *wearing* the letter *A,* or are they *hitting* you with it?"

His mother wouldn't come see him throw himself under a train in Miss Wurtz's rendition of *Anna Karenina,* either. ("I'll ask Caroline to take more pictures, Jack.") There was no end to the wronged women in Caroline Wurtz's instructive repertoire. And how brilliant was The Wurtz's choice of Emma Oastler for the role of Count Vronsky? Emma even had the requisite mustache for the part!

After school—in Jack's room, or just hanging out in the backseat of the Town Car while Peewee stole a look at Emma's legs—Emma controlled their topics of conversation, as before. Jack could not take command of *that* stage, where he and Emma were engaged in an improvisational performance of the kind he needed to learn vastly more about.

"This is perfect, Jack—we're having a love affair!"

"We *are*?"

"Onstage, I mean."

"But what are we having *here*?" he asked—meaning the backseat of the Town Car, where he lay pinned, with one of Emma's heavy legs thrown over him, much in the impulsive, half-asleep manner that his mom occasionally threw a leg over him; or on the bed in his room, where Emma told Lottie she was helping Jack with his homework and not to bother them.

"He's fallen behind, Lottie. I can help him catch up, if I can just get him to listen to me."

How could he *not* listen to her? In the first place, she simply overpowered him on the backseat *or* on his bed. And she knew he couldn't resist her mustache; she would brush her silky upper lip against him. She ran her mustache over the back of his hand while she imitated Connie Turnbull's French kiss, which she did a better job of than Connie; or against his cheek, or even (after she'd untucked his shirt) over his bare belly, pausing to give special consideration to his navel. "Do you ever *wash* this thing, Jack? It's got lint in it, you know."

It was all prelude—whether she was pretending she was Count Vronsky and Jack was Anna, or whether she was herself, Emma Oastler, who would never be a minor character, not in Jack's life. Everything led up to the "end line," as Miss Wurtz was fond of saying. "Hit your end line so that your audience of one remembers it, Jack. Say your end line so that no one can forget it, okay?"

"How's the little guy doing? What's he up to, Jack?" Emma always got around to asking.

It was a crucial time—they were in rehearsals for *Anna Karenina* but had not yet been subjected to Miss Wurtz's plans for *Sense and Sensibility.* Emma and Jack were doing "homework" on his bed. Lottie could be heard banging around below them in the kitchen. To Emma's question regarding what his penis was *up to,* Jack answered as he often did: "Not much."

"Let's have a look, baby cakes." He showed her. He heard such sorrow in Emma's sigh, or maybe he'd been thinking too much about Anna and the train. He didn't want to go on disappointing Emma forever.

"Sometimes it dreams," Jack began.

"Dreams what? Who's in the dreams, Jack?"

"*You* are," he answered. (This seemed safer to admit than the Miss Wurtz part.)

"What am I doing in the dreams, Jack?"

"It's mainly your mustache," he admitted.

"You little pervert, you squirrel dink, Jack—"

"And Miss Wurtz is wearing just her underwear," he blurted out.

"I'm with The Wurtz? *Jesus,* Jack!"

"It's more like Miss Wurtz is alone, with your mustache," Jack confessed. "And the underwear."

"*Whose* underwear?" Emma asked.

He sneaked along the upstairs hall to Lottie's room and brought Emma the latest edition of Lottie's mail-order catalog. "You dork, Jack—I wouldn't be caught dead in this stuff. *I'll* show you some underwear!"

He had seen her previous *training* bra—her present bra was only a little bigger. But when Emma removed the bra, there was a more noticeable shape and substance to her breasts than before; and when she took her panties off and held them against the pleats of her skirt, the lace that rimmed the waistband was a new experience for Jack *and* the little guy.

"It moved," Emma said.

"*What* moved?"

"You know what, Jack." They both looked at the little guy, who was not as little as before. Emma leaned over his penis. "Miss Wurtz," she said. "Shut your eyes, Jack." Of course he did as he was told. "Caroline Wurtz," Emma whispered to his penis. "I'm gonna bring you some *real* underwear, little guy." Even with his eyes closed, Jack knew that the little guy liked this idea.

"I think we're finally getting somewhere, Jack."

"Can I undo your braid, Emma?"

"*Now?*"

"Yes." She allowed him to do this, never taking her eyes from his penis. Her hair fell all around his hips; he felt it touch his thighs. "It's working, baby cakes," Emma reported. "You had the right idea."

"Kettle's boiling!" Lottie called from the kitchen.

"Let me be sure I understand you," Emma said, ignoring Lottie. "It's basically The Wurtz with my mustache and Lottie's underwear."

"Not Lottie's—it's the underwear from her catalog." (The thought of Miss Wurtz in *Lottie's* underwear was unappealing.)

"Whose hair?" Emma asked.

"Yours, I think. It's long hair, anyway."

"Good," Emma said. He couldn't see her; her hair, now undone, completely hid her face. "We seem to be zeroing in on a few priorities."

"Zeroing in on *what*?"

"Clearly you have a hair thing, honey pie. And the usual older-woman thing."

"Oh." (Nothing about his older-woman thing, not to mention his mustache-and-braid fixation, felt the least bit *usual* to Jack.)

"Oh, my God, now we're *really* getting somewhere!" Emma announced; she threw back her hair. Jack had a hard-on like he'd never seen before. If the little guy had stood up any taller, he would have cast a shadow all the way to Jack's belly button—lint and all.

"Jesus, Jack—what are you gonna do with it?"

Jack was at a loss. "Do I have to *do* something with it?" he asked.

Emma hugged him to her bare breasts; his enlarged penis brushed against her scratchy wool skirt. Jack shifted slightly in the big girl's embrace, until the little guy was more comfortably touching Emma's bare thigh. "Oh, Jack," Emma told the boy, "that's the sweetest thing to say—you're just too cute for words. No, of course you don't *have* to do anything with it! One day you'll know what you *want* to do with it! That's gonna be some day."

He touched one of her breasts with his hand; she held his face more tightly there. The next thing was the little guy's idea, entirely. Emma and Jack were sitting on his bed, hip to hip—they were hugging each other—but his penis had somehow not lost contact with her thigh. And if Jack could feel her thigh, Emma must have been able to feel his penis. He was eight; she was fifteen. When Jack swung one of his legs over her far hip, he found himself lying on top of her with the little guy in her lap—now touching both her thighs.

"Do you know what you're doing, Jack?" Emma asked. (Of course he didn't.) Her gum was a mint flavor. Jack could feel her breath on the top of his head. "Maybe the little guy knows," she said, answering herself. Jack's arms could not reach around her hips, but he held her there—his right hand touching the lace waistband of her panties, which Emma had spread on top of her skirt. "Show me what the little guy knows, baby cakes." Her tone of voice indicated that she was teasing him—the *baby cakes* was an affectionate appellation, but faintly mocking in the way Emma usually said it.

"I don't know what the little guy knows," he admitted, just as the little guy and Jack made an astonishing discovery. There was *hair* between Emma Oastler's thighs!

The instant the tip of his penis touched this hairy place, Jack thought that Emma was going to *kill* him. She scissored her legs around his waist and rolled him over onto his back. The little guy was all bunched up in her itchy wool skirt. Emma had some difficulty finding it with her hand, with which Jack feared she might yank it completely *off*—but she didn't. She just held his penis a little too roughly.

"What was *that*?" he asked. He was more afraid of the hair he had felt than he was of the way Emma held him.

"I'm not showing you, honey pie. It would be child molestation."

"It would be *what*?"

"It would freak you out," Emma said. Jack could believe it. He had no desire to see the hairy place. What Jack, or the little guy, strangely wanted was to *be* there. (Jack was actually afraid of what it might look like.)

"I don't want to see it," he said quickly.

Emma relaxed her scissors-hold around his waist; she held his penis a little more gently. "You got a hair thing, all right," she told him.

"The tea is going to get too *strong*!" Lottie hollered from the kitchen.

"Then take out the tea bags or the stupid tea ball!" Emma shouted back.

"It's getting *cold,* too!" Lottie called to them.

When Emma pulled her panties back on, she turned her back on Jack; conversely, she put on her bra and buttoned up her shirt while she faced him. It was clear that the little guy had touched a private place, but why was there *hair* there?

"How's the *homework* going?" Lottie cried. She was verging on the kind of hysteria that implied to Jack she was reliving the horror of her haywire epidural.

"What kind of life does Lottie have?" Emma asked Jack, but she was looking at his penis. The little guy was returning to normal size before their very eyes. "You gotta watch this guy every second, Jack—it's like having your own little miracle. Or *not*-so-little miracle," Emma added. "Oh, *cute*! Look! It's like it's going *away*!"

"Maybe it's sad," the boy said.

"Remember that line, Jack. One day you can use it." He couldn't imagine under what circumstances an admission of his penis's sadness would be of any possible use. Miss Wurtz knew a lot about lines. Somehow Jack sensed she would disapprove of this one—too improvisational, maybe.

* * *

In a week's time, Emma would bring him one of her divorced mom's bras—a black one. It was more like half a bra, Jack observed, with hard wire rims under the cups, which were small but surprisingly aggressive-looking. It was what they called a "push-up" bra, Emma explained. (It was about as assertive as a bra could be—or so Jack imagined.) "What's it want to push your breasts up *for*?" he asked.

"My mom has small boobs," Emma said. "She's trying to make more out of them." But the bra was curious for another reason: it smelled strongly of perfume, and only slightly less powerfully of sweat. Emma had snitched it from the laundry—it wasn't clean. "But that's better, isn't it?" she asked.

"Why?"

"Because you can *smell* her!" Emma declared.

"But I don't know your mom. Why would I want to *smell* her?"

"Just try it, baby cakes. You never know what the little guy might like." Boy, was *that* the truth! (Too bad it would take years for Jack to find that out.)

It would be a while, too, before someone told him that the Chinaman's tattoo shop on the northwest corner of Dundas and Jarvis was never open late at night. The basement tattoo parlor, which you entered from the sidewalk on Dundas, usually closed in the late afternoon. Jack would forget who told him. Maybe it was some old ink addict, a collector, in one of those tattoo shops on Queen Street—around the time his mom opened her own shop there.

Queen Street in the seventies would never have supported the likes of Daughter Alice—it was a greasers' hangout, full of anti-hippie, whisky-drinking, white-T-shirt people. Whoever told Jack was possibly one of them, but it sounded true. The Chinaman's unnamed shop was closed at night, or maybe it stayed open a little longer on Friday and Saturday evenings—though never past eight or nine.

So where was she—out late, almost every night, in Jack's years at St. Hilda's? He hadn't a clue. It was only with hindsight, which is never to be wholly trusted, that Jack concluded his mother might have been trying to break her possessive attachment to her son. As he grew older, he looked more and more like his dad; maybe the more Jack resembled William, the more Alice sought to distance herself from the boy.

That Emma Oastler brought him her mother's push-up bra may have had something to do with it. It was inevitable that Alice would find it. Jack slept with the stupid bra every night—he even took it into his mom's bed on those nights he slept with her. And it was one of those nights when she threw a leg over Jack and woke him up. This night, something woke her up, too. The mystery bra was mashed between them; Alice must have felt the hard wire rims under the cups. She sat up in bed and turned on the light.

"What's this, Jack?" she asked, holding up the stinking bra. The way she looked at her son—well, he would never forget it. It was as if she'd discovered Emma's *mother* in the bed between them; it was as if she'd caught Jack *in flagrante delicto,* the little guy in intimate contact with that hairy, private place.

"It's a push-up bra," he explained.

"I know what it is—I mean *whose.*" Alice sniffed the bra and made a face. She pulled back the covers and stared at the little guy, who was protruding, at attention, from the boy's pajamas. "Start talking, Jack."

"It belongs to Emma Oastler's mom—Emma stole it and gave it to me. I don't know why."

"I know why," Alice said. Jack started to cry. His mom's visible disgust was withering; the little guy was looking withered, too.

"Stop sniveling—don't *snivel,*" Alice said. He needed to blow his nose. His mom handed him the bra, but Jack hesitated. "Go on—*blow!*" she ordered. "I'm going to wash it before I give it back to her, anyway."

"Oh."

"You can start anytime, Jack. The whole story. What games are you playing with Emma? You better begin there."

He told her everything—well, maybe not everything. Possibly not the part about Emma baring her breasts; probably not *every* time Emma asked to have a look at the little guy; certainly not the part about his penis making actual contact with Emma's hairy, private place. But his mother must have had a pretty good idea of what was going on. "She's *fifteen,* Jack—you're *eight.* I'll have a little talk with Mrs. Oastler."

"Is Emma going to get in trouble?"

"I sincerely hope so," Alice said.

"Am *I* in trouble?" he asked.

What a look she gave him! Jack hadn't known what she meant when she'd said they were "becoming like strangers." Now he knew. His mom looked at him as if he were a stranger. "You're going to be in trouble soon enough," was all she said.

11

His Father Inside Him

Compared to the drama unfolding between Jack and Emma, and what lay ahead between Alice and Mrs. Oastler, the inability of Miss Wurtz to manage her grade-three classroom was minor; yet there was drama there as well, however improvisational.

Lucinda Fleming, whom Jack couldn't see over, sat at the desk in front of his. She would routinely and deliberately whip his face with her huge ponytail, which hung halfway down her back and was as thick as a broom. In exasperation, Jack would respond by grabbing it with both his hands and pulling it. He could barely manage to pin the back of her head to the top of his desk. Jack found he could restrain her there by pressing his chin against her forehead, but it hurt. Nothing appeared to hurt Lucinda, except her alleged proclivity to hurt herself, which Jack was beginning to doubt. Maybe Lucinda had despised playing Dimmesdale to Jack-as-Hester, or she hated being a head taller than he was; possibly she believed that by whipping Jack with her ponytail, she could make him *grow*.

Caroline Wurtz never saw Lucinda lash out at Jack with her broom of hair. Miss Wurtz only became aware of the situation *after* he'd pinned Lucinda's head to his desk. "Please, Jack," Miss Wurtz would say. "Don't *disappoint* me."

In his dreams, when The Wurtz would say "Don't *disappoint* me," her tone of voice was deeply seductive. Not so in the grade-three classroom. In reality, disappointing Miss Wurtz was a bad idea—she did not handle it well. Yet the grade-three children often disappointed her deliberately. They resented what a well-organized tyrant she was in her *other* capacity, as their drama teacher; that she couldn't maintain order in the classroom was a weakness they exploited.

Gordon French once released his pet hamster into his hostile twin's hair. From Caroline's reaction, one might have guessed that the hamster was rabid and bit her. But all the stupid hamster did was race around and around her head, as if it were running on its incessant wheel. Miss Wurtz, perhaps fearful that the hamster would be harmed, began to cry. Crying was the last resort of her disappointment, and she resorted to it with tiresome frequency. "Oh, I never thought I'd be *this* disappointed!" she would wail. "Oh, my feelings are hurt more than I can *say*!" But when Miss Wurtz began to cry, the kids stopped paying attention to what she said. They were concentrating on what they knew would happen next, for which there was no preparing themselves. The Gray Ghost's sudden appearances, even when they were anticipated, were always startling.

There was only one door to the grade-three classroom, and despite her reputedly supernatural powers, Mrs. McQuat could not pass through walls; yet even though the children saw the doorknob turning, they could not protect themselves from the shock. Sometimes the door would swing open, but no one would be there. They would hear The Gray Ghost's labored breathing from the hall, while Jimmy Bacon moaned and the two sets of twins sounded their predictable alarms. At other times, Mrs. McQuat seemed to leap inside the classroom before the doorknob so much as *twitched*. Only Roland Simpson, the class's future criminal, purposely closed his eyes. (Roland *liked* being startled.)

According to Mrs. Wicksteed, The Gray Ghost had lost a lung in the war, *What* war and *which* lung were unknown to Jack. Mrs. McQuat had been a combat nurse, and she'd been gassed. Hence her labored breathing; The Gray Ghost was always out of breath. Gassed *where* and with *what* were also a mystery to Jack.

The third graders could have written Mrs. McQuat's dialogue for her. Upon her unpreventable sudden appearance, The Gray Ghost would address the class as if she were a character in a dramatization Caroline Wurtz had scripted. In her cold-as-the-grave, out-of-breath voice, Mrs. McQuat would ask: "Which of you . . . made Miss Wurtz . . . *cry*?"

Without hesitation, the children identified the guilty party. They would betray *anyone* when asked that terrifying question. At that moment, they had no friends, no loyalties. Because here is the dark heart of what they believed: if Mrs. McQuat had been gassed and lost a lung, wasn't it possible that she had *died*? Who could say for certain that she *wasn't* a ghost? Her skin, her hair, her clothes—gray on gray on gray. And why were her hands so cold? Why did no one ever see her arrive at school, or leave? Why was she always so suddenly *there*?

Jack would long remember The Gray Ghost asking Gordon French: "You put . . . a *what* . . . in your sister's . . . hair?"

Gordon answered: "Just a hamster, a *friendly* one!"

"It felt like a small dog, Gordon," Caroline said. Gordon knew the drill. He stood like a soldier in the aisle beside his desk, immobilized by his foreknowledge of what he was about to endure.

"I hope . . . you didn't . . . *hurt* the hamster . . . Caroline," Mrs. McQuat said, granting Gordon brief reprieve.

"It's no fun having one in your hair," Caroline replied.

"Where *is* the hamster?" Miss Wurtz suddenly cried. (That her first name was also Caroline was confusing.)

"Please *find* . . . the hamster . . . Caroline," The Gray Ghost said. But before Caroline French could begin to look, Miss Wurtz dropped to all fours and crawled under Caroline's desk. "Not *you* . . . dear," Mrs. McQuat said reprovingly. All the children had joined Miss Wurtz on the floor.

"What's its name, Gordon?" Maureen Yap asked.

The Gray Ghost was not letting Gordon off so easily. "You'll come with me . . . Gordon," Mrs. McQuat said. "Pray your hamster isn't lost . . . for it will *surely die,* if it's lost."

The kids watched Gordon leave the classroom with The Gray Ghost. Everyone knew that Mrs. McQuat was taking Gordon to the chapel. Often it was empty. But even if one of the choirs was practicing, she took the offending child to the chapel and left him or her there. The child had to kneel on the stone floor in the center aisle next to one of the middle rows of pews and face backward, away from the altar. "You have . . . turned your back on God," The Gray Ghost would tell the child. "You better hope . . . He isn't looking."

As Gordon would recount, it was a bad feeling to have turned his back on God and not know if He was looking. After a few minutes, Gordon felt sure that someone was behind him—in the vicinity of the altar or the pulpit. Perhaps one of the four women attending to Jesus—saints, now ghosts themselves—had stepped out of the stained glass and was about to touch him with her icy hand.

The grade-three class was interrupted in this fashion so frequently that they often couldn't remember who'd been banished to the chapel and had turned his or her back on God. Mrs. McQuat never brought you back from the chapel—she just took you there. (Roland Simpson virtually *lived* in the chapel with his back turned to God.) Time would pass, and someone—often The Yap—would ask: "Miss Wurtz, shouldn't someone check to see if Gordon is all right in the chapel?"

"Oh, my goodness!" Miss Wurtz would cry. "How *could* I have forgotten!" And someone would be sent to release Gordon (or Roland) from the certifiably lonely terror of kneeling in the chapel backward. It felt wrong to be looking the wrong way in church, like you were really asking for trouble.

But the third graders were well prepared for fourth grade; Mrs. McQuat, of course, was the teacher for grade four. The only fourth graders who were ever in need of being disciplined in the chapel were *new* students who'd not had the pleasure of witnessing The Wurtz's emotional meltdowns. The Gray Ghost had no trouble managing *her* classroom; it was Miss Wurtz's class that repeatedly called upon Mrs. McQuat's ghostly skills.

The third graders continued to get in trouble, and they often ended up in the chapel facing backward, because—despite their fear of The Gray Ghost—there was something *irresistible* about how The Wurtz fell apart. The kids both loved the way she cried and hated her for it, because—even in grade three—they understood that it was Miss Wurtz's weakness that brought Mrs. McQuat's punishment upon them. (Miss Wurtz's *weakness* was not infrequently on display in Jack's dreams of her in Mrs. Oastler's push-up bra—which were not thwarted by Alice returning the bra to Mrs. Oastler.)

Gratefully, Jack never dreamed about The Gray Ghost. In his young mind, this gave further credibility to the theory that Mrs. McQuat was dead. She was, however, very much alive in the grade-three classroom, where her sudden appearances became as commonplace as The Wurtz bursting into tears. Hence, when Jimmy Bacon exposed himself to Maureen Yap—when he raised his ghost-sheet to demonstrate that, indeed, he wore no underwear beneath his Halloween costume—Miss Wurtz's feelings were again hurt more than she could *say*. (She bitterly expressed how she never thought she'd be so *completely* disappointed.) And when The Gray Ghost left Jimmy in the chapel facing the wrong way, Jimmy pooed in his bedsheet like the frightened ghost he was. If Mrs. McQuat's sudden appearance had started Jimmy pooing, his overwhelming conviction that Jesus had *disappeared* from the stained glass above the altar finished the job.

"A poor costume choice, Jimmy," was all The Wurtz would say about the beshitted sheet.

No matter how many times Lucinda Fleming provoked Jack with her ponytail and he pinned her head to the top of his desk, it was never *that* dispute between them that reduced Caroline Wurtz to tears. In all their fights, Lucinda and Jack stopped short of causing Miss Wurtz's sobs. They may have been foolish enough to imagine that they would be spared The Gray Ghost's sudden appearance.

But Lucinda was led by her ear to the chapel over *another* issue: she erased the answers on Roland Simpson's math test while Roland was turning his back on God in the chapel. (All the other kids were surprised that Lucinda had bothered; in all probability, the answers on Roland's math test were wrong.)

Mrs. McQuat took Jack to the chapel only once, but memorably. He drove Miss Wurtz to tears *not* by grabbing Lucinda Fleming's ponytail and pinning her head to his desk, but by kissing her. It was Miss Wurtz Jack *imagined* kissing, of course, but he kissed Lucinda Fleming on the back of her neck instead.

Only one person could have prompted him to do such a repugnant thing—Emma Oastler. Emma was angry at Jack for "ratting" on her to his mother, although the return of Mrs. Oastler's bra hardly amounted to a day of reckoning for Emma. Emma's mom was unmoved by Alice's assertion that Emma had "molested" Jack. In Mrs. Oastler's opinion, it was not possible for a woman or a girl to molest a man or a boy; whatever games Emma had played with Jack, he'd probably liked them, Mrs. Oastler maintained. But Emma was disciplined in some minor fashion. She was "grounded," she told Jack; she was to come directly home from school for a month.

"No more cuddling in the backseat, baby cakes. No more making the little guy stand at attention."

"It's only for a month," Jack reminded her.

"I don't suppose there's anyone in grade three who turns you on," Emma inquired. "I mean *besides* The Wurtz."

Jack made the mistake of complaining about Lucinda Fleming—how she tortured him with her ponytail, but he was always the one who got in trouble. In her present mood, Emma probably liked the idea of getting Jack in trouble.

"Lucinda wants you to kiss her, Jack."

"She *does*?"

"She doesn't know it, but she does."

"She's bigger than I am," he pointed out.

"Just kiss Lucinda, Jack—it'll make her your slave."

"I don't want a *slave*!"

"You don't know it, but you do," Emma told him. "Just imagine you're kissing The Wurtz."

The discovery, that same week, of Gordon's dead hamster in the chalk box should have forewarned Jack. Talk about an ill omen! But he didn't heed it. If, for what seemed the longest time, he *didn't* dare to kiss Lucinda Fleming, he also couldn't dispel the idea of doing it. Sitting behind her, watching her swish her whip of a ponytail back and forth—well, suffice it to say her neck was often exposed. And one day, when Miss Wurtz was writing the new vocabulary words on the blackboard, Jack stood on tiptoe and leaned across his desk and—lifting her ponytail—kissed Lucinda Fleming on the back of her neck.

There was no response from the little guy—another ill omen, this one not lost on Jack. And what bullshit it was—that the children were ever told to be on their guard for Lucinda's so-called silent rage. There was nothing *silent* about it! Lucinda never made a sound when Jack pulled her ponytail or pinned her head to the top of his desk, but when he kissed her, you would have thought she'd been bitten by the avenging ghost of Gordon's dead hamster. (Not even in Jack's wildest dreams had Miss Wurtz, in a variety of bras and restraining devices, once responded to his kisses with *half* of Lucinda's demented energy.)

Lucinda Fleming screamed until she was red in the face. She lay in the aisle beside her desk and kicked her legs and flailed her arms and thrashed her head *and* ponytail back and forth, as if she were being devoured by rats. This was a challenge well beyond The Wurtz's limited capacity. She must have thought that Lucinda was warming up for a suicide attempt. "Oh, Lucinda, who has *disappointed* you so?" Miss Wurtz cried—or some such idiotic utterance, because The Wurtz always said something amazingly inappropriate. Maybe the kids couldn't resist misbehaving just to see what she would say.

In crafting dramatizations from her beloved novels, Miss

Wurtz had an ear for the best lines—many of which she robbed for her own voice-over. In introducing Jack-as-Elinor in *Sense and Sensibility,* she set him-as-her up perfectly. (Jack was the reasonable sister.) Miss Wurtz said of Elinor, in voice-over: " 'She had an excellent heart; her disposition was affectionate, and her feelings were strong; but she knew how to govern them: it was a knowledge which her mother had yet to learn, and which one of her sisters had resolved never to be taught.' "

Alas, in Jack's grade-four year, Miss Wurtz would cast him as the immoderate sister, Marianne, whom he detested. It was the meddlesome mother, Mrs. Dashwood, whom he wanted to play, but Miss Wurtz, who conveniently overlooked the fact that she'd cast Jack as blind Rochester, maiden-no-more Tess, *A*-on-her-breast Hester, *and* under-the-train Anna, said that he didn't look *old enough* to be a woman who'd had three daughters.

Though Miss Wurtz seemed at a loss about what to say when something spontaneously just *happened,* she always spoke with authority, her diction and enunciation perfect, even if what she said revealed a total misunderstanding of the situation. This the children found very confusing.

Hence, when Lucinda Fleming suddenly went stiff as a board and began to bang the back of her head on the floor, Miss Wurtz asked the class: "Which of you thoughtless children has caused Lucinda such anguish and pain?"

"*What?*" Maureen Yap asked.

"Lucinda is *peeing!*" Caroline French observed.

Indeed, Lucinda lay in a spreading puddle—her skirt stained a darker gray. In a doomed effort to keep time with the floor-thumping of Lucinda's head, the French twins began the all-too-recognizable patter of their heels; they were not unlike the rhythm section of a band in need of practice. The anticipated blanket-sucking sounds of the Booth twins were ominously replaced by their identical imitations of *gagging.* They were more like blanket-*strangulation* sounds; yet, as accompaniment to the spectacle of Lucinda Fleming methodically banging her head in a pool of her own urine, the sounds were more suitable than anything Miss Wurtz had to say.

"Lucinda is having one of her *bad moments,* children," Miss Wurtz needlessly informed the grade-three class. "What might we do to make her feel better?" Jimmy Bacon, of course, moaned.

Jack wanted to help, but *how*? "I just *kissed* her," he tried to explain.

"You *what*?" Miss Wurtz said.

"On the neck."

Jack saw the eyes roll up in Lucinda Fleming's head; she appeared to be passing to another world. Lucinda emitted a strangling sound of her own—as if she meant to comfort the Booth twins, long separated from their kindergarten blankets. Even Roland Simpson, destined for reform school and ultimately jail, was instantly afraid and (for the moment) law-abiding. And if Jimmy Bacon had been wearing his bedsheet—well, there's no need to spell it out.

Caroline French suddenly looked like a girl with a *hundred* hamsters rushing through her hair. Those utter boneheads Grant Porter and James Turner *and* Gordon French—in fact, *all* the boys in the class, Roland Simpson and Jimmy Bacon included—were absolutely disgusted with Jack. He had kissed Lucinda Fleming, evidently a mentally retarded girl. (Now *there* was a disgrace to live down!) Perhaps fearful of *never* being kissed, The Yap began to cry—although nowhere near as noticeably as The Wurtz.

Had Lucinda Fleming swallowed her tongue? Was *that* the reason for the choking sound she was making? "Now she's *bleeding*!" Caroline French cried. Indeed, Lucinda was bleeding in the area of her mouth. But it was not her tongue—she had bitten through her lower lip.

"She's *eating* herself!" Maureen Yap screamed.

"Oh, Jack, this disappoints me more than I can *say*," Miss Wurtz sobbed. By the commotion she made, you would have thought he'd gotten Lucinda *pregnant*. Clearly his time in the chapel was nigh. This was what could come from *kissing*: the urine, the blood, the impressive pantomime of rigor mortis—and to think he'd kissed only her *neck*!

That was when Jimmy Bacon fainted. The Gray Ghost's sudden appearance was so spectacular, Jimmy must have been too frightened to poo. None of the children had seen her coming. Suddenly Mrs. McQuat was kneeling over Lucinda. The Gray Ghost pried Lucinda's teeth apart, thereby rescuing her mangled lower lip. Mrs. McQuat then stuck a book in Lucinda's mouth. "Bite that . . . Lucinda," The Gray Ghost said. "You've done *enough* to your lip . . . already."

Jack would remember the book. Unfortunately, his memorization skills couldn't always distinguish between the trivial and the important, although Edna Mae Burnham's *Piano Course: Book Two,* which he'd often seen on Lucinda's desk, was not exactly trivial to Jack Burns. He assumed it was a book his dad had used. Jack was sure William had taught from that very book—he'd probably assigned it to someone, back in those days when he was fooling around with two girls at St. Hilda's. Possibly one (or both) of the girls had been an Edna Mae Burnham reader!

It was all too much for The Yap, beginning with the kissing. Maureen fainted, less spectacularly than Jimmy. It might have been that The Gray Ghost's sudden appearance, especially her kneeling over Lucinda, made it appear to Maureen that Mrs. McQuat was the Angel of Death. But of course The Gray Ghost would know how to attend to someone who'd bitten through her lip. (If she'd been a combat nurse, in whichever war, surely she'd seen more blood than that.)

Miss Wurtz, naturally, could not stop crying—thus the inevitable ensued. "Which of you," Mrs. McQuat began in her breathless way, "made Miss Wurtz . . . *cry?*"

"I did," Jack answered. Everyone seemed astonished that he had answered for himself—that simply wasn't done. Only The Gray Ghost looked unsurprised that he'd spoken up. "I'm *sorry,*" he added, but Mrs. McQuat turned her attention elsewhere.

Lucinda Fleming was on her feet, albeit unsteadily, blood oozing from her gashed lip; her shirt and tie were soaked. And then there was the urine—Lucinda didn't seem to notice it. The unnatural serenity of her smile was intact, as before.

"You need . . . *stitches* . . . Lucinda," The Gray Ghost was saying. "Take her to . . . the nurse's office . . . Caroline." Miss Wurtz once more thought that Mrs. McQuat meant *her,* but Caroline French understood that she was the designated helper. "Not *you* . . . dear," The Gray Ghost told Miss Wurtz. "This is your class . . . you *stay.*"

The Booth twins were instructed to accompany Maureen Yap to the nurse's office as well. Not entirely revived from her swoon, Maureen looked dizzy. Jimmy Bacon wasn't completely recovered from his fainting spell, either. He was down on all fours, as if he were still searching for Gordon's deceased hamster. Grant Porter and James Turner were assigned the task of taking Jimmy to the nurse. (They were such dolts, Jack doubted that they knew where the nurse's office was.)

As for Jack, he was surprised by how gently Mrs. McQuat took hold of his ear. Her thumb and index finger, which pinched his earlobe, were ice-cold, but when The Gray Ghost led him from the classroom, he was not in pain. And in the corridor, where she released his ear—her cold hand still steering him by the back of his neck—they struck up quite a cordial conversation, considering the circumstances.

"And what is . . . Miss Wurtz's problem . . . *this* time?" Mrs. McQuat whispered.

He'd been afraid that the issue of the kiss itself might come up, but he hesitated only a second. To lie to The Gray Ghost was unthinkable. "I kissed Lucinda Fleming," Jack confessed.

Mrs. McQuat nodded, seemingly unsurprised. "Where?" she whispered.

"On the back of her neck."

"That's not . . . so bad," The Gray Ghost said. "I expected . . . much worse."

There was no one in the chapel, where Jack regarded the prospect of turning his back on God with the greatest trepidation. But Mrs. McQuat steered him into one of the foremost pews. They sat down together, facing the altar. "Don't you want me to turn around?" Jack asked.

"Not you, Jack."

"Why not?"

"I think you need to face . . . the right way," The Gray Ghost said. "Don't you *ever* turn your back on God, Jack . . . in your case, I'm sure . . . He's looking."

"He *is*?"

"Definitely."

"Oh."

"You're . . . only eight, Jack. You're . . . already kissing girls at eight!"

"It was just on the neck."

"What you did was nothing . . . but you saw . . . the consequences." (Urination, bleeding, rigor mortis, *stitches*!)

"What should I do, Mrs. McQuat?"

"Pray," she said. "You should be . . . facing the right way for prayers."

"Pray *what*?"

"That you can . . . control your urges," The Gray Ghost said.

"Control my *what*?"

"Pray for the strength to . . . restrain yourself, Jack."

"From kissing?"

"From . . . worse than that, Jack."

From his father inside him, Mrs. McQuat might as well have said. When she'd added, "Pray for the strength to . . . restrain yourself," she hadn't been able to look him in the eye—she was staring at his *lap*! She meant the little guy, and all that he might be up to. Whatever was worse than kissing, Jack prayed for the strength to resist it. He prayed and prayed.

"Excuse me for . . . interrupting your prayers, Jack, but I have . . . a question."

"Go ahead," he said.

"Have you ever done . . . worse than kiss a girl?"

"What would be worse?"

"Something . . . *more* than kissing . . . perhaps."

Jack prayed that The Gray Ghost would forgive him if he told her. "I slept with Mrs. Oastler's bra."

"*Emma* Oastler? She gave you . . . her bra?"

"Not Emma's—it was her mom's bra."

"But Emma . . . gave it to *you*?"

"Yes. My mom took it back."

"Mercy!" Mrs. McQuat said.

"It was a *push-up* bra," he explained further.

"Go back . . . to your prayers, Jack."

In her ghostly way, she left—genuflecting in the aisle and making the sign of the cross. In her kindness to him, Jack couldn't help but feel that she was more alive than he first thought; yet the message Mrs. McQuat had left with him was as chilling as an admonition from the grave.

God was watching Jack Burns. If Jack turned his back on God, He would see. And if God was looking so closely at him, this was because He was certain Jack would *err*. (The Gray Ghost seemed fairly certain of this herself.) Whether the fault lay with his father inside him, or with the independence of mind and imagination already exhibited by the little guy, Jack seemed as predestined for sexual transgression as Emma Oastler had predicted.

He prayed and prayed. His knees were sore, his back was aching. Moments later, he recognized the smell of chewing gum in the pew behind him—this time, it was a fruity flavor. "What are you doing, baby cakes?" Emma whispered.

Jack didn't dare turn around. "Praying," he answered. "What's it look like I'm doing?"

"I heard you kissed her, Jack. It took four stitches to close her lip! Boy, have we got our homework cut out for us! You can't kiss a girl like she's a *steak*!"

"She bit herself," he explained, to no avail.

"Passion of the moment, eh?" Emma asked.

"I'm *praying,*" Jack said, still not turning around.

"Prayers won't help you, honey pie. Homework will."

Thus did Emma Oastler distract him from his prayers. If Emma hadn't found him in the chapel, he might have followed The Gray Ghost's instructions to the letter. And if he'd successfully prayed for the strength to restrain himself, which of course meant restraining the little guy, too—well, who knows what Jack Burns might have been spared, or what he might have spared others?

12

Not Just Another
Rose of Jericho

Years later, Lucinda Fleming would still include Jack among the bored recipients of her Christmas letter. He didn't know why. He never kissed her again. He hadn't kept in touch.

Emma Oastler's theory was that Jack's third-grade kiss on Lucinda's neck was her first and best—possibly her last. But given the sheer number of children Lucinda Fleming would have— they were mentioned by name, together with their ages, in those repetitive Christmas letters—Jack would be inclined to refute Emma's theory. Spellbound as he was by Lucinda's prodigious childbearing, Jack could conclude only that her husband had been kissing her—even happily. And in all likelihood, the husband who had spent the better part of his life kissing Lucinda Fleming had *not* caused her to bite through her lower lip and pee all over herself.

Looking back, Jack wouldn't miss Lucinda—or the rage she saved seemingly just for him. It was The Gray Ghost he would miss. Mrs. McQuat had done her best to help him not become like his father. It wasn't her fault that Jack didn't pray hard enough, or that he lacked the strength to control what The Gray Ghost called his "urges"; that he turned his back on God was more Jack's failure than Mrs. McQuat's *or* his dad's.

He had a ton of homework in grade four. Emma genuinely helped him with it. Jack's *other* homework, his sexual education, remained Emma's responsibility; she was tireless in her role as his self-appointed initiator.

As his grade-four teacher, Mrs. McQuat stayed after school two days a week to help Jack with his math. He actually concentrated on the math; with The Gray Ghost, there were no distractions, no conflicting desires to breathe her in. He never dreamed about Mrs. McQuat in *anyone's* underwear. In fact, Jack should have thanked her for the sympathy she showed him—not only for what she said to him in the chapel, but the degree to which she tried to counteract the command Caroline Wurtz took of the boy whenever she turned him loose onstage. (Or turned him not-so-loose, as was more often the case with Jack's performances under The Wurtz's uptight direction.)

He was cast as Adam in Miss Wurtz's cloying rendition of *Adam Bede.* THEY KISS EACH OTHER WITH A DEEP JOY, the stage directions read. Overlooking the disastrous results of the Lucinda Fleming kiss, which afforded no joy of any kind, Jack devoted himself to the task. Given that The Wurtz had cast Heather Booth as Dinah, the kiss was indeed a daunting one. Not only did Heather make her disturbing blanket-sucking sounds when he kissed her, but her twin, Patsy, made identical sucking sounds backstage.

Miss Wurtz had cast Patsy as Hetty, the woman who betrays Adam. And what a god-awful misinterpretation of *Adam Bede* it turned out to be! Jack-as-Adam eventually *marries* the identical twin of the woman who cheats on him! (George Eliot must have rolled around in her grave over such a liberty as that!)

And The Wurtz was overfond of the passage at the end of Chapter 54. Following her own inclinations, as ever, Miss Wurtz gave the passage to Jack as dialogue, even though it is actually George Eliot's narration. Looking into Heather Booth's love-struck eyes as he delivered his weighty lines didn't help. " 'What greater thing is there for two human souls, than to feel that they are joined for life—to strengthen each other in all labour, to rest on each other in all sorrow, to minister to each other in all pain, to be one with each other in silent unspeakable memories at the moment of the last parting?' " Jack-as-Adam asked Heather-as-Dinah, while she persisted in making barely audible sucking sounds in the back of her throat—as if his kiss had made her ill and she were readying herself to vomit.

"Jack," Mrs. McQuat said, when she saw his performance, "you must take everything Miss Wurtz says with a grain of salt."

"A what?"

"It's an expression—'with a grain of salt' means not to take someone or something too seriously."

"Oh."

"I wouldn't agree that there is no greater thing for two so-called human souls than to be joined for life. Frankly, I can't think of a comparable horror."

Jack would conclude that Mrs. McQuat was unhappily married—or else, if her husband had died and she was a widow who still called herself *Mrs.*, The Gray Ghost and the late *Mr.* McQuat had not enjoyed many silent unspeakable memories at the moment of *their* last parting.

Naturally, he took no end of shit from Emma Oastler for kissing Heather Booth WITH A DEEP JOY in front of the older girls. "Did you use your tongue?" Emma asked him. "It looked like you French-kissed her."

"Used my tongue *how*?"

"We'll get to that, honey pie—the homework is piling up. All the math you're doing is causing you to fall behind."

"Behind in what?"

"It sounded like you were *gagging* her, you dork."

But the Booth twins had made those terrible blanket-sucking sounds since kindergarten—Emma should have remembered that. (Emma's sleepy-time stories were the probable *origin* of the twins making those awful sounds!)

"Just wait till you get to *Middlemarch,* Jack," The Gray Ghost consoled him. "It's not only a better novel than *Adam Bede;* Miss Wurtz has not yet found a way to trivialize it."

Thus, in grade four, did he encounter in Mrs. McQuat a necessary dose of perspective. He would regret that she wasn't his mentor for his remaining years in school, but Jack was indeed fortunate to have her as his teacher in his last year at St. Hilda's.

Perspective is hard to come by. Caroline Wurtz was one of those readers who ransacked a novel for extractable truths, moral lessons, and pithy witticisms—with little concern for the wreck of the novel she left in her wake. Without The Gray Ghost's prescription of a grain of salt, who knows for how long Jack might have misled himself into thinking that he'd actually read *Jane Eyre* or *Tess of the d'Urbervilles*—or *The Scarlet Letter, Anna Karenina, Sense and Sensibility, Adam Bede,* and *Middlemarch.* By grade four, he had *not* read these wonderful books—he'd only acted in Miss Wurtz's purposeful plundering of them.

Of course Jack was familiar with the bulletin boards at St. Hilda's, where praise of women was rampant; there among the usual announcements was some humorless observation of Emerson's. ("A sufficient measure of civilization is the influence of good women.") And before Jack was cast as Dorothea in Miss Wurtz's dramatization of *Middlemarch,* he had seen George Eliot quoted among a variety of bulletin-board announcements. At the time, of course, Jack thought George Eliot was a *man.* Possibly a man-hating one, at least on the evidence of a most popular bulletin-board assertion of *Mr.* Eliot's—or so Jack believed. ("A man's mind—what there is of it—has always the advantage of being masculine—as the smallest birch-tree is of a higher kind than the most soaring palm—and even his ignorance is of a sounder quality.") *What does* that *mean?* he used to wonder.

As Dorothea, "with all her eagerness to know the truths of life," Jack radiated (under Miss Wurtz's direction) "very child-like ideas about marriage." No kidding—he was a child!

" 'Pride helps us,' " Jack-as-Dorothea prattled, " 'and pride is not a bad thing when it only urges us to hide our own hurts—not to hurt others.' " (Once again, this was *not* written as Dorothea's dialogue, or anyone else's, in the novel.)

To Miss Wurtz's assessment of his talents onstage—namely, that there were no boundaries to his "possibilities" as an actor— Mrs. McQuat countered with her own little scrap of truthfulness she had found in the pages of *Middlemarch.* " 'In fact, the world is full of hopeful analogies and handsome dubious eggs called possibilities,' " The Gray Ghost whispered.

"George Eliot?" Jack asked. "*Middlemarch*?"

"You bet," Mrs. McQuat replied. "There's more in that book than dramatic *homilies,* Jack."

To Miss Wurtz's prediction that he would one day be a great actor—if, and only if, he dedicated himself to a precision of character of the demanding kind The Wurtz so rigorously taught— The Gray Ghost offered another *un*dramatized observation from *Middlemarch.* " 'Among all forms of mistake, prophecy is the most gratuitous.' "

"The most what?"

"What I'm saying, Jack, is that *you* must play a more active role in your future than Miss Wurtz."

"Oh."

"Don't you see what's wrong with The Wurtz, baby cakes?" Emma Oastler asked.

"What's *wrong* with her?"

"Obviously The Wurtz is unfulfilled, Jack," Emma said. "I must have been wrong about her having a boyfriend. Maybe someone in her family bought her nice clothes. You don't imagine she has a sex life, or ever had one, do you?" Only in his dreams, Jack hoped. He had to admit, if not to Emma, that it was confusing—namely, how much he was learning from Miss Wurtz, which stood in contrast to how obviously flawed she was.

Like Caroline Wurtz roaming randomly in a novel, Jack searched the St. Hilda's bulletin boards for gems of uplifting advice; unlike Miss Wurtz at large in a novel, he found little that was useful there. Kahlil Gibran was a favorite of the older girls in those years. Jack brought one of Gibran's baffling recommendations to The Gray Ghost for a translation.

> Let there be spaces in your togetherness,
> And let the winds of the heavens dance between you.

"What does that mean?" Jack asked Mrs. McQuat.

"Poppycock, hogwash, bunk," The Gray Ghost said.

"What?"

"It doesn't mean anything at all, Jack."

"Oh." Mrs. McQuat had taken the quotation from him. He watched her crumple it in her cold hand. "Shouldn't I put it back on the bulletin board?" he asked.

"Let's see if Mr. Gibran can find his way back to the bulletin board all by himself," The Gray Ghost said.

Jack trusted her. He dared to ask her things he was afraid to ask anyone else. There were a growing number of things he *wouldn't* ask his mother; her distancing herself from him was a warning, but of what Jack wasn't sure. He had tired of the when-you're-old-enough answer, no matter what the reason for her aloofness.

Lottie was Lottie. As much as she had mattered to him once—maybe most of all when he'd been in those Baltic and North Sea ports and had missed her—now that he was older, Lottie didn't hold him chest-to-chest to compare their beating hearts. At his age, that was a game Jack preferred to play with Emma. (As Emma put it: "You can tell that the most interesting part of Lottie's life is over.")

And Mrs. Wicksteed was old and growing older; when she

warmed her increasingly uncooperative fingers over her tea, her fingers would dip in and out of the tea, with which she occasionally sprinkled Jack's shirt and tie. She'd become an expert at doing a necktie during the years of her late husband's arthritis. "Now I have his affliction, Jack," Mrs. Wicksteed told the boy. "I ask you. Does that seem fair?"

The fairness question was one that had occurred to Jack in other areas. "It's not fair that I should turn out to be like my father," he said frankly to Mrs. McQuat. (He was in a phase of being slightly less than frank with Emma on this subject.) "Do *you* think it's fair?" Jack asked The Gray Ghost. He could see she'd really been a combat nurse—notwithstanding what truth, or lack thereof, resided in the story of her having one lung because she'd been gassed. "Do *you* think I'm going to turn out like him, Mrs. McQuat?"

"Let's take a walk, Jack."

He could tell they were headed for the chapel. "Am I being punished?" he asked.

"Not at all! We're just going where we can think."

They sat together in one of the foremost pews, facing in the right direction. It was a minor distraction that a grade-three boy was kneeling in the center aisle with his back turned on God. Although The Gray Ghost had positioned him there—however long ago—she seemed surprised to see him in the aisle, but she quickly ignored him.

"*If* you turn out to be like your father, Jack, don't blame your father."

"Why not?"

"Barring acts of God, you're only a victim if you choose to be one," The Gray Ghost said. From the look of the frightened third grader kneeling in the center aisle, he clearly thought that Mrs. McQuat was describing him.

Thank goodness Jack never asked Emma Oastler his next question, which he addressed to Mrs. McQuat in the chapel. "Is it an act of God if you have sex on your mind every minute?"

"Mercy!" The Gray Ghost said, taking her eyes from the altar to look at him. "Are you serious?"

"Every minute," he repeated. "It's all I dream about, too."

"Jack, have you talked to your mother about this?" Mrs. McQuat asked.

"She'll just say I'm not old enough to talk about it."

"But it seems that you *are* old enough to be thinking and dreaming about little else!"

"Maybe it will be better in an all-boys' school," Jack said. He knew that an all-boys' school was his mother's next plan for him. Just up the road from St. Hilda's—within easy walking distance, in fact—was Upper Canada College. (The UCC boys were always sniffing around the older of the St. Hilda's girls.) And it was no surprise that Mrs. Wicksteed "knew someone" at Upper Canada College, or that Jack would have good recommendations from his teachers at St. Hilda's—at least academically. He'd already been to UCC for an interview. Coming from the gray-and-maroon standard at St. Hilda's, he thought there was entirely too much blue in the school colors at Upper Canada— their regimental-striped ties were navy blue and white. If you played a varsity sport, the first-team ties (as they were called) were a solid-blue-knit variety—navy blue with square bottoms. Alice had found it ominous that the jocks were singled out and idolized in this fashion. In Jack's interview, his mother freely offered that her son was not athletic.

"How do you know?" Jack asked her. (He'd never had the opportunity to *try*!)

"Trust me, Jack. You're not." But he trusted his mother less and less.

"Which all-boys' school are you thinking of?" The Gray Ghost asked him.

"Upper Canada College, my mom says."

"I'll have a word with your mother, Jack. Those UCC boys will eat you alive."

Given his respect for Mrs. McQuat, this was not an encouraging concept. Jack expressed his concern to Emma. "Eat me alive *why*? Eat me *how*?"

"It's hard to imagine that you're a jock, Jack."

"So?"

"So they'll eat you alive, so what? The sport of *life* is gonna be your sport, baby cakes."

"The sport of—"

"Shut up and kiss me, honey pie," Emma said. They were scrunched down in the backseat of the Town Car again. It was a fairly recent development that Emma could give Jack a boner in a matter of seconds—or *not,* depending on the little guy's unpredictable response. Emma was in grade ten, sixteen going on thirty or forty, and—to her considerable rage—she had newly acquired braces. Jack was a little afraid of kissing her. "Not like *that*!" Emma instructed him. "Am I a baby bird? Are you feeding me some kind of *worm*?"

"It's my tongue," he told her.

"I know what it is, Jack. I'm addressing the more important subject of how it *feels*."

"It feels like a *worm*?"

"Like you're trying to choke me."

She cradled his head in her lap and looked down at him with impatient affection. Every year, Emma got bigger and stronger. At the same time, Jack felt he was barely growing. But he had a boner, and Emma always knew when he had one. "That little guy is like a coming attraction, honey pie."

"A what?"

"At the movies, a coming attraction—"

"Oh."

"You're soon to be all over the place, Jack. That's what I'm saying."

"This girl is just jerking your wire, mon," Peewee said.

"Just shut up and drive, *mon*," Emma said to Peewee. He was, as Jack was, in her thrall.

Jack would wonder, after his mom had returned the push-up bra to Mrs. Oastler, what possibly could have transpired between the two mothers that had led to him being left alone with Emma *again*. And Jack and Emma were alone a lot; they were even alone, for an hour or more at a time, in Emma's house. Whether Emma's mom was at home or not, they were left alone there—no Lottie banging around in the kitchen below them, screaming some nonsense about tea.

The Oastler house in Forest Hill was a three-story mansion bequeathed to Mrs. Oastler by her ex-husband; the alimony settlement had made Emma and her mother rich. Women who scored big in their divorces were treated with immeasurable scorn in the Toronto tabloids, but Mrs. Oastler would have said it was as good a way to get rich as any.

Emma's mom was a small, compact woman—as her push-up bra would suggest. As Emma's mustache would imply, her mother was surprisingly hairy—at least for a woman, and a small woman at that. Emma's mom would have had a more discernible mustache than her daughter, but (according to Emma) Mrs. Oastler frequently had her upper lip waxed. She would not have been rash to consider waxing her arms as well, but the only other *visible* preventative measure taken against her hairiness was that she had her sleek black hair cut as short as a boy's in an elfish pixie. Despite her prettiness, which was petite in nature, Jack thought that Mrs. Oastler looked a little like a man.

"Yes, but an *attractive* one," Alice said to her son. She thought that Emma's mother was "very good-looking," and that it was a pity Emma "took after" her father.

Jack never met Emma's dad. After every winter break from St. Hilda's, Emma returned to school with a tan. Her father had taken her to the West Indies, or Mexico; that was virtually the only time they spent together. Emma also spent a month of every summer at a cottage in Georgian Bay, but most of that time she was in the care of a nanny or a housekeeper—her dad came to the cottage only on weekends. Emma never spoke of him.

That Mrs. Oastler thought Emma was too young to have her mustache waxed was a source of contention between mother and daughter. "It's hardly noticeable," Emma's mom would tell her. "Besides, at your age, what does it matter?" And there were other issues between them, as one might expect of a divorced woman raising a "difficult" only child—a sixteen-year-old daughter who was physically bigger and stronger than her mother, and still growing.

Mrs. Oastler also thought that Emma was too young to have a tattoo—an intolerable hypocrisy, in Emma's opinion, because her mom had recently been tattooed by Daughter Alice. This was news to Jack, but so was almost everything Emma told him. "What's her tattoo? A tattoo *where*?" he asked.

Well, what a surprise! Emma's mom had been tattooed to conceal a scar. "She had a Cesarean," Emma said. *That old business again,* Jack thought. "It's a scar from her C-section," Emma told him. And to think he'd once believed this was the ward for difficult births in a hospital in Halifax! "She had a bikini cut," Emma explained.

"A what?"

"A horizontal incision, not the vertical kind."

"I still don't get it," Jack said.

This necessitated a trip to Mrs. Oastler's bedroom. (Emma's mother was out.) There Emma showed Jack a pair of her mom's panties—black bikini briefs, no doubt a fetching match to the push-up bra. Mrs. Oastler's scar was called a bikini cut because the incision was below the panty line of the briefs.

"Oh. And what's the tattoo?"

"A stupid rose."

Jack thought not. He was pretty sure he knew what kind of rose it was, in which case it would have been too big to be completely concealed under the panty line of Mrs. Oastler's bikini briefs. "A Rose of Jericho?" he asked Emma.

It was, for once, her turn to be uninformed. "A Rose of *what*?"

This was not the easiest thing for a nine-year-old to explain. Jack made a fist. "It's about this big, maybe a little bigger," he began.

"Yes, it is," Emma said. "Go on, Jack."

"It's a flower with the petals of *another* flower hidden inside it."

"*What* other flower?"

There were so many words he'd heard and remembered—not that he understood them. *Labia* was one, *vagina* another—they were like flowers, weren't they? And the other flower hidden in a Rose of Jericho was like the petals, or the labia, a *woman* had—a vagina concealed in a rose. Jack couldn't imagine what a mess he made of this explanation to Emma, but of course Emma knew what he was *trying* to say.

"You must be kidding, Jack."

"You have to know what you're looking for in order to see it," the boy said.

"Don't tell me you know what a vagina looks like, honey pie."

"Not an actual one," Jack admitted. But he had seen a Rose of Jericho—many, in fact. He had examined the petals of *that* flower. He'd spotted "the lips" within the rose, as Ladies' Man Madsen had called them—the oh-so-peculiar-but-discernible *something* that made a Rose of Jericho not quite like any other rose. "Maybe you haven't looked closely enough," he said to Emma, who seemed not herself—she was paralyzed with disbelief. "I mean at the *tattoo*."

Emma took Jack by the hand and led him back to her bedroom. In her other hand, Emma was still holding her mom's bikini briefs; it was as if Jack Burns were destined to bear to his grave the burden of a life-changing relationship with Mrs. Oastler's underwear.

Emma's bedroom was everything you would expect of that passage from childhood through puberty to concupiscence. The neglected teddy bears and other stuffed animals occupied positions of no particular importance on the king-size bed; there was a poster from a Beatles concert, and one from a Robert Redford movie. (It might have been *Jeremiah Johnson,* because Redford had a beard.) And everywhere, on the floor, on the bed—in one case, as if strangling a teddy bear—Emma's bras and panties were flagrantly displayed. The underwear of a woman-in-progress, which Emma clearly was, indicated (albeit not to Jack) that Emma was in more of a hurry on her journey to womanhood than most girls her age.

In comparison, Jack was in no hurry on his journey to becoming a young man. He just happened to have met Emma Oastler, who knew his father's story; despite the seven years between them, Emma was eager to see him catch up to her. "So you know what a vagina looks like," Emma was saying, as she lay down among her discarded panties and bras and teddy bears.

"I know what one looks like in a Rose of Jericho," Jack replied. She'd not let go of his hand. He had no choice but to lie down on the bed beside her.

"So a vagina is familiar to you—the labia, the whole business," Emma was saying, as she lifted her short pleated skirt and wriggled out of her panties. Her mom's bikini briefs could never have accommodated Emma's hips. Consistent with the general sloppiness of dress (and undress) of the older girls at St. Hilda's, Emma didn't bother to take her panties entirely off; she kicked one leg free but left her panties dangling on one ankle, where their whiteness stood in contrast to her gray kneesocks, which were typically pushed down below midcalf, as if the socks were also indications of Emma's preference for half-dress (or half-undress).

"You have big feet," Jack observed.

"Forget the feet, Jack. You're looking at your first vagina, and you're telling me you're not surprised?" The *hair* was again a surprise—though not nearly so much as when he'd first felt it, unseen. But the rest of the business—well, he was prepared for it to be complicated. The intricate folds ("the lips," as Ladies' Man Madsen had called them) were of a certain healthiness of pink that no tattoo pigment could imitate; yet this ornate door, for a vagina was clearly an opening, was recognizable from his mom's

Rose of Jericho, of which Jack had seen a hundred. Having seen Emma's, he would have no trouble (in the future) finding that other flower in the rose, but for how many nine-year-old boys is it no big deal to see your first actual vagina? "Cat got your tongue, Jack?" Emma said.

"The hair's different—there's no hair on the tattoo," he told her.

"You're saying only the *hair* is special? You're saying you've seen the rest of it?"

"It's a Rose of Jericho," Jack said. "I would recognize it anywhere."

"It's a *vagina,* honey pie!"

"But it's also a Rose of Jericho," he insisted. "You just need to take a closer look at your mom's—at her *tattoo,* I mean."

"Maybe the little guy has more of an interest in the real thing than you do, Jack." Alas, the little guy did not look interested enough to merit Emma's approval. "Jesus, baby cakes, I think there's something wrong." At nine going on ten, Jack simply wasn't old enough. The unpredictability of his penis—aroused one minute, indifferent the next—wasn't half as disappointing to him as it was to Emma. "Kiss me," Emma demanded. "That sometimes works."

Not this time. Jack would have admitted that the kiss was more aggressive than usual on Emma's part, and that—notwithstanding how she'd criticized him for inserting his tongue in her mouth and wiggling it like a *worm*—the probing use she made of *her* tongue was beginning to get the little guy's attention. But at the very moment his pinkie of a penis demonstrated a growing interest, which Emma might have called "promising," he snagged his lower lip on a loose wire in Emma's newly acquired braces. Before either of them noticed, Jack had bled all over Emma and himself—*and* her bed, several stuffed animals, and the aforementioned bra. (The one that appeared to be strangling a teddy bear.)

There was blood everywhere; more alarming, Emma and Jack were still attached. While Emma searched her messy bedroom for a hand mirror, they were clumsily—in Jack's case, painfully—linked. His lower lip was hooked to her wired teeth. And the hand mirror, when Emma finally found it, offered a confusingly reversed view. They were caught in the act of failing to disengage his lip from her braces when Emma's mom came home and skillfully, in a matter of seconds, separated them. "Maybe you *should* get your upper lip waxed, Emma," Mrs. Oastler said.

Did he need *stitches*? Jack wanted to know. There was every bit as much blood as when Lucinda Fleming had attempted to eat herself. Dangerous kissing was not new to Jack Burns!

"It's just a puncture wound," Emma's mom said, pinching his lower lip between her thumb and index finger. She didn't seem to mind the blood. Jack recognized her perfume from his many nights with her push-up bra. Mrs. Oastler, the instant he remembered her stolen bra, spotted her black bikini briefs on Emma's bloodstained bed. "I wish you'd play these games with your own underwear, Emma," Mrs. Oastler said. By the evidence of Emma's white panties with the lace waistband, which were still wrapped around Emma's left ankle and draped over her left foot, it was clear that Emma and Jack *had* been playing a game with her underwear as well. But Mrs. Oastler took more of an interest in recovering her black bikini briefs. "You're evidently a precocious boy, Jack," Emma's mom said.

"Jack knows all about tattoos," Emma told her. "He knows all about *yours,* anyway."

"Really? Is that true, Jack?" Mrs. Oastler asked.

"If it's a Rose of Jericho, I know something about it," he said.

"Go on—show him," Emma told her mom.

"I'm sure Jack doesn't need to see another Rose of Jericho. I'll bet he's already seen his share," Mrs. Oastler said.

"Well, I'd like to take a closer look at it myself," Emma told her mother. "Now that I know what it is."

"Maybe later, Emma," Mrs. Oastler said. "We can't send Jack home all covered with blood."

"You've got a *vagina* above your vagina, and you won't let me get a butterfly on my *ankle*!" Emma screamed.

"Ankles hurt," Jack offered. "Tattoos hurt where there's nothing but bone."

"It seems that Jack *does* know all about tattoos, Emma. You should listen to Jack."

"I just want a *butterfly*!" Emma screamed.

"Here's what we're going to do, Jack," Mrs. Oastler said, ignoring her daughter. "I'm going to take you to my bathroom, where you can wash up. Emma can wash up in her bathroom." Emma's mom took Jack's hand and led him down the familiar path to her bedroom, which was connected to a large bathroom with wall-to-wall mirrors. In her other hand, Mrs. Oastler carried her black bikini briefs, which she twirled around and around her index finger. In the slight breeze made by her swinging panties, Jack became more aware of her perfume than before.

She removed his bloodstained shirt and tie and filled her bathroom sink with warm water; with a wet washcloth, she wiped his face and neck, being careful to gently pat his punctured lip, which was still bleeding, if only a little. While Jack washed the blood from his hands in the sink, Mrs. Oastler rubbed his shoulders with her cool, silky hands. There wasn't any blood on Jack's shoulders, but Emma's mom seemed almost as comfortable touching him as her daughter was. "You're going to be a strong boy, Jack—not very big, but strong."

"Do you think so?" he asked.

"I know so," Mrs. Oastler said. "I can tell."

"Oh." He realized why her hands felt so cool and silky. She was rubbing his back and shoulders with her black bikini briefs.

"You're obviously very mature for your age," Emma's mom continued, "whereas Emma, although she's a big girl, is somewhat *immature* in other areas. She's not at all at ease with boys her own age, for example."

"Oh," Jack said again. He was drying his hands with a towel while Mrs. Oastler continued rubbing his back and shoulders with her panties. In the mirror, he could see her intense, serious face, framed by her pixie haircut.

"As for you, Jack, you seem quite comfortable around older girls and women." He felt somewhat less comfortable when Emma's mom ran her silky underwear over the back of his neck and placed her panties on his head, like a hat—like a curiously misshapen beret. His ears protruded from her bikini briefs, where her thighs would normally be. "What on earth will we tell your mom about your *lip*?" she asked. Before Jack could think of an answer, Mrs. Oastler said: "I get the feeling Alice isn't quite ready for the idea of you kissing a sixteen-year-old."

So his mom was "Alice" to Mrs. Oastler, which was only a mild surprise. He should have known. A Rose of Jericho is a fairly lengthy procedure, several hours under the best circumstances—and in this case, on such an intimate area of the body. Jack could easily imagine his mom and Mrs. Oastler having quite the conversation. Lying face-up on a bed or a table, for hours at a time, having a Rose of Jericho tattooed a few inches above your vagina—well, what subjects *wouldn't* you feel free to discuss? People became fast friends in less than half the time it took to tattoo a Rose of Jericho. Alice had spent hours staring at Mrs. Oastler's pubes; in such a situation, how could they *not* get to know each other? But while Alice had apparently gone along with Mrs. Oastler regarding Jack and Emma's behavior, that he had cut his lip in a *kissing* accident might just nip Alice's friendship with Mrs. Oastler in the bud. In any case, it made perfect sense to Jack not to tell his mother how he'd hurt himself kissing Emma.

"You could say it was a staple, Jack. I was trying to separate two pages of paper that had been stapled together, and you tried to help me. You opened the staple with your teeth."

"Why would I use my teeth?" he asked.

"Because you're a kid," Mrs. Oastler said. She patted her bikini briefs, which Jack still wore as a hat; then she plucked her panties off his head and threw them across the bathroom into an open laundry hamper. It was a good shot. She had a kind of athletic grace, boyish in nature. "I'll find you a T-shirt, something to wear home. Tell your mom I'm sending your shirt and tie to the dry cleaner's."

"Okay," he said.

Emma's mom was in her bedroom, opening a drawer. Jack kept looking at himself, bare-chested, in her bathroom mirror above the sink—as if he expected to start growing in some observable fashion. Mrs. Oastler came back with a T-shirt. It was all black, like her bikini briefs, and with the sleeves for the upper arms cut short and tight, the way women liked them. Emma's mom was so small, her T-shirt was only a little loose on Jack. "It's one of mine, of course. Emma's clothes," she added, disapprovingly, "would be too big."

His lower lip had finally stopped bleeding, but it was swollen and you could see the pinprick where the wire from Emma's braces had stabbed him. Mrs. Oastler gently rubbed some lip gloss over the wound. Emma walked into the bathroom while her mom was doing this. "You look like a girl in that T-shirt, Jack," Emma said.

"Well, Jack's pretty enough to be a girl, isn't he?" Mrs. Oastler asked. There was a noticeable measure of shame in Emma's resentful expression and slouched posture, as if she'd taken her mother's point to heart. (Jack may have been pretty enough to be a girl, but—in her mom's estimation—Emma wasn't.) "We're telling Jack's mother that he cut himself on a staple. He was trying to open a staple with his teeth, silly boy."

"I want to see the fucking Rose of Jericho," Emma said. "I want Jack to see it, too."

Without a word, Mrs. Oastler, who wore a tight-fitting pair of black jeans with a silver belt, untucked her long-sleeved cotton turtleneck, which was also black. She unbuckled the belt and wriggled the jeans over her slim hips. Jack could see only the top half of the Rose of Jericho above the panty line of her black bikini briefs. She hooked her thumbs under the waistband of her panties, but before she slid them down, she said: "*This,* Jack, would be in the category of needlessly upsetting your mom—maybe even worse than kissing a sixteen-year-old, if you know what I mean."

"Oh," he said, as she pulled her bikini briefs down.

There it was. (*Not* the Rose of Jericho. Jack didn't need to waste a second of his time looking at another one. His mom was a pro; he assumed that Daughter Alice's Rose of Jericho was the same every time.) While Emma saw, with a gasp, the unmistakable *other* flower within the rose, Jack took a long, careful look at the real thing—his second sighting of an actual vagina in one day. Emma's pubic hair was as unruly as she was, but Mrs. Oastler's pubes were neatly trimmed. And if Jack ever doubted Emma's authority—that he had an older-woman thing, as she put it—he didn't doubt it now. If Emma's vagina had left the little guy largely unimpressed, what was Jack to make of the quantum leap the little guy made in response to Emma's mom?

"That's *disgusting*!" Emma said. (She meant the tattoo.)

"It's a Rose of Jericho, like any other," Jack insisted. "My mom does a good one."

While he went on staring at her vagina, Mrs. Oastler rumpled his hair and said: "You bet she does, Jack—you bet she does."

Emma suddenly hit him so hard that he took a short flight across the bathroom tiles and landed in the vicinity of the laundry hamper. Jack instinctively put a finger to his lower lip, to be sure he wasn't bleeding again. "You weren't looking at the *tattoo,* baby cakes."

"Boys will be boys, Emma," Mrs. Oastler told her daughter. "Be nice to Jack. Please don't make him bleed again."

Emma yanked him to his feet by grabbing hold of her mom's skimpy T-shirt. In one of the bathroom's many mirrors, Jack caught a glimpse of Mrs. Oastler pulling up her bikini briefs and wriggling her hips back into her jeans. "What's the little guy think of my mom's Rose of Jericho?" Emma asked Jack in her vaguely threatening way.

Mrs. Oastler, of course, didn't realize that Emma was referring to Jack's penis. She probably assumed that her daughter was being disparaging about the boy's smaller size. "Don't bully him, Emma," Mrs. Oastler said. "It's unbecoming."

As Jack was leaving, he found it confusing that both Emma and her mom kissed him good-bye—Mrs. Oastler on his cheek, Emma on his undamaged upper lip. In the category of unnecessarily upsetting his mother, Jack was determined he would make no mention of his confusion to her—nor would he tell her about the rest of his eventful day at the Oastler mansion in Forest Hill.

Jack went to bed that night in Mrs. Oastler's black T-shirt, although Lottie said she liked him better in his own pajamas. Lottie wrapped an ice cube in a washcloth and held it to his lower lip while she said her prayers over him. "May the Lord protect you, Jack, and may He keep you from harming others," Lottie always began. Jack thought the latter was a ridiculous concern. Why would he ever harm others? "May the Lord keep Mrs. Wicksteed alive a little longer," Lottie went on. "May I please be permitted to die in Toronto, and never go back to Prince Edward Island."

"Amen," Jack usually tried to say at this point, hoping that would be the end of it.

But Lottie wasn't finished. "Please, Lord, deliver Alice from her inclinations—"

"Her what?"

"You know what, Jack—her tendencies," Lottie told him. "Her choice of friends."

"Oh."

"May God keep your mother from hurting herself, not to put too fine a point on it," Lottie continued. "And may the Lord bless the ground you walk on, Jack Burns, so that you are ever mindful of temptation. May you become the very model of what a man *should* be, Jack—not what most men are."

"Amen," he said again.

"That's for me to say and for you to say *after* me," Lottie always told him.

"Oh, right."

"Thank you, Mrs. Wicksteed," Lottie whispered, at the end—almost as if Mrs. Wicksteed were God and Lottie had been addressing Her from the beginning. "Amen."

"Amen."

She took the ice cube in the washcloth away from his lip, which was numb. But Jack was wide awake, and as soon as Lottie left, he went to his mother's room and got into her bed, where he eventually fell asleep. (Jack had many vivid memories of his two-vagina day; it was impossible to fall asleep right away.)

It was his mom's leg across his body that woke him; it was the T-shirt that woke *her*. Alice turned on the light to have a better look. "Why are you wearing Leslie's shirt, Jack? Is Emma stealing her mom's T-shirts now?"

So Mrs. Oastler was "Leslie"—another mild surprise. Even the T-shirt was more familiar to his mom than Jack had thought. He carefully explained that Mrs. Oastler had given him her T-shirt to wear because his clothes were all bloody—they'd been sent off to the dry cleaner's—and any shirt of Emma's would have been too big. Jack showed his mom his puffy lower lip, where he had poked himself with a staple he'd tried to undo with his teeth.

"I thought you were smarter than that," Alice said.

Jack very slowly, and even more carefully, said that he understood his mom had tattooed Mrs. Oastler—it sounded like a Rose of Jericho from Emma's description, he unconvincingly explained—but the tattoo was in such a private place that Emma's mom wouldn't show it to him.

"I'm surprised she didn't show you," Alice said.

"I don't need to see another Rose of Jericho," Jack went on. (Even to himself, he sounded too cavalier.) "What's so special about hers?"

"Just the place, Jack—it's in a special place."

"Oh." He must have moved his eyes away from hers. His mom was such a good liar, she was tough to lie to.

"Not every woman shaves her pubic hair in quite that way," his mother said.

"Her what?"

"The hair is called *pubic* hair, Jack."

"Oh."

"You don't have any yet, but you will."

"Do you shave your pubic hair that way?" Jack asked his mom.

"That's not your business, young man," she told him, but he could see she was crying. He didn't say anything. "*Leslie*—Mrs. Oastler, to you— is a very . . . *independent* woman," Alice started to say, as if she were beginning to read out loud from a long book. "She's been through a divorce, a bad time, but she's very . . . *rich*. She's determined to seize control of everything that happens to her. She's a very . . . *forceful* woman."

"She's kind of small—smaller than Emma, anyway," Jack interjected. (He had no idea what his mother was struggling to say.)

"You want to be careful around Mrs. Oastler, Jack."

"I'm pretty careful around *Emma*," he ventured.

"Yes, you should be careful around Emma, too," Alice said, "but you want to be *more* careful around Emma's mom."

"Okay."

"It's all right that she showed you," his mother said. "I'm sure you didn't ask to see it."

"Emma asked her to show me," he said.

"Now tell me about your lip."

Jack was learning that adults were better at concealing things than kids were, and he was increasingly aware that his mom knew a lot she wasn't telling him. Mrs. Wicksteed's health, for example: Jack knew she had arthritis because he could see it for himself, and because Mrs. Wicksteed had told him. But no one told him she had cancer, not until the day she didn't get up in time to do his tie—and then Lottie told him, not his mother. (Maybe his mom had been too busy; it might have been the same week she'd been tattooing Mrs. Oastler.)

Suddenly there was no one in the house who knew how to do a necktie, except Mrs. Wicksteed, who was dying! "Is she dying of *arthritis*?" Jack asked Lottie.

"No, dear. She has cancer."

"Oh." So that was why Lottie prayed every night for the Lord to keep Mrs. Wicksteed alive a little longer.

Peewee did Jack's tie that morning. He was a limo driver; he did his own tie every morning. He tied Jack's in a very matter-of-fact fashion, not making half the fuss that Mrs. Wicksteed had—even before her arthritis. "Mrs. Wicksteed is dying, Peewee."

"That's too bad, mon. What's the lady with the limp going to do then?" So that was why Lottie prayed to be permitted to die in Toronto. Everyone, including Peewee, knew that Lottie didn't want to go back to Prince Edward Island.

Maybe everyone had a Rose of Jericho hidden somewhere, Jack thought. Perhaps it wasn't always the kind of tattoo you could see, but another kind—like a free tattoo. No less a mark for life, just one not visible on the skin.

13

Not Your Usual
Mail-Order Bride

Out of concern for Mrs. Wicksteed, Jack asked Miss Wurtz if he could be excused from *Jane Eyre* rehearsals the rest of that week; after all, he'd played Rochester before. (He could do the part blind, so to speak.) But Connie-Turnbull-as-Jane had been replaced with Caroline French. Jack had never embraced a girl his own height. Caroline's hair got in his mouth, which he found disagreeable. In the throes of that passionate moment when Jack-as-Rochester tells Caroline-as-Jane that she must think him an "irreligious dog," Caroline nervously thumped her heels. Backstage, Jack could imagine her dim-witted twin, Gordon, thumping his heels, too. And when Caroline-as-Jane first took Jack-as-Rochester's hand and mashed it to her lips, Jack was overcome with revulsion—both Caroline's hand and her mouth were sticky.

It wasn't only because Mrs. Wicksteed was dying that he wanted to miss a week of rehearsals; Miss Wurtz was reduced to tears all that week. Jack's mom told him that Mrs. Wicksteed had helped Miss Wurtz out of a "tight spot" before. Whether the so-called tight spot had been the source of The Wurtz's tastefully expensive clothes—the boyfriend Emma no longer believed in—Jack never learned. He was permitted to miss rehearsals. Caroline French was forced to imagine him in her sticky embrace.

His availability was of little use to Mrs. Wicksteed, who was hospitalized and enduring a battery of tests. Lottie assured Jack that he didn't want to see the old lady that way. Jack's mother, though she told him almost nothing of what she was feeling, was noticeably distraught. If, upon Mrs. Wicksteed's death, Lottie

would soon be on a boat back to Prince Edward Island, Alice confided to Jack in the semidarkness of her bedroom that they were out on the street. Jack inquired if, in lieu of the street, she and room for them in the Chinaman's tattoo parlor.
"No needles again," was all his mother

Was their enemy Mrs. Wicksteed's divorced daughter? She had never cared for their status as her mother's rent-free boarders. But wasn't she alleged to be Mrs. Oastler's friend? Hadn't she and Leslie Oastler attended St. Hilda's together? Now that Leslie and Alice were friends, Jack suggested that maybe Mrs. Oastler would speak to Mrs. Wicksteed's daughter on their behalf. All Alice said was that Mrs. Wicksteed's daughter and Leslie Oastler weren't the best of friends anymore.

It was only natural that Jack turned to The Gray Ghost for guidance in this troubling time, but Mrs. McQuat knew something she wasn't telling him. Her strongest recommendation was that they pray together in the chapel, which meant only that they prayed together *more*. And when he asked The Gray Ghost if she'd been successful in persuading his mother that he would be "eaten alive" by those boys at Upper Canada College, Mrs. McQuat's answer was out of character. It was not like a former combat nurse to be evasive. "Maybe UCC . . . wouldn't have been . . . so bad, Jack."

What did the "wouldn't have been" mean? "Excuse me, Mrs. McQuat—" Jack started to say.

"You're a bit . . . *young* to be a boarder . . . Jack . . . but there are schools—mostly in the States—where boarding is . . . the norm."

"The what?"

They were in the second pew, to the left of the center aisle— the altar bathed in a golden light, the stained-glass saints administering to Jesus. What a lucky guy, to have four women fussing over him! Mrs. McQuat put her cold hand on Jack's far shoulder and pulled him against her. She put her dry lips to his temple and gave him the faintest trace of a kiss. ("She gives him a paper kiss," Jack would read in a screenplay, years later, and remember this moment in the chapel.)

"For a boy in your . . . *situation,* Jack . . . maybe a little . . . *independence* is the best thing."

"A little what?"

"Talk to your mother, Jack."

But having tried to open that door without looking out the to Emma Oastler instead. Emma was Mrs. Oastler called it. mother's mansion *in Forest Hills,* guest bedrooms—the guest bedrooms, each with its own bathroom; it was There were three bedrooms, each with its own bathroom; it was a *wing,* all right. "Horestly," Emma was saying, "I can't understand why you and your mom don't just move in *here.* I think it's stupid to send you away."

"Away where?"

"Talk to your mom. It's her idea. She thinks you and I are a bad combination. She doesn't want you going through puberty in the same house with me."

"Going through what?"

"It's not like we'd have to sleep in the same bedroom," Emma said, pushing him down on the biggest of the guest-room beds. "Your mom and mine have the prevailing St. Hilda's mentality. Girls get to see boys until the boys are *nine-year-olds*—then the boys disappear!"

"Disappear *where*?"

Emma was engaged in one of her periodic checks on the progress of his penis, which seemed to render her melancholic. She'd pulled down his pants and underwear and was lying with her heavy head on his bare thigh. "I have a new theory," Emma said, as if she were speaking exclusively to the little guy. "Maybe you *are* old enough. Maybe it's *me* who's not old enough—I mean I'm not old enough for *you.*"

"Disappear *where*?" Jack asked her again. "Where am I being sent away?"

"It's an all-boys' school in Maine, baby cakes. I hear it's kind of *remote.*"

"Kind of what?"

"Possibly the little guy likes even older women than I first supposed," Emma was saying. His penis lay still and small in the palm of her hand. Jack was being sent to *Maine,* but the little guy didn't care. "I've talked to a couple of girls in grade thirteen, and one in grade twelve. They know everything about penises," Emma went on. "Maybe they can help."

"Help what?"

Not Your Usual M...oney ...s. We can't get you into

"The problem is that th...ing. How hard was it for him to
their residence unless ...ugh, as Mrs. Oastler had observed—
Jack should have ...e performances at St. Hilda's, he'd been a
be a girl? He was ...
and in his many... than he'd been a man.
woman more ...
Much aga...st Miss Wurtz's wishes, he'd recently been cast as
a woman... in the senior-school production of *A Mail-Order Bride*
in the M...in the ...tories—a nineteenth-century melodrama
that The Wurtz despised. Jack was the pathetic child bride. Because of the play's subject matter—it was annually performed
for the senior school *exclusively*—he'd needed his mother's permission to accept the part. Alice, in her fashion, had acquiesced.
She'd never read the play. Not growing up in Canada, Alice
hadn't been subjected to *A Mail-Order Bride in the Northwest Territories* in her girlhood—as almost every Canadian
woman of Alice's generation had. (As almost every Canadian
girl of Emma's generation would be.)

In those days—at St. Hilda's, especially—the senior girls were
fed a steady diet of Canadian literature. Miss Wurtz was outraged that many novels of international stature—the classics,
which she adored—were popularly replaced by Can Lit, as it
was called. Canada had many wonderful writers, Miss Wurtz
declared—on those occasions when she was not raving about
the so-called classics. (Robertson Davies, Alice Munro, and
Margaret Atwood were her favorites.) Years later, as if she were
still arguing with Jack about *A Mail-Order Bride in the Northwest Territories,* Miss Wurtz would write him and tell him to
read Alice Munro's "A Wilderness Station"—a terrific story
about a mail-order bride. The Wurtz didn't want Jack to assume
that the *subject matter* of mail-order brides had prejudiced her
against the annual senior-school play.

Abigail Cooke, the playwright, who'd been an unhappily married woman in the Northwest Territories, was certainly not among
Canada's better writers. (She was no Alice Munro.) That Abigail
Cooke's *A Mail-Order Bride in the Northwest Territories* was required reading in the senior school at St. Hilda's was, in Miss
Wurtz's view, "an abomination"; that the play was performed
every year was, in her well-enunciated words, "a theatrical trav-
esty." The play was published by a small, obscure press that specialized in scholastic books. (Miss Wurtz, with uncharacteristic

vulgarity, once referred to the C... *Girls*
nis Press; she immediately apolog... blisher as Beaver Pe-
nis.) The play, Miss Wurtz assured Ja... ck for the word *pe-*
as an actor; it was nothing short of an ...neath his talents
himself before an audience of older girls. ...on to humiliate

Much to Jack's relief, *The Gray Ghost* offere... ...m her grain-
of-salt perspective. It *was* a dreadful play, Mrs. McQuat agreed—
"the fantasies of an amateur writer an... certi... ...in
1882, Abigail Cooke had murder... her allegedly abusive husband and then shot herself: h... play, which was discovered in her
attic, was published posthumously in the 1950s. There were
those St. Hilda's Old Girls, Mrs. Wicksteed among them, who
thought of the author as a feminist ahead of her time.

Mrs. McQuat advised Jack that the only interesting role was
the one he'd been offered—the mail-order bride. *The Gray
Ghost* believed it was an opportunity for Jack to express himself
"more freely," by which Mrs. McQuat meant that Miss Wurtz
would *not* be the director. In the senior school, the maven of the
dramatic arts—and the only other male teacher at St. Hilda's besides Mr. Malcolm—was the mercurial Mr. Ramsey. He was
what in those days they called "a confirmed bachelor." Only five
feet, two inches tall, with a spade-shaped blond beard and long
blond hair—like a child Viking—Mr. Ramsey was head and
shoulders shorter than many of the girls in the senior school, and
(in some cases) ten or fifteen pounds lighter. His voice was as
high-pitched as a girl's, and his enthusiasm on the girls' behalf
was both shrill and a model of constancy. Mr. Ramsey was an
unrestrained advocate of young women, and the older girls at St.
Hilda's loved him.

In an all-boys' environment, or even in a coeducational
school, Mr. Ramsey would have been taunted and mistreated;
that he was obviously a homosexual was of no concern at St.
Hilda's. If a student had been so crude as to call him a "fairy" or
a "fag," or any of the common pejoratives boys use to bully other
boys, the senior-school girls would have beaten the culprit to a
pulp—and rightly so.

Notwithstanding Mr. Ramsey's embarrassing fondness for *A
Mail-Order Bride in the Northwest Territories,* he was a refresh-
ing presence for Jack—his first truly creative (as opposed to restraining) director.

"Is it *the* Jack Burns? We don't deserve to be *this* lucky!" Mr. Ramsey cried, with open arms, at the first rehearsal. "*Look* at him!" Mr. Ramsey commanded the older girls, who had been looking at Jack for some time; they didn't need Mr. Ramsey's encouragement. "Is this not a child bride *born* to break our hearts? Is this not the precious innocence and flawless beauty that, in darker days, led so *many* a mail-order bride to her brutal fate?"

Jack was familiar with "fate"—he'd already played Tess. *A Mail-Order Bride in the Northwest Territories* was hardly a tale of the same literary magnitude; yet the heroine of the play was, as Mr. Ramsey correctly observed, a reliable heartbreaker for an audience of pubescent (and often hysterical) girls.

In the rugged Northwest Territories, where men are men and women are scarce, a pioneer community of fur trappers and ice fishermen sends a sizable amount of money, "for traveling expenses," to a mail-order service called Brides Back East. The poor brides are chosen from among unadoptable orphans in Quebec; many of them don't speak English. Some of the girls, at the time they set out for the Northwest Territories to meet their mail-order husbands, are *pre*pubescent. The play is set in the 1860s; it's a long, hard trip from Quebec to the Northwest Territories. It is presumed that most of the girls will be old enough for marriage, or more than old enough, by the time they arrive. Besides, the fur trappers and ice fishermen aren't asking for older girls. The play's principal fur trapper, Jack's future husband, Mr. Halliday, says, in sending for his mail-order bride: "I want a wife on the younger side. You got that?"

In the play, four young girls make their way west in the company of a cruel chaperone, Madame Auber, who sells one of the girls to a blacksmith in Manitoba and another to a cattle rancher in Alberta. Both of these unfortunate brides speak only French. Madame Auber, though French herself, has nothing but contempt for them. Of the two girls who make it to the Northwest Territories, one, Sarah, a bilingual stutterer, loses her virginity to her mail-order husband on a dog sled; thereafter, she wanders off in the snow and freezes to death in a blizzard.

Jack plays the other one who makes it, Darlin' Jenny, who successfully prays for the delay of her first period—her "menses," as they are called throughout the play. She is aware that when she starts bleeding, she'll be old enough to be Mr. Halliday's bride—

at least in Halliday's crude opinion. Thus, aided only by prayer, Jenny wills herself not to start. It was this plot point that required Alice's permission for her son to accept the role and necessitated Jack's perplexing visit to the nurse's office, where the school nurse, the young Miss Bell, informed him of "the facts of life"— but only the facts that pertained to *girls,* menstruation foremost among them.

Having seen his first two vaginas in a single day, Jack was not surprised to learn that such a complicated place of business was given to periodic bleeding, but imagine the consternation this caused him when he mistakenly thought that *this* was the long-awaited event Emma Oastler expected to find evidence of in his bedsheets. To Jack's knowledge, his penis had not yet "squirted"; it alarmed him to imagine that Emma had meant he would squirt *blood.*

Jack's confusion understandably upset the school nurse. Miss Bell had talked to many girls about their first periods; while she was awkward in discussing menstruation with a nine-year-old boy, she was at least prepared to do so. But the area of male nocturnal emissions was way off Miss Bell's map. She was aghast that Jack could confuse a wet dream with menstrual bleeding, but she was at a loss to explain the difference to him. "In all probability, Jack, you won't even know the first time you ejaculate in your sleep."

"The first time I *what*?"

Miss Bell was young and earnest. Jack left the school nurse's office knowing more than he needed to know about menstruation. As for the specter of his first wet dream, he was in terror. A nocturnal emission sounded like something one might encounter at the bat-cave exhibit in the Royal Ontario Museum. If, in all probability—as Miss Bell had said—Jack wouldn't even *know* the first time he ejaculated in his sleep, this meant to the boy that he might bleed to death without ever waking up!

In the play, the most impressive hulk among the grade-thirteen girls, Virginia Jarvis, was cast as Jack's mail-order husband, Mr. Halliday. Ginny Jarvis looked like a fur trapper. She was both big and womanly—in the manner of Emma Oastler and Charlotte Barford, but Ginny was older. She had a more developed mustache on her upper lip than Emma had, and Mrs. Oastler's push-up bra could never have contained her. Prior to Jack's first rehearsal, Emma informed him that Ginny Jarvis was one of the two grade-thirteen girls who knew everything about penises; the other one was Ginny's best friend, Penny Hamilton, who was cast as the evil chaperone, Madame Auber. (Penny had lived for a time in Montreal and did a killer French accent, of the kind everyone in Toronto found very funny.)

As for the grade-twelve girl who, according to Emma, also knew everything about penises—the third boarder—that was Penny's younger sister, Bonnie. Penny Hamilton was a good-looking girl, and she knew it. Bonnie Hamilton had been in an automobile accident; innumerable surgeries had failed to correct her limp. (It was worse than Lottie's.) Something permanently twisted in her pelvis caused Bonnie Hamilton to lead with her left foot while dragging her right leg behind her, like a sack. Jack did not find her limp unattractive, but Bonnie did.

Bonnie Hamilton wasn't in *A Mail-Order Bride in the Northwest Territories;* she refused to be in any plays, because of her limp. But Jack thought Bonnie was more beautiful than Penny. During rehearsals for *A Mail-Order Bride in the Northwest Territories,* he saw Bonnie only when she was sitting down. She was the prompter. In a folding metal chair, with the script open in her lap, Bonnie held a pencil ready to make note of the errors. Naturally, she didn't limp when she was sitting down.

In the first rehearsal, when Ginny-Jarvis-as-Mr.-Halliday asked Jack-as-Darlin'-Jenny if she'd "started *bleedin'* yet," the sheer coarseness of the moment evoked an awkward, embarrassed silence from the rest of the cast. "I know, I know—it's an *unforgivable* question, but that's the point," Mr. Ramsey said.

Jack answered in character; he already knew his lines. Bonnie Hamilton didn't need to prompt *him.* "What do you *mean*?" Jenny screams at Halliday. "Why should I be *bleedin'*?" But Jenny knows exactly what Halliday means.

Halliday grows impatient. He can't believe how long it's taking for his child bride to become a woman. One evening, when Jack-as-Jenny is singing a nostalgic song on a porch swing, Ginny-as-Halliday assaults her. Clever girl that she is, Jenny has stolen Madame Auber's pistol—a prop Mr. Ramsey borrowed from the Upper Canada College boys' track team. It was a starting gun that fired blanks. At the end of Act Two, Jack-as-Jenny shoots Ginny-as-Halliday with the starting gun. He-as-she fires two very loud blanks into her-as-his chest, and Ginny Jarvis—

a star on the St. Hilda's field-hockey team—falls on the stage with an athletic thud.

Act Three is Jenny's trial for Halliday's murder. Her defense is that she was only a child when she was forced to marry the fur trapper, and that she is still a virgin. The "miracle"—namely, that Jenny hasn't yet begun her menses—is disputed by the prosecution. Jenny refuses to be examined by the community's only doctor, because he's a man. The few women in the community—only two women are on the jury—are tolerant of her refusal. (They despise the male doctor.)

Jenny's fate appears to be in the hands of a female physician who has been summoned from Yellowknife. But before the lady doctor arrives, Jenny is saved by another miracle of her own making—once again, the power of prayer. While testifying about shooting Mr. Halliday, Jenny suddenly stands, screams, and begins to bleed. A prop more creative than the UCC track team's starting gun is employed for the bleeding. Jack wears a plastic bag filled with water and red food coloring under his dress. His wrists are bound together at his waist. When he stands, he clutches his lower abdomen as if in pain—bursting the bag of colored water, which soaks his dress and hands blood-red.

Darlin' Jenny's piercing scream indicates to the jury that this *must* be her first period. She has been telling the truth. She is innocent. Trial over! But Jack was able to practice bursting the plastic bag—at the time, filled with just water—only once before the first performance. He thought that more practice might have helped.

Meanwhile, backstage, after the dress rehearsal, Emma Oastler, Penny and Bonnie Hamilton, and Ginny Jarvis stealthily dressed Jack in a school uniform they had scrounged from one of the bigger grade-six girls—a short gray skirt and knee-highs. Since Jack already had makeup on—a little rouge, some stage lipstick, which showed redder than it was in the footlights—it was only necessary to adjust the wig he wore as Darlin' Jenny. Flanked by Penny Hamilton and Emma, with Ginny Jarvis leading the way and Bonnie Hamilton (accompanied, as always, by her limp) taking a rearguard position, Jack-as-a-girl marched straight-away to the older girls' residence. In the after-school hours, their entrance from the second floor of the junior school was unobserved.

The Hamilton sisters shared a room. Ginny Jarvis occupied the room across the hall from them. There were no locks on the residence doors, but the matron was not inclined to check on the girls until after supper—when they had to be accounted for and were supposed to be studying. Jack was invited to lie down on a bed. He must have looked anxious, because Emma bent over him and whispered in his ear: "Don't worry, honey pie, I won't let anyone touch you." But Jack was in the presence of girls who were older than Emma; he was frightened.

"Which one of us do you like looking at the best, Jack?" Ginny Jarvis asked. By the indifferent way she raised the question, Ginny seemed resigned to the fact that she wouldn't be the boy's first choice. Penny Hamilton was staring at him with an intimidating self-confidence. Bonnie Hamilton wouldn't look at him; she stood at some distance from the bed, her left foot forward.

"I think Bonnie is beautiful," Jack said.

"You see?" Ginny asked the assembled girls. "There's no predicting what turns on men or boys." Jack could tell he'd made Penny angry by not choosing her, which under the circumstances made him more anxious than before. "Get closer to him, Bonnie," Ginny directed. "Let him see more of you."

Bonnie lurched forward, left foot first. Jack was afraid she was going to fall on him, but she dropped to her knees beside him—catching her balance with both hands on his chest. She still wouldn't look at him. She knelt next to him, putting her hands on her thighs and staring at her lap; ever the prompter, it was as if she were waiting for someone to flub a line. Jack was suddenly shy about looking at her, because Bonnie wouldn't look at him. He could feel Ginny Jarvis lift his skirt and pull down his underpants. At least he assumed it was Ginny—Penny Hamilton seemed too peeved with him to take an interest. No one touched him. "It's *little*, all right," Penny said, when Ginny had exposed him.

"We'll see about that," Ginny replied.

"What's happening?" Jack asked Emma.

"Nothing, baby cakes. Don't you worry."

"*Less* than nothing," Penny Hamilton said.

"He's frightened. This isn't right," Bonnie Hamilton said. "He's too young—he's just a *kid*!" She leaned over Jack. When Bonnie looked at him, it was in the same way that she scrutinized the text in her capacity as prompter—as if his face were the only true map of the unfolding story and Bonnie Hamilton was the absolute authority on what he might be feeling.

Bonnie's limp compelled Jack to look at her and imagine her accident. It was his first understanding that physical attraction, even sexual desire, was stimulated by more than the perfection of a body or the beauty of a face. He was drawn to Bonnie's *past*, to everything traumatic that had happened to her before he met her. Her crippling accident drew Jack to her. This was worse than what Emma had correctly identified as his older-woman thing. He was attracted to how Bonnie had been damaged; that she'd been hurt made her more desirable. The thought was so troubling to Jack that he began to cry.

"I've had it with penises," Ginny Jarvis was saying.

"Maybe it's asleep or something," Penny Hamilton suggested.

"Don't let them frighten you, Jack," Bonnie Hamilton said.

It surprised him that *she* was the one who looked stricken with fear, as if she were a prisoner in the passenger seat and saw the fast-approaching collision seconds before the driver could react to it. Bonnie pinched her lower lip with her teeth and stared at Jack as if she were transfixed—as if *he* were the upcoming accident and, even though she saw him coming, she couldn't turn away. "What's wrong?" he asked her. "What do you *see*?" Bonnie's eyes welled up with tears.

"Don't *cry* on the kid, Bonnie—*you're* the one who's frightening him," Penny Hamilton said.

"*Something's* working," Ginny Jarvis observed. "Maybe it's the crying."

"Keep crying. See if I care," Penny told her sister.

"If Jack is frightened, we should stop," Emma said.

"I think *Bonnie's* frightened," Penny said with a laugh.

"If Bonnie is frightened, we should stop," Jack said—not that he was aware of what they had started. Bonnie Hamilton looked *terrified* to him. He felt increasingly afraid of whatever was frightening *her*.

"This is a frightened little boy!" Bonnie Hamilton cried.

"I'm here, baby cakes," Emma said. She leaned over Jack and kissed him on the mouth. He wouldn't remember if she used her tongue; his fixation was with her upper lip. It must have been her mustache that made Jack hold his breath.

"Keep kissing him, Emma," Ginny Jarvis said.

"Something's *definitely* happening," Penny Hamilton more closely observed.

It wasn't that he couldn't breathe; he'd simply stopped. He saw a multitude of streaming stars, the speckled glow of northern lights—the aurora borealis, that radiant emission beloved by all Canadians. "Better let him breathe, Emma," he heard Bonnie Hamilton say.

"*Whoa!* Look out!" Ginny Jarvis cried. His ejaculation caught Penny Hamilton as she was taking a closer look—too close, as it turned out. (And to think that no one had touched him!)

"You got her smack between the eyes, honey pie," Emma told him later. "I'm so proud of you! I felt responsible that you were afraid. Never again are those girls getting anywhere near you, Jack. I'm taking better care of you from now on."

At the time, Bonnie Hamilton's eyes were locked onto Jack's; she couldn't stop staring at the boy. "What do *you* see?" she asked him. "Jack, what *is* it?"

"You're the most beautiful of all the girls," he told her, still gasping for breath.

"He's delirious—he doesn't know what he's saying," Emma said cruelly, but Bonnie didn't seem to hear her; she just went on looking at Jack. Her sister, Penny, was furiously wiping her forehead with a wad of tissues. Naturally, Jack asked to see the blood.

"The *what,* baby cakes?"

"He must think he's Darlin' Jenny!" Ginny Jarvis said. "Boys are truly sick."

Emma Oastler took him by the hand. They left the older girls' residence traipsing through the junior school the way they'd come. They went to the theater, where Jack dressed in his own clothes backstage. He wanted to practice bursting the blood bag, but Mr. Ramsey had gone home for the day.

Jack and Emma found Peewee sleeping in the Town Car. They went to the house on the corner of Lowther and Spadina, because Lottie was spending most of her time at the hospital, where she said Mrs. Wicksteed was "at death's door," and Alice was either at the Chinaman's or with Mrs. Oastler. Jack was touched that Emma had stood up for him, and that she'd promised to keep the older girls away from him, but for how much longer? Wasn't he being sent to Maine for his fifth-grade year? (Who would keep the older *boys* away?)

Also troubling was Emma's discovery that she, upon entering grade eleven, would become a *boarder*. Why? Jack wondered. Emma lived at home. She could *walk* to school! "My mom doesn't want me around," was all Emma would say. She was even more sullen than usual at the prospect of being a boarder.

They were in Jack's bedroom, where Emma was examining the little guy. "No signs of wear and tear," she said. "I don't suppose you remember what you were thinking." Jack could barely remember not breathing, but he was wondering—after his near-death ejaculation—if Mrs. Wicksteed would see that radiant emission of northern lights when she passed away. He was also struggling to articulate to Emma exactly what had attracted him to Bonnie Hamilton—not just the limp but her overall aura of damage, of having been *hurt*. Jack couldn't quite express it, nor could he convey to Emma how Bonnie had looked at him—how he'd recognized that she was smitten, although Bonnie herself might not have known it.

Jack even tried to talk about it with The Gray Ghost—without letting on to her that he'd had a near-death ejaculation in the older girls' residence, of course. "This was one of the older girls?" Mrs. McQuat asked. "And she looked at you *how*?"

"Like she couldn't look away, like she couldn't help herself," he said.

"Tell me who this was, Jack."

"Bonnie Hamilton."

"She's in grade *twelve*!"

"I told you she was older."

"Jack, when an older girl looks at you like that, you just look away."

"What if I can't look away or help myself, either?"

"Mercy!" Mrs. McQuat exclaimed. Thinking she was changing the subject, she asked: "How's it going with the mail-order-bride business?"

"The blood is the tricky part," he said.

"There's *blood* this year, *actual* blood?"

"It's red food coloring with water—it's just a prop."

"A *prop*! I think I like blood better when I have to imagine it. Maybe I should have a word with Mr. Ramsey." But if The Gray Ghost ever had a word with Mr. Ramsey, nothing of their conversation was reflected in the premiere performance of *A Mail-Order Bride in the Northwest Territories*. On Saturday night, the St. Hilda's theater was packed. To Jack's surprise, not only was The Wurtz in attendance, but The Gray Ghost sat in the front row beside her. Maybe Mrs. McQuat believed that her encouraging presence would serve to mitigate Miss Wurtz's scathing condemnation of the play.

More surprising still, and also occupying front-row seats, Alice had come with Mrs. Oastler and Emma. (Lottie, Jack knew, was maintaining her vigil at Mrs. Wicksteed's deathbed—otherwise Lottie would have been at the theater, too.) And most surprising of all, *Peewee* was there! He must have overheard Emma and Jack talking about the play in the backseat of the Town Car. A strikingly beautiful black woman was with him. Peewee had a wife or girlfriend! Whoever she was, Peewee's date seemed stunningly overdressed among the divorced moms and dads who were the usual audience for a senior-school play at St. Hilda's. *Mrs.* Peewee wore a flowery dress with a plunging neckline; from Jack's backstage perspective, her hat resembled a stuffed parrot.

It was a most impressive audience, especially by the junior-school standards Jack was familiar with from Miss Wurtz's dramatizations. But some of the cast suffered from stage fright. Penny-Hamilton-as-Madame-Auber, whose French accent was such a hit with Torontonians, had a fit getting into her evil-chaperone costume. (In retrospect, Jack would like to think that Penny was distracted from the task of dressing herself by her memory of his jism nailing her in the forehead.)

Sandra Stewart, a grade-nine girl who was small for her age, played Sarah, the bilingual stutterer—who ended up freezing to death after losing her virginity on a dog sled. Sandra threw up backstage, which prompted Mr. Ramsey to say: "It's just butterflies."

Ginny-Jarvis-as-Mr.-Halliday, sweating in her fur-trapper costume, said: "That looks like worse than butterflies." (Naturally, Jack thought that Mr. Ramsey and Ginny were referring to the *contents* of Sandra's vomit.)

For the first two acts of the play, Jack kept stealing looks at Bonnie Hamilton, whose eyes not once met his. Jack caught only a few backstage glimpses of the audience. Peewee seemed to be enjoying himself. Mrs. Peewee had removed the stuffed parrot from her head. The Wurtz spent much of the evening scowling and muttering to Mrs. McQuat. The Gray Ghost was in character, unreadable most of the time. Mrs. Oastler looked bored—she had no doubt seen better theater in her sophisticated life. Emma fidgeted in her seat; she'd been to most of the rehearsals and was interested only in what would happen with the blood.

When Jack-as-Darlin'-Jenny shot Ginny-as-Halliday twice with the starting gun, Peewee jumped to his feet and pumped both fists in the air. (Miss Wurtz, knowing the shots were coming, had covered her ears.) Alice, who hadn't read the play and had only the dimmest idea of its heavy-handed subject, looked growingly appalled. When the gun went off, she flinched as if she'd been shot.

The curtain fell at the end of Act Two; the houselights came up and revealed more of the audience. But from backstage, Jack's attention lingered on the first row. Peewee was still excited about the shooting. Emma was chewing gum. Miss Wurtz appeared to be delivering a lengthy critique of the play, and no doubt the entire subject of menstruation, to a taciturn Mrs. McQuat. Alice and Mrs. Oastler were holding hands.

Why were they holding hands? Jack wondered. He knew that this was fairly common among Dutch women and other Europeans, but he'd not seen any *Canadian* women holding hands—some of the girls at St. Hilda's excluded. *Young* women or girls occasionally held hands, but not women the age of Alice and Leslie Oastler. Furthermore, Emma's mom had kicked off her shoes. With one bare foot, smaller than Emma's, she was stroking Alice's bare calf. Jack looked uncomprehendingly upon this curious behavior. He had not yet made the leap, which Emma would make before him, regarding *why* his mother and Mrs. Oastler wanted to live alone in such a big house; that Emma and Jack were a "bad combination" was only part of the reason.

Mr. Ramsey interrupted Jack's scrutiny of the audience from backstage—it was time for him to tie the blood bag around the boy's waist, and for Jack to put his trial dress on. Maybe Jack was supposed to resemble Joan of Arc, although (despite getting his first period onstage) he would fare better than poor Joan. The dress was a sackcloth sheath, as beige as a potato. The blood, Mr.

Ramsey assured him, would be most vivid against such a neutral background. The clamminess of the plastic bag, which flopped against Jack's bare abdomen, was at first disconcerting under the dress. While it wasn't a very big bag, Mr. Ramsey worried that it might make Jack-as-Jenny look *pregnant*. Mr. Ramsey loosened the knot at the top of the bag to release any excess air. This may have precipitated the slow leak, which Jack didn't notice until he sat down in the witness box to give his testimony. He thought he was sweating. But the trickle down one leg was blood, or water with red food coloring—not sweat. Given Jack's near-death ejaculation, he first feared that his *penis* was bleeding. When he realized that the bag of colored water was leaking, he wondered if there would be sufficient blood left in the bag for the all-important *bursting* scene.

After the performance, Mr. Ramsey would praise what he called Jack's "preparation" for the standing, screaming, bleeding extravaganza—the way the boy squirmed in the witness chair as if, unbeknownst to him, his first period was already starting. But it *was*!

Jenny faltered in her testimony, a hesitation Mr. Ramsey later termed "brilliant"—but one that caused the faithful prompter, Bonnie Hamilton, to look up from her lap and regard Jack-as-Jenny with the utmost concern. (Jack could read his as-yet-unspoken lines on her lips.) He could see that the audience was growing anxious; he hoped that no one in the audience could see the trickle of blood. But Peewee saw it. The poor man was not a regular theatergoer; he'd come out of fondness for Jack. Peewee knew nothing of props—the gun had taken him totally by surprise. And now he saw that Jack was *bleeding*—the strain of the moment, or something hemorrhoidal, or a stab wound inflicted by one of the older girls backstage? Jack was only a couple of lines away from his big moment when Peewee rose from his seat and pointed at the boy. "Jack, you are *bleeding,* mon!" he cried.

It was everything The Wurtz feared—it was *improv.* Jack spontaneously decided to edit his remaining testimony, which made Bonnie Hamilton gasp. But he was already bleeding. Wasn't the blood, and his reaction to it, his best witness? Jack jumped to his feet and struck the leaking bag of colored water with both fists. The bag had lost more blood than he'd realized; it was not full enough to burst easily. Darlin' Jenny struck herself in the lower abdomen again and again. The last time, she hit herself a little too hard; Jack-as-Jenny doubled over at the force of the blow. The bag burst with the sound of a tendon snapping, the blood exploding under the potato-colored dress.

"Jack, you are making it *worse,* mon!" Peewee cried.

But Jack was at that moment in his performance when his audience of one took over completely. He screamed and screamed. He raised his bound wrists above his head, his hands dripping blood; the blood dripped on his face. What was meant to represent a first and long-withheld period suddenly looked like a terminal hemorrhage. Someone on the jury (one of the two women) was supposed to say that this clearly had to be Jenny's first experience with menstruation, but Jack-as-Jenny didn't hear the line. The audience couldn't have heard it, either. Even Bonnie, the prompter, had stopped prompting. Jack was wailing like a banshee.

He was being sent away, to *Maine!* He had managed to ejaculate not only because he was drawn to Bonnie Hamilton's pain, but also because of his enduring infatuation with Emma Oastler's mustache—and holding his breath while kissing Emma had almost *killed* him! Mrs. Wicksteed lay dying. Lottie was taking the boat back to Prince Edward Island. Jack's world was changing, once again. He couldn't stop screaming. Jack-as-Jenny bled enough for a young woman having her first *five* periods!

Miss Wurtz had on her enraptured face an expression of stunned enlightenment; in her literary snobbery, she'd underestimated both Jack's improvisational powers and the theatrical potential of *A Mail-Order Bride in the Northwest Territories.* The entire cast was frozen. Backstage, Sandra Stewart vomited again. (Ginny Jarvis, now the murdered Mr. Halliday, said this was all Jack's doing.)

Emma had stopped chewing her gum with her mouth open. Even Mrs. Oastler seemed impressed by all the blood and screaming. Mrs. Peewee was clutching her hat as if she were strangling the parrot. Jack barely noticed that Peewee had rushed onstage to attend to him. He just went on screaming and bleeding. Jack was only distracted from his audience of one when he looked at his mother.

It had not been an easy time for Alice lately. She had recently caught Jack under the covers trying to sneak a look at the scar from her C-section. In the semidarkness of her bedroom, Jack couldn't see it. He explained that he was curious as to whether she had a bikini cut, like Leslie Oastler, or if her incision had been the vertical kind.

"It's private, Jack—it's not your business!" his mom cried. But why had she been so upset about it?

In the front row at the St. Hilda's theater, maybe Alice was remembering that awkward moment—or the passing of Mrs. Wicksteed, or losing Lottie. (Or the future—moving in with Mrs. Oastler, among other things.)

Even as he went on screaming and bleeding onstage, Jack realized that his mom, like Peewee, was not much of a theatergoer. She may have thought she'd seen him "act" before, but this was nothing she'd been prepared for. Her mouth was as open as Emma's, her hands were fists pressed against her temples, her knees were clamped as tightly together as if *she* were the one who was hemorrhaging. And because Jack was screaming, he couldn't hear her crying. He saw the tears flow down her cheeks. She cried and cried, without restraint; she was hysterical. Jack saw Leslie Oastler trying to comfort her. Emma had stopped looking at Jack and was staring at Alice instead.

"I'm all right," Jack said to Peewee, who had picked him up and was shouting for a doctor. "It's a *play,* Peewee!"

"Mon, you have bled enough for *both* of us!" Peewee said; but Jack was transfixed by his mother.

"Oh, Jackie, Jackie!" she was crying. "I'm sorry, Jack—I'm so sorry!"

"I'm okay, Mom," he tried to tell her, but she didn't hear him. There was now the applause to contend with—it had swelled to a standing ovation. (Even The Wurtz was applauding.) The entire cast was onstage with Peewee and Jack. It was time for their bows, but Peewee wouldn't put Jack down.

"It's just water with red food coloring, Peewee," Jack whispered in the big man's ear. "It was a *prop.* I'm not bleeding."

"Shit, mon," Peewee said, "what am I supposed to do with you then?"

"Try bowing," the boy told him. Still holding Jack-as-Jenny in his arms, Peewee bowed.

On Monday, Mr. Ramsey would inquire if he could ask Peewee to be there for the remaining performances, but it was not an experience Peewee wanted to repeat. (Years later, Peewee told Jack that he never got over it.)

Jack saw that The Gray Ghost had magically materialized at his mother's side. Faithful combat nurse that she was, Mrs. Mc-Quat was doing her best to calm Alice down, but not even The Gray Ghost was effective. Alice's sobs were lost in the uproar, but Jack could still see her stricken face. He could read her lips—his name, over and over again, and she kept repeating that she was sorry.

Jack had meant to ask her if they were to become Mrs. Oastler's rent-free boarders—and, on the subject of "free," had his mom given Emma's mom a free tattoo? But seeing his mom so dissolved by his performance as Darlin' Jenny, Jack knew better than to ask. Without fully understanding his mother's relationship with Leslie Oastler, he guessed that nothing in this world (nothing that mattered) was ever *free*.

Despite the applause, Jack would have begun to scream again—had not the curtain come down and he found himself backstage, still in Peewee's arms. Peewee had only momentarily viewed the falling curtain as another unscripted calamity. Once the sea of girls had surrounded them, Peewee calmed himself and congratulated Jack on his performance. He finally put the boy down.

"Jack Burns!" Mr. Ramsey was calling. "Every mail-order bride in the world is in your debt!" Jack saw that Mr. Ramsey had a camera; he was taking a picture of Jack-as-Jenny.

"You can shoot me anytime, Jack," Ginny Jarvis said too loudly in his ear.

Penny Hamilton, who overheard her—and whose unfortunate forehead had been in the way of his near-death ejaculation—said: "Yeah, Jack, the odds are that you're not shooting blanks."

"What?"

"Leave him alone," Emma Oastler said. She'd managed to make her way backstage and had thrown a protective arm around him.

Also backstage was the haunted face that would stalk Jack's future. Bonnie Hamilton was looking at him from a distance, as if her heart couldn't bear coming any closer. She had stopped prompting, but he could still read her trembling lips.

"You *see*?" Jack whispered in Emma's ear. "You see how Bonnie's looking at me—*that's* what I mean."

But in the clamor of the moment, Emma didn't hear him—or else she was too preoccupied, fending off the older girls. "You know what, baby cakes?" Emma was saying. "It might not be the world's worst idea that you're going to an all-boys' school in Maine."

"Why?"

There was his makeup to remove, and the stage lipstick—not to mention all the blood. The director, Mr. Ramsey, the child Viking, could not stop bouncing on the balls of his feet. "Just when I was beginning to think that Abigail Cooke might be a pinch *dated,*" he was saying to Miss Wurtz, who'd come (with tears in her eyes) to offer her congratulations.

Emma's old friends Wendy Holton and Charlotte Barford had come backstage to join them. "If I ever had a period like that, I think I'd *die,*" Wendy told Jack. Charlotte Barford kept eyeing him as if he were a neglected hors d'oeuvre.

Somehow, despite his considerable size—not to mention his last-minute contribution to the production—Peewee had managed to slip away. In the happy chaos following the successful opening night, Jack allowed his mother's visible distress to drift to the back of his mind. But if he ever had a conscience at St. Hilda's, her name was Mrs. McQuat. Not to be outdone by Jack's success, The Gray Ghost staged a characteristic sudden appearance that took the boy's breath away. If he'd had any blood left in him, he would have started bleeding afresh. If his throat weren't raw from screaming, he would have screamed again—only louder.

Jack was going home with Emma. "Our first *sleepover,* honey pie!" Emma had declared. She'd left the backstage area to go find her mom, who was waiting with Alice. Jack was, albeit briefly, still backstage but miraculously alone. Even his beloved prompter had slipped away, her limp for once unnoticed.

That was when The Gray Ghost appeared at his side—her cold hands taking Jack by both wrists, exactly where they'd been bound together. "Good show, Jack," Mrs. McQuat breathed on him. "But you have work to do. I don't mean . . . onstage," she whispered.

"What work?" he asked.

"Look after your *mother,* Jack. You'll blame yourself . . . if you don't."

"Oh." (Look after her *how*? he wanted to ask. Look after her *why*?) But The Gray Ghost, who was almost always in character, had disappeared.

As he would discover again, later in his life, Jack found that it can be a dark and lonely place backstage—after the audience and the rest of the cast have gone. In no way was Jack Burns a mail-order bride, but that pivotal and blood-soaked performance in Mr. Ramsey's histrionic production had *launched* him.

14

Mrs. Machado

Boys, as a rule, did not attend their class reunions at St. Hilda's. You can't really have a class reunion if you don't graduate, and the St. Hilda's boys left the school at the end of grade four—without ceremony.

Lucinda Fleming was a tireless organizer of her class reunions at St. Hilda's—Jack's graduating class, had he been a girl. Maureen Yap, whose married name would remain a mystery, attended the reunions regularly—even in her nonreunion years. The Booth twins were regulars as well; they were always together. But Lucinda's Christmas letters never mentioned the twins' identical blanket-sucking sounds. (Jack would wonder if the Booths still made them.)

Caroline French was a no-show at the reunions. If Caroline still thumped her heels on occasion, she was doing it alone. Her adversarial twin, Gordon, was killed in a boating accident—not long after he left St. Hilda's, when Jack was still in school elsewhere. As Jack would discover, it's remarkable how you can miss people you barely knew—even those people you never especially liked.

Jack's last day of school, in the spring of 1975, was marked by the unusual occasion of both Emma Oastler and Mrs. McQuat accompanying him to the Lincoln Town Car, which Peewee had dutifully parked with the motor running at the Rosseter Road entrance. It had been Mrs. Wicksteed's dying wish that Peewee continue to be Jack's driver for the duration of the boy's time at St. Hilda's.

Emma and Jack slipped into the backseat of the Town Car as if their lives were not about to change. Peewee was in tears. *His* life was about to change—actually, upon Mrs. Wicksteed's death, and Lottie's abrupt departure for Prince Edward Island, it already had. The Gray Ghost leaned in the open window, her cool hand brushing Jack's cheek like a touch of winter in the burgeoning spring. "You may . . . *write* to me, Jack," Mrs. McQuat said. "In fact, I . . . *recommend* that you do so."

"Yes, Mrs. McQuat," the boy said. Peewee was still sobbing when the Town Car pulled away.

"You better write to me, too, baby cakes," Emma was saying.

"You just watch your ass, mon," Peewee blubbered. "You better grow eyes in the back of your head, just to keep watching your ass!"

Jack sat in the backseat, not talking—much as he had on the way to and from Mrs. Wicksteed's funeral. All the while, his mother kept saying that the summer ahead would be "no vacation." She said she was dedicating herself to the task of getting Jack ready to go away to school. "You have to learn how to deal with *boys,* Jack."

Alice, whose estimation of her son's lack of athletic prowess was exaggerated but largely true, sought the services of four men she had tattooed to instruct Jack in the manly art of self-defense. What form of self-defense he chose was up to him, his mom said.

Three of the tattooed men were Russians—one from Ukraine and two from Belarus. They were wrestlers. The fourth man was a Thai kickboxer, an ex-champion—the former Mr. Bangkok, whose fighting name was Krung. Mr. Bangkok and the wrestler from Ukraine—his name was Shevchenko, but Alice called him "Chenko"—were both older men, and bald. Krung had chevron-shaped blades tattooed on both cheeks, and Chenko had a snarling wolf tattooed on his bald pate. (When Chenko bowed to an opponent, there was the unfriendly wolf.)

"A Ukrainian tattoo, I guess," Alice told Jack, with evident distaste. Krung's facial blades were "a Thai thing," Alice said. Both men had broken hearts tattooed on their chests. Daughter Alice's work—no one had to tell Jack that.

The grungy old gym on Bathurst Street was marginally more frequented by kickboxers than by wrestlers. Blacks and Asians were the principal clientele, but there were a few Portuguese and Italians. The two boys from Belarus were young taxi drivers who'd been born in Minsk—"Minskies," Chenko called them. Boris Ginkevich and Pavel Markevich were sparsely tattooed, but they were serious wrestlers and Chenko was their coach and trainer.

Boris and Pavel had tattoos where some wrestlers like them—high on the back between the shoulder blades, so that they are visible above a wrestler's singlet. Boris had the Chinese character for luck, which Jack recognized as one of his mom's newer tattoos. Pavel had a tattoo of a surgical instrument (a tenaculum) between his shoulder blades—a slender, sharp-pointed hook with a handle. As Pavel explained to Jack, a tenaculum was mainly used for grasping and holding arteries.

The walls of the old gym were brightened by some of Daughter Alice's and the Chinaman's flash—one of the few places in Toronto where the Chinaman's tattoo parlor was advertised. Even the weight-training mirrors were outlined with Alice's broken hearts, and her Man's Ruin was on display in the men's locker room, but the gym's decor was dominated by Chinese characters and symbols. Jack recognized the character for longevity, and the five bats signifying the so-called five fortunes. And there was the Chinaman's signature scepter, the short sword symbolizing "everything as you wish."

Jack had told his mom that it was his favorite of the Chinaman's tattoos—she said, "Forget about it." The boy also liked the finger-shaped citron known as Buddha's Hand, which either Alice or the Chinaman had tattooed on Krung's thigh.

In the old gym, too, there were the Chinese characters for deer and the lucky number six—and the peony symbol, and a Chinese vase, and the carp leaping over the dragon's gate. The so-called dragon's gate is a waterfall, and the carp leaps upstream, over the waterfall; by so doing, it becomes a dragon. This was a full-back tattoo—it took days, sometimes weeks. Alice said that some people with full-back tattoos felt cold, but Tattoo Ole had argued with her on this point. Ole claimed that only people with full-*body* tattoos felt cold, and not all of them did. (According to Alice, *most* full-bodies felt cold.)

There was also a moon goddess in the Bathurst Street gym, and the so-called queen mother of the west—in Taoist legend, she has the power to confer immortality. And the Chinese character for double happiness, which Alice refused to tattoo on anyone; it was synonymous with marriage, which she no longer believed in.

The old gym itself had once been a rug store. The large display windows, which faced the Bathurst Street sidewalk, attracted the more curious of passersby. In the neighborhood, the former Mr. Bangkok's kickboxing classes were famous. Krung, despite the chevrons emblazoned on his cheeks and the Buddha's Hand on one thigh, was a popular teacher. There were kickboxing classes for all levels. Jack was enrolled in a beginner class, of course; given the boy's age and size, his only feasible sparring partners were women.

His mother had put him in Mr. Bangkok's able hands (more to the point, his able *feet*) so that Jack might learn to defend himself from bullies, which boys of a certain age—especially in an all-boys' school—are reputed to be. But Jack once more found himself in a situation where his most dangerous adversaries were older women. When the boy asked a Jamaican lady with a big bottom if she was acquainted with his friend Peewee, she said: "You keep your peewee to yourself, mon." Jack was relieved that she was too big to be his sparring partner.

He was paired instead with a Portuguese woman in her forties, Mrs. Machado, who informed him that her grown children had moved away, leaving her unprotected from the random assaults of her ex-husband. According to Mrs. Machado, she was forced to keep changing the locks on her apartment. Her ex-husband still held her accountable for her wifely duties, even though she was no longer his wife. Because he repeatedly returned to her apartment, either to force sex upon her or beat her up, Mrs. Machado was learning to fight.

For not dissimilar motives, the women in Krung's beginner class were particularly interested in mastering the high-groin kick. (In Jack's case, this meant that Mrs. Machado kicked him in the area of his chest and throat.) In the opinion of the former Mr. Bangkok, the high-groin kick was "impure"; yet Jack *and* the women in Krung's beginner class had reasons beyond the *purity* of kickboxing for mastering a high-groin maneuver. If he was going to be bullied by older boys, Jack was not opposed to learning a high-groin kick.

Mrs. Machado was a challenging sparring partner. A short, heavyset woman with coarse, glossy black hair and pendulous, low-slung breasts, she blocked most of the boy's kicks with her ample thighs, or by turning sideways to him and receiving his kicks with her wide hips. And as short as she was, Jack was shorter. He was four feet, eight inches tall and weighed seventy-five pounds. Mrs. Machado was five feet two and weighed one-fifty. She could kick a lot harder than he could.

"You'd be better off *wrestling* her," Chenko advised Jack. "You just don't want to end up *underneath* her."

Chenko respected Krung and the more skilled kickboxers in the gym, but he had contempt for the women in Krung's beginner class—Mrs. Machado included. She was a hard kicker, but she wasn't very agile. In Chenko's opinion, Mrs. Machado could never defend herself from her ex-husband by kicking him. She would have to cripple him with the first kick; if she missed her mark, the fight would be over. Chenko thought that Mrs. Machado would be better off learning to wrestle.

As for Jack's eventual self-defense, Chenko believed that the boy would have scant success defending himself—either kickboxing *or* wrestling—until he grew a few more inches and put on another fifty or seventy-five pounds. "I don't see that your mom is getting her money's worth *yet,*" Chenko told Jack—this was when Jack and Mrs. Machado had been kicking each other for about a week.

But wasn't it Mrs. Oastler's money? (She was getting *her* money's worth, Jack suspected.) Leslie Oastler would drive him to the gym on Bathurst Street before his mother was out of bed in the morning. Jack was there all day. He kickboxed with Mrs. Machado, he hopped on one foot for five minutes at a time, he stretched and stretched—the objective being to kick consistently above your height at shoulder level without losing your balance.

Jack rolled out the mats with Chenko, and disinfected them, and wiped them dry. He brought clean towels, fresh water bottles, and oranges cut into quarters to the kickboxers and the wrestlers. When the Minskies came in the midafternoon, Jack sat at matside with Chenko and watched Boris and Pavel pummel each other. They were both about Mrs. Machado's weight, but lean—two very tough taxi drivers in their late twenties or early thirties. Chenko had the worst cauliflower ears, but Boris and Pavel had similar no-necks with little more than scar tissue for eyebrows, and the Minskies' ears were unmatched lumps of dough—barely more recognizable (as ears) than Chenko's.

The wrestling Jack learned was rudimentary—much of it defensive. A Russian arm-tie and front headlock, a three-quarter nelson and a cross-face cradle. On top, Boris had a mean cross-body ride; from the feet, Pavel had a good duck-under, a better arm-drag, and an outstanding ankle-pick. Chenko was a high-crotch man, but Boris and Pavel preferred an outside single-leg. Chenko liked the lateral drop, but only if your opponent was close to your height. There was no one Jack's height in the Bathurst Street gym. In wrestling, he had no actual opponent—he just drilled the moves repeatedly with Chenko, Pavel, and Boris.

Occasionally, after Mrs. Machado had landed her best high-groin kicks in the area of Jack's chest and throat—especially when she'd knocked his wind out—he could persuade her to "roll around" with him on the wrestling mat. She was the wrong height for the lateral drop, but Jack could ankle-pick her all day, which Mrs. Machado found frustrating—and when he managed to get her down on the mat, he could keep her down with a cross-body ride. She couldn't get away from him.

To be fair, Chenko taught Mrs. Machado a snap-down; when she snapped Jack down on all fours, he couldn't get away from her. (She would just lie on the boy with her seventy-five-pound weight advantage, breathing heavily.) "Ha!" she would cry, when she got him down—the exact same exclamation Mrs. Machado favored when she landed her best high-groin kicks.

If Jack was making any progress in defending himself, he had no accurate means of testing it. At the end of the day, Emma would relentlessly attack him—on the living-room couch or rug, or in her bedroom or one of the guest bedrooms, two of which Jack and his mom occupied for the summer. Now seventeen, Emma was both taller and heavier than Mrs. Machado. Emma could destroy Jack. Nothing he had learned worked with her, which was a sizable blow to his confidence.

In mid-June, Mrs. Oastler sent Emma to what she described as a weight-management program in California. "The fat farm," Emma called it. Jack never thought of Emma as fat, but Mrs. Oastler did. Emma's self-esteem may have been further under-mined by Alice's slim and attractive appearance, although Alice was by no means as small as Leslie Oastler.

It was a two-week weight-loss program—poor Emma—during which time Mrs. Machado was hired to give Jack dinner and be his babysitter until his mom and Mrs. Oastler came home (usually long after Mrs. Machado had put the boy to bed). Thus

Jack's kickboxing sparring partner and occasional wrestling opponent became his nanny—Lottie's unlikely replacement.

At his appointed bedtime, Mrs. Machado and Jack would spar a little—no full contact, "no finishing the moves," as Chenko would have said—and Mrs. Machado would put him to bed with the door to the guest-wing hall open, and the light at the far end of the corridor left on. Before he fell asleep, Jack often heard her talking on the telephone. She spoke in Portuguese—he assumed to one or another of her grown children, who had moved "away." They must have been living somewhere in Toronto; given the length of these conversations, they were surely local calls. Not infrequently, the calls ended with Mrs. Machado in tears.

Jack would fall asleep to the sound of her crying, while she padded barefoot through the beautiful rooms in the downstairs of the Oastler mansion—her feet occasionally squeaking on the hardwood floors as she pivoted sharply on the ball of one foot while raising her kicking foot above shoulder level. At such times, Jack knew that Mrs. Machado was kicking the shit out of her imagined ex-husband—or some other assailant. After all, he was familiar with the exercise—including the sound of the footwork.

On one of the first warm nights of the summer, near the end of June, Mrs. Machado was crying and pivoting and kickboxing loudly enough for Jack to hear her over the ceiling fan. (The Oastler mansion was air-conditioned, but not the guest wing—Jack and his mom had ceiling fans.) For the warm weather, Alice had bought Jack several pairs of what she called "summer pajamas"—namely, his first boxer shorts. They were a little big for him.

The boy got out of bed in a checkered pair of boxers that hung to his knees. Fittingly, the checks were gray and maroon—the familiar St. Hilda's colors. He followed the light to the far end of the guest-wing hall, and went downstairs to offer what comfort he could to Mrs. Machado. Jack could see her in the front hall, circling the grandfather clock as if the clock were her opponent. When she balanced on her left foot, he was impressed by the perfect, bent-knee position of her kicking leg; her elevated foot was held at a right angle to her ankle, like the flared head of a cobra.

Jack should have said something, or at least cleared his throat, but Mrs. Machado was concentrating so fiercely that he was afraid he might startle her if he spoke. She was also breathing too hard to hear the boy's descending footsteps on the stairs—her breaths catching on short, choked-back sobs. Tears bathed her face, she was sweating, her black tank top had become untucked from her powder-blue gym shorts, and her heavy, low-slung breasts swayed as she rocked back and forth on her left foot, which Krung called "the pivot foot"—her strenuously maintained point of balance.

Mrs. Machado must have seen Jack's partial reflection in the glass door of the grandfather clock—a half-naked man, her height or a little taller, sneaking up on her from behind. Jack was still two or three steps upstairs from the front hall when she saw him, which is why Mrs. Machado misjudged his height. (And maybe it was just like her ex-husband to take off most of his clothes before he attacked her.) The sharp squeak of her pivot foot froze Jack on the stairs. Her high-groin kick would have made Mr. Bangkok proud—notwithstanding Krung's purist disapproval of such kicks. Because Jack was standing on the stairs, Mrs. Machado's aim was a little lower than he expected; her full-contact kick caught him in the balls. "Ha!" she cried.

Jack crumpled like a pair of boxer shorts with no one inside them. He lay curled in a fetal position in the front hall. His testicles, which he imagined were suddenly the size of grapefruits, felt as if they had risen to the back of his throat. "Oh! Oh! Oh!" Mrs. Machado was crying, still hopping on one foot.

Jack wanted to die, or at least throw up, but neither option for relief was forthcoming. "I am coming *queeckly* to the rescue with *ice,* lots of *ice*!" Mrs. Machado was calling from the kitchen.

She then helped him to his feet and half carried him up the stairs; a plastic bag full of ice cubes dangled from her mouth. "Jack, Jack—my poor *dahleen* Jack!" Mrs. Machado managed to say through her clenched teeth.

She spread a bath towel on his bed and made him take off his boxers. Having shown the little guy to Emma and her friends, Jack was more anxious about the ice than he was embarrassed. However, Mrs. Machado seemed agitated by how small his penis was. Maybe she'd had daughters. (Or if she'd had sons, perhaps it was long ago when they'd been little boys; maybe Mrs. Machado had forgotten the ridiculous size of their balls and penises.) "Ees eet *smaller*?" she asked in alarm.

"Smaller than what?"

"Smaller than eet was before I *keecked* you!"

Jack quickly took a look himself, but everything appeared to be the same. His balls ached, his penis throbbed, and the little guy might have been shrinking at the thought of the ice, which Mrs. Machado packed around Jack's balls and penis as he lay on his back on the towel. "It's cold. It hurts *more,*" he told her.

"Eet will hurt more for just a few meenutes, Jack."

"Oh. How long do you ice it?"

"Feefteen meenutes."

That seemed long enough to *freeze* a penis, Jack was thinking. "Have you ever iced a penis before?" he asked Mrs. Machado.

"Not *thees* way," she answered.

His penis was so cold that Jack started to cry. Mrs. Machado lay down beside him and rocked him in her arms. She sang a Portuguese song. In ten minutes, Jack was still shivering, but his teeth had stopped chattering. To make the boy warmer, Mrs. Machado stretched out on top of him; her breasts felt like a sofa cushion wedged between them. "I can feel the ice, too, you know," Mrs. Machado told him, after a minute or two. "Eet's not so bad." The pain had subsided; his balls were numb and he couldn't feel his penis at all.

After fifteen minutes, Mrs. Machado removed the bag of ice. Jack was afraid to look at himself in case he had disappeared. He listened to Mrs. Machado pouring the ice water and the remaining cubes into the bathroom sink. She came back to the bed and sat beside him. "Eet's very red," she observed.

"I have no feeling. I think it died," Jack told her.

She gently patted the little guy with the towel. "I theenk eet will come back to life," Mrs. Machado said, holding the towel against his penis. Jack could feel the heat of her hand through the towel. She sat in profile to him. Her coarse, glossy black hair was pulled back from her face in an unruly ponytail—her "fighting hairdo," Mrs. Machado called it. Jack could see that the skin under her chin and on her throat was loose and sagging, and her breasts drooped to her thick waist. She had never been pretty. But when you're ten years old and a woman is holding your penis, nothing else matters.

"Ha!" Mrs. Machado said, removing the towel. "Meester Penis has come back to life with *beeg* plans!" The little guy was unused to being treated with such respect. (Mister Penis was more familiar with expressions of disappointment—even disparagement and reproach.) Clearly flattered by Mrs. Machado's attention, the little guy had more than recovered from the high-groin kick; Jack's penis rose to the occasion with the stiffening determination of a war hero. "My *goodness,* Meester Penis!" Mrs. Machado exclaimed. "Are you just showing off, or ees there something you want?"

Of course there is always something penises want—not that Jack, at age ten, could articulate exactly what his penis wanted. But Mrs. Machado must have been a mind reader. "What ees Meester Penis *theenking*?" she asked the little guy.

"I don't know, Mrs. Machado," Jack answered truthfully.

When the back of his hand brushed her hip, the contact was incidental—but it was no accident that Mrs. Machado pressed her hip against him, pinning Jack's hand to his side. She reached behind her head and undid her ponytail in one quick motion, her hair hiding her face as she leaned over his penis. The little guy could feel her breath. "I theenk I know what Meester Penis wants," Mrs. Machado said.

Jack felt the weight of her breasts on his stomach as she slid his penis into her mouth. Looking back, Jack would concede that Mister Penis had been a bit reckless ever since. The corresponding movement of Jack's hips was involuntary, but his excitement wasn't entirely pleasurable. (The boy was afraid that Mrs. Machado might *swallow* him!) "What's happening?" he asked her.

Perhaps Chenko had been wrong to assume that Mrs. Machado wasn't very agile, because she shifted her weight and changed her position so suddenly that Jack was unable to respond with any movement of his own. Surely Mrs. Machado was not a magician, but Jack didn't see her take off her tank top or her bra—and how she managed to remove her powder-blue gym shorts and her panties would remain a mystery to him. He got only a glimpse of the *huge* hairy place between her legs—that is, *huge* in comparison to his earlier sightings of Mrs. Oastler's and Emma's places of business. And if his mother's tattoo of a Rose of Jericho was artistically consistent—that is, the flower within the rose was always the same—Jack realized (at the moment Mrs. Machado mounted him) how the real thing was remarkably different in each case. On the irrefutable evidence of these formative examples, it would be Jack Burns's unfortunate fate to believe that every vagina was unique.

When Mrs. Machado straddled him, holding his hips between her thighs, he asked again but more urgently: "What's *happening*?" Jack would have been more frightened (when she guided the little guy inside her) had he not been so familiar with those intricate folds of the flower hidden in a Rose of Jericho. At least he knew where he was going. The boy's remaining fear was that *all* of him would somehow slip inside Mrs. Machado—he felt that small.

His hips still suffered the involuntary urge to move, but he couldn't move with Mrs. Machado's weight on him. A rivulet of sweat ran between her breasts, which surrounded his face. "What ees happening, my dahleen Jack, ees that Meester Penis ees going to *cry.*"

"Cry *how*?" he managed to ask, although his voice was muffled between her breasts.

"Tears of joy, leetle one," Mrs. Machado said.

Jack was familiar with the expression, but its application to his penis was alarming. "I don't want Mister Penis to cry," he said.

"Eet ees happening any meenute, dahleen. Don't be afraid—eet won't hurt."

But Jack *was* afraid. (Hadn't Chenko warned him about ending up *underneath* her?) "I'm scared, Mrs. Machado!" he cried.

"Eet's almost feeneeshed, Jack."

He felt something leave him. If he had tried to describe the feeling to The Gray Ghost, she would have told him that he'd lost his soul. Something momentous had departed, but its departure went almost unnoticed—like childhood. Jack would imagine, for years, that this was the moment he turned his back on God—without meaning to. Maybe God had slipped away when Jack wasn't looking.

"What was that?" he asked Mrs. Machado, who had stopped grinding against him.

"Tears of joy. Eet's your first time, I theenk."

Not his first time, in fact. (The first time, Jack's tears of joy had hit Penny Hamilton in the forehead.) "It's my second time," the boy told Mrs. Machado. "But the first time I forgot to breathe. This time was better."

"Ha!" Mrs. Machado cried. "You can't keed me, dahleen."

He didn't try to persuade her. When a hundred-and-fifty-pound woman is sitting on you, and you weigh only seventy-five pounds, you don't argue. Besides, Jack was fascinated to watch Mrs. Machado dress herself. She did such a leisurely job of it, especially when you consider how quickly she had *un*dressed. Mrs. Machado continued to sit on him while she put on her bra and tank top; finally she had to get off him when she put on her panties and the powder-blue gym shorts.

There was a wet spot on the bed, which Mrs. Machado wiped away with the towel. She put the towel in the laundry hamper and filled the bathtub only half full, instructing Jack to wash himself—Mister Penis in particular. Jack was aware of a strong, unfamiliar smell, which went away in the bath. What was strange about the smell was that he couldn't decide if he liked it.

The wet spot was still damp when Jack got back in bed, but Mrs. Machado had fetched a pair of clean boxers, which she told him to put on. He lay down—not on the wet spot, but near enough to it that he could touch it with his hand. The spot was cold, and Jack felt a chill—as if he were kneeling on the stone floor of the chapel with his back turned to God, or maybe one of those women attending to Jesus in the stained glass above the altar had slipped into bed with him.

He knew that the stained-glass woman was a saint, because she was invisible. Mrs. Machado couldn't see her, but Jack could feel the coldness coming off her unseen body, which was as hard as the stone floor of the chapel and as forbidden to touch as the stained glass above the altar, where she had come from.

"Don't go," he whispered to Mrs. Machado.

"Eet's time to sleep, my dahleen."

"*Please* don't go!" the boy begged her.

Jack was somehow sure that the stained-glass saint was waiting for Mrs. Machado to leave. He didn't know what plans the saint had for him. He touched the cold, damp spot in the bed again, but he didn't dare reach beyond it, not knowing what he might feel.

"Tomorrow we'll wrestle like crazy," Mrs. Machado was saying. "No more keecking, just wrestling!"

"I'm afraid," Jack told her.

"Does eet hurt, dahleen?"

"Does *what* hurt?"

"Meester Penis."

"No, but it feels different," he said.

"Eet *ees* different! Meester Penis has a *secret.*"

"*What* secret?"

"What happened to Meester Penis is our secret, dahleen."

"Oh."

Had he agreed to share Mrs. Machado's secret? He felt the saint slip away, or maybe it was Jack himself who slipped away. Had the saint turned back into stained glass? (Or was it Jack's *childhood* he felt slip away?)

"*Boa noite,*" Mrs. Machado whispered in Portuguese.

"What?"

"Good night, leetle one."

"Good night, Mrs. Machado."

From the bedroom doorway, she was backlit by the light at the far end of the guest-wing hall. Seeing her squat, thick silhouette made Jack remember Chenko's observation of Mrs. Machado's stance as a wrestler—namely, that she stood like a bear on its hind legs, as if Mrs. Machado might have felt more at home on all fours.

From the hall, as if to remind him of their secret, Mrs. Machado whispered one more time: "*Boa noite,* Meester Penis."

Jack didn't sleep well; he had dreams, of course. Was he worried that the stained-glass saint would slip back into his bed while he slept—or more worried that she had turned her back on him, as he feared he had turned his back on God?

Jack was aware that his mother and Mrs. Oastler had come home, not because he woke up when his mom came into his bedroom and kissed him—at least his mom *said* she came into his room and kissed him, every night—but because the lights in the hall had changed. No longer was there a light on at the far end of the corridor, but the door to his mother's room was ajar and the light from her bathroom glowed dimly in the hall. The light in Jack's bathroom was also on, and it cast a thin, bright line of light under the door.

Jack was aware of his wet dream, too, because the cold, damp area of his bed had dried—but near it was a *wetter* spot, still warm, where the little guy had shed a few more tears of joy. Maybe he'd been dreaming about Mrs. Machado. He wondered if he would tell Emma about his wet dream, which Emma had anticipated for so long. (Jack Burns wondered if he would ever tell *anyone* about Mrs. Machado.)

He got out of bed and crossed the hall to his mother's room, but his mom wasn't there; her bed wasn't even turned down. Jack went looking for his mother in the dark mansion. Mrs. Machado must have gone home, because the downstairs lights were off. The boy wandered from the guest wing into the hallway that led past Emma's empty bedroom. There was a flickering light; it came from under Leslie Oastler's bedroom door.

Maybe Mrs. Oastler and his mom were watching television, Jack was thinking. He knocked on the door, but they didn't hear him. Or maybe he forgot to knock and just opened the door. The TV was off—it was a candle on the night table that was flickering.

He thought at first that Mrs. Oastler was dead. Her body was arched as if her spine were broken, and her head was hanging off the side of the bed so that her face was turned toward Jack—but her face was upside down. The boy could tell that she didn't see him. She was naked and her eyes were wide and staring, as if the dim light from the hall had made Jack invisible—or else *he* was the one who was dead and Mrs. Oastler was looking right through him. Maybe he'd died during his wet dream, Jack imagined. (It would not have surprised him to learn that the experience with Mrs. Machado had killed him—not just the high-groin kick, but all the rest of it.)

Alice sat up suddenly and covered her breasts with both hands. She was naked, too, but Jack had not seen her in the bed until she moved. She sat bolt-upright with Leslie Oastler's legs wrapped around her. Mrs. Oastler hadn't moved, but Jack saw that her eyes had regained their focus; he was greatly relieved that she saw him.

"I didn't die, but I had a dream," Jack told them.

"Go back to your room, Jack—I'll be right there," his mom told him.

Alice was looking for her nightgown, which she found tangled in the sheets at the foot of the bed. Leslie Oastler just lay there naked, staring at Jack. In the candlelight, the rose-red, rose-pink petals of her Rose of Jericho looked like two shades of black—black and blacker.

Jack was in the hall, going back to his room, when he heard Mrs. Oastler say: "You shouldn't still be sleeping in the same bed with him, Alice—he's too old."

"I only do it when he's had a bad dream," Alice told her.

"You do it whenever Jack wants to do it," Mrs. Oastler said.

"I'm sorry, Leslie," Jack heard his mother say.

The boy lay in his bed, not knowing quite what he should do or say about the wet spot. Maybe nothing. But when his mother got into bed with him, it didn't take her long to discover it. "Oh, it was *that* kind of dream," she said, as if this hardly counted as a nightmare.

"It's not blood, it's not pee," the boy elaborated.

"Of course it isn't, Jack—it's *semen.*"

Jack was thoroughly confused. (He failed to see how a wet dream could have anything to do with *sailors*!) "I didn't mean to do it," he explained. "I don't even remember doing it."

"It's not your fault, Jackie—a boy's wet dreams just happen."

"Oh."

He wanted her to hold him; he wanted to snuggle against her, the way he used to snuggle against her after bad dreams when he was smaller. But when he tried to get closer to her, he unintentionally touched her breasts and she pushed him away. "I think you're too old to be in bed with me," she said.

"I'm not too old!" Jack told her. How could he go from being *not old enough* to being *too old* in such a hurry? He felt like crying, but he didn't. His mom must have sensed it.

"Don't cry, Jack—you're almost too old to cry," she said. "When you go away to school, you can't cry. If you cry, the boys will tease you."

"Why am I going away to school?" he asked her.

"It's better for everyone," his mother said. "Under the circumstances, it's just better."

"*What* circumstances?"

"It's just better," she repeated.

"It's not better for *me*!" Jack cried. She put her arms around him and let him snuggle against her. It was the way he used to fall asleep when he was four and they were in Europe.

Jack should have told his mom about Mrs. Machado. (If he'd told his mother about Mrs. Machado, maybe Alice would have realized that he was still not old enough—that there was *nothing* too old about him.) But Jack didn't tell her. He fell asleep in her arms, like the old days—or almost like the old days. Something about her smell was different; his mother's face had a funny odor. Jack realized it was the same strong smell he had noticed in his bath. Maybe the odor had come from Mrs. Machado. As before, it was strange not knowing if he liked the smell. Even in his sleep, the smell persisted.

How long had Leslie Oastler been there in Jack's bedroom with them, just sitting on Alice's side of the bed? When Jack woke up and saw her, he didn't know at first that it was Mrs. Oastler. Jack thought it was the stained-glass saint. She'd come back to claim him! (Maybe that was how a woman saint took possession of you, by taking all her clothes off first.)

Leslie Oastler was naked, and she was rubbing Alice on that spot between her shoulder blades where Boris had a tattoo of the Chinese character for luck and Pavel had a tattoo of a tenaculum.

Jack must have woken up only a split second before his mom did. "You should put some clothes on, Leslie," Alice was saying.

"I had a dream," Mrs. Oastler replied. "A bad one."

"Go back to your room, Leslie—I'll be right there," Alice said. Jack watched Mrs. Oastler leave his room; she was awfully proud of her body, the boy thought. His mother kissed him on the forehead. There was that smell again; he shut his eyes, still trying to decide if he liked it. His mom kissed him on his eyelids. It was a hard smell to like; nevertheless, he thought he liked it.

"I'm sorry, Jack," his mom said. He kept his eyes closed and listened to her bare feet padding down the hall after Leslie Oastler.

He couldn't wait for Emma to get back from the fat farm in California. Surely Emma would help him understand these new and troubling "circumstances"—to use his mother's word for her relationship with Mrs. Oastler.

With Mrs. Machado as his regular workout partner, Jack's wrestling noticeably improved—although not as noticeably as hers. She was a feisty competitor—even Chenko was impressed—and she was twice his weight, an advantage he couldn't overcome. Jack still managed to hold her down with a cross-body ride, but he had trouble taking her down in the first place; she controlled their tie-ups on the feet, to the degree that he couldn't ankle-pick her anymore. An arm-drag to an outside single-leg was the only offensive takedown he occasionally got on her, and Mrs. Machado was impossible to pin unless he caught her in a cross-face cradle. She was just too strong for him, especially in the area of hand control. But Jack knew he was getting better.

Mrs. Machado knew it, too, and she encouraged him. Two thirds of the points they scored were hers, but she was the one who needed to rest. He wasn't the one who got tired.

Wrestling was a weight-class sport, Chenko kept reminding him. If or when he ever got the opportunity to wrestle a kid his own size, both Boris and Pavel agreed that Jack would pound him. But there was no one Jack's size in his life, at least not for the remainder of that summer.

When Emma came home from the fat farm, she'd lost ten pounds—but neither her disposition nor her eating habits had improved. "They just fucking *starved* me," was how she put it.

Emma still outweighed Mrs. Machado, whom Emma briefly replaced as Jack's nanny. Emma was in Toronto less than a week before she had to leave for her father's cottage in Georgian Bay for all of July. Still, in the few nights they were alone together, Jack could have told Emma about Mrs. Machado. He didn't. It was upsetting enough that he told her about her mom and his, about discovering them in bed together. What upset Jack most was that Emma was unsurprised. "Well, I've seen them do everything but *lick* each other," she said with disgust. "It's no wonder they're sending you to fucking *Maine* and making me a goddamn *boarder*!"

"Lick *what*?"

"Forget it, Jack. They're *lovers*, okay? They like each other in the way girls usually like boys, and vice versa."

"Oh."

"I don't care what they're doing!" Emma cried. "What pisses me off, baby cakes, is that they won't *talk* to us about it. They're just getting rid of us instead!"

Jack decided that he had a right to be pissed off about the issue of not talking about it, too. It seemed a further injustice that there were photographs of Emma and Jack, often together, all over the Oastler house. Surely these pictures were evidence that they were a family, that Emma and Jack belonged there—yet they were being sent away!

And if Jack's mother wouldn't talk to him about *her* lover, why should he tell his mom about Mrs. Machado? It was *Emma* he should have talked to about Mrs. Machado—that is, sooner than he did. But before Jack knew it, it was July. Emma was off in Georgian Bay, and Mrs. Machado was once again his sparring-partner nanny.

15

Friends for Life

If what Mrs. Machado did to Jack qualified as "abuse," why didn't he feel abused at the time? It wouldn't be long before Jack had other relationships that he *knew* were sexual; the things he did and the things that were done to him only then registered as experiences he'd previously had with Mrs. Machado. But at the time it was happening, he had no frame of reference to understand how inappropriate she was with him.

She sometimes physically hurt him, but never intentionally. And he was repulsed by her, but many times—on occasion, simultaneously to being repulsed—Jack was also attracted to her. He was often frightened, too. Or at least Jack didn't understand what she was doing to him, and why—or what she wanted him to do to her, and how he was supposed to do it.

One thing was certain: she cared for him. He felt it at the time; no later reconstruction of his pliable memory could convince Jack that she didn't, in her heart, adore him. In fact, however confusingly, Mrs. Machado made him feel loved—at a time when his mother was sending him to Maine!

Interestingly, it was only when Jack asked Mrs. Machado about *her* children that she was ever short-tempered with him. He presumed that they had simply grown up—that this was why they'd moved "away"—but it was a sore point with her.

It was Mrs. Machado's fondest hope, or so she said, that Mister Penis would never be taken advantage of. But by whom? By willful girls and venal women?

Jack was an adult when he saw his first psychiatrist, who told him that many women who sexually molest children believe that they are protecting them—that what the rest of us might call abuse is for these women a form of mothering. ("Too weird," as a girl Jack hadn't yet met would say.)

What he noticed most of all, at the time, was that he changed overnight from someone who could keep nothing from his mother to someone who was determined to keep *everything* from her. Even more than he submitted to having sex with Mrs. Machado, he absolutely embraced the secrecy of it—most of all, the idea of keeping Mrs. Machado a secret from his mom.

Alice was so involved with Leslie Oastler, which was a parallel pursuit to Alice distancing herself from Jack, that the boy could have kept anything a secret from her. That Mrs. Machado was obsessed with doing the laundry—not only Jack's sheets and towels and underwear, and his workout clothes, but also Alice's and Mrs. Oastler's laundry—was nothing Alice or Leslie appeared to notice. (If he'd gotten Mrs. Machado *pregnant*—if he actually could have—it's doubtful that Alice or Mrs. Oastler would have noticed that!)

When Emma came home from Georgian Bay in August—with her body all tanned, and the dark hair on her arms bleached blond by the sun—*Emma* noticed that something had changed in him, and not only because her mom and Jack's were lovers. "What's wrong with you, baby cakes?" Emma asked. "What's with all the *wrestling*? Anyone would think you were *fucking* Mrs. Machado!"

In retrospect, Jack would wonder why Chenko—or Boris, or Pavel—didn't suspect something. They certainly observed that many of the women in Krung's kickboxing classes were inordinately interested in watching him wrestle with Mrs. Machado. And after Emma returned from Georgian Bay, she once again became Jack's nighttime nanny. Surely Chenko and Boris and Pavel were aware that he regularly left the gym in Mrs. Machado's company—for an hour or two almost every day, in either the late morning or the early afternoon.

"Thees ees a growing boy, and eet's August in the *ceety*! He needs to breathe some fresh air!" Mrs. Machado announced.

They went to her apartment, which was within walking distance on St. Clair—a dirty, dark-brown building, in which Mrs. Machado barely maintained a sparsely furnished walk-up on the third floor. There was a partial view of the ravine that ran behind Sir Winston Churchill Park and the St. Clair reservoir, and in the building's small courtyard, where the grass had died, were an unused jungle gym and swing set and slide—as if *all* the children in Mrs. Machado's apartment building had grown up and moved "away," and no more children had been born to replace them.

The air was no fresher in Mrs. Machado's small apartment than in the Bathurst Street gym, and Jack was struck by the absence of family photographs. Well, it was no surprise that pictures of Mrs. Machado's ex-husband were absent—because he was alleged to assault her periodically. Why would she want a picture of *him*? But of her two children there were only two photographs—she had one photo of each boy. In the photographs, they were both about Jack's age, although Mrs. Machado said they were born four years apart and they were "all grown up now." (She wouldn't tell Jack their present ages—as if the numbers themselves were unlucky, or she was simply too upset to acknowledge that they were no longer children.)

It was a one-bedroom apartment, to be kind, with only a chest of drawers and a queen-size mattress on the floor of the bedroom. There was a combination kitchen and dining room, with no living room—and not even a hutch or sideboard for dishes. There was little evidence of kitchenware, which suggested to Jack that Mrs. Machado, if she ate at all, ate *out*. As to how she might have fed her family, when she'd had a family, he had no clue; there wasn't even a dining-room table, or chairs, and there was only *one* stool at the strikingly uncluttered kitchen counter.

It looked less like an apartment where Mrs. Machado's children had grown up than a place where Mrs. Machado had just recently moved in. But they came there only for the purpose of having sex, and to have a quick shower. Jack didn't think to ask her where her children had slept. Or why she still called herself *Mrs.* Machado, or why the nameplate by the buzzer in the foyer of the building said *M.* Machado—as if the *Mrs.* were, or had permanently become, her first name. (Given her ex-husband's reported hostility, why was she still a *Mrs.* at all?)

It was these trysts in her apartment, in the less-than-fresh air of August, that finally took their toll on Jack—not the wrestling. He was tired all the time. Chenko was concerned that he had lost five pounds—his mother's response was that Jack should drink more milk—and his wet dreams, which had started that summer, suddenly stopped. (How could he have wet dreams when he was getting laid almost every day?)

Jack had other dreams instead—bad ones, as Leslie Oastler might have said. Moreover, he had taken it to heart when his mom told him he was too old to be in bed with her. He knew he wasn't welcome to crawl into bed with his mother and Mrs. Oastler, and if he could—albeit only occasionally—persuade his mom to get into his bed with him, she wouldn't stay long. Jack knew that Leslie would come and take her away.

Their "family dinners," which Emma spoke of with mounting scorn, were an exercise in awkwardness. Alice couldn't cook, Mrs. Oastler didn't like to eat, and Emma had put back on the weight she'd lost in California.

"What did you expect would happen to me in Georgian Bay?" Emma asked her mom. "Does anyone lose weight eating *barbe-cue*?" For dinner, they usually went to a Thai place or ordered takeout. As Emma put it: "In my mind, it always comes down to Thai or pizza."

"For God's sake, Emma," Mrs. Oastler would say. "Just have a *salad*."

It was over one such gastronomical event—takeout pizza *and* salad—that Alice and Leslie discussed the dilemma of delivering Jack to his new school in Maine. It seemed he had no certain means of getting there, nor was it an easy place to get to. The boy would fly to Boston and take a smaller plane to Portland; from Portland, one had to rent a car and drive, and Alice wasn't a driver. Mrs. Oastler could drive, but she was ill disposed to go to Maine.

"If Redding were on the coast, I'd consider it," Leslie said. But Redding, which was the name of the town *and* the all-boys' school, was in southwestern Maine—*inland* Maine, not coastal Maine. (There was, Jack would learn, a difference.)

"For Christ's sake, I've got my driver's license—I can take him," Emma said. But Emma, at seventeen, was too young to be permitted to rent a car in Portland—and even Emma agreed that Redding was far too long a drive from Toronto.

Emma was reading a Maine road map in lieu of eating her salad. "Redding is north of Welchville," she said. "It's south of Rumford, east of Bethel, west of Livermore Falls. God, it really is *nowhere*!"

"We could hire Peewee to go with him and be the driver," Mrs. Oastler proposed.

"Peewee is a Canadian citizen, but he was born in Jamaica," Alice pointed out. (Were the Americans touchy about foreign-born Canadians seeking entry into the United States?)

"Boris and Pavel could drive me," Jack suggested. "They're taxi drivers." They were also *wrestlers,* he was thinking. He knew he would be safe with them. But Boris and Pavel were not yet Canadian citizens; they had only recently applied for refugee status.

Chenko couldn't drive a car, and Krung, who drove wildly, was a scary-looking Thai with chevron-shaped blades tattooed on his cheeks. Given that the war in Vietnam had ended only a few years before, Leslie Oastler and Alice didn't think that U.S. Customs would look welcomingly upon Mr. Bangkok.

"Maybe Mrs. McQuat would take me," Jack suggested. His mother stiffened as if she'd been slapped.

"One shouldn't bother teachers in the summer," Mrs. Oastler said—mysteriously, it seemed to Jack. He sensed that his mom had other reasons for not considering The Gray Ghost; maybe Mrs. McQuat had made clear her disapproval of his mother's plans to send Jack away.

Miss Wurtz, Jack knew, spent part of her summer in Edmonton—not that he relished the prospect of The Wurtz delivering him to Redding. (The very journey itself would be *dramatized,* of that he had little doubt.)

"What about Mrs. Machado?" Alice asked. Only Emma noticed that this caused Jack to lose his appetite.

"I doubt she can drive," Leslie Oastler said dismissively. "That woman is so stupid—she can't put the laundry back in the right drawers."

"Don't you like the pizza, honey pie?"

"Jack, please finish your milk—even if you're full. You have to stop losing weight," Alice said.

"If you don't want the rest of that pizza, I'll eat it," Emma said.

"What about that little faggot, your drama teacher?" Mrs. Oastler asked Jack. "What's his name?"

"Mr. Ramsey," Emma answered. "He's nice—he's a good guy! Don't call him a *faggot.*"

"He *is* one, dear," Emma's mom told her. "I'm sure he's entirely *safe,*" Leslie said to Alice. "If he'd so much as *touched* a boy at St. Hilda's, someone would have blown the whistle on him."

"What about not bothering teachers in the summer?" Jack asked.

"Mr. Ramsey wouldn't mind," Mrs. Oastler said. "He obviously worships the ground you walk on, Jack."

"Well, I don't know—" Alice began.

"You don't know what, Alice?" Leslie Oastler asked.

"It's just that he *is* a homosexual," Alice replied.

"It's not *guys* who are inclined to mess around with Jack," Emma observed.

"I *like* Mr. Ramsey—he would be *fine,*" Jack said.

"If he can see over the steering wheel, baby cakes."

"I guess it wouldn't do any harm to *ask* him," Alice said. "Maybe Mr. Ramsey wants a tattoo."

"He's a teacher, Alice—he makes no money," Leslie told her. "Mr. Ramsey doesn't need a free tattoo; he needs *money.*"

"Well—" Alice said.

When Alice and Mrs. Oastler went out to a movie, Emma was left to do the dishes and put Jack to bed. Emma ate the remaining pizza off everyone's plate. Jack understood why she was hungry—she hadn't touched her salad.

"Put on some music, honey pie."

Emma liked to sing when she was eating. She did her best Bob Dylan imitation with her mouth full. Jack put on the album called *Another Side of Bob Dylan*—loud, the way Emma liked it—and went upstairs to get ready for bed. Even with the water running in the bathroom sink, when he was brushing his teeth, he could hear Emma singing along with "Motorpsycho Nightmare." It must have put him in a mood.

When Jack undressed, he had a look at his penis, which was a little red and sore-looking. He thought of putting some moisturizer on it, but he was afraid the moisturizer would sting. He put on a clean pair of "summer pajamas"—his boxer shorts—and lay in bed waiting for Emma to come kiss him good night.

Jack was thinking that he missed saying prayers with Lottie. The only prayer he sometimes said by himself was the one he used to say with his mom, who had stopped saying prayers with him—another feature of his being too old, apparently. Besides, that familiar Scottish prayer seemed inappropriate—given his new life with Mrs. Machado. "The day Thou gavest, Lord, is ended. Thank You for it." (Most nights, Jack didn't feel like thanking anyone for the day he'd had.)

As for Lottie, she'd sent the boy a postcard from Prince Edward Island; from the look of the fir trees, the gray rocks, the dark-blue ocean, you wouldn't know that anything was wrong.

"No, no, no, it ain't me, babe," Emma was singing. *"It ain't me you're lookin' for, babe."*

Jack was obsessing about Mr. Ramsey taking him to Maine, which also put him in a mood. He was feeling sorry for himself, which is fertile territory for bad dreams. The Bob Dylan album was still playing when he fell asleep. He imagined that his mother and Mrs. Oastler had returned from the movie before Emma had come upstairs to kiss him good night. He was lying there wondering if his mom or Emma would kiss him good night first, but of course it was a dream—he was only dreaming that he was lying in bed, awake.

Bob Dylan was still wailing away, or he was wailing away in Jack's dream. *"Perhaps it's the color of the sun cut flat / An' cov- 'rin' the crossroads I'm standing at,"* Emma sang along with Bob. *"Or maybe it's the weather or something like that, / But mama, you been on my mind."* (*There* was an understatement!)

Someone came into Jack's bedroom. He opened his eyes to see if it was Emma or his mother, but it was Leslie Oastler and she was naked. She pulled back the covers and got into bed with him. Given how small she was, there was more room in the bed for her than there ever had been for Mrs. Machado—and Mrs. Oastler smelled better. She made a sound in the back of her throat, a kind of growl—as if she were feral, or as if she might bite. Her long, painted nails scratched Jack's chest; her nails skittered over his stomach. Her small, fast hand shot inside his boxers. One of her nails nicked his penis; she just happened to scratch him on a spot where the little guy was sore. Jack must have flinched.

"What's wrong—you don't *like* me?" Leslie whispered in his ear. Her small hand closed around his penis. He was paralyzed in Mrs. Oastler's clinging embrace.

"No, I like you—it's just that my penis hurts," Jack tried to say, but the words wouldn't come. (In dreams, he was always tongue-tied—he could never speak.)

Jack could feel the little guy getting bigger in Leslie's hand. *Mrs. Oastler's hand is no bigger than my own!* he was thinking, while the music played. *"It don't even matter to me where you're wakin' up tomorrow,"* Emma was singing, *"but mama, you're just on my mind."*

"Where Mister Penis is going, it won't hurt anymore," Mrs. Oastler whispered in Jack's ear.

But how did Leslie know about Mister Penis? the boy wondered—and how did she know his penis hurt, when he couldn't even *talk*? "What did you say?" Jack tried to ask her, but he couldn't hear his own words—only Mrs. Oastler, repeating herself.

Her voice had changed. It was definitely Leslie Oastler's hard, thin body that was grinding against Jack's, but her voice was Mrs. Machado's voice—or a perfect imitation. "Where Meester Penis ees going, eet won't hurt anymore." (Jack was surprised she didn't call him "dahleen.")

"Please don't. My penis really hurts. Please stop," Jack kept trying to say. But if he couldn't hear himself, how could Mrs. Oastler hear him? (He knew it was pointless to think that his *mother* might hear him, or that she would come save him if she did.)

If Bob Dylan ever stopped singing, maybe *Emma* would hear him and come to his rescue, Jack was thinking. He couldn't hear the music anymore, but this didn't necessarily mean that Bob had shut up. The way Leslie Oastler was breathing in his ear, Jack couldn't have heard Bob Dylan if Bob had been singing his brains out in the bedroom.

"You're forgetting to breathe again, baby cakes," Jack distinctly heard Emma say. He'd thought it was Mrs. Oastler who was kissing him, but it was *Emma*! "You can keep kissing me, but you gotta breathe, too."

"I was dreaming," he told her.

"You're telling me! You were pulling your pecker off, honey pie—I'm not surprised it hurts."

"Oh."

"Better show me the little guy, Jack," Emma said. "Let's see what's the matter."

"Nothing's the matter," he told her. (He was ashamed to let her see the damage.)

"Jack, it's *me*, for Christ's sake. I'm not going to hurt you." Both the bathroom light and the lamp on the night table were on. Emma took a good look at Mister Penis. "It's kind of sore-looking—it's all *chafed*!" she said.

"It's *what*?"

"Jesus, Jack, you've rubbed yourself *raw*! You gotta leave it alone for a night or two. When did this start?"

"I haven't been rubbing it," he told her.

"Don't bullshit me, baby cakes. You've been whacking off so much that the little guy looks positively *abused*!"

"What's 'whacking off'?"

"You clearly know what it is, Jack. You've been *masturbating*."

"What?"

"You've been giving yourself a hand job, Jack!"

"I didn't do it to myself," he said.

"Jack, you were doing it to yourself in your *dream*!" That was when Jack started to cry. He wanted Emma to believe him, but he didn't know how to tell her. "Don't cry, honey pie. We'll make it all better."

"How?"

"We'll put some moisturizer on it or something. Don't worry, Jack. This is what boys do—they beat off. I was wrong to think you were too young to be doing it."

"I'm *not* doing it!" Jack insisted. He had to shout because she'd gone across the hall into his mother's bathroom. She came back with some moisturizer. "Will it sting?" he asked her.

"Not this kind—only the kind with stuff in it stings."

"What stuff?"

"Chemicals," Emma said. "Perfume, unnatural shit, other stuff." She was rubbing the lotion on his penis; it didn't hurt, but he couldn't stop crying. "You gotta get hold of yourself, honey pie. Beating off is no big deal."

"I'm not beating off. It's Mrs. Machado," he told her.

Emma let go of the little guy in a hurry. "Mrs. Machado is touching you, Jack?"

"She does lots of things," Jack said. "She puts Mister Penis inside her."

"Mister Penis?"

"Mrs. Machado says *Meester*," he told Emma.

"She puts you inside her *where*, baby cakes? In her *mouth*?" Emma asked, before he could answer her.

"In her mouth, too," he said.

"Jack, what Mrs. Machado is doing is a *crime*!"

"A what?"

"It's *wrong,* honey pie. I don't mean you—*you* haven't done anything wrong. But *she* has."

"Please don't tell my mom," the boy said.

Emma put her arms around Jack and hugged him. "Honey pie," she whispered, "we have to stop Mrs. Machado from doing this. We have to stop her."

"*You* can stop her," Jack suggested. "I bet you could stop her."

"Yes, I bet I could," Emma said darkly.

"Don't go!" he begged her. He held her as tightly as he could. He knew she could hold him much tighter, but Emma went on holding him as before. She rubbed his back, between his shoulders, and she kissed his eyelids, which were still wet from crying, and she kissed his ears.

"I've got you, baby cakes. You just go to sleep, Jack. I'm not going anywhere."

He fell into one of those dreamless sleeps, so deep he almost didn't wake up for the argument. "He had a nightmare, for Christ's sake," Jack heard Emma saying. "I was just holding him until he went to sleep. I fell asleep, too. What do you *think* I was doing? *Fucking* him with all my clothes on?"

"You shouldn't be in bed with Jack, Emma," Mrs. Oastler was saying. "You were under the covers, not to put too fine a point on it."

"I think it's all right. I think Jack is fine," Alice was saying.

"Oh, you think he's *fine.* Well, I'm so fucking *relieved* to hear that!" Emma shouted.

"Don't you use that tone of voice with Alice, Emma," Mrs. Oastler said.

"Jack, are you awake?" Emma asked.

"I guess so," he said.

"You have any bad dreams, you just let me know," Emma told him. "You know where to find me."

"Thank you!" Jack called after her as she was leaving.

"Emma—" Mrs. Oastler started to say.

"Let her go, Leslie," Alice said. "I can tell that nothing happened."

"Are you sure you're okay, Jack?" Leslie asked.

"Sure I'm sure. I'm okay," he told her. Jack looked at his mom as if she were his audience of one, although he knew that she wasn't. "Nothing at all has happened," he told her. Miss Wurtz would have approved of the boy's enunciation. To Jack's surprise, the lie was as simple to say as any line he'd ever delivered; for the first time, lying to his mother was actually easy to do.

Jack could hear Mrs. Oastler going down the hall. He heard the door to Emma's room slam shut long before Leslie got there. He knew that his mom and Mrs. Oastler had made Emma madder than they made him, which was pretty mad—all things considered.

Jack smiled when his mother kissed him good night. He knew which of his smiles his mom liked best, and he gave it to her. He was tired and upset, but somehow he knew he would have a good night's sleep. Mrs. Machado would meet her match in Emma Oastler—of that Jack had no doubt.

The following morning, Emma woke Jack before her mom was up. (Jack's mother was *never* up in the morning; Mrs. Oastler always drove him to the Bathurst Street gym.) The boy usually got up and fixed himself a bowl of cereal or a piece of toast, and he drank a glass of milk and a glass of orange juice—by which time Leslie had come downstairs and made herself some coffee.

Mrs. Oastler was friendly to Jack in the mornings, but she wasn't talkative. She smoothed the boy's hair or patted the back of his neck with her hand, and she made him a sandwich for his lunch, which also included an apple and some cookies—especially if Leslie wanted to keep the cookies away from Emma.

But on this mid-August morning, Jack woke up with the ceiling fan going full speed. He saw Emma stuffing a pair of her shorts and socks and a T-shirt into his gym bag, where he carried his wrestling gear. "We're getting to the gym early today, baby cakes. I'm your new workout partner, from now on. But I want to go over some moves with Wolf-Head before we start."

"With Chenko?" Jack asked her.

"Yeah, with Wolf-Head," Emma said.

"But why do we have to be early?" he asked.

"Because I'm a big girl, honey pie. Big girls gotta warm up."

"Oh."

There was already a note on the kitchen table when they padded downstairs in their bare feet—they were trying to be as quiet as they could. Emma must have written the note the night before. (*"I'm taking Jack to the gym,"* or a message to that effect.)

Emma and Jack walked to Forest Hill Village and had breakfast in a coffee shop on Spadina. He had a scone with raisins in it, and his usual glass of milk and glass of orange juice. Emma just had coffee, and a big bite of Jack's scone.

They cut over to St. Clair and he pointed out the dirty, dark-brown apartment building where Mrs. Machado lived. He was a little afraid of how purposefully Emma kept walking; it wasn't like her to not say anything. She seemed so angry that Jack thought he should tell her a *nice* story about Mrs. Machado—something sympathetic. To his shame, he basically *liked* Mrs. Machado. (He would recognize only later that this was part of the problem.)

"Mrs. Machado has to keep changing the locks on her apartment door, because her ex-husband keeps breaking in," Jack told Emma.

"Did you see the new locks?" Emma asked.

Now that Jack thought about it, he hadn't. "I can't remember seeing any," he said.

"Maybe there *aren't* any new locks, baby cakes."

It wasn't the conversation he'd had in mind.

They were at the Bathurst Street gym so early that Krung hadn't yet arrived. A couple of pretty good kickboxers were going at each other. Chenko was sitting on the rolled-up wrestling mats, drinking his coffee. "Jackie boy!" he said, when he saw Emma. "Did you bring your girlfriend?"

"I'm Jack's new workout partner," Emma told him. "Jack's too young to have a girlfriend."

Chenko stood up to shake Emma's hand. The Ukrainian was in his early sixties—a little thick in the waist, but the muscles in his chest and arms were well-defined slabs, and he was very light on his feet for a man who weighed one-eighty or one-ninety and was only five feet ten.

"This is Emma," Jack said to Chenko, who bowed his head to her when he shook her hand. Emma regarded the snarling wolf on Chenko's bald pate as if it were a family pet. (Jack had told her all about it.)

"You must be five-eleven, Emma," Chenko said.

"Five-eleven-and-a-half," Emma told him. "But I'm still growing."

Emma and Jack helped Chenko roll out the mats before they went to their respective locker rooms to change into their workout gear. Emma didn't have any wrestling shoes, just socks. "I'll find you some wrestling shoes, Emma," Chenko said. "You'll slip on the mat in those socks."

"I don't slip a whole lot," Emma told him.

"What does she weigh, do you suppose?" Chenko whispered to Jack—the Ukrainian was finding Emma a pair of shoes—but Emma heard him.

"I weigh one-sixty-five, on a good day," she answered.

"On a good day," Chenko repeated, watching her put on the shoes.

"Maybe one-*seventy*-five today," Emma said.

"You're a little out of Jack's weight class, Emma," Chenko said.

"I'll start with you," Emma told Chenko. "You look big enough."

"Well—" Chenko started to say, but Emma was out on the mat; she was already circling him.

"I suppose you should start by telling me the rules," Emma said. "If there are any rules, I guess I should know them."

"There are *some* rules, not many," Chenko began. "You can't poke your opponent in the eyes."

"That's too bad," Emma said.

Chenko started with a little hand fighting—just grabbing Emma's wrists and controlling her hands—but she got the idea and peeled his fingers off her wrists, grabbing his hands and wrists instead. "That's the way," Chenko said. "You seem to have a feeling for hand control. You just have to remember to grab a whole fistful of fingers at a time, at least three or four. No grabbing a thumb or a pinkie by itself and bending it."

"Why not?" Emma asked.

"You can break someone's finger that way," Chenko told her. "It's illegal. You have to grab a *bunch* of fingers."

"There's no biting, I suppose," Emma said. (She sounded disappointed.)

"No, of course not!" Chenko said. "And no pulling hair, no grasping clothes. And no choke holds," Chenko added.

"Show me a choke hold," Emma said.

He put her in a front headlock, jerking her head down and holding the back of her neck against his chest with his forearm across her throat. "This is an *illegal* headlock," Chenko explained, "because I don't have your arm, too." He incorporated one of Emma's arms in the headlock; this kept Chenko's forearm off her throat. "You headlock someone, you have to take his arm, too. You can't wrap your arm around someone's neck and just choke him."

"That's too bad," Emma repeated.

Chenko showed her a proper stance and a pretty basic knee-pick. He showed her an underhook and a double-underhook, and how you get from a collar tie-up into a front headlock. "*With* the arm," Chenko made a point of repeating. He showed Emma a lateral drop; he even let her do a lateral drop on him. (Jack could tell that Chenko landed a little harder than he expected, with all of Emma's weight on him.) "You've got good—" Chenko started to say; then he stopped. He was pointing at the middle of her body.

"Hips?" Emma said.

"Good hips, yes," Chenko said. "Your hips are the strongest part of your body."

"I always thought so," Emma replied.

They were down on the mat—Chenko was showing Emma an arm-bar—when Jack noticed that Mrs. Machado had come out on the mat in her workout gear. She was just stretching, but he could tell she had her eye on Emma. "Who ees the beeg girl, dahleen?" Mrs. Machado asked him.

Jack was as tongue-tied as he was in any dream; he couldn't speak. Emma was still rolling around on the mat with Chenko. "Mrs. Machado is molesting Jack," Emma told the Ukrainian. "She made his little penis sore." Chenko had rolled into a sitting position; he was staring at Jack and Mrs. Machado. Emma was already on her feet and walking toward them.

"Jack, did you tell thees beeg girl our *secret*?" Mrs. Machado asked.

It was no contest, Chenko would tell Boris and Pavel later. Emma poked Mrs. Machado in the eyes, in *both* her eyes. Mrs. Machado cried out in pain and covered her face with her hands. Emma grabbed the pinkie on Mrs. Machado's right hand and bent it back, breaking it. The finger stood up at a right angle from the back of her hand. Mrs. Machado screamed as if she'd been stabbed.

Emma slapped a collar tie-up on Mrs. Machado and snapped

her neck forward, putting her into an illegal front headlock—
without the arm. Emma dropped her weight on the back of Mrs.
Machado's head; with Emma's forearm across her throat, Mrs.
Machado couldn't breathe.

Jack realized only then that Krung was there. The former Mr.
Bangkok may have noticed the wrestling because Emma and
Mrs. Machado had rolled off the mat, but Emma hadn't let up
with her choke hold. Mrs. Machado couldn't breathe but her legs
were still thrashing.

"Who's the new girl?" Krung asked Chenko.

"She's a fast learner, isn't she?" Chenko said. Emma had hit
three illegal moves in under ten seconds; it was hard to imagine a
faster learner. No wonder she wanted to know the rules!

"Aren't you going to stop it?" Krung asked the Ukrainian.

"In a minute," Chenko said. Mrs. Machado was flat on her
belly; her legs had almost stopped moving, but one foot was fee-
bly kicking. She didn't have a high-groin kick left in her.

"I guess this has gone far enough," Chenko said to Jack. He
knelt beside the wrestlers and put a three-quarter nelson on
Emma. "You can't believe how I had to crank on her to get her to
let go of that headlock!" he would tell Pavel and Boris that afternoon when he introduced them to Jack's new workout partner.

Mrs. Machado never said a word. By the time the defeated
woman left the Bathurst Street gym, which was as soon as she
was able to stand up and walk, her throat was so sore that she
couldn't speak. Emma did the talking. It may have been lost on
Mrs. Machado when Emma called her "not exactly mail-order-
bride material," but she understood what Emma meant when
Emma called herself "Jack's *only* workout partner." However
this registered with Mrs. Machado, both Krung and Chenko were
suitably impressed—albeit a trifle afraid for the boy.

Mr. Bangkok tried to interest Emma in a kickboxing class, but
Emma said she would stick to the wrestling. "I only like kicking
something when it's on the ground," she told Krung, who ultimately looked relieved, even grateful, that Emma was committed
to the mat.

When Pavel and Boris came to the gym to wrestle that afternoon, Emma rolled around with them, too. Jack needed a break
by that time. He had a mat burn on his cheek and a sore shoulder—
Chenko had shown Emma a fireman's carry, which she had a natural feeling for—and Jack was nursing his first cauliflower ear.

When Emma saw that Pavel and Boris had cauliflower ears that were almost as bad as Chenko's, she insisted that Jack get his cauliflower ear fixed. It was news to Jack that one *could* fix a cauliflower ear, but although Chenko and the Minskies disapproved of "draining" cauliflower ears, they knew how.

"I'm sorry, baby cakes—this may hurt, but it would be criminal to let you grow up with ears like these poor guys. You're gonna be too good-looking to ruin your prospects for the future with dog-turd ears."

Jack could tell that Chenko and Pavel and Boris were offended. Their cauliflower ears were badges of honor, not dog turds! But Emma Oastler had made Jack's future her business, and she was not to be denied.

A so-called cauliflower ear is caused by fluid; when the ear gets rubbed on the mat, or against your opponent's face, it bleeds and swells. When the fluid hardens, you have a lump where you used to have an indentation. The trick is not to let the fluid harden. You drain it with a needle and a syringe. Then you take some gauze, dipped in wet plaster, and press it into the contours of the ear. When the plaster hardens, your ear can't swell—it can't keep filling with fluid. The original shape of the ear is retained.

"It's a little uncomfortable," Chenko forewarned Jack.

"It's better than a sore penis, honey pie." (Even the Minskies agreed with Emma about that.) So Jack went home with a gauze plaster on one ear and a mat burn oozing on the opposite cheek.

"Look at your Jackie, Alice," Leslie Oastler said, when they were eating takeout that night. "Those thugs at the Bathurst Street gym are going to *kill* him."

"It's better than a sore penis," Jack said.

"Not to mention the *language* those Russians are teaching him," Mrs. Oastler said.

"Jack, I'll ask you to watch your language," his mother said.

The next night, Emma had a cauliflower ear. Jack and Emma were pretty proud of their matching gauze plasters. He'd caught her in a cross-face cradle, and while he was grinding his right temple against her left ear, she kicked out of the cradle and pinned him with a reverse half nelson.

"You can't cradle someone who's built like her, not if you're built like *you*," Chenko told Jack.

True enough, but Jack knew that it was good for him to have a workout partner as tough as Emma Oastler. The wrestling turned out to be good for Emma, too. She lost eight pounds in a week. Jack knew that Boris and Pavel had impressed her—if not their ears, at least their diet. The Minskies were disciplined—not only their workouts, but what they ate. "You could have saved your money by sending me to the Bathurst Street gym instead of the fucking fat farm," Emma told her mom.

"I'll ask you to watch your language, too, young lady," Mrs. Oastler said.

"Penis, penis, penis—" Jack chanted.

"That about covers it," Leslie Oastler said.

"Go to your room, Jack," his mom told him.

But Jack didn't care. He wanted to say, "You're making Emma be a miserable *boarder* and you're sending me to fucking *Maine,* and you want us to watch our *language*!" Instead, he said, "Penis, penis, penis," all the way up the stairs.

"That's really mature, Jack!" his mother called.

"Don't be angry with him, Alice—he's just upset about going away to school," Jack heard Leslie Oastler say.

"No shit—that's fucking brilliant," Emma said.

"Go to your room, Emma," Mrs. Oastler told her.

"Enjoy washing the dishes!" Emma said as she stomped upstairs. (Emma was usually the dishwasher.)

Emma and Jack were workout partners in more ways than one. They had at last become true friends—in part because their mothers were separating them. With each mat burn, split lip, black eye, or cauliflower ear that they gave each other, Emma and Jack thoroughly convinced Alice and Mrs. Oastler that the contact between them—whatever it was—wasn't sexual. Jack could get up in the middle of the night and go to Emma's room and get into bed with her—or she could come to his room and get into bed with him. Their mothers said nothing.

The summer was almost over anyway. What did Alice and Leslie Oastler care if Emma and Jack beat each other up at the Bathurst Street gym all day? (Not that Jack ever "beat up" Emma, but he succeeded with a shot or two.)

"It's just hormones, in Emma's case," Mrs. Oastler said. In Alice's mind, Jack was still about the business of learning how to defend himself from *boys*.

In two weeks, Emma had lost twelve pounds—and it was

clear that she would lose more. It wasn't just the workouts; her eating habits had changed. She liked Chenko. "Everything but his ears." With the exception of their ears, Emma liked Boris and Pavel, too.

When Jack lay next to Emma in her bed, or when she held him in her arms in his, it pained him to ask her who she was going to work out with—he meant after he had gone to Maine.

"Oh, I daresay I'll find someone else I can beat the shit out of, baby cakes."

Jack had learned how to kiss her and keep breathing, although the temptation to hold his breath until he fainted was strong. And Emma's attention to the little guy never wavered; true to her word, his penis had healed. A combination of the moisturizer, which Emma continued to apply to the little guy—long after Jack could discern any visible need for it—and the welcome cessation of Mrs. Machado's attention to his penis, which evidently had been excessive.

"Do you miss her, Jack?" Emma asked him one night. He had been thinking that he missed some of the things Mrs. Machado did, but not that he missed *her.* He felt awkward telling Emma about the things he missed. Jack didn't want her to feel that he was ungrateful to her for saving him from Mrs. Machado. But they were true friends and workout partners. Emma understood him. "It sounds like you were excited but frightened," Emma said.

"Yes."

"I shudder to think what kind of trouble the little guy can get into in *Maine,*" Emma said.

"What do you mean, Emma?"

They were in her room. Emma had a king-size bed, if you didn't count the stuffed animals. Jack was wearing just his boxers, and Emma was wearing a T-shirt that Pavel or Boris had given her. It was from a wrestling tournament in Tbilisi, but you had to be able to read Georgian to know where it was from; more to Emma's liking, the T-shirt was faded and torn and it had old bloodstains on it.

"Take off your boxers, honey pie." Emma was removing her T-shirt under the covers, which created a little chaos among the stuffed animals. "I'm going to show you how *not* to get in trouble, Jack." She took his hand and placed it on his penis. "Use your other hand, if you prefer," Emma told him. "Just do whatever's comfortable."

"Comfortable?"

"Just beat off, Jack! You can do that, can't you?"

"Beat *what*?"

"Don't tell me this is your first time, honey pie."

"It's my first time," he admitted.

"Well, take your time—you'll get the hang of it," Emma told him. "You can kiss me, or touch me with your other hand. Just do *something*, Jack—for Christ's sake!"

Jack was trying. At least he wasn't frightened. "I think my left hand works better," he told her, "even though I'm right-handed."

"It's not as complicated as a Russian arm-tie," Emma said. "We don't have to discuss it."

He hugged her as hard as he could—she was so strong, so solid. When she kissed him, Jack remembered to breathe—at least at the beginning. "I think it's working," he said.

"Try not to make a mess all over the place, baby cakes," Emma said. "I'm just kidding," she quickly added.

It was becoming difficult to kiss her and keep breathing—not to mention *talk*. "What exactly are we doing? What *is* this?" he asked Emma.

"This is how you survive Maine," Emma told him.

"But you won't be there!" he cried.

"You have to imagine me, baby cakes, or I'll send you pictures." Oh, that aurora borealis—those northern lights! "Well, if *that* isn't 'all over the place,' I don't know what is," Emma was saying, while Jack practiced breathing again. "Just look at this mess. I never want to hear you say I don't love you."

"I love you, Emma," the boy blurted out.

"You don't have to make a commitment or anything," Emma said. "That you're my best friend is enough of a miracle."

"I'm going to miss you!" Jack cried.

"*Shhh*, don't cry—they'll hear you. Don't give them the satisfaction."

"The what?"

"I'm going to miss you, too, honey pie," she whispered. She was putting her T-shirt back on—more stuffed animals were getting out of her way, in whatever way they could—when Jack heard his mother in the hall. Emma's bedroom door was partially open.

"Was that *you*, Jackie?" his mom was calling. (No doubt he'd been making unusual sounds.)

Both Emma and Jack knew he hadn't put his boxers back on. He didn't even know where they were; he hoped they were under the covers. His head was on Emma's shoulder; one of her arms was thrown loosely around his neck. The "loosely" made it not yet a headlock, but there was no question that they were snuggled together, under the covers, when Alice came into the room.

"I had a dream," Jack told his mom.

"I see," she said.

"There's more room for him to have a bad dream in my bed than in his," Emma told Alice.

"Yes, I see that there is," Alice replied.

"It was that dream about the moat," Jack said. "You remember the littlest soldier."

"Yes, of course," Alice said.

"It was that one," he told her.

"I didn't know you still had that one," his mother said.

"All the time," he lied. "More than usual, lately."

"I see," his mom said. "Well, I'm sorry."

There were stuffed animals scattered everywhere, as if there'd been a massacre. Jack kept hoping his boxers weren't lying among them. Alice started to leave Emma's bedroom, but she paused in the doorway to the hall and turned back to face them.

"Thank you for being such a good friend to Jack, Emma," Alice said.

"We're gonna be friends for life, Alice," Emma told her.

"Well, I hope so," Alice said. "Good night, you two," she called softly, as she went down the hall.

"Good night, Mom!" Jack called after her.

"Good night!" Emma called. Under the covers, her hand found and held the little guy, who appeared to have fallen asleep.

"How quickly you forget," Emma whispered to his penis.

Like old times, Jack thought, as he was falling asleep—without ascertaining very clearly what had been good about the aforementioned "old times" and what hadn't. It was even a comfort to listen to Emma snoring.

Emma had shot a whole roll of photographs of Jack with Chenko in the Bathurst Street gym. Various angles of Chenko's wolf-head tattoo; Jack sitting cross-legged on the wrestling mat beside the old Ukrainian; Chenko's arm around Jack's shoulders in what the boy thought of as a *fatherly* way.

Jack lay listening to Emma snoring, just visualizing those photographs. Soon he would be in Maine, but he was no longer frightened. As he drifted away, Jack believed there was nothing in Maine that could scare him.

Jack Burns would miss those girls, those so-called older women. Even the ones who had molested him. (Sometimes *especially* the ones who had molested him!) He would miss Mrs. Machado, too—more than he ever admitted to Emma Oastler.

Jack even missed the girls who never abused him—among them Sandra Stewart, who had played the bilingual stutterer, the *vomiter,* the mail-order bride who gets fucked on a dog sled and wanders off and freezes to death in the snow, in a histrionic blizzard! How sick was it that he remembered *her*?

He would miss each one, every major and minor character in his sea of girls. Those girls—those *women,* at the time—had made him strong. They prepared Jack Burns for the terra firma (and not so firma) of the life ahead, including his life with boys and men. After the sea of girls, what *pushovers* boys were! After Jack's older-women experiences, how easy it would be to deal with *men*!

III

Lucky

16

Frost Heaves

In those hectic last days before Jack left for Maine, his mother devoted herself to sewing name tags on his new clothes. Mrs. Oastler had taken him shopping. There were no school uniforms at Redding, no special colors, but the boys wore jackets and ties, and either khakis or wool-flannel trousers—not jeans. With Leslie Oastler choosing his clothes, Jack would be one of the best-dressed boys at the school.

Alice should have talked to him; she should have told Jack everything. But in lieu of conversation, she sewed.

It made no sense to Jack: when he was four, they'd spent the better part of a year searching those Baltic and North Sea ports for his runaway dad; yet in Jack's five years at St. Hilda's, Alice rarely spoke of William. At ten, Jack was increasingly curious about his father; that William had been demonized made the boy afraid of himself and who he might become. But his mom would not indulge Jack's questions about his dad. Alice was rarely cruel to Jack, but she could be cold, and nothing drew the coldness out of her as predictably as Jack asking her about his father.

Alice must have closed the door on that conversation a hundred times. "When you're old enough," she would usually say— a door-closing line if the boy had ever heard one.

He'd once spoken to Mrs. McQuat about it. "Don't complain about a woman who knows how to keep a secret," The Gray Ghost replied.

Since Emma had a list of grievances against her mother, Jack felt comfortable complaining to Emma about *his*. "I just want to know what kind of guy he was, for Christ's sake!"

"Watch your language, baby cakes."

Emma and Jack had both read the *School Philosophy Handbook* that Redding sent to new students and their families. So-called proper language was a big deal in the student code. Mr. Ramsey, who'd agreed to take Jack to Maine, had eagerly read the *School Philosophy Handbook,* too; he'd found the student code "very challenging."

The day before Jack and Mr. Ramsey left for Maine, Emma and Jack got matching haircuts at a barbershop in Forest Hill Village. Jack's wasn't so bad, although it was shorter than the floppy mops most boys had for haircuts in 1975. But short hair on Emma was arguably a mistake. It wasn't a buzz cut, but it was very much a *boy's* haircut, which left her neck exposed. While she'd continued to lose weight, Emma's neck had gotten noticeably bigger—all those neck-bridges, three or four times a week, with a flat twenty-five-pound weight on her chest. She had a neck like a linebacker, and her short haircut served to exaggerate one's unfortunate first impression of her, which was that Emma Oastler had no neck at all. From behind, she looked like a man.

Jack got the first haircut and then stood beside Emma's chair while the barber was cutting her hair. "Your mom's going to kill you for this," Jack told her.

"*How?*" Emma asked.

She had a point—Emma could have snapped Mrs. Oastler like a Popsicle stick. Not even Chenko was tough enough for her, as the Ukrainian would soon discover. After Jack went to Maine, Chenko stepped in as Emma's workout partner. He was in good shape for a man his age, and he had twenty-five or thirty pounds on her—this in addition to his considerable experience as a wrestler. But Jack knew you could get hurt when you were trying too hard not to hurt your opponent; in wrestling, it was not natural to hold back.

Chenko caught Emma leaning on him; he was in position to hit her with a lateral drop, but he hesitated, afraid he might hurt her. While he was waiting, Emma executed a perfect lateral drop on him. Emma separated Chenko's sternum when she landed on his chest. That was a slow-healing injury, especially for someone in his sixties.

Emma's only recourse was to work out with Boris and Pavel; at least they were young enough to risk getting hurt.

In the barbershop mirror, examining their matching haircuts, Jack could see in advance that St. Hilda's had been crazy to admit Emma as a boarder. She had the wrong attitude for it, not to mention her hulking shoulders and her seventeen-inch neck.

"An inch for every year of your age," Chenko had told her.

It would come as no surprise to Jack that Emma lasted only a year as a boarder at St. Hilda's. He was a little surprised she lasted that long. To the school's great relief, and with Mrs. Oastler's reluctant consent, Emma moved back home and finished grades twelve and thirteen as a day student. She would take over what had been the guest wing, moving into Alice's old bedroom, which was across the hall from Jack's room—not that he would get to use his room to any significant degree in the upcoming years.

Alice, of course, abandoned all pretense and moved into Leslie Oastler's bedroom. (According to Emma, this happened within a week of Jack's departure for Maine.) Emma's choice to occupy the guest wing was motivated less by her desire to sleep as far away from them as she could than by her irritation that neither her mom nor Jack's ever talked about their relationship. But talking about things was not Alice's style, and Mrs. Oastler had closed the door on too many conversations with Emma to realistically expect her daughter to *allow* her to open that door again. Alice had closed the door on too many conversations with Jack, too. When she was ready to talk, whenever that might be, Jack had already decided he wouldn't listen.

In Maine, he heard more from Emma than from his mother—including the news about Mrs. Machado. She'd been arrested in Sir Winston Churchill Park for sexually soliciting a minor, a ten-year-old boy. It turned out that her own children had *not* grown up and moved "away"; at ages eleven and fifteen, they lived in another part of Toronto with their father, who'd happily remarried. There was a restraining order against Mrs. Machado, who'd molested her fifteen-year-old son when he was ten.

Of course there'd been no assaults against Mrs. Machado by her ex-husband, no need for her to change the locks on her apartment door. Quite possibly, the *M.* in *M.* Machado didn't mean *Mrs.*—at least not anymore. And whoever she was, her reasons for wanting to learn how to kickbox and wrestle would forever remain unclear.

Alice made no mention to Jack of this news, although she probably knew about it. Emma said it was in all the newspapers, "with pictures and everything." Maybe Alice never imagined that Mrs. Machado might have molested Jack. More likely, she didn't want to think about it—or she felt secure in the fiction that, had anything been wrong, Jack would have told her.

As Emma said, sarcastically: "Yeah, like if anything had been wrong with *her,* she would have told *you!*"

Jack was not as faithful a correspondent to The Gray Ghost as she was to him. Mrs. McQuat was a wise woman, but Emma was Jack's principal advice-giver now. How strange that the boy's earlier misunderstanding of prostitutes as advice-givers was not that far off the mark. Emma was no prostitute, but sex and advice-giving were seemingly interchangeable to her.

Jack would also be intermittent in his correspondence with Miss Wurtz. It was more than his mail-order-bride role that linked him to Mr. Ramsey. The boy's first trip to Maine, in Mr. Ramsey's company, was so formative an experience that Mr. Ramsey replaced The Wurtz as Jack's mentor in that all-important area of the dramatic arts.

Jack didn't stop *dreaming* of Miss Wurtz, underwear and all, but he had come to a crossroads in his life, where *listening* to Mr. Ramsey took center stage and made more sense—this despite the fact that there was often more theatricality than meaning in what Mr. Ramsey had to say. (As an actor, Jack would be a hypocrite to love Mr. Ramsey any the less for that.)

As their plane touched down in Portland, Mr. Ramsey clasped Jack's hands in his. "Jack Burns!" he cried, so loudly and suddenly that the boy thought the plane was crashing. "For better or worse, you are in *Maine!*" Jack looked anxiously at the swiftly passing tarmac. "Just remember, Jack—no school with a motto like Redding's can be all bad. Let me hear you say it!"

"Say what?"

"Your school motto!"

Jack had already forgotten it. Unlike Mr. Ramsey, the boy had spotted a militant heartiness in Redding's *School Philosophy Handbook*. The word *character* was repeated in every imaginable context. "Decency is the norm," the handbook had declared. Maybe *that* was the motto.

" 'Decency is the norm'?" Jack asked Mr. Ramsey.

"Well, of *course* it is!" he replied impatiently. "But that's not the motto. Jack Burns, with your remarkable capacity for memory, I'm surprised at you!"

Jack could recall the bit in the handbook about "interacting" with his fellow students. "Eschew the *d*-words!" the handbook had advised. While he remembered this unusual command, he had enough sense to know it wasn't the school motto—though it might have sufficed. They were instructed not to treat their school-mates in a *d*ismissive or *d*erogatory manner. And at the heart of the student code was a "character contract" signed by every student, saying that self-respect was impossible without an abiding respect for others. Jack had signed his name, but this didn't sound like motto material to him.

"A hint, Jack. It's in *Latin*." As if that helped!

The air was clear, but still summery, in Portland—not as bracing as Jack had expected Maine to be, though it soon would be. The airport was as rudimentary as the tarmac.

"Labor omnia vincit!" Mr. Ramsey called to a couple of passing pilots. They clearly thought he was insane. "You haven't heard a motto until you've heard Jack Burns say it," he told a surprised stewardess, an attractive woman in her thirties.

"Labor omnia vincit," Jack said, with authority—putting more emphasis on the *vincit*.

"Tell her what it means, Jack," Mr. Ramsey said, but the stewardess ignored him; she had eyes only for Jack. Here he was in a foreign country—in Maine, of all places—and while he couldn't remember his new school's motto *or* what it meant, he could read the mind of a flight attendant. She was recognizably older-woman material to Jack. All the boy did was smile at her, but he knew everything she was thinking.

"It's a good thing he's not traveling as an unaccompanied minor," the stewardess told Mr. Ramsey, never taking her eyes off Jack.

"This is Jack Burns," Mr. Ramsey said to her. "He's got the memory of an elephant, but not today."

"Labor omnia vincit," Jack repeated, trying to remember the correct translation.

"Work—" Mr. Ramsey started to say, but Jack cut him off. The translation had come back to him.

"Work conquers all things," the ten-year-old told the flight attendant.

"Silly me—I thought it was *love* that conquered everything," she said.

"No, it's *work*," Jack told her firmly.

The stewardess sighed, ruffling the boy's hair. She kept looking at Jack, but she spoke to Mr. Ramsey. "I'll bet you can't count the hearts he's going to break," she said.

It was still light as they drove north-northwest to Redding in the rental car; they'd left the ocean behind them in Portland. After Lewiston, there wasn't a lot to see. West Minot was not memorable, nor were East Sumner and West Sumner—although the absence of a Sumner proper got Mr. Ramsey's attention. "Maine is not a state at the forefront of intelligently naming towns—or so it would seem, Jack."

The surrounding wilderness in the approaching sunset was more than a little tinged with desolation. Earlier Mr. Ramsey had led Jack into a rousing conversation on the possible application of Mrs. Wicksteed's be-nice-twice philosophy to those hostile students the boy might encounter at Redding, but not now. The forlorn landscape prompted even as ebullient a fellow as Mr. Ramsey to speak of the unmentionable. "Jack, I am tempted to say this looks like *mail-order-bride* territory." Jack's heart sank. Mr. Ramsey tried to change the subject. "I would guess— wouldn't you, Jack—that most of the students at Redding are boarders?"

"I guess so," the boy said.

Redding was a private (or so-called independent) school, grades five through eight. While Mrs. Oastler could afford Jack's tuition—"without batting an eye," as Alice had said—the towns and no-towns, the less-than-villages they drove through, suggested to Mr. Ramsey and Jack that few local families could afford to send their boys to Redding. The school did offer scholarships, though not more than fifteen or twenty percent of the students received any kind of financial aid. Redding was not generously endowed.

Mr. Ramsey also shared with Jack his between-the-lines interpretation of Redding's *School Philosophy Handbook;* he shrewdly noted the defensiveness or oversensitivity of the handbook's opening sentence: "First of all, not all students who attend Redding have problems."

Naturally, this suggested to Mr. Ramsey that most or many of the students attending Redding *did* have problems, and he speculated out loud to Jack about what these problems might be. "They come from troubled families, I suppose, or they've been thrown out of other schools."

"For what?" Jack asked.

"Let's just say there aren't a lot of boarding schools, even in New England, that admit students as young as fifth graders as *boarders*. But I suspect that a boy like Jack Burns will *flourish* at such a place!" Mr. Ramsey declared.

"Flourish at what?"

"Let's just say that this is a school that values *attitude* over *aptitude,* Jack. I believe it will be to your advantage that you have both." Jack Burns had more attitude than aptitude, and Mr. Ramsey knew it—but the good man pressed ahead. His enthusiasm on Jack's behalf knew only one speed and direction: fast-forward. "And it strikes me that so-called character-based education might be pursued with fewer distractions at a single-sex institution—I mean fewer distractions for a handsome lad like Jack Burns!"

"You mean no girls."

"Precisely, Jack. Don't even *think* about girls. Your objective is to be a hero among your fellow young men—or, failing that, at least *look* like a hero."

"Why be a hero?" Jack asked.

"At an all-boys' school, Jack, there are heroes and there are foot soldiers. It's happier to be one of the heroes."

Emma had been right: Mr. Ramsey had some difficulty seeing over the steering wheel. He was as short as Mrs. Machado, and twenty pounds lighter. That he'd made himself a hero at an all-girls' school did not hide from Jack the likelihood that Mr. Ramsey had played the role of foot soldier in an earlier life. His neatly trimmed, spade-shaped beard was the size of a child's sandbox shovel; his little feet, in what Jack guessed were size-six loafers, could barely reach the brake and accelerator pedals. "Where will you spend the night?" Jack asked. The thought of Mr. Ramsey driving back to Portland—alone, in the dark—made the boy afraid for him. But Mr. Ramsey was a brave soul; his only fears were for Jack.

"If there's trouble, Jack, gather a crowd. If there's more than one bully, go after the toughest one first. Just be sure you do it publicly."

"Why publicly?"

"If he's killing you, maybe someone in the crowd will stop him."

"Oh."

"Never be afraid to take a beating, Jack. At the very least, it's an acting opportunity."

"I see."

Thus they drove through southwestern Maine. The loneliness of the place was heart-stopping. When they were almost at the school, Mr. Ramsey pulled into a gas station. Jack was relieved to imagine him driving back to Portland with a full tank. It was the sort of rural gas station that sold groceries—mostly chips and soda, cigarettes and beer. A blind dog was panting near the cash register, behind which a hefty woman sat on a stool. Even sitting down, she was taller than Mr. Ramsey. Being a wrestler had made Jack an expert at guessing people's weight. This woman weighed over two hundred pounds.

"For better or worse, we're on our way to Redding," Mr. Ramsey informed her.

"I could have told you that," the big woman said.

"We don't look like we're from Maine, eh?" Mr. Ramsey guessed. The woman didn't smile.

"Seems a shame to send a boy away to school before he's even *shaving,*" she said, nodding in Jack's direction.

"Well," Mr. Ramsey replied, "there are many difficult circumstances that families find themselves in these days. There's not always a *choice.*"

"There's *always* a choice," the woman said stubbornly. She reached under the cash register and brought out a handgun, which she placed on the counter. "For example," she continued, "I could blow my brains out, hoping someone would find the dog in the morning—not that anyone would take care of a blind dog. It might be better to shoot the dog first, *then* blow my brains out. What I'm saying is, it's never not complicated—but there's always a *choice.*"

"I see," Mr. Ramsey said.

The big woman saw Jack looking at the gun; she put it away under the cash register. "It's kind of early *tonight* to shoot anyone," she said, winking at the boy.

"Thank you for the gas," Mr. Ramsey said. Back in the car, he remarked: "I forgot that everyone is *armed* in this country. It would be cheaper and safer if they all took sleeping pills, but I suppose you need a prescription for sleeping pills."

"You don't need a prescription for a gun?" Jack asked.

"Apparently not, Jack, but what seems worse to me is that *owning* a gun must to some degree encourage you to *use* it—even if only to shoot a blind dog!"

"The poor dog," Jack pointed out.

"Listen to me," Mr. Ramsey said, just as the Redding campus rose out of the river mist—the red-brick buildings suggesting the austerity and correctional purpose of a prison, which Jack thought it might have been before it became a school. Redding actually had once been Maine's largest mental asylum, a state facility that had lost its funding to the war effort in the forties. (That there were still bars on the dormitory windows was what gave the place the appearance of a penitentiary.)

"Jack Burns," Mr. Ramsey intoned, "if you ever feel like running away from this place, think twice. The environment into which you escape might be more hostile than the school itself, and quite clearly the citizens have *weapons*."

"I would be shot down like a blind dog. Is that what you mean?" the boy asked.

"Well said, Jack Burns!" Mr. Ramsey cried. "A most prescient view of the situation, and spoken like a leading man!"

Jack bore scant resemblance to a leading man when he said a tearful good-bye to Mr. Ramsey in the corridor of his dormitory. Mr. Ramsey wept as he bid the boy adieu.

Jack's roommate was a pale, long-haired Jewish kid from the Boston area, Noah Rosen, who was kind enough to distract Jack from the urge to weep by expressing his considerable indignation that their room had no door. Only a curtain gave them some measure of privacy from passersby in the hall. Jack instantly shook Noah's hand and expressed his indignation about the curtain, too. They were engaged in the overpolite exercise of offering each other the choice of the desk with a window view, or the best bed, which was obviously the one farther from the curtain and the traffic in the corridor, when the curtain was flung open (without warning) and into their room stepped an aggressive-looking older boy—a seventh or eighth grader, Jack assumed—and this rude fellow asked, in a loud voice, a question of such offensiveness and hostility that Jack almost abandoned Mrs. Wicksteed's be-nice-twice philosophy. "Which of you faggots has the little fag for a father?"

"His name is Tom Abbott," Noah told Jack. "I met him in the washroom half an hour ago, and he called me a 'kike.'"

"Hi, Tom," Jack said, holding out his hand. "My name's Jack Burns. I'm from Toronto." That was being nice once, Jack was thinking, but he foresaw that the math could get confusing in a hurry. (Even when he was an adult, numbers would be his undoing.)

"Was that little fag with the blond beard your father?" Tom Abbott asked Jack.

"Actually, no. He's a friend of the family," Jack replied. "He's a former teacher of mine, my drama coach—a great guy." Jack turned to Noah and said: "Please help me keep count. I've been nice twice. That's it for nice." He walked past Tom Abbott, pushing open the curtain on his way into the hall.

"What did you say, faggot?" Abbott asked; he followed Jack into the corridor. "You think someone out here is going to help you?"

"I don't want any help," Jack told him. "Just an audience."

There was a kid who looked like another fifth grader; he was sitting on a steamer trunk in the hall. His roommate stood in the doorway to their room, holding the curtain open. "Hi, I'm Jack Burns—from Toronto," he told them. "There's probably going to be a fight, if you're interested." Jack kept his back turned to Tom Abbott, calling to a couple of boys down the hall. "Talk about *derogatory*! How about calling someone a 'kike'? How about 'faggot'? Doesn't that sound *derogatory* to you?"

Jack felt a hand on his shoulder; he knew it wasn't Noah's. When someone touched you from behind, there was usually a way they expected you to turn. Chenko had told Jack to turn the opposite way—it caught your opponent a little flat-footed. Jack turned the opposite way and stepped chest-to-chest with Tom Abbott, the top of Jack's head not quite touching Abbott's chin. Tom Abbott had four or five inches and about thirty or forty pounds on Jack, but Abbott was no wrestler; he leaned into Jack with all his weight.

Jack caught him with an arm-drag and Abbott dropped down on all fours; Jack drove Abbott's head to his knee and locked up the cross-face cradle. Tom Abbott wasn't a third as strong as Emma Oastler; at best, he was only two thirds as strong as Mrs. Machado. It was as tight a cradle as Jack had ever had on anyone before. Tom Abbott's nose was flat against his knee; he was breathing like he had a sinus problem. That was when Jack heard someone say, "That's a halfway decent cross-face cradle."

"What's wrong with it?" Jack asked. He couldn't see who'd spoken, but it had been an older boy's voice.

"I could show you how to make it *tighter,*" the older boy told Jack. The surrounding faces of the kids seemed like fifth-grade faces. Jack had the feeling that the older boy was standing directly behind his head. Jack knew that Tom Abbott couldn't talk—Abbott could barely breathe. Jack just kept cranking the cradle as hard as he could; he waited. "You can let him up now," the boy with the older-sounding voice said.

"You shouldn't call people faggots or kikes," Jack said. "It's *derogatory.*"

"Let him up," the older boy said. Jack let Tom Abbott go and got to his feet. "What are you doing in a fifth-grade dorm, Tom?"

Jack had a look at the older boy who was talking. Jack didn't yet know that the boy was the proctor on their floor, but it was evident he was a wrestler. He was no taller than five-eight or five-nine; by his build, he was in Emma's weight class or a little heavier. And while his cauliflower ears were mere trifles in comparison to Chenko's—they weren't even as bad as Pavel's or Boris's—you could tell he was proud of them.

Tom Abbott still wasn't talking. He seemed resigned to his fate—namely, that the proctor was going to show Jack how he might improve his cross-face cradle. "You want to see *tighter?*" the proctor asked Jack.

"Yes, please," Jack said.

The proctor put Tom Abbott in another cross-face cradle. He stuck one of his knees in Abbott's ribs, which had the effect of driving Tom's hips in a diagonally opposed direction from his head and neck. "Not only tighter but more uncomfortable," the proctor explained.

His name was Loomis—everyone called him by his last name. He was an eighth grader from Pennsylvania, and he'd been wrestling for ten years. Loomis had some kind of learning disability; he'd repeated both second and fourth grade. He was only a couple of years younger than Emma.

Jack didn't know that Redding had a wrestling team, but it made perfect sense at a school where *character* counted—where effort was regarded as more reliable than talent.

In Redding's point system, you lost a point for every *derogatory* or *dismissive* thing you said to another boy, and, like a profane word, every act of unkindness cost you as well. For example, Tom Abbott had three points against him—one for calling Noah a kike, another for calling Jack and Noah faggots, and a third for picking a fight with Jack. ("He touched me first," Jack told Loomis, who seemed unsurprised.)

Tom Abbott had another point against him for being an upper-classman in a fifth-grade dorm. You needed permission from the proctor on the floor to visit with a younger kid. You had a limit of four points against you per month. More than four and you were expelled—this was nonnegotiable. Tom Abbott had four points against him on the first day of school; he wouldn't last at Redding past the second week.

It was hard to come to Redding as an older boy. Abbott was a transfer student from another school. Kids admitted in grade five had a better chance of making it through grade eight. Loomis was a four-year boy, like most of the surviving eighth graders.

If you did the work—both your homework and your work-job, because everyone had a work-job at Redding—you were okay. And you had to treat the other kids respectfully; you had to be nice from the start, a tougher philosophy than being nice twice. Mrs. Wicksteed would have respected Redding.

Swearing was a half-point against you, a half-point for every word. For example, it was better to say "Fuck!" or "Shit!" than "Fucking shit!" (Emma would not have done well at Redding.)

They were not all boys with "problems," but they were all boys who were not welcome to live at home. Loomis's parents and older sister had been killed in an automobile accident; his grandparents had wanted him out of their house before the puberty business started.

"Fair enough," Loomis always said. That could have been a motto at Redding, too, though it wasn't as resonant as *Labor omnia vincit*.

In the wrestling room, Jack discovered another motto; it was printed on the ceiling, where you could read it only if you were being pinned.

NO WHINING

The academic expectations of the school were fairly modest; the homework was less demanding than it was repetitive. A lot of memorization, which was okay with Jack. A duck-under, an arm-drag, an ankle-pick, an outside single-leg—as Chenko had taught the boy, these things were essentially undemanding, but they required repetition. Jack felt right at home at Redding.

And neither Miss Wurtz nor Mr. Ramsey would have questioned the value of memorization. At Redding, nothing was inspired—everything was a drill. Smart boys, not that there were many, lay low; hard work was all that mattered. The more you had to overcome, the better your efforts were appreciated.

The headmaster, whose main role at the school was fundraising, was away a lot. His wife reported his whereabouts to the boys at Morning Meeting. "Mr. Adkins, bless his heart, is in Cleveland," she would say. "We have a few successful alumni there, and Mr. Adkins has already met a needy boy or two."

So they were "needy"—they didn't mind. "Redding's first purpose," Mr. Adkins told them, on one of the rare occasions when he was home, "is to prepare you for a better school than Redding."

Once Redding showed the boys how to work hard, the thinking was, another school, a better one, would educate them. Jack learned that the least utilitarian thing about Redding was those bars on the dormitory windows. No one wanted to run away from the school—they just longed to be in a better one.

The wrestling coach, Mr. Clum, had come to Maine from Colorado. He'd wrestled somewhere in the Big Ten, but he made a point of telling the team that he'd never been a starter. "For four years, I was a backup to someone better," Coach Clum said. "Every year it was a different guy, but he was always better."

Inferiority was their advantage; that they believed they were inferior, in combination with their zeal for hard work, made them formidably tenacious boys.

Coach Clum designed a wrestling schedule that purposely overmatched them. Redding's wrestling team never had a winning season, but the boys were unafraid to lose—and when they won an occasional match, they were elated. Jack found out only later, when he was at a better school, that everyone hated to wrestle Redding. Redding boys relished taking a pounding— they were often beaten but rarely pinned—and, boy, were they *nice*.

"When you lose, tell your opponent how good he is," Loomis instructed the younger boys on the team. "When you win, tell him you're sorry—say you've been in his situation, even if you haven't."

They were competing against a school in Bath, Maine, when Jack won his first match. He was wrestling a strong but clumsy kid who'd never seen a cross-face cradle before. Jack was making the cradle tighter, the way Loomis had shown him, when the kid from Bath bit him. He sank his teeth into Jack's forearm, drawing blood. Jack could see the boy's face; there was no malevolence or awareness of wrongful conduct in the Bath wrestler's eyes, only fear. Possibly the kid from Bath was afraid of losing, especially of being pinned—more likely, he was terrified of being hurt. He was fighting for his life, the way a captured animal would fight.

Jack let him go. The bite-wound was obvious—wrestlers from both teams solemnly had a look at it—and the kid from Bath was disqualified for unsportsmanlike behavior, which amounted to the same number of points for Redding that Jack would have won for a fall.

"I'm sorry," Jack told the biter. "I've been in your situation." The kid from Bath looked humiliated, inconsolable.

Loomis was shaking his head. "What?" Jack asked him.

"You don't say you've been in his situation to a *biter,* Jack."

So there were rules to be learned at Redding; learning the rules was what made Jack feel at home there.

Mrs. Adkins, a virtual widow to her husband's fund-raising trips on behalf of the school, taught English and served as casting director for the school's weekly Drama Night. She was a severely depressed woman in her fifties—an unhappy-looking, washed-out blonde. Her pallor was gold-going-gray, a fair-turning-to-slate complexion. Her clothes seemed a size too large for her, as if she suffered from a disease that was shrinking her.

Her gift for casting was a profoundly restless or roving one—causing her to visit, unannounced, classes in all manner of subjects. Mrs. Adkins would just walk into the classroom and pace among the students, while the class continued in as undistracted a fashion as possible.

"Pretend I'm not here," she would say to the fifth graders. (Mrs. Adkins assumed that the older boys already knew to ignore her.)

There might be a note in your school mailbox after her appearance in your class:

See me.—Mrs. A.

In Jack's fifth- and sixth-grade years, he was usually cast as a woman. He was by far the prettiest of the boys at Redding, and—from the glowing recommendations of Miss Wurtz and Mr. Ramsey—Mrs. Adkins knew he had female acting credentials.

By the time Jack was in seventh and eighth grade, and he was more than occasionally picked for a male role, Mrs. Adkins had dispensed with leaving notes in his mailbox. Her touch on his shoulder was, he knew, a see-me touch.

Yes, Jack slept with her—but not until his eighth-grade year, when he was thirteen going on fourteen and the deprivations of a single-sex school had made him nostalgic for his earlier life as a sexually molested child. By then, Mrs. Adkins had given him three-plus years of the best speaking parts, and he was old enough to be attracted to her permanent air of sadness.

"There will be no points against you for this," she told Jack the first time. But he foresaw that, after Redding, the world might hold him accountable to another system for keeping score. Jack Burns would hold Mrs. Adkins as a point against him.

The Nezinscot River ran through Redding, and most of the year one would have to make a considerable (even a *ludicrous*) effort to drown in it. But some years after Jack left Redding, Mrs. Adkins managed to drown herself in the Nezinscot. It would have happened in the spring—in such measure as there *was* a spring in Maine.

There was a glimmer of Miss Wurtz's perishable beauty about Mrs. Adkins; in her capacity as casting director for Drama Night, there was also something of The Wurtz's eccentricity for *dramatization* about her. The boys did not do entire plays or dramatizations of novels at Redding; the rehearsals would have taken too much time away from the nuts-and-bolts business of what was at heart a no-nonsense school. But almost as an echo of the school's mantra to memorization, Mrs. Adkins desired to make thespians of them all.

They were costumed in character, and Mrs. Adkins supervised their makeup. The women's clothes, Jack gradually discovered, were Mrs. Adkins's castaways—or the unexciting donations of the almost uniformly dowdy faculty wives. (Mrs. Adkins was one of only two female teachers at the school.)

The weekly Drama Night at Redding consisted of speeches and skits, excerpts from short stories or plays, recitations of poems—often only *parts* of poems—and such challenging feats of memorization as could be found in the monologues of inspired statesmen.

In fifth grade, Jack recited Anne Bradstreet's "To My Dear and Loving Husband." Dressed in Mrs. Adkins's prim but faded clothes, he managed to convey the hardships of early colonial life and the duties of a Puritan housewife, which Mrs. Bradstreet had so stoically endured.

Jack was also the ravishingly beautiful ghost (the guillotined young woman) in Washington Irving's gothic story "Adventure of the German Student." His black dress had been Mrs. Adkins's nightgown once—possibly at a time when *Mr.* Adkins had traveled less.

He was the poisoned Beatrice in Hawthorne's "Rappaccini's Daughter"; befitting his death in a garden, Jack wore something summery, which Mrs. Adkins remembered wearing to an old friend's wedding. He was in sixth grade when he did "Sigh No More, Ladies"—that little ditty from *Much Ado About Nothing*. Shakespeare was a favorite of Mrs. Adkins. Jack wore one of her pleated skirts when he sang "Under the Greenwood Tree" from *As You Like It*.

He would remember her saying: "Why, that skirt looks so nice on you, Jack. I just might wear it again!"

On his first Drama Night as a *boy,* it was a mild surprise that—even then—Mrs. Adkins dressed him in her clothes. (Black slacks, a long-sleeved white blouse with a ruffled collar.) Jack did "O Mistress Mine" from *Twelfth Night,* and Mrs. Adkins scolded him for saying his end line to *her*—not to the audience:

Youth's a stuff will not endure.

Indeed not; Mrs. Adkins seemed to sense that this was so. She made Jack sing "Take, Oh, Take Those Lips Away" from *Measure for Measure*. (His voice had not yet changed, but it was changing.)

By the seventh grade, Jack was getting a little too muscular for Mrs. Adkins's clothes. But even when Jack was in the eighth grade, no boy at Redding was a better girl. He had pubic hair early, but his facial hair came late and his beard would never be heavy. He missed Emma, and faithfully thought of her when he masturbated. He couldn't get used to taking showers with boys; Jack didn't like looking at the other boys' penises. When he admitted this to Mrs. Adkins, she told him to memorize a poem and say it to himself in the shower.

On those weekends when Mr. Adkins was away, Jack visited Mrs. Adkins in the headmaster's house, where she would dress him in her clothes—the ones she was not yet ready to donate to Drama Night. An ivory camisole with a built-in shelf bra; a bouclé lace turtleneck; a velour cardigan; a crinkled silk shirt; a satin-trimmed wrap sweater. For a small woman, Mrs. Adkins. had big feet—Jack could wear her beaded jade mules.

She never touched him first, nor did she once need to tell him to touch her. While she dressed him—often in the clothes she was wearing at the time, which meant that Mrs. Adkins undressed herself first—she stood so close to him, and she smelled so nice, that he could not resist touching her. The first time he did so, she closed her eyes and held her breath—compelling him to touch her more. It was a seduction quite the opposite of Mrs. Machado's assertive kind; yet Jack was aware that he had the confidence to touch Mrs. Adkins because Mrs. Machado had shown him how. Mrs. Adkins never asked him how, at thirteen, he knew *where* to touch her.

Maybe she should have had a daughter, Jack found himself thinking once—when Mrs. Adkins was dressing him in her favorite velvet top. (For fun, she put lemons in the underwire bra—being a small-breasted woman herself.) Jack would learn, much later, that Mrs. Adkins and her husband had had a son and lost him. The boy's death was an underlying reason for the permanent air of sadness that had first attracted Jack to Mrs. Adkins, although Jack didn't know this at the time.

"I love you in my clothes," was all she told him.

Having cast Jack in his seventh-grade year as Mildred Douglas in Eugene O'Neill's *The Hairy Ape,* Mrs. Adkins loved him so much as Mildred that she perversely cast him the following year as Mildred's cantankerous aunt. In that, his final year at Redding, when Jack was lying in her arms, Mrs. Adkins liked to test his memory of cue lines in the dark. In the husky voice of the

Second Engineer in *The Hairy Ape,* she said: " 'You'll likely rub against oil and dirt. It can't be helped.' "

Rubbing against her, Jack-as-Mildred replied: " 'It doesn't matter. I have lots of white dresses.' " All *hers;* every dress he wore on Drama Night had once been worn by Mrs. Adkins. How at home he felt in her clothes.

Except when he was wrestling, Jack took few trips away from Redding. Since Toronto was so far, he would generally spend American Thanksgiving in Boston—actually in nearby Cambridge—with his roommate, Noah. Jack went back to Toronto for Christmas, and for the misnomered spring break, which was in March or April—when it was barely more spring-like in Toronto than it was in Maine. (It was *never* spring in Maine.)

But as a wrestler, he got to see a lot of New England. Coach Clum once took the team as far as New York State, to a tournament where even Loomis lost. It was the only time Jack saw Loomis lose, although Loomis—in addition to losing his parents and older sister—had other losses ahead. He would be expelled from Blair Academy for getting a referee's underage daughter pregnant. Loomis gave up an opportunity for a college wrestling scholarship because of it. He became a Navy SEAL instead. He was stabbed to death somewhere in the Philippines, while on a perilous undercover mission, perhaps, or drunk and rowdy in a bar—in either case, his killer was reputed to be a transvestite prostitute.

But Loomis was the model Jack aspired to on the Redding wrestling team. Jack was never as good a wrestler as Loomis was, although in Jack's last two years at Redding, he managed to win more matches than he lost.

If someone had been taking his picture on Drama Night, Jack would have known it, but he wouldn't have known if someone was watching or taking pictures when he was wrestling—he wouldn't have heard the *click* of the camera shutter or the noise of the crowd. When Jack was wrestling, he even lost sight of his audience of one. In a wrestling match, either you take command of your opponent or you lose; you wrestle in an empty space, to an audience of none. And after Loomis left Redding, Jack was the team leader—for the first time, he had responsibilities.

He was the leader on the team bus, too. His teammates were

either asleep and farting—or doing their homework with flash-lights and farting. (They were instructed to create a minimum of distractions for the bus driver.)

Sometimes Jack would tell stories on the way back to Red-ding. He told the one about the littlest soldier saving him from the Kastelsgraven, and the one about putting the bandage on In-grid Moe's breast after his mom tattooed her there. He told the one about Saskia's bracelets, including how horribly one of her customers had burned her—but *not* the one about his mom breaking her pearl necklace in her efforts to be an advice-giver to that young boy in Amsterdam. And nothing about Mrs. Machado, of course.

Jack bragged that his "stepsister," Emma, could beat anyone on the Redding wrestling team, with the exception of Loomis, who at that time hadn't yet been kicked out of Blair. (Everyone at Redding, except Noah and Mrs. Adkins, thought that Jack's mother was a famous tattoo artist who lived with a guy named *Mr.* Oastler, who was Emma's *dad.*)

Possibly Jack told these stories because he missed not only Emma but also his mother and Mrs. Oastler—even Mrs. Machado, or at least her roughness, which was nowhere to be found in the gentler persuasions of Mrs. Adkins. Maybe he missed Mrs. Machado's crudeness, too.

Jack also told the story of his greatest onstage triumph to date, which was his role in *A Mail-Order Bride in the Northwest Terri-tories.* This was a dangerous story to tell on the team bus. Coach Clum objected to the word *menstruation;* once when Jack used it, the coach put down a half-point against the boy.

In his eighth-grade year, when Jack was co-captain of the wrestling team, they had a lightweight named Lambrecht—a new sixth grader from Arizona. He had grown up in the desert and had never seen snow before, let alone a road sign saying FROST HEAVES.

He must have had some difficulty reading in the dark, and the road signs out the window of the moving bus went by very fast at night, because Lambrecht asked, of no one in particular: "What's a frost heavy?" His question hung there in the semidark bus; the sleepers and nonstop farters never stirred. Jack was memorizing Matthew Arnold at that moment. He turned off his flashlight and waited to see if anyone would answer Lambrecht. "We don't have frost heavies in Arizona," Lambrecht continued.

"Frost heavies are hard to see at night," Jack told Lambrecht. "They're so low to the ground that the headlights don't reflect in their eyes, and they're the color of the road."

"But what *are* they?" Lambrecht asked.

Those bus rides were pure *improv*! "Look, just don't go out of your dorm at night, Lambrecht—not at this time of year. Frost heavies are nocturnal."

"But what do frost heavies *do*?" Lambrecht asked. He was getting agitated, in the peculiar way that lightweights express their agitation—his voice was pretty shrill under *normal* circumstances. That must have been what prompted Mike Heller, the team's heavyweight, to put an end to Jack's game. Heller was a humorless soul. He was a grumpy guy with too much baby fat to be a legitimate heavyweight; he never won a match, at least not one Jack saw.

"For Christ's sake, Lambrecht, can't you *read*?" Heller asked. "The sign says frost *heaves,* not frost *heavies.* You know *heaves,* like *heaves* in the road? Fucking *potholes,* you moron!"

"That's one and a half points against you, Mike—correction, make that *two,*" Coach Clum said. (He was never really asleep.) "A half-point for *Christ,* a half-point for *fucking,* and one full point for *moron,* which you truly are, Lambrecht—but moron is a *derogatory* word, if I ever heard one."

"Damn!" Heller said.

"Make that two and a *half,*" Coach Clum said.

"So frost heaves are just bumps in the road?" Lambrecht asked.

"I'm surprised you don't have frost in Arizona," Jack said.

"In parts of Arizona, we do," Lambrecht replied. "We just don't have the road signs—or the *heaves,* I guess."

"*Jesus,* Lambrecht!" Heller cried.

"That's *three,* Heller," Coach Clum said. "You're not having a very good road trip."

"When does Heller *ever* have a good road trip?" Jack asked. He had no points against him for the month. He knew he could afford one.

To Jack's surprise, Coach Clum said: "That's *two* against you, Burns. It is *derogatory* of you to call our attention to Heller's losing record, but it's also *dismissive* of Lambrecht's intelligence to encourage him to imagine that frost heavies exist, that they have eyes and are low to the ground—"

"—and they're the color of the fucking *road*!" Lambrecht interrupted him.

"That's a half-point against *you,* Lambrecht," Coach Clum said.

They were somewhere in Rhode Island, or maybe it was Massachusetts. They were a long way from Maine, Jack knew. How he loved those nights! He turned his flashlight back on and redirected his thoughts to the task of memorizing "Dover Beach"—not a short poem, and one with an overlong first stanza.

" '*The sea is calm tonight,*' " Jack read aloud, thinking it magnanimous of him to change the subject.

"Save it for Drama Night, Burns," Coach Clum said. "Just memorize it to yourself, if you don't mind."

He wasn't a bad guy, Coach Clum, but he never accepted what he presumed was the *vanity* of Jack having his cauliflower ears drained. When Mike Heller called Jack a "sissy" for not wanting to go through the rest of his life with cauliflower ears, Coach Clum not only awarded a point against Heller for *sissy,* which was clearly *derogatory*—the coach made Heller get his next cauliflower ear drained. "Does it hurt, Mike?" Coach Clum asked the heavyweight, standing over him while the fluid from the damaged ear was being extracted in the training room.

"Yeah," Heller answered. "It hurts."

"Well, then, the right word for Burns wouldn't be *sissy,* would it?" the coach asked. "*Vain,* maybe," Coach Clum said, "but not *sissy.*"

"Okay, Burns is *vain,* then," Heller said, wincing.

"Right you are, Mike," Coach Clum said. "But *vain* is a point against you, too."

One night on the team bus, when Coach Clum and Jack were the only ones awake, Jack had a somewhat philosophical conversation with him. "I want to be an actor," he told his coach. "I wouldn't say it was *vain* for an actor not to want cauliflower ears. I would say it was *practical.*"

"Hmm," Coach Clum said. Maybe he wasn't really awake, Jack thought. But Coach Clum was just thinking it over. "Let me put it to you this way, Jack," he said. "*If* it turns out that you're a movie star, I'll tell everyone that you were one of the most *practical* wrestlers I ever had the privilege to coach."

"I see," Jack said. "And if I don't make it as an actor—"

"Well, *making it* is the point, isn't it, Jack? If you don't turn out to be a movie star, I'll tell everyone that I never coached a wrestler as *vain* about his ears as Jack Burns."

"I'll bet you it turns out being a *practical* decision," Jack told him.

"What's that, Jack?"

"I'll bet you a whole dollar that I make it as an actor," the boy said.

"Since we're the only ones awake," Coach Clum whispered, "I'll pretend I didn't hear that, Jack." It was the school philosophy again. As Mr. Ramsey (who had read the handbook more carefully than Jack) could have told him, there was no gambling at Redding. Jack shut his eyes and prayed for sleep, but Coach Clum went on whispering in the dark bus. "Memorize this, Jack," the coach whispered. "If I had to guess—*guess,* I say, not *bet*—you're going to end up being a *starter* somewhere."

"You can count on it," Jack told him.

That was Redding. To Jack's surprise, and Emma's—not to mention how shocked Alice and Mrs. Oastler were—he *loved* the place. It was what such schools are, or can be, to some boys. You travel to what seems, or is, a foreign country; your troubles may travel with you, but nonetheless you fit in. Jack Burns had never fit in before.

17

Michele Maher, and Others

Jack did not *fit in* at Exeter, where he was admitted on the strength of Redding's reputation for building character—with the additional support, in the admissions office, of Exeter's wrestling coach, who knew that Coach Clum's boys were "grinders." Jack was a *grinder*—a hard-nosed kid, if little more—and while he was good enough to wrestle on the Exeter team, he was not at all prepared for how difficult a school Phillips Exeter Academy was.

That Noah Rosen was also admitted to Exeter (Noah *deserved* to be) was Jack's salvation. Coach Hudson, the Exeter wrestling coach, further intervened on Jack's behalf: the coach arranged for Noah to be Jack's roommate, and Noah helped Jack with his homework. Jack's memorization skills notwithstanding, Exeter was so academically demanding, so intellectually rigorous, that his abilities at mere mimicry just couldn't keep up. The memorization helped him, both as a wrestler and as an actor-to-be, but Noah Rosen kept him in school.

Jack rewarded Noah by sleeping with his older sister, who was a college student at Radcliffe at the time. Jack had met Leah Rosen at one of the Thanksgivings he spent with Noah and his family in Cambridge. Leah was four years older than Noah and Jack; she was at Andover while they were at Redding, and she entered Radcliffe when they began at Exeter. She was not especially pretty, but she had wonderful hair and a Gibson girl's bosom—and she was attractive to Jack in what was becoming a familiar, older-woman way.

Noah was his best friend; a nonathlete, he was nevertheless closer to Jack than any of Jack's wrestler friends. When Leah dropped out of Radcliffe for a semester—not just to have an abortion but to worry obsessively about it—Noah didn't know Jack was the father.

After he'd stopped sleeping with Leah and was having an affair with a married woman who worked as a dishwasher in the academy kitchen—Mrs. Stackpole was a short, stout woman with several mercifully faded tattoos—Jack learned from Noah that Leah was depressed and seeing a psychiatrist. Jack still didn't tell him.

Unlike at Redding, where everyone had a work-job, the only work-jobs at Exeter were done by the scholarship students. Noah was a scholarship kid at Exeter. Once, when Noah was sick, Jack took his work-job in the school dining hall; he collected the used trays from the cafeteria and carried them into the kitchen, which is how and when he came to know Mrs. Stackpole.

He visited Mrs. Stackpole midmornings, between classes, in her small, shabby house near the gasworks. Jack came and went in a hurry, because Mrs. Stackpole's husband worked in the gasworks and always ate his lunch at home. The lunch, a leftover from the previous evening's supper, was warming in the oven while Mrs. Stackpole spread a towel on the living-room couch and she and Jack engaged in a combative kind of lovemaking—reminiscent of the boy's initiation to sex with Mrs. Machado. The dishwasher's heavy breathing was accompanied by a whistling sound, which Jack first thought was coming from the husband's mystery lunch; perhaps it was about to explode in the oven. But Mrs. Stackpole suffered from a deviated nasal septum, the result of a broken nose her husband had given her. (Possibly because of an unsavory lunchtime experience—Mrs. Stackpole never explained the circumstances to Jack.)

He couldn't imagine that she'd ever been attractive, nor could he have articulated why he was attracted to her (in part) for that reason—her glum, expressionless face, the downturned corners of her sullen mouth, her oily skin, the bad tattoos, and what she referred to as the "love handles" girdling her thick waist—but the dishwasher was passionate about certain sexual positions, wherein Mrs. Adkins had merely sighed or taken some evident pains to endure. Among these was Mrs. Stackpole's preference for the top position, which allowed her to look down on Jack while she mounted and rode him.

"You're too good-lookin' for a guy," she told him once, during one such rough ride.

The husband's lunch sent forth an odor of cauliflower, caraway seeds, and smoked sausage—maybe kielbasa. Something too powerful to be contained in the oven, anyway. Strong stuff—like Mrs. Stackpole herself, Jack was thinking.

"I wonder," Jack said to Noah once, in their senior year at Exeter, "if older women can look at younger boys and know the ones who are attracted to them—even if no one else is."

"Why would you wonder about that?" Noah asked.

Jack then told him almost everything—about Mrs. Machado, too. But somewhere, maybe from his mother, he'd learned to be selective about telling the truth. He *didn't* tell Noah that he'd slept with Leah, or even about Mrs. Adkins. (Jack knew that Noah loved his sister, and Noah had been awfully fond of Mrs. Adkins.)

Jack's mistake was that Noah simply told the truth; he wasn't at all selective about it. Noah told Leah that Jack had an unusual older-woman thing; he told his sister about the dishwasher and about Mrs. Machado, too.

At Exeter, where his fellow students were absorbing all manner of requisite information—at the highest level of learning—Jack chiefly learned how one can fuck up a friendship by telling the truth selectively, which of course amounts to *not* telling it. It was Leah, not Jack, who told Noah that she'd been pregnant with Jack's child; she told her brother about the abortion, too. So when Leah dropped out of Radcliffe again—this time, for good—Jack knew he thoroughly deserved to lose Noah Rosen as a friend.

Jack had spent what felt like a lifetime in childhood, but his adolescence passed as quickly and unclearly as those road signs out the window of his wrestling team's bus. Jack Burns had no better understanding of women, or what might constitute correct behavior with them, than poor Lambrecht did of frost heaves—or that it was sorrow and boredom that drove Mrs. Adkins and Mrs. Stackpole *and* Leah Rosen to sleep with Jack, when they knew he was nothing but a horny boy.

When Jack graduated from Exeter in the spring of 1983, Noah Rosen wouldn't shake his hand. For years, Jack couldn't bear to think of him. In essence, Jack had obliterated Noah from his life—at a time when Noah was the warmest presence in it.

Both of Noah's parents were academics, theorists in early-childhood education. From their appearance, and that of their

Cambridge household—not to mention Noah's scholarship to Exeter, and Leah had gone to Andover *and* Radcliffe on scholarships—Jack guessed that there was little money to be made in early-childhood education. (A pity, because it was inarguably very *formative* to Jack.)

The Rosens had a high regard for education at every level; it must have devastated them that Leah left Radcliffe. She went to Madison, Wisconsin, and got into some trouble there. It wasn't drug trouble; it was something political—the wrong bunch of friends, Noah implied. "There was a succession of bad boyfriends," Noah told Jack, "beginning with you."

Leah Rosen ended up dead, in Chile. That's all Jack knew. At least there wasn't any water involved—not the absurd Nezinscot, the so-called river that claimed Mrs. Adkins.

Jack hadn't *meant* these people any harm! Not Mrs. Stackpole, either; her body was found in the Exeter River, below the falls. Above the falls, the river was freshwater and not very deep. Below the falls, the water was brackish—the lower river was tidal—and Mrs. Stackpole was discovered in the salt water, in the mudflats at low tide. The water had receded enough for a golfer to spot the body, or maybe it was a rower on the Exeter crew. Distracted by his impending graduation, Jack couldn't remember. In either case, the academy's former dishwasher was unrecognizable; she'd been underwater too long.

She'd been strangled, the town newspaper said, and then dumped in the river—she hadn't drowned. Had Mrs. Stackpole told her husband about Jack? Had her husband somehow found out? Was there someone else she was seeing, in addition to Jack? As so often happened in New Hampshire, everyone suspected the husband who worked in the gasworks and came home for lunch. But he was never charged.

Nor was Jack charged, except by Noah Rosen—and not even Noah accused Jack of the actual murder. "Let's just say you probably *contributed* to it," Noah said.

He might have said worse, had Leah died in Chile before Mrs. Stackpole was found in the Exeter River. But Leah was still in Madison, Wisconsin, though no doubt she was already in a Chile frame of mind.

In those years away at school, Jack extended the distance between his mother and himself—a process Alice had initiated when Jack was still at St. Hilda's. But what little he saw of Emma was always elevating, and their fondness for each other grew. He was too young—and too inclined to think of women as novelties—to acknowledge that he adored Emma.

Only Emma understood why, for four years at Exeter, which was a coed school, Jack never really had a girlfriend. Emma knew he liked older women; the Exeter girls were just girls. When Jack was in grade nine, when he was fourteen going on fifteen, some of the Exeter seniors, who were seventeen or eighteen, attracted him, but he was no longer a pretty little boy. He was a gawky young teenager; in his first two years at Exeter, the older teenage girls ignored him.

Naturally, Jack saw something of Emma in those years—and not only over school vacations or for parts of every summer. Upon her graduation from St. Hilda's, Emma had gone to McGill in Montreal, which Mrs. Oastler, who was a fiercely loyal Torontonian, considered an un-Toronto (or an anti-Toronto) thing to do.

Emma was quickly bored, not by McGill but with the Quebecois. She was always an excellent student, although French wasn't her favorite subject; she discovered that she liked French movies better with subtitles. It was movies themselves that Emma decided she liked.

She got into NYU, where she declared herself a film major. Her grades had been good at McGill; she was able to transfer all her credits, and she loved living in New York. When Jack began at Exeter, in the fall of 1979, Emma was starting her second year of university but her first at NYU. On her invitation, Jack traveled to New York to see her for a weekend that fall. It wasn't much of a weekend. Exeter had a half-day of classes on Saturday; getting from New Hampshire to New York City took the rest of the day, and Jack was required to be back at the academy by eight o'clock Sunday night.

Nevertheless he had a thrilling Saturday night and Sunday morning with Emma and her film-major friends. They went to an all-night cinema that was playing Billy Wilder movies. Jack wasn't that familiar with Wilder, although he'd seen *Some Like It Hot* in Toronto with his mother; he must have been nine or ten. When Marilyn Monroe sang "I Wanna Be Loved by You" in that sequined dress, Jack got a boner and made the mistake of showing it to his mom. (Alice's sarcasm toward her son's penis could be brutal. She didn't *say,* "Just like your father," but the look she gave Jack said it for her.)

In New York, the first film Emma and her friends and Jack saw was *Five Graves to Cairo,* but Jack would remember only the beginning: that ghost tank transporting dead soldiers through the desert. After the tank, he forgot everything that happened to Franchot Tone—largely because Emma put her hand in his lap and held his penis for the rest of the movie. It was not until years later that Jack realized Erich von Stroheim had been Rommel.

There was more penis-holding through *The Lost Weekend,* during which Jack got the idea that Ray Milland looked like his father—or like what he imagined his dad might look like if William were drunk.

Jack had fallen asleep on Emma's shoulder for the whole of *Sunset Blvd.;* then he woke up and although he had to pee, he watched every minute of *Ace in the Hole.* On Sunday morning, over breakfast, Emma's film-major friends said Jack should have slept through *Ace in the Hole* and stayed awake for *Sunset Blvd.*

"That's what I love about you, honey pie—don't listen to them," Emma said. Jack didn't like her friends very much, but being with Emma was worth every minute of that long trip.

He would never be a Billy Wilder fan, although Wilder was born in Vienna and Jack could see what was European about even the most American of his films. It was the European filmmakers who first interested Jack, and it was Emma Oastler who introduced him to them. Whether with Emma on weekends in New York, or with Noah on weekends in Cambridge—when they would see all the foreign films in Harvard Square—Jack became a fan of films with subtitles. With the exception of Westerns, he didn't like American movies at all.

On the subject of *not* being like his father, it would occur to Jack that if William had met Emma when he was a young man, he probably would have had sex with her—and from everything she'd heard about Jack's father, Emma agreed that she would have submitted to his charms.

"That's one reason you can be happy that we *haven't* had sex," Emma told Jack. As to how she felt about not having sex with Jack, Emma didn't say.

Every winter term at Exeter, Jack's weekends were taken up by wrestling. Emma would often rent a car and come to see his matches; she herself had stopped wrestling and was once again struggling with her weight. Emma was a binge eater, but she was a binge weightlifter, too. She would take up smoking, quit smoking, start overeating, stop, and then go kill herself in the gym. When the cycle began again, Emma seemed powerless to interrupt its predictable course.

What she needed was Chenko, her favorite workout partner, but Chenko was not only far away in Toronto—he was waiting for a hip replacement. Boris had gone back to Belarus. "A family matter," was all Pavel, who had moved to Vancouver, would say. He'd married a woman from British Columbia—someone he met in his cab.

Jack's second year at Exeter, when he was fifteen going on sixteen, Emma was twenty-two. After the wrestling matches, most Saturdays, Emma took Jack to the movie theater in Durham, New Hampshire. Durham was an easy drive from Exeter, and it was a university town; they had an art-house kind of cinema, where they showed both old and current foreign films. At Exeter, they showed only the old ones.

Jack loved Fellini's *La Strada,* which he saw (more than once) with Emma holding his penis. They both believed that Chenko could have kicked the crap out of the Anthony Quinn character, but only in those days before Chenko needed a new hip. Jack wasn't as crazy about *La Dolce Vita.* The Marcello Mastroianni character was the playboy Jack imagined his father to be—the sex-seeker Jack feared he would become. And he didn't like *8½* at all—Mastroianni again.

Fellini won Jack Burns back with *Amarcord.* Emma had already seen the film in New York, but she made a point of taking Jack to Durham to see it. She wanted to witness his response to the tobacconist with the huge hooters. With her hand in Jack's lap, Emma knew the little guy's reaction almost before Jack knew it. "How's *that* for an older woman, baby cakes?"

They committed to memory the little-known name of the actress who played the big-breasted tobacconist from Rimini. When Emma called Jack in his dorm at Exeter, she would occasionally adopt an Italian accent and say to whoever answered the phone: "Pleeze tell-a Jack Burns—eet's Maria Antonietta *Beluzzi* on da fon-a!"

More often, when Emma phoned, she just said she was Jack's

sister. Jack had stopped calling Emma his *step*sister; he referred to her as his *older* sister instead.

No one at Exeter was insensitive enough to comment on the lack of a family resemblance—with the exception of Ed McCarthy, Jack's wrestling teammate, who was hit-and-miss in his attention to details. At wrestling practice, McCarthy once forgot to wear a jock; his penis slipped out of his shorts and lay like a slug on the mat, where his workout partner, a fellow one-hundred-and-seventy-seven-pounder, stepped on it.

Jack felt like stepping on McCarthy's penis the day he made an unkind remark about Emma. "It's too bad you got all the good looks in your family, Burns. Your sister looks more like a wrestler than you do."

They were in the locker room—wooden benches, metal lockers, cement floors—getting dressed for practice. Jack underhooked one of McCarthy's arms and collared the bigger boy's neck with his right hand, snapping him forward. When McCarthy pulled away, his weight shifting to the heel of his right foot, Jack caught him with a foot-sweep and McCarthy fell on his bare ass on the cement floor—hitting his back on an open locker door and giving his elbow a whack on the bench on his way down.

Jack assumed that McCarthy would get to his feet and beat the shit out of him, but McCarthy just sat there. "I could kick the crap out of you, Burns," he said.

"Do it then," Jack told him.

Even in his senior year, Jack never once wrestled above one-forty-five. After he stopped growing, he was five-eight, but only if he stood on his toes—and he competed better at one-thirty-five than he did at one-forty.

Jack was one of Exeter's better wrestlers in his final two years at the academy. Ed McCarthy would never be better than unexceptional as a wrestler. Jack *might* have beaten McCarthy in a wrestling match, but not in a fight. Even a mediocre one-seventy-seven-pounder can take a halfway decent one-thirty-five-pounder, and McCarthy knew it. He got to his feet, rubbing his back and his sore elbow.

As Mr. Ramsey had advised Jack, although this time it was unintentional, he had an audience. "You shouldn't call anyone's sister ugly, Ed," one of the lightweights said.

"Jack's sister *is* ugly," McCarthy replied.

That's what saved Jack—not McCarthy's belligerence but his insistence on the word *ugly*. While there were no rules regarding niceness at Exeter, no points off for saying something *derogatory* or *dismissive*—in fact, the intellectual fashion at the school favored everything negative and *derisive*—it was true that, for a few sentimental souls, sisters were sacred, especially if they weren't good-looking. And with Emma, who had just missed being pretty, there was also the problem with her weight.

"Who got all the good looks in *your* family, McCarthy?" the team's heavyweight asked. His name was Herman Castro; he was a scholarship kid from El Paso, Texas, and while he was a halfway decent wrestler, he might have stolen a few matches by frightening his opponents. He was so scary-looking that one was ill advised to use the word *ugly* within his hearing.

"I wasn't speaking to you, Herman," Ed McCarthy said.

"You are now," Herman Castro told him, and that was the end of it. Or it would have been, if Jack had let it be the end of it. His loyalty to Emma was fierce.

Ed McCarthy wasn't ugly—although his *penis* was, especially after that guy had stepped on it—but he wasn't at all handsome, either. He didn't have a girlfriend till his senior year, and the best he could do was a startled-looking girl with red hair and freckles who was only in grade ten. The redhead had just turned sixteen; McCarthy was eighteen. It was almost certainly not a sexual relationship, but it was probably the first relationship of any kind for both of them.

Jack toyed with the idea of seducing her—certainly not to have sex with her, because she was far too young and startled-looking for him, but simply to turn her against McCarthy, who'd said such cruel things about Emma.

Jack found Ed McCarthy's girlfriend in the cafeteria—she was at the salad bar. During wrestling season, Jack lived on salad; he could not weigh in at one hundred and thirty-four and a half pounds and eat much else. (He had a bowl of oatmeal for breakfast, sometimes with a banana; salad for lunch; salad for supper, occasionally with another banana.)

The redhead with the freckles became even more startled-looking than usual when Jack spoke to her. "Is he treating you okay?" Jack asked.

Her name was Molly—he didn't know her last name—and she was staring at him as if she expected some unknown and uncontrollable reaction from her body, as if he'd just injected one of her veins with a hallucinogenic drug.

He touched her hand, which, unbeknownst to her, had slipped into the stainless-steel bin of raw mushrooms, where it lay like something severed. "I mean McCarthy," Jack said. "He can be cruel to women, and superficial. I hope he's not like that with you."

"Did he hurt someone you know?" Molly asked; she seemed truly frightened of McCarthy.

"I suppose he only hurt my feelings—about my older sister," Jack said.

As he had taught himself to do, his eyes welled up with tears. All those movies, with Emma holding his penis, had conditioned him to imagine the close-up. By then Jack had seen Anthony Quinn in tears maybe half a dozen times. If Zampanò, the strongman, could cry, so could he.

Jack had not done much acting at Exeter. He had too much schoolwork to take part in most of the productions chosen by the school's dramatic association, the Dramat.

He was neutral to *Death of a Salesman,* which was the fall play in his ninth-grade year. Jack knew he was too boyish-looking to play Willy Loman, and too small to be either of Willy's sons, Happy or Biff. He bravely auditioned for the part of Linda, beating out a bunch of girls in the process—two seniors who were fourth-year members of the Dramat among them. But in Jack's first experience with dramatic criticism, *The PEAN,* the school yearbook, described Jack's performance as "overly distraught," and *The Exonian,* the school newspaper, stated that Linda was miscast—"resulting in the kind of sexual parody audiences must have been forced to endure in those dark ages when Exeter was an all-boys' school." *What do* they *know?* Jack thought. *Try telling* Linda *that she's "overly distraught"!*

After that, when Jack realized how hard the academic workload was for him, he pretended to be disdainful of what the Dramat chose for its plays. For the most part, this wasn't hard; many of the choices reflected the taste of the dated hippie who was the dramatic association's faculty adviser. More to the point, Jack was saving himself for the occasional Shakespeare, which not even amateurs could seriously harm.

His fellow thespians in the Dramat had resented his female impersonation of Linda in *Death of a Salesman.* They tried to force male roles on him, urging him to audition for *Mister Roberts*—as if the movie hadn't been bad enough. Talk about dated! Jack evoked Wendy Holton. "I'd rather die," he said.

This was excellent for his reputation as an actor—playing hard-to-get worked. (And what was the risk?)

He decided to surprise everyone by volunteering for a small role in *The Teahouse of the August Moon*. Jack knew that the part of Lótus Blossom, a geisha girl, would cement his hold on any future female role he wanted. The part he really desired was in the spring play his penultimate year at the academy. Jack was *Lady* Macbeth, of course—and just who was going to give him shit about it? Another wrestler? (One senior girl in the Dramat rationalized that the part called for a "domineering" woman— hence a more "masculine" choice might work.)

When the Dramat at last thought they had him figured out— Burns likes Shakespeare, Burns wants to do everything *in drag*—he surprised them one more time. Jack auditioned for *Richard III*, but only if he could be Richard. *Let them fart around with* Our Town *till the cows come home,* Jack thought. He wanted that football, his choice for a humpback, behind his neck.

It was the winter of Jack's senior year—wrestling season, when he was especially gaunt. He would show them a "winter of discontent" like they'd never seen; he would offer his "kingdom for a horse" and make them believe it, which he did.

Jack's tears now fell on Molly's hand, in the mushrooms; his tears fell on the broccoli and on the sliced cucumbers, too. A radish rolled off his plate. He didn't even try to catch it.

Molly led him to one of the cafeteria tables. Other students made room for them. "Tell me everything," Molly said, clutching his hand. Her eyes were a diluted, washed-out blue; one of the freckles on her throat looked infected.

"I didn't ask to be born good-looking," Jack told her. "My sister wasn't so lucky—my *older* sister," he added, as if Emma's advanced age were a telltale indication that she would never have a boyfriend. (In truth, Emma fooled around a lot—mostly with boys who were Jack's age, or younger. She claimed that she *didn't* have sex with them—"not exactly.")

"Your sister doesn't look like *you*?" Molly asked Jack.

"McCarthy says my sister is ugly," he told her. "Naturally, I don't see her that way—I *love* her!"

"Of *course* you do!" Molly cried, clutching his hand harder.

She was not only not pretty; at sixteen, Molly was probably as appealing as she would ever be. She'd never liked looking in a mirror—and she would like it less and less as she grew older, Jack imagined. That her boyfriend had called *another* girl ugly must have hit too close to home.

Jack had cried enough; the overacting had left his salad a little wet. Another close-up came to mind, that of the slightly quivering but stiff upper lip. "I'm sorry I brought this up," he said. "There's nothing anyone can do about it. I won't bother you again."

"No!" she said, grabbing his wrist as he tried to take his tray and go. A raw carrot fell off his plate; a little iced tea spilled from his glass. Jack drank so much iced tea in the wrestling season, he was bouncing off the walls. His fingers always trembled, as if he were riding on a speeding train.

"I better go, Molly," Jack said; he left her without looking back. He knew that she and Ed McCarthy were finished. (He also knew that Ed would be having his lunch soon.)

Jack wandered back over to the salad bar; he was basically starving. The prettiest girl in the school was there—Michele Maher, a fellow senior. She was a slim honey-blonde with a model's glowing skin and—in McCarthy's crude appraisal—"a couple of high, hard ones."

Michele was over five-ten—she had two inches on Jack. She was in the Dramat. Jack had beaten her out for Lady Macbeth, but she'd been a good sport about it—one of the few who had. Despite her good looks, everyone liked her; she was smart, but she was also nice to people. She'd done the early-acceptance thing at Columbia, because she was from New York and wanted to be back in the city; so, unlike most of the seniors, she wasn't thinking about where she might end up in college—she already knew.

"Jack Burns, looking lean and mean," Michele said.

"That's me," he told her. "I'm a starving heart of darkness."

"Where's your hump, Dick?" she asked. It was a *Richard III* joke—everyone in the Dramat kept asking him.

"It's in the costume closet, and it's just a football," Jack said, for maybe the hundredth time.

"Why don't you have a girlfriend, Jack?" Michele asked. She was just kidding around, or so he thought.

"Because I get the feeling you're not available," Jack told her.

It was just a line. Jack was still acting—he didn't mean it. He saw at once he'd made a mistake, but he couldn't think fast enough to correct it. All that iced tea on an empty stomach was giving him a buzz.

Michele Maher lowered her eyes, as if the salad bar had consumed her interest. Her posture, which was generally excellent, crumpled; for a moment, Jack was almost as tall as she was.

Hey, it was just a line, he almost said—he should have said. But Michele was faster. "I had no idea you were interested in me, Jack. I didn't think you were interested in *anyone.*"

The problem was, Jack liked her; he didn't want to hurt her feelings. And the truth is, if he'd told Michele Maher he was banging Mrs. Stackpole, Michele wouldn't have believed him. Mrs. Stackpole was so ugly, to use McCarthy's word—so unfortunate-looking in the world of women, even in the world of *much* older women—that the dishwasher herself had expressed disbelief that Jack Burns was banging her.

"Why me?" Mrs. Stackpole had asked him once, with all her weight crushing the breath out of him. He couldn't speak, not that he knew the answer. There was an urgency about Mrs. Stackpole's need to be with him; boys like Jack Burns had never even looked at her. How could Jack have been forthcoming about that to a beauty like Michele Maher?

"How can anyone not be interested in you, Michele?" Jack asked.

Maybe if he'd made that his end line, and walked away, it would have been all right. But he was too hungry to take a step away from the salad bar. When someone grabbed him, Jack first thought it was Michele. He *hoped* it was Michele.

"What the fuck did you say to Molly, asshole?" McCarthy asked him.

"Just the truth," Jack replied. "You said my sister is ugly—isn't that what you said?"

Jack hadn't meant to make Michele Maher fall for him, but she was standing next to him. And what could Ed McCarthy do? Jack was a Redding boy. McCarthy knew that Jack could take a beating. And what would Coach Hudson do to McCarthy if he hurt Jack, and one of the Exeter wrestling team's best lightweights missed several matches at the end of the season?

Also, Herman Castro would have kicked the crap out of Ed

McCarthy if McCarthy had laid a hand on Jack. Jack had made a friend for life of Herman Castro, just by standing up for ugliness.

"Ed thinks my older sister, Emma, is ugly," Jack explained to Michele Maher. He saw that it was hopeless to bring her back; she was too far gone already. "Naturally, I don't see Emma that way, because I love her."

Ed McCarthy's best move—under the circumstances, perhaps his only move—was to walk away; even so, Jack was a little surprised when McCarthy did so. McCarthy had just lost his pathetic girlfriend—and the only way, for the rest of his life, he would ever breathe the same air as the Michele Mahers of this world was if he were standing beside the likes of Jack Burns. It was the Jack Burnses of this world who got the Michele Mahers—in Jack's case, without half trying.

One weekend, in the spring of their senior year, Michele took Jack home with her to New York. It was the first time Jack felt he was being unfaithful to Emma, not because he was with Michele but because he didn't tell Emma he was going to be in the city. Michele was so pretty, Jack was afraid it would hurt Emma's feelings to meet her—or that Emma would treat Michele badly. (The whole Maher family was beautiful, even the dog.)

Besides, Jack rationalized, would it really matter to Emma if he was in town and didn't tell her? Emma had graduated from NYU and was a fledgling comedy writer for a late-night New York TV show. She hated it. She'd come to the conclusion that, at least in her case, the hallway to making movies did not pass through television; she wasn't even sure she still wanted to make movies.

"I'm going to be a writer, honey pie—I mean novels, not screenplays. I mean literature, not journalism."

"When are you going to write?" he'd asked her.

"On the weekends."

Thus Jack gave himself the impression that he might disturb Emma's *writing* if he bothered her on a weekend.

Michele's parents had an apartment on Park Avenue; it took up half a building and was bigger than Jack's fifth-grade dorm at Redding. He'd not known that people had apartments with "fine art" that they actually owned. He didn't even know that people could privately own fine art. Maybe that was a particularly Canadian underestimation of the power of the private sector, or else he'd been in Maine and New Hampshire long enough to have been deprived of his city sensibilities.

There was a small Picasso in the guest-room bathroom; it was low on the wall, beside the toilet, where you could see it best when you were sitting down. Jack was so impressed by it, he almost peed on it when he was standing up. For some reason, his penis produced an errant stream.

He thought there was something wrong with his penis—a little gonorrhea, maybe. Jack knew it was entirely possible that he'd caught the clap from Mrs. Stackpole. (Who knew who else she was fucking, or who else her husband was fucking?) Now, after almost pissing on the knee-high Picasso, Jack convinced himself that he had a venereal disease—something he might pass on to Michele Maher. Not that he imagined Michele would have sex with him. It was their first time away from Exeter together. Yes, he had kissed her—but he hadn't once felt what Ed McCarthy crudely called her "high, hard ones."

Just Jack's luck—Michele's beautiful parents went off to some black-tie event, leaving Jack and Michele in the vast Park Avenue apartment with the beautiful dog. They began by watching the TV in Michele's bedroom, after her mom and dad had left. "They'll be gone all evening," Michele said.

Jack was prepared to make out, but he'd never imagined that Michele Maher was the kind of girl who would "go all the way"—to use one of Alice's prehippie expressions. "I just hope you don't know any girls who *go all the way,* Jack," was what his mom had said when he was back in Toronto, in the snow, for his last so-called spring break.

Michele Maher *wasn't* the kind of girl who went all the way, but she wanted to talk about it. Perhaps she'd been wrong not to do it.

"No, I think you've been right," Jack quickly told her.

Short of telling her that he might have caught the clap from an Exeter dishwasher, he didn't know what else to do but claim to be an advocate of *not* going all the way himself.

It was a John Wayne night on one of the TV channels, beginning with *The Fighting Kentuckian.* Leading a regiment of Kentucky riflemen, John Wayne wears what looks like an entire raccoon on his head. Jack liked John Wayne, but Emma had undermined Jack's enthusiasm for Wayne's kind of heroics; she'd been feeding him a strict diet of Truffaut and Bergman films. Jack liked Truffaut, but he *loved* Bergman.

It was true that he'd been bored by *The Four Hundred Blows,* and had said so. Emma was so disappointed in him that she stopped holding his penis; she picked it up again for *Shoot the Piano Player,* a film Jack adored, and held it without once letting go through *Jules and Jim,* while Jack imagined that Jeanne Moreau, not Emma, was holding his penis.

As for Ingmar Bergman, there was never enough. *The Seventh Seal, The Virgin Spring, Winter Light, The Silence*—those were the films that sold Jack Burns on the movies and made him want to act in films rather than the theater. *Scenes from a Marriage, Face to Face, Autumn Sonata*—those were the movies that inspired him. He couldn't stop imagining his expression in close-up with those Bergman women. With every line he spoke, not neglecting the slightest gesture, Jack imagined that the camera was so tight on him that his whole face filled the giant screen—or just the fingers of his hand, making a fist, or even the tip of his index finger coming into frame alongside a doorbell.

Not to mention the *sex* in Bergman's films—oh, those older women! And to think that Jack met all of them while Emma Oastler held his penis in her hand! (Bibi Andersson, Gunnel Lindblom, Ingrid Thulin, Liv Ullmann.) Meanwhile, Alice hoped that Jack didn't know any girls who went all the way! What was she *thinking*?

"What's wrong, Dick? Lost your hump?" Michele Maher asked. It was another *Richard III* joke.

Jack usually answered, "No, it's just *deflated.*"

He couldn't claim he was distracted by *The Fighting Kentuckian,* not for a moment. Michele and Jack made out through *Rio Grande,* too. John Wayne is at war again, this time with the Apaches. He is also at war with his estranged, tempestuous wife—Maureen O'Hara with her hooters. But Jack had eyes only for Michele Maher. God, she was beautiful! And nice, and smart, and funny. How he wanted her.

Michele Maher wanted him that night, too, but he refused to have sex with her—notwithstanding that he couldn't take his eyes off her. He couldn't stop himself from kissing her, touching her, holding her. He kept repeating her name. For years he would wake up saying it: "Michele Maher, Michele Maher, Michele Maher."

"Jack Burns," she said, half-mocking in her tone. "Richard the Humpback, also known as *Third,*" she said. "*Lady* Macbeth," she teased him. She was the best kisser he would ever encounter, hands down—not forgetting that Emma Oastler could kiss up a storm. No one could hold a candle to Michele Maher in the kissing department.

Why, then, didn't Jack simply tell her the truth? That he was afraid he had a dose of gonorrhea; that he might have caught the clap from an adulterous dishwasher, a woman old enough to be his mother! (It sounded like the subject of a play the Dramat might have chosen—or, more likely, a sequel to *A Mail-Order Bride in the Northwest Territories.*)

Why didn't Jack tell Michele that he loved her, and that he wanted most of all to protect her from everything he imagined or knew to be bad about himself? He should have made up a story—God knows, he could act. He could have told Michele Maher that his workout partner had stepped on his penis in the wrestling room, a surprisingly common but little-discussed injury among wrestlers. Under the circumstances, he was simply too *sore* to have sex with her—or so he could have claimed.

But, no, Jack was such a fool, he proposed *masturbating* with Michele Maher—this instead of having sex with her! "It's the safest sex there is," Jack told her, while a bloody Indian war raged around them—the Apaches were whooping and dying. John Wayne was fighting for his life while Jack was committing suicide with Michele Maher. "You know, we take our clothes off, but I just touch myself, and you touch yourself," he went on, digging his grave. "We keep looking at each other, we kiss—we just *imagine* it, the way actors do."

The tears in Michele Maher's eyes would have broken hearts on the big screen; she was a girl who could withstand the tightest close-up. "Oh, Jack," she said. "All this time, I've defended you. When people say, 'Jack Burns is just too weird,' I always say, 'No, he isn't!'"

"Michele—" Jack started to say, but he could see it in her eyes. He had watched her fall for him; now he saw how irreversibly he'd lost her. The John Wayne Western on the TV was wreathed with a funereal dust—fallen horses, dead Apaches.

Jack left Michele Maher alone in her bedroom; he was sensitive enough to know that she wanted to be alone. The beautiful dog stayed with her. In his guest bedroom, with its fine-art bathroom, Jack was alone with the knee-high Picasso and his own TV. He watched *The Quiet Man* by himself.

John Wayne is an Irish-American prizefighter who gives up boxing when he unintentionally kills an opponent in the ring. He goes to Ireland and falls in love with Maureen O'Hara and her hooters (again). But Maureen's brother (Victor McLaglen) is an asshole; in what is arguably the longest and least believable fist-fight in Ireland's history, Wayne has to put up his dukes again.

In the throes of Jack's self-pity, he concluded that Victor McLaglen would have kicked the crap out of John Wayne. (McLaglen was a pro; he fought Jack Johnson, and gave Johnson all he could handle. Wayne wouldn't have lasted a round with McLaglen.)

It was a long, largely silent trip back to Exeter with Michele Maher. Jack made matters worse between them by professing that he loved her; he declared that he'd only suggested mutual masturbation as an indication of his *respect* for her.

"I'll tell you what's weird about you, Jack—" Michele started to say, but she burst into tears and didn't tell him. He was left to finish her thought in his imagination. For almost twenty years, Jack Burns would wish he could have that weekend back.

"If I had to guess," Noah Rosen ventured, "it didn't work out between you and Michele because you couldn't stop *looking* at each other."

Jack was only a week or two away from telling Noah about Mrs. Stackpole, which led Noah to tell his sister—and that would be the end of Jack's friendship with Noah. A painful loss—at the time, more devastating to Jack than losing Michele Maher. But Noah would fade; Michele would persist.

Michele did nothing wrong. She was Jack's age, seventeen going on eighteen, but she had the self-restraint and dignity not to tell her closest friends that Jack was a creep—or even that he was as weird as some of them thought he was. In truth, she went on defending him from the weirdness charge. Herman Castro later told Jack that Michele always spoke well of him, even after they'd "broken up." Herman said: "When I think of the two of you together—well, I just can't imagine it. You both must have felt you were models in a magazine or something."

Herman Castro would go on to Harvard and Harvard Medical School. He became a doctor of infectious diseases and went back to El Paso, where he treated mostly AIDS patients. He married a very attractive Mexican-American woman, and they had a bunch of kids. From Herman's Christmas cards, Jack would be relieved to see that the children took after *her*. Herman, as much as Jack loved him, was always hard to look at. He was slope-shouldered and jug-shaped, with a flattened nose and a protruding forehead; above his small, black, close-together eyes, his forehead bulged like a baked potato.

Herman Castro was the wrestling team's photographer. In those days, heavyweights always wrestled last; Herman took pictures of his teammates wrestling even when he was warming up. Jack used to think that Herman liked to hide his face from view. Maybe the camera was his shield.

"*Hey, amigo,*" the note on Herman Castro's Christmas card traditionally said, "*when I think of your love life—well, I just can't imagine it.*"

Little did Herman know. Over time, Jack Burns would believe that he lost the love of his life on the night he lost Michele Maher. It would be small consolation to him to imagine that his father, at Jack's age, would have fucked her—clap or no clap.

And he *didn't* have the clap! Jack had himself checked at the infirmary when he got back from New York. The doctor said it was just some irritation, possibly caused by the change in his diet since the end of the wrestling season.

"It's not gonorrhea?" Jack asked in disbelief.

"It's nothing, Jack."

After all, he'd been screwing a one-hundred-seventy-pound dishwasher for months on end—sometimes as often as four or five times a week. No doubt there was sufficient *irritation* to make Jack piss sideways at a knee-high Picasso—not to mention ruin his chances with "la belle Michele," as Noah Rosen called Michele Maher.

Michele and Jack were in only one class together—fourth-year German. Many of the students who took German at the academy imagined that they might become doctors. German was said to be a good second language for the study of medicine. Jack had no such hope—he wasn't strong in the sciences. What he liked about German was the word order—the verbs all lay in wait till the end of the sentence. Talk about end lines! In a German sentence, all the action happened at the end. German was an actor's language.

Jack liked Goethe, but he loved Rilke, and in German IV, he loved most of all Shakespeare *in German,* particularly the love sonnets, which the teacher, Herr Richter, claimed were better *auf Deutsch* than they were in English.

Michele Maher, bless her heart, disagreed. "Surely, Herr Richter, you would not argue that 'Lascivious grace, in whom all ill well shows,' is *improved* by '*Mutwillige Anmut, reizend noch im Schlimmen*'!"

"Ah, but Michele," Herr Richter intoned, "surely *you* would agree that '*Sonst prüft die kluge Welt der Tränen* Sinn, *Und höhnt dich um mich, wenn ich nicht mehr* bin' is a considerable improvement on the original. Would you say it for us in English, Jack? You say it so well."

" 'Lest the wise world should look into your *moan,*' " Jack recited to Michele Maher, " 'And mock you with me after I am *gone.*' "

"You see?" Herr Richter asked the class. "It's a sizable stretch to make *gone* rhyme with *moan,* isn't it? Whereas *bin* with *Sinn*—well, I rest my case."

Jack could not look at Michele, nor she at him. To imagine that his last words to her might be the sizable stretch of trying to make *gone* rhyme with *moan*—it was too cruel.

In their last class together, Michele handed Jack a note. "Read it later, please," was all she said.

It was something by Goethe. Michele liked Goethe better than Jack did. *"Behandelt die Frauen mit Nachsicht."* He knew the line. "Be lenient when handling womankind."

If he'd had the courage to give Michele a note, Jack would have chosen Rilke. *"Sie lächelte einmal. Es tat fast weh."* But Michele Maher would have said it was too prosaic. "She smiled once. It was almost painful."

One small measure of pride Jack took in his academic efforts at Exeter was that he managed to pass four years of German without Noah Rosen's assistance. German was the only subject Noah couldn't and didn't help him with. (Quite understandably, as a Jew, Noah felt that German was the language of his people's executioners and he refused to learn a word of it.)

Noah couldn't help Jack with the SATs, either. There Jack was on his own; there *aptitude* was a far superior tool to *attitude.*

Jack's effort notwithstanding, his talent lagged behind that of his Exeter classmates. He had the lowest SAT scores in the Class of '83.

"Actors don't do multiple choice," was the way Jack put it to Herman Castro.

"Why not?" Herman asked.

"Actors don't *guess*," Jack replied. "Actors *do* have choices, but they know what they are. If you don't know the answer, you don't guess."

"If you don't mind my saying so, Jack, that's a pretty stupid approach to a multiple-choice examination."

Because of his miserable SAT scores, Jack wouldn't be joining Herman Castro and Noah Rosen at Harvard. He wouldn't be attending any of the so-called better colleges or universities. His mother begged him to return to Toronto and go to university there. But he didn't want to go back to Toronto.

Having initiated the distance between them, Alice suddenly wanted Jack to be close to her again. He wanted nothing to do with her. Jack was way over "the lesbian thing," as Emma called it—Emma was way over it, too. They no longer cared that Alice and Mrs. Oastler were an item; in fact, both Emma and Jack were pleased, even proud, that their mothers were still together. So many couples *weren't* still together, both the couples they'd known among their friends *and* the parents of so many of their friends.

But Jack couldn't forget that he'd been sent away from Toronto—and from Canada, his country. For eight years, he'd been living in the United States; his fellow students, for the most part, were Americans, and the films that made him want to be an actor in the movies were European.

Jack applied to, and was accepted at, the University of New Hampshire. Emma was all over him. "For Christ's sake, baby cakes, you shouldn't choose UNH because of how much you like the local movie theater!" But he'd made his decision. He liked Durham *and* that movie theater, which was never the same, Jack would admit, when Emma Oastler *wasn't* sitting beside him holding his penis.

That trip to the North Sea and the Baltic with his mother had formed Jack Burns. St. Hilda's had established what Emma would correctly call his older-woman thing, and the school had given him some pretty basic acting techniques—also a belief in himself that he could be convincing, even as a girl. Redding had taught him how to work hard. Mrs. Adkins had drawn him to her sadness. And at Exeter he'd discovered that he was not an intellectual, but he had learned how to read and write. (At the time, Jack didn't know how rare and useful this knowledge was—no more than he could have defined the vulnerability Mrs. Stackpole had exposed in him.)

The female faculty at Exeter struck Jack as sexually unapproachable, in that older-woman way. Whether Jack was right or wrong in that assumption, they were certainly not as approachable as Mrs. Stackpole—her crude, suggestive urgency had captivated him. Redding was a wilderness where women went and became weary, or at least weary-looking. At Exeter, on the other hand, there were some attractive faculty wives who captured the boys' attention—if only at the fantasy level. (Jack wouldn't have dreamed of approaching a single one of them; they all looked too happy.)

Least approachable of them all was Madame Delacorte, a French fox who worked in the library and whose husband taught in the Department of Romance Languages. *Romance* was not what Madame Delacorte brought to mind. There wasn't a boy at Exeter who could look her in the eye—nor was there a boy who ever visited the library without searching longingly for her.

Madame Delacorte looked as if she'd just been laid but wanted more, *much* more. (Yet, somehow, the first sweaty encounter had not mussed her hair.) Madame Delacorte was as commanding a presence as Jeanne Moreau in *Jules and Jim;* not even her husband could approach her without stuttering, and he was from Paris.

Jack was cramming for his history final in the library one spring night; he had a favorite carrel on the second floor of the stacks. He'd burned his bridges with Noah Rosen *and* Michele Maher, and he was feeling resigned about his next four years in Durham, New Hampshire.

Emma Oastler was moving to Iowa City. She'd sent some of her writing to Iowa and had been admitted to the Writers' Workshop there. Jack had never heard of the place. He knew only that Iowa was in the Midwest, and that he would miss Emma.

"You can come visit me, honey pie. I'm sure they have movie

theaters there, despite all the writers. They probably have the movie theaters to purposely drive the writers *crazy*."

In this context, Jack wasn't worried about his history final—he was just a little depressed. When Madame Delacorte came to his carrel, he'd been plowing through a bunch of books he was supposed to have read already. He'd made a pile of the ones he was finished with; among them was a dusty tome about Roman law, which Madame Delacorte said someone had been looking for. She wanted him to return the book to the stacks on the third floor. The classics were kept there—all the Greek and Latin.

"Okay," Jack said to Madame Delacorte. He could never look at her above her slender waist; her waist alone was enough to undo him. He went off to the third floor with the book about Roman law.

"Come right back, Jack," Madame Delacorte called after him. "I don't want to be responsible for distracting you." As if she, or Jack, had any control of that!

It seemed that, as usual, there was no one in the stacks on the third floor. Jack quickly found where the book belonged, but—above the moldy bindings, in the next aisle—a pair of disembodied eyes regarded him. "Michele Maher isn't the girl for you," the voice that went with the eyes said. "You're already good-looking. What do *you* need a good-looking girl for? You need something else, something *real*."

Another dishwasher? Jack wondered. But he recognized the voice and the diluted, washed-out blue of the eyes. It was Molly whatever-her-name-was, Ed McCarthy's ex-girlfriend. (*Penis* McCarthy, as Herman Castro less-than-lovingly called him.)

"Hi, Molly," Jack said; he came around into her aisle and stood next to her.

"*I* should be your girlfriend," Molly told him. "I know you love your sister, and she's ugly. Well, I'm ugly, too."

"You're not ugly, Molly."

"Yes, I am," she said. She was demented, clearly. She also had a cold; the rims of her nostrils were red and her nose was running. Molly whatever-her-name-was leaned back against the stacks and closed her eyes. "Take me," she whispered.

Jack didn't know whether to laugh or cry. He did neither. On an impulse largely meant to do her minimal harm, he fell to his knees and lifted her skirt. He pushed his face into her panties;

with both his hands on her buttocks, he pulled the waistband of her panties down.

Jack Burns actually *licked* a tenth-grade girl, a sixteen-year-old, in the stacks on the third floor of the Exeter library! From Mrs. Machado and Mrs. Stackpole, he knew exactly how to do it; the difference was, this time he initiated it. He could feel Molly's fingers in his hair; she was pulling his head into her. He could feel her slumping against the stacks as she came on his face—not one's usual library experience. And the worst of it was that he didn't know her last name; he couldn't even write her a letter of explanation.

Jack left her standing in the stacks, or barely standing. Unlike Michele Maher, Molly was short enough that he could kiss her on her forehead—as if she were a little girl. When he left her, with nothing to say for himself except that he had to cram for a history final, it seemed to him that her knees were buckling.

Jack found a drinking fountain, in which he washed his face. When he returned to his carrel on the second floor, he was aware he'd been away for what may have struck Madame Delacorte as a long time—not to mention that he'd suffered a major distraction. Maybe he was a little wild-eyed, or there was something in the aftermath of impromptu cunnilingus that caught Madame Delacorte's eye.

"My word, Jack Burns," she said. "What on earth have *you* been reading? Not Roman law, clearly."

The lilt in her voice was more mischievous than scientific. Was Madame Delacorte flirting with him? He finally got up the nerve to look at her, but Madame Delacorte was as unreadable as Jack's future. He knew only that the rest of his life had begun, and that he would begin it without Michele Maher—his first, maybe his last, true love.

18

Enter Claudia;
Exit Mrs. McQuat

Jack Burns saw his college years through a telescope, the way you do when the object of your desire is not of the moment—the way you do when you're biding your time. The University of New Hampshire was like a layover in an airport—a stop on Jack's journey *elsewhere.* He got good grades, the kind he never could have gotten at Exeter—he even graduated *cum laude*—but he was detached the whole time.

In the student theater, Jack got every part he auditioned for, but there weren't many he wanted. And he saw all the foreign films that came to Durham in those years, sometimes but not usually by himself; if he took a girl with him, she had to be someone who would hold his penis. There were only a couple of girls like that.

It was most often Claudia, who was a theater major. There was also a Japanese girl named Midori; she was in one of Jack's life-drawing classes. He was the only male model for *all* of the life-drawing classes. As Mr. Ramsey would have said, it was an acting opportunity—and Jack got paid for it. Modeling for life drawing was not an occasion when he thought so fixedly of his audience of one, as Miss Wurtz had instructed him; rather it was an exercise in imagining the close-ups he was preparing for. He hoped there would be many.

Modeling for life drawing was an exercise in mind-over-matter, too, because Jack willed himself not to get an erection; what was more tricky, but he got pretty good at it, was allowing a hard-on to start and then stopping it. (It might have been that exercise that made a moviegoer out of Midori.)

"Set us free, O God, from the bondage of our sins," Lottie

used to pray. But Jack had stopped hearing from Lottie, even by postcard. He never learned what happened to her on Prince Edward Island—maybe nothing.

Emma had taught Jack how to drive—illegally, in keeping with her nature, but at least Jack got his driver's license at the earliest opportunity. He didn't own a car; hence he developed a possessive fondness for Claudia's Volvo. He liked Claudia, but he *loved* her car.

Claudia was an aspiring actress—she and Jack were in several student plays together—and her willingness as a penis-holder was for the most part unshakable. Yes, he had sex with her, too, which made the penis-holding less strange (albeit arguably less exciting) than with Emma. Claudia also drove Jack where he wanted to go, and once he had his license, she was generous about lending him her Volvo.

Jack drove to Exeter a few times a week, just to work out with the wrestling team and run on the sloped, wooden track in the indoor cage. He had no interest in wrestling in college; it had never been the competition that mattered to him. He'd wanted to stay in halfway decent shape and to be able to protect himself, and he owed the sport a debt he didn't mind repaying. He made himself an extra coach in the Exeter wrestling room, mostly demonstrating moves and holds for the wrestlers who were beginners— much as Chenko, Pavel, and Boris had done for him as a child, and Coach Clum and Coach Hudson later on.

Unlike Coach Clum, Coach Hudson hadn't looked down on Jack's habit of having his cauliflower ears drained in the training room. Unlike Coach Clum, Coach Hudson was a good-looking guy; he understood why Jack might not want to look like a wrestler for the rest of his life, especially if he wanted to be an actor.

"Given what I hope will be my career, wouldn't you say it is *practical* of me to have my cauliflower ears drained?" Jack asked him.

"*Very* practical," Coach Hudson replied.

There was another wrestling coach at Exeter in those years. Coach Shapiro taught Russian at the academy; later he would be made dean of students.

Once, when Jack brought Claudia with him to the wrestling room, she sat sullenly on the mat with her back against the padded wall—just watching the wrestlers with hostile, womanly suspicion, as if she might any second pull out a gun and shoot one of them. There was something vaguely dangerous about Claudia—a secret she kept to herself, perhaps, or her plans for a future she wouldn't disclose. Or was she, like Jack, always *acting*?

Coach Shapiro remarked that Jack's friend was both "arrestingly beautiful" and "Slavic-looking." Jack knew that Claudia was attractive, although every woman's claim to beauty was diminished, in his mind's eye, by the incomparable Michele Maher. But he hadn't thought of Claudia as particularly *Slavic*-looking. On the other hand, Coach Shapiro was a Russian scholar; he obviously knew what he was talking about. He knew his wrestling, too. Coach Shapiro and Jack had a few of Chenko's old tricks in common.

This amounted to Jack's male company in his years in Durham—those wrestling coaches at his old school, and the younger of those Exeter wrestlers who were just learning how.

Jack was in his second year at UNH before he was forced to choose between his Slavic-looking beauty, Claudia, and his conquest from life drawing—his personal jewel of the Orient, Midori, with whom he had first seen Kurosawa's *Yojimbo*. (An exciting film to see with a Japanese girl holding your penis in her hand!) Jack must have been in the United States long enough to have succumbed to American materialism, because he chose Claudia—not only because she had a car; she also had her own apartment. It was off-campus, in Newmarket—more or less between Durham and Exeter. And because Claudia was an actress, she and Jack were interested in the same kind of summer jobs. Summer stock, everyone called it. (Claudia used to say that the phrase reminded her of cows.)

New England had uncounted summer-stock theaters, some better than others, and while graduate students were more often hired for the paying jobs—these were people in MFA theater programs, for the most part—some gifted undergraduates could find internships, and some, including Claudia and Jack, were even paid.

Claudia liked the theater better than Jack did. She knew Jack wanted to be a movie actor, but films failed to impress her. She once told Jack that she would have walked out of most of the movies she saw with him, except that she was holding his penis in her hand.

Claudia was heavy-breasted and self-conscious about her hips, but her creamy-smooth skin, and her prominent jaw and cheekbones, gave her a face made for close-ups. She should have liked movies better than she did, because the camera would have loved her—not least her eyes, which were a yellowish brown, like polished wood. But Claudia believed she would be "hopelessly fat" before she was thirty. "Then only the theater will have me, and only because I can act."

In March of their sophomore year, Claudia and Jack drove halfway across the country in her Volvo to spend their spring vacation with Emma. Jack had decided to take Claudia to Toronto the following fall, and Emma thought she and Jack should prepare "poor Claudia" for the eventual meeting with Alice and Mrs. Oastler. Jack wasn't taking Claudia to Toronto solely for the purpose of meeting his mother, although such a meeting was to be expected. His mom knew they lived together; naturally, both Alice and Leslie Oastler were eager to meet Claudia.

Jack's principal reason for going to Toronto was to take Claudia to the film festival and attempt to pass her off as a Russian actress who didn't speak a word of English; he was looking at the trip as what Mr. Ramsey would have called an "acting opportunity" for both of them. Also Claudia and Jack were a little desperate for some city time, which is what living in New Hampshire did to people.

To Jack's surprise, Emma liked Claudia, maybe because Claudia also struggled with her weight. Though Claudia was beautiful, her self-deprecating view of herself won Emma over completely. (Quite possibly, Emma also knew that Claudia and Jack wouldn't last.)

Jack was less certain than Emma that Claudia's view of herself *was* self-deprecating. Her criticism of her body may also have been an acting opportunity, because Claudia had no lack of confidence in her attractiveness to men—nor could she have failed to notice Jack's appreciation of her full figure. And Claudia had overheard Jack saying to Emma, on the phone, that the road trip to Iowa in the spring was first and foremost a "motel opportunity."

"Just what did you mean by that?" Claudia had asked him, when he hung up the phone.

"You're the kind of girl who makes me think about finding a motel," he'd told her; he wasn't acting.

But Claudia may have been acting when she replied—that was what was a little dangerous or unknowable about her. "With you, I wouldn't need a motel, Jack. With you, I could do it standing up."

They had tried it that way—both of them conscious, at first, of how they might have looked to an audience, but in the end they gave themselves over to the moment. At least Jack did; with Claudia, he could never be sure.

There were indeed motel opportunities on their trip to the Midwest and back, and Jack was also pleased that, unlike New England, Iowa had a real spring; the surrounding farmlands were lush. Emma and three other graduate students in the Writers' Workshop were renting a farmhouse a few miles from Iowa City; the other students had gone home for the holiday, so Emma and Claudia and Jack had the farm to themselves. They drove into town to eat almost every night—Emma was no cook.

Emma wanted Claudia to understand "the lesbian thing" between Jack's mom and hers, which Emma said was actually *not* a lesbian thing.

"It's *not*?" Jack asked, surprised.

"They're not *normal* lesbians, baby cakes—they're nothing at all like lesbians, except that they sleep together and live together."

"They sound a *little* like lesbians," Claudia ventured.

"You gotta understand their relationship *in context*," Emma explained. "Jack's mom feels that her life with men began and ended with Jack's dad. *My* mom simply hates my dad—and other men, by association. Before my mom and Jack's mom met each other, they had any number of bad boyfriends—the kind of boyfriends who are in the self-fulfilling-prophecy category, if you know what I mean."

"Yes, I know," Claudia said. "You think men are assholes, so you pick an asshole for a boyfriend. I know the type."

"That way," Emma went on, "when your boyfriend dumps you, or you dump him, you don't have to change your mind about what assholes men are."

"Yes, exactly," Claudia agreed.

Jack didn't say anything. It was news to him that his mother had "had any number of bad boyfriends" before she met Mrs.

Oastler, and it struck him that Emma and Claudia might have been describing *Emma's* love life—what little he knew of it. There'd been a lot of boyfriends, most of them one-night stands—all of them bad, in Emma's estimation, yet she'd never experienced the slightest difficulty in getting over any of them. (Most of them *young,* in Jack's opinion—at least the ones he'd met.)

In an effort to change the subject, albeit slightly, Jack asked Emma a question about his mother that had been on his mind for years. It was easier to ask the question with a third party present; out of respect for Claudia, Jack hoped that Emma might hold back a little something in her answer.

"I don't know about your mom, Emma," he began, "but I would be surprised if my mother wasn't still interested in men—in *young* men, anyway. If only occasionally."

"I wouldn't absolutely trust my mom around young men, either, honey pie, but I *know* your mom is still interested in men—in young men *especially.*"

Jack wasn't surprised, but this was the first confirmation he'd had. And, recalling one of Emma's sleepy-time tales, Jack wondered if the bad boyfriend in the squeezed-child saga might have been an ex-boyfriend of Mrs. Oastler's—someone who'd turned Emma off older men, or even men her own age.

As for Alice, she had left the Chinaman and moved into her own tattoo shop on Queen Street. When Alice opened her shop, which was called Daughter Alice, she got in on the ground floor of a trend. (No doubt Leslie Oastler had helped her buy the building, Jack thought.)

In later years, Queen Street would be too trendy to stand, with stores with cute names and an overabundance of bistros. Daughter Alice was located west of that, where Queen Street began to get a little seedy—and, in Emma's opinion, "a lot Chinese."

From the moment Alice moved in, her clientele was "way young"—to use Emma's description. But Jack never knew if the young people came because of his mom or because Queen Street was full of young people most of the time. Emma said it was chiefly young men who went to Daughter Alice. Occasionally they went with their girlfriends, who got tattooed, too, but Jack already knew that young men liked his mother, and that she was attracted to them.

Emma also said that Leslie Oastler was "not a Queen Street

person." Mrs. Oastler didn't much care for the atmosphere *or* the clientele in Daughter Alice. But after all her years as someone's apprentice, Alice loved working for herself. The tattoo parlor was always full; people were happy to wait their turn, or just watch Alice work. She had her flash on the walls, nobody else's; she had her notebooks full of her stencils, which her customers could look through while they waited. She made tea and coffee, and always had music playing. She had tropical fish in brightly lit aquariums; she'd even arranged some of her flash underwater, with the fish, so that the fish appeared to be swimming in a tattoo world.

"That shop is a *happening*," Emma told Claudia.

Jack knew that, but the emphasis on the young men had escaped him—or he just hadn't wanted to think about it. The thought of his mother with boys his age, or younger, was disturbing. Jack was much happier imagining his mom in Leslie Oastler's arms, where she'd looked safe to him—if not exactly happy.

"And what do you suppose your mom thinks of my mom's young men, if there are any?" Jack asked Emma.

"For the most part—" Emma said; she stopped herself and then resumed, speaking more to Claudia than to Jack. "For the most part, I think my mom is glad Jack's mom isn't a *man*."

It was always hard for Jack to dispute Emma's authority, especially on the subject of his mother and Mrs. Oastler. Since '75, when he'd gone off to Redding, Emma had spent more time with their moms than Jack had. Toronto wasn't his city, not anymore.

All he'd really known of Toronto was Mrs. Wicksteed's old house on Spadina and Lowther, and the St. Hilda's area of Forest Hill. Well, okay—there was the Bathurst Street gym, and what little he could see of the ravine near Sir Winston Churchill Park from Mrs. Machado's apartment on St. Clair. But Jack had never known downtown Toronto very well, especially not that area of Jarvis and Dundas, where the Chinaman's tattoo parlor was—and he was a virtual stranger to Queen Street West and his mom's *happening*, as Emma called it, at Daughter Alice.

Between Emma and Jack, Emma was the true Torontonian—even when she was in Iowa City, and later, when she was living in Los Angeles.

Alice had finally tattooed Emma. Jack couldn't imagine the negotiations this had entailed, not only with his mother but with

Mrs. Oastler. The butterfly Emma had once wanted was replaced by her latest heart's desire, a smaller version of Alice's famous Rose of Jericho.

"Don't give me any shit about it," Emma told Jack she had said to her mom. "If you'd let me get a stupid butterfly on my ankle when I wanted one, you wouldn't be faced with a vagina today."

The problem was that Emma didn't want to conceal the vagina. This was no flower hidden in a rose—this was just the petals of that most recognizable flower. Granted it was small, but it was clearly a vagina. (Oh, Jack thought—to have been a fly on the wall for these mother-daughter discussions!)

Alice had smoothed the way for the tattoo to happen. "It's a question of where it is, Emma," Alice said. "I refuse to tattoo a vagina on your *ankle*."

Naturally, Emma was "way beyond" (as she put it) wanting a tattoo on her ankle—and Alice would no longer put a tattoo on a woman's coccyx. She'd read in a tattoo magazine that an anesthesiologist wouldn't give you an epidural if you were tattooed there. (Possibly this had something to do with the ink getting into the spinal column, although the danger of that happening sounded unlikely.)

"What if you have a child and you need an epidural?" Alice asked Emma.

"I'm not ever going to have children, Alice," Emma told her.

"You don't *know* that," Alice replied.

"Yeah, I know that, Alice."

"I'm not giving you a vagina on your coccyx, Emma."

Even Emma had to admit that her coccyx would have been a confusing place for a vagina. Alice finally agreed to put the tattoo on Emma's hip, just below the panty line; that way, Emma could see it without looking in a mirror *and* she could see it in a mirror as well. "Which hip?" Alice asked her.

Emma considered this, but not for long. "My right one," she replied.

According to Emma, the tattoo was already a vagina-in-progress when Alice asked her: "Why the *right* hip?"

"I generally sleep on my left side," Emma told her. "If I'm sleeping with a guy, I want to be sure he can see the vagina—the *tattoo,* I mean."

Emma said she appreciated Alice's thoughtful reply, although she had to wait for it. Jack could imagine this exactly: his mother never taking her foot off the foot-switch, the needles in the tattoo machine going nonstop, the flow of ink and pain as steady as hard rain. At first, Emma was vague about the music that was playing at the time. "It might have been 'Mr. Tambourine Man,' " she said.

> *Though I know that evenin's empire has returned into sand,*
> *Vanished from my hand,*
> *Left me blindly here to stand but still not sleeping.*
> *My weariness amazes me, I'm branded on my feet,*
> *I have no one to meet*
> *And the ancient empty street's too dead for dreaming.*

"There were the usual creepy guys hanging around the tattoo parlor," as Emma remembered her experience. Jack felt certain these guys would have had more than a passing interest in the expanse of Emma's hip that was exposed, not to mention her tattoo-in-progress.

"Come to think of it, it was Dylan, but it was 'Just Like a Woman,' " Emma suddenly recalled. Jack could imagine this, too.

> *Ah, you fake just like a woman, yes, you do*
> *You make love just like a woman, yes, you do*
> *Then you ache just like a woman*
> *But you break just like a little girl.*

"Let me be sure I understand you, Emma," Alice said, after a lengthy pause. "If you're sleeping with a guy, you want him to be able to see this tattoo—even when you're asleep?"

"He may forget me, but he'll remember my tattoo," Emma said.

"Lucky fella," Alice said. It seemed to Emma that Alice was keeping time to Bob Dylan with the foot-switch as she tattooed on.

"My mom's a bitch, but you're gonna *love* Alice," Emma told Claudia. "Everyone loves Alice."

"I used to," Jack said.

He walked outside to have a look at the Iowa farmland. It was stretched out flat, as far as he could see—nothing like the tree-dense hills of Maine and New Hampshire. Emma followed him outside.

"Okay, so I lied—not quite *everyone* loves your mother," Emma said.

"I used to," Jack said again.

"Let's go see a movie, baby cakes. Let's take Claudia to the picture show."

"Sure," Jack said.

If he'd had half a brain, he might have anticipated the problem inherent in watching a movie with Emma *and* Claudia. It was most unlike him not to remember the movie; he even remembered bad movies. But from the moment Jack sat down in the theater, with Claudia seated to his left and Emma to his right, the problem—namely, which of them would hold his penis—presented itself. Any thoughts he might have had about the film vanished.

Emma, who was left-handed, put her hand in Jack's lap first; she had no sooner unzipped his fly than Claudia, who was right-handed, made contact with his penis, which Emma already held in her hand. No heads turned; the three of them stared unblinkingly at the screen. Claudia politely withdrew her hand, but no farther than the inside of Jack's left thigh. Emma, in a conciliatory gesture, prodded his penis in Claudia's direction until the tip touched the back of Claudia's hand. Claudia put her hand back in his lap, holding both his penis and Emma's hand. Watching the film in this fashion gave Jack a two-hour erection.

After the movie, they went out and drank some beer. Jack didn't really like to drink. Emma bought the beer, but either Claudia or Jack could have. No one ever carded Claudia; although she was only nineteen, she looked like an older woman, not a college student. And ever since Jack had seen *Yojimbo*, no one had carded him. He was nineteen, almost twenty, but he'd adopted Toshiro Mifune's disapproving scowl, and he used a fair amount of gel in his hair. Emma approved of the look, the scowl especially, but Claudia occasionally complained about his shaving only every third day.

It was Toshiro Mifune's indignation that Jack chose to imitate—particularly in the beginning of *Yojimbo*, when the samurai comes to town and sees the dog trot by with a human hand in its mouth. Jack loved that outraged look Mifune gives the dog.

Emma had too much to drink, and Jack drove her car back to the farmhouse, with Emma and Claudia holding hands and making out in the backseat. "If you were back here, honey pie, we'd make out with you, too," Emma said.

Jack was used to Emma's lawlessness, her willingness to bend the rules, but Claudia's seeming complicity unnerved him. Though Emma was complicated—and she could be difficult—it was Claudia Jack couldn't figure out. Like him, she seemed to be biding her time; she held herself back, she seemed detached, she was always a little hard to read. Or was Claudia merely holding a mirror up to Jack, stymieing him in the same ways he stymied her?

Back at the farmhouse, after Emma had passed out, Claudia helped Jack carry Emma to her bedroom, where they undressed her and put her to bed. Emma was already snoring, but this failed to distract Claudia and Jack; they couldn't help noticing the perfect vagina tattooed on Emma's right hip.

"Exactly what is your relationship with Emma?" Claudia asked.

"I don't really know," Jack replied honestly.

"Boy, I'll say you don't!" Claudia said, laughing.

When they were in bed, Claudia asked him: "When did the penis-holding start? I mean with Emma. I know when it started with me."

Jack pretended not to remember exactly. "When I was eight or nine," he said. "Emma would have been fifteen or sixteen. Or maybe it was a little earlier. I might have been seven. Emma was maybe fourteen."

Claudia went on holding his penis, not saying anything. When he was almost asleep, she asked him: "Do you have any idea how weird that is, Jack?"

Michele Maher had made him sensitive to his alleged weirdness—as in *too* weird. Jack harbored no illusion that Claudia had mistaken him for the love of her life; surely Claudia was too smart to imagine for a moment that Jack thought *she* was the love of *his* life. But it hurt him that Claudia thought he was weird.

"*Too* weird?" Jack asked her.

"That depends, Jack."

He didn't like this game. *Depends on what?* he knew she wanted him to ask her. But he wouldn't ask—he already knew the answer. He held her breasts, he nuzzled her neck, but just as his penis was coming to life in her hand, Claudia let it go. "Why doesn't Emma want to have children?" she asked.

Well, Jack Burns was an actor—he knew a loaded question when he heard one. "Maybe she doesn't think she'll be a good mother," Jack ventured, still holding Claudia's breasts. The question was really about *him,* of course. Why didn't *he* want children? Because, if he turned out to be like his father, he would leave, he had told Claudia once. He didn't want to be the kind of father who left.

But this answer hadn't satisfied Claudia. Jack was well aware she wanted to have children. As an actress, Claudia hated her body; that she had "a body designed to have children" was the only positive thing she ever said about herself. She said this as if she meant it, too. To Jack, it didn't sound like an act. Clearly, in her mind, the kind of father Jack would turn out to be was Jack's problem.

"It depends on whether or not you want children, Jack," Claudia said.

Jack let go of her breasts and rolled over, turning his back to her in the bed. Claudia rolled toward him, wrapping her arm around his waist and once more holding his penis.

"We don't graduate from college for another two years," Jack pointed out to her.

"I don't mean I want children *now,* Jack."

He'd already told Claudia that he *never* wanted children. "Not till the day I discover that my dad has been a loving father to a child, or children, he *didn't* leave." That was how Jack had put it to her.

Was it any wonder Claudia held herself back from him?

Yet they had fun together—in summer stock, especially. The previous summer, they'd done *Romeo and Juliet* in a playhouse in the Berkshires. The older, veteran actors got all the main parts. Claudia was Juliet's understudy. The dull, flat-chested robot they cast as Juliet never missed a night's performance—not even a matinee. Jack had wanted to be Romeo—or, failing that, Mercutio—but because he'd been a wrestler and looked confrontational, they made him Tybalt, that cocky asshole.

Claudia was always taking their picture; maybe she thought that if there were sufficient photographic evidence of them as a couple, they might stay together. She had a camera with a delayed-shutter mechanism; she would set the timer and then run to get in the photo. (The obsessive picture-taking sometimes made Jack wonder if Claudia just *might* have mistaken him for the love of her life.)

After their visit to Emma, Claudia and Jack did a García Lorca play—*The House of Bernarda Alba*—at a summer playhouse in Connecticut. The setting was Spain, 1936. Claudia and Jack both played women. Jack had eaten some bad clams and was food-poisoned for one evening performance. There was no intermission. The director, who was also a woman, told him to "suck it up and wear a longer skirt." His understudy had a yeast infection, and the director was more sympathetic to her ailment than she was to Jack's. (There were nine women in the cast, plus Jack.)

He had terrible stomach cramps and diarrhea. In the grip of an alarmingly explosive episode, he flinched so violently that one of his falsies slipped out of his bra; he managed to trap it against his ribs with his elbow. Claudia later told him that he looked as if he were mocking the moment of the playwright's assassination in the Spanish Civil War; Jack was thankful García Lorca was not alive to suffer through his performance.

"What a learning experience!" Mr. Ramsey responded, when Jack wrote him about the long night of the bad clams.

Miss Wurtz would have been proud of him; never had he concentrated with such pinpoint accuracy on his audience of one. He could almost see his father in the audience. (It was the perfect play for William, Jack was thinking—all women!)

Claudia and Jack were both understudies that summer in *Cabaret,* their first musical. He was the understudy to the Emcee, a Brit who told Jack pointedly on opening night not to get his hopes up; he'd never been sick a day in his life. Jack's heart wasn't in the Emcee role, anyway. He would have been a better Sally Bowles than the woman who was cast as Sally—even better than Claudia, who was her understudy.

But it would have been too aggressive a moment in their relationship—had Jack auditioned for the Sally Bowles character and beaten out Claudia for the part. They spent a month singing "Tomorrow Belongs to Me" and "Maybe This Time" to each other—in the privacy of their boudoir, where all understudies shine.

But he and Claudia were cast as Kit Kat Girls in *Cabaret,* so they got to strut their stuff to an audience. Given the scant costume, not to mention the period—Berlin, 1929–30—Jack was a somewhat transparent transvestite, but the audience loved him. Claudia said she was jealous because he looked hotter than she did.

"You better be careful, Jack," Claudia warned him. It was the summer they were both twenty. "If you get any better in drag, no one's going to cast you as a guy anymore." (Under the circumstances, Jack thought it was better not to tell her how badly he had wanted the Sally Bowles part.)

How well he would remember that summer in Connecticut. When Sally Bowles and the Kit Kat Girls sang "Don't Tell Mama" and "Mein Herr," Jack was looking right at the audience; he saw their faces. They were staring at him, the transvestite Kit Kat Girl—not at Sally. They couldn't take their eyes off him. Every man in that audience made his skin crawl.

Both Claudia and Jack were good enough students to skip a few classes in order to attend the film festival in Toronto that September. Their teachers permitted them to write about the movies they saw, in place of the work they would miss—Jack's first and last adventure in film criticism, except at small dinner parties.

When he took Claudia to Daughter Alice to meet his mother for the first time, Jack was questioning Claudia's claim that she had seen Raul Julia coming out of a men's room at the Park Plaza. Alice immediately took Claudia's side. Jack knew that film festivals were full of such real or imagined sightings, but he wanted his mom and Claudia to like each other; he held his tongue.

Alice was tattooing a small scorpion on a young woman's abdomen. The scorpion's narrow, segmented tail was curled up over its back. The venomous stinger, at the tip of the tail, was directly under the girl's navel; the arachnid's pincers were poised above her pubic hair. The young woman was obviously disturbed—she would be a handful under the best of circumstances, Jack thought, although he held his tongue about that, too. He could see that Claudia was enthralled with the atmosphere of the tattoo parlor; he didn't want to be the voice of disbelief, about either the Raul Julia sighting or the forbidding location of the scorpion tattoo.

The film festival was good for Daughter Alice's business. Alice told them she'd been tattooing a guy who was a die-hard moviegoer when she saw Glenn Close walk by on the Queen Street sidewalk. Jack seriously doubted it. He didn't think Queen and Palmerston was a Glenn Close part of town, but all he said was: "I'm surprised Glenn didn't stop in for a Rose of Jericho."

Claudia, who was instantly fond of Alice—as Emma had said she would be—was angry at Jack for what she called his disrespectful tone of voice. This created some tension between Claudia and Jack, and they had different reactions to *My Beautiful Laundrette,* which Alice and Mrs. Oastler and Claudia loved. Jack didn't *hate* the film. All he said was: "I was expecting the laundrette to be a beautiful *woman.*"

"That would be a *laundress,* dear," his mom said.

"I thought the word for the place was a *launderette,* not a *laundrette,*" Jack said.

"God, you're *picky,*" Claudia told him.

"Talk about a 'disrespectful tone of voice'!" he said.

And Jack was less than thrilled to see *Desert Hearts,* which even Leslie Oastler described as a lesbian love story—she'd been dying to see it. (Alice visibly less so.) The film drew a crowd of women holding hands. Claudia, who wouldn't hold Jack's penis at *any* film they attended with Alice and Mrs. Oastler, wouldn't even hold his hand at *Desert Hearts.* It was as if Claudia were contemplating her own trip to Reno, without him; maybe Claudia imagined discovering herself with Helen Shaver, or something.

All Jack said was: "The characters are a little sketchy." This was enough to turn all three women against him: he was homophobic; he was threatened by lesbians. "I *like* Helen Shaver," he kept saying, but this didn't save him.

The festival marked the beginning of an Asian boom, some guy hitting on Claudia told her at a screening party. Jack thought it was cool to say nothing; he just kept his hand on Claudia's ass, in a clearly nonplatonic way. When Claudia went to the women's room, Jack gave the Asian-boom asshole his Toshiro Mifune scowl. The guy slunk away.

Alice and Leslie lit into Jack about being "too possessive." They loved Claudia, they told him. No woman likes to be touched in public—not to the degree that Jack touched Claudia, they said. (This advice from the couple who'd held hands and played footsie during Jack's groundbreaking performance in *A Mail-Order Bride in the Northwest Territories*!)

Jack had had it with going to the movies and the parties with his mother and Mrs. Oastler. That night, in bed, he complained to Claudia about it. They were staying in Emma's room. ("The bed's bigger—as you know, dear," his mom had reminded him.)

Claudia thought that Alice and Leslie were a cute couple. "It's obvious that they adore you," Claudia said. Perhaps Jack lacked the perspective to see this.

He decided to take Claudia to St. Hilda's—not only so she could see his old school, which had been so formative of his older-woman thing, but also to meet his favorite teachers. What a mistake! All the girls looked preternaturally young. (Of *course* they did—Claudia and Jack were *twenty*-year-olds!)

Jack took Claudia first to meet Mr. Malcolm, who always left school in a hurry—wheeling Mrs. Malcolm in her wheelchair ahead of him. Wheelchair Jane, who couldn't see Claudia, reached out and touched Claudia's hips, her waist, even her breasts. (A blind woman's audacity is like no other's, maybe.) "Following in his father's footsteps, isn't he?" she asked her husband.

Jack was still trying to explain this reference to Claudia when they encountered Mr. Ramsey emerging from the boys' washroom. "Jack Burns!" he cried, zipping up his fly. "Patron saint of mail-order brides!" *This* reference, Jack realized, would take somewhat longer to explain. Claudia seemed unnerved by her close proximity to a man so small who never stopped bouncing on the balls of his feet.

Mr. Ramsey insisted on bringing them to his after-school drama rehearsal of the day; the senior-school girls were doing *The Diary of Anne Frank*, which Jack knew brought bitter memories to Claudia. In junior high school, she had auditioned for the part of the doomed girl, but she had already looked too old. (Her boobs were too big—even then.)

Mr. Ramsey presented Jack to the girls as the best male St. Hilda's actor in memory—despite the fact that his reputation rested on his female roles. Claudia was introduced as Jack's actress friend. "They're here for the film festival!" Mr. Ramsey exclaimed, which led the star-struck girls to imagine that Claudia and Jack were promoting a new movie. Mr. Ramsey made it seem as if they were up-and-coming names in the industry.

Jack was reminded of his irritation with Claudia for refusing to let him pass her off as a famous Russian film star of the not-English-speaking variety. Her courage was not of the improvisational kind—without lines, she was lost. And not only did she always seem older than she was; she was also inclined to lie about her age. "I'm in my early thirties, and that's all I want to say about it," she would say. It was a good line, but it was bullshit—by ten years, and counting.

The St. Hilda's girls looked forlorn. Jack Burns was very much an object of their keenest desire, but he was with this voluptuous *woman* who made them feel sexually retarded. To make matters worse, Mr. Ramsey wanted Claudia and Jack to *perform* something. (Jack had written him that he and Claudia had been in plays together.)

Against Jack's better judgment, he let Claudia persuade him to sing a Kit Kat Girl number. "Mein Herr" was Claudia's choice, not Jack's; it was a little raunchy for St. Hilda's, he told her later. (In retrospect, in the context of the play the girls were rehearsing, the insensitivity of Claudia and Jack singing a song from that sleazy Nazi nightclub in Berlin took Jack's breath away.) And to make "Mein Herr" more confounding, they both sang it as if they were Sally Bowles, causing Claudia finally to realize how much Jack had wanted her part.

When they finished the lascivious song, Mr. Ramsey was a virtual pogo stick of enthusiasm. The poor girls swooned, or died of envy and embarrassment. Claudia said that she and Jack should let them all get back to *The Diary of Anne Frank.*

But Mr. Ramsey was pained to let them go. He wanted to know what they thought of the festival and the films they had seen. "Have you seen the Godard? *Hail Mary* or something," Mr. Ramsey said. "The Pope has condemned it!"

"Jack has condemned it without seeing it," Claudia said. "He hates Godard." Jack tried to look friendlier than Toshiro Mifune, if only for the sake of the mortified girls.

The young girl cast as Anne Frank was pushed forward to meet them. Claudia seemed fixated on her flat chest. Jack observed that the poor girl was terrified of them, as if they represented a blatant contradiction of Anne Frank's most memorable observation, which Claudia knew by heart and recited (without a hint of sarcasm) on the spot. " 'It's really a wonder that I haven't dropped all my ideals, because they seem so absurd and impossible to carry out. Yet I keep them, because in spite of everything I still believe that people are really good at heart.' "

"Marvelous!" Mr. Ramsey cried. "A trifle *deadpan* for Anne, perhaps, but marvelous!"

"We have to go," Claudia told him, mercifully.

The girls were all looking at Jack as if Claudia had been holding his penis in front of them. Claudia was looking at Jack as if not even Godard's *Hail Mary* could be as excruciatingly boring as this journey through time on his old stomping grounds.

Jack was actually tempted to see the Godard film, because the Catholics were up in arms about it and had threatened to protest the Toronto screening. But Claudia didn't like Godard any better than he did. (*Hail Mary* was an update of Christ's birth, this time to a virgin gas-station attendant and her cabdriver boyfriend.)

It was in this disturbed frame of mind—Claudia hating Jack for bringing her to his old school, Jack wishing that he had not come (or that he'd come alone)—that the sudden appearance of The Gray Ghost startled Claudia and Jack, just as Jack was about to show Claudia the chapel. Claudia made such an immediate impression on Mrs. McQuat that Jack's former fourth-grade teacher ushered them both up the center aisle and into the foremost pew, where she insisted they sit down; at least she didn't make them *kneel*.

Claudia was not religious and later told Jack she was offended by the stained-glass images of "those servile women attending to Jesus." Mrs. McQuat held Claudia's hand and Jack's; she asked them in a low whisper when they were going to be married. That Claudia and Jack were still *students* was a point lost on The Gray Ghost, who'd heard a rumor spreading like a forest fire through the girls at St. Hilda's—namely, that Jack Burns had been seen at the film festival in the company of an American movie star, apparently Claudia. He'd brought her to St. Hilda's to show her the chapel. The rumor was that Jack wanted to be married in the chapel of his old school, where he'd had such a formative experience.

"We haven't really made any plans," Jack said, not knowing how else to answer Mrs. McQuat's question.

"I'm never going to marry Jack," Claudia told The Gray Ghost. "I'm not marrying anybody who doesn't want to have children."

"Mercy!" Mrs. McQuat exclaimed. "Why . . . wouldn't you want to have . . . *children* . . . Jack?"

"You know," he answered.

"He says it's all about his father," Claudia told her.

"You're not . . . *still* worrying . . . you'll turn out like him . . . are you, Jack?" The Gray Ghost asked.

"It's a reasonable suspicion," he said.

"Nonsense!" Mrs. McQuat cried. "Do you know . . . what *I* think?" she asked Claudia, patting her hand. "I think it's just an excuse . . . not to marry *anybody*!"

"That's what I think, too," Claudia said.

Jack felt like Jesus in the stained glass; everywhere he went in Toronto, women were ganging up on him. He must have looked like he wanted to leave, because The Gray Ghost took hold of his wrist in that not-uncertain way of hers.

"You aren't leaving without seeing . . . Miss *Wurtz* . . . are you?" she asked him. "Mercy, she'll be . . . *crushed* if she learns you were here . . . and you didn't see her!"

"Oh."

"You should take Caroline . . . to the film festival, Jack," Mrs. McQuat went on. "She's too *timid* to go to the movies . . . by herself."

The Gray Ghost was always the voice of Jack's conscience. Later he would be ashamed that he never told her how much she meant to him, or even what a good teacher she was.

Mrs. McQuat would *die* in the St. Hilda's chapel—after having disciplined one of Miss Wurtz's misbehaving third graders, whom she'd faced away from the altar with his back turned to God. Mrs. McQuat dropped dead in the center aisle, a passageway she had made her own, with her back turned to God and with only God's eyes and those of the third grader who was being punished to see her fall. (That poor kid—talk about a *formative* experience!)

Miss Wurtz must have come running as soon as she heard—*crying* all the way.

Jack didn't go to The Gray Ghost's funeral. He learned she had died only *after* the funeral, when his mother told him something about Mrs. McQuat that he was surprised he hadn't guessed. She was no *Mrs.* anybody; no one had ever married her. Like Miss Wurtz, she was a *Miss* McQuat—for life. But something in her combat-nurse nature refused to acknowledge that she was unmarried, which in those days obdurately implied you were unloved.

Jack used to wonder why The Gray Ghost had trusted his mom with this secret. They weren't friends. Then he remembered Mrs. McQuat telling him not to complain about a woman who knew how to keep a secret—meaning Alice. (Meaning herself as well.)

It was only a mild shock to discover that The Gray Ghost had been a Miss instead of a Mrs. In retrospect, Jack wouldn't have been surprised to learn that Mrs. McQuat—as she preferred to be called—had been a *man*.

Alice and Mrs. Oastler attended The Gray Ghost's funeral, which was in the St. Hilda's chapel. Being a St. Hilda's Old Girl, Leslie was informed of all the school news. As for Alice, she told Jack she went out of "nostalgia," which he would remember thinking at the time was an uncharacteristic word for her to use—not to mention an uncharacteristic feeling for her to have.

Alice was vague about who else was in attendance. "Caroline, of course." She didn't mean Caroline French—she meant Miss Wurtz. The *other* Caroline didn't attend, and Jack knew that her twin, Gordon, was absent. (Gordon was dead—the aforementioned boating accident had precluded his attendance.)

Jack asked his mother if she'd been aware of blanket-sucking sounds, or moaning, during the funeral; by his mom's puzzled response, he knew that the Booth twins and Jimmy Bacon had skipped the event, or they'd been out of town.

Lucinda Fleming, with or without her mysterious rage, made no reference to The Gray Ghost's passing in her annual Christmas letter; if Lucinda had gone to the funeral, Jack was sure she would have told everyone about it. And he knew Roland Simpson wasn't there—Roland was already in jail.

The faculty who were in attendance are easily imagined. Miss Wong, mourning in broken bits and pieces, as if the hurricane she was born in showed itself only in squalls—or only at funerals. Mr. Malcolm, guiding his wife in her wheelchair; the poor man was forever trying to steer Wheelchair Jane around the looming obstacles of her madness. Mr. Ramsey, too restless to sit in a pew, would have been bouncing on the balls of his feet at the back of the chapel. And Miss Wurtz—my goodness, how she must have cried!

"Caroline was *overcome*," Alice told Jack.

He could see Miss Wurtz *overcome* as clearly as if she were still leaning over his incorrect math and he were still breathing her in. (In Jack's dreams, The Wurtz's mail-order bra and panties were always properly in place—no matter how *overcome* she was.)

Yet how could Miss Wurtz have gone on being the St. Hilda's grade-three teacher? How could she have managed her classroom without The Gray Ghost there to bail her out?

It was Leslie Oastler who told Jack that, upon Mrs. McQuat's death, Miss Wurtz became a *better* teacher; finally, Miss Wurtz had to learn *how.* But at The Gray Ghost's funeral, there was no stopping The Wurtz. She cried and cried without hope of rescue. Miss Wurtz must have cried until all her tears were gone, and then—one breakthrough day in her grade-three classroom—she never cried again.

Jack thought Caroline Wurtz must still be saying in her nightly prayers, "God bless you, Mrs. McQuat."

As Jack occasionally remembered to say in his, although not as often—and never as fervently—as he used to say, without cease, "Michele Maher, Michele Maher, Michele Maher."

19

Claudia, Who Would Haunt Him

Jack would never entirely forgive The Gray Ghost for suggesting that he and Claudia take Miss Wurtz to the film festival in Toronto in the fall of 1985. The Wurtz was in her forties at the time—not that much older than Alice in years, but noticeably older in appearance and stamina. Possibly she had always been too thin, too fragile, but now what was most *Wurtz*-like about her was a gauntness Jack associated with illness. Miss Wurtz was still beautiful in her damaged way, but she not only looked a little unhealthy; she seemed ashamed of something, although Jack couldn't imagine what she had ever done to be ashamed of. Perhaps there'd been a long-ago scandal—something so fleeting that it was barely remembered by others, although the memory of it was alive and throbbing in The Wurtz.

Her appearance seemed contrary to her restrained, even abstemious character, because what Caroline Wurtz most resembled was an actress of a bygone era—a once-famous woman who'd become overlooked. At least this was the impression Caroline made at the film festival, where Claudia and Jack took her to the premiere of Paul Schrader's *Mishima*. "Remind me who Mishima is," Miss Wurtz said as they approached the theater.

The ever-persistent photographers, who often snapped pictures of Claudia—because Claudia was such a babe and the photographers had convinced themselves that she must be *someone*—turned their attention to Miss Wurtz instead. She was overdressed for the film-festival crowd, like a woman who found herself at a rock concert when she'd thought she was going to an opera. Jack was wearing black jeans and a black linen jacket with a white T-shirt. ("An L.A. look," in Claudia's estimation, though she'd never been to Los Angeles.)

The younger photographers, especially, assumed that Caroline Wurtz was *someone*—possibly someone who'd made her last movie before any of them had been born. "You'd have thought she was Joan Crawford," Claudia said later. Claudia was poured into a shimmery dress with spaghetti straps, but she was a good sport about the photographers being all over The Wurtz.

"Goodness," Miss Wurtz whispered, "they must think you're already famous, Jack." It was sweet how she believed the fuss was about *him*. "I'm completely convinced you soon will be," The Wurtz added, squeezing his hand. "And you, too, dear," she said to Claudia, who squeezed her hand back.

"I thought she was *dead*!" an older man said. Jack didn't catch the name of the actress from yesteryear for whom Miss Wurtz had been mistaken.

"Is Mishima a dancer?" Caroline asked.

"No, a writer—" Jack started to say, but Claudia cut him off.

"He *was* a writer," Claudia corrected him.

And an actor, a director, and a militarist *nutcase,* which Jack didn't have time to say. They were swept inside the theater, where they were ushered to the reserved seats—all because of the prevailing conviction that Caroline Wurtz was not a third-grade teacher but a movie star.

Jack heard the word "European," probably in reference to Miss Wurtz's dress, which was a pale-peach color and might have fit her once—perhaps in Edmonton. Now it appeared that The Wurtz was diminished by the dress, which would have been more suitable for a prom than a premiere. The dress was something Mrs. Adkins might have donated for Drama Night at Redding, yet it had a gauzy quality, like underwear, which reminded Jack of the mail-order lingerie he had dressed Miss Wurtz in—if only in his imagination.

"Mishima is Japanese," Jack was trying to explain.

"He *was*—" Claudia interjected.

"He's no longer Japanese?" Caroline asked.

They couldn't answer her before the movie began—a stylish piece of work, wherein the scenes from Mishima's life (shot in black and white) were intercut with color dramatizations of his fictional work. Jack had never cared much about Mishima as a writer, but he liked him as a lunatic; his ritualistic suicide, in 1970, was the film's dramatic conclusion.

Throughout the movie, Miss Wurtz held Jack's hand; this gave him a hard-on, which Claudia noticed. Claudia would not hold his penis, or venture anywhere near his lap; she sat with her arms folded on her considerable bosom, and never flinched at Mishima's self-disemboweling, which caused Caroline to dig her nails into Jack's wrist. In the flickering light from the movie screen, he regarded the small, fishhook-shaped scar on her throat, above her fetching birthmark. In her preternatural thinness, Miss Wurtz had a visible pulse in her throat—an actual heartbeat in close proximity to her scar. This was a pounding that could only be quieted by a kiss, Jack thought—not that he would have dared to kiss The Wurtz, not even if Claudia hadn't been there.

"Goodness!" Caroline exclaimed as they were leaving the theater. (She was as breathless as Mrs. McQuat, as desirable as Mrs. Adkins.) "That was certainly . . . *ambitious!*"

It was about four o'clock in the afternoon when they exited into the mob of Catholic protesters who'd come to the wrong theater. The protesters were there on their knees, chanting to an endless "Hail Mary" that repeated itself over a ghetto blaster. Jack knew in an instant that the kneeling Catholics thought they were emerging from a screening of Godard's *Hail Mary;* the Catholics had come to protest *Mishima* by mistake.

Not only was Miss Wurtz unprepared for the spectacle; she didn't understand that the protests were in error. "Naturally, the suicide has upset them—I'm not surprised," she told Claudia and Jack. "I once knew why Catholics make such a fuss about suicide, but I've forgotten. They were all in a knot about Graham Greene's *The Heart of the Matter,* as I remember. But I think they got themselves all worked up over *The Power and the Glory* and *The End of the Affair,* too."

Claudia and Jack just looked at each other. What was the point of even mentioning the Godard film to Caroline?

A TV journalist wanted to interview her, which Miss Wurtz seemed to think was perfectly normal. "What do you think of all this?" the journalist asked Jack's former grade-three teacher. "The film, the controversy—"

"I thought the film was quite a . . . *drama,*" The Wurtz declared. "It was overlong and at times hard to grasp, and not always as *satisfying* as it was *engaging*. The cinematography was beautiful, and the music—well, whether one likes it or not, it was *sweeping*."

This was more than the journalist had bargained for; he was clearly more interested in the kneeling Catholics and the ceaseless "Hail Mary" on the ghetto blaster than he was in the *Mishima* movie. "But the *controversy*—" he started to say, trying to steer Miss Wurtz to the fracas of the moment (as journalists do).

"Oh, who cares about that?" Caroline said dismissively. "If the Catholics want to flagellate themselves over a suicide, let them! I remember when they had a hissy fit about fish on Fridays!"

It would be on the six o'clock news. Alice and Leslie Oastler were watching television, and there was Miss Wurtz holding forth in her pale-peach dress—Claudia and Jack on either side of her. It was almost as much fun as passing Claudia off as a Russian film star, and Caroline was thoroughly enjoying herself, though she wasn't in on the joke.

The moviegoers, meaning the *Mishima* crowd, were in no mood to be greeted by kneeling Catholics and "Hail Mary"— not with Mishima's disembowelment fresh on their minds. (Nor would Mishima have been amused, Jack thought; at least when he was disemboweling himself, he looked like a pretty serious guy.)

Claudia and Jack took Miss Wurtz to a party. They had no trouble crashing parties; the bouncers wouldn't have kept Claudia out of a men's room, if she'd wanted to go into one. Claudia said they got into parties because Jack looked like a movie star, but Claudia was the reason. With Miss Wurtz in tow, it was clear they got in because of *her*. In fact, they were leaving one such party when a young man approached Caroline in a fawning fashion; he'd snatched a flower from a vase on the bar and pressed it into her hand. "I love your work!" he told her, disappearing into the crowd.

"I freely admit I don't remember him at all," Miss Wurtz told Jack. "I can't be expected to recognize every grade-three boy I ever taught," she said to Claudia. "They were not all as memorable as Jack!"

Claudia and Jack were quite certain that the young man had not been referring to Caroline's *teaching* career. But how to explain all this to The Wurtz—well, why would Claudia or Jack have bothered?

In the lineup of limos outside a restaurant, Jack recognized an old friend among the drivers. "Peewee!" he cried.

The big Jamaican got out of his limo and embraced Jack on the sidewalk, lifting him off his feet. That was when the *Hail Mary* protesters must have assumed that Jack was the cabdriver boyfriend in the Godard film—the Joseph character—which made Claudia, in their demented eyes, the pregnant gas-station attendant who was an updated version of the Virgin Mary. (God knows who they thought Miss Wurtz was.)

"Jack Burns, you are *already* a star, mon!" Peewee exclaimed, hugging him so hard that he couldn't breathe.

The Catholics, crawling around on their knees, were an unsettling experience for Claudia, and Caroline was fed up with their zealotry. "Oh, why don't you go home and read his *books*!" Miss Wurtz told one of the kneelers. She was a young woman whose face was streaked with grime and tears. Jack could see her thinking: *Christ was a writer?*

The other Catholics kept repeating the infuriating "Hail Mary."

"Quick, get in the car, Jack!" Peewee said. He was already holding the door open for Claudia and Caroline.

"It's Mrs. Wicksteed's driver, dear—don't be alarmed," Miss Wurtz told Claudia. (As if Mrs. Wicksteed were still in need of a driver!) But Claudia was having her legs held, at the thighs, by a kneeling Catholic. "Let her go, you craven imbecile," Caroline told the Catholic. "Don't you get it? He killed himself because he wanted his life to merge with his art."

Miss Wurtz meant Mishima, of course, but the Catholic who reluctantly released Claudia thought that Caroline was talking about *Christ.* He was an indignant-looking man—bald, middle-aged—in a long-sleeved white dress shirt of a thin see-through material, with a pen that had leaked in his breast pocket. He looked like a deranged income-tax auditor.

Peewee managed to get Claudia into the car, but Miss Wurtz was facing down the mob of kneelers. "The man was Japanese and he wanted to off himself," she told them in a huff. "Just get over it!"

To a one, the Catholics looked as if no number of repetitions of "Hail Mary" could redeem such a slur on the unfortunate Christ as this. Jesus was *Japanese*?

Jack put an arm around Caroline's slender waist as if she were his dance partner. "Miss Wurtz, they're all insane," he whispered in her ear. "Get in the car."

"My goodness—you've become so worldly, Jack," she told him, stooping to get into the backseat of the limo. Claudia caught her by the hand and pulled her inside; Peewee shoved Jack inside after her, closing the door.

One of the protesters had wrapped her arms around Peewee's knees, but when he began to walk with her, dragging her to the driver's-side door of the limo, she thought better of it and let him go. Jack had no idea which *actual* movie star had Peewee for a limo driver that evening—Peewee claimed that he couldn't remember—but Peewee drove Miss Wurtz home first, then Claudia and Jack.

Jack had never known where The Wurtz lived, but he was unsurprised when Peewee stopped the limo at a large house on Russell Hill Road, which was within walking distance of St. Hilda's. Jack *was* somewhat surprised when Miss Wurtz asked Peewee to drive around to the back entrance, where an outside staircase led to her small, rented apartment.

Where had the money for Caroline's once-fashionable clothes come from? If it had been family money from Edmonton, it must have been spent. Had she ever had a suitor, or a secret lover with good taste? If there'd ever been a well-to-do ex-boyfriend—or more improbably, an ex-husband—he was long gone, clearly.

Miss Wurtz would not let Jack accompany her up the stairs to her modest rooms. Possibly she did not think it proper to bring a young man to her apartment; yet she allowed Claudia to go with her. Jack sat in the limo with Peewee and watched them turn on some lights.

Later, when Jack pressed Claudia to describe The Wurtz's apartment, Claudia became irritated. "I didn't snoop around," she said. "She's an older woman—she has too much stuff, things she should have thrown away. Out-of-date magazines, junk like that."

"A TV?"

"I didn't see one, but I wasn't looking."

"Photographs? Any pictures of *men*?"

"Jesus, Jack! Have you got the *hots* for her, or something?" Claudia asked.

They lay in Emma's bed—bereft of the stuffed animals, which either Emma or Mrs. Oastler had disposed of. Jack couldn't remember a single one of them—nor could he dispel from his memory that Emma had taught him how to masturbate as he lay in her arms in the very same bed.

Given Claudia's bitchy mood, Jack decided to spare her *that* detail.

The parties and intrigues of the film festival notwithstanding, Claudia and Jack spent the lion's share of their time in Toronto at Daughter Alice—at least Claudia did. Jack frequently escaped the tattoo parlor, preferring the clientele in the nearby Salvation Army store to many of his mother's devotees.

Aberdeen Bill had been a maritime man—like Charlie Snow and Sailor Jerry, like Tattoo Ole and Tattoo Peter and Doc Forest. They were Alice's mentors. But the tattoo world had changed; while Daughter Alice still did the occasional Man's Ruin, or the broken heart that sustains a sailor for long months at sea, a new vulgarity exhibited itself on the skin of young men seeking to be marked for life.

Gone was the romance of those Baltic and North Sea ports— and the steady sound of his mom's tattoo machine, which had lulled Jack to sleep as a child. Gone were those brave girls in the Hotel Torni: Ritva, whose breasts he never saw, and Hannele's unshaven armpits and her striking birthmark—that crumpled top hat over her navel, the color of a wine stain, the shape of Florida.

Jack had once been so bold as to march up to anyone and ask: "Do you have a tattoo?" In the restaurant of the Hotel Bristol, he'd told that beautiful girl: "I have the room and the equipment, if you have the time." (And to think it was *his* idea for his mom to offer the littlest soldier a free tattoo!)

In his sleep, Jack heard the vast organ in the Oude Kerk playing to the prostitutes at night; even awake, if he shut his eyes, he could feel the thick, waxed rope and the smooth, wooden handrail on the other side of the old church's twisting stairs.

But (especially in Claudia's company) the tattoo culture on display at Daughter Alice made Jack ashamed of his mother's "art"; and many of her customers, the seeming lowlifes of Queen

Street, filled him with foreboding. The old maritime tattoos, the sentiments of sailors collecting souvenirs on their bodies, had been replaced by tasteless displays of hostility and violence and evil. The skinheads with their biker insignia—skulls spurting blood, flames licking the corners of the skeletons' eye sockets.

There were naked, writhing women who would have made Tattoo Ole blush; even Ladies' Man Madsen might have looked away. (More than an inverted eyebrow indicated their pubic hair.) And there was all the tribal memorabilia. Claudia was fascinated by some pimply kid from Kitchener, Ontario, getting a full *moko*—the Maori facial tattoo. On her hip, which she proudly bared for Claudia, the kid's emaciated girlfriend had a *koru*—those spirals like the head of a fern.

Jack took Claudia aside and said to her: "Generally speaking, attractive people don't get tattooed." But this wasn't strictly true; Jack was speaking *too* generally. His dislike of the scene at Daughter Alice caused him to overstate his case.

No sooner had he spoken than a gay bodybuilder appeared; he must have been a fashion model. He gave Claudia the most cursory once-over and flirted shamelessly with Jack. "I just stopped in for a little *alteration,* Alice," the bodybuilder said, smiling at Jack. "But if I knew in advance when your handsome son was going to be here, I would come by and be altered every day."

His name was Edgar; Alice and Claudia thought he was charming and amusing, but Jack made a point of looking away. Tattooed on one of the bodybuilder's shoulder blades was the photographic likeness of the cowboy Clint Eastwood with his signature thin cigar. On Edgar's other shoulder blade was the tattoo in need of altering—an evidently Satanic rendition of Christ's crucifixion, in which Jesus is chained in figure-four fashion to a motorcycle wheel. The alteration Edgar required was some indication that Christ had been "roughed up"— a scratch and a drop of blood on one cheek, perhaps, or a wound in the area of the rib cage.

"Maybe both," Alice said.

"You don't think that would be too vulgar?" Edgar asked.

"It's your tattoo, Edgar," Alice replied.

Possibly it was Claudia's love of all things theatrical that enamored her to Daughter Alice's world. To Jack, if Edgar wasn't ugly, his tattoos were—and Edgar himself was certainly *vulgar.* To Jack, almost everything at Daughter Alice was uglier than ugly, and the ugliness was intentional—your skin not merely marked for life but *maimed.*

"You're just a snob," Claudia told him.

Well, yes and no. The tattoo world, which had not once frightened Jack when he was four, terrified him at twenty. Here was Jack Burns, affecting Toshiro Mifune's scowl—the samurai's condemning look at a dog trotting past with a human hand in its mouth—while the tattoo scene at Daughter Alice reflected far worse behavior than that dog's.

Once upon a time, the maritime world had been the gateway to all that was foreign and new; but this was no longer true. Now tattoos were drug-induced—psychedelic gibberish and hallucinogenic horror. The new tattoos radiated sexual anarchy; they worshiped death.

"*May you stay forever young,*" Bob Dylan sang, and Alice had more than sung along with Bob; she'd embraced this philosophy without realizing that the young people around her were not the hippies and flower children of her day.

Of course there were the collectors, the sad ink addicts with their bodies-in-progress—the old crazies, like William Burns, on the road to discovering the full-body chill—but Jack chiefly detested *his* generation, now in their late teens or early twenties. He hated the pierced-lip guys—sometimes with pierced eyelids and tongues. He loathed the girls with their pierced nipples and navels—even their *labia*! The people *Jack's* age who hung out at Daughter Alice were certifiable freaks and losers.

But Alice made them tea and coffee, and she played her favorite music for them; some of them brought their own music, which was harsher than hers. Daughter Alice was a hangout. Not everyone was there to get a tattoo, but you had to have been tattooed to feel comfortable hanging around there.

Jack saw Krung once—he stopped in for a cup of tea. The Bathurst Street gym was gone; it had become a health-food store.

"Gym rats always gotta find a new ship, Jackie," Krung said. He sized up Claudia with a lingering glance; he told Jack that he thought she had the hips to be a formidable kickboxer.

Another day, Chenko came by; he walked with a cane, but Jack was happy to see him and wished he'd stayed longer. Even with the cane, Chenko was more protection to Alice than she had most of the time.

Chenko was courteous to Claudia, but he made no mention to Jack of her potential as a wrestler. He would never get over Emma, Chenko said sadly—meaning more than the fact that his separated sternum had not entirely recovered from her lateral drop.

The lost kids with no money came to Daughter Alice and watched Alice work; they were trying to find the cash and making up their minds about which tattoo they would get next. The old ink addicts dropped in to show themselves off; some of them appeared to be rationing what remained of their bodies, because they had little skin left for another tattoo. (It drove Jack crazy that Claudia called them "romantics.")

"The saddest cases," Alice said, "are the *almost* full-bodies."

But were they *almost* cold? Jack wondered. He couldn't look at them without imagining his dad. Did William Burns have any skin left for that one last note?

Jack could have predicted that Claudia would get a tattoo, but he pretended to be surprised when she announced her decision. "Just don't get one where it will show onstage," he said.

There was a movable curtain Alice rolled around on casters; like those enclosures for hospital beds in recovery rooms, this curtain sealed off the customer who was being *intimately* tattooed. Claudia wanted her tattoo high up—on the inside of her right thigh, where she chose the Chinaman's signature scepter. It was Jack's personal favorite, Claudia knew, symbolizing "everything as you wish."

"Forget about it," his mom had told him, when he'd said it was the best of the tattoos she'd learned from the Chinaman. But Alice raised no objection to giving one to Claudia.

When Jack was at Redding, he'd briefly benefited from the exotic impression he gave his fellow schoolboys of his mother—the *famous* tattoo artist. (As if, if she *weren't* famous, there could be little that was exotic about her profession.) Now his mom *was* famous—in her small, Queen Street way—and Jack was embarrassed by Daughter Alice and the general seediness, the depraved fringe, that tattooing represented to him.

But what else could his mother have done? She had tried to protect Jack from the tattoo world. She'd made it clear that he wasn't welcome at the Chinaman's, and it hadn't been Alice's fault that Jack became her virtual apprentice when she tattooed her way through those Baltic and North Sea ports in search of William—excepting those nights when Ladies' Man Lars tucked the boy into bed in Copenhagen.

Now, ironically, at the same time Alice seemed to be proud of her work—and of being her own boss in her own shop—Jack was growing ashamed of her. Claudia was right to criticize Jack for this, but Claudia hadn't been there in those years when his mother was turning her back on him.

Jack made matters worse by objecting to his mom's apprentice observing Claudia's tattoo-in-progress. What was the curtain *for,* if this guy was permitted to see the scepter? The tattoo almost touched Claudia's *pubes*!

He was a young guy from New Zealand. "Alice's kiwi boy," Mrs. Oastler called him. Leslie didn't like him, nor did he appeal to Jack. He was from Wellington, and he taught Alice some Maori stuff. Like her other young apprentices, he wouldn't stay long—a couple of months, at most. Then another apprentice would come; he was always someone who could teach her one or two things, while she had much more to teach him. (That was how the tattoo business worked; that part hadn't changed.)

Well before the end of the 1980s, because of AIDS, every knowledgeable tattoo artist in Canada and the United States was wearing rubber gloves. Jack could never get used to his mom in those gloves. Her shop was not an especially sanitary-looking place, yet here she was with her hands resembling a doctor's or a nurse's. When everything went right, tattooing wasn't exactly blood work.

But at Daughter Alice, some things stayed the same: the pigment in those little paper cups, the many uses of Vaseline, the strangely *dental* sound the needles made in the electric machine, the smell of penetrated skin—and the coffee, and the tea, and the honey in that sticky jar. And over it all, *Bob,* still howling—still complaining about this or that, prophesying doom or the next new thing.

"Like the pigment of a tattoo," Alice said, "Bob Dylan gets under your skin."

While Claudia was getting her scepter, Alice was playing "It's All Over Now, Baby Blue." Gritting her teeth, Claudia probably didn't notice; to Jack, a part of her mystery was that Claudia had not let Bob (or anyone else) get under *her* skin.

Some pothead was putting honey in his *coffee;* maybe he thought it was tea. His head was bobbing up and down like one of those distracting dashboard toys. He was from "somewhere in the Maritimes," he told Jack—as if the exact city or town had disowned him, or he'd banished it from what was left of his drugged memory. He had a tattoo of a green-and-red lobster on one forearm. The creature looked half cooked—therefore inadvisable to eat.

Bob wailed away.

> *Yonder stands your orphan with his gun,*
> *Crying like a fire in the sun.*

The sign in the Queen Street window that advertised Daughter Alice was painted wood. "As cheerful as sunny Leith, where the sun never shines," Alice said of the colorful sign. It had a seaside feeling to it, as if Daughter Alice were the name of a ship or a port of call. "Daughter Alice is a maritime name," Alice always said—coming, as it did, from Copenhagen and Tattoo Ole.

"*All your seasick sailors, they are rowing home,*" Bob Dylan sang.

Or they're rowing *here,* Jack thought. He went to have a look at Claudia behind the curtain; she smiled at him, clenching her fists to her sides. "The scepter is a Buddhist symbol," Alice was saying softly, while the tattoo needles danced on Claudia's thigh and she winced in pain. (Jack knew that the inner side of limbs hurt more than the outer.) "The shape of the scepter is modeled on the magic fungus of immortality," Alice went on.

A mushroom of immortality! What next? Jack turned away. The rubber gloves really bothered him. He preferred to watch the pothead from the Maritimes; the guy looked as if he were getting high on the honey in his coffee. This was the trip to Toronto that would convince Jack Burns it would never be his true home.

"*Forget the dead you've left, they will not follow you,*" Bob sang—as always, with the utmost authority. Bob got a lot right, but he was wrong about that. As Jack would discover, *everything* followed you.

The scepter high on her inner thigh made lovemaking uncomfortable for Claudia during their remaining days in Toronto, but

Jack was increasingly aware of Claudia holding him in disfavor; even without the new tattoo, Claudia might have been disinclined to make love to him. (That they were sleeping in Emma's bed didn't help.) They left Toronto before the film festival's closing night.

Jack could tell that Claudia was disheartened; the pettiness of their bickering had worn them both down. And her new tattoo chafed when she walked. With Mrs. Oastler's permission, Claudia had borrowed one of Emma's skirts; it was way too big for her, but she could walk in it with her legs wide apart, as if she were wearing a diaper.

Looking back, Jack found the retrospective material at the film festival more interesting than most of the featured competition. The one movie that Claudia and Jack had seen alone was Fassbinder's *The Marriage of Maria Braun*. Jack loved that film.

Hanna Schygulla is the soldier's wife who makes such a success of herself in postwar Germany. There are worse things than watching Hanna Schygulla while a woman holds your penis. The problem was, although this was the first and only occasion at the film festival when Claudia held his penis, Jack had seen *The Marriage of Maria Braun* with Emma when he was fourteen. (They were in the cinema in Durham; it was his first year at Exeter.)

The comparison was disconcerting, and it was a premonition of a life-changing experience: Jack realized that he liked the way Emma held his penis better than he liked the way anyone else held it. (Of course he still had hopes for Michele Maher one day.)

"Is it me or Hanna?" Claudia had whispered in his ear, noting the little guy's enthusiastic response. But Jack knew it was neither Claudia nor Fräulein Schygulla who provoked such an uplifting of the little guy's spirits. It was his memory of Emma holding his penis when he was all of fourteen.

Jack knew from that moment in *The Marriage of Maria Braun* that he and Claudia were merely marking time; they were just going through the paces, like a married couple who knew the divorce was pending.

His parting of the ways with Claudia had been set in motion by that trip to Iowa to visit Emma the previous spring. "The children conversation," as Claudia called it. They had continued on a downward path at the Toronto film festival. And when they drove back from Toronto, things got even worse.

They went home a different route than they'd come; it wasn't the best way to go, but it was a boring drive no matter how you did it. They drove to Kingston, Ontario, and crossed the St. Lawrence at Gananoque; the bridge took them into New York State at Alexandria Bay. At U.S. Customs, Jack presented his student visa and his Canadian passport. Claudia handed the customs guy her American passport. Jack was driving the Volvo. Claudia's new tattoo was bothering her; she didn't want to drive.

She was still wearing Emma's overlarge skirt, which Mrs. Oastler had insisted she take with her. "Emma will be several sizes too big for it the next time she's home, anyway," Leslie had said pessimistically. "You look better in it than Emma does, Claudia—even though it's *enormous* on you."

For most of the ride, Claudia sat with the skirt pulled up to her waist—airing the Chinese scepter, which she kept rubbing with moisturizer. Her skin was a little red around the edges of the tattoo, and she was tired of hearing that the inner skin of limbs is tender.

When Jack stopped the car at the border crossing, Claudia properly lowered Emma's skirt. The customs agent looked them over. "We were visiting my mother, who lives in Toronto," Jack told him, unasked. "We saw some movies at the film festival."

"Are you bringing anything back from Canada?" the customs agent inquired.

"Nope," Claudia said.

"Not even some Canadian beer?" the guy asked Claudia; he smiled at her. She was fantastic-looking, really.

"I don't usually drink beer, and Jack is always watching his weight," Claudia told him.

"So you've got nothing to declare?" the customs agent asked Jack, more sternly.

Jack didn't know what got into him. ("I just felt like fooling around," he would tell Claudia later, but there was more to it than that.)

It was a close-up opportunity—Jack gave the guy his furtive look. He did furtive pretty well; it was a look he'd acquired from observing certain kinds of dogs, especially craven and sneaky dogs. "Well—" Jack started to say, interrupting himself by looking *furtively* at Claudia. "We don't have to declare the Chinese scepter, do we?" he asked her. Oh, what a look she gave him!

"The *what*?" the customs agent said.

"A royal mace, or sometimes it's a staff—in this case, a short sword," Jack went on. "It's a ceremonial emblem of authority."

"It's *Chinese*?" the guy asked. "Is it very *old*?"

"Yes, *very*—it's *Buddhist,* actually," Jack told him.

"I better have a look at it," the customs agent said.

"It's a tattoo," Claudia told him. "I don't have to declare a *tattoo,* do I?"

Why had Jack done this to her? He loved Claudia—well, he *liked* her, anyway. Jack had not seen Claudia look so disappointed in him since she discovered the photographs of Emma naked; these were the old photos Emma sent to him when he was regularly beating off at Redding. They were photos of Emma at seventeen. Charlotte Barford had taken them. Claudia made Jack throw them away, but he kept one.

"Let me be sure it's just a tattoo," the customs guy said to Claudia. "I've never seen a Chinese scepter."

"Do you have a female colleague?" Claudia asked the guy. "*She* can see it."

"It's in a rather *intimate* location," Jack pointed out.

"Just a minute," the customs agent said. He left them sitting in the car and went off to find a female colleague; there was a building with what looked like offices, where the agent momentarily disappeared.

"You are so immature, Jack," Claudia said. He remembered that evening in the Oastler mansion when his mom had made a similar point.

"Penis, penis, penis—" Jack started to say, but he stopped. The customs guy was returning with a stout black woman. Claudia got out of the car and went into the office building with the female customs agent while Jack waited in the car.

"What did you do that for?" the customs guy asked him.

"We haven't been getting along lately," Jack admitted.

"Well, this'll really help," the guy said.

When Claudia came back to the car, she gave Jack her violated look and they drove on. For those first few miles, when they were back in the United States, Jack felt exhilarated without knowing why.

Canada was Jack's homeland, his country of origin, yet he

was elated to be back in America, where he felt more at home. Why was that? he wondered. Wasn't he Canadian? Was it Jack's rejection of his mother and her tattoo world that made him turn his back on his native land?

Claudia wouldn't speak to him for about three hundred miles. She had once again hiked Emma's skirt to her waist, exposing the tattoo of the Chinese scepter on her right inner thigh, where Jack could see it with a downcast, sideways glance at her lap. It was one of very few tattoos he ever saw that he was tempted to get himself, but not on his inner thigh. He was thinking about where on his body he might one day get a tattoo of that very same Chinese scepter, when Claudia, finally, spoke.

By that time, they were in Vermont—about a hundred miles from where they were going, in New Hampshire. When Claudia saw Jack glance at her crotch—at her brand-new Chinese scepter, specifically—she said: "I got the damn tattoo for you, you know."

"I know," Jack said. "I *like* it. I really do." Claudia knew that he liked the tattoo *and* the special place she put it. "I'm sorry about what I did at the border," Jack told her. "I really am."

"I'm over it, Jack. It took a while, but I'm over it. I'm sorrier about other things," she said.

"Oh."

"Is that all you can say?"

"I'm sorry," he repeated.

"It's not just that you'll never have children," she told him. "You'll go on blaming your father's genes for the fact that you'll never stay with the same woman—not for long, anyway."

It was Jack's turn to say nothing for the next hundred miles. And to make a point of not responding to someone is another acting opportunity.

Jack soon would make a point of not responding to The Gray Ghost, too. A letter came from her not long after he and Claudia were back in New Hampshire. The Gray Ghost made merely a passing reference to Claudia's "extraordinary beauty"—Mrs. McQuat also referred to Claudia as his "reluctant bride." But neither Claudia herself nor Jack's reluctance to have children was the true subject of The Gray Ghost's letter. Mrs. McQuat was writing to remind him that he must pay closer attention to his mother, whom she felt certain he was neglecting.

"Don't neglect her, Jack," The Gray Ghost said.

Well, hadn't she told him before? Jack threw her letter away without answering it. Later, when he learned that Mrs. McQuat had died, he wondered if he'd had a premonition of her death. Not only would he *not* pay closer attention to his mother; by not answering The Gray Ghost's letter, it was as if he'd sensed that Mrs. McQuat was already dying—a death-in-progress, so to speak—and that when she was gone, the voice of Jack's conscience would leave him, too.

They were just a few miles outside Durham, not far from Claudia's apartment in Newmarket, before Claudia broke the silence. "God damn you, Jack," she said. "After I die, I'm going to haunt you—I promise you I will—I might even haunt you *before* I die."

Well, Jack Burns was an actor—he should have known an end line when he heard one. He should have committed Claudia's warning to memory more deeply than he did.

20

Two Canadians in the City of Angels

Despite their growing estrangement, Jack and Claudia would live together their final two years at UNH. It was more than inertia that bound them; they were actors-in-training, learning the tricks of concealment. By what they managed to hide of themselves, they instructed each other. They became keen but sullen observers of their innermost secrets, their hidden characters.

The summer following their Toronto trip, they again did summer stock, this time at a playhouse on Cape Cod. The artistic director was a gay guy whom Jack liked a lot. Bruno Litkins was a tall, graceful man who *swooped* onstage; waving his long arms, he looked like a heron making an exaggerated if misguided effort to teach other, smaller birds to fly.

To Bruno Litkins, a musical based on a play or a novel was something to be tampered with—to be reinvented in a shockingly different way with each new production. The original text might be sacred to Bruno, but once someone had made a musical out of the material, there were no limits regarding how the story and the characters could be altered further.

Announcing auditions for *The Hunchback of Notre Dame*—in which Claudia had her heart set on the role of the beautiful Gypsy girl, Esmeralda—Bruno Litkins said that *his* Esmeralda was a beautiful *transvestite* who would liberate the reluctant homosexuality that flickered in the heart of Captain Phoebus like a flame in need of air. Esmeralda, the Gypsy drag queen of Paris, would *wrestle* the gay captain out of his closet. She was the oxygen Captain Phoebus needed in order to awaken his homosexual self!

The wicked Father Frollo, who first imagines he is in love

with Esmeralda, ultimately wants her to be put to death—not only because Esmeralda doesn't love him but because Esmeralda is a *guy*. (Father Frollo is a French homophobe.) Quasimodo, who also falls in love with Esmeralda, is in the end *relieved* that Esmeralda is in love with Captain Phoebus.

"It's a better story," Bruno Litkins told the shocked ensemble, "because Quasimodo isn't sad to give up Esmeralda to the soldier." (His hunchback notwithstanding, Quasimodo is *straight*.)

"What would Victor Hugo say?" Claudia asked. Poor Claudia saw that her cherished role was gone; at least onstage, Jack Burns was *born* to be a transvestite Esmeralda.

"Keep the audience *guessing*!" Bruno Litkins, flapping his long arms, liked to say. "Is Esmeralda a woman? Is she a man? Make them *guess*!"

There was, of course, another beautiful Gypsy girl in the play—Quasimodo's murdered mother, who has a brief but moving part. And there were other plays in that Cape Cod summer season—not all of them musicals that opened themselves to new, gay interpretations. Claudia would have bigger and better roles. She was the eponymous Salomé in Bruno Litkins's production of the Oscar Wilde play—Bruno revered Wilde and wouldn't change a purple word he'd written. Claudia was one hot Salomé. Her absurd dance of the seven veils was Wilde's fault, not Claudia's—although the Chinese scepter on her inner right thigh required a lot of makeup to conceal. (Without the makeup, the scepter might have been confusing to the audience—possibly mistaken for a birthmark, or a wound.)

Jack had the smaller part in *Salomé*—the prophet Jokanaan, good old John the Baptist, whose decapitated head Salomé kisses. That was some kiss. (Jack was kneeling under a table with a hole cut in the top for his head; the tablecloth hid not only his hard-on, but all the rest of him.) Yet the damage to his relationship with Claudia had already been done; not even that kiss could undo their drifting apart.

The gay version of *The Hunchback of Notre Dame* merely served to further the distance between them. In retrospect, Jack didn't blame Claudia for her one-night stand with the handsome actor who played the gay Captain Phoebus, but he blamed her at the time. (Jack knew that Claudia had every right to repay him for cheating on her with a tango teacher that previous spring.)

Claudia's luck was bad. The actor who played Captain Phoebus gave her *and* Jack the clap. Jack would never have found out about the affair otherwise, unless Claudia eventually told him— and given her unrepentant lies about her age, Jack had no reason to think that she ever would have let him in on her little secret. It was the captain's gonorrhea that gave her away.

Naturally, Jack pretended it was much more painful than it was, dropping to his knees and screaming upon every act of urination—while Claudia called from the bedroom, "I'm sorry, I'm sorry, I'm *sorry!*"

In Bruno's brilliantly choreographed scene where Jack-as-the-transvestite-Esmeralda reveals to Captain Phoebus that he is, below the waist, a man, Jack is singing his heart out to the captain while Phoebus both acquiesces and retreats. (The captain is attracted to Jack, but the idiot still thinks Jack is a *girl*— hence his reluctance.)

Jack seizes one of the captain's hands and holds it to one of his falsies; Phoebus looks underwhelmed. Jack seizes the captain's other hand and holds it to his crotch; Phoebus gives the audience an astonished look while Jack whispers in his ear. Then they both sing the song Bruno Litkins wrote for his gay version of *The Hunchback of Notre Dame*—"Same As Me, Babe," to the tune of Dylan's "It Ain't Me, Babe." (Jack knew his Bob; he sang it well.)

But the night of the performance after Jack learned he had gonorrhea—and Claudia confessed where it came from—Jack had something *real* to whisper in Captain Phoebus's ear while he held the captain's hand against his pecker. "Thanks for the *clap,* babe," Jack whispered.

It was quite a good look Phoebus gave the audience every night—it usually brought the house down. Such a look of recognition—Esmeralda has a *penis!* Of course the audience already knows. Jack-as-Esmeralda had earlier shown Father Frollo, thinking it would make Frollo stop hitting on him—never realizing that Frollo is such an *overreactor* that he'll insist on having Esmeralda hanged!

But that memorable night Captain Phoebus held Esmeralda's penis and Jack-as-Esmeralda thanked Phoebus for giving him the clap was a showstopper for the handsome soldier. The look he gave the audience *that* night interrupted the performance for a full minute or more; the audience spontaneously rose as one and gave Captain Phoebus a standing ovation.

"Maybe take a little something *off* the look, Phoebus," Bruno Litkins told the actor after that performance.

Jack just gave the captain his best Esmeralda-as-a-transvestite smile. Phoebus knew Jack could kick the crap out of him if he wanted to.

In truth, Jack was grateful to Captain Phoebus for making Claudia feel guilty; Phoebus had made Jack feel a little *less* guilty about the fact that he and Claudia were drifting apart.

The summer following their graduation from the University of New Hampshire, Claudia and Jack finally went their separate ways. She was going the graduate-student route—an MFA theater program at one of the Big Ten universities. (Jack would make a point of forgetting which one.) It seemed sensible for them to apply to different summer-stock playhouses that summer. Claudia was at a Shakespeare festival in New Jersey. Jack did a *Beauty and the Beast* and a *Peter Pan and Wendy* at a children's theater workshop in Cambridge, Massachusetts.

He might have been feeling nostalgic about his lost friend Noah Rosen—or Noah's more irrevocably lost sister, Leah—but Jack fondly recalled those foreign films in the movie theaters around Harvard Square. A summer of subtitles—and audiences of children, and their young mothers—somehow suited him.

Claudia said—and if these weren't *truly* her last spoken words to him, they were the last words he would remember—"What do you want to perform for *children* for? You don't want any."

Jack played the Beast to an older-woman Belle; she was also one of the founders of the children's theater workshop, and she'd hired him. Yes, he slept with her—they had a summer-long affair, not a day longer. She was way too old to play Wendy to Jack's Peter Pan, but she was a reasonably youthful-looking Mrs. Darling—Wendy's mom. (Imagine Peter Pan screwing Wendy's *mother,* if only for a summer.)

Jack needed to go to graduate school, to continue to be a student, or else get a real job—hence a green card—if he didn't want to go back to Canada, and he didn't. Emma, once again, would save him. She'd been out of Iowa for two years, living in Los Angeles and writing her first novel, which sounded like a contradiction in terms. Who went to L.A. to write a *novel*? But being an outsider had always suited Emma.

She'd found a job reading scripts at one of the studios; like

Jack, she was still a Canadian citizen and had only a Canadian passport, but Emma also had a green card. The script-reading job was more the result of her year as a comedy writer for New York television than it was anything she'd prepared herself to do at the Iowa Writers' Workshop. She was writing her novel, which Emma said was to be her revenge on the time she'd wasted as a film major—and all the while she was, as she put it, "working for the enemy and getting paid for it."

Why didn't he come live with her? Emma asked Jack. She'd find him a job in the movie business. "There are some good-looking guys out here, baby cakes—it's tougher competition than you'd have in Toronto. But there aren't that many good-looking guys who can act as well as you."

So that was Jack's plan, to the extent that he had one. He'd had it with the theater—and no wonder, when you consider the pre-ponderance of musicals. It was fine with him if his last onstage performance was as Peter Pan, taking Wendy Darling and her brothers off to Neverland—while in the wee hours of the morning, long after the curtain fell, he was banging Wendy's mom, Mrs. Darling.

"What would J. M. Barrie say?" Claudia might have asked, had she known. It made Jack sad to think about her.

The thing about Los Angeles, Jack would learn, is that it's unimpressed by you—no matter who you are. Eventually, the city tells you, your comeuppance will come; exclusivity fades. But Jack Burns wasn't moving in exclusive circles when he first went to L.A.—he wasn't famous yet. In the fall of 1987, when he moved in with Emma, the nearest landmark representing the sundry entertainments that the future held in store was that garish playground of possibilities, the Santa Monica Pier.

All that Jack and Emma really cared about was that they were bathed in the warm Pacific air; it didn't matter that they were breathing in an ocean spiked with smog. They were living together again—not in Toronto, and not with their mothers.

Emma, who was twenty-nine, looked considerably older. Her struggles with her weight were apparent to anyone who knew her, but a different, interior battle had been more costly to her; her shifting ambitions were at war with her obdurate determination. That Emma was a restless soul was obvious, but not even

Jack (not even *Emma*) was aware that something was seriously wrong with her.

Numbers were never Jack's strong suit. Living with Emma in L.A., he couldn't remember how much their rent was, or what day of the month they were supposed to pay it.

"Your math sucks, honey pie, but what do you need to know math for? You're gonna be an actor!"

At St. Hilda's, Jack had needed Miss Wurtz bending over him—as if breathing her in were a substitute for learning his numbers. And while it's true that Mrs. McQuat had helped him, even more than Miss Wurtz, he had never mastered math.

Mrs. Adkins had assisted him with his algebra at Redding— she who'd dressed him in her old clothes, she who'd made love to him with such a morbid air of resignation. (It was as if Mrs. Adkins were undressing to drown herself in the Nezinscot, or at least practicing for that loneliest of moments in her future.)

"You shouldn't trust yourself to count past ten," Noah Rosen had once cautioned Jack.

Mr. Warren, Jack's faculty adviser at Exeter, had been more kind but no less pessimistic. "I would advise you, Jack, never to rely on your *numerical* evaluation of a situation."

Jack Burns would live in Los Angeles for sixteen years. He liked all the driving. He and Emma first shared one half of a rat-eaten duplex in Venice. It was on Windward Avenue, downwind of a sushi place on the corner of Windward and Main—more to the point, downwind of the restaurant's Dumpster. Hama Sushi was good. Emma and Jack ate there a lot. The fish was really fresh—less fresh, alas, was whatever ended up in the Dumpster.

Jack's first girlfriend in L.A. was a waitress he met at Hama Sushi. She shared an overused house with some other girls on one of those small streets off Ocean Front Walk—Eighteenth, Nineteenth, or Twentieth Avenue. He could never remember the number. He went one night to the wrong house, possibly on the wrong avenue. There were a bunch of girls who welcomed him inside when he pushed the buzzer, but his waitress friend was not among them. By the time Jack realized it was the wrong bunch of girls, he'd met someone who interested him more than the sushi waitress. Numbers, once again, had misled him.

"You oughta carry a calculator," Emma told him, "or at least write everything down."

He liked Venice—the beach, the gyms, the underlying grubbiness of it. After Emma had a bad experience at Gold's Gym— she'd met a bodybuilder there who had beaten her up—she got Jack and herself a membership at World Gym; she said she liked the gorilla on the World Gym T-shirts and tank tops. A big gorilla standing on the planet Earth, the size of a beach ball, with a barbell in his hairy hands—the barbell had to weigh three or four hundred pounds, not that this was a credible explanation for why the bar was bending.

The World Gym tank tops were cut low; they had a scoop neck and a lot of space under the arms. They weren't made for women to wear—at least not the ones Emma bought, which were all in workout-gray with Day-Glo orange lettering. The tank tops showed a lot of cleavage, and Emma's breasts would occasionally fall out at the sides, but she only got the World Gym tank tops to wear as nightshirts or when she was writing.

Emma and Jack had their own bedrooms in the duplex, but most nights, when they didn't have "dates," they slept in the same bed—not really doing anything. Emma would hold Jack's penis until one of them fell asleep—that is, if they even went to bed at the same time, which they didn't often. Jack would occasionally hold her breasts, nothing more. He never once masturbated in the bed when she was there.

Emma and Jack had had their one time; they seemed to know this without discussing it. She had taught him how to beat off; she'd even invited him to imagine her when he did it. But this was entirely for Jack's self-preservation in prep school, especially at Redding, and although she'd sent him photographs of herself naked—and, unbeknownst to Emma, Jack still had one of them—it was their mutual understanding in Los Angeles that they were more than friends, and certainly a little different from other brothers and sisters, but they were *not* lovers. (The penis-holding notwithstanding—and no matter how many times they were undressed in each other's company, without seeming to think twice about it.)

Emma met another bodybuilder—this one at World Gym—and he didn't beat her up. He worked as a waiter at Stan's, which was on the corner of Rose and Main.

Stan's was one of those places that wouldn't last long in Venice. The waiters weren't as brash as they were in a New York steakhouse, like Smith & Wollensky, and for steaks and chops and Maine lobsters, which was all they served, the white table-cloths seemed out of place; yet the waiters wore white dress shirts with their sleeves rolled up, and no ties, and those starched white aprons that made them look like butchers who'd not yet made contact with any meat. It's hard to feel superior in a steak-house, but the waiters at Stan's (there were no waitresses) took naturally to superiority. It was as if they'd been born in those starched white aprons—remarkably, without a drop of blood be-ing shed in the process.

The waiter Emma knew who worked at Stan's had a name like Giorgio or Guido; he could bench-press three hundred pounds. Emma managed to persuade him that Jack was an experienced waiter, and Giorgio or Guido reluctantly introduced Jack to Don-ald, the maître d' at Stan's—a headwaiter of intimidating snotti-ness.

Admittedly, Jack had had no experience as a waiter, but Emma had skillfully revised Mr. Ramsey's written recommen-dation of Jack's training as an actor, which repeatedly cited his "vast potential." The studio in West Hollywood where, every morning, Emma turned in her notes and picked up an armload of new screenplays—she read and critiqued three or four scripts a day—had lots of fancy copying equipment, with which Emma slickly executed Mr. Ramsey's edited recommendation of Jack.

The word *actor* was replaced with *waiter,* and the names of certain plays or dramatizations (even the musicals) were pre-sented to the clueless American reader as the names of trendy Toronto restaurants, in which Mr. Ramsey extolled the virtue of Jack's "performance"—an oft-repeated word, which Emma left unaltered, except she sometimes changed it to a verb.

Hence Jack had "performed" superbly at an alleged bistro called Mail-Order Bride (there was another restaurant called Northwest Territories) and at what was probably a French place, d'Urbervilles, and at several restaurants of note in the northeast-ern United States, among them The Restaurant of Notre Dame and Peter and Wendy's—not to mention what must have been a Spanish eatery, Bernarda Alba.

Mr. Ramsey's letterhead—namely, that of St. Hilda's—which stated he was Chairman of English and Drama, had been tweaked to identify him as Chairman of the Hotel and Restau-rant of that oddly religious-sounding name. Mr. Ramsey's opening sentence described St. Hilda's (he meant, of course, the school) as "one of Toronto's best."

But Donald was an imperious prick—a headwaiter from Hell. "When I'm recommending a hotel with a good restaurant in Toronto, I always recommend the Four Seasons," he told Jack. He then challenged Jack to take a minute or two to memorize the specials.

"If you give me ten minutes, I can memorize the whole menu," Jack told him.

But Donald didn't give him the chance. The maître d' later told Giorgio or Guido that Jack's attitude had offended him. He had sized up Jack as "a hick from Toronto via New Hampshire"—or so he said to Giorgio or Guido. Jack had already decided he didn't want the waiter job—not in such a self-important *steakhouse*. But when Donald offered him an opportunity in the restaurant's valet-parking department, Jack accepted. He was a good driver.

It wasn't that Emma thought the job was beneath him; her objection was political. "You can't be a parking valet, baby cakes. English is your first language. You're taking a job from some unfortunate illegal alien."

But Giorgio or Guido looked relieved. He didn't want Jack to be a fellow waiter at Stan's. He'd had enough difficulty accepting Jack as Emma's roommate, no matter how many times Emma had told him that she and Jack didn't have sex together. (Jack wondered what Giorgio or Guido's problem was. How could you bench-press three hundred pounds and be *that* insecure?)

Jack didn't last long as a parking valet; he was fired from the job his first night—in fact, he never got to park his first car.

It was a silver Audi with gunmetal-gray leather seats, and the guy who flipped Jack the keys was a young, arty type who appeared to have been quarreling with his young, arty wife—or his girlfriend, Jack had thought, before he'd driven less than a block and the little girl sat up in the backseat. Her face, which was streaked with tears, was perfectly framed in the rearview mirror. She was maybe four, at the most five, years old, and she wasn't sitting in a booster seat. Evidently the backseat was her bed for the evening, because she was wearing pajamas and clutching both a blanket and a teddy bear to her chest. Jack saw a pillow propped against the armrest on the passenger side of the backseat; the booster seat was on the floor, kicked out of the way.

"Are you parking in a garage or outdoors?" the little girl asked him, wiping her nose on the sleeve of her pajamas.

"You can't stay in the car," Jack told her. He stopped the Audi and put on the hazard blinkers; she had scared the shit out of him and his heart was pounding.

"I'm not well enough behaved to eat in a grown-up restaurant," the little girl said.

Jack didn't know what to do. Maybe the young, arty couple had been arguing about leaving the little girl in the backseat, but he thought not. The girl had the look of a valet-parking veteran. "I like the garages better than parking on the street," she explained. "It will be dark soon," the little girl observed.

Jack drove down Main to Windward, where a gang of rowdies— noisy singles, though it was early in the evening—were crowding the entrance to Hama Sushi, waiting for tables. He left the Audi running at the curb and rang the buzzer to the half of the ratty duplex he shared with Emma; then he went back to the car and waited beside it. The little girl was never out of his sight.

"Is this where we're parking?" she asked.

"I'm not leaving you alone, not anywhere," he told her.

Emma opened the door and came out on the sidewalk; she was wearing one of her World Gym tank tops and nothing else. Because she looked more than usually pissed off, Jack guessed she'd been writing her novel.

"Nice car, honey pie. Does it come with the kid?" Jack explained the situation while the little girl observed them from the backseat. She'd probably never seen anyone quite like Emma in her World Gym tank top. "I told you—you shouldn't be parking cars," Emma said. She kept looking at the little girl. "I'm not babysitter material, Jack."

"I usually sleep on the floor, if I think anyone can see me sleeping on the backseat," the little girl said.

The "usually" made up Jack's mind for him—that and what Emma said before she walked back inside to continue what must have been one of the angrier passages in her novel-in-progress. "Nothing good can come of this job, baby cakes."

Jack put the little girl in the middle of the backseat and fastened a seat belt around her, because he couldn't figure out how the stupid booster seat worked. "It's probably hard to understand if you don't have children," the little girl told him forgivingly. Her name was Lucy. "I'm almost five," she said.

When Jack returned to the corner of Rose and Main, he pulled up at the curb in front of Stan's; his fellow valet parkers looked surprised to see him. "*¿Qué pasa?*" Roberto asked, when Jack handed him the keys.

"Better not park the Audi just yet," Jack told him, taking Lucy into the restaurant. She wanted to bring her blanket and her teddy bear, but not the pillow, which was okay with Jack.

The asshole maître d', Donald, was standing at his desk as if it were a pulpit and the book of reservations a Bible. Lucy, seeing all the people, wanted Jack to pick her up, which he did. "*Now* we're going to get in trouble," the child whispered in his ear.

"You're going to be fine, Lucy," Jack told her. "*I'm* the one who's going to get in trouble."

"You're already in trouble, Burns," Donald said, but Jack walked past him into the restaurant. Lucy spotted her parents before Jack did. It was still early, a soft light outside; the tables weren't full yet. (Maybe the tables were never full at Stan's.)

Lucy's mother got up from her chair and met them halfway to her table. "Is something wrong?" she asked Jack. What a question. And women (not only Claudia) gave Jack a hard time when he said he wasn't ready to be a parent!

"You forgot something," Jack said to the young, arty mom. "You left Lucy in the car." The woman just stared at him, but Lucy held out her arms and her mother took her from Jack— teddy bear and blanket and all.

Jack hoped that would be the end of it, but Donald, the head-waiter from Hell, wouldn't let him leave. "There is no St. Hilda's, hotel *or* restaurant, in Toronto," he hissed. "There is no Mail-Order Bride—"

"So you're from Toronto," Jack interrupted him. The way Donald had said, "*T'ronto,*" had given him away. Jack should have known. Donald was another undiscovered Canadian work-ing as a waiter in L.A.

Naturally, the young, arty husband and bad father wouldn't let Jack leave Stan's without giving him his two cents' worth. "I'm gonna get you fired, pretty boy," the guy said.

"It's a good job to lose," Jack told him, making note of the line.

Giorgio or Guido was hovering around, to the extent that a bodybuilder who can bench-press three hundred pounds can *hover.* "You better get *outta* here, Jack," he was saying.

"I'm *trying* to get out of here," Jack said.

He was abreast of the reservation desk when he spotted the telephone; it occurred to him to call 911 and report a clear case of child neglect, but he thought better of it. Jack didn't know the license plate of the silver Audi. He would have to write it down if he wanted to remember it—damn numbers again.

But the bad father was too angry to let Jack go. He stepped in front of Jack and blocked his way; he was a medium-tall young man, and his chin was level to Jack's eyes. Jack waited for the guy to touch him. When he grabbed Jack's shoulders, Jack stepped back a little and the young man pulled Jack toward him. Jack let him pull, head-butting him in the lips. Jack didn't butt him all that hard, but the guy was a big bleeder.

"I'm calling nine-one-one the second I'm home," Jack said to Giorgio or Guido. "Tell Donald."

"Donald says you're fired, Jack," the bodybuilder said.

"It's a good job to lose," Jack repeated. (He knew that line would have legs.)

Out on the sidewalk, Roberto was still holding the keys to the silver Audi. That's when Jack remembered he had the parking chit in his shirt pocket; he'd already written down the license-plate numbers. "You'll have to write out a new chit for the Audi," he told Roberto.

"No problem," Roberto said.

Jack walked along Main to Windward. It was a nice evening, only now growing dark. (When you've grown up in Toronto, Maine, and New Hampshire, when *isn't* it a nice evening in L.A.?)

Emma was writing away when Jack got home, but she overheard his 911 call. "What did you do with the kid?" she asked him, after he'd hung up.

"Gave her to her parents."

"What's that on your forehead?" Emma asked.

"A little ketchup, maybe—I've been in a food fight."

"It's *blood,* baby cakes—I can see the teeth-marks."

"You should've seen the fucker's lips," he told her.

"Ha!" Emma said. (Shades of Mrs. Machado—that exclamation always gave Jack the shivers.)

They went out to Hama Sushi. You could talk about anything at Hama Sushi—it was so noisy. Jack really liked the place, but it was partly what Emma called "*l'eau de* Dumpster" (her Montreal French) that eventually drove them away from their Windward Avenue duplex.

"So what did you learn from your brief experience as a parking valet, honey pie?"

"I got one good line out of it," Jack said.

What convinced Emma that Jack should be a waiter at American Pacific, a restaurant in Santa Monica not far from the beach, was neither the location nor the menu. She went there on a date one night and liked what the waiters were wearing—blue Oxford cloth button-down shirts with solid burgundy ties, khakis with dark-brown belts, and dark-brown loafers. "It's very Exeter, baby cakes—you'll fit right in. I stole a dinner menu for you. Just think of it as an acting opportunity, as Mr. Ramsey would say."

Emma meant that memorizing the menu was an acting opportunity. It took Jack the better part of a morning. Counting the salads and other starters together with the main courses, there were about twenty items.

Jack then called Mr. Ramsey in Toronto and alerted him to the modifications Emma had made in Mr. Ramsey's recommendation for Jack; just in case someone phoned Mr. Ramsey to verify Jack's credentials as a waiter, Jack wanted his beloved mentor to know that Mail-Order Bride was supposed to be a fabulous bistro.

"You have to make reservations a *month* in advance!" Mr. Ramsey responded, with his usual enthusiasm. "Jack Burns, I know you'll go far!" (Maybe, Jack thought—if only as a waiter.)

Jack showed up that afternoon at American Pacific; it still sounded more like a railroad than a restaurant to him, but the maître d', a handsome fellow named Carlos, was a welcome sight. Jack knew at once that Carlos was no Canadian. When Carlos looked at Jack's letter of recommendation, he nodded as if he'd eaten at Mail-Order Bride many times.

The specials were on a blackboard by the bar. "I'll bet you can memorize them in a heartbeat," Carlos said.

"I've already memorized the menu," Jack told him. "You want to hear it?" That got the attention of the other waitstaff. It was only about five-thirty in the afternoon—no customers as yet—but Jack had his audience. He skipped the veal chop with the gorgonzola mashed potatoes, just to make them think he'd forgotten something—only to surprise them by mentioning the veal chop at the end of his recitation. He forgot nothing. He'd already dressed as if he had the job, and he knew he'd nailed the audition. Carlos didn't ask him to recite the specials.

It was to be the first in a long line of auditions for Jack—not counting the aborted one with Donald—but all of Jack's other auditions would be as an actor instead of a waiter; he was at American Pacific until he no longer needed a job waiting tables.

Emma had arranged for Jack's head shots with a photographer she knew; they were ridiculously expensive. Emma carried them around with her. At the studio in West Hollywood, she occasionally met an agent or a casting director. But she was more likely to meet someone important on a date, or in any of several restaurants in West Hollywood and Beverly Hills.

Some young hotshot at Creative Artists wanted to bang Emma in the worst way. There wasn't an agent at C.A.A. who would represent a nobody like Jack Burns, but the guy told Emma he would negotiate a contract for Jack—if Jack managed to get an acting job. (Just how Jack might do that *without* an agent wasn't made clear.)

Emma took advantage of the young agent's lust and brought him one night to American Pacific. His name was Lawrence. "Not *Larry*," he told Jack, with an arched eyebrow.

Not much came of that meeting, but Lawrence made a few calls on Jack's behalf. These were calls to other agents, not at C.A.A. but on Lawrence's personal B-list—or more likely his *C*-list.

Someone whose name Jack confused with Rottweiler (the dog) told him that his recommendations and college acting experiences were basically worthless. "Ditto the summer stock," Rottweiler said, "except for Bruno Litkins." Bruno had a Hollywood connection: casting directors occasionally consulted him on roles related to transvestism. "Or transvestitism," Rottweiler said. "Whatever the fuck you call it."

Jack's toe in the door, albeit an odd one, was that he had found favor with Bruno Litkins for his creation of the gay transvestite Esmeralda in Bruno's transformation of *The Hunchback of Notre Dame.* "Not what I'd call super-marketable," Rottweiler informed Jack. (Not that Jack was at all sure he wanted to be marketed exclusively for roles related to transvestism *or* transvestitism.)

Another of the agents on Lawrence's B- or C-list sent Jack to an audition for a movie in Van Nuys. The place looked like a private home, but doubled as a film set. When the woman who did hair or makeup told Jack the name of the movie, *Muffy the Vampire Hooker 3,* Jack thought it was a joke. He didn't understand the situation until the producer introduced herself and asked to see his penis.

"Small schlongs need not apply," she said. Her name was Milly. She was wearing a slate-gray pin-striped pantsuit, very businesswoman-banker chic, which stood in seeming contradiction to her old-fashioned pearl necklace—of a kind worn by ladies who belong to bridge clubs. Her hair was huge—a silver-blond bubble, like a motorcycle helmet sans insignia.

Jack said there'd been a misunderstanding and started to leave. "You might as well show me your schlong," Milly said. "It's a free opportunity to find out if you measure up." That got the attention of a bodybuilder-type with a ponytail and a busty young woman who looked like a vampire. They were sitting on a couch, watching a movie on a VCR. It was footage of themselves, probably from *Muffy the Vampire Hooker 2*—a long, unvarying blow job, in the throes of which the eponymous Muffy occasionally bared her vampiric canines. One would hope that when she was moved to bite the bodybuilder and suck his blood, she would do so in his *throat.* Jack saw that Muffy did not have the bloodsucking canines inserted while she watched the movie on the couch; she was innocently chewing gum.

The guy with the ponytail paused the blow job on the VCR, and the three of them had a look at Jack's penis. While this was not specifically the film career Jack sought, most men are curious to know how their penises compare; after all, here was a panel of experts.

"It's okay, buddy," the bodybuilder told Jack.

"Cut the crap, Hank," Milly said.

"Yeah, Hank," Muffy the vampire hooker said.

Hank went back to the couch and started up the blow job on the VCR again. "His dick looks fine to me," Hank said.

"It's cute," Muffy told Jack, "but in this business, cute doesn't quite cut it."

"Forget *quite,*" Milly said. She was in her fifties, maybe sixty—a *former* porn star, one of the cameramen had told Jack, but the cameraman must have been kidding. Except for the big hair, Milly reminded Jack of Noah Rosen's mother.

"It's cute, and it doesn't *matta* how big it is," Muffy whispered in Jack's ear. She went back to the couch and plopped down next to Hank.

"It doesn't cut it, period. And it *does* matter how big it is," Milly said. "It doesn't matter if it's *cute.*"

"Thank you," Jack told them, zipping up.

Hank, the big guy getting the endless blow job from Muffy on the VCR, followed Jack to the car; there was nothing cute about Hank's schlong, which Jack had noticed was enormous. "Don't be discouraged," Hank said. "Just eat healthy. I'd stick to low-fat, low-sodium, low-carb stuff, if I were you."

"Hank, are you *ready*?" Milly was screaming from inside the house.

"This job isn't for everyone," Hank admitted to Jack. "There's a lotta pressure." He had a high, nasal voice—a mismatch with his hulking presence.

"Hank!" Muffy called. She was standing in the open doorway of the house, baring her teeth in a broad-mouthed grin. She had inserted the bloodsucking canines; Muffy was ready for the next shot, whatever it was.

"Coming!" Hank called back to her. "It might have worked out differently if I'd met Mildred's sister," he said, "but I met Milly first."

"She has a sister?" Jack asked.

"Myra Ascheim is legit," Hank said. "Mildred is the porn-producer side of the Ascheim family."

Jack saw that Mildred Ascheim had joined Muffy the vampire hooker in the doorway. "Stop stalling, Hank!" Milly yelled.

"What is Myra Ascheim legit at?" Jack asked.

"She's some kind of agent," Hank told him. "She used to represent Val Kilmer, or maybe it was Michael J. Fox—lots of people like that, anyway. It's all about who you meet out here," he added. Hank was walking back to the house like a man about to have nonstop sex with a vampire hooker. He looked less than thrilled.

"Good luck!" Jack called to him.

"I'll look for you on the big screen," Hank said, pointing skyward—as if the big screen, in both their minds, lay in a heavenly direction.

"Good luck, little schlong!" Milly called to Jack.

Hank stopped and walked back to Jack for a minute. "If you ever meet Myra, don't tell her you've met Mildred," he warned Jack. "That would be the kiss of death."

"It's not as if I actually *auditioned*," Jack said.

"This was an audition, kid. I'll look for you," Hank said again.

Jack would look for him, too, although he didn't tell Hank that at the time. His porn name was Hank Long—a big, handsome guy, no stranger to a weight room, always with minimal dialogue, no doubt because of his high, nasal voice. Jack would see him in fifteen or twenty "adult" movies after their first meeting—for the most part, nothing memorable by title or plot.

Jack could have recognized Hank's penis all by itself—Emma could have, too. They watched Hank Long movies together, after Jack's not-exactly-an-audition in Van Nuys.

"Never go to Van Nuys," he told Emma, when he got home. "There are a lot of guys with huge schlongs out there."

"Like that would really keep me away," Emma said somewhat ambiguously.

Jack told her the whole story—how his penis, in Mildred Ascheim's estimation, didn't cut it; how he was "cute," according to Muffy the vampire hooker, but not in a league with Hank Long.

"I wouldn't say you were *tiny,* baby cakes, but I've seen bigger." More than Milly's small-schlong assessment, Emma's bluntness left Jack a little crestfallen. "For Christ's sake, you're not trying to be a *porn* star!" Emma said, trying to cheer him up.

She called Lawrence at C.A.A. immediately, beginning the conversation by telling him she would never fuck him. "Let's get *that* out of the way," was how Emma put it. "Do you have any other brilliant ideas about which agents Jack should see?" Emma covered the mouthpiece of the telephone and turned to Jack. "He says no," she reported.

"Ask him if he knows Myra Ascheim," Jack said.

Emma got a quick answer to her question over the phone. "Lawrence says she's a has-been, honey pie. She's been let go by everyone. She doesn't even have an assistant anymore."

"She sounds like a good place to start," Jack said. "Ask Lawrence if he'll make a call—just *one* call."

Emma asked the bastard. "Lawrence says Myra doesn't even have an *office*."

"She sounds perfect for me," Jack said.

Emma conveyed Jack's feelings to Lawrence over the phone. "He says not to mention Myra's *sister*," Emma told Jack.

"I know," Jack said. "It's *Myra,* not Mildred. I know, I know."

That night there were three messages on the answering machine when Jack got back from American Pacific. He was anxious that one of the messages might have been from a housewife he'd been banging in Benedict Canyon. The woman was insane; she claimed that from her bedroom she could see part of the estate on Cielo Drive where Sharon Tate had been murdered, but Jack couldn't see it. When the Santa Anas were blowing, she said she could hear the screams and moans of Ms. Tate and the other victims—as if the murders were ongoing.

She called Jack frequently, often to reschedule their rendezvous. Usually the postponement had something to do with her husband or one of her children, but the last time the family dog had been to blame. The unfortunate animal had eaten something it shouldn't have; the complications were so severe that the vet had promised to make a house call.

Emma said that Jack should learn to read between the lines—clearly the housewife was also sleeping with the vet. Emma loved listening to all the reasons the Benedict Canyon woman found not to sleep with Jack, or at least to postpone the illicit act. But Emma had been writing; she'd not answered the phone that night. She and Jack listened to the answering machine together after Jack came home.

Both Lawrence and Rottweiler said they had called Myra Ascheim and told her she should meet Jack; they'd given her his phone number. The third message was from Myra. Her voice was alarmingly like her sister's. Jack first thought it was Mildred, calling to further abuse his small schlong.

"There's two people, both assholes, who say I should meet you," Myra Ascheim's message began. "So where the fuck are you, Jack Burns?"

That was the message—not very elegant, and she didn't even leave her name. Jack knew it was Myra only because he'd met Milly and recognized the sisterly voice. (It was a voice with more Brooklyn in it than L.A.)

Emma must have noticed the despondency in Jack's expression when he replayed the three messages, again and again. That some word from the insane housewife in Benedict Canyon was not among the messages appeared to pain him. Only Emma knew Jack well enough to guess that, although he was relieved to let the relationship slip away, he missed the woman's madness.

Emma Oastler's first novel was called *The Slush-Pile Reader*, which was almost entirely based on Emma's job—not that "slush-pile reader" was her job's official title. (With an uncustomary dignity, as if her job were a pinnacle of the profession, the studio called Emma a "first" reader—a part of the process also called "screenplay development.")

Emma read not only unsolicited manuscripts; she read the scripts submitted by agents who were less than name brands, and the occasional script by a marquee screenwriter whose agent had recently jerked the studio around. Very few screenplays were eventually produced—and most of those had more important first readers than Emma, but Emma would eventually read those scripts, too.

What bothered Emma about her job was not how many screenplays she had to read, or even how badly written most of them were. Emma's principal gripe was with the studio execs— they read her notes but not the screenplays. Emma discovered that for the majority of scripts she read, she was the *only* reader. This inclined her to be overgenerous in her notes, even in the case of bad screenplays; she didn't want to be the sole reason a film wasn't produced, even though Emma's foremost complaint about many of the movies she saw was that they should never have been made in the first place.

"But why would a studio hire a script reader, especially for the slush pile, if the studio execs *wanted* to read a bunch of bad screenplays?" Jack asked her. It seemed perfectly natural to him that, in most cases, a first reader *meant* an only reader.

Not to Emma; she was both indignant and unreasonable about it. "The execs should still *read* them, even if they're bad," she insisted.

"But they hired you, Emma, so they wouldn't have to read all the junk!"

"Someone *wrote* that junk, baby cakes. It took hours and hours."

Emma surely exaggerated what she called wasting her time as a film major. What was the point of learning to appreciate good films? Emma argued. The way the movie industry worked had nothing to do with film as an art form. Jack thought that Emma's motive for revenge was misguided; it was the machinations of the movie industry that had wasted her time, not her having been a film major.

Emma insisted that the studio execs were responsible for making many terrible movies that should never have been made; therefore, to make some small measure of atonement for their crimes, they should read their fair share of bad screenplays.

Jack argued that Emma should have been more upset about what happened in that rare case of an unknown screenwriter who wrote a script the studio execs actually read and *liked*. On only two occasions had Emma *loved* an unsolicited screenplay; both times, she'd managed to persuade the execs to read it. In each case, they promptly bought the rights and offered the screenwriter a fee to write a second draft; they rejected the second draft, paid off the screenwriter, and hired an established writer to reconstruct the story in all the usual, conventional ways. Whatever quality had been good enough to catch Emma's attention (in the original script) was lost, but the studio now owned and continued to develop what they called "the property."

This didn't upset Emma at all. "It's the writer's fault—the writer caved to the money. That's what the damn writers do. You want to maintain control of your screenplay, you take no money up front—you don't even let the fuckers buy you lunch, honey pie."

"But what if the writer *needs* the money?" Jack asked. "The writer probably needs *lunch*!"

"Then the writer should get a day job," Emma said.

Arguing with Emma drove Jack crazy. It also worried him about Emma's novel—that the writing would descend to a level of autobiographical complaining; that it would be an *un*imagined story, without an iota of invention, full of rantings and accusatory anecdotes he'd heard before. That the main character of *The Slush-Pile Reader* was a young Canadian woman—a newcomer to L.A. who'd gone to school "back East" and had Emma's job—did not, Jack thought, bode well. But it turned out that Emma had invented a character who seemed most unlike herself; she'd actually imagined a story, one that was far more interesting than her own. And, sentence by sentence, she wrote well—she'd taken the necessary pains to revise herself.

Furthermore, Emma had envisioned a *heroic* character—one capable of touchingly unselfish gestures—notwithstanding that

Emma was generally too cynical to be heroic herself. The main character of *The Slush-Pile Reader,* the eponymous reader, is not a cynic. On the contrary, Michele Maher (of all names!) is a pure-hearted optimist with an indestructibly sunny disposition. Michele Maher—that is, Emma's character—is such a good girl that her purity survives her most degrading experiences, and she has a few.

Unlike Emma, Michele is a preternaturally thin young woman who has to force herself to eat. She haunts gyms and health-food stores, gagging on protein powder and popping all the dietary supplements that bodybuilders use, but she never manages to put on a pound. Despite all her weightlifting, she looks like a wire. Michele Maher has the body and metabolism of a twelve-year-old boy.

Also unlike Emma, Michele is conscience-stricken by the bad scripts she reads. The worst, most self-deluded screenwriters break her heart. Michele wants to help them be better writers; to that futile end, she writes them encouraging letters on the studio letterhead. These letters are very different in content and tone from the notes Michele submits to the studio execs; in those notes, she is critical in the extreme. In short, Michele does her job well: she tells her bosses all the reasons why they shouldn't waste their time reading this crap.

But to the rock-bottom writers themselves, Michele Maher is an angel of hope; she always finds something positive to say about their most abhorrent excrescences. In the first chapter of *The Slush-Pile Reader,* Michele writes a warm, enthusiastic letter to a heavily tattooed bodybuilder and porn star named Miguel Santiago. His porn name is Jimmy.

In his pathetic screenplay, which is the story of his life, Santiago describes himself as a porn star who hates his work. The only way Santiago can have sex on command is to imagine he is a young James Stewart falling in love with Margaret Sullavan in *The Shopworn Angel,* or submitting to the sentimental bliss of domestic life with Donna Reed in *It's a Wonderful Life.* Santiago manages to stay the course through such epics as *Bored Housewives 4* and *Keep It Up, Inc.,* by imagining he is the one and only Jimmy Stewart in these black-and-white soap-opera masterpieces.

There's no story: we see Miguel Santiago lifting weights and getting tattooed, we see him memorizing lines from *The Shop-*

worn Angel and *It's a Wonderful Life,* and of course we see him performing as the *other* Jimmy. In her notes to the studio execs, Michele Maher states that such a film is "not makable"—easily a third of it would be a porn movie! But in her letter to Miguel Santiago, Michele calls his screenplay "a bittersweet memoir." And her letter takes a personal turn: she asks Miguel where he works out.

Santiago, of course, imagines that Michele Maher is a studio exec—not a slush-pile reader. Little does he know that she goes to the video store and rents all four of the *Bored Housewives* movies. In one of her more self-degrading moments, Michele masturbates to *Keep It Up, Inc.;* sexually repressed, she goes to the gym where Miguel Santiago (alias Jimmy) trains, just to watch him work out. In this respect, Michele Maher is like Emma: she has a thing for bodybuilder-types. But unlike Emma, Michele doesn't usually act on her cravings. And what bodybuilder would ever hit on Michele? She's built like a pencil.

What makes *The Slush-Pile Reader* moving is that Miguel Santiago is a dim-witted but genuinely nice guy. When Michele Maher gets up the nerve to introduce herself to him, she confesses she's no exec—she's just a first reader who felt sorry for him. They begin a relationship that one reviewer of *The Slush-Pile Reader* would call "L.A. dysfunctional"—this was in praise of the novel, which generally got terrific reviews. "More *noir* than *noir,*" said *The New York Times.*

Miguel and Michele end up living together—"within breathing distance of a sushi Dumpster in Venice." (Jack knew where that came from.) They don't have sex. His schlong is too big for Michele—it hurts. She just holds it. (Jack knew where that came from, too—if not the "too big" part.)

Over time, out of his growing and abiding love for her, Miguel introduces Michele to other bodybuilders he knows at the gym; he's seen them in the shower, so he knows who's got the small schlongs. Michele sleeps with them. "A muted pleasure," as she puts it to Miguel. Holding his porn-movie penis with mixed emotions, she tells him she's happy.

As for Miguel Santiago—a.k.a. Jimmy, the penile phenomenon—he gets all the sex he wants or needs at his day job, which he stoically endures. He accepts his relationship with Michele for what it is. Michele sleeps with the occasional small schlong, but she always goes home to Miguel and they lie in bed together, she holding his huge, unacceptable penis—the two of them not saying anything—while they watch *Waterloo Bridge* on the VCR, the 1940 remake with Vivien Leigh and Robert Taylor. It's Miguel's kind of movie, a real tearjerker.

At the end of Emma's novel, Michele Maher and Miguel Santiago are still living together. Michele doesn't write letters of encouragement to bad screenwriters anymore; she restricts her comments to the notes she gives the studio execs, who never read the screenplays she reads. The worst scripts still break her heart, but she doesn't talk about her day when she comes home to Miguel; naturally, he doesn't talk about his. They consume some protein powder and dietary supplements, and they go to the gym. He says he likes it when she sleeps in a World Gym tank top—her small, almost nonexistent breasts are easy to touch under the angry gorilla holding the bending barbell.

"There are worse relationships in L.A.," Emma writes; it was a line quoted in a lot of her reviews, and a pretty good setup to the novel's last sentence: "If you or your partner is in a bad movie, or in any number of bad movies—even if you're perpetually in the act of rewriting the *same* bad movie—there are worse things to be ashamed of."

Jack liked the novel's first sentence better: "Either there are no coincidences in this town, or everything in this town is a coincidence."

Take the message on the answering machine from Myra Ascheim, for example. Jack didn't know that Emma already knew who *Mildred* Ascheim was, not to mention that Emma had been watching porn films day and night—"research" for *The Slush-Pile Reader,* she later called it—and this was *before* he happened to meet Hank Long on the set of *Muffy the Vampire Hooker 3* and Jack and Emma started watching Hank Long movies together.

Jack told Emma that he couldn't read about Miguel Santiago without seeing Hank Long in the part, but Emma objected to his premature conclusion that her novel would one day be a film. "Spare me the movie talk, baby cakes," was how she put it. "You're getting ahead of yourself."

Jack first read *The Slush-Pile Reader* while the manuscript was still making the rounds of New York literary agents; Emma had decided she was more American than Canadian and she wanted to sell the U.S. rights before she even showed the novel to a Toronto publisher—notwithstanding that Charlotte Breasts-with-*Bones*-in-Them Barford, her old pal from St. Hilda's, was a young up-and-comer in Canadian publishing.

"Did you have to call her Michele Maher?" Jack asked Emma. "I adored Michele Maher, I *worshiped* her. I will always worship her. You never even met her, Emma."

"You kept her away from me, Jack. Besides, Michele is a very positive character—in the book, I mean."

"Michele is a very positive character *in real life!*" Jack protested. "You've given her the body of a twelve-year-old boy! You've made her this pathetic creature who's enslaved to body-builders!"

"It's just a name," Emma said. "You're overreacting."

Naturally, Jack was sensitive about the small-schlong business, too—that part about sleeping with a guy with a small penis being "a muted pleasure."

"It's a *novel,* honey pie—a work of *fiction.* Don't you know how to read a novel?"

"You've been holding my penis for years, Emma. I didn't know you were making a *size* assessment."

"It's a *novel,*" Emma repeated. "You're taking it too personally. You've missed the point about penises, Jack."

"What point is that?"

"When they're too big, it hurts, baby cakes. I mean, it hurts if the woman is too small."

Jack thought about it; he hadn't known that a woman *could* be too small. (Too *big,* maybe, but not too small.) Did Emma mean that "a muted pleasure" was preferable to pain? Was that the point? Then he saw that Emma was crying. "I *liked* the novel," he told her. "I didn't mean that I didn't like it."

"You don't get it," Emma said.

Jack thought she was talking about *The Slush-Pile Reader,* which he believed he'd understood fairly well. "I get it, Emma," he said. "It may not be exactly my cup of tea—I mean it's hardly an old-fashioned novel with a complicated plot and a complex cast of characters. It may be a little contemporary for my taste— a psychological study of a relationship more than a narrative, and a dysfunctional relationship at that. But I *liked* it—I really did. I thought the tone of voice was consistent—a kind of sarcastic understatement, I guess you'd call it. There was a deadpan voice in the more emotional scenes, which I particularly liked. And the relationship, imperfect though it is, is better than *no* relationship. I get that. They don't have sex, they *can't* have sex, but—for different reasons—not having sex is almost a *relief* for them."

"Oh, shut the fuck up!" Emma said; she was still crying.

"What don't I get?" he asked.

"It's not the *novel* you don't get—it's *me*!" she cried. "*I'm* too small, Jack," Emma said softly. "Even not-very-big guys hurt me."

Jack was completely surprised. Emma was such a big girl, such a strong young woman, and she was always battling her weight; she was much taller and heavier than Jack. How was it possible that she was too small? "Have you seen a doctor?" he asked.

"A gynecologist—yes, several. They say I'm *not* too small. It's all in my mind, apparently."

"The pain is in your mind?" he asked her.

"No, that's not where the pain is," she said.

Emma's condition had an uncomfortable-sounding name. Vaginismus, Emma explained, was a conditioned response; often a spasm of the perineal muscles occurred if there was any stimulation of the area. In some women, even the anticipation of vaginal insertion could result in muscle spasm.

"You want to avoid penetration?" Jack asked Emma.

"It's involuntary, honey pie. I can't help it—it's chronic."

"There's no treatment?"

Emma laughed. She'd tried hypnosis—an attempt to retrain the muscles to relax instead of involuntarily contracting. But even the psychiatrist had forewarned her that this worked with only a small percentage of sufferers, and it hadn't worked with Emma.

On the advice of a Toronto gynecologist, Emma had experimented with a treatment known as systematic desensitization—or the Q-tip method, as her Los Angeles gynecologist disparagingly called it. By inserting something as narrow as a Q-tip—and when this was accomplished, progressively inserting slightly larger objects—

"Stop," Jack told her; he didn't want to know all the treatments she'd tried. "Has anything *worked*?" he asked Emma.

The only thing that worked (and this didn't work every time) was the absolute cooperation of a partner. "I have to be on top, baby cakes, and the guy can't move at all. If he makes even one move, I get a spasm." Emma had to be in complete control. All the moves were her moves; only that worked. It went without saying that such a willing partner was hard to find.

Jack was thinking many things, most of them unutterable. How Emma's attraction to bodybuilders wasn't the best idea; how her long-standing interest in boys much younger than herself made more sense. And he remembered how adamant Emma was about not having children. No doubt the vaginismus was a reason—a more compelling one than fearing she'd be a bad mother, or like *her* mother.

It would have been insensitive to ask her if she'd inquired about a surgical solution to her problem. Emma felt squeamish in a doctor's office; she dreaded everything medical, most of all surgery. Besides, it didn't sound as if there was a surgical solution to vaginismus—not if it was all in her mind.

Jack didn't have the heart to tell Emma that she should consider revising *The Slush-Pile Reader.* He thought that the vaginismus would make a better story than all the small-schlong, big-schlong business—not to mention the unlikelihood of the Michele Maher character having a vagina that was too small. But he understood that Emma's fiction was a purer choice—a fable of acceptance, and as close as Emma could allow herself to approach her problem. A life in the top position; a lifetime looking for the unmoving partner. It seemed too cruel. Or would this method eventually train her perineal muscles to relax?

"What *causes* vaginismus?" Jack asked, but Emma might not have heard him, or she was distracted. Maybe she didn't know what caused it—maybe nothing did—or else she didn't want to discuss it further.

They took off their clothes and went to bed. Emma held his penis. Jack got very hard—unusually hard, it seemed to him—but all Emma said was, "You're not really all that small, Jack. Small*ish,* I would say. If I were you, honey pie, I wouldn't worry about it."

Emma didn't exactly say she'd seen smaller—he'd only heard her say she'd seen *bigger*—but Jack didn't press her. It was enough that she held his penis. He was awfully fond of the way she held it.

"We should move," Emma said sleepily.

"Maybe roommates aren't the best readers," Jack ventured to say, touching her breasts.

"I didn't mean we should stop living together, Jack. I meant I'm sick of Venice."

That struck Jack as too bad, but he didn't say anything. He would miss Venice—even *l'eau de* Dumpster from Hama Sushi. He had grown fond of World Gym, and—despite Emma's bad experience—he occasionally went to Gold's, though Jack Burns was no bodybuilder; in both gyms, when he wanted to use the free weights, he did his lifting at the women's end of the weight room.

"You're going to be a strong boy, Jack—not very big, but strong," Leslie Oastler had told him.

"Do you think so?" he'd asked her.

"I know so," Mrs. Oastler had said. "I can tell."

Jack lay there remembering that, with his small*ish* penis as hard as a diamond in Emma's big, strong hand. Jack had small hands, like his mother. He lay there thinking how strange it was that he hadn't thought of his mom in months. Maybe Jack didn't like to think of her because he believed he more and more re-minded her of his father; and while it wasn't his *physical* resemblance to his dad that bothered Jack, surely *any* resemblance he bore to William would have been upsetting to Alice. Jack just got the feeling that his mother didn't like him.

Jack was also wondering where he and Emma might move. He'd once mentioned the Palisades to Emma. It was like a vil-lage; you could walk everywhere. But Emma said the Palisades was "swarming with children"—it was, in her view, "a place where formerly sane people went to *breed.*" Jack guessed that they wouldn't be moving there.

Clearly Beverly Hills was too expensive for them; besides, it was too far away from the beach. Emma said she liked to see the ocean every day—not that she ever set foot on the beach. Malibu maybe, Jack was thinking, or Santa Monica. But given Emma's revelation that sex hurt her—quite possibly, it hurt her most of the time—it would have been insensitive of Jack to pursue a con-versation about where they might move. Save it for another time, he thought.

"Say it in Latin for me," he said to Emma.

She knew what he meant—it was the epigraph she'd set at the

beginning of her novel. She went around saying it like a litany, but until now Jack had not realized she meant *them*.

"*Nihil facimus sed id bene facimus*," Emma whispered, holding his penis like no one before or since.

"We do nothing but we do it well," Jack said in English, holding her breasts.

It was the fall of 1988. *Rain Man* would be the year's top-grossing film and would clean up at the Academy Awards. Jack's favorite film that year was *A Fish Called Wanda*. He would have killed to have had Kevin Kline's part, for which Kline would win an Oscar for Best Actor in a Supporting Role.

Jack Burns was twenty-three. Emma Oastler was thirty. Boy, were their lives about to change!

Jack met Myra Ascheim at a breakfast place on Montana, shortly after he and Emma had moved to a rental in Santa Monica. Emma, who bought all Jack's clothes, dressed him for his meeting. A coffee-colored, long-sleeved shirt—untucked, with the top two buttons unbuttoned—medium-tan chinos, and the dark-brown loafers he wore as a waiter. His hair was a little long, with more gel in it than usual, and he hadn't shaved for two days—all of which was entirely Emma's decision. She said he was "almost feminine" when he was clean-shaven, but three days' growth made him "too Toshiro Mifune." The shirt was linen. Emma liked the wrinkles.

Jack was reminded of Mrs. Oastler buying his clothes for Redding—later, for Exeter—and he commented to Emma that he felt remiss for never thanking her mother. Emma was spreading the gel through his hair with her hands, a little roughly. "*And* she paid my tuition at both schools," Jack added. "Your mom must think I'm ungrateful."

"Please don't thank her, honey pie."

"Why not?" he asked.

"Just *don't*," Emma said, yanking his hair.

It was evident that no one had dressed Myra Ascheim as attentively as Leslie Oastler and Emma had dressed Jack. He first mistook Myra for a homeless person who'd wandered east on Montana from that narrow strip of park on the Pacific side of Ocean Avenue. She was smoking a cigarette on the sidewalk in front of the Marmalade Café—a woman in her late sixties, maybe seventy, wearing dirty running shoes, baggy gray sweatpants, and a faded-pink, unlaundered sweatshirt. With her lank, dirty-white hair—in a ponytail that protruded from an Anaheim Angels baseball cap, from which the halo had fallen off the letter *A*—Myra bore no resemblance to her younger and far more stylish sister, Mildred.

She even toted an overstuffed shopping bag, in which she carried an old raincoat. Jack walked right by her. It wasn't until Myra spoke to him that he recognized her, and then it was only because she had Milly's porn-producer voice. "You should lose the stubble," she said, "and go easy on the gel in your hair. You look like you've been sleeping under a car."

"Ms. Ascheim?" he asked.

"What a bright boy you are, Jack Burns. And don't listen to Lawrence—you're not too pretty."

"Lawrence said I was too pretty?" Jack asked, holding the door for her.

"Lawrence is a fink and a liar. You can't be too pretty in this town," Myra Ascheim said. "Or too successful."

The issue of how successful, or not, Myra Ascheim had ever been was never made clear to Jack—or, to his knowledge, to anyone else. No one had either corroborated or repudiated the Hollywood legends attached to Myra, all of them stories about who she *used* to be. Was she once an agent whom I.C.M. wooed away from William Morris, or did C.A.A. woo her away from I.C.M.? Was she eventually fired from all three agencies, or did she go off on her own of her own volition? Did she once represent Julia Roberts? Was it Sharon Stone she was supposed to have "discovered," or was that Demi Moore? And was Myra truly the first person to refer to Demi as *Gimme* Moore?

Jack later ran into Lawrence at the bar of Raffles L'Ermitage— not Jack's favorite hotel in Beverly Hills, but a watering hole Lawrence loved. Lawrence told Jack that Demi Moore's nickname of "Gimme" was his idea, not Myra's. But Myra was right—Lawrence was a fink and a liar. And whether or not Myra Ascheim *ever* represented Julia Roberts, Myra had maintained her contacts with casting directors—almost all of whom liked her. Even if Myra no longer represented *anyone,* casting directors still returned her calls.

Bob Bookman, who was Emma's agent at C.A.A. before he became Jack's, told Jack a story about Myra's identifying baseball cap. She wasn't an Anaheim fan—she didn't even like baseball. She liked the *A* on the hat, but she detested the halo. "It's an A-list hat, but I'm no angel," she liked to say.

According to Bob Bookman, Myra bought an Angels cap every year and removed the halo with a pair of fingernail clippers. "I saw her do it over lunch," Bookman said. "Myra snipped off the halo while she was waiting for her Cobb salad." The Cobb salad made the story ring true; aside from breakfast, a Cobb salad was all Jack ever saw Myra eat.

Alan Hergott—who became Jack's entertainment lawyer—said that Myra always left the same message on his answering machine. "Call me back or I'll sue your pants off." That sounded like Myra.

"In this town, you get tired of hearing something you already know," Alan told Jack. "You're supposed to sound or at least look interested, but you know more about the story than the guy who's telling you the story does. Myra's different. She always knows something you don't know. True or not—it doesn't matter."

In Hollywood, there were as many Myra Ascheim stories as there were stories about Milton Berle's penis. And to think that Jack Burns met her because his schlong was small, or small*ish*— and only because he met her porn-producer sister, Milly, first! In fact, if it hadn't been for Lawrence, Jack might never have met the Ascheim sisters, and he met Lawrence only because the fink wanted to bang Emma. (Knowing Emma, she probably had an instinct that steered her away from Lawrence—maybe his schlong was all wrong for her, or she knew that Lawrence would never relinquish the top position.)

"Actually, I'm no longer an agent," Myra told Jack over their breakfast at Marmalade. They were sitting at a kind of picnic table—communal dining in Santa Monica. "My sister and I have created a talent-management company." This information confused Jack, given his limited (albeit specific) knowledge of the *other* Ascheim. But he would make a point of never trying to grasp how the industry worked. From the beginning, Jack Burns realized that his job was getting a job. He already knew how to be an actor.

A man had spread a newspaper over one end of the picnic table; he sat on the bench beside Jack, muttering, as if he bore a lifelong grudge against the news. At the other end of the table, nearer to Myra than to Jack, was a family of four—a young, harried couple with two quarreling children.

Like Rottweiler, Myra Ascheim had plucked Bruno Litkins from Jack's résumé. "The gay heron," as Jack had called Bruno, was the only marketable name among Jack's earliest supporters. "I don't suppose you *are* a transvestite—you just know how to look like one," Myra said.

"I just know how to look like one," Jack concurred.

"I'll let you know, Jack, when I sense a surfeit of transsexual roles."

The children at Myra's end of the table were bothering her. A little boy, maybe six or seven, had ordered the oatmeal with sliced bananas; then he picked all the bananas out. He wanted some of his older sister's bacon instead, but she wouldn't give him any. "If you wanted bacon, you should have ordered it," the children's mother kept telling him.

"You can have my bananas," the boy told his sister, but the bacon was not negotiable—not for bananas.

"Look—there's a lesson here," Myra said crossly to the little boy. "You want her bacon, but you've got nothing she wants. That's not how you make a deal."

In the movie business, Jack was learning, meeting people was an audition. You didn't even have to know which part you were auditioning for; you just picked a part and played it, *any* part. Jack looked at the little girl who had the bacon. She was nine or ten; she had three strips of bacon. She was his audience of one, for the moment, but Jack was auditioning for Myra Ascheim, and Myra knew it.

In *Blade Runner,* Rutger Hauer plays the blond android—the last to die. He holds Harrison Ford's life in his hands, but Rutger is dying; he'd rather have someone to talk to than die alone. "I've seen things you people wouldn't believe," Rutger Hauer says. That was the moment Jack had in mind.

That was the tone of voice Jack adopted when he spoke to the girl about her bacon. "I have a younger brother," Jack-as-Rutger-Hauer began. "He was always asking me for my stuff—he wanted my bacon, just like your brother wants yours. Maybe I should have given him the bacon, at least one strip."

"Why?" the girl asked.

"I was in a motorcycle accident," Jack said. When he touched his side, he winced; his sudden intake of breath made the little boy squish one of his banana slices. "The handlebars went in here—they went right through me."

"Not while we're eating," Myra Ascheim said, but the children and Jack-as-Rutger-Hauer ignored her.

"I thought I was going to be okay—I lost only one kidney," Jack explained. "We have two," he told the little boy. "You have to have at least one."

"What's wrong with the one you've got?" the little girl asked.

Jack shrugged, then winced again; after the handlebars, apparently it hurt to shrug, too. (He was thinking of the way Rutger Hauer says, "All those moments will be lost in time, like tears in rain.") Jack said: "My one remaining kidney is failing."

" 'Time to die,' " Myra Ascheim said, with a shrug. (Those are Rutger Hauer's last words in *Blade Runner.* Myra obviously knew the movie, too.)

"Of course I could ask my brother for one of *his* kidneys," Jack went on. "Only a brother's body-part would work inside me—only a brother's or a sister's, and I don't have a sister."

"So ask your brother!" the girl said excitedly.

"I suppose I *better* ask him," Jack agreed. "But you see the problem. I never gave him my bacon—not even one strip."

"What's a kidney?" the boy asked.

His sister carefully placed a strip of bacon beside his banana-less bowl of oatmeal. "Here—take this," she told him. "You don't need a kidney."

"I'll let you know, Jack, when I sense a surfeit of Rutger Hauer roles," was all Myra Ascheim said, but Jack knew he'd nailed the audition.

The girl sat watching her brother eat the bacon; Jack could tell she was still thinking about the accident. "Can I see the scar, from the handlebars?" she asked.

"Not while we're eating," Myra said again.

Jack had been so focused on his audience of one, he'd not noticed when the man with the newspaper had left. In any performance, even a good one, somebody always walks out. But after breakfast, out on Montana, Myra was critical of Jack's audition. "You lost the newspaper guy. He didn't buy the handlebars, not for a minute."

"The girl was my audience," Jack said. "The girl and you."

"The girl was an easy audience," Myra told him. "You kind of lost me with the handlebars, too."

"Oh."

"Lose the '*Oh*'—it's a meaningless exclamation, Jack."

Jack realized that he wasn't sure what a talent-management company did, or how what Myra did was different from what an agent did. "Don't I need an agent?" he asked her.

"Let me find you a movie first," Myra said. "A movie and a director. The best time to get an agent is when you don't really need one."

Jack would often think how his career, and his life, might have turned out differently if Myra Ascheim had found a different movie from the one she found for him—or at least a different director. But he knew that one thing you were powerless to change was your first break, and you could never calculate the influence of that initial experience on what happened to you next.

Every young actor imagines there is a special part—a groove in which he or she is a perfect fit. Well—Jack's advice to young actors would be: Hope you never get the perfect part. The groove that Myra Ascheim found for Jack Burns (his first film) became a rut.

"*Principiis obsta!*" Mr. Ramsey would write to him, quoting Ovid. "Beware the beginnings!"

21

Two Candles, Burning

Ultimately, Jack Burns owed his success to William "Wild Bill" Vanvleck, who was also called The Mad Dutchman and The Remake Monster—the latter for his deplorable habit of stealing his stories from classics of the European cinema and crassly reinventing them for American movie audiences.

Hence the brilliant *Knife in the Water,* Roman Polanski's first feature film, which was made in Poland in 1962, was remade by Vanvleck in 1989 as *My Last Hitchhiker*—about a couple with a troubled relationship who go off for a weekend of skiing, not sailing, and pick up a *transvestite* hitchhiker. Jack Burns was born to be that cross-dressing hitchhiker.

William Vanvleck was both a screenwriter and a director. *Variety* once wrote that The Remake Monster never knew a film or a gender he couldn't change for the worse. But if Wild Bill was a rip-off artist, he had a survivor's abundance of common sense; he stole only good stuff. And Vanvleck brought a European kinkiness, if not art, to American sex and violence—always with a lavishness of deceit or duplicity that Bill, and many movie audiences, loved.

For example, there was a section of Route 40 between Empire and Winter Park, Colorado—a steep road with lots of S-turns, it climbed over Berthoud Pass. In the winter, they closed the road when they blasted avalanches, and you could see back-country skiers and snowboarders hitching rides to wherever they parked their cars.

In the opening shot of *My Last Hitchhiker,* we see a pretty female skier wearing a backpack, her skis over her shoulder; she's hitching a ride on Route 40. As everyone would find out, it's not a real girl—it's Jack Burns, and he looks fantastic.

The reason Jack got the part was not only that he had the

Bruno Litkins, transvestite-Esmeralda connection; The Mad Dutchman also liked the idea of the hitchhiker being an unknown.

The couple in the car take a good look at Jack-as-a-girl. (Almost anyone would.) "Keep driving," the woman says.

The man brakes, stopping the car. "My last hitchhiker," he says. "I promise."

"You promised before, Ethan," she tells him. "It was a pretty girl the last time, too."

As Jack is putting his skis on the roof rack of their car, they take a closer look at him. Ethan stares at the pretty girl's breasts; the wife or girlfriend is more interested in Jack's dark, shoulder-length hair. When Jack gets into the backseat, Ethan adjusts the rearview mirror so he can see the hitchhiker better; the woman notices this, with mounting irritation.

"Hi—I'm Jack," he tells them, taking off the wig and wiping the mauve lip gloss off his lips with the back of his ski glove. "You probably thought I was a girl, right?"

The woman turns to watch Jack put the wig in his backpack. Jack unzips his parka, which fits him like a glove, and removes (to Ethan's horror) his breasts, putting the falsies in his backpack with the wig. Granted, it's a B-movie—inspiring a cult of followers—but it's a great opening.

"Hi—I'm Nicole," the woman in the front seat says to Jack; she's suddenly all smiles.

Justine Dunn played Nicole; it was her last movie before her disfiguring, career-ending car crash—that famous five-car smash-up where Wilshire Boulevard tangles with the 405.

In the movie, when Ethan sees that Jack is a guy, he tells him to get out of the car.

"You picked him up, Ethan. Give the guy a ride," Nicole says.

"I didn't pick up a *guy,*" Ethan tells her.

Jack is looking over his shoulder, out the rear window, at the S-turn behind them. "This isn't a very safe place to stop," he says.

"Get out of the car!" Ethan shouts.

A quick cut to the inside of a black van navigating the S-turn; some stoned snowboarders are passing a joint around. (Nicole's line—"If he gets out, Ethan, I'm getting out with him"—plays as voice-over.)

Back on Ethan and Nicole in their stopped car: he prevents

her from undoing her seat belt. The hitchhiker has already taken his skis off the roof rack; he taps on the passenger-side window, which Nicole lowers. Suddenly all-guy, Jack says: "I'm sorry for the trouble, but I catch more rides as a girl." Then he steps back from the car. Here comes the black van!

The van skids past the stopped car in a four-wheel drift—one of the stoned snowboarders frantically giving Ethan and Nicole and Jack the finger. Ethan and Nicole are visibly shaken by the near-collision, but Jack never even flinches.

The movie went downhill from there. When they showed film clips from *My Last Hitchhiker,* they always showed those first two close-ups of Jack.

When the film was released, Jack was twenty-four. Justine was twelve years older—an attractive older woman to Jack's transvestite hitchhiker.

They have one really hot scene later in the movie. Jack-as-a-girl is in the women's room at a ski-resort restaurant, fussing with his makeup in the mirror. Justine-as-Nicole comes out of a stall, straightening her dress. They both look pretty good, but Justine is thirty-six, and it's no secret who looks better.

"What ride are you trying to catch now?" she asks Jack.

"It's called dinner," he replies.

"Do you buy your own lift tickets?" she asks.

"Skiing is an expensive sport," Jack says, with a shrug. "I try not to buy my own dinner."

Justine is looking Jack over when she says, "And what do you do *after* dinner?"

"I talk him out of it," he tells her. "What do *you* do after dinner?"

At this point in the film, Justine-as-Nicole is still with Ethan—and she's not happy about it. "I *try* to talk him out of it," she admits, a little sadly.

That's when Jack kisses her on the lips. It's disturbingly unclear if he's kissing her as a woman or as a man. But what does it matter? *My Last Hitchhiker* would wind up being a favorite of Justine Dunn fans. After she was so tragically disfigured and disappeared from the big screen, Justine gathered an *army* of fans. Crazies, for the most part—the kind of moviegoers who made heroes out of people killed or maimed in stupid accidents.

As for Jack, it was the start of something he felt powerless to stop. As an ex-wrestler, he knew how to lose weight, and how to keep the pounds off—he had kept himself small. He was a light-weight, a former one-thirty-five-pounder; he had a lean-and-mean look, as Michele Maher (the *real* one) had observed.

"Androgyny seems to suit you, Jack," Myra Ascheim would tell him, after Wild Bill Vanvleck had made Jack an aberrant sex symbol—a sexy guy who was, if not to every taste, arguably more sexy as a girl.

Jack's role as the transvestite hitchhiker was three years before Jaye Davidson's debut as Dil in *The Crying Game*—and though Neil Jordan was a first-rate writer and director, and everyone knew Wild Bill Vanvleck was *not,* Jack Burns did it before Jaye Davidson did.

Granted, it was not a role Jack could count on growing old in. (Hollywood didn't exactly have a plethora of parts for foxy but graying Mrs. Doubtfires.) Nevertheless, it was a good start. Jack wasn't as famous as Emma, whose first novel had been a *New York Times* bestseller for fifteen weeks before *My Last Hitchhiker* opened in "select theaters." And Emma was far more famous in Toronto, where there was no one more famous than a natural-born Canadian who made it big in the United States. But to hear Jack's mother talk, not to mention Mr. Ramsey, you would have thought that Jack Burns had eclipsed Jeff Bridges (as a transvestite, anyway) and was even bigger box office than Harrison Ford.

My Last Hitchhiker was an awful movie, but Jack's two close-ups caught on—the parody on *Saturday Night Live* didn't hurt—and the candlelight vigil outside the UCLA Medical Center, where Justine Dunn lay in a coma from her awesome wreck, made a talk-show celebrity out of Wild Bill Vanvleck, who spoke glowingly of Jack Burns.

Of course he did. Myra Ascheim had committed Jack to making another movie with The Mad Dutchman. By singing Jack's praises for what had been less than a supporting-actor role, Wild Bill was promoting his next film, which, alas, would not achieve the cult-classic status of *My Last Hitchhiker.* Although Jack was the male (*and* female) lead in this one, his second B-movie for The Remake Monster, there was no Justine Dunn counterpart—no celebrity actor or actress who suffered a well-timed car crash and lasting, career-ending disfigurement. (No unmerited publicity, in other words.)

Meanwhile, before his follow-up appearance as a cross-dresser in another Vanvleck remake, Jack was the beneficiary of *Emma's* publicity for *The Slush-Pile Reader,* which was considerable. A *People* magazine piece, in which Emma referred to Jack as her roommate, included photographs of them looking cozy together—these in addition to that familiar movie still of Jack transforming himself from a woman to a man, the telltale smudge of pale-purple lip gloss lending to that corner of his pretty mouth the wanton look of someone who's been roughly kissed.

"It's platonic love," Emma was quoted as saying. "We're just roommates." In another interview, Emma said: "I like taking pictures of Jack. He's so photogenic." (This was published with a photograph of Jack, asleep.)

Maybe only Alice and Mrs. Oastler believed that Emma and Jack weren't lovers, and Jack knew that Leslie had her doubts. Lawrence, that fink, had his doubts, too. Emma told Jack that she ran into Lawrence having lunch at Morton's. Lawrence had lost his job at C.A.A., but not to hear him tell it; he bullshitted Emma about starting his own talent-management company and wanting to be "unencumbered." (Like Myra Ascheim, whom he'd so confidently called a has-been.)

Lawrence was "unencumbered" at lunch, Emma observed; he was just a liar who was out of a job. Morton's—the enduring and expensive celebrity hangout on Melrose, in West Hollywood—was not a place where you wanted to be eating lunch alone. No deals were going down for Lawrence, Emma concluded; maybe that's why he got a little crude with her. "Do you still claim you're not banging your boyfriend?" he asked, meaning Jack. "Does Jack go on dates as a girl?"

Emma knew she could kick the crap out of him, but she let it pass. "You're such a loser, Lawrence," was all she said. It was sufficiently gratifying to her that Lawrence didn't seem to know he was in one of the least prestigious booths.

Emma had resigned from her studio job as a script reader a couple of months before *The Slush-Pile Reader* was published. "Screenplay development just isn't for me," she'd told them, but one of the studio execs got hold of a set of her galleys. There was a kind of code in Hollywood, too vague and virulently denied to be a rule: you were not supposed to call an asshole an asshole, not in writing. It was the dim understanding of this studio exec that Emma had violated the code. To punish her, the exec copied Emma's script notes and distributed them to the rejected writers' agents. But the punishment backfired: once you start making copies, *everyone* sees them. The execs at other studios read Emma's notes; after all, many of the screenplays in question were still making the rounds.

A few of those scripts were now films in production; a couple were in post-production, meaning they'd miraculously been shot, and one had recently been released, to tepid reviews. Naturally, the reviews weren't as insightful or well-written as Emma's notes on an earlier draft of the screenplay. Even the rejected writers' agents liked Emma's notes—two of them offered her a job.

A celebrity talk-show host at an L.A. radio station asked Emma's permission to read some of her script notes on the air. "Sure," Emma said. "Everyone else has read them." (More publicity for *The Slush-Pile Reader*—not that Emma needed it.)

This didn't win Emma many friends among screenwriters, but what really insulted the industry was that Emma said she wasn't interested in writing a screenplay herself—especially not an adaptation of *The Slush-Pile Reader.* In the novel, she'd already made the point that the story was one third porn film; no one would attempt to make a serious movie out of that material. To virtually assure herself that no one would, Emma entangled the film rights to her novel with the kind of approvals never granted to writers—not to first novelists, anyway. She again asserted that she had no interest in adapting *The Slush-Pile Reader* herself, yet she insisted on retaining script approval, should anyone else be enough of a fool to write a screenplay, and she insisted on having cast approval and director approval—even final cut. *The Slush-Pile Reader* couldn't be made as a movie under those outrageous terms.

When Emma showed up at all the usual places—she took Jack with her, more and more—it was widely assumed that she was doing research for another Hollywood novel, but Jack didn't know (at the time) that this was the case. He thought she just liked to eat and drink. But Emma saw herself as a specter sent to remind the studio execs that there was such a thing as a script reader who could *write.*

In the movie business, they were already speaking admiringly of *The Slush-Pile Reader* as "not makable," which could be quite a compliment in the industry—provided you didn't make a habit of it.

Jack worried about Emma. She had bought the house they'd been renting in Santa Monica, for no good reason. The move from Venice had irritated her; she said she didn't want to move again. But if the house in Santa Monica was no prize to rent, it was just plain stupid to *buy* it.

It was a two-story, three-bedroom house on the downhill end of Entrada Drive—near where Entrada ran into the Pacific Coast Highway. You could hear the drone of traffic on the PCH over the air-conditioning. Furthermore, as if Emma and Jack were permanently drawn to the perfume of restaurant Dumpsters, the driveway of the house intersected the alley behind an Italian restaurant. It wasn't sushi they smelled—it was more like old eggplant parmigiana.

But they were living on Entrada Drive when Emma's first novel was published, and she became what she called (with no small amount of pride) "a self-supporting novelist." Her revenge on having wasted her time as a film major was complete; she had made it in the industry's hometown by writing, of all things, a *novel.* Staying in the house on Entrada, even buying the stupid place, was another way of thumbing her nose at the industry. Emma had come to L.A. as an outsider; it meant a lot to her to *stay* an outsider.

"I'm not moving to Beverly Hills, baby cakes."

"Yeah, well—we sure do a lot of *eating* there," Jack reminded her.

It was a lot of late-night eating, for the most part. Jack didn't drink, so he was always the driver. Emma could drink a bottle of red wine by herself—usually before she finished her dinner. She had a special fondness for Kate Mantilini in Beverly Hills.

"Kate Mantilini is quite a distance to travel for a steak sandwich and mashed potatoes," Jack complained; he didn't eat bread, not to mention mashed potatoes. But Emma loved to eat at the long bar that ran the length of the restaurant. The industry crowd all knew her and asked her how the new novel was coming.

"It's coming," was all Emma would say. "Have you met my roommate, Jack Burns? He was the chick in *My Last Hitch-hiker*—I mean the hot one."

"I was the *hitchhiker*," Jack would explain. Despite Myra Ascheim telling him to lose the stubble, he was usually growing a little something on his face—anything that might mitigate his androgynous first impression.

Monday nights, Emma and Jack went to Dan Tana's in West Hollywood. You could watch *Monday Night Football* on the TV at the bar, yet the waiters wore tuxedos. There was a mostly hip Hollywood crowd—people in the biz, or trying to be, but in the curious company of assorted gangsters and hookers. There were red-vinyl booths and red-and-white-checkered tablecloths, and the items on the menu were named for film-industry celebs.

"You're gonna have a lamb loin named after you one day, honey pie," Emma would tell Jack. She usually ordered the Lew Wasserman veal chop. After Wasserman died, Jack felt funny about eating there—as if the veal chop in his name were a piece of Lew himself. Emma also liked the steak à la Diller, but Jack ate light—often just a salad. He was back on iced tea big-time, as during his days cutting weight as a wrestler. With a half-gallon of tea on an empty stomach, Jack could dance all night.

Emma liked late-night music, too. She was crazy about a place in West Hollywood on Sunset Boulevard—Coconut Teaszer. It was a bit sleazy—lots of rock 'n' roll and fast, sweaty dancing. Very young kids went there. Emma would occasionally pick up a boy and bring him home. Jack made an effort not to watch them making out in the backseat. "Listen," she would always say to the kid. "You gotta do *exactly* what I tell you." Jack tried not to listen.

He also tried not to imagine Emma in the top position. He didn't like to think about her vaginismus, but he would remember the night he found her in tears in the bathroom—doubled over in pain. "He said he wouldn't move," she was crying. "He *promised* he wouldn't—the little fucker!"

The mornings after Emma brought home some kid from Coconut Teaszer were the only ones when she wouldn't get up early to write her next Hollywood novel. (*"Number Two,"* as she would refer to it—as if that were the title.) Emma was disciplined, even driven, but the pressure was off; she'd published her first novel and seemed confident that someone would publish the second.

To a lesser degree, the pressure was off Jack, too. That he had made his first film with William Vanvleck—and worse, was under contract to make another movie with him—didn't impress anyone at C.A.A. (Or at I.C.M. or the William Morris Agency.) Perhaps, when Jack was free of any future obligation to Wild Bill, one of those agencies would consider representing him. But for now, Myra Ascheim was looking after him—he was instructed to call Myra his *manager*.

When Jack quit his job at American Pacific, there were no hard feelings; he'd slept with only two of the waitresses, and one of them had quit before he did. Even working for The Remake Monster beat being a waiter.

Emma wanted Jack to read her fan mail before he showed it to her. She had no tolerance for anything negative; Jack was under orders to throw the criticism away. "And don't show me the death threats, Jack—just send them to the F.B.I." There weren't any death threats; most of Emma's mail was positive. The worst of it, in Jack's opinion, was how many of her readers insisted on telling Emma their life stories. It was amazing how many dysfunctional people wanted her to write about *them*.

Emma read Jack's fan mail before he saw it, but he read all of his mail eventually—good and bad. He didn't get a *twentieth* of the mail Emma received, and most of his was both vaguely and not so vaguely insinuating. Letters, always with photographs, from transsexuals—"chicks with dicks," according to Emma—and letters from gay men, inquiring if Jack was gay. There was only the occasional letter from a young woman—usually, but not always, stating that she hoped he was straight.

Jack was more interested in Emma's mail than he was in his, because he kept thinking that Michele Maher would write to her—demanding to know why Emma had used her name. But there was no letter from Michele Maher about *The Slush-Pile Reader*.

It killed Jack that he knew nothing about Michele; worse, he imagined she had seen *My Last Hitchhiker* and found his performance as a transvestite to be resounding confirmation that he was "too weird."

"Just wait till Michele sees the next one, baby cakes—talk about *too weird*!" They'd both read Vanvleck's screenplay, which had prompted even Emma to say: "Words fail me."

It was a magical but unknown movie that Wild Bill had ripped off this time; he'd stolen a little gem from a fellow Dutchman, Peter van Engen, who died of AIDS shortly after his first and only feature film was made. Called *Lieve Anne Frank* (in English, *Dear Anne Frank,* as you might begin a letter to the dead girl), it won a prize at some film festival in the Netherlands—and it was dubbed for distribution in Germany, but nowhere else. Outside Holland, almost no one saw it; yet William Vanvleck had seen it, and he'd traduced *Lieve Anne Frank* to such a degree that poor Peter van Engen couldn't possibly have recognized his own movie—not even from the all-seeing perspective of his grave.

"*Lieve Anne Frank,*" the voice-over begins. It is the voice of a young Jewish girl, living in Amsterdam today; she is about the same age Anne Frank was when Anne was caught by the Nazis and taken to the death camp.

Emma and Jack saw the original Dutch film in William Vanvleck's home screening room. The Remake Monster had an ugly mansion on Loma Vista Drive in Beverly Hills. Wild Bill liked whippets; they ran free in the mansion, slipping and falling on the hardwood floors. Vanvleck had his own chef and his own gardener—a Surinamese couple, a child-size woman with a similarly miniature husband.

" 'Dear Anne Frank,' " Wild Bill translated for Emma and Jack; he had a smoker's cough. " 'I believe that you live in me, and that I have been born to serve you.' "

Rachel is her name. Weekdays after school, and on weekends, she works as a tour guide in the Anne Frank House—Prinsengracht 263. The house is open, as a museum, every day of the year except Yom Kippur.

"The Anne Frank House is beautiful in a sad way," Rachel says to the camera—as if we (the audience) were tourists and Rachel our guide. We see samples of Anne's handwriting, facsimiles from her diary, and many photographs. Rachel has cut her hair to look as much like Anne as she can; she despises contemporary fashion and dresses herself, whenever possible, in clothes Anne might have worn.

We see Rachel shopping in flea markets and secondhand clothing stores; we see her at night, hiding from her parents in her bedroom, imitating poses and expressions we recognize from photographs of Anne.

"They could have gotten away," Rachel keeps repeating. "Her father, Otto, could have stolen a boat. He could have steered a course from the Prinsengracht, the canal, to the Amstel—a river, broader than the canal. *Not* to the sea, of course, but somewhere safe. I *know* they could have gotten away."

By this point in the film, nothing had really happened, but Emma was already in tears. "You see—it's good, isn't it?" Vanvleck kept asking. "Isn't it *great*?"

Rachel is obsessed with the idea that she is Anne Frank come back to life; she believes she can rewrite history. On Yom Kippur, when the Anne Frank House is closed, Rachel unlocks the door and lets herself inside. She dresses herself as Anne— *transforms* herself, actually, because the likeness is more than a little creepy—and the next morning, when the tourists are waiting to get in, Rachel-as-Anne simply walks out of the Anne Frank House *as if she were Anne Frank*. Some of the tourists scream, believing she's a ghost; others follow her, taking her picture.

She goes to the canal, the Prinsengracht, where her father, Otto, is waiting with a boat. Absurdly, it's a kind of gondola— more suited to Venice than to Amsterdam—and Otto is a most unlikely, un-Italian-looking gondolier. Anne boards the boat, waving to her admirers.

There's a beautiful shot from the golden crown of the Westerkerk of the boat passing on the Prinsengracht—crowds of wellwishers run to the bridges, waving. There's a shot of the little boat entering the broader water of the Amstel; more crowds, more cameras clicking.

How the fantasy dies is almost entirely done with sound—the sound of soldiers' boots on the cobblestone streets; the sound of the boots on the stairs of the Anne Frank House, which we see is empty. Some furniture has been tipped over; Anne's writing has been scattered here and there. She hasn't escaped.

Emma was bawling her eyes out. As Jack sat there in that tasteless mansion on Loma Vista Drive, the sound of The Mad Dutchman's whippets dashing everywhere was somehow intercut in Jack's mind with the sound of the storm troopers' boots. He couldn't imagine what a mess Wild Bill Vanvleck was going to make of *Dear Anne Frank*.

As it turned out, The Remake Monster's screenplay would leave Emma and Jack depressed for days.

"I think I'll go to the gym," Jack told Emma when he first read it.

After she said, "Words fail me," Emma took a deep breath and announced she was going back to work. "I should have known when we saw the movie," Emma told Jack later. "There was no way you were gonna be Anne Frank."

But that day they read the remake, which was their first understanding of what would become of *Dear Anne Frank*, all Jack could do was go to the gym and punish his body; all Emma could do was go back to work on her next Hollywood novel. The Mad Dutchman's screenplay was god-awful.

Being successful had made Emma even more of a workaholic. She usually got up with the rush-hour traffic on the PCH and drank several cups of strong coffee, sometimes with her eyes closed but always with the music playing—something too loud and metallic for Jack's taste, although it was a welcome change from the generally uninspired music out on the highway.

Emma wrote all morning—the coffee was what she called her "appetite suppressant of choice." When she was famished, she drove herself out to lunch. She didn't drink at lunch, although she was a big eater—both at lunch *and* at her late-night dinners.

She liked Le Dome on Sunset Strip. It had a stodgy, Old Hollywood feeling, but it was still a happening place for executives and agents and entertainment lawyers. Emma also liked Spago in West Hollywood—the original Spago, up the hill on Sunset Boulevard. And while it was too expensive even for the most successful of first novelists, Emma needed a weekly fix of The Palm on Santa Monica Boulevard, where she said there were more agents than steaks and lobsters.

She was burning the candle at both ends, because she'd go to the gym after lunch and lift weights most of the afternoon. After the weightlifting, when she said she had "digested," she would do a hundred or more crunches for her abs. Nothing aerobic. (Dancing and whatever sex she could manage in the top position were Emma's aerobics.)

It was a lot for a big girl to put her body through, and Jack didn't like to think of her driving—not even in the daytime, when she hadn't been drinking. Emma was a fast driver, but the speed was only a small part of what bothered Jack.

Emma loved Sunset Boulevard. Even in Toronto, as a schoolgirl at St. Hilda's, she used to dream of driving on Sunset Boulevard. Emma tried to drive everywhere on Sunset—out to Beverly Hills and West Hollywood and Hollywood, *all* on Sunset.

It was when she was driving back to Santa Monica that Jack worried about her. He knew she'd had a big lunch and had crazily worked it off, or not, in the gym. He worried about the curves on Sunset. And when Emma took that left on Chautauqua, just before the Palisades, it was a steep, twisting downhill to the PCH. You had to get into the far-left lane and make what amounted to a U-turn on West Channel.

It would be late afternoon, rush-hour traffic, and Emma was drained from her workout in the gym—two or three liter-size bottles of Evian later. With the traffic barreling down Chautauqua, into that last long curve, Emma would be three quarters of the way through the turn before she could see the ocean. Jack knew Emma, even her driving. She wouldn't be watching the cars—not when she could see that first, dazzling-blue glint of the Pacific. She was, after all, a Toronto girl. L.A. affected you in direct proportion to where you came from; there were no views of the Pacific in Toronto.

Jack would wait in the Entrada house for Emma to come home. Then she would write. That was when Jack went to the gym. (He never told her he occasionally went to Gold's.)

It was a good time to work out; mostly the nondrinkers, and a few noneaters, were there. Jack met some pretty pumped women doing free weights, but the ones on the cardiovascular machines were the ultra-skinny girls, and at dinnertime, many of the skinny girls were anorexics. One girl—she spent an hour every night on the stair-climber—told Jack she was on "an all-smoothie diet."

"How's your energy?" he asked her.

"Berries, teaspoon of honey, nonfat yogurt—every third day, a banana. Just put everything in the blender," she told him. "Your body doesn't need anything else."

She fell off the treadmill one night and just lay there. One of the yoga instructors speculated that her colon had collapsed on itself. Jack would remember a bunch of bodybuilders standing outside the gym; when they saw the ambulance, they waved it down with their towels.

Jack was on his usual diet—mostly proteins, maybe a little light on the carbs for all the time he spent on the cardiovascular machines. He was taking it easy with the free weights: nothing heavy, just lots of reps. He wasn't trying to bulk up. His job,

meaning getting one—the next role, and the role after that—
depended on his staying lean and mean.

Jack was light-headed with hunger by the time he left the gym
every night, when he went back to get Emma and they drove out
again to eat—and his stomach was falling in on itself every
morning. You could say that Jack was burning the candle at both
ends, too—but not like Emma.

One night, when she was wolfing down her mashed potatoes
at Kate Mantilini, Emma noticed that Jack hadn't finished his
salad. He'd stopped eating and was watching her eat; his expression was one of concern, not disgust, but Jack should have
known that Emma would have found his disgust more acceptable.

"Are you thinking I'm gonna die young?" she asked him.

"No!" he said, too quickly.

"Well, I am," she told him. "If my appetite doesn't kill me, the
vaginismus will."

"The vaginismus can't kill you, can it?" Jack asked her, but
Emma's mouth was full; she just shrugged and went on eating.

22

Money Shots

Batman and *Lethal Weapon 2* were among the top-grossing movies of 1989, but the Oscar for Best Picture would go to *Driving Miss Daisy.* Jack's second film with William Vanvleck was called *The Tour Guide;* it wouldn't win any awards.

The Anne Frank House has been reinvented in Las Vegas. A tacky shrine to a dead rock-'n'-roll star clearly modeled on a prettier Janis Joplin—that would be Jack—draws morbid fans of the late sexpot, who, earlier in the movie, chokes to death on her own vomit following a drunken binge. The dead singer's name is Melody; her group, Pure Innocence, gets its start in the beatnik haunts of Venice and North Beach in the early 1960s. They abandon their folk-jazz-blues roots for psychedelic rock, finding an audience and a home for themselves among the flower children in San Francisco in 1966.

Everything in a William Vanvleck remake was stolen from something else; Pure Innocence and Melody's leap to fame coincides with when Janis Joplin started singing with Big Brother and the Holding Company. Melody's first hit single, "You Can't Handle My Heart Like It Was Somethin' Else," sounds suspiciously like Big Mama Thornton's "Ball and Chain." Jack didn't sing it half badly.

Jack-as-Melody promptly dumps Pure Innocence and goes solo. By '69, Melody's albums have gone gold and platinum and triple-platinum. She returns to being a blues singer with her last hit single, "Bad Bill Is Gone," an ode to an abusive ex-boyfriend—the former lead guitarist in Pure Innocence, whom the tabloids allege Melody once tried to kill by lacing his favorite marijuana lasagna with rat poison. (That "Bad Bill Is Gone" sounded like "Me and Bobby McGee" couldn't be a coincidence.)

Jack-as-Melody dies passed-out drunk and choking on his-as-her puke in a Las Vegas hotel room, following a concert there—hence the shrine to Melody's short life and intense fame opens as yet another rock-'n'-roll museum, this one at the Mandalay Bay end of the strip. The crass display of Melody's less-than-innocent underwear is out of place and easy to overlook among those casinos and hotels on the strip, but The Mad Dutchman had always wanted to make a movie in Las Vegas, and *The Tour Guide* was it.

Certainly Wild Bill could have found a better singer for Melody, but maybe not a hotter girl. ("You were hot, baby cakes," Emma told Jack. "Your singing lacked a little something, but you were hot—I'll give you that.") Jack wasn't bad as the guy, either—the eponymous tour guide himself.

"Let's keep it simple," Wild Bill Vanvleck told Jack. "Let's call the tour guide Jack."

Jack-as-Jack is a devoted fan of Pure Innocence, in the group's short-lived Melody years. Jack is still in college when Melody splits from the group; he has only recently graduated when the singer dies. His adoration of Melody is deeper than the after-her-death kind. (In the film, Jack appears to be dancing when he walks—"Bad Bill Is Gone" or "You Can't Handle My Heart Like It Was Somethin' Else" is pounding in his head.)

The sleazy manager of the Melody Museum, as the shameless shrine is called, hires Jack-as-Jack as a tour guide, but Jack is disapproving of some of the displays, which he sees as exploiting Melody—not that the slut singer didn't do plenty to exploit herself. Her collected musical instruments are innocent, as are the photos of her tours and the music itself. But there are "compromising" photographs—of Melody consorting with the lead guitarist who beat her, of Melody drunk and passed out on various motel-room beds. And there are her clothes, especially her "intimate apparel"; no one should see or paw over her underwear, Jack believes. Jack also disapproves of the collection of empty wine bottles; some of the dates on the labels indicate that Melody died before the wines were bottled.

The manager, a precursor of the Harvey Keitel character in *Holy Smoke,* tells Jack that the wine bottles are for "atmosphere"; as for the displayed underwear, a pink thong, among others—these items are "essential."

Just as Rachel imagines that Anne Frank could have gotten

away, Jack convinces himself that Melody didn't have to die. If only he'd been around and had known her, he could have saved her. Jack believes that the shrine to Melody is a betrayal of her; the seedier of her collected things are mocking her.

One night, when the Melody Museum is closed, Jack lets himself in—he has a key. He brings a couple of empty suitcases and packs up the items he considers too intimate, or too damaging to Melody's reputation; the latter, apparently, is sacred only to him. Two cops in a patrol car see lights in the closed building and investigate. But Jack-as-Jack has transformed himself into Jack-as-Melody. Dressed as the dead singer, he carries the suitcases past the stunned policemen—out onto the Vegas strip. (Not every guy can get away with emerald-green spangles on black spandex.) It is The Mad Dutchman's sole directorial touch of genius: until the scene when Jack-as-Melody walks out of the Melody Museum, toting the suitcases, the audience has never seen the strip at night in its garish neon splendor.

Inexplicably, the cops let Jack-as-Melody go. Do they think he's Melody's ghost? (They don't look frightened.) Do they know he's a guy in drag? (They don't look as if they care.) Or do the cops—like Jack, like the audience—recognize that the Melody Museum is a twisted place? Do they think the shrine *ought to be* robbed?

Wild Bill Vanvleck doesn't explain. It's the image The Re-make Monster cares about—Jack-as-Melody walking up the strip in emerald-green heels and that hot dress, lugging those obviously heavy bags. As Jack is leaving, disappearing into the night—reborn as Melody, maybe, or just looking for an afford-able hotel—the sleazy manager sees him-as-her walking away. Jack looks so perfect that the manager doesn't try to intervene. He merely shouts: "You're fired, Jack—you bitch!"

In Melody's voice, Jack says: "It's a good job to lose." (Jack Burns's contribution to Vanvleck's god-awful script—he was right about that line having legs.)

The Tour Guide was by no means the *worst* movie of the year. (Or of the following year, which produced *Teenage Mutant Ninja Turtles* and *Die Hard 2*.) And the shot of Jack Burns in drag, when he's saying, "It's a good job to lose"—well, *everyone* would remember that. The film may have been forgettable, but not that shot—not that line.

At the 1991 Academy Awards, Billy Crystal was the host. He was good, but he may have been a bit too fast with one of his jokes. It was a pretty knowing audience at the Shrine Civic Auditorium, but most of them missed the joke. Not Jack, who was watching the show on TV; he got it, but that's because it was his line.

Billy Crystal was talking about the possibility of being replaced as the host of the Academy Awards. The audience groaned in protest at the very idea; most of them then missed Billy saying, in a pointedly *feminine* way, "It's a good job to lose."

That was when Emma and Jack knew he had made it. "Shit, did you hear that, baby cakes?" They were in Mrs. Oastler's house—Emma and Jack were back in Toronto, visiting their mothers—but Alice and Leslie were whispering to each other in the kitchen; they missed Billy Crystal's homage to Jack's famous end line in *The Tour Guide,* and they would go to bed before *Dances with Wolves* won the Oscar for Best Picture.

Jack had not only heard Billy Crystal's joke; he was genuinely impressed by Billy's imitation of Jack-as-Melody. "Christ," he said.

"No more Mad Dutchman, honey pie," Emma said. "I can't wait for your next movie." Jack and Emma were on the couch in the grand living room of what he used to think of as the Oastler mansion. (That was before he'd seen some of those *real* mansions in Beverly Hills.) If Jack looked over Emma's shoulder, he could see the foyer at the foot of the main staircase, where Mrs. Machado had landed her high-groin kick with such devastating results.

Emma had sold her second novel for big bucks. She'd taken the manuscript to Bob Bookman at C.A.A. before she submitted it to her publisher. She had no intention of making the film rights unsalable this time. Bookman got her a movie deal before the novel was published, which was just the way Emma wanted it.

Called *Normal and Nice,* Emma's second Hollywood novel was about what happens to a young couple from Iowa who go to Hollywood to fulfill their dreams of becoming movie stars. The husband, Johnny, gives up his dream before his wife, Carol, gives up hers. Johnny is too thin-skinned to make it as an actor; a couple of rough auditions and he packs it in. Besides, he's a real clean liver—a nondrinker, an overall straight arrow. With boyish charm and a spotless driving record, Johnny gets a job as a limo driver; soon he's driving a stretch.

Given Emma's knack for irony, Johnny ends up driving movie stars. His lingering desire for the actor's imagined life is reflected by his ponytail, Johnny's sole emblem of rebellion among limo drivers. His ponytail is neat and clean, and not very long. (Emma describes Johnny as "attractive in a delicate, almost feminine way.") Long hair suits him; Johnny feels fortunate that the limousine company lets him keep the ponytail.

His wife, Carol, isn't so lucky. She goes to work for an escort service—much to Johnny's shame but with his reluctant approval. Carol tries one service after another, in alphabetical order—Absolutely Gorgeous, Beautiful Beyond Belief, and so on.

Johnny draws the line at Have You Been a Bad Boy? But it doesn't matter; as Carol discovers, they're all alike. Whether at Instant Escorts or Irresistible Temptations, what's expected of her is the same—namely, everything.

At one escort service, Carol might last a week or a month or less than a day. It all depends on how long it takes for her to meet what Emma calls an "irregular" customer. Once Carol starts refusing to do what a client wants, her days at that particular escort service are numbered.

Not unlike *The Slush-Pile Reader, Normal and Nice* reveals Emma's sympathy for damaged, deeply compromised relationships that somehow work. Carol and Johnny never stop loving each other; what holds them together is their absolute, unshakable agreement concerning what constitutes normal and nice behavior.

Carol does outcalls only. She always phones Johnny and tells him where she's going—not just the hotel but the customer's name and room number—and she calls Johnny again when she gets to the room, and when she's safely out. But *irregular* requests are commonplace; Carol loses her job at one service after another.

Finally, Johnny has a suggestion: Carol should have her own listing in the Yellow Pages. The best thing Carol ever has to say about a client is that he was "nice." Nice means "normal"—hence Carol calls her escort service Normal and Nice.

Emma writes: "She might have attracted more customers with

a service called Maternity Leave. Who calls an escort service for normal and nice?"

Johnny starts pimping for Carol. He has some regular limo clients, people Johnny feels he knows—movie stars among them. "You're probably not interested," Johnny says to the outwardly nicer of the gentlemen he drives around in his stretch, "but if you're ever tempted to call an escort service, I know one particularly *nice* woman—*normal* and nice, if that's what you like. Nothing *irregular,* if you know what I mean."

The first time Johnny says this to a famous actor, it is heartbreaking. The reader already knows that, instead of becoming a movie star, Johnny is driving them. Now Carol is *fucking* them!

It seems that only older men are interested; most of them aren't movie stars, either. They're character actors—villains in the great Westerns, now with ravaged faces and unsteady on their feet, old cowboys with chronic lower-back pain. As children, Carol and Johnny had seen these classic Westerns; they were the movies that made them want to leave Iowa and go to Hollywood in the first place.

At home, in their half of a tacky duplex in Marina del Rey—close enough to hear and smell the L.A. airport—Carol and Johnny play dress-up games, their roles reversed. She puts her blond hair in a ponytail and dresses in his white shirt and black tie; this prompts Johnny to buy Carol a man's black suit, one that fits her. She dresses as a limo driver, then undresses for him.

Johnny lets Carol dress him in *her* clothes; she later buys him his own bra, with falsies, and a dress that fits him. She brushes out his shoulder-length hair and makes him up—lipstick, eye shadow, the works. He rings the doorbell and she lets him-as-her in; he pretends to be the escort, arriving in a stranger's hotel room. "This is their only opportunity to act—together, in the same movie," Emma writes.

A veteran cowboy actor is in town to promote his new film—what Emma calls a "nouvelle Western." Lester Billings was born Lester Magruder in Billings, Montana; he's an actual cowboy, and nouvelle Westerns offend him. It's a sore point with Lester that Westerns have become so rare that young actors don't know how to ride and shoot anymore. In the so-called Western that Lester is promoting, there are no good guys, no bad guys; everyone is an anti-hero. "A *French* Western," Lester calls it.

Johnny sends Carol to Lester's hotel room—after Lester confesses to a hankering for a nice, normal woman. But Lester really *is* a cowboy; he climbs on Carol. ("There was nothing *too* irregular—at first," she assures Johnny.) Then, while they're proceeding in the regular way, Lester puts a gun to his head. It's a Colt .45—only one chamber of the revolver is loaded. Lester calls this cowboy roulette.

"Either I die in the saddle or I live to ride another day!" he hollers. As Lester pulls the trigger, Carol wonders how many girls in L.A. escort services have heard the *click* of that hammer striking an empty chamber, while Lester lived to ride another day. Not this time. It's Lester's day to die in the saddle.

In the midafternoon, there aren't many guests in The Peninsula Beverly Hills to hear the gunshot. Besides, the hotel doesn't cater to an especially youthful crowd; maybe the guests in nearby rooms are napping or hard of hearing. Emma describes The Peninsula as being "sort of like the Four Seasons, but with a few more hookers and businessmen."

Because the hotel is adjacent to C.A.A., possibly an agent hears Lester Billings blow his brains out, but nobody else. And what would an agent care about a gunshot?

Carol calls Johnny. She knows that no one noticed her crossing the lobby and getting on the elevator, but what if someone sees her *leave*? She is understandably distraught; she believes that she *looks* like a hooker. She doesn't, really. Carol has always dressed like a studio exec having lunch; in keeping with normal and nice, she *doesn't* look like a call girl.

Johnny saves her. He comes to Lester's hotel room with the requisite changes of clothes, for Carol and himself. The limo driver's suit for Carol, together with the dress and bra and falsies Carol bought for him; by the time Carol has applied his makeup and brushed out his shoulder-length hair, Johnny looks a lot more like a prostitute than Carol *ever* has.

He tells her where the limo is parked. It's not far—nor is it parked within sight of the entrance to The Peninsula. He says he'll come find her.

When Johnny-as-a-hooker leaves The Peninsula, he makes sure he's noticed. Johnny has used a little bottle of bourbon from the minibar in Lester's hotel room as a mouthwash. He struts up to the front desk, where he-as-she seizes a young clerk by his coat lapels and breathes in his face. "There's something you should know," Johnny-as-a-hooker says in a husky voice.

"Lester Billings has checked out. I'm afraid he's really left his room a *mess.*" Then Johnny-as-a-hooker releases the young man and sways through the lobby, leaving the hotel. He and Carol drive home to Marina del Rey, where they change into their regular clothes.

At the end of the novel, they've stopped for the night in a motel room off Interstate 80 somewhere in the Midwest. They're on their way back to Iowa to find normal jobs and live a nice life. Carol is pregnant. (Maternity Leave, as an escort service, might have been wildly successful, but Carol wants no part of the business—not anymore—and Johnny is through with driving movie stars.)

In the motel room off the interstate, there's an old Lester Billings movie on the TV—an *authentic* Western. Lester is a cattle rustler; he dies in the saddle, shot dead on his horse.

Normal and Nice turned out to be a better movie than a novel, and Emma knew it would be. The film was already in production while the novel was still on the *New York Times* bestseller list. Many book reviewers complained that the novel was written with the future screenplay in mind. Naturally, Emma wrote the screenplay, too; among film critics, there was some speculation that she might have written it before she wrote the novel. Emma wouldn't say.

Jack didn't know the details of the deal she made with Bob Bookman at C.A.A., but while Bookman didn't normally represent actors, he agreed to represent Jack. Whether it was in writing—or something that was said over lunch, or in a phone call—it was understood that Emma *and* Jack were attached to the movie that would be made from *Normal and Nice.* Emma would write the script and Jack would be Johnny. Of course Emma had Jack in mind for the part from the beginning—a *sympathetic* cross-dresser. And this time his shoulder-length hair would be real, not a wig.

Mary Kendall played Carol—as innocent an escort as you'd ever see. Jake "Prairie Dog" Rawlings played Lester Billings—his first role in a long time, and his only screen appearance *not* in a Western.

When Mary Kendall and Jack are holding hands in that Interstate 80 motel room, just watching TV, they have no dialogue. In the same scene in the novel, watching Lester Billings get shot,

Carol says, "I wonder how many times he got killed in his career."

"Enough so he wasn't afraid of it," Johnny says.

But Emma thought it was better if they didn't say anything in the film. It's more of a movie moment—to just see them watching the old cowboy die. Their dreams, to be movie stars, have died, too; something of that is visible in Carol's and Johnny's resigned expressions. That green or blue-gray light from the television screen flickers on their faces.

But Jack would have liked to say the line. ("Enough so he wasn't afraid of it.")

"Maybe you'll get to use it later," Emma told him, "but not this time. This time, *I'm* the writer."

Emma was more than that. She was the architect of Jack's future in film, the reason he would make the leap from Wild Bill Vanvleck to more-or-less mainstream. Of course Jack Burns was still best known in drag, but suddenly he was *serious*.

It was quite a surprise when Jack was nominated for an Academy Award; he hadn't thought of the cross-dressing limo driver as being *that* sympathetic a part. It was no surprise that Jack wouldn't win that year. It was Mary Kendall's first Oscar nomination, too, and she wouldn't win, either. But they were both nominated, which was more than they'd ever imagined.

The Silence of the Lambs would win Best Picture, and Jodie Foster and Anthony Hopkins Best Actress and Best Actor, respectively—it was their year.

Emma wasn't nominated. Screenwriters were nominated by screenwriters; Emma's famous script notes still rankled. Emma went to the Oscars as Jack's date, which made it fun. They generally agreed who the assholes were; identifying the assholes was an important activity at an event like that.

Billy Crystal, again the host, made a joke about the evening being delayed—"because Jack Burns is still changing his bra."

Emma had a very noticeable hickey on her throat. Jack had given it to her, at her request. She hadn't gone out with anyone in a long time, she thought she was ugly, and she hated her Oscar dress. "At least make it look like someone's kissing me, honey pie."

Mrs. Oastler spotted Emma's hickey on TV in Toronto. "Couldn't you have put a little concealer on it?" Leslie asked Emma.

It was March 30, 1992—the first time Mrs. Oastler and Alice stayed up to watch the entire Academy Awards show, although Jack told them not to bother. He knew Anthony Hopkins was going to win Best Actor, but Leslie and Alice stayed up to watch Jack not win, anyway.

They always showed a film clip of the nominated actors. Jack knew the shot he wanted them to use for him. It's his face at the wheel of the limo—Jack-as-Johnny glances once in the rearview mirror at his wife, Carol, who's all alone in the long backseat of the stretch. Carol is trying to put her hair and lipstick in order; she's looking a little messy from a hotel-room groping by an overeager tourist at the Beverly Wilshire. Jack's eyes go briefly to the rearview mirror, then back to the road. It's a look between stoic and *noir;* he was proud of that close-up.

But with marketing, there's no such thing as too obvious. The film clip they showed instead was the call-girl shot: Jack-as-a-hooker is breathing bourbon into the face of the front-desk clerk at The Peninsula Beverly Hills. "There's something you should know," Jack-as-a-hooker tells the clerk in that husky voice. "Lester Billings has checked out. I'm afraid he's really left his room a *mess.*"

"The money shot," Myra Ascheim called it, when Emma and Jack ran into her at the Oscar party at Morton's. It had taken ages to get in; the limos were backed up on Robertson as far as they could see.

Jack was unfamiliar with the phrase. "The money shot," he repeated.

"He's Canadian," Myra explained. Jack saw that she was sitting with her sister, Mildred.

"Two tough old broads in a power booth," Emma would say later.

"In a porn film," Milly Ascheim explained, without looking at Jack, "the money shot is the male-ejaculation moment. You don't get it, you got nothin'. Either the guy delivers the goods, or he can't."

"What's it called when you don't deliver, or you can't?" Emma asked the porn producer.

"Crabs in ice water," Milly said. "You *gotta* deliver the money shot."

"The equivalent of that shot of you as a hooker, Jack," Myra said condescendingly. Perhaps she was peeved with him because he hadn't recognized her. (She wasn't wearing her baseball cap.)

"I get it," Jack told the Ascheim sisters. He was anxious to leave. Emma was holding his hand; Jack could tell she wanted to leave, too. The two tough old broads were looking her over, and it wasn't a friendly assessment.

"It doesn't matter that you didn't win, Jack," Myra continued, staring at Emma.

"It *only* matters when you win," Milly corrected her.

"Well, we gotta go—there's another party," Emma said. "A *younger* one."

"Nice hickey," Mildred Ascheim told Emma.

"Thanks," Emma said. "Jack gave it to me—it's a real doozy."

Mildred shifted her examining gaze to Jack. "He's cute, isn't he?" Myra asked her sister. "You can see what all the fuss is about."

Jack could tell that Milly Ascheim was thinking over the word *cute.* In her world, Jack knew, *cute* didn't cut it. "I think he's cuter as a girl," Mildred Ascheim said; she was scrutinizing Emma again, ignoring Jack. He thought that Milly was weighing whether or not to expose him.

That was when Myra said, "You're just jealous, Milly, because I met Jack first."

Uh-oh—here it comes, Jack thought. But Mildred Ascheim surprised him. She gave Jack a withering look, just to let him know she remembered how small his schlong was; yet she didn't give him away. It was not a reassuring look—on the contrary, Milly wanted Jack to know that she hadn't forgotten a single disappointing detail of his *audition* in Van Nuys. This just wasn't the time for her to bear witness.

"For Christ's sake, Myra, it's Oscar night," Milly told her sister. "We oughta let these kids enjoy it."

"Yeah, we gotta go," Emma said again.

"Thank you," Jack told Mildred Ascheim.

Milly was looking at Emma once more; she just waved to Jack with the back of her hand. He anticipated that Milly would say something as he and Emma were walking away, a parting shot. ("So long, small schlong"—or words to that effect.) But Milly held her tongue.

"Mark my words, Mildred—Jack Burns has a world of money shots ahead of him," Jack heard Myra Ascheim say.

"Maybe," Milly said. "I still say he's cuter as a girl."

"Don't let those old bitches bother you, baby cakes," Emma told him when they were back in their limousine.

They were drifting in a sea of limos. Jack didn't know or care which party they were going to next. He always let Emma be in charge.

After a night like that, Jack would have expected to hear from everyone he ever knew—even though he lost. (Maybe especially because he lost.) But not that many people reached out to him. Caroline Wurtz called Alice, though. "Please tell Jack I think he should have won," Miss Wurtz said. "Imagine giving an Oscar to someone for *eating* people!"

When Jack and Emma got back to their place in Santa Monica, Mr. Ramsey's was the first message on the answering machine. "Jack Burns!" he cried. That was all; it was enough.

Jack's old wrestling friends contacted him more slowly. Coach Clum, from Redding, wrote: *"You made the right call, Jack. Cauliflower ears wouldn't have worked on a girl."*

Coach Hudson and Coach Shapiro sent Jack their congratulations, too. Hudson said he hoped that Jack wasn't taking any of those female hormones, and that Jack's boobs hadn't been implants—just falsies. Shapiro was curious to know what had become of the Slavic-looking beauty, whose name he had forgotten; he'd been hoping to catch a glimpse of her at the Academy Awards.

Coach Shapiro meant Claudia, of course. Jack didn't hear from her. Not a word from Noah Rosen, either—not that Jack expected to hear from him. And not a sound from Michele Maher, who had vanished without a peep. Herman Castro thought she'd gone to medical school, but after that he'd lost track of her. Naturally, Jack heard from Herman, but it was just a note. *"Way to go, amigo—you got to the finals."*

Yes, it felt like that—he had gotten to the finals and lost, no contest. There was no telling if or when he might get there again; maybe the Oscar opportunity had been a one-shot deal.

Both *Terminator 2: Judgment Day* and *The Naked Gun 2½: The Smell of Fear* did much bigger box office than *Normal and Nice,* but that little film and the Academy Award nomination gave Jack Burns a face that was recognized everywhere. As a man *or* as a woman, maybe; as a man, without a doubt. (Jack hadn't, as yet, tried going anywhere as a woman—except in the movies.) He was a celebrity now.

Emma seemed determined that he take the utmost advantage of his fame. To that end, she persuaded Jack to say he was writing something—though of course he wasn't. "Keep it non-specific, baby cakes. Just say you're *always* writing." This amounted to a conversation-stopper in many of Jack's interviews. It sounded vaguely sinister, as if the alleged something he was *always* writing were an exposé. But of *what*? "It makes you more mysterious," Emma told him. "It adds to your *noir* thing." Did she mean that being a writer somehow enhanced his sexually ambiguous reputation as an actor?

Some interviewers *only* wanted to talk about what Jack was writing; it drove them crazy that he wouldn't say. For this reason alone, it seemed worth repeating. "I'm not interested in settling down, getting married, having kids—not right now," he would usually begin. "Now's the time to concentrate on my work."

"You mean your acting?"

"Well, sure. *And* my writing."

"What are you writing?"

"Something. I'm just *always* writing."

Even his mother wanted to know what Jack was writing. "Not a memoir, I hope!" Alice said, laughing nervously.

Leslie Oastler regarded Jack with regret—as if, if she'd known he was going to become a *writer,* she wouldn't have shown him her Rose of Jericho.

Emma said her mom never stopped asking her if she'd read any of Jack's writing. Emma thought her lie was very funny. Not Jack. He didn't see the point of it.

When Myra Ascheim died—Jack read her obituary in *Variety;* no one called him—Bob Bookman said that Jack didn't need a talent manager, anyway. Having an agent at C.A.A. would suffice. Jack already had an agent *and* an entertainment lawyer— Alan Hergott. "You need a *money* manager, not a talent manager," Alan told him.

Because he wanted to support his mother, Jack found a money manager in Buffalo, New York—Willard Saperston. Coming from Buffalo, Willard had connections in Toronto. Jack was getting killed by Canadian taxes. For starters, Willard told him that he had to become an American citizen, which Jack did. He also became an "investor" in Daughter Alice; that way, his mom wouldn't pay "taxes up the wazoo" for every U.S. dollar he gave her.

It crossed Jack's mind that his mom might just sell Daughter Alice and stop being a tattoo artist; it also occurred to him that *if* his mom's relationship with Mrs. Oastler was based on Leslie's financial support, which he'd once thought it was, Alice might leave Leslie.

But Jack's mother felt at home in the tattoo world—it was her one area of expertise—and whatever Jack had once believed were Alice's reasons for moving in with Mrs. Oastler, he'd been wrong to think that his mother wasn't Leslie's willing partner. They were a couple who would go the distance. As Tattoo Ole had first indicated, Jack's mother *was* Daughter Alice; she was both an old hippie and a maritimer, and she'd lived up to her tattoo name.

Jack might have spent more time in Toronto if he could have made peace with that—that and the fact that his missing father would never be a topic of conversation between him and his mom.

That Jack Burns was the son of a tattoo artist, and that he'd never known his father—well, anyone could imagine how these things would figure in various interviews and profiles of the successful young actor. The movie media never tired of an exotic childhood; nor did entertainment journalists release their grip on every bone of dysfunction in a celebrity's life. In the words of one reporter, Jack had a "tattooed past." (The latter observation was made all the more intriguing by the fact that neither Jack nor his mom was tattooed.)

Canadian television always asked to interview Jack and his mother in Daughter Alice. And soon after the American media published a picture of Jack with this or that date—except for Emma, they were never Canadians, and Emma (also for tax purposes) had become an American citizen—there would be someone from CBC-TV in Daughter Alice, asking Alice if she knew the woman Jack was "seeing" and if the relationship was "serious."

"Oh, I don't bug Jack about his personal life," Alice would say with the unhurried insouciance of the perpetually stoned. (Bob Dylan would be yowling away in the background.) "And Jack doesn't bug me about mine."

* * *

Jack met a meat heiress in New York. Samantha was an older woman; she liked dressing Jack in her clothes. (Not to go out—he never once went out as a woman in New York, and he wasn't with Samantha very long.)

He had a fling with an older woman in London, too—Emma's English publisher. Corinna was fascinated that Jack was writing something; naturally, he never told her what it was. For a publisher, she had very sexy clothes, but Jack wasn't with her for long, either.

Both of these older women were jealous of his enduring relationship with Emma, and Jack felt he wasted too much time flying from London and New York to L.A. Emma basically refused to leave their crappy house on Entrada, and Jack missed her too much when he was away.

Besides, by not moving from Santa Monica, Emma and Jack could afford to buy a really good car. They bought a silver Audi with gunmetal-gray leather seats, the same model Jack had once driven as a parking valet in his brief employment at Stan's. Emma understood the symbolism of it. "Just so long as it doesn't come with a kid in the backseat, baby cakes."

Having a car like that made Jack glad he didn't drink—not that he drove appreciably faster. According to Emma, Jack was as irritatingly slow and overcareful a driver as ever. But Emma wasn't slow or overcareful. "It might have been *safer* to buy a *house* in Beverly Hills," Jack used to tell her. He meant that Emma might have done less driving.

So they went out, and they came home (or not)—and, of course, they met people. Jack was never "with" someone for more than a month or two, at most. There was no one Emma was "with"—not for more than a night, like the pretty boys she met dancing at Coconut Teaszer.

Jack kept his hair long, almost shoulder-length, which made his occasional cross-dressing more natural—if only in the privacy of a boudoir. As a guy, he still favored a little stubble; he stayed lean and mean, because that was his job.

Jack's roles didn't always require him to transform himself from a man to a woman, but the potential remained obdurately a part of his character—an element of his *noir* thing, as Emma called it.

On-screen, Jack was "with" just about everyone: Elisabeth

Shue before she did *Leaving Las Vegas;* Cameron Diaz in a stupid chick flick; Drew Barrymore in a Stephen King screamer. He was Nicole Kidman's *slowly* dying husband—it took three quarters of the film for Jack to die. Nicole Kidman was much taller than Jack Burns, but that wasn't evident from the movie, in which Jack never got out of bed.

Jack was the guy Julia Roberts wisely didn't marry. He told the lie that made Meg Ryan leave him. He suffered as a smitten waiter, the one who spilled the vichyssoise down Gwyneth Paltrow's back.

Bruce Willis kicked the crap out of him. Denzel Washington arrested him. And Jack was, albeit briefly, a Bond girl—the one who was killed by a poisonous dart from a cigarette lighter when 007 deduced Jack was a guy.

Myra Ascheim had been right: a world of money shots lay ahead of him. If Jack had to pick a favorite, it would be that bit with Jessica Lee. "The almost cross-dressing moment," some critic in *The New Yorker* called it.

Jessica is a beautiful heiress. Jack is a thief, and he's just slept with her. She's taking a shower while Jack is alone in her bedroom, taking inventory of her assets. There's pricey stuff everywhere. He's just wandering around her bedroom in his boxer shorts while we hear Jessica singing in the shower.

When Jack comes to her wardrobe closet, he is enraptured by her clothes. It's an inside joke—Jack Burns fingering through a closet full of women's clothes. Not even the jewelry has attracted *this* much attention from the thief in his boxers. It's clear that Jack loves her clothes. He's so mesmerized that he doesn't hear the shower shut off; Jessica has stopped singing.

When the bathroom door opens, and Jessica is standing there in that terry-cloth robe—her wet hair wrapped in a towel—her image is reflected in the mirror on the wardrobe-closet door. It's a great shot: Jessica appears to be standing beside Jack when he holds up her dress to his half-naked body and takes a look at himself (and at her) in the mirror.

He is one cool thief. "Boy, I'll bet this looks great on you," Jack says to Jessica Lee. In the film, Jessica's character is completely taken in. (Because that's the story: she's in love with the thief.) But they had to shoot that scene ten times. Jessica herself wasn't taken in. The first time she saw Jack Burns holding up a dress to his body, Jessica turned pale. It wasn't in the script. She saw something she didn't like—something about Jack. It took her ten takes to get over whatever it was she saw; it took Jack a few takes, too.

"What was it? What did you see?" he asked her later.

"I don't know what it was, Jack," Jessica said. "You just gave me the willies."

Jessica Lee's *willies* notwithstanding, the final take was a keeper. In any retrospective of Jack Burns, his collected film clips, there was that one of him and Jessica in the mirror. He's holding up the dress and saying, "Boy, I'll bet this looks great on you." She's in the doorway to the bathroom, smiling that smile. Jessica's smile is wide enough to fall into, big enough to consume you. But Jack could never see that clip without remembering the *first* look she gave him. Jessica wasn't smiling the first time, and she wasn't acting.

Moments like that made Jack even more of an outsider. When you know you've spooked someone, you learn to be careful. What Emma called Jack's *noir* thing was a bit creepy. Bankable, yes, but *likable*?

Jack Burns had found a close-up all his own; it was more disquieting than Toshiro Mifune's scowl. Jack couldn't really see himself, only his effect on others. Was it a sexually disturbing look? Yes, definitely. Was it more threatening than *noir*? Well— it was beyond mischievous, anyway.

"It's unpredictable, honey pie—that's your look."

"That's just acting," he told her. (*That's just keeping my audience of one on his toes,* Jack thought.)

"No, that's *you,* baby cakes. You're unpredictable. That's what's scary about you, Jack."

"I'm not scary!" he insisted. Jack thought that *Emma* was the scary one.

He would remember where they were when Emma said he was scary. They were on Sunset Boulevard in the silver Audi. Jack was driving. They were in Hollywood—Château Marmont territory, where John Belushi died—and Jack was trying to figure out what it was that had scared Jessica Lee. "Maybe the dress was all wrong for me," he said to Emma. "I wish I could just forget about it."

"Boy, am I sick of the Bar Marmont," was all Emma said.

Because Jack was famous, he was always admitted to the Bar Marmont, which was adjacent to the hotel. It was big and noisy, a scene—lots of fake boobs and aspiring talent managers, very trendy, ultra young. There were usually about thirty people outside, being denied entrance; on this particular night, Lawrence was among them. Emma looked the other way, but Lawrence caught Jack's wrist.

"You're not a girl tonight? You're just a guy? How disappointing to your fans!" Lawrence cried.

Emma caught him in the nuts with her knee; then she and Jack went inside together. Lawrence was lying in a fetal way, his knees drawn up to his chest in a kind of birthing position—not that anything was forthcoming. Jack would remember thinking that if *he'd* kneed Lawrence in the balls, there would have been a lawsuit, but Emma could get away with it. (That's why he thought *she* was the scary one.)

The Château Marmont—the hotel itself—was another story. Jack didn't go to that lobby to be with a crowd, but he often saw actors having meetings there. Jack would have a bunch of meetings in that lobby—the lobby was really a bar.

He preferred to have his meetings, when he could choose, in the bar at the Four Seasons Hotel in Beverly Hills. In Jack's opinion, this was where the classiest meetings happened. He was convinced that famous ghosts would one day haunt the Four Seasons in Beverly Hills—actors whose meetings went awry. But, for Jack, it was the only place where he felt like an insider.

For the most part, like Emma, he was still an outsider; they were notoriously uncool. The U.S. wasn't their country. L.A. wasn't their town. Not that they were Canadians, either. Toronto didn't feel like home.

Redding had been the first and last place Jack had fit in. Somehow he and Emma knew they would *never* fit in in L.A. It wasn't a matter of being famous; that was only what other people saw. With the money they'd made, Emma and Jack could have moved from Entrada, but Jack was more and more persuaded by Emma's determination to remain an outsider. For them, Los Angeles was a working town; whatever else they were, Emma and Jack were workers. L.A. was their *job*.

Being seen—being *spotted*—was part of the job. (Part of Jack's, anyway; Emma didn't care who saw her.)

In their own way, they were gods, Emma and Jack—uncool Canadian gods in the city of angels. And like the gods, they were remote. They didn't see themselves all that clearly; typical of the movie business, they registered their performances by how they were received. But in his heart, Jack Burns knew that Donald, that prick maître d' at Stan's, had been right. Donald had seen through him: Jack was a hick from Toronto via New Hampshire. Yes, he was a U.S. citizen and a legal resident of Santa Monica, California, but Jack wasn't truly living anywhere—he was just biding his time. (At least he knew how to do that. He'd done it before, with Claudia.)

Naturally, Jack was making a ton of money. Yet Jack knew that wasn't all there was, or all that he was supposed to be.

Jack was in Toronto—unwillingly, as usual. Emma wasn't with him, though she generally spent more time there than he did; being a writer was such a big deal in Canada.

"Life is a call sheet," Emma wrote in *The Slush-Pile Reader*. "You're supposed to show up when they tell you, but that's the only rule."

Hanging out with his mom in Daughter Alice, Jack started arguing with her about tattoo conventions. There never used to *be* tattoo conventions, but lately Alice had been going to one every month. She'd attended one in Tokyo and another in Madrid, but mostly she went to the conventions in the United States. They were everywhere.

The rare times Alice came to Los Angeles were usually in the fall, and not exclusively to visit Jack. Not so coincidentally, that was the time of the annual Inkslingers Ball—the L.A. tattoo and body-piercing convention. It was allegedly the world's largest; they held it in the Hollywood Palladium on Sunset Boulevard, a former swing-era dance hall.

The New York tattoo convention, where Daughter Alice was also a regular, was held in the Roseland Ballroom on West Fifty-second Street—that one was in the spring. The one in Atlanta was also in the spring. There was even one in Maine—in *February*! Despite her promises, Jack's mom never once came to Maine to visit him at Redding, but she wouldn't miss the Mad Hatter's Tea Party in Portland.

Alice went to the Hell City Tattoo Festival—this being in Columbus, Ohio, in a Hyatt Regency Hotel. (That one was in June, if Jack remembered correctly.) He thought his mom liked Philadelphia the best. She had a photograph of herself with

Crazy Philadelphia Eddie; he always wore a yellow sports jacket and had his hair so stiff with gel that it stood up like a rooster's comb.

Wherever the convention was—Dallas or Dublin, the so-called Meeting of the Marked in Pittsburgh, the annual Man's Ruin in Decatur, Illinois—Daughter Alice went.

She had been to Boston and to Hamburg, Germany. To her great disappointment, Herbert Hoffmann had retired, but she met Robert Gorlt in Hamburg. "He's six-nine and played basketball in Canada," she told Jack.

Tattoo artists from all over the world came to these conventions: from Tahiti, Cyprus, Samoa; from Thailand and Mexico, and from Paris, Berlin, and Miami. They even came from Oklahoma, where tattooing was illegal. (There was nowhere Alice wouldn't go to meet with her colleagues—including some Sheraton in the Meadowlands.) And it was always the same people who went.

"If it's always the same weirdos, why go?" Jack asked his mother. "Why go again and again?"

"Because we *are* the same weirdos, Jack. Because we are what we do. We don't change."

"For Christ's sake, Mom, do you have any idea what sort of shit can happen to you in a Hyatt Regency in Columbus, Ohio, or in a fucking Sheraton in the Meadowlands?"

"If Miss Wurtz could hear you, Jack," his mother said. "If poor Lottie, or Mrs. Wicksteed—may she rest in peace—could hear you. It's so sad what's happened to your *language*. Is it California or the movie business that's done this to you?"

"Done *what* to me?"

"Maybe it's Emma," Alice said. "It's living with that foul-mouthed girl—I know it is. It's *for Christ's sake* this and *fucking* that. To hear you talk, you'd think that *shit* were an all-purpose noun! And you used to speak so well. You once knew how to talk. You *enunciated* perfectly."

She had a point, but it was just like Alice to change the subject. Here Jack was, trying to impress upon her—a middle-aged woman—that these tattoo conventions were freak shows, and his mother got all in a knot about his *language*. The conventions were absolutely terrifying. The full-body wackos turned up; they had *contests*! Ex-convicts were tattooed—*prison* tattoos were a genre as distinctive as biker tattoos. Strippers were tattooed, not to mention porn stars. (Jack's "research," meaning countless Hank Long films, had taught him that.)

Just who did Daughter Alice think these conventions were *for*? Jack had seen those angry voodoo dolls and the slashed heart with the dagger in it—the latter inscribed NO REGRET—at Riley Baxter's Tabu Tattoo in West L.A. (On Baxter's business card, under one such voodoo doll, it said DISPOSABLE NEEDLES.)

Alice's waist had thickened, but she'd not lost her pretty smile; her hair, once an amber or maple-syrup color, was streaked with gray. But her skin was surprisingly unwrinkled, and her choice in clothing took noticeable advantage of her full breasts. She liked dresses with an empire waist, and usually a scoop or square neckline. At her age, she wore an underwire bra—she liked red or fuchsia. That day in Daughter Alice, she wore a peasant-style dress with a neckline that dropped from the apex of her shoulders; her bra straps were showing, but they usually were. Jack thought that she liked her bra straps to show, although she never wore a dress or blouse with a revealing décolletage. "My cleavage," Alice liked to say, "is nobody's business." (Strange, Jack used to think—how his mom wanted everyone to know she had good breasts, but she never bared even a little bit of them.)

And what was a woman who *wouldn't* bare her breasts doing at tattoo conventions? "Mom—" Jack tried to say, but she was fussing with a pot of tea; she'd turned her back on him.

"And the *women,* Jack. Do you know any *nice* girls? Or have I just not met them?"

"Nice?"

"Like Claudia. She was nice. What's happened to Claudia?"

"I don't know, Mom."

"What about that unfortunate young woman who had an entry-level job at the William Morris Agency? She had the strangest lisp, didn't she?"

"Gwen somebody," he said. (That was all he remembered about Gwen—she lisped. Maybe she was still at William Morris, maybe not.)

"Gwen is long gone, is she?" his mom asked. "Do you still take honey in your tea, dear?"

"Yes, Gwen is long gone. No, I don't take honey—I never have."

"Actresses, waitresses, office girls, *meat heiresses*—not to mention the hangers-on," his mom continued.

"The what?"

"Do you call them groupies?"

"I don't know any groupies, Mom. There are more groupies in your world than there are in mine."

"What on earth do you mean, dear?"

"At the tattoo conventions, there must be," he said.

"You should go to a tattoo convention, Jack. Then you wouldn't be so afraid."

"I took you to the Inkslingers Ball," he reminded her.

"Yes, but you wouldn't go inside the Palladium," she said.

"There was a motorcycle gang *outside* the Palladium!"

"You said it was bad enough to see a bunch of fake boobs at night—you weren't going to hang around a bunch of fake boobs in broad daylight. That's exactly what you said. Honestly, your *language*—"

"Mom—"

"That Brit you were with in London—she was as old as I am!" Alice cried. Jack watched her put honey in his tea.

The door to Queen Street opened and a little bell tinkled, as if Daughter Alice were a shop selling lace doilies or birthday cards. The girl who came in was suffering some kind of inflammation from her latest piercing; an object that looked like a cuff-link made her lower lip stick out. She had a ball and chain attached to one eyebrow, which was shaved, but only her lower lip was inflamed.

"What can I do for you, dear?" Alice asked her. "I just made some tea. Would you like some?"

"Yeah, I guess," the girl said. "I don't usually do tea, but that's okay."

"Jack, fix the young lady some tea, please," his mother said.

The girl was eighteen—maybe twenty, tops. Her dark hair was dirty; she was wearing jeans and a Grateful Dead T-shirt. "Shit, you look kinda like Jack Burns," she told Jack, "except you look like a normal guy."

Alice had put some music on—Bob, of course. "Jack is my son," Alice told the pierced girl. "This *is* Jack Burns!"

"Oh, wow," the girl said. "I'll bet you've been with a lot of women, eh?"

"Not too many," he told her. "Do you take honey in your tea?"

"Yeah, sure," she said; she kept touching her sore-looking lower lip with the tip of her tongue.

"What sort of tattoo are you interested in, dear?" Alice asked her. (There was a sign in the window of Daughter Alice: NO PIERCING. The girl had to have come for a tattoo.)

The girl unzipped her jeans and hooked her thumbs under the waistband of her panties, exposing a fringe of pubic hair, above which a honeybee hovered. The bee's body was no bigger than the topmost joint of Jack's little finger; its translucent wings were a blur of yellow. The little bee's body was a darker shade of gold.

"Gold is a tricky pigment," Alice said—perhaps admiringly. Jack couldn't tell. "I take a bright yellow and mix it with brick red, or you can use what they call English vermilion—same as mercuric sulfide. I mix that with molasses." Jack was pretty sure this was three quarters fabrication. Alice would never tell just anyone how she made her pigments—especially a nonprofessional.

"Molasses?" the girl said.

"I cut it with a little witch hazel," Alice told her. "It's tricky to get a good gold." Jack believed that the witch-hazel part was true.

The girl was looking at her honeybee with new eyes. "I got the bee in Winnipeg," she told them.

"At Tattoos for the Individual, I suppose," Alice said.

"Yeah, do you know those guys?" the girl asked.

"Sure, I know them. You can't exactly get lost in Winnipeg. So you want a flower for the bee?" she asked the girl.

"Yeah, but I can't decide what *kinda* flower," the girl said.

Jack was edging toward the door. He thought he'd take his chances out on Queen Street; a fan (or a lunatic) would probably recognize him, but Jack Burns didn't need to see someone get another tattoo.

"Where are you off to, Jack?" Alice asked, not looking at him. She was laying out her flash of flower choices, to show the honeybee girl.

"You don't hafta go," the girl said to Jack. "You can watch— no matter where she puts it."

"That depends," Alice told her.

"I'll see you back at home," Jack said to his mom. "I'll take you and Leslie out to dinner."

Both Alice and the girl looked disappointed that Jack was leaving. Bob Dylan was yowling away. ("Idiot Wind." Jack would always remember that song.) Jack wasn't thinking about the girl; he was trying to decipher more exactly the look of disappointment on his mother's face. *What is it about me that bothers you?* Jack wanted to ask her, but not with the honeybee girl there.

"*Someone's got it in for me,*" Bob complained. Every time Jack came to Toronto, he felt that way. "*They say I shot a man named Gray and took his wife to Italy,*" Bob sang away. "*She inherited a million bucks and when she died it came to me.*"

Jack sang the next line out loud, with Bob—never taking his eyes off his mother. "*I can't help it if I'm lucky,*" he sang—because *that* was the principal ingredient in the look his mom was giving him. She thought he'd been lucky!

"So far, Jack—so far!" Alice called after him, as he stepped out on Queen Street and closed the door to Daughter Alice.

IV

Sleeping in the Needles

23

Billy Rainbow

Jack was on a press junket in New York. ("Following Mira-max's marching orders," as Emma put it.) The only thing memorable about this particular interview was not the opening question itself, which he'd been asked a hundred times before, but the sheer clumsiness of how the journalist worded the question—that and the fact that Emma called in the middle of his oft-repeated answer, and it was the last time Jack would hear her voice.

His interviewer, a matronly woman with a baffling accent, was the same journalist, from the Hollywood Foreign Press, who, in a previous press junket, had asked Jack if he was modeling his appearance on that of a young Martin Sheen in *Apocalypse Now.* She was drinking a Diet Coke and smoking a mentholated cigarette, her artificially sweetened breath wafting over him like smoke from a fire in a mint factory.

"Captain Willard has short hair," Jack had answered her that previous time.

"Cap-ee-tan who?"

"The Martin Sheen character in *Apocalypse Now*—Captain Willard," he'd said. "I'm not a hundred percent sure about his rank."

"I didn't mean-a hees hair," the journalist had said.

"I'm not consciously modeling myself on a young Martin Sheen," Jack had told her. "I'm not trying to kill Marlon Brando, either."

"You mean-a *young* Marlon Brando?" the lady from the Hollywood Foreign Press had asked him.

"In the movie you mentioned," he had explained to her, slowly, "the young Martin Sheen character is sent to kill Marlon Brando—remember? Not a young Marlon Brando, either."

"Forget eet," she'd said. "Let's-a move on."

This time her question was breathtaking in its awkwardness, but she had at last moved on from Martin Sheen. "Are you a person who-wa, though not a homosexual, psychologically identifies weeth the opposite sex-sa? I mean-a weeth *wee*-men."

"Am I a transvestite, do you mean?"

"Yes!"

"No."

"But-a you are always dressing as a *woo*-man—or you seem to be theenking about eet, I mean-a dressing as a woo-man, even when-a you are dressed as a *man*."

"I'm not thinking about dressing as a woman right now," Jack told her. "It's just something I occasionally do in a movie—you know, when I'm *acting*."

"Are you *writing* about eet?"

"About dressing as a woman?"

"Yes!"

"No."

His cell phone rang. Ordinarily he didn't answer his phone in the middle of an interview, but Jack could see that the call was from Emma and she'd been depressed lately. Emma was losing the fight with her weight; every morning since he'd been away, Emma called to tell him what she weighed. It was almost lunchtime in New York, but Jack knew that Emma was just getting up in L.A.

He'd told her that he was being interviewed around the clock—Emma knew very well what press junkets were for. In mild exasperation, Jack handed his cell phone to the lady from the Hollywood Foreign Press. "This woman won't leave me alone," he said to his interviewer. "Try telling her I'm in the middle of an interview. See how far you get."

If nothing else, Jack hoped this might interrupt the chain of thought that the journalist from the Hollywood Foreign Press was pursuing. He already knew that his interviewer would have no luck interrupting Emma from *her* train of thought.

"Hello-a?" the woman who thought he looked like a young Martin Sheen said.

It suddenly sounded like *Emma* was speaking Italian—of course Jack recognized her spiel. "Pleeze tell-a Jack Burns—eet's Maria Antonietta *Beluzzi* on da fon-a!"

"I'm-a sorry. Jack Burns ees in the meedle of an interview," the lady from the Hollywood Foreign Press said.

"Tell heem I mees-a holding hees *pee*-nis!" Emma said.

"Eet's a Ms. *Beluzzi,*" his interviewer said, handing him back his cell phone. "Eet sounds urgent."

"So what do you weigh this morning?" Jack asked Emma.

"Two hundred and fucking *five!*" Emma wailed—loudly enough for the journalist to hear her.

"You have to go on a diet, Emma," he told her, for what had to be the hundredth time.

Jack Burns was thirty-two in 1997—Emma was thirty-nine. He had a better metabolism than she had, and he'd always watched what he ate. But now that Jack was in his thirties, even he had to be more strict with his diet.

Emma didn't understand dieting. Her one bottle of red wine a night had become two; she had pasta for *lunch.* Here she was, pushing forty, and her favorite food was still gorgonzola mashed potatoes. Jack kept telling her: she could spend all day on the ab machine at the Four Seasons in Beverly Hills—she could be bench-pressing her own weight—and not work off those kinds of carbs.

Jack could see that the journalist from the Hollywood Foreign Press was writing everything down—including, as he would later read in her interview, the "two hundred and fucking *five.*" She even spelled Maria Antonietta Beluzzi correctly; naturally, it turned out that the journalist was Italian.

"Emma—" Jack started to say.

"*He calls her Emma and brutally tells her to go on a diet,*" the lady from the Hollywood Foreign Press would write.

"Fuck you and your diet, Jack," Emma said sharply on the phone. "I want you to know I've taken good care of you in my will." Then she hung up.

"Your-a girlfriend?" his interviewer asked. "I mean-a *one* of them."

"Kind of," Jack replied.

"Ees Ms. Beluzzi an actress?"

"She's a voluptuous tobacconist," he said. Although the journalist didn't write this down, *voluptuous* would somehow make it into her interview—but in reference to *Emma.*

"I suppose-za you have, or have-a had, *many* girlfriends," Jack's interviewer said.

"Nobody serious," he said, for what had to be the hundredth time—with apologies to Michele Maher.

Jack was tired. He'd had too many interviews, with too many prying and insinuating journalists. But that was no excuse. He shouldn't have lost control of this interview. He shouldn't have so recklessly, even deliberately, allowed this lady from the Hollywood Foreign Press to imagine anything she might want to imagine—but he did.

Of course it wasn't the interview that would bother him; such things aren't truly damaging, not for long. But that Emma's last words to Jack were about her *will*—well, that would hurt him forever.

By the time the interview was published, Emma would be dead—and the Italian journalist from the Hollywood Foreign Press had figured out that he couldn't have been having a relationship with Maria Antonietta Beluzzi, the big-breasted tobacconist in Fellini's *Amarcord*. (Ms. Beluzzi would be old enough to be Jack's grandmother!)

It had to have been Emma Oastler Jack was talking to, the journalist wrote—he and Emma, who were "just roommates," were known to be living together—and anyone who'd seen the famous author recently knew at a glance she was overweight, if not that she weighed as much as two hundred and five pounds. (In this context, Jack's use of the word *voluptuous* appeared to mock Emma for becoming so fat.)

Besides, the Italian lady concluded, Emma was said to have been depressed that her third novel—after many years, it was still only a work-in-progress—was growing too long.

"How long *is* it?" all the journalists would ask Jack, after Emma's death. But by then he had learned, the hard way, to be more careful with the press.

That trip to New York, Jack was staying at The Mark. He had registered in the name of Billy Rainbow—the character he played in the soon-to-be-released film he was promoting at the press junket. He usually registered in hotels in the name of the character he was playing in his most recent, not-yet-released movie. That way, the Jack Burns fans couldn't find him.

They weren't all exactly fans. Some of the "chicks with dicks" had taken offense that Jack repeatedly denied he was a transsexual or a transvestite. In almost every interview, Jack said he was a cross-dresser only occasionally—and only in the movies. *Real* transsexuals and transvestites were offended; they said that Jack was "merely acting." Well—of course he was!

So Jack was registered at The Mark as Billy Rainbow; the front desk screened all his calls. Jack always told his mom where he was staying—and who he was, this time—and of course Emma knew, and his agent, Bob Bookman, and his lawyer, Alan Hergott. And the publicist for whichever studio was making his most recent movie, in this case Erica Steinberg from Miramax. Naturally, Harvey Weinstein knew, too. If you were making a Miramax movie, Harvey knew where you were staying *and* under what name.

At the time, Jack was sleeping with the well-known cellist Mimi Lederer, so she knew where he was staying, too. In fact, he was in bed with her—asleep at The Mark—when Emma died.

That night, after dinner, Mimi had brought her cello back to his hotel room; she'd played two solos naked for him. It had been awkward at dinner, because Mimi wouldn't check her cello. The big instrument, in its case, occupied a third chair at their table; Mimi would look at it from time to time, as if she expected the cello to say something.

Jack didn't tell Mimi that he'd met another cellist when he was a little boy—Hannele, a music student at Sibelius Academy and one (of two) of his father's girlfriends in Helsinki. Hannele had shared a tattoo with her friend Ritva. Hannele got the vertical left side of a heart torn in two; it was tattooed on her heart-side breast. And Hannele's armpits were unshaven—Jack would always remember that.

When Mimi Lederer was playing for Jack in his hotel room at The Mark, it made him shudder to remember how Hannele had sat for her tattoo—like Mimi, maybe like *all* female cellists, with her legs spread apart. That was when Jack wondered if Hannele had ever played naked for his dad, which again caused him to wonder if he was like William. (The way William was with women, especially.)

Jack would remember what Mimi Lederer played for him that night at The Mark, when Emma was still alive—a cello solo, part of something from a Mozart trio. (Jack had made a point of learning as little as he could about classical music because it reminded him of organ music, or church music, which reminded him of his derelict dad.)

"Divertimento—E Flat Major," Mimi Lederer whispered to him, before she began to play. Like Hannele, maybe like *all* female cellists, Mimi was tall with long arms and small breasts. Naturally, Jack wondered if your breasts got in the way when you were playing a cello.

The second piece Mimi played naked for him was part of something from a Beethoven string quartet. "*Razumovsky* Opus Fifty-Nine," Mimi murmured to him, "Number One." Just the names of pieces of classical music made Jack's teeth ache. Why couldn't composers think of better titles? But it was wonderful to witness Mimi Lederer's control of that big instrument she so confidently straddled.

They were still asleep when the phone rang. It was way too early in the morning for it to be Emma—that was Jack's first thought. Toronto, like New York, was on Eastern time; that was the second idea to pop into his head. He saw it was a little after six in the morning—too early for it to be his mother, either, or so Jack thought.

Erica Steinberg was both too nice and too tactful to call him this early in the morning, and Erica knew that Jack was sleeping with Mimi Lederer—Erica knew everything. Jack thought maybe it was Harvey Weinstein on the phone. He would call you when he wanted to; he'd called Jack early in the morning before. Maybe Jack had said something in one of his interviews that he shouldn't have said.

Mimi Lederer and Jack had to get up early, anyway—although not quite this early. Jack had another day to go on the press junket, and Mimi was teaching a class at Juilliard; then she had to catch a plane. Mimi was a member of some trio or quartet; they had a concert in Minneapolis, or maybe it was Cleveland. Jack didn't remember.

"It must be room service," Mimi said. "It's probably about your breakfast order. I told you last night, Jack—you should order a normal breakfast."

Mimi had made an issue of Jack's breakfast order—his "breakfast manifesto," she'd called it. The room-service staff at The Mark (as in most New York hotels) was struggling with English as a second language. Jack should have just *checked* what he wanted for breakfast, Mimi had said; he should not have written a "thesis" on the little card they hung on the door.

But you have to be specific about a soft-boiled egg, Jack had argued—and how complicated is it to understand "nonfat yogurt or *no* yogurt"?

"It's Harvey Weinstein," Jack told Mimi, *finally* picking up the telephone. "Yes?" he said into the mouthpiece.

"It's your mother, Mr. Rainbow," the young man at the front desk said.

In the movie, Billy Rainbow doesn't have a mother, but Jack said, "Please put her through." *Where* is *she?* he was wondering. (According to Mimi Lederer, he was still half asleep.)

There'd been a tattoo convention in Santa Rosa. Had his mom come to see him in Los Angeles on her way to it, or on her way home from it? She'd been on her way home, Jack dimly recalled—she'd told him all about the convention.

It had been at the Flamingo Hotel, or maybe it was the *Pink Flamingo*. She'd said something about a blues band—possibly the Wine Drinkin' Roosters. She'd told Jack everything about everyone who was there.

By his mother's own admission, it had been a three-day party; tattoo artists party like underage drinkers. Alice was a wreck on her way back from Santa Rosa. How could Jack have forgotten her telling him about Captain Don's sword-swallowing act? Or Suzy Ming, the contortionist, writhing her way into indelible memory—if not exactly art. (So his mom *wasn't* calling from Santa Rosa.)

Paris, perhaps—that would explain the earliness of her call. It was the middle of the day in Paris; maybe Alice had miscalculated the time difference. But hadn't she come home from Paris, too?

Yes, Jack remembered—she had. She told him she'd met up with Uncle Pauly and Little Vinnie Myers, among other tattoo artists. It hadn't been a convention, not exactly; it had been about *planning* a Mondial du Tatouage in Paris. The whole thing had probably been Tin-Tin's idea; he was the best tattoo artist in Paris, in Alice's view. Stéphane Chaudesaigues from Avignon would surely have been there, and Filip Leu from Lausanne—maybe even Roonui from Mooréa, French Polynesia.

They'd all stayed at some hotel in the red-light district. "Just down the street from the Moulin Rouge," Alice had told Jack. Le Tribal Act, a body-piercing group, had provided one memorable evening's entertainment: they'd hoisted some fairly remarkable household items with their nipples and penises, and other pierced parts.

But this was weeks (maybe months) ago! Jack's mother was calling from Toronto, where it was as early in the morning as it was in New York. Jack really must have been out of it.

"Oh, Jackie, I'm sorry—I'm *so* sorry!" his mother cried into the phone.

"Mom, are you in Toronto?"

"Of course I'm in Toronto, dear," she said, with sudden indignation. "Oh, Jackie—it's so *awful!*"

Maybe she'd passed out, drunk or stoned at Daughter Alice. She'd just woken up—after a night of sleeping in the needles, Jack imagined. Or one of her colleagues in the tattoo world had died, one of the old-timers; maybe a maritime man was *eternally* sleeping in the needles. Her old pal Sailor Jerry, possibly—her friend from Halifax and fellow apprentice to Charlie Snow.

"It makes me *sick* to have to tell you, dear," Alice said.

It crossed Jack's mind that Leslie Oastler had left her—for another woman! "Mom—just tell me what it is, for Christ's sake."

"It's *Emma*—Emma's gone, Jack. She's *gone.*"

"Gone *where,* Mom?"

But he knew the second he said it—the telephone suddenly cold against his ear. Jack saw that dazzling-blue glint of the Pacific, the way you see it for the first time—turning off Sunset Boulevard, barreling down Chautauqua. Below you, depending on the time of day, the dead-slow or lightning-fast lanes of the Pacific Coast Highway, sometimes a sea of cars, always a tongue of concrete—the last barrier between you and the fabulous West Coast ocean.

"Gone *how*?" Jack asked his mother.

He didn't realize he was sitting up in bed and shivering—not until Mimi Lederer held him from behind, the way she held her cello. She wrapped her long arms around him; her long legs, wide apart, gripped his hips.

"Leslie's already left for the airport," Alice went on, as if she hadn't heard him. "I should have gone with her, but you know Leslie—she wasn't even crying!"

"Mom—what happened to Emma?"

"Oh, no—not *Emma*!" Mimi Lederer cried. She was draped over Jack like a shroud; he felt her lips brush the back of his neck.

"Jack—you're not alone!" his mother said.

"Of *course* I'm not alone! What happened to Emma, Mom?"

"It looks like you should have been with her, Jack."

"*Mom—*"

"Emma was *dancing,*" Alice began. "She met a boy dancing. Leslie told me the name of the place. Oh, it's *awful*! Something like Coconut Squeezer."

"*Teaszer,* not Squeezer, Mom—Coconut Teaszer."

"Emma took the boy home with her," Alice said.

Jack knew that if Emma had brought some kid from Coconut Teaszer back to their dump on Entrada Drive, she hadn't died *dancing.* "What did Emma die of, Mom?"

"Oh, it's *awful*!" Alice said again. "They said it was a heart attack, but she was a young woman."

"Who said? Who's *they*?" Jack asked.

"The police—they called here. But how *could* she have had a heart attack, Jack?"

In Emma's case, he could imagine it—even at thirty-nine— considering the food, the wine, the weightlifting, and the occasional kid from Coconut Teaszer. But Emma didn't do drugs. There'd been more kids from Coconut Teaszer lately. (Both Emma and Jack had thought the kids were safer than the bodybuilders.)

"There will probably be an autopsy," Jack told his mother.

"An *autopsy*—if it was just a heart attack?" Alice asked.

"You're not *supposed* to have a heart attack at thirty-nine, Mom."

"The boy was . . . *underage,*" Alice whispered. "The police won't release his name."

"Who cares about his name?" Jack said. There'd been more and more kids who looked *underage* to him. Poor Emma had died fucking a minor from Coconut Teaszer!

As for the kid himself, Jack could only imagine that it must have been a traumatizing experience. He knew that Emma liked the top position, and that she would have told the boy not to move. (Maybe he'd moved.) If the boy had been a virgin—and Emma would have picked him only if he looked *small*—what would it have been like to have a two-hundred-and-five-pound woman *die* on you, your first time?

"The boy called the police," his mother went on; she was still whispering. "Oh, Jack, was Emma *in the habit of*—"

"Sometimes," was all he said.

"You must meet Leslie in Los Angeles, Jack. She shouldn't have to go through this alone. I know Leslie. She'll break down, *eventually.*"

Jack couldn't imagine it, but he was uncomfortable with the idea of Mrs. Oastler alone in the Entrada Drive house. What kind of stuff would Emma have left lying around? The notion of Leslie discovering Emma's collection of porn films wasn't as disturbing as the thought of her reading Emma's *writing*—whatever Emma hadn't finished, or what she didn't want published. Jack had not seen a word of Emma's work-in-progress—her third novel, which was reportedly growing too long.

"I'll leave New York as soon as I can, Mom. If Leslie calls, tell her I'll be in L.A. before dark."

He knew that Erica Steinberg was a good soul; Jack assumed she would release him from his interviews at the press junket.

Everyone who knew Jack knew that Emma had been part of his family. As it turned out, Miramax arranged everything for him—including the car to the airport. Erica got him his ticket; she even offered to fly with him. It wasn't necessary for her to come with him, Jack told her, but he appreciated the offer.

There was another call to Jack's room at The Mark that morning. Mimi Lederer had been right—room service was confused by his breakfast order. Although he'd stopped shivering, Mimi had gone on holding him as if he were her cello, until the phone rang that second time.

"I don't give a rat's ass about the yogurt," Mimi heard Jack say into the phone. "*Any* kind of yogurt will do."

"Are you okay, Jack?" Mimi asked.

"Emma's dead," he snapped at her. "I guess I can worry about the fucking yogurt another day."

"Are you acting?" she asked him. "I mean even now. Are you still acting?"

Jack didn't know what she meant, but she was covering herself with the bedsheet as if he were a total stranger to her. "What's wrong?" he asked.

"What's wrong with *you,* Jack?"

They were both sitting up in bed, and Jack could see himself in the mirror above the dresser. There was nothing wrong with him, but that was the problem. Jack didn't look as if his best friend had died; on the contrary, he looked as if nothing had happened to him. His face was a clean slate—"more *noir* than *noir*," *The New York Times* might have said.

Jack couldn't stop staring at himself—that was a problem, too. Mimi Lederer said later that she couldn't stand the sight of him, not at that moment. "You're not in a movie, Jack," Mimi started to say, but Jack looked at her as if he really were Billy Rainbow. "Why aren't you crying?" Mimi Lederer asked him.

Jack couldn't answer her, and he was good at tears. When his part called for crying, he would usually start when he heard the A.D. say, "Quiet, please."

"Rolling," the cameraman would say; Jack's eyes were already watering away.

"Speed," said the sound guy—Jack's face would be bathed in tears.

When the director (even Wild Bill Vanvleck) said, "Action!"— well, Jack could cry on-camera like nobody's business. His eyes would well with tears just reading a script!

But that morning at The Mark, Jack was as tough-guy *noir* as he'd ever been—on film or off. He was as deadpan as Emma when she wrote, "Life is a call sheet. You're supposed to show up when they tell you, but that's the only rule."

That was what Jack Burns was doing—he was going to L.A., just to show up. He would probably hold Mrs. Oastler's hand, because he was *supposed to*—those were just the rules.

"Jesus, Jack—" Mimi Lederer started to say; then she stopped. Jack realized, as if he'd missed something she'd said, that she was getting dressed. "If you didn't love Emma, you never loved *anyone*," Mimi was saying. "She was the person closest to you, Jack. *Can* you love anyone? If you didn't love *her*, I think not."

That was the last Jack saw of Mimi Lederer, and he liked Mimi—he really did. But she didn't like him anymore after that morning at The Mark. Mimi said when she left that she didn't know who he was. But the scary thing was that *Jack* didn't know who he was.

As an actor, he could be anybody. On-screen, the *world* had seen Jack Burns cry—as a man *and* as a woman. He'd made his mascara run many times—*anything* for a movie! Yet Jack couldn't cry for Emma; he didn't shed a single tear that morning at The Mark.

It was still pretty early when he left the hotel for the airport.

The front-desk clerk was a young man Jack hadn't seen before—probably the same young man who'd put through Alice's call. Of course the clerk knew it was *the* Jack Burns—everyone did. But as Jack was leaving, the clerk called out—his voice full of the utmost sincerity, of the kind that young people express when they genuinely want to please you. "Have a nice day, Mr. Rainbow!"

As it turned out, Jack had been wrong to envision Emma's death as a heart attack, which typically has some familiar symptoms antecedent to death—like sweating, shortness of breath, light-headedness, and chest pains. But Emma Oastler died of a heart condition called Long QT Syndrome; an inherited disease, it affects the sodium and potassium channels in the heart. (This, in turn, leads to abnormalities in the heart's electrical system.) Emma died of a sudden arrhythmia—ventricular fibrillation, her doctor told Jack. Her heart suddenly stopped pumping; Emma died before she was even aware of not feeling well.

With Long QT Syndrome, often sudden death is the first indication of a problem. In sixty percent of patients, a resting EKG would indicate an abnormality, which would alert a doctor to the possibility of the condition. But the other forty percent would have completely normal examinations—unless exercise EKG's were used. (Emma's doctor told Jack that Emma had never had one.)

Her doctor went on to tell him that a fatal episode could be triggered by a loud noise, extreme emotion, exertion, or an electrolyte imbalance—which, in turn, could be caused by drinking alcohol or having sex.

The boy from Coconut Teaszer—whose name would never be made public—said that Emma had collapsed on him so spontaneously that he'd thought it was simply the way she liked to have sex, which he was having for the first time. He'd done exactly what Emma had told him to do; he hadn't moved. (He was probably too afraid to move.) After he'd managed to extricate himself from Emma's last embrace, the kid called the police.

Given the genetic nature of the syndrome, Emma's surviving family would eventually be screened for it. Leslie Oastler was the sole survivor, and she showed no signs of the abnormality. Her ex-husband, Emma's father, had died several years earlier—apparently, in his sleep.

"What a pisser," as Leslie would put it.

Jack arrived home before he had time to prepare himself for Mrs. Oastler. On the plane, he'd been thinking about Emma— not Leslie. (He'd been considering his lack of emotion, if that was the right word for what he lacked.)

Leslie Oastler was all over Jack, like a storm. "I know Leslie," Alice had said. "She'll break down, *eventually*." But Mrs. Oastler's grief was not yet evident—only her anger.

Leslie greeted him at the door. "Where the fuck is Emma's novel, Jack? I mean the new one."

"I don't know where Emma's novel is, Leslie."

"Where's *your* novel, Jack? Or whatever the fuck it is that you're supposed to be writing—you don't even have a computer!"

"I don't work at home," he answered. This was not exactly a lie—regarding the writing part of his life, Jack didn't work *any-where*.

"You don't even have a *typewriter*!" Mrs. Oastler said. "Do you write in longhand?"

"Yes. I happen to *like* writing by hand, Leslie." This wasn't ex-actly a lie, either. What writing he did—shopping lists, script notes, autographs—was always in longhand.

Mrs. Oastler had been all through Emma's computer. She had searched for Emma's novel under every name she could think of; nothing on Emma's computer had a name that contained the word *novel,* or the number three, or the word *third.* There was nothing resembling a title of a work-in-progress, either.

The boy from Coconut Teaszer must have been very believ-able, because the police never treated the house on Entrada as a crime scene. And because Emma was a famous author—not that the boy even knew she was a writer—both the police and Emma's doctor had concluded their business promptly, and with-out making much of a mess.

Mrs. Oastler, on the other hand, had ransacked the house. Whatever damage had been done by Emma spontaneously dying on top of the kid from Coconut Teaszer was minimal in compari-son to Leslie's frenzied searching, which resembled a drug-induced burglary—drawers and closets flung wide open, clothes strewn about. She'd found a couple of pairs of Jack's boxers in Emma's bedroom, and a pair of Emma's panties and two of her bras under Jack's bed; she'd found Emma's cache of porn films, too. "Did you watch them together?" Mrs. Oastler asked.

"Sometimes—for research," Jack said.

"Bullshit!"

"We should get out of here, Leslie—let me take you to dinner." Jack was trying to imagine what else Mrs. Oastler might have discovered in her search.

"Were you fucking each other or not?" she asked him.

"Absolutely not," he told her. "Not once."

"Why not?" Mrs. Oastler asked. Jack had no good answer to that question; he said nothing. "You slept together but you didn't do it—is that the way it was, Jack?" He nodded. "Like the script reader and the porn star in Emma's depressing novel?" Leslie asked.

"Kind of," was all he could say. Jack didn't want to give Mrs. Oastler the impression that he was too *big* for Emma, which would imply they had *tried.* But Leslie had come to her own conclusions—at least in regard to how Emma had handled her vaginismus. (Top position; young boys she could boss around, usually.)

Jack had been right to ask Emma if her vaginismus had a *cause*—of course it did, not that Emma could ever have told him. She'd been sexually abused when she was nine or ten—one of her mother's bad boyfriends had done it. He would be Mrs. Oastler's last boyfriend. Emma had been so traumatized that she'd missed a year of school. "Some problem at home" was all Jack remembered hearing about it; he'd assumed that this had something to do with Leslie's divorce.

Mrs. Oastler's final boyfriend gave new meaning to Emma's saga of the squeezed child; at twelve, perhaps this had been her first attempt to fictionalize her personal grievances. "Of course there were any number of traumatic visits to doctors' offices, beginning with Emma's first gynecological examination," Leslie told Jack. "And she *hated* her father—naturally, *he* was a doctor."

Jack didn't know that Emma's dad had been a doctor. Whenever Emma or her mother mentioned him, the word *asshole* was dominant. The word *doctor,* if Jack had ever heard it, had been drummed out of his memory by *asshole.*

"Let me take you to dinner, Leslie," Jack repeated. "Let's go someplace Emma liked."

"I hate to eat," Mrs. Oastler reminded him.

"Well, I usually have just a salad," Jack said. "Let's go somewhere and have a salad."

"Which one of you liked the Japanese condoms?" Leslie asked. (She'd even found Jack's Kimono MicroThins!)

"Those are mine," he told her. "They have great salads at One Pico." His old boss—Carlos, from American Pacific—was now working as a waiter there. Jack called and asked Carlos for a table with a view of the ocean and the promenade.

There were a lot of messages on the answering machine, but Mrs. Oastler assured Jack they were not worth listening to—she'd already done so. Condolences from friends—even Wild Bill Vanvleck had called. (The Mad Dutchman hadn't made a movie in years. Jack had worried that he might be dead.)

The only thing even mildly interesting, Leslie said, was the call from Alan Hergott—informing Jack that he'd been named literary executor in Emma's will. (Alan was also Emma's lawyer.) And Bob Bookman, their agent, had called; it was important, Bookman said, that he and Jack meet with Alan to discuss Emma's will. (Jack had only recently learned—from his last, unpleasant conversation with Emma—that she had a will, and that she'd supposedly taken good care of him in it.)

"I'll bet she's left you *everything*," Mrs. Oastler remarked, with an encompassing wave of her thin arm—indicating the ransacked ruin of the wretched house on Entrada Drive. "Lucky you."

While Leslie had a shower and changed her clothes, Jack played the messages on the answering machine at low volume. Both Bob Bookman and Alan Hergott made him think that his role as "literary executor" was a bigger deal than he might be anticipating; their voices had an unexpected urgency, which Mrs. Oastler had missed or chosen to ignore.

Leslie had changed into a sexy backless dress with a halter-type neckline. Only nine years older than Alice, Mrs. Oastler had just turned sixty, but she was so sleek and unwrinkled that she looked ten years younger—and she knew it. Her dark, boyish pixie was dyed to its roots, her small breasts didn't droop, her small bottom looked firm. Only the veins on the backs of her hands betrayed her, and her hands were never at rest—as if to deny you a lingering look at them.

Leslie announced that Emma's bedroom had the ambience of a crime scene, and that she wouldn't sleep there. Jack offered her his bedroom, or the guest room, but Mrs. Oastler told him that she had reserved a room for them at Shutters. After all, they were going to eat at the restaurant there. "We might as well spend the night," she said.

"*We?*" he asked her.

"I shouldn't be left alone," she told him. "If you slept with Emma and didn't do it, I guess you can sleep with me and *not* do it, too, Jack."

He put her small carry-on bag in the backseat of the Audi and drove her to Shutters. The sun had set, but a faded-pink glow served as a backlight to the Santa Monica Pier; the lights on the Ferris wheel were on. On the promenade below One Pico, people on Rollerblades swept past incessantly. Leslie drank a bottle of red wine with her salad; Jack had about a gallon of iced tea with his.

"I wonder what you're the literary executor *of,*" Mrs. Oastler remarked. (Carlos had told him, while she'd gone off to register in the hotel, that Leslie was the best-looking date he'd seen Jack with in a long time.)

"Her novel, maybe," Jack said.

"In which case, what would *you* do with it, Jack?"

"Maybe Emma wanted me to decide if it was fit to publish or not," he replied.

"It doesn't exist, Jack. There *is* no third novel. It wasn't her novel that was growing too long—it was the period of time in which she'd written *nothing,*" Leslie said.

"Emma told you that?" he asked, because it suddenly sounded true.

Mrs. Oastler shrugged. "Emma never told me anything, Jack. Did she talk to you?"

"Not about her third novel," he admitted.

"There *is* no third novel," Leslie repeated.

It turned out that Mrs. Oastler had called Alan Hergott. Alan said something vague to her: the proceedings were "of a literary nature"; in fact, Emma had specified that her mother be excluded from the process. Even the reading of the will was a private matter, Alan told Mrs. Oastler; only Bob Bookman and Jack were allowed to hear what Emma wanted done with her estate.

"But are you guessing, or do you *know* there's no third novel—not even a work-in-progress?" Jack asked Leslie.

"I'm only guessing," Mrs. Oastler admitted. "With Emma, I was always guessing."

"Me, too," he said.

Surprisingly, Mrs. Oastler held his hand. He looked at her pretty face—her bright, dark eyes, her thin-lipped mouth with that seductive smile, her perfectly straight little nose—and wondered how a creature of Emma's outsize dimensions could ever have come forth from such a lean, taut body.

What Mrs. Oastler said surprised him. "Emma's death was not your fault, Jack. You were the only person she cared about. She told me once that taking care of you was all that mattered to her."

"She never told me that," he admitted. It would have been a good time to cry, but he still couldn't. And if, in his mother's estimation, Leslie Oastler would *eventually* break down, now was apparently not her moment to fall apart, either.

"Let's get the check," Leslie said. "I can't wait to see what sleeping with you and *not* doing it is like."

Jack thought they should tell his mother where they were spending the night. Alice would be worried about Leslie—and about Jack, to a lesser degree. What if his mom called the house on Entrada and got only the answering machine? Alice would be calling him on his cell phone all night.

"I'll call her while you use the bathroom," Mrs. Oastler said.

He'd forgotten to bring a toothbrush. For a host of historical reasons, Jack was disinclined to use Leslie's toothbrush, but he took a dab of her toothpaste and smeared it on his teeth with his index finger.

"Please feel free to use my toothbrush, Jack," Mrs. Oastler said through the closed bathroom door. "In fact, if you have any expectations of kissing me, please *do* use it."

He had *no* expectations of kissing Leslie Oastler—that is, not until she brought it up. Against his better judgment, Jack used her toothbrush to brush his teeth.

When he exited the bathroom, Mrs. Oastler had already undressed. She was naked except for her black bikini-cut panties— a sinister match to the bikini cut of her C-section scar and Alice's signature Rose of Jericho. Leslie crossed her arms over her small, perfect breasts as she slipped past Jack, into the bathroom, with a modesty that was as unexpected as her kisses a few minutes later.

She was an intimidating kisser, excitable and feral—without once closing her bright, watchful eyes. But Jack had the feeling that everything about her was an experiment, that she was merely conducting a test.

When they'd kissed to the point of exhaustion—either they had to stop or they had to progress to a more serious level of foreplay—Mrs. Oastler calmly asked him: "You did this with Emma, didn't you? I mean you *kissed.*"

"Yes, we kissed."

"Did you touch each other?"

"Sometimes."

"How?" He took Mrs. Oastler's breasts in his hands. "Is that all?" she asked.

"That's the only way I touched Emma," he told her.

"Where did she touch you, Jack?"

He couldn't say *penis*—with all the penis-holding in his life, God knows why. Jack let go of Leslie's breasts and rolled over, turning his back to her. Mrs. Oastler didn't hesitate; her thin arm snaked around Jack's waist, her small hand closing on his penis, which was already hard. "Like that," was all he said to her.

"Well, *that's* not very big," Leslie said. "I don't think Emma would have had an involuntary muscle spasm over *that.* Do you, Jack?"

"Maybe not," he said.

Mrs. Oastler went on holding him. He tried to will his erection away, but it endured. Leslie Oastler would always have a certain power over him, he was thinking. She had entered his childhood at a vulnerable time, first with her push-up bra—before he even met her—and later by showing him her Rose of Jericho, when Jack was of such a young age that the way she trimmed her pubic hair would become the model of the form for him.

In this way, in increments both measurable and not, our childhood is stolen from us—not always in one momentous event but often in a series of small robberies, which add up to the same loss. For surely Mrs. Oastler was one of the thieves of Jack's childhood—not that she necessarily meant to hurt him, or that she gave the matter any thought one way or another. Leslie Oastler was simply someone who disliked innocence, or she held innocence in contempt for reasons that weren't even clear to her.

She'd been disillusioned by her doctor ex-husband, whose great wealth was family money, which both he and Mrs. Oastler took for granted. (*Dr.* Oastler didn't make all that money as a doctor—not in Canada.) As a result, Mrs. Oastler had dedicated herself to the task of disillusioning others; and because Leslie met Alice, Jack just happened to fall under Leslie's spell.

In any case, when Emma had held his penis, his erection always subsided before long—not so with Mrs. Oastler. Jack was sure he had a hard-on that would last as long as she held him, and Leslie gave no indication that she was about to let go. He attempted to distract her with conversation of an inappropriate kind, but this only inspired her to alter her grip—or to alternately stroke and pull his penis in a maddeningly indifferent way.

"I feel that I never thanked you properly," Jack began. His betrayal of Emma's strongly expressed wish—namely, that he *not* thank her mother—made him feel as disloyal to his dear, departed friend as his continuing erection in her mother's hand.

"Thanked me for *what*?" Mrs. Oastler asked.

"For buying my clothes—for Redding, and for Exeter. For paying my tuition at both schools. For taking care of us—I mean my mother *and* me. For all you did for us, after Mrs. Wicksteed—"

"Stop it, Jack." He would have stopped without her telling him to do so, because her grip on his penis had tightened—painfully. Leslie Oastler pressed her open mouth between his shoulder blades, as if she were preparing to bite him; maybe she was smothering a scream. But all she said was, "Don't thank *me.*"

"But why not, Leslie? You've been very generous."

"Me, *generous*?" Mrs. Oastler asked. He felt her hand relax at last; her fingers lightly traced an imaginary outline of his penis, which had not relaxed at all.

Jack remembered a lull between customers at Daughter Alice, when his mom had said to him—as if it were part of an ongoing conversation, which it wasn't, and not out of the blue, which it was—"Promise me one thing, Jack. Don't ever sleep with Leslie."

"Mom, I would never do such a thing!" he'd declared.

And there was that night at the Sunset Marquis, a small West Hollywood hotel where Jack had been banging a model; she had a private villa on the grounds, not one of those cheap rooms in the main building. A noisy bunch of musicians—rock-'n'-rollers and their groupies—were partying in an adjacent villa, and

Jack's model wanted to crash their party. Jack just needed to crash, but not there—he wanted to go home. To prevent him from leaving, the model flushed his car keys down the toilet.

Jack could have gone to the front desk and asked someone to call him a taxi, but he didn't want to leave the Audi at the Sunset Marquis overnight; bad things had happened there. Besides, except for her bra, the model had dressed herself in Jack's clothes and gone off to the musicians' party. He would have had to leave the hotel wearing *her* clothes, and they weren't a good fit. (She was a size six, or something.)

Jack had called Emma, who was writing. He'd begged her to take a taxi and bring him the spare set of keys to the Audi; they were in the kitchen drawer, by the telephone, he was explaining, when she interrupted him. "Promise me one thing, Jack. Just don't ever sleep with my mother."

"Emma, I would never do such a thing!"

"I'm not so sure, baby cakes. I know *she* would."

"I promise," he'd told her. "Please come get me."

The model had gone off with Jack's wallet, which was in the left-front pocket of his suit pants, so he had to crash the rock-'n'-rollers' party and find her. He made himself up pretty well—the lipstick, the eye shadow, the works. Her bras were so small that Jack mistook one for a thong, but he managed to stuff each cup with half a tennis ball; he'd cut the ball in two.

The model had "twitches" in her fingers—the result of some deficiency in her diet, probably—and her personal trainer had prescribed squeezing a tennis ball as a remedy. There were tennis balls all over the villa; Jack had used her nail scissors to cut one in half.

He crammed himself into a lime-green camisole with a bare midriff, which unfortunately exposed the line of dark hair that ran from his navel below his waist. But Jack shaved this off with the model's razor. At the same time, he shaved his legs in her sink—cutting one shin. He stuck a piece of toilet paper on the cut and painted his toenails a blood-red color, which matched his wound.

Jack found a pair of peach-colored panties with a lace waistband, but the leg holes would have cut his circulation off if he hadn't snipped them with the nail scissors. Naturally, he couldn't close the zipper on the short navy-blue skirt, but the half-zipped look, which revealed the lace waistband of his panties, more or less went with the overall portrait. He looked very trashy, but so did half the hangers-on and groupies who hung out at the bar at the Sunset Marquis.

In the full-length mirror, Jack saw that he'd painted his nails in too hasty a fashion—it appeared that he'd had a barefoot accident with a lawn mower. The skirt fell off one hip, and he'd torn one side of the camisole, which exposed the tight, twisted back strap of the ivory-colored bra. Jack's tennis-ball breasts were noticeably smaller than his biceps. He looked like a field-hockey player, maybe three or four months pregnant, just starting to show.

He would have forgone the toenail polish if he could have worn his shoes, but the model had used them to weigh down his suit jacket, which was under about four inches of water in the bathtub.

It was just a musicians' party—Jack didn't expect that the dress code would be very severe. He thought it was adequate that he'd used a gob of the model's extra-body conditioner and then blow-dried his hair. He looked like a slightly pregnant *former* field-hockey player (now a hooker) who'd been struck by lightning, but compared to the girls who were the usual groupies with the rock-'n'-rollers at the Sunset Marquis, Jack was head and shoulders above the competition.

Except for the model—she was hot. She'd stripped off Jack's suit pants and the white dress shirt; she was dancing up a storm in his boxers and her bra. The musicians and their entourage were so wasted that Jack could have been Toshiro Mifune in drag, and no one would have noticed him. All but one guy, who appeared to be giving mouth-to-mouth resuscitation to his harmonica. He stopped playing and stared at Jack—well, at Jack's tennis ball in two halves, specifically.

"Did you come with her?" he asked Jack, nodding to the dancing model.

"I recognize the boxers and the bra," Jack said. It was a Jack Burns kind of line—it gave him away.

"You could pass for Jack Burns," the harmonica player said. "I'm not shitting you."

"Really?" Jack asked him. "Any idea where the honey in the boxers ditched the rest of her clothes?"

The harmonica player pointed to a couch, where a tall young

woman was stretched out; she was asleep or passed out or dead. (Unmindful of the din, whichever the case.) She'd covered herself with Jack's white dress shirt, which either she or the model had used to blot her lipstick. Jack found his suit pants and took the wallet out of the left-front pocket. There was no point in keeping the pants—not with the suit jacket under water in the model's bathtub—and he had a hundred white dress shirts. It was the kind of night when you cut your losses and left.

The model was still dancing. "Tell her she can keep the boxers, but I want my bra back," Jack said to the harmonica player, who was yowling away on his instrument like a runover cat; he barely nodded in Jack's direction.

There was a bouncer-type who'd not seen Jack come in. The bouncer followed Jack out, into the semidark grounds, where there were other villas—some lit, some not. There was already dew on the grass. "Hey," the bouncer said. "Someone said you were that weirdo Jack Burns."

Jack's face came up to the broad chest of the bouncer's Hawaiian shirt; he was blocking Jack's way. Ordinarily Jack would have sidestepped him; he could have easily outrun him to the lineup at the velvet rope out in front of the bar. The bouncer wouldn't have messed with Jack in a crowd. But Jack's skirt was so tight that his knees were brushing together when he walked; he couldn't have run anywhere.

"Is that you, honey pie?" he heard Emma say. The bouncer stepped aside and let him pass. "Just look at you—you're half unzipped!" Emma said to Jack. She threw her big arm around his hip, pulling him to her. She kissed Jack on the mouth, smearing his lipstick. "What happened to your shoes, baby cakes?" she asked.

"Under water," Jack explained.

"They better not have been your Manolo Blahniks, you bad girl," Emma said, putting her big hand on Jack's ass.

"Dykes!" the bouncer called after them.

"I've got a dildo that would make you cry like a little baby!" Emma yelled at the bouncer, who looked suddenly pale in the bad light.

A tall, floppy guy, like a scarecrow, had fallen on the velvet rope in front of the bar; he was draped over it like a coat over a clothesline.

"I think it's illegal to drive barefoot in California," Emma was telling Jack.

"I promise I won't sleep with your mother," he whispered to her.

Jack was almost asleep, with his penis still stiff in Mrs. Oastler's hand, when Leslie spoke to him. "I had to promise your mom I wouldn't sleep with you, Jack. Of course, we're not *really* sleeping together—not the way Alice meant—are we?"

"Of course not," Jack told her.

One of Mrs. Oastler's fingernails nicked the tip of his penis, and he flinched against her. "I'm sorry," she said. "I haven't played with anyone's penis in quite some time."

"It's okay," he said.

"You gotta talk to your mom, Jack," Leslie said, the way Emma might have said it.

"Why's that?" he asked.

"Talk to her while there's still time, Jack."

"Still time for what?"

"Emma and I didn't talk enough," Mrs. Oastler said. "Now we're out of time."

"Talk to my mom about *what*?"

"You must have questions, Jack."

"She never answered them!" he told her.

"Well, maybe now's the time," Mrs. Oastler said. "Ask her *again*."

"Do you know something I don't, Leslie?"

"Definitely," she said. "But I'm not telling you. Ask your mom."

Outside, someone was screaming—probably in the parking lot near the hotel, but at Shutters on the Beach you could hear someone screaming all the way from the Santa Monica Pier. Perhaps it was the screaming that did it, but Jack's erection finally subsided.

"Oh, *cute*!" Mrs. Oastler said. (She was making a considerable effort to bring his penis back to life.) "It's like it's going *away*!"

"Maybe it's sad," he suggested.

"Remember that line, Jack," Emma had told him. "You can use it." And to think he hadn't been able to imagine under what circumstances an admission of your penis's sadness would be of any possible use!

But the word *sad* affected Leslie Oastler in a way Jack wouldn't have predicted. She let go of his penis and rolled over, turning her back to him. He didn't know she was crying until he felt the bed tremble; she was crying without making a sound. Jack guessed that this was the *eventually* his mother had meant when she'd said that Leslie would break down, but—even in the act of falling apart—Mrs. Oastler was contained. Her small body shook, her face was wet with tears, her breasts were cool to his touch, but she never said a word.

When Jack woke up, he could hear Mrs. Oastler in the shower; room service had come and gone, unbeknownst to him. The pot of coffee, which was all that Leslie had ordered, was lukewarm. She'd already packed her small suitcase, and had laid flat (at the foot of the bed) the clothes she would wear on the plane— a black pantsuit, her bikini-cut panties, the little push-up bra. On her pillow, Mrs. Oastler had left a surprise for Jack: that photograph of Emma, naked, the one he'd kept. Leslie must have found it in the Entrada house; she wanted him to know she'd seen it.

The photo regarded Jack critically—Emma at seventeen, when Jack was ten and heading off to Redding. She had never been fitter. There was evidence of a matburn on one of her cheeks; probably Chenko, or one of the Minskies, had given it to her.

When Leslie Oastler came out of the bathroom, she was wearing a Shutters bathrobe and her hair was still wet. "Cute picture, huh?" Mrs. Oastler asked.

"Charlotte Barford took it," he said.

"Then she probably took more than one—didn't she, Jack?"

"An ex-girlfriend made me throw them away," he told her.

"She probably thought you threw *all* of them away, Jack."

"Right," he said.

"A famous guy like you shouldn't have pictures like that lying around," Mrs. Oastler told him. "But I'm not going to throw it away for you. I'm not likely to throw *any* photographs of Emma away—not now."

"No, of course not," he said.

Jack went and stood naked at the window, overlooking the parking lot; there was a partial view of the dead, motionless Ferris wheel, which resembled the skeleton of a dinosaur in the bleached-gray light. Santa Monica wasn't an early-morning town.

Mrs. Oastler came and stood behind him, holding his penis in both her hands; he had a hard-on in a matter of seconds. It seemed like such a betrayal of Emma—all of it. That was when Jack began to cry. He could tell that Leslie was naked because she was rubbing herself against his bare back. If she'd wanted to make love, he would have; that was probably why he was crying. The promises he'd made to Emma and his mother meant nothing.

"Poor Jack," Leslie Oastler said sarcastically. She let him go and dressed herself; her hair was so short, she could dry it easily with a towel. "You're going to have a busy day, I'm sure," she told him, "doing whatever literary executors do." Jack could have cried all day, but not in front of her. He stopped. He found his clothes and started to get dressed, putting Emma's photo in his right-front pocket. "Your mother will no doubt call you before I'm back in Toronto," Mrs. Oastler was telling him. "She'll want to know all about our night together—how we *didn't* sleep together, and all of that."

"I know what to say," he told her.

"Just be sure you *talk* to her, Jack. Ask her everything, while there's still time."

Jack finished dressing without saying anything. He went into the bathroom and shut the door. He tried to do something about his hair; he washed his face. He was grateful to Mrs. Oastler for leaving him her tube of toothpaste, if not her toothbrush, which he presumed she'd packed. He smeared a dab of toothpaste on his teeth with his index finger and rinsed his mouth in the sink. Jack heard the hotel-room door close before he was finished in the bathroom; when he came back out into the room, Leslie was gone.

He had some trouble leaving Shutters. Mrs. Oastler had paid the bill, but the paparazzi were waiting for him. Thankfully, they'd missed Mrs. Oastler. Someone had spotted Jack Burns having dinner with a good-looking older woman at One Pico; someone had figured out that they'd spent the night at Shutters.

"Who was the woman, Jack?" one of the photographers kept asking.

There were a few more paparazzi waiting for him at Entrada

Drive, but that was to be expected. Jack wondered why they hadn't been there the night before; they could have followed him and Leslie to Shutters. He stripped Emma's bed and put her linens and towels in the washing machine; he straightened up the place a little. His mom called before he'd managed to make himself any breakfast. He told her that Leslie was already on the plane, and that they'd had a comforting night together.

"*Comforting?* You didn't sleep with her—did you, Jack?"

"Of course not!" he said with indignation.

"Well, Leslie can be a little *lawless,*" Alice said.

Jack could only imagine how Mrs. Oastler might have reacted to that. He would have guessed that, in their relationship, his mom was the more *lawless* of the two. But he didn't say anything. Jack knew he was supposed to talk to his mother, but he didn't know what to say.

"Leslie said I should talk to you, Mom. She said I should ask you everything, while there's still time."

"Goodness, what a morbid night you two must have had!" Alice said.

"Mom, *talk* to me."

"We *are* talking, dear."

She was being coy. Jack simply turned against her. There was a time when he'd *tried* to ask her everything, and she'd wanted no part of it. Now he didn't want to give her the opportunity to unburden herself. What did Jack care about any of it now—what did it matter? When he was a kid, when it would have mattered, she was silent. Jack was the one who was silent now.

"If there's anything you want to ask me, dear, ask away!" his mother said.

"Are you faithful to Leslie?" he asked. "Isn't she more faithful to you than you are to her?" That wasn't what Jack really cared about—he was just testing his mother's willingness to give him a straight answer.

"Jackie—what a question!"

"What kind of guy was my dad? Was he a good guy or a bad one?"

"Jack, I think you should come home to Toronto for a few days—so we can talk."

"We *are* talking, Mom."

"You're just being argumentative, dear."

"Please tell Leslie that I *tried* to talk to you," Jack said.

"You didn't sleep with her, *really*?" his mom asked.

Jack almost regretted that he hadn't *really* slept with Leslie Oastler, but all he said was: "No, Mom, I did not."

After that, their conversation (such as it was) slipped away. When Jack told his mother that he'd thanked Mrs. Oastler for all she'd done for him—for *them,* he meant—his mom responded with her usual "That's nice, dear."

He also should have said that Leslie was funny about his thanking her, but he didn't.

Jack was on the cordless phone, looking out the window at a TV crew in his driveway. They were filming the exterior of the Entrada Drive house, which really pissed Jack off. He was distracted and didn't understand what his mom was saying about some tattoo convention in Woodstock, New York.

Out of the blue, Jack asked her: "Do you remember when I was at Redding? One year, you were going to come see me in Maine, but something happened and you couldn't come. I was at Redding for four years, but you never came to see me."

"Well, that's quite some story—why I didn't come to Redding. Of *course* I remember! I'll have to tell you that story sometime, Jack. It's a good one."

Somehow this didn't strike him as what Mrs. Oastler meant by *talking* to his mother. They were talking in circles. Jack had lived with Emma for ten years; now Emma was gone, and he and his mom couldn't talk to each other. They never *had*. It was pretty clear that she didn't want to tell him anything, ever.

Alice wanted to know what was entailed in being a literary executor—not that Jack knew. "I guess I'll find out what's involved," was all he could say.

Jack was surprised to see that there was only one message on the answering machine, which he played while his mom was still on the phone. It was Mildred ("Milly") Ascheim, the porn producer, calling with her condolences. Her voice was so much like Myra's that, for a moment, Jack thought that Myra was summoning him from the grave. "Dear Jack Burns," Milly Ascheim said, as if she were dictating a letter to him. "I'm sorry you've lost your friend."

She didn't leave her number or say her name, but she must have known that he knew the Ascheim sisters spoke with one voice. He was touched that she'd called, but once again he was distracted from what his mom was saying—something about Mrs. Oastler, again.

"Jack, are you alone?"

"Yes, I'm alone, Mom."

"I heard a woman's voice."

"It was someone on television," he lied.

"I asked you if Leslie kept her clothes on, Jack."

"Well, I think I would have noticed if she'd taken them off," he told her.

"Actor," Alice said.

"Mom, I gotta go." (It was the way Emma would have said *gotta,* they both noticed.)

"Good-bye, Billy Rainbow," his mother said, hanging up the phone.

24

The Button Trick

A St. Hilda's Old Girl, like Leslie Oastler, would often choose to have her funeral or memorial service in the school's chapel, where the Old Girls had both fond and traumatizing memories of their younger days, many of which had not been spent in the contaminating presence of boys—except for those *little* boys, who were neither a threat nor a temptation to the much more grown-up girls. (Except for Jack Burns.)

It's unlikely that Emma would have chosen the chapel at St. Hilda's for her memorial service, but she had left her mother no instructions regarding how she wanted to be "remembered." That Mrs. Oastler chose the St. Hilda's chapel was only natural. After all, it was in Leslie's neighborhood and she had already chosen it for her own service.

Alice called Jack to convey Leslie's request: Mrs. Oastler wanted him to "say a little something" at Emma's service. "You're so good with words, dear," Jack's mother said. "And for how many years now have you been writing something?"

Well, how could he refuse? Besides, Jack's mom and Mrs. Oastler had no idea how the myth of his *writing something,* which Emma had so presciently set in motion, was now a reality.

In her will, Emma had indeed left him *everything.* ("Lucky you," Leslie had remarked—little knowing just how lucky he would soon be.) Jack was Emma's "literary executor" in more ways than one—the exact terms of which would never be known to anyone other than Bob Bookman, Alan Hergott, and Jack Burns himself—for if ever a will were ironclad, that would aptly describe how Emma had set him up.

Upon her death, the film rights to *The Slush-Pile Reader,* which Emma had so entangled with the kind of approvals never granted to writers—cast approval, director approval, final cut—

462 | *Sleeping in the Needles*

were passed unencumbered to Jack. He could make the movie of her novel as he saw fit, provided that he wrote the script. What only Bob Bookman, Alan Hergott, and Jack knew was that Emma had already written a rudimentary adaptation of *The Slush-Pile Reader*—her screenplay was a rough first draft. There were also her notes, addressed to Jack—suggestions as to what he might want to change or add or delete. And there were gaps in the story, some substantial, where it fell to him to fill in the blanks. Or, as Emma put it: "Write your own dialogue, baby cakes." She had intended, all along, that Jack would play the porn star in the film.

Were he to reject this flagrant plagiarism—should Jack not accept the falsehood that he was the sole screenwriter of *The Slush-Pile Reader*—the movie could not be made until a requisite number of years had passed (under existing copyright law) and Emma's novel had at last entered the public domain.

As for Emma's *third* novel, Mrs. Oastler had been right—it did not exist. But Emma hadn't suffered from writer's block; she'd simply been busy adapting *The Slush-Pile Reader* as a screenplay by Jack Burns.

He learned from Bob Bookman—whose other clients included directors and writers, not actors—how Emma had persuaded Bob to accept Jack as a client. In her words: "Jack Burns is a writer, not an actor; he just doesn't know it yet."

The royalties from Emma's backlist—the paperback sales of *The Slush-Pile Reader* and *Normal and Nice*—were also left to Jack. This would more than compensate him for his time spent "finishing" Emma's screenplay. In short, Emma had made Jack declare himself a writer to the media while she was alive; in death, she had given him the opportunity to become one.

Both the unfinished draft of the screenplay for *The Slush-Pile Reader* and Emma's notes to Jack had been removed from her computer. She hadn't saved any copies on disk, and she'd deleted the files from her hard drive. The only printed copy, which Alan Hergott kept safely in his office—where he and Bob Bookman explained to Jack the terms of Emma's will—needed to be transcribed into Jack's handwriting. From interviews he'd given, most of them bullshit, everyone knew that Jack Burns wrote in longhand; even Leslie Oastler knew that he didn't own a computer or a typewriter, and that he allegedly *liked* to write by hand.

Bob and Alan thought that Jack should do the copying into

longhand as soon as possible. He could take all the time he needed to "revise."

"But should I really do this?" Jack asked them. "I mean—is it right?"

"It's what Emma wanted, Jack, but you don't *have* to do it," Alan said.

"Yeah, it's entirely your decision," Bookman told him. "But it's a pretty good script."

Jack would read it and concur; if Emma had taken charge of him in life, he saw no reason to resist her efforts to control him from the grave.

That Mrs. Oastler wanted Jack to "say a little something" in remembrance of Emma in the chapel at St. Hilda's, where Mrs. McQuat had first warned him of the dangers of turning his back on God, seemed appropriate to the kind of writer he'd become.

The public impression—namely, that Emma Oastler had suffered from a writer's block of several years' duration and had, as a result, become grossly overweight—was further fueled by the report of that Italian journalist from the Hollywood Foreign Press. According to Jack's interviewer, Emma's allegedly platonic but live-in relationship with the actor Jack Burns showed signs of recent strain; yet the bestselling author had been extremely generous to him in her will. It had been known, for years, that Jack was "a closet writer"—as Emma's obituary notice in *Entertainment Weekly* would say. Now he was said to be "developing" a screenplay of *The Slush-Pile Reader*. (Emma, "mysteriously," had not wanted her novel to be made into a movie while she was alive.)

What guilt Jack might have had—that is, in accepting Emma's gift to him as rightfully his—was overshadowed by the certainty that, even if he were to tell the truth, the *truth* was not what Emma had wanted. She had wanted to get *The Slush-Pile Reader* made as a movie—more or less as she'd written it. But with *her* name on the script, the film, as she wrote it, would never have been made. Jack Burns, Emma knew, was a movie star; with *his* name on the screenplay, he could control it.

Thus, at one of the better addresses he knew—in the Beverly Hills offices of Bloom, Hergott, Diemer and Cook, LLP, Attorneys-at-Law—Jack Burns transcribed Emma's rough draft of *The Slush-Pile Reader* into his handwriting, and faithfully copied her notes as well. With the first small change he made, which was not even as big an alteration as the choice of a different *word*—Jack used the contraction "didn't" where Emma had written "did not"—he discovered how it was possible for a would-be writer to take at least partial possession of a real writer's work. (And with subsequent changes, deletions, additions, his sense of rightful ownership—though false—only grew.)

This should not have surprised him. After all, Jack was in the movie business; he had seen how scripts were changed, and by how many amateur hands these alterations were wrought. In another draft or two, the screenplay of *The Slush-Pile Reader* would feel—even to Jack—as if he'd written it. But the structure of the script and its prevailing tone of voice were entirely Emma's. As an actor, Jack knew how to imitate her voice.

Not all art is imitation, but imitating was what Jack Burns did best. With a little direction—in Emma's case, she gave him quite a lot—writing (that is, *re*writing) the script of *The Slush-Pile Reader* was just another acting job. Jack did his job well.

The decision to make Michele Maher (the character) the movie's voice-over was Emma's. The idea to make the penultimate sentence of the novel the opening line of voice-over in the film was Jack's. ("There are worse relationships in L.A.") We see Michele, the script reader, in bed with the porn star—just holding his penis, we presume, under the covers. It's all very tastefully done. The story of how they meet (when she reads the porn star's atrocious screenplay) is a flashback. Naturally, we never see his (that is, Jack's) penis.

Jack took a similar liberty with the novel's first sentence, which had always been his favorite; he made it the end line of Michele's voice-over, where he thought it had more weight. ("Either there are no coincidences in this town, or everything in this town is a coincidence.") It was too good a line to waste on the opening credits.

For the most part, Jack followed Emma's instructions. The Michele Maher character remains an angel of hope to talentless screenwriters; she is conscience-stricken by the awful scripts she reads, an impossible optimist in the cynical world of screenplay development.

Emma recommended that Jack give the porn star, Miguel Santiago, a more Anglo-sounding name. ("You don't look Hispanic, honey pie.") Jack decided on James Stronach. The last name would make his mom happy, and James was a natural for "Jimmy"—the unhappy actor's porn name in *Bored Housewives* (one through four), *Keep It Up, Inc.,* and countless other adult films, for which Jimmy is famous.

James ("Jimmy") Stronach's homage to James Stewart is an essential aspect of his character; Jack-Burns-as-James-Stronach memorizing Jimmy Stewart's lines in *The Shopworn Angel* and *It's a Wonderful Life* would be among Jack's most sympathetic moments in the movie.

Jack didn't look like a bodybuilder before they filmed *The Slush-Pile Reader,* but he had time to change his diet and step up the weightlifting. In truth, he would never look like a body-builder; he just had to look like he belonged at the male end of the weight rack in the free-weights section of the gym. (His tattoos, in the movie, would be fakes.)

Emma had taken some of her best lines from the novel and given them to Michele Maher as voice-over. "I lived within breathing distance of a sushi Dumpster in Venice"—that kind of thing. She'd left Jack a note about dropping the mutual-masturbation scene. "There's already too much masturbation, or *implied* masturbation, for a movie."

Emma was right to go easy on the masturbation—although *The Slush-Pile Reader* would release, as a film, in the same year that another masturbation movie, *American Beauty,* cleaned up at the Academy Awards. (Miss Wurtz, who was dismayed at Anthony Hopkins's winning an Oscar for Best Actor for *eating* people, would be silent on the subject of Kevin Spacey's winning an Academy Award for beating off in a shower.)

And Jack decided to cut Michele Maher's misadventure with the Swedish power lifter, Per the Destroyer. (Per too closely resembled the bodybuilder at Gold's who had beaten Emma up.) Instead Jack added a scene with James Stronach scouting the locker room at World Gym for bodybuilders with small schlongs. James makes a mistake. Someone he introduces to Michele isn't as small as James thinks. Michele gets hurt.

"He was bigger than you thought," is all Michele says in the movie. (The words *schlong* and *penis* are never used.)

"Couldn't you tell him it hurt? Didn't you ask him to stop?" Jack-as-James asks her.

"I asked, but he wouldn't stop," Michele tells him.

Naturally, Jack-as-James gets the guy back at the gym. (Jack added that scene, too.) The not-so-small schlong asks James to spot for him when he's bench-pressing three hundred pounds; it's too good an opportunity to pass up.

"I've got it!" James tells him, as if Jack-as-James could possibly hold three hundred pounds; he drops the barbell on the big schlong's chest, breaking his clavicle.

Emma herself cut the line about Michele's assessment of the small schlongs she sleeps with as "a muted pleasure"—and there's no frontal nudity, no actual porn-film parts. For the most part, we see the porn stars between takes or going through the motions of their private lives. (The horny men in motel rooms with the television light flickering on their riveted faces—well, those are the *implied* masturbation scenes that Emma referred to in her notes.) The film would still pull an R rating.

When James and Michele are holding each other, not talking, at the end of the picture—"just breathing in the sushi perfume of the Dumpster," as Michele's voice-over puts it—Jack thought he'd been as true to Emma's novel and the rough draft of her screenplay as he could have been.

Jack did *not* incorporate Emma's feelings that the reason screenwriters lost control of their scripts was that they caved to the money, as he'd heard Emma say a hundred times. It was Emma's triumph—in her novel, if not in real life—that the Michele Maher character was a whole lot more sympathetic to screenwriters than Emma was.

The film itself became a kind of tribute to the unread screenplay, the unmade movie. And both Emma and Jack were careful to be kind to porn stars; to that end, Jack would insist that Hank Long have a part. James ("Jimmy") Stronach needed a buddy, didn't he? Besides, Jack had used Hank Long's unnaturally high voice as the model for his stutter in the movie. (The stutter was Emma's idea—to make it clear why James's only career choice is in so-called adult films.)

Muffy, that special kind of vampire, had retired by the time they made *The Slush-Pile Reader,* but Jack was instrumental in casting her as the single-mom porn star—a woman with a couple of uncontainable children, both hyperactive boys. Muffy organizes barbecue lunches on the weekends; the male porn stars, like Hank and Jack-as-James, handle the outdoor grill and play catch with Muffy's kids.

Emma advised Jack to involve Mildred Ascheim in the picture, too—if only in an advisory role. Not even Bob Bookman or Alan Hergott knew why. Milly (and Hank, and Muffy) had seen Jack's small schlong. For Jack to be cast as a porn star could have given rise to some ugly rumors, but not if the industry's only professional witnesses were part of the movie.

What *hadn't* Emma Oastler done for Jack Burns? How hard could it be to "say a little something" in memoriam at the St. Hilda's chapel? Surely he owed Emma that much.

In the front pew, in a side-aisle seat, Miss Wong sat as still as a hard-boiled egg. She'd positioned herself directly beneath the pulpit, where Jack spoke, and had drawn her knees tightly together—as if the alleged weirdness of Jack's Hollywood reputation might spontaneously force her legs apart.

It must have been Emma who'd first called her Miss Bahamas. Why else would Miss Wong have come? Possibly Emma's fictional depictions of extreme yet acceptable dysfunction had eased Miss Wong's disappointment with her life. To have been born in a hurricane, only to find herself becalmed at an all-girls' school—well, one can imagine how this might have left her feeling let down.

Was an Old Girl's death always commemorated by the attendance of the existing faculty at St. Hilda's? Jack didn't remember such a turnout in remembrance of Mrs. Wicksteed, but she had been old. And Miss Wong was not the only front-pew attendant among the faculty. Mr. Malcolm, who'd also ensconced himself there, had planted the unseeing Mrs. Malcolm in the center aisle. Mr. Malcolm sat beside his deranged wife with his hand on the armrest of her wheelchair, lest she be moved by Jack's words to charge the altar or go after his mother and Mrs. Oastler, who were seated directly across the aisle from the Malcolms.

In a side-aisle seat, at some distance from the pulpit, Miss Caroline Wurtz appraised Jack's performance from her audience-of-one perspective.

The chapel was not quite full. There were a few bare spots in the side-aisle pews, and plenty of standing room in the vicinity of the rear entrance, where Mr. Ramsey paced and bounced on the balls of his feet—as if his grief for Emma, whom he'd barely known, had left him too agitated to sit down.

Had Emma been a more popular girl than Jack had first supposed? Of course Wendy Fists-of-Stone Holton had a center-aisle seat in a pew near the front. A gaunt woman with a washed-out complexion and flyaway, silver-blond hair, Wendy had been recently divorced from an ear, nose, and throat doctor who'd declared himself gay upon the accusation that he'd impregnated his nurse. (Wendy had spoken to Jack before Emma's service; she said it would be nice to have a coffee, "or something," if he had the time.)

In the pew behind Miss Wong sat the very personification of a hurricane preparing to consume the Bahamas—all two-hundred-plus pounds of Charlotte Breasts-with-*Bones*-in-Them Barford, Emma's Canadian publisher. Charlotte had offered Jack her editorial assistance, purely for the privilege of reading whatever it was he was alleged to be writing—a novel or a memoir, perhaps titled *A Penis at St. Hilda's*. (Or so Charlotte might have dreamed.) Before the service, she'd hinted to Jack that it must have been "a bitch" to interrupt his *other* writing to write an adaptation of *The Slush-Pile Reader*.

"Indeed," he'd managed to say—his voice, like Hank Long's, unnaturally high. In the company of grown women among whom Jack remembered being a little boy, he was again a child.

The Hamilton sisters were there; notably, they were not sitting together. Penny, between whose eyes he had once ejaculated, watched him with the innocent eagerness of a soccer mom—sperm the farthest thing from her mind, not to mention her forehead. She'd brought her children, two terribly well-behaved and well-dressed little girls; her husband, Penny told Jack, was having "an all-boys' weekend away." (Golf, Jack imagined. He didn't ask.)

As for Penny's sister, Bonnie, who was in grade twelve when Jack was in grade four, she'd managed to enter the chapel without his seeing her limp to her pew—assuming that Bonnie still limped. Her proximity to the rear entrance, where Mr. Ramsey continued to make a moving target of himself, suggested to Jack that Bonnie's pelvis was irreparably twisted; her dead right leg would forever trail behind her while she lurched forward on her leading left foot.

The eight years between them seemed of no consequence now. She'd never married, Jack's mother had told him. Bonnie Hamilton was the most sought-after real estate agent in Toronto, Mrs. Oastler had said. "With that limp," Leslie had added, "it must hold things up to have her show you a property with lots of *stairs*."

Ever the prompter, Bonnie sat in the back and moved her lips before Jack spoke—as if she already knew what he was *supposed* to say about Emma, as if he'd actually written something and Bonnie had miraculously read and memorized it before he began to speak. She was forty, but the fatalistic tug Jack had felt when he was nine (and Bonnie seventeen) was pulling them together still. As he'd tried to tell Emma, but had managed to tell only Mrs. McQuat, Bonnie Hamilton was an older woman who, when she looked at him, couldn't look away.

For a moment, Jack thought that *all* the older women of his childhood were there.

Connie Turnbull, who'd run up to Mrs. Oastler and Alice and Jack—this was immediately after Connie had parked her car, with a big dog in it—had clearly been practicing her lines from Miss Wurtz's long-ago dramatization of *Jane Eyre*. " 'It is in vain to say human beings ought to be satisfied with tranquillity,' " Connie said, breathlessly—holding Jack's shoulders and assessing him, as if she were measuring him for a coffin or a suit.

" 'Dread remorse when you are tempted to err,' " Jack began; then, sensing how deeply Connie Turnbull was dissatisfied with tranquillity, he stopped.

Jack had come up to her breasts when they'd last engaged in this dialogue—when he'd played a grade-three Rochester to her grade-six Jane. Now, in her two-inch heels, Connie was only a forehead taller than Jack was. " 'You think me, I daresay, an irreligious dog,' " he started to say.

On cue, Connie took his hand and kissed it. Her lips were parted, and she made the usual contact with her teeth and tongue—only this time there was no applause. Alice and Mrs. Oastler looked on, aghast; they clearly didn't know their *Jane Eyre*. What must they have thought? That Jack had arranged an assignation with Connie Turnbull *after* Emma's memorial service; possibly that he'd slept with Connie the night *before*?

"Nice job, Jack," Connie whispered in his ear—her hair faintly redolent of dog-breath, which at a glance he could see was fogging up the windows of her parked car.

Thank goodness Ginny Jarvis wasn't there. It was as if the gun he'd shot her with—onstage, in *A Mail-Order Bride in the Northwest Territories*—hadn't been firing blanks. But Jack was unprepared for those *other* Old Girls who'd come to honor Emma. Or had they? Many of them were unknown to him.

"It's *you*, baby cakes," he could imagine Emma saying in her husky whisper. "The old broads are here to get a look at *you*." Maybe so. How else to explain the presence of Jack's classmates? There were four of them, all girls.

The Booth twins, Heather and Patsy, whose identical blanket-sucking sounds had been born in the terrors of Emma Oastler's sleepy-time stories, when they were in kindergarten together and Emma was in grade six—*they* couldn't have come out of respect for their old tormentor. Likewise Maureen Yap, whose married name would forever elude Jack; Maureen must have remembered how Emma had abused her.

As alert as an endangered squirrel, Maureen had chosen a center-aisle seat in the back of the chapel, lest she should feel the sudden need to flee—from some reference Jack might make to the bat-cave exhibit in the Royal Ontario Museum, perchance, not to mention his reminding her of Emma's divorced-dad story. ("He has just passed out from too much sex.")

It was Maureen Yap who'd asked Emma: "What is too much sex?"

"Nothing you'll ever have," Emma had answered her dismissively.

After Emma's service, at what Mrs. Oastler would describe as "a kind of wake," which was held in the Great Hall, Maureen Yap approached Jack. A strand of her hair had strayed to a corner of her mouth, where there also lingered a remnant of cheese. Little cubes of cheddar, skewered on toothpicks, were the only food served—and these were washed down by white wine, which Alice said was warm, or by sparkling water, which Jack would have described as "room temperature at best."

Whether it was the speck of cheese or the strand of hair—or her miserable conviction that Emma's prophecy, which denied Maureen Yap the possibility of ever having too much sex, was incontrovertibly true—Maureen was difficult to understand.

"I blame the delay on Pam Hoover," Jack thought she said, as she nervously spilled her wine.

He sipped some tepid sparkling water and considered what Maureen might have meant. *All* the women at Emma's memorial service—the ones Jack recognized and the many he did not—had looked better in their school uniforms. But maybe Jack had looked better then, too. "I must have misheard you, Maureen," he replied, bringing tears to her eyes.

"I came all the way from Vancouver," Maureen Yap repeated. "I'm staying at the Four Seasons, under my maiden name."

Jack was staying at the Four Seasons, too—a source of some friction between him and his mom. Jack wasn't sure what Leslie Oastler thought of his defection to a hotel. Maybe Mrs. Oastler, if not his mom, understood why he wouldn't have wanted to spend the night in Emma's bed, or even in what had been Jack's designated bedroom, where Emma had more than once held him in her arms—where Mrs. Machado had taken such indelible advantage of him.

That they each had a room at the Four Seasons did not mean Jack was doomed to sleep with Maureen Yap. She would never find him, he was thinking; he was registered under a new name. Because the Billy Rainbow film had already been released, Jack was Jimmy Stronach now. As he'd newly invented the porn star's name, and not even Bob Bookman or Alan Hergott had read his many revisions of Emma's script, truly *no one* knew who Jack Burns was.

Those women who came to the St. Hilda's chapel had come to see *him*—Jack Burns, the movie star. He failed to recognize the majority of them, but they were mostly in their thirties and forties. If they hadn't known Jack as a little boy, they'd probably seen him around the school—and without a doubt they had seen his films. Their husbands (if they had husbands) weren't with them; their children occasionally were. To be sure, the women wore black or navy blue, but their attire struck Jack as more suitable for a dinner party than a funeral. Maybe this was underscored by Emma's memorial service being held at the cocktail hour on a Sunday evening.

And the fourth of Jack's classmates to attend the service had not entered St. Hilda's in kindergarten. Lucinda Fleming had been a new student when he'd first met her in grade one; she'd never experienced Emma's sleepy-time tales. Lucinda, and what Miss Wong once referred to as her "silent rage," had never been intimate with Emma Oastler.

What had urged Lucinda to include Jack on her Christmas-letter list? What had made her such a tireless organizer of the class reunions at St. Hilda's, despite *everyone* remembering her violent overreaction to being kissed? (Her biting herself so badly that she required stitches, her lying in a puddle of her pee on the third-grade floor!)

If Lucinda Fleming had known how Emma hated Christmas letters *and* the people who wrote them, she wouldn't have come to pay her last respects. If she'd had any idea of the contempt Emma felt for the repeated announcements of childbearing, which caused Emma to denounce Lucinda's Christmas letters as "breeding statistics"—well, Lucinda Fleming (had she known Emma *at all*) wouldn't have been moved to pray for Emma's soul.

But it was *Jack's* soul Lucinda and the others were after—and while he might have been a movie star in those women's eyes, he instantly lost the essential contact with his audience of one in their company. In the St. Hilda's chapel, where even Jesus was depicted as surrounded by women—saints maybe, but women *definitely*—he didn't feel like Jack Burns, the actor. He felt like Jack Burns, the little boy—lost again in a sea of girls. No matter that they were grown women now. In reentering their world, Jack had returned to his childhood and its fears—and, like a child, he felt as frightened and as unsure of himself as he'd ever been.

How could Jack "say a little something" about Emma to this audience of older women—among them, those grown-up girls and older women who had *formed* him? How could he feel at ease in this holy place—where, even as a little boy, he had turned his back on God?

Jack gripped the pulpit in both hands, but he couldn't speak; the words wouldn't come. The congregation waited for him; the chapel was as still as Emma's heart.

It's awful how your mind can trick you when you're scared, Jack thought. Among those women's faces, all of them looking up at him, Jack could have sworn he saw Mrs. Stackpole—the long-dead dishwasher from his Exeter days. If he'd dared to search among their faces, he might have come upon Mrs. Adkins, so long ago immersed in the Nezinscot—or Claudia, who had threatened to haunt him, or Leah Rosen, dead in Chile, or even Emma herself, who no doubt would have been disappointed in Jack for failing to say what he'd come to say.

Jack tried to look beyond their faces, focusing on no one—except maybe Mr. Ramsey, who was always so encouraging. But Mr. Ramsey had disappeared from sight. Actually he'd been swallowed up in the sea of late arrivals—young girls, students at

St. Hilda's, who all wore their school uniforms, as if this special Sunday-evening service were just another day at school.

In Jack's state of mind, he mistook the girls for ghosts, but they were boarders—the only St. Hilda's students on campus on a Sunday. They must have mustered the courage to come to the chapel en masse from their residence. They hadn't been invited, although they were the age—seventeen or eighteen—of Emma Oastler's most adoring fans. (Young women had been Emma's biggest readers.)

It was a shock to see them there, standing at the rear of the chapel in their universal postures of sullenness and exultation and prettiness and slouching disarray—as Jack had seen them at the age of four, when he first felt compelled to hold his mother's hand. The girls made him remember his fear of their bare legs— with their kneesocks pushed down to their ankles, as if to reveal their interior unrest. The cant of their hips, their untucked shirts, their unbuttoned buttons, their bitten lips and willfully unattended hair—well, there they were, these unnamed girls, some of them carrying well-worn paperbacks of Emma's first or second novel, *all* of them signifying to Jack the gestures of an emerging sexuality he had so skillfully imitated as an actor. (Even as a *man*!)

They took Jack's breath away, but they brought him back to the task at hand. He found his voice, though it was weak—barely above a whisper—and he spoke as if only to them, those young-girl boarders. They were probably in grades twelve and thirteen.

"I remember," Jack began, "how she held my . . . *hand.*"

Without Mrs. Oastler's sigh of relief, he wouldn't have known she'd been holding her breath. A spontaneous shudder shook Miss Wong's shoulders; her knees unclenched, her legs lolled apart.

"Emma Oastler looked after me," Jack continued. "I didn't have a father," he told them—not that they didn't already know that! "But Emma was my *protector.*"

The word *protector* animated Maureen Yap like a jolt of electricity; her hands flew up from her lap, her palms held open and apart like the pages of a prayer book or a hymnal. (Jack half expected her to sing.) Lucinda Fleming curled her lower lip and seized it between her teeth. There was a sound like the binding of a new book breaking—Wendy Fists-of-Stone Holton cracking her knuckles against her flat chest.

Then Jack's tears came, unplanned—he wasn't acting. Without making a noise, he just started to cry—he couldn't stop. He'd had more to say, but what was the point? Wasn't this the performance they'd all been hoping for? JACK BURNS BREAKS DOWN, OR WAS IT AN ACT? one of the tabloids would say. But it wasn't an act.

Those heartbreaking young girls (the abandoned boarders with their collected loneliness) were what released him—the way they just stood there without once standing still. They shook their hair, they shrugged their shoulders—they stood first on one leg, then the other. They cocked a hip here, an elbow there. They scratched their bare knees and looked under their nails, the tips of their tongues touching their upper lips or the corners of their open mouths—as if Jack Burns were in a movie on a giant screen and they watched him from the dark, safe and unseen.

Jack simply stopped talking and let his tears fall, not at first knowing that this would have an unleashing effect on the assembled congregation. He never meant to make them cry, but that was the unavoidable result.

Mrs. Malcolm rocked uncontrollably back and forth in her wheelchair, as if a third accident—either crippling or blinding, or both—had befallen her. It must have been something Mr. Malcolm, in his grief, was powerless to ward away. Alice's face, ageless when bathed in tears, was tilted up to Jack. He could read her lips. ("I'm so sorry, Jackie!")

"Jack Burns!" Mr. Ramsey cried, choking back a sob.

Miss Wurtz had covered her face with a white handkerchief, as if she were less than stoically facing a firing squad.

Caroline French, usually a no-show at the class reunions, was a no-show at Emma's memorial service as well. Jack was sorry to miss the sound of her heel-thumping, as Caroline must have missed the once-resonant heel-thumps of her deceased twin, Gordon—gone to a boater's watery grave. Dire moaning from Jimmy Bacon would have fit right in at Emma's service, but Jimmy was also absent. Fortunately, the Booth twins didn't disappoint Jack—Heather and Patsy with their identical blanket-sucking sounds, which were now intermingled with the congregation's spontaneous grieving.

A wail escaped Wendy Horton, who pressed her temples with her fists of stone. A bellow broke forth from Charlotte Barford; she clutched her breasts with *bones* in them, as if her hammering heart could not otherwise be contained.

They all would have wept themselves silly, if Jack hadn't said something; they would *still* be weeping, if he hadn't thought of something to say. "Let us pray," Jack said, as if he'd known all along what he was doing. (They were in a church—they were *supposed* to pray!)

"You've had a bad day, and you're very tired," Emma had intoned, in his kindergarten class. But this didn't sound like an appropriate prayer. "For three of you," Emma always said, before concluding her squeezed-child saga, "your bad day just got worse." But this lacked closure, and the tone was threatening—not at all *prayerlike* in the usual, uplifting sort of way.

And so Jack Burns said the only prayer he could remember at that moment. It was the one he and his mother had stopped saying together; it usually made him sad to think about it, because it signified everything he and his mom didn't say to each other, but it had the virtue of being short.

The heads bowed before him were quite a sight, although he'd not spotted Chenko in the row directly behind his mother until Chenko bowed his head. There on his bald pate was the familiar Ukrainian tattoo—a snarling wolf, which (no matter how many times Jack had seen it) was always unnerving.

"The day Thou gavest, Lord, is ended," Jack said to the only face looking back at him—the wolf's. "Thank You for it." *Now what?* he wondered, but Jack was saved by the organist, whom he never saw. (He or she was behind Jack.) The organist knew how and when to fill a silence, and—at St. Hilda's—with what to fill it. The hymn that came crashing down upon them was one they knew by heart. Even those castaway boys who'd left the school and its morning chapel at the end of grade four—they'd not forgotten it. Certainly all the Old Girls, of whatever age, had committed these quatrains to memory; they doubtless murmured their beloved William Blake in their sleep.

And what about the teenage boarders standing restlessly in the rear of the chapel, where Mr. Ramsey became their instant choirmaster? What about those young women yearning for a life out of their school uniforms, but fearful of what that life might be—as girls of that blossoming age are? Boy, could they ever belt out that hymn! They'd sung it every week, or twice a week, in their seemingly interminable time at St. Hilda's.

The tune of "Jerusalem"—Hymn 157, a dog-eared page in the St. Hilda's hymnals—resounded triumphantly in every Old

Girl's heart. They were William Blake's words, set to song—that odd belief that Jesus came to England, where Blake imagined a spiritual Israel.

"*And did those feet in ancient time/Walk upon England's mountains green?*" the congregation sang.

Jack came down the altar stairs, where he was momentarily accosted by Wheelchair Jane; wailing like a banshee, she blocked the center aisle. But Mr. Malcolm never hesitated; he darted into the aisle and wheeled his startled wife a hundred and eighty degrees around, propelling her wheelchair ahead of him. Jack followed the Malcolms up the aisle—pausing only a second for Mrs. Oastler, Emma's grieving mother, to take his arm and allow him to escort her. Chenko, perhaps the only member of the congregation who *wasn't* singing—Ukrainian wrestlers weren't familiar with William Blake—was still weeping when Alice ushered him up the aisle beside her. (Chenko hobbled on his cane.) Pew by pew, from front to back, the congregation followed them.

"*Bring me my bow of burning gold!/Bring me my arrows of desire!/Bring me my spear! O clouds unfold!/Bring me my chariot of fire,*" sang the multitude.

Even Penny Hamilton's little girls were singing. (Of course they were—they were probably students at St. Hilda's!)

As Jack neared the rear entrance to the chapel, one of the seventeen- or eighteen-year-olds—a pale-skinned, blue-eyed blonde, as thin as a model—appeared to swoon or faint or trip into her fellow boarders' arms. From the look of her, this might have been more the result of a starvation diet than her near-enough-to-touch proximity to Jack Burns, a movie star—not that Jack hadn't seen girls her age swoon or faint or trip in his presence before. Or it might have been the overstimulating effect of the soaring hymn.

The falling-down girl distracted Jack from the more immediate object of his desire. Bonnie Hamilton had not only managed to slip into a pew at the back of the chapel without his seeing her limp to her seat. She'd likewise managed to slip away—ahead of the recessional hymn and the wheelchair-bound Mrs. Malcolm, who still led their lamenting retreat. How had Bonnie escaped Jack's notice? (With a limp like hers, maybe she knew instinctively when to leave.)

Out into the corridor, marching to the Great Hall, the girls' and women's voices bore them along; as they retreated from the chapel, the organ grew less reverberant, but the closing couplet of the hymn's final quatrain roared in their midst loud and strong.

"*Till we have built Jerusalem / In England's green and pleasant land,*" sang the throng.

"I gotta hand it to you, Jack," Leslie Oastler whispered in his ear—the word *gotta* very much the way her daughter would have said it. "There's not a dry eye, or a dry pair of panties, in the house."

Jack wasn't sure that wakes were a good idea. Possibly the fault lay in the concept of mixing mourning with wine and cheese. Or mixing *women* with wine and cheese—maybe the mourning had nothing to do with it.

Lucinda Fleming was the first to inform him that the St. Hilda's reunion cocktail parties were held in the gym, not in the Great Hall, which was not great enough to contain the Old Girls who'd come to pay their last respects to Emma—or to gawk at, or hit on, Jack Burns.

Most of the women wore high heels, of one kind or another. They'd seen Jack only when he was a little boy or on the big screen; they were unprepared for how short he was. Those women who (in their heels) were taller than Jack were inclined to remove their shoes. Hence they stood seductively before him, either barefoot or in their stocking feet—their high heels in one hand, the plastic cup of white wine in the other, which left no hand free to handle the toothpicks with the little cubes of cheese.

From Hollywood parties, which some actors view as auditions, Jack was in the habit of eating and drinking nothing. He didn't want all manner of disgusting things to get stuck between his teeth; he didn't want his breath to smell like piss. (To a nondrinker, white wine on the breath smells like gasoline—or some other unburned fuel—and the Old Girls at Emma's wake were breathing up a firestorm.)

There were especially desperate-looking women in their late thirties or early forties. More than a few of them were divorced; their children were spending the weekend with their fathers, or so Jack was repeatedly told. These women were shamelessly aggressive, or at least inappropriately aggressive for a *wake.*

Connie Turnbull, whom Jack-as-Rochester once had taken in

his arms while declaring, " 'Never, never was anything at once so frail and so indomitable,' " contradicted her Eyre-like impression by whispering in Jack's ear that she was "*entirely* domitable."

Miss Wurtz, whom Jack had not seen since he and Claudia had escorted her to the Toronto film festival more than a decade before, had dramatically covered her head with a black scarf—very nearly a veil. She resembled a twelfth-century pilgrim from an order of flagellants. She was thinner than ever, and her perishable beauty had not altogether disappeared but was diminished by an aura of supernatural persecution—as if she suffered from stigmata, or another form of unexplained bleeding.

"I shan't leave you alone, Jack," The Wurtz whispered, in the same ear that Connie Turnbull had whispered in. "No doubt you've met your share of loose women in California, but some of these Old Girls have a boundless capacity for looseness, which only women who are unaccustomed to being loose can have."

"Mercy," he said. There was only one Old Girl who, whether or not she stood on the threshold of looseness, interested him—Bonnie Hamilton. But despite her identifying limp, she appeared to have slipped away.

As for the teenage boarders, Mrs. Malcolm had herded them together with her wheelchair; she'd driven the cowed girls to a far corner of the Great Hall, where Mr. Malcolm was attempting to rescue them from his demented wife. Wheelchair Jane, Jack could only imagine, was intent on keeping these young women safe from him. In Mrs. Malcolm's mind, or what was left of it, Jack Burns was the evil reincarnation of his father; in her view, Jack had returned to St. Hilda's for the sole and lewd purpose of deflowering these girls, whose sexual awakening could be discerned in the dishevelment of their school uniforms.

Jack noticed that the young woman who'd fainted or swooned, or just tripped, had lost one of her shoes. She walked in circles, off-balance, scuffing her remaining loafer. Jack purposely made his way to these students; they were the only ones who'd brought copies of Emma's novel, probably for him to sign.

The girls gave no indication of sexual interest in him—they weren't the slightest bit flirtatious. Most of them couldn't meet Jack's eyes when he looked at them, and those who could look at him couldn't speak. They were just *kids,* embarrassed and shy.

Mrs. Malcolm was crazy to think they needed to be protected from Jack! One of them held out a copy of Emma's first book for him to sign.

"I wanted Emma to sign it," she said, "but maybe you wouldn't mind." The other girls politely waited their turn.

To the thin, unsteady-looking young woman with one shoe, Maureen Yap said something clearly unkind but incomprehensible. It sounded like, "Did you just have major bridgework?" But Jack knew Maureen; he was sure she'd said, "Don't you have any homework?"

Before the poor girl struggled to answer The Yap—before she fainted or swooned or tripped, again—Jack took her by her cold, clammy hand and said, "Let's get out of here. I'll help you find your missing shoe."

"Yeah, let's get outta here," another of the boarders chimed in. "Let's go look for Ellie's shoe."

"Someone stepped on my heel as I was leaving the chapel," Ellie said. "I didn't want to see who it was, so I just forgot about it."

"I hate it when that happens," Jack told the young women.

"It's so rude," one of them said.

"It *sucks*," he said. (It might have been the word *sucks* that turned Maureen Yap away.)

Jack went with the girls down the corridor, back toward the chapel, looking for the lost loafer; he signed copies of Emma's books on the way. "I haven't been with a bunch of *boarders* since a few girls sneaked me into their residence when I was in school here," he told them.

"How old were you?" a girl who reminded Jack of Ginny Jarvis asked.

"I guess I was nine or ten," Jack said.

"And the boarders were *how* old?" Ellie asked.

"They would have been your age," Jack told her.

"That's *sick*!" Ellie said.

"Nothing happened, did it?" one of the boarders asked Jack.

"No, of course not—I just remember being frightened," he replied.

"Well, you were a little boy," one of them pointed out. "Of course you were frightened."

"Look, there's my stupid shoe," Ellie said. The loafer lay kicked aside, against the corridor wall.

480 | *Sleeping in the Needles*

"How will you ever make a movie of *The Slush-Pile Reader*?" one of the young women asked him.

"It's potentially so *gross,*" another of the girls said.

"The film won't be as explicit as the novel," Jack explained. "The word *penis* won't ever be mentioned, for example."

"What about *vagina*?" one of the girls asked.

"Not that, either," he said.

"Why didn't she just get her vagina *fixed*?" Ellie asked. Of course Jack knew she meant the Michele Maher character, but his thoughts went entirely to Emma.

"I don't know," Jack answered.

"There must have been some *psychological* reason, Ellie," one of her fellow boarders said. "I mean it's not exactly knee surgery, is it?"

The young women, Ellie among them, nodded soberly. They were such sensible girls—children at heart but, in so many other ways, more grown up than Emma at that age, not to mention Ginny Jarvis and Penny Hamilton (or Charlotte Barford, or Wendy Holton). Jack wondered what had been so different or wrong about him that those girls had ever thought it was acceptable to abuse him.

These girls wouldn't have harmed a little boy. Jack felt, in their company, like a nine- or ten-year-old again—only he felt safe. So safe, and like *such* a little boy, that he suddenly announced: "I have to pee." (It was exactly the way a nine- or ten-year-old would have said it.)

The young women were unsurprised; they responded to his announcement in a strictly practical fashion. "Do you remember where the boys' washroom is?" Ellie asked him.

"There's still only one," another of the young women said.

"I'll show you where it is," Ellie told Jack, taking his hand. (It was exactly the way she would have taken a nine- or ten-year-old by the hand; for some reason, it broke Jack's heart.)

It had all been *his* fault, he thought—the way those older girls in his time at St. Hilda's had taken such an unnatural interest in him. It must have been something they detected in him. Jack was convinced that he was the unnatural one.

Jack pulled his hand away from Ellie. He didn't want her or her friends—these incredibly healthy, *normal* young women—to see him cry. Jack felt he was on the verge of dissolving into tears, but in that unembarrassed way that a nine- or ten-year-old might cry. He was suddenly ashamed of what the *real* Michele Maher might have called his weirdness.

"I can certainly find the boys' washroom by myself," Jack told them—laughing about it, but in an *actorly* way. "I believe I could find that washroom from the darkness of my grave," he added, which made it sound like his journey to the boys' washroom was a heroic voyage—meant to be undertaken alone, and in full acceptance of such perils as one might encounter along the way.

Jack was soon lost in an unfamiliar corridor; perhaps the old school had been repainted, he was thinking. The stairwells were the likely haunts of ghosts, he believed—Mrs. McQuat, his departed conscience; or even Emma, disappointed by the brevity of his prayer. The voices of the boarders no longer accompanied him on his journey; Jack wasn't followed, or so he thought.

Ahead of him, not far from a bend in the corridor, was the dining hall—all closed up and dark. Did a figure, old and stooped, emerge from the shadows there? It was an elderly woman, no one Jack recognized but surely not a ghost; she looked too solidly built for a spirit. A cleaning woman, from the look of her, he thought. But why would a cleaning woman be working at St. Hilda's on a Sunday, and where were her mop and pail?

"Jack, my *dahleen*—my *leetle* one!" Mrs. Machado cried.

To see her, to know it was really her, had the effect on Jack of her high-groin kick of so many years ago. He couldn't move or speak—he couldn't *breathe*.

He'd recognized that Leslie Oastler had a certain power over him, and always would have. But in all his efforts, conscious and unconscious, to diminish his memories of Mrs. Machado, Jack had underestimated her implacable authority over him. He'd never defeated her—only Emma had.

Gone was her waist—what little she'd ever had of one. Mrs. Machado's low-slung breasts protruded from the midriff of her untucked blouse with the over-obviousness of an amateur shoplifter's stolen goods. But what she'd stolen from Jack was more obvious; Mrs. Machado had robbed him of the ability to say no to her. (Or to anyone else!)

"This is a frightened little boy!" Bonnie Hamilton had told her sister and Ginny Jarvis, when those older girls were trying to get Jack's penis to respond.

In Mrs. Machado's company, Jack was still a frightened little boy. She circled him in the corridor as if she were setting up her customary single-leg attack; she underhooked his left arm, the thick fingers of her left hand closing tightly around his right wrist. Jack knew the takedown she appeared to be looking for, but he couldn't overcome his inertia; he made no move to defend himself.

Mrs. Machado pressed her forehead against his chest. The top of her head—entangled with gray, wiry hair—touched his throat. Jack was surprised by how short she was, but of course he'd been shorter when they last did this dance together—with Chenko repeating his familiar litany, like a call to prayer. "*Hand*-control! Circle, circle! Don't *lean* on her, Jackie!"

It wasn't wrestling that Mrs. Machado had in mind. With her insistent grip on Jack's right wrist, she guided his hand under her blouse; with her broad nose, Mrs. Machado nudged his necktie out of her way and unbuttoned the second button of his shirt with her teeth. Jack thought he detected the smell of anchovies in her hair. It was the contact his right hand made with her sagging breasts, which was quickly followed by the feeling of her tongue on his chest, that filled him with revulsion and gave him the strength to push her away.

Until that moment, he'd never believed in so-called recovered memory—namely, that various acts of abuse or molestation from one's childhood are mercifully erased, only to return with a vengeance, *vividly,* many years down the road. As Jack recoiled from Mrs. Machado in the semidark Sunday corridor of his old school, he remembered the button trick. How she had unbuttoned and unzipped him with her teeth—and all the other clever things she'd managed to do with her mouth, which he'd blanked from his memory.

"Don't be cruel, Meester Penis," Mrs. Machado whispered, as Jack retreated from her. She was shuffling after him, in her laceless running shoes, when she suddenly halted. It wasn't Jack's feeble resistance that had stopped her. Her gaze had shifted. She was peering around him, or behind him—and the second he turned to look where she was looking, Mrs. Machado was gone.

She must have been in her late sixties or early seventies. How could she have been that agile, that quick on her feet? Or was the bend in the corridor closer to them than Jack had thought? It was more probable, of course, that Mrs. Machado had never been there at all.

In any case, Jack hadn't heard the wheelchair behind him; the wheels on that smooth linoleum floor didn't make a sound. (He was, after all, on haunted ground.) "Jack," the woman in the wheelchair said, "you look like you've seen a ghost."

He'd expected to be confronted by Mrs. Malcolm—ever the protector of those girls, whose violation, she imagined, Jack sought. But the woman in the wheelchair was an attractive, forty-year-old real estate agent in a black pantsuit.

Bonnie Hamilton had managed to park her wheelchair in some out-of-sight place, near the back of the chapel, and limp to and from her pew unseen. She'd been successful in the real estate business, she would tell Jack later, because she always left her wheelchair at the front entrance and limped with her clients from room to room—even, as Leslie Oastler had cruelly suggested, up and down stairs. "My clients must feel sorry for me," Bonnie would joke. "Nobody wants to disappoint a cripple—to add insult to injury, as they say."

But at public events, or whenever there was a crowd, Bonnie Hamilton was also successful at keeping her limp to herself; she had a knack for sneaking in and out of her wheelchair without anyone seeing her. In the wheelchair, she looked elegant; she was as beautiful to Jack as she'd been when they were students together.

Jack was still speechless from his encounter with Mrs. Machado, real or not—and how grotesquely he now recalled the lost details of everything Mrs. Machado had done to him. It was too much for him, on top of all that—to be rescued by Bonnie Hamilton, who'd tried her hardest to protect him from her sister and Ginny Jarvis when he'd been nine or ten.

Jack dropped to his knees and burst into tears. Bonnie, wheeling closer, pulled him headfirst into her lap. Bonnie must have thought that *she* had made him cry; it must have been Jack's memory of being *coerced* to ejaculate on her sister's forehead that was traumatizing him still! (That terrible loss of his innocence in the big girls' residence when he'd been a frightened little boy—this in addition to his losing Emma, no doubt, had undone him.)

"Jack, I think about what an awful thing we did to you—every day of my life, I think of you!" Bonnie cried. Jack tried to shake his head in her lap, but Bonnie probably thought he was attempting to get away from her; she held him tighter.

"No, no—don't be afraid!" she urged him. "I'm not surprised

it makes you cry to look at me, or that you dress up as a woman or do other weird things. After what we did to you, why *wouldn't* you be weird? Of *course* you're weird!" Bonnie cried.

She's completely crazy, Jack thought, struggling to breathe; she gripped his hair with both hands, squeezing his face between her thighs. Bonnie Hamilton felt very strong; she clearly worked out a lot. But you can't *wrestle* a woman in a wheelchair; Jack just let her hold him as hard as she wanted to.

Bending over him, Bonnie whispered in his ear: "We can put it all to rest, Jack. I've talked to a psychiatrist about the best way to get over it. We can just move on."

She didn't hear him ask, "How?" in her lap; Jack's voice was muffled between her thighs. Her fingers, combing through his hair, stroked the back of his neck.

"*Normal* sex, Jack—*that's* the best way to get over an upsetting experience," Bonnie Hamilton told him.

How Jack wished Emma had been alive to hear this! Wouldn't she have gotten a kick out of the very idea of *normal* sex?

Wasn't it destiny, after all? Hadn't Bonnie and Jack once looked at each other and been unable to look away? And that had been when he was in fourth grade and she in twelfth!

Besides, he was Jack Burns. Wasn't he supposed to sleep with everybody? Just how would it have made Bonnie Hamilton feel if he *hadn't* slept with her, a cripple?

Still, it gave Jack pause—she was definitely nuts. Bonnie must have seen the reservation on his face when she finally released his head from her lap. Her confidence wavered; she became unbearably shy. "Don't feel that I'm *forcing* you, Jack. You poor boy!" she cried. "You've been forced enough!"

She backed her wheelchair away from him; it was a disturbing image. Jack had the idea that they were rewinding a film; they were returning in time. At any second, Mrs. Machado would reappear; he could sense her coming around the bend in the corridor, reemerging from the shadows.

Under the circumstances, Jack chose to leave with Bonnie.

All night, at the Four Seasons, Bonnie Hamilton never once limped for Jack. She didn't limp when she was lying down. Once, when she got out of bed to use the bathroom—and again, when she got dressed in the morning—she asked him to look away.

Jack never fell asleep. He was too afraid of the nightmares Mrs. Machado might give him. In the dark, when he felt the first nightmare approaching—even though he was wide awake— Jack asked Bonnie if she'd seen the short, stout woman he'd been talking to in the corridor. Jack's body might have blocked Bonnie's view; down low in her wheelchair, she'd had the impression that he was talking to himself. "I thought maybe you were *acting,*" she said.

This didn't prove that Mrs. Machado was a ghost, or that he'd only imagined her. There was a hair on Jack's necktie; he saw it when he undressed for bed. (More gray and wiry than a hair belonging to Bonnie Hamilton or Jack, and no one else had put her head on his chest.) And then there was the second button of his shirt: it was already unbuttoned when Jack undressed that night. This made him shiver.

Naturally, the button trick was the source of the nightmares Jack feared would beset him—not because of the trick itself, which for so many years he'd happily forgotten, but because of what it led to. All those *other* games Mrs. Machado had played!

It was compassionate of Bonnie Hamilton to stay awake with him. Of course she thought of their night together as *therapy,* and maybe it was. For that night, if not all the others that followed it, Bonnie held the button trick at bay.

25

Daughter Alice Goes Home

Alice and Leslie Oastler were perturbed with Jack for leaving Emma's wake at St. Hilda's without saying good-bye. A tough bunch of Old Girls—actually, Mrs. Oastler's former classmates at the school—had invited Leslie and Alice out to dinner. Jack was expected to join them, or at least not run off with a woman in a wheelchair. (Given Jack's older-woman reputation, his mother and Mrs. Oastler first thought that he'd absconded with Wheelchair Jane!)

No doubt the description of Jack's emotional departure with Bonnie Hamilton was exaggerated by several eyewitnesses—that lip-biter Lucinda Fleming among them. Lucinda, probably in a silent rage, had observed Peewee folding Bonnie's wheelchair and stowing it in the trunk of the limo. And while Alice and Leslie Oastler were wondering out loud what on earth Mrs. Malcolm and Jack had done with poor *Mr.* Malcolm, Penny Hamilton had a hissy fit in front of her own children—those darling little girls. "I *knew* it!" Penny cried, clawing at her pretty hair. "Jack Burns is fucking my crippled sister—that *slut!*"

Miss Wurtz, who'd managed to shed an uplifting light on *Tess of the d'Urbervilles,* now put a positive spin on Penny Hamilton's announcement. "Thank goodness *that's* been clarified!" Caroline told Alice and Mrs. Oastler.

"Jack Burns!" Mr. Ramsey was overheard murmuring, in faithful appreciation.

The Old Girls, to a one, were stunned silent. Only the boarders, those irrepressible seventeen- and eighteen-year-olds, continued to carry on a conversation, which they conducted in a kind of shorthand—comprehensible only to them.

The Wurtz, in her ongoing effort to cheer up Alice and Mrs. Oastler, said: "Well, it would have been more predictable, but not nearly as much fun, if Jack had left *as* a woman instead of *with* one."

Jack checked out of the hotel pretty early the next morning—if not as early as Bonnie Hamilton, who had a seven o'clock appointment in Rosedale. They told him at the front desk that there'd been about fifty calls for Jack Burns, and no small number of increasingly irritable requests for Billy Rainbow, but no one had known to ask for Jimmy Stronach. He and Bonnie hadn't been disturbed.

Jack took a taxi to Forest Hill. He fully expected that his mother would still be asleep and that Mrs. Oastler would have been up for hours. Leslie surely would have made some coffee. He wasn't wrong about the coffee.

Mrs. Oastler told him that his mom had left the house before seven—an unheard-of hour for Alice to be up, much less dressed and going anywhere. (No one wanted a tattoo the first thing in the morning.)

Leslie looked as if she'd just got up. She was wearing one of Emma's old T-shirts, which fit her like a baggy dress; evidently she'd slept in it. The T-shirt almost touched her knees, the sleeves falling below her elbows. Jack followed her into the kitchen, where the coffee smelled fresh. There were no dishes in the sink, and not a crumb on the kitchen table; it didn't look as if Alice had eaten any breakfast.

Mrs. Oastler sat down at the neat table, her hands trembling a little as she drank her coffee. Jack poured himself a cup and sat down beside her.

"I had a bet with your mom, Jack. I said you were gonna get gang-banged by that bunch of boarders. Alice thought you were gonna go home with that overenthusiastic woman with the big dog. Nobody bet on the crip."

"Where did Mom go, Leslie?"

"Another MRI," Mrs. Oastler said. "*Imaging,* they call it."

"Imaging for what?"

"Come on, Jack. Have you talked to her lately? I don't get the impression that you've talked at all."

"I've tried," he told her. "She won't say anything to me."

"You haven't asked her the right questions, Jack."

There was a white envelope on the kitchen table; it stood perfectly straight, propped between the salt and pepper shakers, as innocent-seeming as an invitation to a wedding. If it were something Alice had left for Jack, it would have had his name in big letters on it—it would have had her drawing of a monstrous heart, bursting with motherly love for him, or some other over-the-top illustration of undying affection. But the envelope was unmarked and unsealed.

"Has my mom been sick, Leslie?"

"Envelope? *What* envelope? I don't see an envelope," Mrs. Oastler said, looking right at it.

"What's in the envelope?" he asked.

"Nothing you're supposed to see, Jack. Surely nothing *I* would ever show you."

Jack opened the envelope, which of course was what Leslie wanted him to do, and placed the four photographs face-up on the clean kitchen table—as if they were playing cards in a game of solitaire with formidably different rules.

The photos were slightly varying views of a young woman's torso, from her pretty navel to her shoulders. She was naked; her breasts, which were fully formed, didn't droop. Her breasts and the smoothness of her skin were what indicated her youthfulness to Jack, but he was drawn above all to her tattoo. It was a good one, of what his mom would have called the old school. It was a traditional maritime heart—torn vertically in two, all in tattoo-blue. The tattoo was all outline, no shading. The heart was tattooed on the upper, outer quadrant of the left breast, where it touched both the breast and the heart side of the rib cage. It was exactly where, in Alice's opinion, a tattoo of a damaged heart could best be hidden—and binding this broken heart together, like a bandage, were the words *Until I find you.* The words were in cursive on a scroll.

The tattoo was good enough to be his mother's work, but Jack knew Daughter Alice's handwriting by heart; the writing wasn't hers. More traditional—instead of the *Until I find you*—was the actual name of the lover who'd left you or deceived you, or otherwise broken your heart.

Jack could easily imagine he was looking at a Tattoo Ole or a Doc Forest or a Tattoo Peter—or possibly Sailor Jerry's work, from Halifax, long ago. The photos looked old enough. But Jack should have been thinking about the young woman, not her tattoo.

"You're looking at the wrong breast, Jack," Leslie Oastler

said. "I don't know why Alice bothered to keep that tattoo a secret from you all these years. The tattoo isn't what's gonna kill
her."

That was when Jack realized he was looking at pictures of his
mother's breasts—in which case, the photographs must have
been taken about twenty years ago. Contrary to her unique reputation as a tattoo artist, not to mention what she'd told him, his
mom had been tattooed—probably when William broke her
heart, or shortly thereafter; certainly when Jack had still been a
child, or even before he'd been born.

Alice's insistence on hiding her tattoo from Jack was something he'd mistaken for modesty, which had never made the
greatest sense alongside the opposite impression he had of her. It
wasn't modesty—not wanting Jack to take a bath with her, never
allowing him to see her naked. (And this had nothing to do with
the alleged scar from her C-section.) It was the tattoo that Alice
hadn't wanted Jack to see—and not only because she *was* tattooed, which contradicted her claim to originality among tattoo
artists. Mainly it was the tattoo itself that she'd needed to conceal. Because the *you* in *Until I find you* must have been his
missing father—it was *William* she'd kept a secret, from the
start! And to mark herself for life *because* of him belied the indifference she pretended to—abandoning her search for William
and refusing to talk to Jack about him.

The two-inch scar on the upper, outer quadrant of Alice's
right, untattooed breast was a thin, surgical line with no visible
stitch-marks.

"She had the lumpectomy when she was thirty-one," Mrs.
Oastler informed Jack. "You were twelve—in grade seven, if I
remember correctly."

"I was at Redding," he remembered out loud. "It was when
Mom said she was going to come see me, but she didn't."

"She had radiation, Jack—and the chemotherapy was repeated every four weeks, for six cycles. The chemo made her
sick for a few days every month—you know, *vomiting*—and of
course she lost her hair. She didn't want you to see her bald, or
with a wig. You can't see the scar in her right armpit in the photographs; it's hard enough to see if you're looking right at it.
Lymph-node removal—rather standard procedure," Leslie explained.

"Did a mammogram detect it, or did she feel the lump?" Jack asked.

"*I* felt it," Mrs. Oastler said. "It was fairly firm, actually hard to the touch."

"Has the cancer come back, Leslie?"

"A recurrence in the other breast is very common," Mrs. Oastler said, "but it hasn't come back in her breast. It could have spread to her lungs, or to her liver, but it's gone to her brain. Not the worst place it could show up—*bones* are awful."

"What do they do for brain cancer?" he asked.

"It's not really brain cancer, Jack. The breast cancer has metastasized in her brain—those are breast-cancer cells. When breast cancer goes somewhere else, I guess there's not much they can do about it."

"So Mom has a tumor in her brain?" Jack asked.

"A 'space-occupying lesion,' I think they call it—but, yeah, it's a tumor to you and me," Leslie said with a shrug. "Any intervention would be futile, they say. Even chemo would be merely palliative, to relieve symptoms—it isn't a cure. There *ain't* a cure," she added—the curious *ain't* (like Leslie's use of *gonna* and *oughta*) being a grieving mother's conscious or unconscious effort to evoke her late daughter's persistent but bestselling abuse of the language.

Mrs. Oastler picked up the photographs and put them in a kitchen drawer. It was where the manuals to the appliances were kept, but it was full of other junk; it was where Emma and Jack, as kids, had searched for Scotch tape or thumbtacks or paper clips or rubber bands.

The photos of her breasts had been Alice's idea; she wanted Leslie to show them to Jack, but not until after she was dead.

"What are the symptoms, Leslie?"

"Despite the anti-seizure medication, she may have a few more seizures. She's had one, anyway—I saw it. I felt the lump, I saw the seizure. There's not much I miss," Mrs. Oastler added.

"Is it like a convulsion, or a stroke?" he asked.

"I suppose so," Leslie answered, shrugging again. "I've also noticed vague changes in her moods, even in her personality."

"Leslie, Mom's *moods* change all the time—her personality has always been *vague*!"

"She's different, Jack. You'll see. Especially if you can get her to talk to you."

Jack called a taxi to take him to Queen Street. He thought he'd go wait for his mom to show up at Daughter Alice. Mrs. Oastler put her arms around Jack and hugged him with her head against his chest. "She's gonna go quickly, Jack. They say it'll be pretty painless, but she's gonna go fast." Jack stood in the kitchen with his arms around Leslie, hugging her back. She wasn't hitting on him; she just wanted him to hold her. "You oughta talk to Maureen Yap, Jack. She kept calling you all night, from the Four Seasons."

"I don't think Maureen wants to *talk* to me," he told Mrs. Oastler.

"I said you oughta talk to *her,* Jack. Maureen Yap is a doctor. She's a fucking oncologist."

"Oh."

In the lobby of the Four Seasons, the front-desk clerks were surprised to see Jack Burns checking in. He'd planned to spend a couple of days in New York before flying back to L.A., but when he registered—again, as Jimmy Stronach—Jack told them that he would be staying in Toronto indefinitely, meaning until further notice. He also asked them, feigning indifference, if Maureen Yap had checked out. (In fact, Dr. Yap had just called room service and ordered her breakfast.)

They gave him back his old room. Because he'd forgotten to take the DO NOT DISTURB sign off the door, and the hotel maids hadn't been informed that he'd checked out, it was almost as if he'd never left the hotel—and never been to Forest Hill and back—except for the news that his mother was dying.

It crossed Jack's mind to call Maureen. "This is room service, Dr. Yap," he might say. "Would you like to have Jack Burns with your breakfast?"

Jack could only imagine Maureen saying, "Yes, please," but he didn't feel like joking around. When Maureen had told him she was staying at the hotel under her maiden name, she hadn't been kidding.

Jack took a quick shower and put on the hotel bathrobe and the stupid white slippers, as if he were on his way to or from the swimming pool. He knew Maureen Yap's room number; his fans at the front desk had told him, although they weren't supposed to. After all, he was Jack Burns; if he'd called the front desk and asked them to send him a pepperoni pizza with two hookers, they'd have had the pizza and the prostitutes at his door in about forty-five minutes.

The movies had taught Jack the power of presenting himself without words, and the little peephole in Maureen Yap's hotel-room door offered Maureen an unexpected close-up of her favorite actor. Her breakfast had arrived only moments before—now here was Jack Burns in a bathrobe!

"I blame the delay on Pam Hoover," Maureen mumbled again as she let Jack in. She was wearing her hotel robe, too—sans the stupid white slippers. (Jack kicked his off at the door.)

"You came all the way from Vancouver for *what*?" he asked, untying her robe.

"To have too much sex with you," Maureen Yap said, untying his. Never mind that it sounded like "To shave my legs for you"; Jack knew what she meant.

She was a tiny woman: the cavity of her pelvis couldn't have been bigger than a thirteen-year-old girl's. The skin on her breasts had the transparency of a child's—a faint bluish tone, as if her veins, although unseen, lent their color to her skin. Jack could touch the fingers of his hands together when he encircled her thigh.

"My femur is smaller than your humerus," Maureen told him; there's no describing what *that* sounded like, but he somehow managed to understand her.

Maureen's husband and son called her in her hotel room at 9:45 A.M.—6:45 in Vancouver, where the father was getting the little boy up for school. Maureen covered one of Jack's ears with her cupped palm—pressing his head, and his other ear, into her flat tummy. He could still hear her endearments to her husband, who was also a doctor, and her young son—not that Jack could follow word-for-word what she told them. Maureen was in tears; Jack could feel the taut muscles in her lower abdomen.

It was the sadness of Emma's memorial service, she told her family—it still made her cry to think about it. Jack heard Pam Hoover's name again—there was mention, he thought, of how Pam seemed "shaken" and was "lately insane." Only after the phone call would Jack figure out that Maureen Yap had said she was "taking a later plane to Vancouver."

It was also after the phone call when Jack reminded Maureen that, from their bed in the Four Seasons, they were very close to the bat-cave exhibit at the Royal Ontario Museum, which prompted Maureen to show him her fruit-bat and vampire-bat imitations. Naturally, this led them to enact Emma's squeezed-child saga—all three endings.

"There is no way to have too much sex with you," The Yap told him later, when he was having some difficulty peeing in her bathroom. He heard this, of course, as: "It is no fair I bathe all bare for you," or something like that.

"My mother has cancer," Jack called from the bathroom. (Not too loudly; the door was open.) "She's dying."

"Come back to bed," Maureen said distinctly. Once they'd moved on to medical matters, he had no trouble understanding her. *Dr.* Yap spoke very clearly.

What would happen to his mother's brain? Jack wanted to know. It must have sounded to Maureen like a child's question, because she held him in her arms, with his head against her breasts, and talked to him as if he were a child. "It probably won't be as bad for her as it will be for you, Jack," she began, "depending on where in her brain the tumor is. You should send me the MRI."

"Okay," Jack said. He noticed he was crying.

"If it's in her visual cortex, she'll go blind. If it's in the speech cortex—well, you get the picture. If the cancer eats through a blood vessel, she will hemorrhage and die without ever knowing or feeling what has happened to her. Or, as her brain swells, she will simply slip away."

"Will she be in a coma?" he asked.

"She could be, Jack. She could die peacefully in a coma—she could simply stop breathing. But along the way, she might think she was someone else. She might have hallucinations—she might smell strange, nonexistent smells. Truly anything is possible. She will go fairly quickly and painlessly, but she may not know who she is when she goes. The hard part for you, Jack, is that you may not know who she is, either."

The hard part for Jack, as he would tell Maureen, was that he'd *never* known who his mother was. The description of her ultimate death seemed almost familiar.

"Do you mind if I call you *Dr.* Yap?" Jack asked Maureen, when they were saying good-bye.

"Not if you call me incessantly," she said.

He wouldn't, of course; Maureen knew that. When Jack sent her his mom's MRI, he already had a pretty good idea of where the tumor was—the so-called space-occupying lesion. Alice knew, too. Dr. Yap's interpretation of the MRI would merely confirm the prognosis. The tumor was in the limbic system—the emotional center of the brain.

"Well, isn't that fucking *great*!" Leslie Oastler would say. "I suppose that Alice will think the whole thing is terribly *funny,* or she'll be laughing one minute and crying the next—an emotional *yo-yo,* either telling grossly inappropriate jokes or drowning in some inexpressible sorrow!"

Of course, from Jack's point of view, his mom had *always* been that way; that a malignant tumor now occupied the emotional center of her brain seemed unremarkable, even normal.

"If it's gone this far, Jack," Maureen Yap had forewarned him, "I'm sure that your mother has already come to terms with dying. Just imagine how much she's thought about it. She even decided, somewhere along the line, not to tell you. That means to me that she's thought about it a lot—enough to have the peace of mind to keep it to herself. It's Mrs. Oastler who can't come to terms with it. And *you*—you won't have time to come to terms with it until she's gone. It'll happen that fast, Jack."

"She's only fifty-one!" he'd cried against her thirteen-year-old's breasts, her child-size body.

"Cancer likes you when you're young, Jack," Maureen had told him. "Even cancer slows down when you're old."

There was no slowing down Alice's cancer; it would run away with her in a hurry, befitting a disease that had a twenty-year head start. Later that same morning—after he'd said good-bye to Dr. Yap—Jack got himself down to Queen Street and once more entered the tattoo world of Daughter Alice, where he and his mother had a little talk. (A little *dance* would more accurately describe it.)

"Do you still take your tea with honey, dear?" his mom asked him, when he walked into the shop. "I just made a fresh pot."

"No honey, Mom. We have to talk."

"My, aren't we serious this morning!" his mother said. "I suppose Leslie spilled the beans in her dramatic fashion. You'd think *she* was the one who's dying—she's so angry about it!"

Jack didn't say anything; he just let her talk, knowing she might clam up at any moment. "Of course Leslie has a right to be angry," Alice went on. "After all, I'm leaving her—and I promised her I never would. She let me go to all those tattoo conventions, where there's a lot of fooling around. But I always came back."

"I guess you're leaving me, too," Jack said. "When were you planning to tell me?"

"The only person I ever wanted to agonize over me was your father, Jack, and he simply refused. He didn't want me—even knowing that, if he rejected me, I would never let him be with you."

Perhaps it was being with Maureen Yap that made Jack wonder if he'd misheard what his mother had said, but he could tell by the way she suddenly gave his cup of tea her complete attention that she might have said a little more than she'd meant to say.

"He *wanted* to be with me?" Jack asked her.

"*I'm* the one who's dying, dear. Don't you think you should ask me about *me*?"

He watched her put a heaping teaspoon of honey in his tea; her hands, like Mrs. Oastler's at the kitchen table, were shaking slightly as she stirred the spoon in the cup.

Jack knew that he'd not misheard her. She'd clearly said that William didn't want her—even knowing that, if he rejected her, *she would never let him be with Jack*. When his mom handed him his cup of tea—looking, for all the world, as if she were *still* the wronged party—Jack imagined there would be no stopping him this time, no turning him away.

"If my dad wanted to be with me," Jack persisted, "why did he flee from us? I mean everywhere we went. In city after city, why had he always left before we arrived?"

"The cancer is in my brain—I suppose you know," his mother replied. "I wouldn't be surprised if my memory is affected, dear."

"Let's start with Halifax," Jack continued. "Did he leave Halifax before you got there? If he was still there when you arrived, he must have wanted to see me be born."

"He *was* still there when I arrived," Alice admitted, with her back turned to Jack. "I wouldn't *let* him see you be born."

"So he wasn't exactly running away from you," Jack said.

"Did Leslie tell you about my mood changes?" his mom asked. "They're not always logical, or what you would expect."

"I'm guessing it's bullshit that I was a Cesarean birth," Jack told her. "The scar from your C-section wasn't why you wouldn't let me see you naked. There was something else you didn't want me to see. Isn't that right?"

"Leslie showed you the photographs—that *bitch*!" Alice said. "You weren't supposed to see them until after I was gone!"

"Why show me at all?" he asked.

"I was beautiful once!" his mother cried. (She meant her breasts, when she was younger—he'd meant her tattoo.)

"I've been thinking about it—I mean your tattoo," Jack told her. "I'll bet it's a Tattoo Ole, from Copenhagen. You had it almost from the start."

"Well, of *course* it's a Tattoo Ole, Jack. Ole preferred only outlining, and I wasn't about to shade myself."

"I suppose you wouldn't let the Ladies' Man shade you," he said.

"I wouldn't let Lars *touch* me, Jack—not even shading. I wouldn't have shown Ladies' Man Madsen my *breasts*!"

"We're getting ahead of ourselves, Mom. Let's talk about Toronto before we talk about Copenhagen. When we got to Toronto, had my dad already left?"

"He got a girl at St. Hilda's in trouble, Jack—he had another girlfriend at the school, and for all I know an affair with one or more of the teachers, too!"

"Mom, I know about the girls."

"He was with other women in Halifax!" she blurted out.

"Mom, you told me. I know he left you. But I never knew he wanted to see me."

"I couldn't stop him from *seeing* you, could I?" she asked. "When you were out in public, I couldn't prevent him from getting a look at you. But if he wasn't going to be with me, why should I have let him be with you?"

"So that I would have a father?"

"Who knows what sort of father he would have been, Jack? With a man like that, you can never be sure."

"Did he see me in Toronto, Mom? Did he get a look at me, when I was a baby—before you drove him away?"

"How dare you!" his mother said. "I never drove him away! I gave him all the looks at you that he could stand! I let him see you—at least from a distance—every time he asked!"

"He *asked*? What do you mean, '*from a distance*,' Mom?"

"Well, I would never let him see you *alone*," she explained. "He wasn't allowed to *talk* to you."

What wasn't he getting? Jack wondered. What didn't add up? Had he been a child *on display* for his father, perhaps to tempt William to accept Alice's terms—namely, to live with her? "Let me get this straight," Jack said to his mother. "You let him see me, but if he wanted further contact with me, he had to marry you."

"He *did* marry me, Jack—but only under the condition that we get *immediately* divorced!"

"I thought it was Mrs. Wicksteed's idea that I have his name—so I would seem less illegitimate," Jack said. "I never knew you *married* him!"

"It was Mrs. Wicksteed's idea that the only *legitimate* way for you to have his name would be if he married me and we were then divorced," his mother told him—as if this were a petty detail of no lasting importance.

"So he must have been around, in Toronto—when we were here—for quite some time," Jack said.

"*Barely* long enough to get married and divorced," Alice said. "And you were still an infant. I knew you wouldn't *remember* him." (She hadn't *wanted* Jack to remember William, obviously.)

"But Mrs. Wicksteed was my *benefactor,* wasn't she?" Jack asked. "I mean we *were* her rent-free boarders, weren't we?"

"Mrs. Wicksteed was the epitome of generosity!" his mother said with indignation—as if he'd been questioning Mrs. Wicksteed's character and good intentions, which he'd never doubted.

"Who paid for things, Mom?"

"Mrs. Wicksteed, for the most part," Alice replied frostily. "Your father occasionally helped."

"He sent money?"

"It was the *least* he could do!" his mom cried. "I never asked William for a penny—he just sent what he could."

But the money had to come from somewhere, Jack realized; she must have known where William was, every step of the way.

"Which brings us to Copenhagen," Jack said. "We weren't exactly searching for him, were we? You must have already known he was there."

"You haven't touched your tea, dear. Is there something wrong with it?"

"Did you take me to Copenhagen to *show* me to him?" Jack asked her.

"Some people, Jack—*men,* especially—are of the opinion that all babies look alike, that infants are all the same. But when you were a four-year-old, you were something special—you were a *beautiful* little boy, Jack."

He was only beginning to get the picture: she'd used him as *bait!* "How many times did my dad see me?" Jack asked. "I mean in Copenhagen." (What Jack *really* meant, in terms familiar to him from the movie business, was how many times she had offered William the *deal.*)

"Jackie—" his mother said, stopping herself, as if she detected in her tone of voice something of the way she'd admonished him as a child. When she began afresh, her voice had changed; she sounded frail and pleading, like a woman with breast-cancer cells taking hold of the emotional center of her brain. "Any father would have been proud of what a gorgeous-looking boy you were, Jack. What dad wouldn't have wanted to see the handsome young man you would become?"

"But you wouldn't let him," Jack reminded her.

"I gave him a *choice!*" she insisted. "You and I were a *team,* Jackie—don't you remember? We were a *package!* He could have chosen us, or nothing. He chose nothing."

"But how many times did you make him choose?" Jack asked her. "We followed him to Sweden, to Norway, to Finland, to the Netherlands. Mom—you gave up only because *Australia* was too fucking far!"

He should have watched his language, which may have seemed especially disrespectful to a dying woman—not that his mother had ever tolerated his use of the word *fucking.*

"You think you're so smart!" Alice snapped at him. "You don't know the half of it, Jack. We didn't follow *him.* I made your father follow *us!* He was the one who *gave up,*" she said—softly but no less bitterly, as if her pride were still hurt more than she could bring herself to say.

Jack knew then that he knew nothing, and that the only questions she would ever answer were direct ones—and he would have to guess *which* direct questions were the right ones to ask. A hopeless task.

"You should talk to Leslie," his mother told him. "Leslie likes to talk. Tell her I don't care what she tells you, Jack."

"Mom, Leslie wasn't there."

He meant in Europe. But his mom wasn't paying attention;

she was pushing buttons on her new CD player, seeking to drown him out with the usual music.

"I want to send your MRI to Maureen Yap," Jack told her. "She's an oncologist."

"Tell Leslie. She'll arrange it, Jack." The door to their conversation was closing once again—not that she'd ever opened it an inch more than she had to.

Jack tried one last time. "Maybe I should take a trip," he said. "I'll start with Copenhagen, where we began."

"Why not take Leslie with you, Jack? That'll keep her out of my hair."

"I think I'll go alone," Jack said.

His mom's exasperation with the CD player was growing. "Where's the remote?" he asked her. "You should use the remote, Mom."

Alice found the remote, pointing it at Jack—then at the CD player—like a gun. "Just do me a favor, *Jackie boy,*" she said. "If you're going to go find him, do it after I'm gone." ·

The CD player was new, but Bob Dylan was familiar—albeit a lot louder than they expected.

> *The guilty undertaker sighs,*
> *The lonesome organ grinder cries,*
> *The silver saxophones say I should refuse you.*

"Jesus, turn it down!" Jack said, but his mother pushed the wrong button—not the volume. The song started over, at the beginning.

"Go find him after I'm gone," Alice said, pointing the remote at Jack—not at the stupid CD player.

"I want to know what really *happened*! I've been asking you about the *past,* Mom. I don't know enough about him to know if I *want* to find him!"

"Well, if *that's* the trip you want to take, go on and take it," his mother told him, pointing the remote in the right direction and turning down the volume, though it was still too loud.

> *The cracked bells and washed-out horns*
> *Blow into my face with scorn,*
> *But it's not that way,*
> *I wasn't born to lose you.*

Thanks to Bob, they didn't hear the little tinkle of the bell as the door to the tattoo parlor swung open. It was warm and stuffy in the shop, but even after he closed the door, the gray-faced man in the doorway kept shivering; he had white shoulder-length hair, like an old hippie. There was a rising sun sewn on his jeans jacket, just above his heart, and he wore a red bandanna around his throat—Richard Harris as a cowboy, or perhaps an over-the-hill rodeo rider.

"Would you like a cup of tea?" Alice asked him.

The man was still too cold to talk, but he nodded. He wore tight black jeans and black-and-purple cowboy boots with a diamondback-rattlesnake pattern; he walked stiff-legged to the couch, which Jack knew was a sofa bed. (His mom occasionally slept there, Mrs. Oastler had told him—probably when Alice and Leslie had been quarreling.) The old cowboy sat down on the couch, as gingerly as you might imagine him settling himself on a bronco.

"*I want you, I want you,/I want you so bad,*" Bob Dylan was wailing. "*Honey, I want you.*"

"You're a full-body, aren't you?" Alice asked the cowboy, who was still shivering.

"Almost," he told her. You couldn't see a tattoo on him—only a relentless chill.

The cowboy was at least a decade older than William Burns would be, Jack thought; yet Jack felt an instant pang, as if his dad were shivering with cold. The old hippie, whose hands were shaking, was having trouble removing one of his cowboy boots. Jack knelt down and helped him get the boot off; the boot was so tight, the cowboy's sock came off with it. His bare foot was star-tlingly white. Descending below the pant leg of his jeans, the skull of a long-horned steer completely covered the cowboy's ankle; the fire-breathing flames from the skeleton's open mouth licked the top of his unmarked foot.

The cowboy made no effort to remove his other boot. (Jack surmised that the other foot was tattooed, like all the rest of him.)

"I got one thing left that's clean," the cowboy hippie said to Alice. "You're lookin' at it."

"Your hands and face are clean," Alice told the cowboy.

"I gotta keep my hands and face clean, lady, if I wanna find any interestin' work."

As Jack had done so often in the past, he just slipped away. He poured his cup of tea down the sink, edging his way to the door.

"I'll see you at home, Mom," he said softly. Jack was pretty sure that their little talk was over; he was enough of a fool to think their dance was done.

"Lie down—let's make you comfortable," Alice told the cowboy, not looking at Jack. The old hippie stretched out on the couch, where Alice covered him with a blanket.

Bob was moaning his way through the refrain again; it's a relentless song, over which Jack could nonetheless hear the cowboy's teeth chattering.

> *I want you, I want you,*
> *I want you so bad,*
> *Honey, I want you.*

"Take Leslie with you, dear," his mother said, as Jack was going out the door; she was still not looking at him, preferring to fuss over the old cowboy. The door was closing when Alice called after her son: "It doesn't matter anymore, Jack. I don't even care if you sleep with her!"

Jack carried his mom's little morsel of anticipation and horror with him as he walked along the south side of Queen Street until he caught a cab heading east, bringing him back to the Four Seasons. There was a small flurry of excitement among Jack's fans at the front desk when he checked out of the hotel for the second time that day. Jack didn't like chaos; it bothered him that he must have appeared disorganized, even directionless, but he had a plan.

He would move into the guest wing in what he had once thought of as Mrs. Oastler's "mansion" in Forest Hill. Jack would sleep in Emma's bedroom, of which—of the bed, in particular—he had mostly fond memories. Jack would move Emma's desk, which was a big one, into what had been his bedroom, where Mrs. Machado had molested him; that room, charged as it was with the loss of Jack's innocence, would become his office. Add his dying mother and Leslie Oastler to the *package,* as Alice might have put it, and he had chosen a terrific climate for completing his (or Emma's) adaptation of *The Slush-Pile Reader.*

The screenplay, and Emma's notes, had already been transcribed in Jack's handwriting. He'd brought the script with him—to work on. All he needed was a little more writing paper and some extra pens. As it would turn out—and this was no surprise, given what a veteran shopper she was—Leslie rushed right out and got the writing supplies for him. (She even bought him a new lamp for Emma's desk.)

Leslie was grateful to Jack for not leaving her alone with his mother, especially with Alice's changes of mood and personality.

At first, it gave Jack pause that he was alone with Mrs. Oastler for the duration of the workday. He had some anxiety that she would throw herself at him in a state of undress. After all, his mother had not only given Jack permission to sleep with Leslie—she also repeatedly *encouraged* Leslie to sleep with Jack. (When Mrs. Oastler was doing the dishes after dinner, for example—when Jack was listening to music in the living room, while his mom was stretched out on the couch.)

"Leslie, why don't you sleep with Jack tonight?" Alice would call out to the kitchen.

"Mom, for Christ's sake—"

"No, thank you, Alice!" Mrs. Oastler would call into the living room.

"You should try it—you might like it," Alice told them over supper one night. "You don't snore, do you, Jack? He won't keep you awake, Leslie—well, not like I do, anyway. He won't keep you awake *all night,* I mean."

"Please stop, Alice," Leslie said.

"How much longer do you *realistically* expect me to sleep with you?" Alice snapped at Mrs. Oastler. "You won't sleep with me when I'm in a *coma,* I hope!"

"Mom, Leslie and I don't *want* to sleep together," Jack said.

"Yes, you do, dear," his mother said. "Don't you want to sleep with Jack, Leslie? Well, of *course* you do!" she said cheerfully, before Mrs. Oastler could respond one way or another.

Jack could only imagine what a dysfunctional stew Emma would have made of their threesome—a relationship as challenging as that of a too-small slush-pile reader and a too-big porn-star screenwriter! Jack was indeed living, as he had hoped, in the *perfect* atmosphere in which to finish his (or Emma's) screenplay.

The script itself was becoming an intense marriage of plagiarism and rightful ownership; a partnership of wily commerce with those near-blinding shafts of light in which familiar but nonetheless amazing dust motes float. ("These ordinary but well-illuminated things are what we remember best about a good film," Emma had said.)

Perhaps because Jack was devoted to the task of making Emma's best book into a movie, but also because he and Mrs. Oastler were both victims of his mother's escalating abuse, Jack lost his fear of Leslie throwing herself at him in a state of undress. For the most part, she left him alone.

When he would venture downstairs into the kitchen, either to make himself a cup of tea or to eat an apple or a banana, Mrs. Oastler would often be sitting at the kitchen table—as if Alice had only recently left the house or was, at any minute, expected to return. Then, in the briefest possible conversation, Mrs. Oastler would convey to Jack some new detail or missing information she remembered about his father.

Mrs. Oastler struck Jack as exhausted most of the time. Her memory of what Alice had concealed from Jack about his dad returned to her unexpectedly and at unplanned moments, which made Jack extremely jumpy in her company—largely because he never knew what secret she might suddenly divulge. Sadly, this had the effect on Leslie of making her appear as if she *had* slept with Jack, which Alice never failed to notice.

"You slept with him, Leslie, didn't you?" his mom would regularly ask, upon coming home from Daughter Alice.

"No, I did not," Mrs. Oastler would say, still sitting—as if she had taken root—at the kitchen table.

"Well, you look as if you did," Alice would tell her. "You look as if *someone's* been banging your brains out, Leslie."

It was too easy to say that this was the tumor talking—too convenient to call Alice's outrageous behavior the cancer's fault. But even her language was changing. Not her diction or enunciation, which were the unstumbling examples of Miss Wurtz's determined eradication of Alice's Scottish accent, but Alice was increasingly vulgar-tongued—as Emma had *always* been, as Leslie *could* be, as Alice unwaveringly criticized *Jack* for being. ("Since California," as his mother put it.)

But Jack's work went on. He even showed a draft of the screenplay to Mrs. Oastler; she'd said she was dying to read it. To Jack's surprise, Leslie was much moved by the script; she found it extremely faithful to the novel. She even took the time to compose a list of the things that were different from what they'd been in the book. These weren't offered as criticisms—Mrs. Oastler merely wanted Jack to appreciate that she'd noticed. Among the many differences, of course, were those things Emma herself had changed—or else she'd suggested that Jack change them. And some of the changes were entirely his.

"But you *like* it?" he asked Leslie.

"I *love* it, Jack," she said, with tears in her eyes.

Jack Burns was a first-time writer; he'd never encountered *literary* approval. Something in his relationship with Mrs. Oastler changed because of it. They were united by more than his mother's dying; they were joined by Emma's giving him the opportunity to make a movie of *The Slush-Pile Reader,* and by his bringing Leslie into the process.

They were brought together, too, by Alice's refusal to talk to Jack about his dad—and the consequent burden of what Mrs. Oastler knew of that subject, which she was now under pressure to tell Jack. Worst—but, in the long run, maybe this was best— Leslie Oastler and Jack were drawn to each other by Alice's relentless and incomprehensible efforts to virtually *force* them to sleep together, which both Leslie and Jack were determined *not* to do, at least not while Alice was alive and she so thoroughly and insensitively *wanted* them to do it. (And of course what made this last part so difficult was that Alice, even in her madness, was right about one thing: increasingly, Leslie and Jack *did* want to sleep together.)

Alice was inarguably crazy, but how much of her craziness was the result of the breast-cancer cells in her brain—or was, more simply, her undying anger at William Burns—Mrs. Oastler and Jack would never know.

There was the night Jack discovered his mother naked and asleep in Emma's bed—in *his* bed, under the new circumstances— and when he woke her, she told him she was staying where she was so that he could sleep with Leslie. Jack went to bed in his old bedroom (his new office) that night, in the bed where Mrs. Machado had so roughly educated him.

This episode was not repeated, but there were other episodes. The police called Mrs. Oastler one day to say that Daughter Alice was "evidently closed"—meaning all the lights were off and the venetian blinds were shut. Yet, inside the shop, Bob Dylan was singing up a storm—even passersby, on the Queen Street sidewalk, were complaining. This was how Leslie and Jack learned that Alice now routinely closed the tattoo parlor almost as soon as she'd opened it; she took an all-day nap on the sofa bed. Lately there were sounds in her brain that kept her awake at night, Alice explained to them. (According to Mrs. Oastler, Alice was either wide awake or snoring.)

"What sounds, Alice?" Leslie asked her.

"Nothing I can understand," Alice answered. "Voices, maybe—not yours, not Jack's. No one I want to listen to." (Hence Bob, at high volume; thus the complaints.)

"If there's a bend in the road to your dying, Alice, you may have gone around it," Mrs. Oastler told her.

"Suddenly she's a *writer*!" Alice cried, hitting Jack's shoulder but pointing derisively at Leslie. "Here I am, living with a *pair* of writers!"

Jack saw in his mind's eye what he'd tried to overlook when he'd found his mother naked and snoring in his (formerly Emma's) bed: the slackness of her breasts in sleep, and how the tattoo of her broken heart had shifted slightly from its perfect placement on her younger left breast and the heart side of her rib cage. It was now a *lopsided* broken-heart tattoo, as if there'd been something irreparably wrong with Daughter Alice's heart *before* William Burns had broken it. Even in her sleep, there were still faint creases where the underwire of her bra had marked both breasts, and in the light cast from the bathroom—the door was ajar—the scar from Alice's lumpectomy shone an unnatural white, as did the scar in that same-side armpit, where the lymph node had been removed. (Jack had never seen that scar before.)

"If you'd only just *fuck* each other!" his mother shouted one night, making a fist and pounding the kitchen table, which made Jack and Mrs. Oastler jump. "If you fucked each other all day, I'll bet you two writers wouldn't be so *poetic*!"

Although the screenplay kept getting better, Jack rarely felt he was *poetic*. It was no surprise, but it hurt nonetheless, that his mother refused to read the script. ("I'll be dead by the time you make the movie, dear," she'd told him.)

If there were a poetic presence in the house in his mother's final days, Jack would have said that it was Leslie, who appeared early one afternoon in the doorway of his makeshift office—an unprecedented interruption. She was naked. By her reddened skin, in the area of her Rose of Jericho, he saw that she'd been scratching at her tattoo. She was sobbing.

"I regret ever getting this tattoo," she said. Her appearance did not have that unmistakable aura of seduction.

"I'm sorry, Leslie."

"Life forces enough final decisions on us," Mrs. Oastler continued. "We should have the sense to avoid as many of the unnecessary ones as we can."

Jack just sat at Emma's old desk while Mrs. Oastler turned away from him and went down the hall. "Can I use that, Leslie?" he called after her. (He was missing some essential voice-over for the Michele Maher character, and there it was.) "What you just said—can I use it?"

"Sure," Mrs. Oastler said, so softly that Jack almost didn't hear her.

When they eventually signed Lucia Delvecchio for the Michele Maher role, Lucia would say it was the voice-over that made her want the part—that and the fact that she knew she'd have to lose twenty pounds to play Michele. Miramax would put that voice-over on the movie poster, and in all the ads for the film: "Life forces enough final decisions on us. We should have the sense to avoid as many of the unnecessary ones as we can."

"Bingo!" Jack shouted down the hall, after Mrs. Oastler. But she'd gone into her bedroom and had uncharacteristically closed the door.

There was also the night when Leslie came to his bedroom, where Jack was sleeping—but there was scarcely an aura of seduction about this visit, either. By now, the remembered bits of information—the lost details of his missing father—were waking Mrs. Oastler at all hours of the night. This happened as regularly as Alice's alternating sleeplessness and snoring would wake Mrs. Oastler, or the more violent occurrences when Alice would beat Leslie's back with her fists—this for no better reason than that Alice had woken up and discovered that Leslie had turned her back on her, which was apparently forbidden in their relationship.

Neither Alice nor Mrs. Oastler could remember when this rule had been established, or even if it had ever been observed, but this didn't deter Alice from attacking Leslie, who was at least grateful that Alice didn't insist on Bob Dylan blaring through the house all night—not the way Bob belted it out all day at Daughter Alice, or so the police duly reported.

"When I start to go, Jack—you take me there," his mom had told him. He knew she meant her tattoo shop. "When I start to go, I'm sleeping in the needles—nowhere else, dear."

It was in this largely sleepless context that Mrs. Oastler crawled into Jack's bed one night; she took hold of his penis so suddenly, but without any indication of seeking more intimate contact, that he at first thought Emma's ghost had grabbed him. (After all, it was Emma's bed.)

"I'm here to talk, Jack," Leslie said. "I don't care if your mother thinks we're fucking. I'm just here to tell you something."

"Go ahead," he said.

She'd already told him that his father had paid the lion's share of Jack's tuition at St. Hilda's; it was Mrs. Wicksteed who had only, to use his mother's words, "occasionally helped." And the clothes he'd believed Mrs. Oastler had bought for him, both for Redding and for Exeter—not to mention the tuition at both schools? "I was just the shopper," Leslie had told him. "The money came from William."

"Even for college—those years in Durham?" he'd asked her.

"Even your first couple of years in L.A.," she'd said. "He didn't stop sending money until you were famous, Jack."

"And what about Daughter Alice? I mean the tattoo parlor, Leslie."

"William bought her the fucking shop."

This was a portrait of a very different dad from the one Jack had imagined—when last heard of, playing the piano on a cruise ship to Australia, on his way to be tattooed by the famous Cindy Ray! Not so, maybe. Mrs. Oastler remembered Alice saying that William had *never* gone to Australia. Leslie had further surprised Jack by telling him she was sure his father was still in Amsterdam when Jack and his mother left. "I think he watched you leave," Mrs. Oastler had said.

Thus, when Leslie slipped into his bed and took hold of his penis—this was almost, in his half-sleep, like old times—Jack was eager to learn which new tidbit of information about his father might have surfaced in Mrs. Oastler's fitful sleep. "It's about her tattoo—I mean the *you* in *Until I find you*," Leslie whispered in his ear. "It's not necessarily William."

"What?" he whispered back.

"Think about it, Jack. She wasn't looking for him—she'd already found him! It's not like William was *lost* or something."

"Where is he now?" Jack asked her.

"I have no idea where he is now. Alice doesn't know, either."

"Stop *whispering*!" Alice cried; she was calling from Mrs. Oastler's bedroom, down the hall, although her voice was so loud that she could have been in Emma's bed with Leslie and Jack. "*Talking* is better than whispering!" his mother shouted.

Jack whispered to Leslie: "Who else could the *you* in *Until I find you* be?"

"The love of her life, possibly. That certain someone who would heal the heart your dad broke. Obviously she never found him. It's certainly not *me*!" Mrs. Oastler declared, as Jack's mom called out to them again.

"*Fucking* is better than talking!" Alice yelled.

"You mean it's a nonspecific *you*?" Jack asked Leslie.

"For Christ's sake, Jack. It's not me, and *maybe* it's not William—that's all I'm saying."

"I want to go home!" Alice called to them.

"For Christ's sake, Alice—you *are* home!" Mrs. Oastler called back.

Jack lay there having his penis held, his thoughts entirely on the *you* in *Until I find you*. (As if there were *anyone* who could have healed his mother's heart—as if she could *conceivably* have met the man, or woman, who had a snowball's chance in hell of healing her!)

"Miss Wurtz!" Leslie whispered, so suddenly that Jack's penis jumped in her hand. "He wrote to Miss Wurtz! Caroline had some kind of correspondence with your dad."

"The Wurtz?" Jack whispered.

"Miss Wurtz herself told me," Leslie whispered back. "I don't think your mom ever knew about it."

Something blocked the light from the bathroom, where the door was ajar—a sudden appearance of the kind The Gray Ghost was once the master of, as if Mrs. McQuat, who had tried to save him, were reaching out to Jack again. Or maybe Mrs. Machado, or *her* ghost, was coming to get him! But it was his mother, naked; she was as close to entering the next world as any ghost.

"I want to go home," Alice whispered. "If you insist on whispering, I'm going to whisper, too," she said, climbing into Emma's bed.

Strangely it was her heart-side breast that looked ravaged—not the breast where she'd had the lumpectomy. Her broken-heart tattoo was the blue-black of a bruise, the *you* in cursive as meaningless as what was written on the toe tag of a total stranger in a morgue.

Mrs. Oastler and Jack hugged Alice between them. "Please take me home," his mother kept whispering.

"You *are* home," Leslie told her—kissing her neck, her shoulder, her face. "Or do you mean Edinburgh, Alice?"

"No, *home,*" Alice said, more fiercely. "You know where I mean, Jack."

"Where do you mean, Mom?" (Jack knew where she meant; he just wanted to see if she could say it.)

"I mean the needles, dear," his mother said. "It's time to take me to my needles." Not surprisingly, that's what Daughter Alice meant by going home.

26

A Faithless Boy

Jack's mother died peacefully in her sleep, much as Maureen Yap had predicted. For five days and nights, she slept and woke up and fell back to sleep on the sofa bed at Daughter Alice. Leslie and Jack took turns staying with her. They had discovered that Alice was less abusive to them if they weren't together, and the sofa bed wasn't big enough for three people.

On the fifth night, it was Leslie's turn. Alice woke up and asked Mrs. Oastler to let her hear a little Bob Dylan. Leslie was aware of the police complaints; she turned up the volume only slightly. "Is that loud enough, Alice?" she asked.

There was no answer. Mrs. Oastler at first assumed that Alice had fallen back to sleep; it was only when Leslie got into bed beside her that she realized Alice had stopped breathing. (It would turn out that a blood vessel in her brain had hemorrhaged, eaten away by the cancer.)

Jack was in bed with Bonnie Hamilton, in Bonnie's house, when the phone rang. He sensed that his mother was sleeping in the needles before Bonnie answered the phone. "I'll tell him," he heard Bonnie say, while he was still trying to orient himself in the darkened bedroom. (He didn't want to get out of bed and stumble into the wheelchair.) "I'll tell him that, too."

"Alice died in her sleep—she just stopped breathing," Mrs. Oastler had announced straightaway. "I think Jack and I should stay with her till morning. I don't want them to take her away in the dark."

Alice had talked to Leslie and Jack about the kind of memorial service she wanted. She'd been uncharacteristically specific. "It should be on a Saturday evening. If you run out of booze, the beer store and the liquor store will still be open."

Jack and Mrs. Oastler had humored her; they'd agreed to a

Saturday evening, although the concept of running out of booze at *any* event originating in the St. Hilda's chapel was unimaginable. Alice wasn't an Old Girl. Maybe a few of the Old Girls would show up, but they would be Leslie's old friends and they weren't big drinkers. The novelty of seeing Jack Burns (so soon after seeing him at Emma's memorial service) would surely have worn off. Out of a genuine fondness for Jack, there'd be a smattering of St. Hilda's faculty. No doubt some of the same boarders would attend, but those girls weren't drinkers, either. Compared to how it was at the service for Emma, Mrs. Oastler and Jack assumed that the chapel would be virtually empty.

"The *wake* part should be in the gym, not in the Great Hall," Alice had instructed them. "And nobody should say anything—no prayers, *just* singing."

"Hymns?" Leslie had asked.

"It should be an evensong service," Jack's mother, the former choirgirl, had said. "Leslie, you should let Caroline Wurtz arrange it. You don't know anything about church music, and Jack doesn't even *like* music."

"I like Bob Dylan, Mom."

"Let's save Bob for the *wake* part," Mrs. Oastler had suggested, in disbelief.

Leslie and Jack completely missed it. The part about running out of booze should have forewarned them—not to mention that Alice had asked them to inform "just a few" of her old friends.

Jack called Jerry Swallow—Sailor Jerry, from Alice's Halifax days, although Jerry had moved to New Glasgow, Nova Scotia. A woman, maybe Jerry's wife, answered the phone. Jack asked her to please tell Jerry that Daughter Alice had died. To his surprise, the woman asked him where and when there was going to be a service. Jack gave her the details over the phone—little suspecting that Sailor Jerry, and all the rest of them, would show up.

Jack didn't call Tattoo Ole or Tattoo Peter—they were both dead. Tattoo Theo wasn't on Alice's list; probably he had also died.

Doc Forest was the second tattoo artist Jack called. Doc was still in Stockholm. Jack recalled Doc's forearms (like Popeye's) and his neatly trimmed mustache and sideburns—his bright, twinkling eyes. Jack remembered what Doc had said to him, too—when Jack and his mom were leaving Sweden. "Come back and see me when you're older. Maybe then you'll want a tattoo."

Doc regretted that he couldn't come such a distance for Alice's service, but he said he would pass along the sad news. Jack thought it must have been simply a courtesy on Doc's part—to even mention undertaking such a journey. Doc had last seen Alice at a tattoo convention at the Meadowlands, in New Jersey. "She was a maritime girl," the former sailor told Jack, his voice breaking—or maybe it was the long-distance connection.

Jack next called Hanky Panky—the tattoo name for Henk Schiffmacher—at the House of Pain in Amsterdam. Schiffmacher had written several books, the famous *1000 Tattoos* among them; many of the illustrations in that book were collected at the Tattoo Museum in the red-light district. Alice had believed that Hanky Panky was one of the best tattoo artists in the world; she'd met him at any number of tattoo conventions, and she'd stayed with him and his wife in Amsterdam. Henk Schiffmacher was sorry he couldn't come all the way to Canada on such short notice. "But I'll pass the word," he said. "I'm sure that a lot of the guys will show up."

It was only later—actually, on the night before Alice's memorial service at St. Hilda's—that Leslie informed Jack that she'd called a *different* threesome of tattoo artists. Alice had given Leslie another list; this one also had "just a few" names to call.

"Who were they?" Jack asked Mrs. Oastler.

"Jesus, Jack—I can't possibly remember their names. You know what their names are like."

"Did you call Philadelphia Eddie?" Jack asked. (Make that *Crazy* Philadelphia Eddie.) "Or maybe Mao of Madrid, or Bugs of London—"

"There were three guys," Leslie informed him. "They were all in the United States. They all said they'd pass the word."

"Maybe Little Vinnie Myers?" he suggested. Or Uncle Pauly, Jack imagined—or Armadillo Red. He'd never met them, but he knew their names.

"Well, they won't come, anyway," Mrs. Oastler said, but she didn't sound so sure.

"What's the matter, Leslie?"

Mrs. Oastler was remembering what one of them had asked her, when she'd given the guy the bad news. "Where's the party?" the tattoo artist had inquired.

"He said '*party*'?" Jack asked Leslie.

"Isn't that all they *do,* Jack? At least that's my impression. All they *do* is party!"

This gave them both a bad night's sleep. About 2:00 A.M. Mrs. Oastler got into Emma's bed with Jack, but she wasn't interested in holding his penis.

"What if they *all* come?" Leslie whispered, as if Alice were still alive or somehow capable of overhearing them. "What will we *do*?"

"We'll have a *party,*" he told Mrs. Oastler, only half believing that it might be true.

In the morning, while Leslie was making coffee, Jack answered the phone in the kitchen. It was Bruce Smuck, a Toronto tattoo artist and a good friend of Alice's; she'd liked his work and had been something of a mentor to him. He'd already called Leslie and offered his condolences; now he was calling to ask what he could bring.

"Oh, just bring yourself, Bruce," Jack answered cluelessly. "We'll be glad to see you."

"Was that Bruce Smuck again?" Mrs. Oastler asked, after Jack hung up the phone.

"He wanted to know if he could *bring* something," Jack said, the gravity of Bruce's offer slowly sinking in.

"Bring *what*?" Leslie asked.

Bruce must have meant *booze,* Jack thought. Bruce was a nice guy—he was just offering to help out. Obviously Bruce expected a *mob*!

Jack called Peewee on his cell phone and increased the original liquor-store order from a case each of white and red wine to three cases of white and *five* cases of red. (From what Alice had told Leslie, the majority of tattoo artists were red-wine types.)

"Tell Peewee to go to the beer store, too," Mrs. Oastler said. "The bikers drink a lot of beer. Better fill the fucking limo with beer—just in case." Leslie was sitting at the kitchen table with her head in her hands, inhaling the steam from her coffee cup; she looked like someone who'd recently quit smoking and desperately wanted a cigarette.

Jack poured himself a cup of coffee, but the phone rang before he could take his first sip. "Uh-oh," Mrs. Oastler said.

It was a Saturday morning—Alice's evensong service was scheduled for five-thirty that afternoon—but Caroline Wurtz was calling on her cell phone from the St. Hilda's chapel, where she and the organist and the boarders' choir were already practicing. When Jack answered the phone, he could hear the organ and the choir better than he could hear Caroline.

"Jack, a *quandary* has presented itself—in *clerical* form," Miss Wurtz whispered. She sounded as if she were in Emma's bed with him—as Jack had so often dreamed—and his mother was within hearing distance, down the hall.

"What *quandary* is that?" Jack whispered back.

"The Reverend Parker—our chaplain, Jack—wishes to lead the congregation in the Apostles' Creed."

"Mom requested no prayers, Caroline."

"I know," she whispered. "I told him."

"Maybe *I* should tell him," Jack said. He'd met the Reverend Parker only once. Parker was a young twit who'd felt excluded from Emma's memorial service; hence he was inserting himself in Alice's.

"I think I can *negotiate* with him, Jack," Miss Wurtz whispered. In the background, the organ was fainter now—the girlish voices from the boarders' choir were less and less distinct. The Wurtz must have been retreating from the chapel with her cell phone; Jack could hear the squeak of her shoes on the linoleum in the hall.

"What might be the terms of your *negotiation*?" he asked.

"Let him lead the congregation through the Twenty-third Psalm, since he evidently wants to lead us through *something*," Caroline said more loudly.

"Mom said nobody should say *anything*. Aren't psalms like prayers?"

"The Reverend Parker is the chaplain, Jack."

"I like the Twenty-third Psalm better than the Apostles' Creed," Jack conceded.

"There appears to be *another* small quandary," Miss Wurtz went on. Jack couldn't hear the organ or the choir at all. Caroline must have walked all the way down the hall to the main entrance, yet he was having trouble hearing her again; this time, it wasn't the organ or the boarders' choir that was causing the interference. "Goodness!" The Wurtz exclaimed over the throttling engines, a near-deafening sound. (*Another* quandary had presented itself—this one, Jack guessed, was not small.)

"What is it?" he asked, although he already knew. At the tattoo conventions, his mother used to tell him, the bikers always arrived early; perhaps they wanted to be sure they had a good place to park.

"My word, it's a *motorcycle gang*!" Caroline cried, loudly enough for Mrs. Oastler to hear her. "What on earth is a motorcycle gang doing at an all-girls' school?"

"I'll be right there," Jack told her. "Better lock up the boarders."

"Your mother has cursed us, Jack—this is just the beginning," Leslie said, still holding her head in her hands.

Caroline and Jack had already had a little talk about Miss Wurtz's correspondence with William. His dad had taken a particular interest in Jack's artistic or creative training. "Your *development*," as The Wurtz had put it.

"When I was at St. Hilda's?" Jack asked.

"Indeed, Jack—when you were in the earliest stages of your *dramatic* education."

"Your dramatizations, you mean—"

"Beginning with, but by no means exclusively, your remarkable success in *female* roles," Miss Wurtz informed him. "I thought that William would be especially pleased with how you and I, in conversation, arrived at the idea that *he*—your father—was your own special audience of one. If you remember—"

"How could I forget?" Jack asked her.

"But he was *not* pleased," Caroline told Jack, gravely. "Your father strenuously objected, in fact."

"He objected to being my audience of one?"

"To the very *idea* of an audience of one, Jack. William was opposed to the concept aesthetically."

"Why?" Jack asked. He'd noticed that she'd now said the name *William* twice.

Caroline sighed. (No more perishable beauty ever existed.) "Well," she said, "I think his theory more aptly applies to *organs*."

"Why *organs*?"

"Your father insisted that you should be taught to play your heart out, Jack. As for your audience—if only in your mind's eye—they were all the wretched, down-on-their-luck and hard-of-hearing souls in the hindmost pews of the church, and *beyond.*"

"Beyond *what*?"

"He meant even the drunks, sleeping it off in the streets and alleys outside the church. That's what William said."

He meant even the prostitutes within hearing of the Oude Kerk, Jack was thinking; indeed, his dad must have meant that Jack should be reaching *vastly* more than an audience of one. (That is, if he was any good.)

"I think I get it," Jack told Caroline.

"I wouldn't call it a *correspondence,* Jack. We exchanged, at most, two or three letters. I wouldn't want you to think that I still hear from him."

"But he taught at the school—however briefly—when you were teaching there, too," Jack reminded her. "You *knew* him, didn't you, Caroline?"

Jack and Miss Wurtz were in a coffee shop on the corner of Lonsdale and Spadina. It was the weekend after Alice had died. Caroline was dressed, as he'd never seen her, in blue jeans and a man's flannel shirt; Jack didn't think she was wearing a bra. Nevertheless, she was absolutely stunning for a woman in her fifties—she was radiant, even *glowing.* Those high cheekbones, her fine jaw cut like crystal, the peachlike blush to her skin—Miss Wurtz was a knockout. She sighed again and ran her long fingers through her wavy hair, which was now completely gray but still lustrous; her hair had the sheen of slate in sunlight.

"Yes, Jack—if you must know—I *knew* him," Caroline said. Staring down at the coffee in her cup, she added softly: "William gave me some of my favorite clothes. He had an eye for women's clothes. They may be a bit old-fashioned by today's standards, but they're still my favorites, Jack."

Naturally, Emma had spotted the clothes. Caroline saw that Jack couldn't speak; she reached across the small café table and touched his face. "He was not just my lover—he was my *only* lover," Miss Wurtz told him. "Well, it didn't *last,*" she said, almost cheerfully. "Too many other women wanted William—women *and* girls," Caroline added, laughing. Jack was surprised that she sounded more amused than bothered by the thought—

maybe because it was so long after the fact. "Your father was far more committed to his music than to our fair sex, Jack," she went on. "And if you ever heard him *play,*" Miss Wurtz whispered, taking Jack's hands in hers. "Well, it suffices to say—no wonder he was more engaged by his music than by *us!*"

No wonder Jack had dressed The Wurtz in mail-order underwear in his dreams! Who could resist the temptation to give her clothes? His father hadn't resisted her!

Jack swallowed his coffee with unusual difficulty. "Did my mom know?" he asked Caroline.

"Your mother knew that William liked the way I *spoke.* That's all she knew," Miss Wurtz told him. "William must have said something to Alice about my voice—my diction, my enunciation. He used to tell me, *admiringly,* that I didn't have an accent."

"So it was *Mom's* idea—to have you teach her how to *talk?*" Jack asked. "I thought it was Mrs. Wicksteed who wanted her to lose the Scottish accent."

"Goodness, no!" Caroline said, with a laugh. "Mrs. Wicksteed was such an old-school Canadian—she *loved* a Scottish accent!"

"But you must have known about the girls—I mean the boarders, Caroline."

"Oh, who *didn't* know about those silly girls!" Miss Wurtz exclaimed. "You know boarders, Jack. If they could get pregnant all by themselves, they'd probably try it."

"But he left you, too, didn't he?" Jack asked her. "You don't sound as if you hate him."

"I never expected him to stay, Jack. Of course I don't *hate* him! William was one of those pleasures every woman wants to have, at least once in her lifetime. With all due respect to Alice, Jack, you have to be deluded to imagine you might *keep* a man like that. Especially at his age at that time—he was so young!"

Jack looked at Caroline Wurtz with everything he had lost visibly written on his face—the way he must have looked when his mother said, "Who knows what sort of father he would have been, Jack? With a man like that," Alice had said, with disgust, "you can never be sure." But Miss Wurtz had used the exact same phrase—*a man like that*—with enduring affection!

"If *you'd* been my mother," he told Caroline, "I would have had a father. At least I would have occasionally *seen* him."

"I haven't heard a word from him, or about him, in years," Miss Wurtz told Jack. "But that doesn't mean you can't find him."

"He may be dead, Caroline. *Mom* is."

The Wurtz leaned across the café table and grabbed hold of Jack's left ear; it was as if she were Mrs. McQuat and he still in grade three, about to be taken to the chapel by The Gray Ghost.

"You faithless boy!" she said. "If William were dead, my heart would have *stopped*! The day he dies, my breasts will shrivel to the size of *raisins* in my sleep—or I'll turn into *linoleum* or something!"

Linoleum? Jack wondered. (The poor woman had been at St. Hilda's too long.) His ear, which she still held, was throbbing. Suddenly Miss Wurtz let him go; she laughed at herself like a young girl. "Well, don't I sound like a brainless *boarder*!" Caroline exclaimed. "You faithless boy," she said to Jack again—this time fondly. "Go find him!"

"Tell me the context, baby cakes," Emma used to say. "Everything comes with a context."

That Saturday in March—it was 1998, and March in Toronto is not reliable motorcycle weather—Jack walked to the circular driveway at the corner of Pickthall and Hutchings Hill Road, where he had once stood holding his mother's hand in a sea of girls.

The motorcycles, their engines off, were parked in a row—with something less than military precision. The day was overcast, there was a raw chill in the air, and the gas tanks of the motorcycles were beaded and glistening in the descending mist—a fine drizzle. In that weather, Jack didn't take the time to count them, but there were about thirty motorcycles—their license plates indicating how far some of their riders had traveled.

North Dakota Dan had driven all the way from Bismarck; he'd hooked up with Lucky Pierre at Twin Cities Tattoo in Minneapolis, and they rode together down to Madison, Wisconsin, where Badger Schultz and his wife, Little Chicken Wing, were waiting. They'd picked up the Fronhofer brothers at Windy City Tattoo in Chicago, and rode together into Michigan; they hit snow in Kalamazoo and Battle Creek, but they still made it to East Lansing in time to have a party with Flipper Volkmann at Spartan

Tattoo. The next morning, they rode with Flipper to Ann Arbor, where Wolverine Wally joined them. They had some understandable difficulty clearing Canadian customs, but they picked up the 401 in Windsor and rode through the rain to Kitchener and Guelph, where they met a couple of Ontario tattoo artists Jack had never heard of. (He still couldn't remember their names.)

There were riders heading north from Louisville, Kentucky, and three cities in Ohio, too. Joe Ink from Tiger Skin Tattoo in Cincinnati, and the Skretkowicz sisters from Columbus—one of whom was the ex-wife of Flattop Tom, who joined up with the sisters in Cleveland.

The contingent from Pennsylvania, too numerous to name, included notables in the tattoo world from Pittsburgh, Harrisburg, Allentown, and Scranton—and Night-Shift Mike, from Sailors' Friend Tattoo, rode the long way north from Norfolk, Virginia. There were motorcycles in the circular St. Hilda's driveway with license plates from Maryland and Massachusetts and New York and New Jersey, too.

From the voices raised in song—one could hear them booming from the chapel, the *male* voices seeming to challenge the organ and overwhelming the boarders' choir—Jack knew that Miss Wurtz hadn't been idle. She'd ushered the bikers inside and made them comfortable at the rehearsal. Hot coffee would soon be available in the gym, Miss Wurtz had told them, which wasn't quite true—not *soon,* anyway.

"But how many of you know 'God Save the Queen'?" The Wurtz had asked them. To the bikers' uncomprehending silence, Caroline had said: "Well, I *thought* so! It seems you could benefit from a little *practice.*"

By the time Jack got to St. Hilda's, she had them singing. Most of the tattoo artists didn't know which queen they were singing to save—but it was for Daughter Alice, which is why they'd come, and the sound of their voices seemed to warm them. They stood dripping in their wet leathers; the smell of the road, oil and exhaust, mixed with the smell of their well-worn gear, their wind-blown beards, their helmet-matted hair. Thrilled, the boarders' choir faced them from the safety of the altar. The girls' voices sounded like those of children among the bikers, who were mostly men.

The organist, a pretty young woman who was as new to St. Hilda's as the twit chaplain, was making mistakes; even Jack could tell she was nervous, and that her errors were increasing with each new mistake she made.

"Calm down, Eleanor," Miss Wurtz told her,. "or I'll have to take over, and I haven't played an organ in *years.*"

While Eleanor took a short breather, Jack introduced himself to his mom's friends. "The good-lookin' Jack Burns," he heard Night-Shift Mike say, appraising him.

"Daughter Alice's little boy," one of the Skretkowicz sisters said.

"I'm the other Skretkowicz," the other sister told Jack. "The one who was never married to Flattop Tom, or to anybody else," she whispered in Jack's ear, biting his earlobe.

"Your mom sure was proud of you," Badger Schultz said. His wife, Little Chicken Wing, was already dissolved in tears—and it wasn't even noon. They had hours to go before Alice's memorial service.

Caroline clapped her hands. "We're still rehearsing—we're rehearsing until I say, 'Stop!' " Miss Wurtz called from the altar area. Eleanor, the organist, seemed almost composed.

"I didn't know you could play the organ, Caroline," Eleanor said—more audibly than she'd meant to, because Jack and the bikers had suddenly stopped talking.

Glancing in Jack's direction, Miss Wurtz blushed. "Well, I had a few memorable *lessons,*" she said.

> *God save our gracious Queen,*
> *Long live our noble Queen,*
> *God save the Queen!*
> *Send her victorious,*
> *Happy and glorious,*
> *Long to reign over us;*
> *God save the Queen!*

Under The Wurtz's direction, they sang and sang. The pure, girlish voices of the boarders' choir were no match for the beer-hall gusto of the bikers, who—as they recovered from the damp chill of the March roads—shed their leathers. Their tattoos rivaled the colors of Jesus and his surrounding saints on the chapel's stained glass.

Jack slipped away. He knew that Miss Wurtz could *dramatize* anything; by the time of the blessed event, Caroline would have polished to perfection both the boarders' *and* the bikers' choir. As Jack was leaving, the tattoo artists were listening reverentially to the girls, who were singing "Lord of the Dance."

> *I danced in the morning*
> *When the world was begun,*
> *And I danced in the moon*
> *And the stars and the sun,*
> *And I came down from heaven*
> *And I danced on the earth,*
> *At Bethlehem*
> *I had my birth.*

Out in the circular driveway, two more riders had arrived; they were parking their motorcycles alongside the others. Slick Eddie Esposito from The Blue Bulldog in New Haven, Connecticut, and Bad Bill Letters from Black Bear Season Tattoo in Brunswick, Maine. Their creased leathers were streaked with rain and they looked stiff with cold, but they recognized Jack Burns and smiled warmly. Jack shook their icy hands.

He'd thrown on some old clothes at Mrs. Oastler's—jeans, running shoes, a waterproof parka that had been Emma's and was way too big for him. "I'm just going home to change my clothes for the service," Jack told the newly arrived bikers. They seemed mystified by the girls' voices coming from the chapel. "The others are inside, practicing."

"Practicing *what*?" Bad Bill asked. It must have been the third or fourth refrain to "Lord of the Dance"; Miss Wurtz had obviously decided to bring the bikers into the chorus. The men's big voices reached them out in the rain.

> *Dance, then, wherever you may be,*
> *I am the Lord of the Dance, said he,*
> *And I'll lead you all, wherever you may be,*
> *And I'll lead you all in the Dance, said he.*

"Come on, Bill—let's go sing with 'em," Slick Eddie said.
"Are you comin' back as a *girl*?" Bad Bill asked Jack.
"Not today," Jack told him.

They were going inside the building when Jack heard Slick Eddie say: "You're an asshole, Bill."

"Of *course* I'm an asshole!" Bad Bill said.

Jack went back to Mrs. Oastler's house and stretched out in a hot bath. Leslie came into the bathroom in her black bikini-cut underwear; she put the lid down on the toilet and sat there, not looking at him. "How many of them are there?" she asked.

"About thirty motorcycles, maybe forty riders," he told her.

"Most of the tattoo artists your mother knew weren't bikers, Jack. The bikers are just the tip of the iceberg."

"I know," Jack said. "We better call Peewee."

"We better call the *police*," Mrs. Oastler replied. "They can't all *sleep* at St. Hilda's—not even in the gym."

"Some of them could sleep here," he suggested.

"Your mother *intended* to do this, Jack. Maybe if we *had* slept with each other, she would have spared us this final indignity."

"I don't know," Jack said. "I get the feeling that Mom couldn't have kept them away."

Peewee called later that afternoon. "I should be driving a *van*, not a limo, mon—there's no room for more booze in the limo, Jack."

"Better make two trips," Jack told him.

"This is the *third* trip, mon! If you and Mrs. Oastler don't get your asses to that chapel, you won't have any place to *sit*!" Peewee was a born alarmist. Jack knew that Miss Wurtz was in charge; he trusted Caroline to save him and Leslie a couple of seats.

The Wurtz did better than that. She stationed Stinky Monkey, like an usher in the aisle, to guard the pew. Bad to the Bones was there, too—and Sister Bear and Dragon Moon. They were *all* there—everyone Jack had imagined, and more.

A group came from Italy. Luca Brusa (from Switzerland) wouldn't have missed it, he told Jack. Heaven & Hell came from Germany, Manu and Tin-Tin from France. The Las Vegas Pricks were there, and Hollywood's Purple Panther.

They crammed the pews, the aisles—even the corridor, halfway to the gym. A small, frightened-looking gathering of Old Girls—Mrs. Oastler's trembling former classmates—were huddled in two front pews on a side aisle, where Ed Hardy, Bill Funk, and Rusty Savage appeared to have appointed themselves as the Old Girls' bodyguards. At least they weren't letting their fellow tattoo artists anywhere near these older women, who were (like the schoolgirls they'd been long ago) holding hands.

Miss Wurtz had marshaled her two choirs—the boarders and the bikers—to take their positions on either side of the aisle, where these disparate groups faced the largely baffled congregation. The tattoo artists who *hadn't* arrived early could make no sense of "God Save the Queen."

"Who's the Queen?" a broad-shouldered man in a bright yellow sports jacket asked Jack. He had so much gel in his hair, which stood straight up, that the top of his head resembled a shark's dorsal fin. Both the bright yellow jacket and the hair were familiar to Jack from the tattoo magazines he'd seen—Crazy Philadelphia Eddie; there could be no doubt.

The Reverend Parker arrived late. "There was no place to park!" the chaplain peevishly complained, before he had a closer look at the congregation—the tie-dyed tank tops, the tattooed arms, the open collars of the Hawaiian shirts, the exposed chests, also tattooed. Real snakes and mythological serpents regarded the chaplain coldly; in the reptilian tattoos, there were creatures that the Garden of Eden and the Reverend Parker had never seen. There were many depictions of Christ's bleeding heart, bound in thorns—lacking the usual Anglican reserve. There were many skeletons—some breathing fire, others speaking obscenities.

In the blaze of all this tattooed flesh, The Wurtz had outdone herself with "Lord of the Dance." The boarders, whom Leslie described as "a choir of not-quite virgins," sang all five verses—the bikers joining them for the five refrains. The wrecked blond boarder who'd lost her shoe at Emma's memorial service sang the fourth stanza solo, and a beautiful soloist she was; though they'd rehearsed this together several times already, she had the bikers in tears.

> *I danced on a Friday*
> *When the sky turned black—*
> *It's hard to dance*
> *With the devil on your back.*
> *They buried my body*
> *And they thought I'd gone,*
> *But I am the Dance,*
> *And I still go on.*

When it was time for the chaplain to read the Twenty-third Psalm, it was warm in the chapel and some of the heavily tattooed types had taken off their shirts. They weren't all tattoo artists—there were many of Alice's clients present. Her signature work was everywhere; Jack recognized more than a few Daughter Alices.

He also noticed that Mrs. Oastler was crying. She slumped against him in the pew, her small body shaking. That was how Alice's colleagues knew who she was. "I've got a sweetie in Toronto," Alice had told more than one of them. (As in: "No, thanks—not tonight. I've got a sweetie in Toronto.")

"The Lord is my shepherd; I shall not want," the Reverend Parker began anxiously. He was thoroughly rattled by the time he got to "Yea, though I walk through the valley of the shadow of death, I will feel no evil—"

" '. . . *fear,*' not *feel,* 'no evil—' " Miss Wurtz corrected him.

". . . *fear* no evil," the chaplain stumbled ahead. "For Thou art with me; Thy rod and Thy staff, they comfort me."

"Your *what*?" someone in the congregation said—a woman's voice. (Jack didn't see who said it, but he would bet it was one of the Skretkowicz sisters.) This was followed by general laughter; one of the Old Girls among Mrs. Oastler's former classmates was in hysterics.

That was when Leslie lost it. "No praying, no *saying* anything!" Mrs. Oastler shouted to the chaplain. "Alice wanted *just* singing!"

"Thou preparest a table before me in the presence of mine enemies—" the Reverend Parker mumbled; then he stopped. He saw the presence of *his* enemies, all around him.

"Just *singing,* pal," Bad Bill Letters said.

"Yeah—sing or shut up," one of the Fronhofer brothers said.

"Sing or shut up!" Flattop Tom repeated.

"Sing or *shut up*!" the congregation shouted.

Eleanor, the organist, was frozen. Caroline sat down on the organ bench beside her. "If you've forgotten how to play 'Jerusalem,' Eleanor," Miss Wurtz said, "the good Lord may forgive you, but *I* won't." Eleanor, bless her timid heart, lurched forward; she attacked the keyboard. The organ was a little louder than expected, but the boarders' and the bikers' choir gave it their best.

> *And did those feet in ancient time*
> *Walk upon England's mountains green?*
> *And was the holy Lamb of God on England's*
> *pleasant pastures seen?*

As they went up the aisle, Mrs. Oastler was swept into the arms of Crazy Philadelphia Eddie; she was overcome with emotion and didn't, or couldn't, resist him. All of Alice's friends had heard of Leslie and wanted to hug her. "It's Alice's *sweetie*," people were whispering.

"Why do they *know* me?" Leslie asked Jack.

"Mom must have told them about you," Jack said.

"She *did*?" asked Mrs. Oastler, who was in tears. They were *all* in tears—all the tattoo artists, all of Daughter Alice's clients, and her friends. (It was a sentimental business, tattooing—as Leslie was only now discovering.)

They were marching up the hall to the gym by the time the boarders and the bikers hit their full stride in the fourth verse; even Eleanor, with Miss Wurtz's encouragement, had kept up.

> *I will not cease from mental fight,*
> *Nor shall my sword sleep in my hand,*
> *Till we have built Jerusalem*
> *In England's green and pleasant land.*

A bathtub-size bucket of ice, full of cold beer, awaited them in the gym; wine corks were popping. Huge slabs of roast beef and platters of sausages weighed down the picnic tables—not the usual cheese-speared-on-toothpicks fare.

"Who ordered all this food?" Jack asked Leslie.

"*I* did, Jack. Peewee had to make a few more trips."

Wolverine Wally and Flipper Volkmann were having a heated argument. "A Michigan matter," Badger Schultz was saying diplomatically, as he forced himself between them. Badger's wife, Little Chicken Wing, had taken Mrs. Oastler's arm. Joe Ink, from Tiger Skin Tattoo in Cincinnati, placed his hand on Leslie's shoulder—the tattoo on the back of his hand was an ace of spades overlapping an ace of hearts.

"If you're ever in Norfolk," Night-Shift Mike was saying to Mrs. Oastler, "I'll show you the town like you wouldn't *believe*!"

"They *loved* her!" Leslie said breathlessly to Jack. "Invite them to stay, Jack," she added. (Slick Eddie Esposito was showing her the Man's Ruin on his belly; it was Daughter Alice's work.)

"Invite *all* of them?" Jack asked Mrs. Oastler. "To stay with *us*?"

"Of *course* with us!" Leslie told him. "Where else can they stay?"

Maybe not the Skretkowicz sisters, Jack thought—maybe not *both* of them, anyway. Why not just the one who *hadn't* been married to Flattop Tom? But he realized you couldn't control a tattoo artists' party; you had to go with the flow, as Alice's generation would say.

Miss Wurtz was in fine form, praising the bikers' first-time performance. Ever the nondrinker, Jack watched over the boarders like a sheep dog. But everyone was extremely well behaved, the dispute between Flipper Volkmann and Wolverine Wally notwithstanding—and not even that Michigan matter had resulted in a fight.

It was a mild surprise that Mrs. Oastler's former classmates appeared to be having a good time, too. The Old Girls had not seen so much *skin* on display in a great while—if ever. The St. Hilda's gym was hopping; there was nonstop Bob Dylan on the CD player.

From his mother's description of Jerry Swallow as a traditionalist, Jack should have recognized him. A pretty woman wearing a nurse's cap was tattooed on one of his biceps; it's hard to be more of a *traditionalist* than that. The writing on Sailor Jerry's shirt was in Japanese, as was the tattoo on his right forearm. "A Kazuo Oguri," he told Jack proudly. So Jerry Swallow had come all the way from New Glasgow, Nova Scotia—not to mention that he'd made over a hundred phone calls.

"Old-timers keep in touch, Jackie."

Jack thanked him for coming such a long way. "*Life* is a long way, young Mr. Burns," Sailor Jerry said. "Nova Scotia isn't all that far."

Later in the evening, when Jack thought he'd introduced himself to everyone—the boarders' choir keeping him company like his not-quite-virgin guards—he spotted a recognizable presence at the far end of the gym. Bob Dylan's "Rainy Day Women # 12 &

35" was booming from the CD player when Jack edged his way toward the shy, stoned figure weaving to the music under the basketball net. His dreamy countenance, the gray wisp of whiskers on his chin—as if, even in his late forties or early fifties, his beard *still* hadn't begun to grow—and something self-deprecating in his eyes, which were perpetually downcast, all reminded Jack of someone whose confidence in his own meager talent had never been high. (Not now, and not when he'd been Tattoo Theo's young apprentice on the Zeedijk.)

"Not another broken heart," Alice had told Robbie de Wit, when she'd said good-bye. "I've had enough of hearts, torn in two or otherwise." Hence Robbie had settled for Alice's signature on his right upper arm—the slightly faded *Daughter Alice* that Robbie revealed as Jack approached him.

"Still listening to der Zimmerman, Jackie?" Robbie said.

Bob's refrain wailed around them.

> *But I would not feel so all alone,*
> *Everybody must get stoned.*

"Still listening to *den* Zimmerman, Robbie."

"I'm really not in the same league with these guys," Robbie de Wit told Jack, gesturing unsteadily toward the rest of the gym. "It didn't work out for me in Amsterdam."

"I'm sorry to hear that," Jack told him.

"I'm in Rotterdam now. Got my own shop, but I'm still an apprentice—if you know what I mean. I'm doing okay," he said, his head bobbing. The receding hairline had fooled Jack at first—as had the egg-shaped forehead and the deep crow's-feet at the corners of Robbie's pale, watery eyes.

"What happened in Amsterdam, Robbie? What happened to *Mom*? What made her leave?"

"Oh, Jackie—don't go there. Let dying dogs die." (Robbie meant "Let sleeping dogs lie," but Jack understood him.)

"I remember the night she was a prostitute. At least she *acted* like one," Jack said to him. "Saskia and Els looked after me. You brought Mom a little something to smoke, I think."

"Don't, Jackie," Robbie said. "Let it go."

"My dad didn't go to Australia, did he?" Jack asked Robbie de Wit. "He was in Amsterdam the whole time, wasn't he?"

"Your father had a *following,* Jackie. Your mom couldn't help herself."

"Help herself *how*?" Jack asked.

Robbie tripped forward, almost falling; he offered Jack the faded *Daughter Alice* on his upper right arm as if he were daring Jack to punch him on his mom's tattoo. "I won't betray her, Jack," Robbie said. "Don't ask me."

"I apologize, Robbie." Jack was ashamed of himself for being even a little aggressive with him.

Robbie put his hand on the back of Jack's neck; bowing, off-balance, he touched his egg-shaped forehead to the tip of Jack's nose. "Your mom loved you, Jackie. She just didn't love anybody, not even you, like she loved *William.*"

The Old Girls, not counting Leslie Oastler, had gone home. The single ones—especially those Old Girls who were divorced, and proud of it—took some of the tattoo artists with them. Mr. Ramsey, bidding Jack his usual adieu—"Jack Burns!"—had taken a tattoo artist home with him, too. (Night-Shift Mike from Sailors' Friend Tattoo in Norfolk, Virginia. Mike was indeed a friend of sailors!)

Even Miss Wong, at last in touch with the hurricane she was born in, danced up a storm—most memorably losing control of herself on the gym floor, jitterbugging with both Fronhofer brothers to "Stuck Inside of Mobile with the Memphis Blues Again." (Miss Wong went home with the better-looking brother.)

Remarkably, the Malcolms stayed late—Mrs. Malcolm being unusually cheered by the presence of Marvin "Mekong Delta" Jones from Tuscaloosa, Alabama. Marvin had lost both legs, and part of his nose, in the Vietnam War; he'd parked his wheelchair alongside Mrs. Malcolm's and had entertained both her and Mr. Malcolm with his hilarious stories, perhaps apocryphal, of trying to get laid when he was wheelchair-bound and had half a nose. ("Not everyone is sympathetic," one story began; he had Wheelchair Jane in stitches.)

Miss Wurtz, who went home at a proper hour—needless to say, The Wurtz went home *alone*—brought the house down by singing along with Bob. Her renditions of "All I Really Want to Do" and "I'll Be Your Baby Tonight" were haunting. Flattop Tom told Jack there was nobody like her in Cleveland; North

Dakota Dan said there was no one like Miss Wurtz in Bismarck, either. (How, Jack wondered, had Edmonton been so blessed?)

The Oastler mansion was a motel that night, the motorcycles stationed like sentinels on the lawn—some of them lurking close to the house, as if they were intruders seeking access through a window.

Lucky Pierre passed out on the living-room couch, where he was covered by so many of the bikers' leathers that no one knew where he was in the morning—that is, until Joe Ink sat on him.

Flipper Volkmann and Wolverine Wally had to be separated—that old Michigan matter again. They put Flipper to bed in Jack's former bedroom and made the Wolverine spend the night in the kitchen, where the less-good-looking of the Fronhofer brothers watched over him—the one who *hadn't* gone home with Miss Wong and the hurricane she carried inside her.

Bad Bill Letters and Slick Eddie Esposito slept head-to-toe on the dining-room table, where their conversation about Night-Shift Mike, the sailors' friend, was overheard throughout the house. "You'd have to have your eyes in your asshole, Bill, to not know Night-Shift was a fag," Slick Eddie said.

"Eddie, if you had your eyes in your asshole, you'd be the first to know Night-Shift was a fag," Bad Bill told him.

"You're an asshole, Bill," Slick Eddie said.

"Of *course* I'm an asshole!" Bad Bill replied. "Tell me somethin' I don't know." But Slick Eddie was fast asleep; he was already snoring. "Sweet dreams, assholes!" Bad Bill cried, as if he were addressing everyone in the house.

"Sweet dreams, assholes!" Badger Schultz and his wife, Little Chicken Wing, called from the laundry room, where they were sleeping on the floor on an antique quilt.

"Great party, huh?" Jack whispered to the Skretkowicz sister he was sleeping with in Emma's bed.

"Yeah, your mom woulda *loved* it!" Ms. Skretkowicz said. She was, alas, the one who'd been married to Flattop Tom. She also had a fabulous octopus tattooed on her ass; it completely covered both cheeks. "Flattop Tom's work," she admitted a little sadly. "Not to take nothin' away from the octopus."

Down the hall, Leslie was in bed with the other Skretkowicz sister. "She was a real sweetie," Mrs. Oastler would tell Jack later. It was no surprise to Leslie that the other Skretkowicz sister had never been married—not to Flattop Tom or to anybody else. (Her biting Jack's earlobe had been insincere.)

Jack was awake for a long time, not only because of the tender ministrations of the former Mrs. Flattop Tom. Emma used to say that Jack's more than occasional sleeplessness was the plight of a nondrinker in a world of drinkers. (Jack doubted this.) It is fair to say that what the heterosexual Skretkowicz sister could do with the octopus on her ass would keep anyone awake for a long time, but Jack had more on his mind than that interesting octopus.

He regretted, again, his bad behavior with Robbie de Wit, who had come all the way from Rotterdam out of his love for Alice. Understandably, Robbie would never *betray* her—to use his word for it. If Jack wanted to know those things his mom had kept from him, or how she'd distorted his dad's story in her telling of the tale, Jack needed to do his own homework—to make his own discoveries.

Jack needed to take that trip he'd threatened to take when his mother was still alive. Not to find William, as Miss Wurtz had urged him—at least not yet. Not *that* trip, but the trip Jack had taken with his mom when he was four.

Allegedly, when Jack was three, his capacity for consecutive memory was comparable to that of a nine-year-old. At four, his retention of detail and understanding of linear time were equal to an eleven-year-old's—or so he'd been told. But what if that wasn't true? What if he'd actually been a *normal* little boy? A four-year-old whose memory was as easy to manipulate as that of any four-year-old, a four-year-old like any other, whose retention of detail and understanding of linear time were completely unreliable.

That was why Jack was wide awake. He suddenly knew it was a joke for him to even imagine he could remember what had happened to him in those Baltic and North Sea ports when he was four, almost thirty years ago! *That* was the trip Jack needed to take—alone, or certainly not with Leslie Oastler. It was not only a trip he'd already taken; it was possibly a trip he'd largely imagined, or it had been under his mother's management and she'd imagined it for him.

It was not the time to look for his father; it was the time to discover if William was worth looking for.

They'd gone to Copenhagen first. His mother hadn't manipulated that; at least Jack knew where their trip had started, and where he would soon be returning. "Copenhagen," he said aloud—not meaning to. As unlikely as this may seem, Jack had forgotten about the Skretkowicz sister, whose strong thigh gripped his waist.

She'd kicked the covers off; maybe the word *Copenhagen* had triggered something, because her hips were moving. Long-distance motorcyclists have a certain authority in their hips—in the case of Jack's Skretkowicz sister, even in her sleep. A green, somewhat startled-looking sea horse was tattooed on her forearm, which was flung across Jack's chest. The sea horse stared unblinkingly into the flickering light from the weather channel on Emma's small TV, which was on mute. The Skretkowicz sisters had a long ride ahead of them in the morning; the former Mrs. Flattop Tom had wanted to know the forecast for Ohio.

There was a storm story on the weather channel. Palm trees were snapped in half, docks had been swept away in high seas, a small boat was smashed on some rocks, breakers were pounding—all without a sound. The blue-green light from the television illuminated the tattoo on Ms. Skretkowicz's hip; the light threw into relief the barbed dorsal spines near the base of a stingray's whiplike tail.

Yes, Jack observed, there was a *stingray* tattooed on his Skretkowicz sister's undulating hip. The tentacles of the octopus (on her ass) appeared to be reaching for the ray, as if the tattoo artist's body were a map of the ocean's floor.

Jack had to arch his back to reach for the remote, which he still couldn't quite reach; it was not the response to her hips that his biker friend had expected. "Don't go," she whispered hoarsely, still half asleep. "Where are you going?"

"Copenhagen," Jack repeated.

"Is it raining there?" she asked him groggily.

It would be April before he could get there, Jack was thinking; there was a good chance it would be raining. "Probably," he answered.

"Don't go," she whispered again, as if she were falling back to sleep—or at least she wanted to.

"I *have* to go," he told her.

"Who's in Copenhagen?" his Skretkowicz sister asked. Jack could tell she was wide awake now. "What's her name?" she said, her biker's thigh gripping him tighter.

It was a *he*, not a *she*, who primarily interested Jack. Since Jack didn't know his name, it would be hard to find him. But there could be little doubt who Jack was thinking of—the littlest soldier who saved him. Not to diminish the importance of Ladies' Man Madsen; it's just that Lars would be easier to find. At least Jack knew his name.

27

The Commandant's Daughter;
Her Little Brother

Jack slipped away from Toronto without telling Miss Wurtz his plans; he never even said good-bye. He was afraid that Caroline would be disappointed in his decision not to go looking for his father straightaway.

He took only his winter clothes with him; Jack thought they'd be suitable for April in the North Sea and the Baltic. His *Toronto* clothes, Mrs. Oastler called them. Leslie had helped him pack. After all, she'd shopped for Jack's clothes—she'd even paid for most of them, during the winter Alice was dying—and Mrs. Oastler had her own opinions regarding how he should dress in those European ports of call.

"I hope you know, Jack—you don't wear the same clothes to a tattoo parlor that you would wear in a church, and vice versa."

He left Leslie with the responsibility of sending his screenplay of *The Slush-Pile Reader* to Bob Bookman at C.A.A. in Beverly Hills. In the long Canadian winter, Leslie had become Jack's partner in the project; a couple of times, he'd come close to telling her that Emma had left him more than her notes for a screenplay. But that wouldn't have been faithful to what Emma had wanted.

In the months he'd spent with his mom in Toronto, Jack's mail had been forwarded from California. Like her late daughter, Mrs. Oastler invariably read Jack's mail before giving it to him. She didn't give *all* his mail to him, either; she was more censorial than Emma. The fan mail from female admirers was not worthy of Jack's interest, Mrs. Oastler said. She refused to show him the photographs of his she-male tormentors, too.

It must have been February when Jack asked Leslie: "Didn't I get any Christmas cards this year?"

"Yeah, you got a *ton* of Christmas cards," Mrs. Oastler answered. "I threw them away."

"You don't like Christmas cards, Leslie?"

"Who needs them, Jack? You're a busy guy."

Somehow the letter from Michele Maher escaped the censor in Mrs. Oastler and made it into Jack's hands, although it was a month or more after Leslie had first read Michele's letter. "This one's interesting," Mrs. Oastler said. "Some doctor in Massachusetts with the name of Emma's character."

Jack must have looked stricken, or overeager to see the letter, because Leslie didn't immediately hand it over. "Someone you *know*?" she asked him.

"Someone I *knew*," he corrected her, holding out his hand. Mrs. Oastler looked the letter over—more carefully than she had the first time. "Emma knew that I knew her," Jack explained. "Emma knew she was using a real person's name."

"Sort of an inside joke—is that what you're saying, Jack?" She still wouldn't give him the letter.

"Sort of," he said.

"Would you like me to read it to you?" Leslie asked. Jack was still holding out his hand. " 'Dear Jack—' " Mrs. Oastler began, promptly interrupting herself. "Well, even your fans address you as 'Jack'—you can see why I never guessed that she actually *knew* you."

"Perfectly understandable," Jack said, his voice remaining calm.

"Dr. Maher—she's a *dermatologist,* of all things—goes on," Leslie continued. " 'I know you were close to Emma Oastler, and I've read that you're adapting her novel, *The Slush-Pile Reader,* as a film. Good luck with the screenplay, and your other projects. That novel is one of my favorites, not only because of the main character's name. With my best wishes, and congratulations on your considerable success as an actor.' Well, that's it," Mrs. Oastler said with a sigh. "It's a typed letter—probably someone else typed it. She just signed her name, 'Michele.' It's her office letterhead—some sort of doctors' office building at Mount Auburn Hospital in Cambridge, Massachusetts. On second thought, it's not *that* interesting a letter; there's nothing *per-*

sonal in it, really. No one reading this would dream that she ever knew you."

Leslie held the letter at arm's length in her hand—not quite as if it were dirty laundry, but something potentially worse, something she sensed Jack *wanted*. "May I see the letter, please?" he asked her.

"It's not the sort of letter one has to *answer*, Jack."

"Give me the fucking letter, Leslie!"

"I guess it wasn't a *funny* inside joke—Emma using Michele Maher's name," Mrs. Oastler said. She made him reach and take the letter from her hand.

The stationery was off-white, almost cream-colored—high quality. The sky-blue letterhead was printed in a large, clear font—Letter Gothic. Nothing *personal* about it, as Leslie had observed. "With my best wishes" didn't exactly convey a lot of warmth or affection.

"Now that I think of it, it's more of a *note* than a letter," Mrs. Oastler was saying, while Jack searched Michele's scrawled, almost illegible signature for some clue of her true feelings for him. "Personally, I don't like to touch anything a dermatologist has touched," Leslie went on. "But her letter's been around here so long—you don't suppose it could still be *contaminated*, do you?"

"No, I don't suppose so," Jack said.

That letter was coming to the North Sea and the Baltic with him; Jack would read it every day. He believed he would keep that distant, uncommitted, even loveless letter *forever*—knowing that it might be the only contact he would ever have with Michele Maher.

Jack couldn't get a direct flight to Copenhagen. He had an early-morning KLM connection out of Amsterdam, following an early-evening departure from Toronto. When it was time for him to go to the airport, Mrs. Oastler was taking a bath. Jack thought he might leave her a note on the kitchen table, but Leslie had other ideas.

"Don't you dare slip away without kissing me good-bye, Jack!" he heard her call from her bath. She always left the door to her bathroom open—usually the door to her bedroom, too.

They'd been alone together in the house for more than a week, after the bikers had left. But there'd been no nighttime visits, not a single trip down the hall. Not only had there been no penis-holding; there'd been no nakedness or near-nakedness in each other's company, either. Maybe Alice had wanted Leslie and Jack to sleep together a little too much. Despite the spell of attraction that existed between them, Jack believed that he and Mrs. Oastler were still resisting his mother; perhaps, he thought, the Skretkowicz sisters had broken the spell.

Anyway, a good-bye kiss was clearly in order. Jack dutifully traipsed upstairs. He tried not to notice the black bikini-cut underwear tossed on Mrs. Oastler's unmade bed. In the bathtub, Leslie's watchful, feral face was all that was visible above the suds of bubble bath. Under the circumstances, Jack imagined, this might turn out to be a fairly *innocent* good-bye kiss.

"You're not getting away from me, Jack," Mrs. Oastler said. "Emma and Alice have left me. You're not going to leave me, too, are you?"

"No, I won't leave you," he answered as neutrally as possible. She puckered up her small mouth and closed her dark eyes.

Jack knelt beside the bathtub and kissed her very lightly on the lips. Her eyes snapped open, her tongue slipping into his mouth. Leslie grabbed his wrist with her soapy hand and pulled his hand into the bathwater, soaking the sleeve of his shirt. If Jack had to guess where his fingers touched her underwater, he would say he made contact with Mrs. Oastler's Rose of Jericho before he could pull his hand away.

The kiss lingered a little longer. After all they'd been through, Jack didn't want to hurt her feelings. He tried not to let Leslie sense his impatience with her, but he was irritated that he would have to change his shirt.

Mrs. Oastler had never had the greatest esteem for Jack as an actor; probably because she'd known him as a child, she could always read his face. "Come on, Jack. I may not be Michele Maher, but it wasn't *that* bad a kiss, was it?"

"I have to change my shirt," Jack said, hoping she wouldn't notice his erection. Keeping his back turned to her, as he went out the open bathroom door, he added: "No, it wasn't bad at all."

"Just remember!" Leslie called after him. "It was what your mom *wanted*!"

Jack Burns carried that thought to Copenhagen; it felt heavier than his suitcase of winter clothes. He checked into the Hotel D'Angleterre—this time not the chambermaids' quarters but a room overlooking the statue in the square. Both the statue and the arch that stood over it were smaller than he remembered them, but Nyhavn was familiar—the boats slapping on the choppy water of the gray canal, the wind blowing off the Baltic. As for what he'd told his Skretkowicz sister, Jack had guessed right: it was raining.

When he unpacked, he found the photos of his mother's tattooed breast. Mrs. Oastler had carefully placed them on top of his clothes; she'd kept two for herself and had given him two, which seemed fair. Jack was happy to have them—not only for the purpose of verification. His mom had lied to him about so many things; maybe her *Until I find you* wasn't a Tattoo Ole, although Jack was pretty sure it was.

The tattoo parlor at Nyhavn 17 was still called Tattoo Ole. Some of the flash on the walls was Ole's, and the little shop still smelled of smoke and apples, alcohol and witch hazel; some of the pigments had special odors, too, although Jack couldn't identify them.

Bimbo was the man in charge; he'd come in 1975 and had trained with Tattoo Ole. Bimbo was short and powerfully built; he wore a navy watch cap. His flash was a lot like Ole's. A maritime man—an old-timer, Sailor Jerry would have said. Like Ole, Bimbo would never have called himself a tattoo *artist*. He was a tattooist or a tattooer of the old school, a man after Daughter Alice's heart.

Bimbo was working on a broken heart when Jack walked in. *Nothing really changes,* Jack was thinking. Bimbo didn't look up from his tattoo-in-progress. "Jack Burns," he said, as if he'd been expecting him; it wasn't the enthusiastic way Mr. Ramsey said Jack's name, but it wasn't unfriendly, either. "When I heard your mom died, I kind of figured you'd be coming," Bimbo said.

The boy getting the broken heart looked frightened. On his reddened chest, you could see his actual heart beating. The zigzag crack across his tattooed heart was horizontal; the wounded organ lay on a single rose, a real beauty. It was a very good tattoo. There was a banner unfurled across the bottom half of the heart—just a banner with no name on it. If the boy was smart, he would wait and add the name when he met someone who could heal him.

"Why did you think I'd be coming?" Jack asked Bimbo.

"Ole always said you'd be coming, with lots of questions," Bimbo explained. "Ole said you were pumped full of more misinformation than most magazines and newspapers, and that's saying something." Jack was beginning to guess that this was true. "Ole said, 'If that kid turns out to be crazy, I won't be surprised!' But you look like you turned out okay."

"I guess you didn't know my mother," Jack said.

"I never met the lady—that's true," Bimbo answered, choosing his words very carefully.

"Or my dad?" Jack asked.

"Everybody *loved* your dad, but I never met him, either."

That everybody *loved* his father came as something of a surprise to Jack. "I don't mean that *nobody* loved your mom," Bimbo added. "She just did some things that were hard to love."

"What things?" Jack asked him.

Bimbo exhaled softly—so did the boy getting the broken-heart tattoo. The boy's lips were dry and parted; he was gritting his teeth. "Well, you should talk to someone who really knew her," Bimbo told Jack. "I just know what I heard."

"Ole had another apprentice—at the same time my mom worked here," Jack said.

"Sure—I know him," Bimbo said.

" 'Ladies' Man,' Ole called him. We also called him 'Ladies' Man Lars' or 'Ladies' Man Madsen,' " Jack said.

"You mean the *Fish* Man," Bimbo corrected him. "He's no Ladies' Man anymore. He's in the fish business—not that there's anything wrong with that."

Jack remembered that the Madsen family's fish business was not an enterprise the Ladies' Man longed to join. Jack recalled how Lars had rinsed his hair with fresh-squeezed lemon juice.

Kirsten had been the tattoo on Ladies' Man Madsen's left ankle, the one entwined with hearts and thorns; in Jack's cover-up, he'd left Lars's left ankle with a confused bouquet. (It looked as if many small animals had been butchered, their hearts scattered in an unruly garden—a shrub of body parts.)

"So Lars went back to the fish business?" Jack asked.

"I wouldn't have let him tattoo me," Bimbo said. "Not even the shading."

"My mom tattooed him," Jack told Bimbo. A blushing-red heart, as Jack recalled; where the heart was torn in two, the jagged edges of the tear left a bare band of skin, wide enough for a name. There'd been some dispute about it, but Jack's mom had given Lars her signature on the white skin between the pieces of his torn heart—her very own *Daughter Alice*.

Jack began to describe the tattoo to Bimbo, but Bimbo cut him off. "I know the tattoo," the old maritimer said. "I covered up the Daughter Alice part."

So what *were* the things Alice did that were hard to love? Clearly *Fish* Man Madsen knew something about them; it seemed that the Ladies' Man had stopped loving Alice for some pretty good reason.

Bimbo said, "Tattoo Ole told me, 'If Jack comes back, tell him not to be too angry.' "

Jack thanked Bimbo for telling him this; Bimbo was also nice enough to interrupt his tattoo-in-progress to draw Jack a little map. Where they were on Nyhavn wasn't far from the Fiske-huset Højbro—the fish shop where Lars Madsen worked, at Højbro Plads 19. There was a statue of Bishop Absalon in the square, which was close to the Christiansborg Slot—the castle now occupied by the Danish Parliament. (Bishop Absalon was the founder of Copenhagen.) Jack could actually see the old castle from the fish market, Bimbo told him. According to Bimbo, the area was quite a popular meeting place nowadays—cafés and restaurants all around.

Jack almost forgot to show Bimbo the photographs, but he remembered as he was leaving. "Have a look at these," Jack said, handing Bimbo the two photos. "Does the tattoo look familiar?"

"I would know Tattoo Ole's work anywhere," Bimbo said, handing the photos back. "Ole told me he tattooed your mom." That was all the verification Jack needed.

Almost everything about the little shop seemed unchanged; even the radio was playing, if not the same radio. But that wasn't the way Bimbo saw things. As Jack was reaching for the door, Bimbo said: "It's all different now. In the late sixties and early seventies, you could recognize everyone's work. Your work was a kind of a signature. But not anymore; there are too many scratchers." Jack nodded. (He'd heard his mom say this—*all* the maritime tattooers said it.) "Twenty years ago," Bimbo said, "we had two ships a day in here. Now there's one a day," he said, as if that defined absolutely everything that was *different*.

"Thank you again," Jack told him.

It was a wet, windy afternoon. The restaurants on Nyhavn were already cooking. Jack could still distinguish the smells: the rabbit, the leg of deer, the wild duck, the roasted turbot, the grilled salmon, even the delicate veal. He could smell the stewed fruit in the sauces for the game, and those strong Danish cheeses. But he couldn't identify the restaurant where Ole and the Ladies' Man had taken him and his mom for their farewell dinner in Copenhagen. There'd been an open fireplace, and Jack thought he'd had the rabbit.

A place called Cap Horn at Nyhavn 21 looked vaguely familiar, but Jack didn't go inside. He wasn't hungry, and he couldn't wait to find Fish Man Madsen. Like Bimbo—even *more* than Bimbo, Jack imagined—the Ladies' Man was sure to be expecting him. And if Lars Madsen had covered up the *Daughter Alice* on his broken heart, he knew something Jack didn't know, and it must have hurt him.

Ladies' Man Madsen was still blond and blue-eyed; he had the same gap-toothed smile and busted nose, too. Jack was happy to see that Lars had lost the pathetic facial hair and had put on a little weight. The Fish Man was pushing fifty, but he looked younger. It seemed that the fish business had agreed with him, despite his earlier apprehensions—as if Alice's rejection had served Lars better than he'd expected, and his failure in the tattoo world had somehow preserved his innocence.

The Ladies' Man was married now; he and his wife had three kids. "You remember Elise?" he asked Jack, sheepishly.

"I remember covering up her name," Jack said.

Elise was the name he'd covered up on Lars's right ankle; she had formerly been attached to a chain-link fence, which Jack had mangled with his signature sprig of holly. (The result had called to mind a destroyed Christmas decoration— "anti-Christmas propaganda," Ole had called it.)

"Well, she came back, Jack," Ladies' Man Madsen said, smiling. "You couldn't cover Elise up for good."

Although the rain had stopped, it was still too damp and windy to sit outside at the sidewalk tables, but the view across the wet cobblestones—the gray castle, now the Parliament building—was just fine from the fish shop.

"Sometimes you were my babysitter," Jack began.

"I thought she was working late, Jack. I didn't know she was seeing the kid—I swear."

"What kid?"

"That poor little boy," Lars said.

"Stop," Jack said. "*What* little boy?"

Ladies' Man Lars looked very distressed. "Ole *said* this would happen!" he blurted out.

"*What* would happen?"

"*This*—you finding me!" Madsen said. "Okay, okay. Let's begin with that, Jack. How hard was it to find me?"

"Not very," Jack told him.

"It's not hard to find *anybody,* Jack—let's begin with that. Your mom was never looking for your dad. She'd already found him before she came here. Do you get that?"

"Yes, I get that," Jack said. "It was never about *finding* him, right?"

"That's right—you've got that right," the Ladies' Man said. "Okay, okay," he repeated. Jack realized that the Fish Man had been dreading this moment for almost thirty years! "Okay, okay. Here we go, Jack."

Because William thought that the news might *finally* persuade Alice to leave him alone—not to mention that he hoped Alice would allow him at least *occasional* visits with his son—Jack's father wrote to Alice in Toronto and told her that he was engaged to be married. The lucky girl was the daughter of the commandant at Kastellet, the Frederikshavn Citadel, where William Burns was apprenticed to the organist, Anker Rasmussen, in the Kastelskirken.

Jack thought he remembered the Ladies' Man telling him and his mom that William was involved with a military man's young *wife,* but William Burns had actually been engaged to a military man's *daughter.* There was no young wife; if Jack had heard of one, it was his mother who'd told him about her, not Lars. Alice had brought Jack to Copenhagen to prevent the marriage from ever taking place.

Hans Henrik Ringhof was the commandant's name. He was a lieutenant colonel. He loved William like a son, Lars Madsen told Jack. Lieutenant Colonel Ringhof had a young son, Niels, who was twelve going on thirteen. Niels's older sister, Karin—William's fiancée—doted on Niels. William was teaching Niels to play the organ; Niels was quite a gifted pianist. Karin was an accomplished organist; her late mother had been a musician. Lieutenant Colonel Ringhof had lost his wife in a car crash. The family had been returning to Copenhagen from a summer holiday in Bornholm when the accident happened.

They were a wonderful family, William wrote to Alice—he felt he was marrying all of them. Once Jack had started school, his father hoped that Jack's mother would allow the boy to spend part of his Christmas vacation in Copenhagen; William thought that Jack would find the atmosphere of the Frederikshavn Citadel stimulating at that time of year. There were Christmas concerts, and what boy wouldn't be excited to spend time in a fortification with all the soldiers?

"But your mother had her own agenda," Ladies' Man Madsen told Jack.

Soon Lieutenant Colonel Ringhof and his daughter were exposed to various sightings of Alice—and the same long-distance *sightings* of Jack that his mom had permitted his dad in Toronto. Nothing had changed in Alice. "She had a keep-me-or-lose-Jack mentality," as the Ladies' Man put it.

In Copenhagen, Alice added a new rule to the conditions she imposed on William: if he wanted to get a look at his son, William had to bring his fiancée with him. *She* had to see Jack, too. Naturally, it was Alice who wanted to get a look at Karin Ringhof, but Karin complied; she loved William and shared his hope that Alice would one day permit the boy to spend time with his father.

Additionally, Lars told Jack, Alice tried to seduce the only men in William's life who mattered to him. Anker Rasmussen, the organist, was justifiably appalled by her behavior—Rasmussen refused to see her. Lieutenant Colonel Ringhof, the widower who loved William almost as much as he loved his own little boy, was also appalled. Lieutenant Colonel Ringhof tried to reason with Alice, to no avail; he most certainly *didn't* sleep with her.

"The situation was at a standoff," Ladies' Man Madsen informed Jack. "Then you fell in the Kastelsgraven—the damn moat!"

"But what did that have to do with it?" Jack asked.

"Because the commandant sent little Niels to rescue you!" Lars told Jack. It was Niels Ringhof, *not* the littlest soldier, who'd saved him! "Until then," the Ladies' Man continued, "everyone had done a good job keeping your mom away from Niels. She barely knew he *existed.* I know that Niels knew nothing about her. But that was how she met him, Jack. Your mom must have said something to the boy; she must have thanked him for saving you, I suppose."

That had been *Jack's* idea—that his mom should offer his rescuer a free tattoo, not that a tattoo was what she offered Niels.

"She seduced the *kid*?" Jack asked Ladies' Man Madsen.

"She sure did, Jack. She got to him, somehow."

Niels Ringhof's clothes had almost fit Jack, but not the soldier's uniform; Niels had obviously borrowed or stolen it. Maybe that was how Alice had got him in and out of the citadel—she'd dressed him like a soldier. And that night she'd sent him back from the D'Angleterre, he must have walked home *alone*!

"He was *how* old? Did you say *twelve*?" Jack asked Lars.

"Maybe twelve going on thirteen, Jack. I'd say thirteen, *tops*."

Their last night in Copenhagen, Tattoo Ole and Lars had taken Jack and his mom to a fancy restaurant on Nyhavn. But William had picked up the tab. That would have been William's last *sighting* of his son in Copenhagen—his *and* Karin's last sighting, because Jack's mom insisted that his father bring Karin to the restaurant, too. ("To see us off," Alice had told William.)

"They were there, in the restaurant?" Jack asked Lars.

"At a table on the same side of the fireplace," the Ladies' Man answered. "You may remember the restaurant, Jack. You had the rabbit."

But Alice had *not* told Niels Ringhof that she was leaving; the twelve- or thirteen-year-old was crushed. Until Jack and his mom left Copenhagen, Karin Ringhof and her father, the commandant, had no idea that the boy had been seeing Alice—not to mention the depth of the child's infatuation with her. William had no idea, either.

"What happened to the kid?" Jack asked. It had started to rain again, which was not a good sign.

"Niels shot himself," Madsen said. "It was a barracks, after all—a military compound. There were lots of guns around. The kid either died of the gunshot wound or drowned in the Kastelsgraven. They found his body in the moat, about where you broke through the ice. He died where he saved you, Jack."

The moat, the Kastelsgraven, looked more like a pond or a small lake. In April, without the ice, the water had a greenish-gray color. Jack didn't think it looked deep enough to drown in, but it might have sufficed when he was four. And Niels Ringhof was only twelve or thirteen, and he'd just shot himself; clearly the Kastelsgraven had been deep enough for Niels.

If there'd been ice on the moat, Jack would have tested it again—this time hoping no one would save him. The wooden rampart, on which the soldiers' boots had made such a racket—putting even the ducks to flight—now looked like a toy road.

Of course Jack knew it hadn't been Anker Rasmussen, the organist, who'd come running with Alice. In all likelihood, there had never been a *soldier*-organist, a *military* musician, at the Kastelskirken. The man in uniform would have been the commandant, Lieutenant Colonel Ringhof; he'd sent for his young son, who was sick in bed, because the commandant knew that the ice would hold Niels but not a soldier.

That Jack still had that nightmare, when he dreamed of death, at last made sense to him on that April morning in Copenhagen. It was still raining, but what did it matter? In Jack's mind, he had already drowned. When he awoke, as he did every time, to a lasting cold, Jack now knew where the cold came from—from the moat, from the Kastelsgraven, where he always met those centuries of Europe's dead soldiers. The little hero who saved him stood out among them—most notably *not* for the disproportionate size of his penis, which Jack had probably exaggerated in his most unreliable memory, but for the stoic quality of his frozen salute.

Jack had correctly remembered the salute; it was not a real soldier's salute, but a young boy imitating a soldier. *Not* the littlest soldier in Jack's imagination, but Niels Ringhof, a twelve-year-old going on thirteen—a thirteen-year-old, *tops*—who'd been sexually abused by Jack's mother. (As surely as Mrs. Machado had molested Jack!)

He'd made an appointment to see the organist at the Kastelskirken, the Citadel Church. That view of the commandant's house from the church square was familiar to Jack; he remembered being carried from the Kastelsgraven to the commandant's house, where he was dressed in Niels Ringhof's clothes. (His *off-duty* clothes, Alice had called them. She'd been a gifted liar.)

The organist at the Citadel Church was Lasse Ewerlöf. A Swedish-sounding name—maybe he was Swedish. At the age of fourteen, he'd studied the sitar, the violin, and the piano; he'd started the organ relatively late, when he was nineteen or twenty. Jack was disappointed that Ewerlöf couldn't keep their appointment—he'd been called out of Copenhagen rather suddenly, to play the organ at an old friend's funeral—but he'd been kind enough to ask the backup organist at the Kastelskirken to meet with Jack instead.

Lasse Ewerlöf knew that Jack was interested in hearing a little Christmas music—just to imagine what he might have heard at those Christmas concerts his dad had thought would be stimulating to the boy. (The concerts he'd never heard.) Ewerlöf had left Jack a list of his Christmas organ favorites, which his backup—an older man, who told Jack he was semiretired because he suffered from arthritis in his hands—volunteered to play.

"But will it hurt your hands?" Jack asked him. The backup organist's name was Mads Lindhardt; he'd been a student of Anker Rasmussen's and had known Jack's father.

"Not if I don't play for too long," Lindhardt said. "Besides, I would consider it an honor to play for William Burns's boy. William was very special. Naturally, I was jealous of him when I first heard him play, because your father was always better than I was. Most unfair, because he's *younger!*"

Jack was unprepared to meet someone at Kastellet who'd actually known his dad—much less thought of William as "special." Jack couldn't respond; all he could do was listen to Mads Lindhardt play the organ. Jack could scarcely tell there was anything the matter with Lindhardt's hands.

They were alone in the Kastelskirken, except for a couple of cleaning women who were mopping the stone floor of the church; the women might have thought it strange to hear Christmas music on a rainy April morning, but the music didn't appear to interfere with their work.

Among Lasse Ewerlöf's Christmas favorites, Mads Lindhardt told Jack, were a few of William's favorites, too. Bach's *Weihnachtsoratorium* and his *Kanonische Veränderungen über das Weihnachtslied,* which Jack already knew his dad liked to play; also Messiaen's *La nativité du Seigneur* and Charpentier's *Messe de minuit,* which were new to Jack.

Jack realized, listening to Mads Lindhardt, that William would have (*many times*) imagined playing the organ for his son. But this had been forbidden, lost among the other things Alice had not permitted.

"It's *Christmas* music, Mr. Burns," Mads Lindhardt was say-

ing gently; only then did Jack notice that the organist had
stopped playing. "It's supposed to make you *happy*." But Jack
was crying. "That boy, Niels, was the darling of the citadel,"
Mads said. "And your father was the darling of the entire Ringhof family—that was why it was such a tragedy. No one blamed
your dad for what happened to Niels. But Karin had adored her
little brother; understandably, she simply could not look at your
father in the same way again. Even the commandant was sympathetic, but he was destroyed; for him, it was like losing *two*
sons."

"Where are they now?" Jack asked.

Lieutenant Colonel Ringhof had retired. He was an old man,
living in Frederiksberg—a place quite close to Copenhagen,
where many retired people went. Karin, the commandant's
daughter, had never married; she'd also moved away. She taught
music in Odense, at a branch of the Royal Danish Conservatory.

The only mystery remaining to the Copenhagen story was
why William had followed Alice and Jack to Stockholm. Jack
understood that it would have been painful—even impossible—
for his father to stay at the Frederikshavn Citadel, but why did
William follow them when Alice had caused him such a devastating loss?

"To see *you*," Mads Lindhardt told Jack. "How else was he
going to get a look at you, Jack?"

"She was crazy, wasn't she?" Jack asked. "My mother was a
madwoman!"

"Here is something Lasse Ewerlöf taught me," Mads Lindhardt said. " 'Most organists become organists because they meet
another organist.' " Lindhardt could see that Jack wasn't getting
his point. "Many women become crazy because they can't get
over the first man they fall in love with, Jack. What's so hard to
understand about that?"

Jack thanked Mads Lindhardt for his time, and for the Christmas concert. Leaving Kastellet, Jack regretted that he had not
seen a single soldier; maybe they didn't march around in the
rain. Leaving the Frederikshavn Citadel—as angry and sad-
dened as Jack now knew his father must have felt when *he* left
that fortification—Jack tried to imagine his dad's state of mind
as he had followed Alice and Jack to Stockholm.

En route to Stockholm—in advance of his second arrival—
Jack also tried to imagine what deceptions and outright deceits

his mother had created for him there. In Copenhagen, it was not the littlest soldier who had saved Jack—and his rescuer had been his mother's *victim*. Now he wondered if he had been saved by a Swedish accountant in Stockholm, or not. And who had been his mother's victim (or victims) *there*?

So much of what you *think* you remember is a lie, the stuff of postcards. The snow untrampled and unspoiled; the Christmas candles in the windows of the houses, where the damage to the children is unseen and unheard. Or what Jack *thought* he re-membered of the Hedvig Eleonora Church—the one with the golden altar in Stockholm, where his memory of meeting Tor-vald Torén, the young Swedish organist, was (Jack was sure) not exactly as it seemed.

Torén was real; Jack recognized him when they met again. But William hadn't slept with a single choirgirl—much less with *three*! Alice had invented Ulrika, Astrid, and Vendela; no won-der Jack had no memory of meeting them. In Stockholm, Jack's dad had been more celibate than a Catholic priest—well, *almost*.

The Hedvig Eleonora was Lutheran, and Torvald Torén had much enjoyed having William Burns as an apprentice; William was older than Torén and had actually taught the younger organ-ist a few pieces to play. Not for long: Alice had wasted little time in poisoning the congregation against William, whom she por-trayed as a runaway husband and father.

"What little I could manage to say in church every Sunday," Torvald Torén told Jack, "could never overturn that image of you and your mom at the Grand. It was a very visible place for her to be *soliciting,* which she was, and it was no life for a young boy like you—to be on *display*, as you were. Whether there, at the Grand, or skating on Lake Mälaren with your father's mistress— you *were* on display, Jack."

"What?" Jack said. Surely Torén couldn't have meant Torsten Lindberg's *wife*! (Agneta Nilsson, as Jack remembered her— because she preferred to use her maiden name.)

Torvald Torén shook his head. "I think you better talk to Torsten Lindberg, Jack," the organist said. Jack had been plan-ning to do so. He just happened to talk to Torén first; after all, it was easy to find him in the Hedvig Eleonora. It wasn't hard to find Lindberg, either—he still ate breakfast every day at the Grand.

Naturally, Agneta Nilsson, Jack's skating coach, had never been married to Torsten Lindberg. (Lindberg, Jack would soon discover, was *gay;* he always had been.) Agneta Nilsson had taught choral music at the Royal College of Music in Stockholm, where William was her favorite student. In his sorrow at the death of Niels Ringhof—not to mention the end of his engagement to Karin Ringhof, with whom William had been very much in love—William found comfort in the older woman's arms.

If Jack's father wanted to see his son in Stockholm—that is, in addition to watching the boy stuff his face at breakfast—Alice insisted that William watch Jack skate on Lake Mälaren with Agneta Nilsson, William's mistress.

"I have the room and the equipment, if you have the time," Jack had committed to memory—in English *and* in Swedish. (*"Jag har rum och utrustning, om ni har tid."*)

What a dance Alice had put them through—both Jack and his dad. "It was all done to torture them—I mean your father and poor Agneta," Torsten Lindberg told Jack, when Jack met him for breakfast at the Grand. "And I'm sure your mother knew that Agneta Nilsson had a bad heart. It was probably your father who told her—innocently, without a doubt."

"Agneta *died*?" Jack asked.

"She's dead, yes. I mean she died *eventually,* Jack. It wasn't overly *dramatic*—that is, it didn't happen on the *ice.* I'm not even suggesting that all the skating hastened her death."

"And the manager at the Grand?" Jack inquired.

"What about him?" Lindberg said.

"Was he *extorting* my mother?" Jack asked.

"Not the word I would use. Surely *she* seduced *him*—and she was the one who made their affair so *public,*" Torsten Lindberg informed Jack. "To disgrace your father, I suppose, but there was never any discernible *logic* that motivated Alice."

Torsten Lindberg was so obviously gay, but (at *four*) how would Jack have known? The accountant was no less thin than Jack remembered, his appetite no less voracious. Jack himself was eating a little more than usual for breakfast. This was not out of any fondness for the memory of eating there with his mom—on *display,* as he could now see—but because Jack was conscious of needing to put on a little weight for what he hoped would be his role as the failed screenwriter and successful porn star in *The Slush-Pile Reader*.

After breakfast, when Jack felt like throwing up, he asked Lindberg if he could see the accountant's Rose of Jericho. Jack thought there were some things in this world he could rely on—a few constants. Jack knew what his mom's Rose of Jericho looked like—surely he could count on that.

"My *what*?" Torsten Lindberg asked.

"Let's start with your fish," Jack said. "On your forearm, if I'm not mistaken, you have a Japanese tattoo of a fish."

"Oh, my fish out of water. *Yes!*" Lindberg cried. "My *tattoos*, you mean. Yes, of *course!*"

They went to Jack's room at the Grand. It was chiefly his mom's Rose of Jericho that Jack wanted to see. He wanted to look at Lindberg's Doc Forest, too. The clipper ship, a three-masted type, with a sea serpent cresting under its bow—that sailing ship on Torsten Lindberg's chest, the Doc Forest tattoo that Alice had said was better than the HOMEWARD BOUND vessel on the breastbone of the late Charlie Snow.

But could Jack believe *anything* his mother had told him? At least the Doc Forest was as Jack had remembered it. (What boy wouldn't recall a clipper ship endangered by a sea serpent?) As for the eyeball on the left cheek of Lindberg's ass, Jack had missed its gay implications the first time—not to mention the pair of pursed lips on the right cheek, like wet lipstick. The fish on Lindberg's forearm was almost exactly as Jack had remembered it—nothing gay intended by it, clearly.

As for Alice's Rose of Jericho, Jack had never seen the finished tattoo—he'd only heard it discussed as a work-in-progress. It was *not* a Rose of Jericho, of course. What would a gay man want with a vagina hidden in a rose? There was a rose, all right, but the penis was not what Jack would describe as hidden in the petals of that unruly flower. It was a penis practically *bursting out* of a rose!

"What did you call it?" Torsten Lindberg asked.

Jack had no idea what to call it—a *Penis* of Jericho, perhaps, but he thought it best to say nothing.

There was one other, lesser error in Jack's so-called memory of Torsten Lindberg's tattoos. Tattoo Ole's naked lady—she with her oddly upturned eyebrow of pubic hair. Well, she *was* one of

Ole's naked ladies—Jack could see that—but this naked lady had a penis, too.

"I've seen all your movies—I can't tell you how many times!" Torsten Lindberg told Jack. "I won't embarrass you, Jack, by telling you what my friends are *always* saying about you. Let's just say they *love* you as a she-male!"

At the Grand, Jack woke every morning to the ships' horns—the commuter traffic from the archipelago. One such morning, he went to see Lake Mälaren. Like the Kastelsgraven, it wasn't frozen—not in April—but it was possible to imagine where William might have stood to watch his son skating with his mistress with the bad heart, Agneta Nilsson.

As for Doc Forest's tattoo shop—the atmosphere was friendly and familiar.

Jack had never seen a photograph of his father. Jack knew only that William was good-looking to women, but that was not the same thing as a physical description. Doc Forest was the first person who actually described Jack's dad. "He had long hair, to his shoulders," Doc said. "He moved like an athlete, but he looked like a rock star—only better dressed."

Torvald Torén had already cast some doubt on the tattoo William was alleged to have gotten from Doc Forest—a piece by Pachelbel, Alice had said. (She'd suspected it might be something called *Hexachordum Apollinis;* she'd mentioned either an aria quarta or a toccata.)

"William played some Pachelbel, of course," Torén had told Jack. "But I never saw your father's tattoos." Mads Lindhardt had told Jack the same thing, not about Pachelbel but about William's tattoos.

Tattoo artists had seen The Music Man's tattoos—and the women William had slept with, surely. But at least two organists who'd known him well, and had liked him, had never seen his tattoos. Strange that his father didn't show them, Jack thought.

And since so much of what Alice had told Jack was bullshit, Jack was prepared—when he went to see Doc Forest—for the fact that his dad's Pachelbel tattoo might be bullshit, too.

There was no bullshit about Doc. He was glad to see Jack again, he said; he'd seen all of Jack's movies, including the ones in which Jack appeared half naked. Doc had been wondering when Jack was going to get a tattoo. It was an honor that Daughter Alice's son had come to Doc Forest for a tattoo, Doc told Jack.

Jack explained that he'd not come to see Doc for a tattoo.

Doc had aged well; he was still small and strong, and his sandy hair had not yet gone gray. For a former sailor who'd acquired his first tattoo in Amsterdam from Tattoo Peter, Doc Forest looked terrific.

Doc would not say an ill word about Alice—those old-timers, the *maritimers,* stuck together—but he had also liked Jack's dad. Doc had even gone to the Hedvig Eleonora to hear William play.

"I was wondering if you remember the tattoo you gave him, or perhaps you gave him more than one," Jack said. "A piece of music by Pachelbel, maybe."

"No music, just words," Doc said. "They might have been words in a song, but not a hymn. Not church music—I can tell you that."

"Do you remember the words?" Jack asked him.

Doc Forest's tattoo shop was as neat and trim as Doc. Sailors had to be organized—the good ones, anyway. It didn't take Doc long to find the stencil.

"Your dad was very particular about his tattoos," Doc Forest said. "He wouldn't let me write on his skin. He said he wanted to see my handwriting on a stencil first. He certainly was *particular* about the punctuation!"

Doc Forest's cursive was uniform and clear. The tattoo artists Jack had known all had excellent handwriting. The stencil was a little dusty, but Jack had no trouble reading the words and the *particular* punctuation.

The commandant's daughter; her little brother

"My first one of those," Doc said, pointing to the semicolon.

"It's not a song. It's more like a story," Jack told him.

"Well, your dad sure liked it. The tattoo, I mean," Doc said.

"How do you know?" Jack asked.

"He cried and cried," Doc Forest said.

With a tattoo, Jack remembered his mother saying, sometimes that's how you knew when you got it right.

28

The Wrong Tattoo

A child's memory is not only inaccurate—it's not reliably linear, either. Jack not only "remembered" things that had never happened; he was also wrong about the order of events, including at least one thing that had actually taken place. When Jack and his mom had gone downstairs for dinner in the Hotel Bristol, it wasn't their *first* night in Oslo—it was their *last*.

A young couple *did* come into the restaurant, just as Jack remembered. He'd thought it was the first time he saw how his mother looked when she encountered a couple in love. The young man was athletic-looking with long hair to his shoulders; he looked like a rock star, only he was better dressed. In fact, he looked exactly as Doc Forest had described William Burns—and his wife or girlfriend couldn't take her eyes or her hands off him. (Jack even remembered the young woman's breasts.)

Jack also recalled how he'd said to his mom that she should give the couple her sales pitch about getting a tattoo. "No," she'd whispered, "not them. I can't."

Jack had boldly taken matters into his own small hands. He'd walked right up to that beautiful girl and said the lines he still said in his bed, to help him sleep. "Do you have a tattoo?"

Well, that young man was Jack's father, of course—not that Jack knew it. Alice was offering William a last look at Jack before she and Jack left for Helsinki. (Jack didn't know who the girl was; not yet.) No one—certainly not Alice, least of all William—had expected Jack to *approach* the young couple, not to mention *speak* to them.

What was the matter with the guy? Jack had wondered. The handsome, long-haired young man looked almost as if it pained him to see Jack; William had regarded Jack as if he'd never seen a child before. But whenever Jack had looked at him, William had looked away.

And there'd been a bitterness in William's voice that made Jack look at him again—most notably when the young father had said to his son, "Maybe some other time."

"Come with me, my little actor," Alice had whispered in Jack's ear, and Jack's dad closed his eyes—William didn't want to see his son go.

It was after he'd checked into the Bristol in April of 1998—Jack was eating dinner alone in that quiet, old restaurant—when he realized he'd actually seen his father in that gloomy room.

"Maybe some other time," William had said; then Jack had reached for his mother's hand, and she'd taken the boy away.

William would have other sightings of Jack—in Helsinki and in Amsterdam, no doubt—but this might have been Jack's first and last look at his dad, and Jack had not known who William was!

But who was the young woman, and why had William brought her? Were they really in love? William must have known he was going to see his son; Jack's father just hadn't expected the boy to speak. William wasn't prepared for that—neither was Alice. Obviously, Jack had surprised them both.

It unnerved Jack to think he'd correctly remembered the meeting, but that he'd been wrong about when it happened; this made Jack not trust the seeming chronology of things. If he'd met his own father—not knowing that William was his father—on Jack and his mom's *last* night in Oslo instead of their *first*, when had his mother encountered Andreas Breivik? When had she offered Andreas a free tattoo? And when had Jack and Alice met the beautiful young girl with the speech impediment, Ingrid Moe?

Jack recognized the Oslo Cathedral when the taxi dropped him at the front entrance to the Bristol—the dome that greenish color of turned copper, the clock tower large and imposing. He decided he would go there in the morning and speak with the organist; that the organist would turn out to be Andreas Breivik was not the only surprise in store for Jack.

There was a new organ now—not the German-made Walcker, which Jack remembered had a hundred and two stops. (Even the organ that replaced the Walcker had been replaced.) The new one was special in its own way; Andreas Breivik told Jack all about it. If Breivik had been sixteen or seventeen when Alice seduced him—or gave him an *invisible* tattoo, as Alice might have put it—he was not a day over forty-five when he spoke with Jack in the Domkirke. But Andreas Breivik had made something of a maestro of himself, and his success had made him pompous.

His blond, blue-eyed good looks had not endured. A man with delicate features had to be careful. Breivik's face was slightly puffy; perhaps he drank. He gave Jack a virtual lecture on the subject of the cathedral's new organ, which had been completed only a month before Jack's arrival in Oslo—by a Finn living in Norway. (Jack couldn't have cared less about the organ, or the Finn.)

With a grandiose gesture to the green-and-gold instrument, which positively shimmered, Breivik said: "We have the funeral of King Olav the Fifth to thank for this. January 1991—I'll never forget it. The old Jørgensen was such a disgrace. The Prime Minister himself insisted that money be raised for a new organ."

"I see," Jack said.

Andreas Breivik had studied choral music in Stuttgart; he'd furthered his organ studies in London. (This hardly mattered to Jack, but he nodded politely; Breivik's education, not to mention his mastery of English, meant a great deal to Breivik.)

"I've seen your films, of course—very entertaining! But you don't seem to have followed in your father's musical footsteps, so to speak."

"No—no musical footsteps," Jack said. "I took after my mother, it seems."

"Are you tattooed?" Breivik asked.

"No. Are you?"

"Good Lord, no!" Andreas Breivik said. "Your dad was a talented musician, a generous teacher, an engaging man. But his tattoos were his own business. We didn't discuss them. I never saw them."

"Mr. Breivik, please tell me what happened. I don't understand what *happened*."

Jack remembered the cleaning woman in the church—how horrified she'd been to see him and his mom. He recalled what little he'd understood of his mom's seduction of Andreas Breivik, and how Ingrid Moe had come to her for a tattoo—how Ingrid had wanted a broken heart and Alice had given the girl a whole one. But why had Alice insisted on talking to Ingrid Moe in the first place, and what information about Jack's father could either Ingrid or Andreas possibly have given Jack's mom? His dad hadn't run away; Alice hadn't been trying to find William. What was there about William that Alice didn't already know?

Andreas Breivik was less pompous in relating *this* story; he wasn't proud of it, nor was it an easy story for him to tell. But the pattern, which Jack had failed to grasp till now, was really rather simple.

Everywhere Jack and his mom went, after Copenhagen, they arrived *ahead* of his dad. Alice not only expected William to follow them—she knew how much William wanted to see his son— but Alice also knew ahead of time where William would be inclined to travel next. You didn't just choose a church and an organ, Breivik told Jack; these appointments took time to arrange. There was always an experienced organist with whom a relatively *in*experienced organist wanted to study next, and the church where that mentor played had its own hierarchical way of choosing apprentices.

No organist wanted more than a few students, and only the most gifted students were chosen. With an organ, because of how many notes there were to play, sight reading was mandatory. Students with very narrow tastes, or those who disliked certain core composers, were generally discouraged; most younger students were irritating, because they liked to practice only loud or flashy music.

"You had to have a few irons in the fire," Andreas Breivik said. He meant that you had to be making plans way ahead of yourself. Where was the *next* organist you wanted to study with? What church? Which organ? In this world, you were both an apprentice and a teacher; as an apprentice, you also needed to go where you'd have students. (Not too many, but enough to pay the rent.)

This was the way it worked: when William was still playing the organ at the Citadel Church in Denmark, he was already thinking about Sweden—about apprenticing himself to Torvald Torén, about playing the organ at the Hedvig Eleonora in Stockholm—and all the while he was in Stockholm, William was planning to come (eventually) to Oslo, where he could study with Rolf Karlsen and play the organ at the Domkirke.

What Alice did, starting in Copenhagen, was to find out which irons in the fire were the hottest—what city was the next in line for William. Jack and his mom would go there, and Alice would establish herself; she would set up shop and wait for William to arrive. Then, systematically, Alice would set out to destroy the relationships William valued most. First of all, those friends he might have made in the church—possibly even the organist who was his mentor. But Alice more often chose easier targets; in the case of Oslo, she chose William's two best students, Andreas Breivik and Ingrid Moe.

Contrary to what Jack had believed for twenty-eight years, his dad *hadn't* seduced Ingrid Moe. She was sixteen at the time, and engaged to be married to young Andreas Breivik. They'd been childhood sweethearts; they even played the same instruments, first the piano and then the organ. And William prized them as students—not only because they were talented and hardworking, but also because they were in love. (Having been in love with Karin Ringhof, William Burns had a high regard for young musicians in love.)

"Your father was more than a terrific organist and a great teacher," Andreas Breivik told Jack. "In Oslo, the story of what had happened to him in Copenhagen preceded him. He was already a tragic figure."

"So my mother seduced you?" Jack asked him.

His once delicate, now slightly puffy features hardened. "I had known only Ingrid," Breivik said. "A young man who's had only one girlfriend is vulnerable to an older woman—perhaps especially to a woman with a reputation. Your mother put it to me rather bluntly: she said—she was teasing me, of course— 'Andreas, you're really just another kind of *virgin,* aren't you?' "

"Where did you tattoo him?" Jack remembered asking his mom.

"Where he'll never forget it," she'd whispered to Jack, smiling at Andreas. (Possibly the sternum, Jack had imagined; that would explain why the young man had trembled at her touch.)

"Just keep it covered for a day," Jack had said to Breivik, as the young organ student was leaving; it looked like it hurt him to walk. "It will feel like a sunburn," Jack had told him. "Better put some moisturizer on it."

But Andreas didn't know anything. After the organ student had gone, Alice had sobbed, "If he'd known anything, he would have told me."

She'd meant that Andreas Breivik didn't know what irons William had in the fire; the boy had no idea where William was thinking of going next. But Ingrid Moe knew, and Alice wasted little time in letting Ingrid know that she'd slept with the girl's fiancé. Ingrid had never felt so betrayed. Her speech impediment isolated her; she'd always been shy about meeting people. Ingrid couldn't forgive Andreas for being unfaithful to her. It didn't help that Alice wouldn't leave the girl alone.

Jack remembered that Sunday when his mom took the shirt cardboard to church—how she'd stood in the center aisle at the end of the service, with the shirt cardboard saying INGRID MOE held to her chest. Jack had thought Rolf Karlsen must have been playing the organ that Sunday, because everyone said Karlsen was such a big deal and the organ sounded especially good.

But the organist that Sunday had been William Burns. It was the one time his father had played the organ for Jack, but—not unlike how the boy had met his dad in the restaurant at the Hotel Bristol—Jack didn't know it, and neither did William.

"I'm sorry he hurt you," Alice had said to Ingrid Moe, when the girl had come to the hotel for her broken-heart tattoo. But the *he* had been Andreas Breivik, who'd slept with Jack's mother—*not,* as Jack had thought, his father, who had *never* slept with Ingrid Moe.

Jack remembered how Ingrid's exquisite prettiness was marred by what an obvious strain it was for her to *speak.* Not that he'd understood her very well; for all these years, Jack had thought of her speech impediment as an agony connected with *kissing.* (When he'd imagined his father kissing the girl, Jack had felt ashamed.)

"I won't do his name," Alice had told Ingrid.

"I don't want his name," the girl had answered—clenching her teeth together when she talked, as if she were afraid or unable to show her tongue. She'd wanted just a heart, ripped in two.

Then Alice had given her a whole heart instead—a perfectly *un*broken one, as Jack recalled.

"You didn't give me what I wanted!" Ingrid Moe had blurted out.

"I gave you what you *have,* a perfect heart—a small one," Alice had told her.

"I'm not telling you anything," the girl had said.

She'd told Jack instead—"Sibelius," she'd said. Not the composer but the name of a music college in Helsinki, where

William's *next* best students would come from. (New students were part of what Andreas Breivik meant by irons in the fire.)

"Ingrid quit the organ," Andreas told Jack. "She went back to the piano, without much success. I stayed with the organ. I kept growing, as you have to," he said, with no small amount of pride. "Ingrid's marriage didn't have much success, either."

Jack didn't like him; Breivik seemed smug, even a little cruel. "What about *your* marriage?" Jack asked him. "Or didn't you get married?"

Andreas shrugged. "I became an organist," he said, as if that were all that mattered. "I'm grateful to your mother, if you really want to know. She saved me from getting married at a time when I was far too young to be married, anyway. I would have had a time-consuming personal life, when what I needed was to be completely focused on my music. As for Ingrid, in all likelihood, she would have chosen a personal life over a career—whether she married me or someone else. And I don't think her personal life would have worked out any better, or differently, if she'd been married to me. With Ingrid, things just wouldn't have worked out—they just *didn't*."

Like some other successful people Jack had known, Andreas Breivik had all the answers. The more Breivik said, the more Jack wanted to talk with Ingrid Moe. "There's one other thing," Jack said. "I remember a cleaning woman in the church—an older woman, well-spoken, imperious—"

"That's impossible," Breivik said. "Cleaning women aren't well-spoken. Are you telling me this one spoke *English*?"

"Yes, she did," Jack replied. "Her English was quite good."

"She couldn't have been a cleaning woman," Andreas said with irritation. "I don't suppose you remember her name."

"She had a mop—she leaned on it, she pointed with it, she waved it around," Jack went on. "Her name was Else-Marie Lothe."

Breivik laughed scornfully. "That was Ingrid's *mother*! I'll say she was *imperious*! You got that right. But Else-Marie wasn't *that* well-spoken; her English was only *okay*."

"Her last name was Lothe. She had a mop," Jack repeated.

"She was divorced from Ingrid's father. She'd remarried," Andreas said. "She had a *cane,* not a mop. She broke her ankle getting off the streetcar right in front of the cathedral. She caught

her shoe in the trolley tracks. The ankle never healed properly—
hence the cane."

"She had dry hands, like a cleaning woman," Jack mentioned
lamely.

"She was a potter—the artistic type. Potters have dry hands,"
Breivik said.

Needless to say, Else-Marie Lothe had hated Alice; she'd
ended up hating Andreas Breivik, too. (Jack could easily see
how that could happen.)

Jack asked Breivik for Ingrid Moe's married name and her address.

"It's so unnecessary for you to see her," Andreas said. "You
won't find her any easier to understand this time." But, after
some complaining, Breivik gave Jack her name and address.

Under the circumstances, it turned out that Andreas Breivik
knew more about Ingrid Moe than Jack would have thought. Her
name was Ingrid Amundsen now. "After her divorce," Breivik
said, "she moved into a third-floor apartment on Theresesgate—
on the left side of the street, looking north. You can walk from
there to the center of Oslo in twenty-five minutes." Breivik said
this with the dispassion of a man who had *timed* the aforementioned walk, more than once. "The blue tram line goes by," Andreas continued, as slowly as if he were waiting for the tram.
"Since the new Rikshospitalet was built, there are three different
lines passing. The noise might have bothered Ingrid to begin
with, but she probably doesn't hear it any longer."

Ingrid Amundsen was a piano teacher; she gave private
lessons in her apartment.

"Theresesgate is quite a nice street," Andreas said, closing his
eyes, as if he could walk the street in his sleep—of course he
had. "Down at the south end, toward Bislett Stadium, which is
only a five-minute walk from Ingrid's, there are a few cafés, a decent bookstore—even an antiquarian bookstore—and the usual
7-Eleven. Closer to Ingrid, on her side of the street, is a large
grocery store called Rimi. There's a nice vegetable store next
to the Stensgate tram stop, too. It's run by immigrants—Turkish,
I think. You can buy some imported specialties—marinated
olives, some cheeses. It's all very modest, but nice." Breivik's
voice trailed away.

"You've never been *inside* her apartment?" Jack asked him.
Breivik shook his head sadly. "It's an old building, four sto-

ries, built around 1875. It's a bit shabby, I suppose. Knowing Ingrid, she probably would have kept the original wooden floors. She would have done some of the renovating herself. I'm sure her children would have helped her."

"How old are her children?" Jack asked.

"The daughter is the older one," Breivik told Jack. "She's living with a guy she met in university, but they don't have children. She lives in an area called Sofienberg. It's a very popular and hip place for young people to live. The daughter can get on a tram in Trondheimsveien and be at her mother's in about twenty minutes; by bicycle, it would take her ten or fifteen. I imagine, if she had children, she'd want to move out of central Oslo—maybe Holmlia, an affordable area, where there are still *almost* as many Norwegians as there are immigrants."

"And Ingrid has a son?" Jack asked.

"The boy is studying at the university in Bergen," Andreas Breivik said. "He visits his mother only during vacations."

Jack liked Breivik a little better after this conversation. Jack nearly told Andreas that he would come see him after he visited with Ingrid—and that he would describe the interior of her apartment to him so that the organist could imagine the *interior* part of Ingrid's life as obsessively as he'd imagined the rest of it. But that would have been cruel. Andreas was probably unaware of what an *investigation* he'd made of his former girlfriend.

Ingrid Moe had been sixteen when Jack had covered the tattoo on her heart-side breast with a piece of gauze with Vaseline on it. He remembered that he'd had some difficulty getting the adhesive tape to stick to her skin, because she was still sweating from the pain.

"Have you done this before?" Ingrid had asked.

"Sure," Jack had lied.

"No, you haven't," she'd said. "Not on a breast."

When he'd held the gauze against her skin, Jack could feel the heat of her tattoo—her hot heart burning his hand through the bandage.

Like Andreas Breivik, Ingrid Amundsen would be about forty-five now.

"What a waste!" Andreas cried out suddenly, startling Jack. "She had such long fingers—perfect for playing the organ. The *piano*," Breivik said contemptuously. "What a *waste*!"

* * *

Jack remembered her long arms and long fingers. He remembered her thick blond braid, too—how it hung down her perfectly straight back, reaching almost to the base of her spine. And her small breasts—especially the left one, which Jack had touched with the tattoo bandage.

When Ingrid Moe (now Amundsen) spoke, she curled back her lips and bared her clenched teeth; the muscles of her neck were tensed, thrusting her lower jaw forward, as if she were about to spit. It was tragic, he'd thought, that such a beautiful girl could be so instantly transformed—that the not-so-simple act of speaking could make her ugly.

Jack was a little afraid of seeing her again. "That girl is a heart-stopper," his mother had said twenty-eight years before.

"You have your father's eyes, his mouth," Ingrid had whispered to Jack, but her speech impediment had made a mess of her whisper. (She'd said "mouth" in such a way that the mangled word had rhymed with "roof.") And Jack had thought he would faint when she kissed him. When her lips opened, her teeth had clicked against his; he remembered wondering if her speech impediment was contagious.

Was there a problem with her tongue? Of course there might have been nothing the matter with Ingrid's *tongue.* Jack had not asked Andreas Breivik about the *source* of Ingrid's speech impediment; naturally, he had no intention of asking Ingrid.

When Jack called her, from the Bristol, he was afraid she wouldn't see him. Why would she want to be reminded of what had happened? But it was stupid to try to deceive her, and Jack didn't do a very good job of it. ("Some actor *you* are!" Emma would have told him.)

When Ingrid Amundsen answered the phone, Jack was completely flustered that she said something in Norwegian. Well, what else would the poor woman speak in *Norway*?

"Hello? I'm an American who finds himself in Oslo for an indefinite period of time!" Jack blurted out, as if there were worse things the matter with him than a speech impediment. "I want to keep up my piano lessons."

"Jack Burns," Ingrid said; the way she spoke, Jack could hardly recognize his own name. "When you speak the way I do," she continued, "you listen very closely to other people's voices. I would know your voice anywhere, Jack Burns. About the only thing I have in common with people who can talk *normally* is that I've seen all your movies."

"Oh," Jack said, as if he were four years old.

"And if *you* play the piano, Jack, you probably play better than I do. I doubt I can teach you anything."

"I don't play the piano," he confessed. "My mother's dead and I don't know my father. I wanted to talk with you about him."

Jack could hear her crying; it wasn't pretty. She couldn't even *cry* normally. "I'm *glad* your mother's dead!" she said. "I think I'll have a party! I would *love* to talk to you about your father, Jack. Please come talk with me, and we'll have a little party."

He remembered watching her walk away from him—down the long, carpeted hall of the Bristol. She'd been sixteen going on thirty, as he recalled. From behind, she didn't look like a child; she'd walked away from him like a woman. And what a voice—that voice had always been sixteen going on forty-five.

Although it was raining, Jack stood for fifteen minutes outside her building on the Theresesgate—fortunately, under an umbrella. The taxi had brought him sooner than he'd expected. Ingrid had invited him at five in the afternoon, which was when her last piano student of the day would be leaving. Jack looked up from his watch and saw a boy about twelve or thirteen coming out of Ingrid's building. He *looked* like a piano student, Jack thought—a little dreamy, a little delicate, a little like it wasn't entirely *his* idea to be doing this.

"Excuse me," Jack said to the boy. "Do you play the piano?" The kid was terrified; he looked as if he were sizing up which way to run. "Forgive me for being curious," Jack said, hoping to sound reassuring. "I just thought you looked very *musical*. Anyway, if you *are* a piano player, keep doing it. Never stop! I can't tell you how much I regret that I stopped."

"Bugger off!" the boy said, walking backward away from him. To Jack's surprise, the boy had an English accent. "You look like that creep Jack Burns. Just bugger off!"

Jack watched him run; the boy went in the direction of the Stensgate tram stop. Jack imagined that the piano student was about the age of Niels Ringhof when Niels had slept with Jack's mother. He rang the buzzer for AMUNDSEN—no first name, no initial.

It was a third-floor walk-up, but even a snob like Andreas Breivik might have enjoyed the view. The kitchen and the two smaller bedrooms overlooked the Stensparken—a clean-looking park situated on a hill. At the south end of the park, Ingrid pointed out the Fagerborg Kirke—the church where she went every Sunday. On Sunday mornings, she told Jack, you could hear the church bells in the whole area.

"The organist at the Fagerborg Church isn't in the same league as your father or Andreas Breivik," Ingrid said, "but he's more than good enough for a simple piano teacher like me."

She'd learned to conceal her mouth with her long fingers when she spoke, or to always speak when her face was turned slightly away. The constant movement of her long arms, as if she were conducting music only she could hear, was very graceful; she was a head taller than Jack, even in her white athletic socks. (She made him take off his shoes at the door.)

Breivik had been right about the floors—she'd saved the original wood. Her son had helped her remove the old layers of lacquer. The kitchen was the best room in the apartment; it had been remodeled in the early nineties. "With cupboards and all the rest from IKEA—nothing fancy," Ingrid said. It was a blue-and-white kitchen with a wooden workbench, and a kitchen table with three chairs around it; there was no dining room.

In the living room, which faced the street, there was an old fireplace, and the original stucco work was intact. The piano faced a wall of photographs—family pictures, for the most part. The biggest of the three bedrooms, which was Ingrid's, also faced the street—not the park.

"I think the park is rather lonely at night," she told Jack, "and besides, my children wanted views of the park from their bedrooms. There have been no difficult decisions in this apartment." She had an interesting way of speaking—that is, in addition to her speech impediment.

The thick braid that had hung to her waist was gone; her hair was slightly shorter than shoulder-length now, but still blond with only hints of silver in it. She wore jeans, and what may have been her favorite among her son's left-behind shirts—a man's flannel shirt, untucked, like Miss Wurtz had once worn.

"I wore this for you, because it's so American," Ingrid said, plucking at the shirt with her long fingers. "I never dress up or wear any makeup in this apartment." (Another not-difficult decision, Jack imagined.) "If I dressed up and wore makeup, it might make my pupils nervous."

Jack said that he thought he'd met one of her pupils, and that he'd probably made him nervous—without meaning to. "An English boy, about twelve or thirteen?" Jack asked.

She nodded and smiled. Many of her students were from diplomats' families; the parents wanted their children to be occupied with cultural things. "To keep them from being at loose ends," Ingrid said. "Not a bad reason for playing the piano."

Jack asked her if she would play for him, but she shook her head. The apartment wasn't soundproofed, she explained. In the old building, her neighbors could hear the piano through the walls. She stopped playing after five in the afternoon, and the first of her students never came to the apartment before nine—more often ten—in the morning.

She and Jack sat in the kitchen, where Ingrid made some tea. Her cheeks were a little sunken in, but she was still beautiful; nothing of what had been baby-faced about her remained, and her long limbs and broad hips had always given her a womanly appearance. She was more handsome than pretty, befitting the mother of two grown children—the children's photos were all over the apartment, not just on the wall behind the piano.

Jack had spotted a nice-looking man with the children, when the kids were younger; he was a sailor in some of the pictures, a skier in others. The children's father, Ingrid's ex-husband, Jack assumed; the man looked *nice* in the way Emma had once defined the word, meaning that he looked *normal.* Everything about Ingrid seemed normal, too—in the best sense of the word.

"I shouldn't have said I was *glad* your mother was dead. That's an awful thing to say about a mother to her son!" she exclaimed. "I'm sorry."

"No, don't be sorry," Jack said. "I understand."

"I hated her twice," Ingrid told him. "For what she did to me, for seducing Andreas—of course I hated her for that. But when I had children of my own—when they were the age *you* were when I met you—I hated your mother all over again. I hated her for what she did to *you.* First I hated her as a woman, *then* as a mother. No woman can have children and continue to think of herself first, but *she* did. Alice wasn't thinking of you—of you not having a father. She was thinking only about herself."

Jack couldn't say anything; everything Ingrid said sounded true. He couldn't argue with her, but he also couldn't agree with her—not with any authority. What did Jack Burns know about having children, and how having children changed you? He finally said: "You have a *third* reason to hate her—for your tattoo. I remember that it wasn't what you asked for."

Ingrid laughed; her laughter was more natural-sounding than the way she had cried on the telephone. She was moving gracefully around the kitchen—opening the refrigerator, putting food on the table. Jack realized that she'd prepared a cold supper—gravlaks with a mustard sauce, a potato salad with cucumber and dill, and slices of very dark rye bread.

"Well, it was *just* a tattoo—it wasn't life-changing," she was saying. "But I was proud of myself for telling her what I wanted. I knew she would hate the idea. 'A whole heart, a perfectly *un*-broken one,' I told her. 'A heart my babies will one day love to touch,' I said. 'There's not a thing the matter with my heart,' I told your mother. 'Maybe just make it a little smaller than average,' I told her, 'because my breast is a little smaller than average, too.' I thought I was so brave to tell her this, when all the while my heart was broken. Andreas and your mother had broken it, but I wasn't going to let *her* know that."

"What did you say?" Jack asked her. It wasn't the speech impediment; he was pretty sure he had understood her. "You didn't *ask* for a broken heart, Ingrid?"

"*Ask?* Who would *want* one?" she exclaimed. "I asked your mother for the kind of heart I had before she fucked Andreas!" Ingrid was lighting a candle; she'd already arranged the place settings. She hadn't turned a light on in the kitchen, preferring the dusk and the view of the Stensparken. "And the bitch gave me a broken heart!" Ingrid said. "As ugly a heart as one could imagine. Well, you put the bandage on it, Jack. *You* remember."

"I remember it the other way around," he told her. She was pouring herself a glass of wine. (Somehow she knew Jack didn't drink; she told him later that she'd read about his being a teetotaler in an interview.) "I remember you asking for a heart ripped in two, and my mom gave you a *good* one."

"She gave me a *good* one, all right," Ingrid said. She stood next to Jack's chair and unbuttoned the flannel shirt; she wasn't wearing a bra. (He thought of Miss Wurtz in a shirt like that, without a bra—unbuttoning her shirt for his father.)

Even at dusk, in the dim candlelight, the tattoo of Ingrid Amundsen's torn heart looked like a fresh wound—the jagged tear cut the heart diagonally in two. The blood-red edges of the tear were darker than the shading of the heart, and more sharply defined than the outline. Jack had not seen his mother do an uglier tattoo, but Ingrid seemed accepting of it.

"Well, guess what?" she said, buttoning her shirt back up. "My babies *loved* it! They *loved* to touch it! And I came to realize that your mother had given me the heart I had—not the heart I *used to* have. How much more cruel it would have been to walk around wearing the heart I *used to* have. Not that Alice was consciously doing me a favor." She sat down at the table and served him. "*Bon appétit,* Jack," she said. "When I see you in the movies, I think of how proud you must make your father—and how it must have hurt your mother to see you."

"*Hurt* her? How?" he asked.

"Because she finally had to *share* you," Ingrid said. "She never knew how to share you, Jack."

The food was very good, and Jack was hungry; it seemed strange that there wasn't any music, but music is never *background* music to musicians.

"Your father was very religious," Ingrid told him when he was helping her do the dishes. "It's hard to play church music in a church and *not* be, although I wasn't. I became more religious when I went back to playing the piano—that is, *not* in a church."

"How was he *very religious*?" Jack asked.

"When Andreas and your mother hurt me, William told me something. He said, 'Find someone; devote yourself to that person; have a child, or children; praise God.' Not that it ever worked out that way for me! But that's what William told me; that's what *he* believed in. Well, I got the children, and I praise God. That's been good enough."

"So you're religious, too?" he asked.

"Yes—but not like your father, Jack."

"Tell me more about the religious part," he said.

"Take your mother, for example," Ingrid said a little impatiently. "Your father forgave her. I didn't."

"He forgave her?"

"He fought back once, but it backfired. I don't think he fought back again," she told him. It was as if her speech impediment had almost gone away, or he'd forgotten it; she was such a healthy person, Jack was thinking.

She'd gone into the living room and had come back to the kitchen with a photograph. "A pretty young woman, don't you think?" she asked, showing him the picture. Jack recognized the beautiful girl in the photograph; it was the woman William had brought with him to the restaurant in the Hotel Bristol.

"I asked her if she had a tattoo," Jack said.

"That was what backfired," Ingrid told him. "Your dad didn't expect you would *speak* to them. He felt awful."

"Who was the girl?" Jack asked.

"My sister, an actress," Ingrid said. "She's not a movie star, like you—but in Norway she's a little bit famous, in the theater. I convinced your father to take her with him. I thought it would serve your mother right. Alice was always telling him how and when he could get a look at you. In Copenhagen, and in Stockholm, she even told him who to have *with* him!"

"Yes, I know," Jack said.

"So I told him to take my sister, the actress, and I told my sister to fall all over him. I said to them both, 'Make the bitch think you're in love with each other. Make her think that all the lies she tells Jack have come true!' But then you went up to them, and they didn't know what to do. Naturally, your mom fell apart, and she took you away again. She was always taking you away."

"Yes," he said.

"Your father told me: 'Maybe forgiveness would have worked better, Ingrid.' But I told him that nothing would work with Alice. Nothing worked—did it, Jack?"

"No, nothing worked," he answered.

"Your father said: 'God wants us to forgive each other, Ingrid.' That's all I know about the religious part, Jack."

It was dark outside—the lonely time of night in the Stensparken—and the candle on the kitchen table was the only light in the darkening apartment. "Look how dark it is, Jack Burns," Ingrid whispered, bending down to touch his ear with her clenched teeth. "You're still a little boy to me. I can't let you go home in the dark."

Even with her speech impediment, she made it sound as if this were another *not-difficult* decision in her fabulous apartment, where there'd been no difficult decisions—not ever.

Kissing Ingrid Amundsen was almost normal; there was an unnatural sound she made when she swallowed, when she was kissing him, but it wasn't unpleasant. Jack held his mom's ripped-heart tattoo on Ingrid's small left breast—exactly where her babies had been delighted to touch her.

Ingrid had no breasts to speak of, and the blue veins in her forearms stood out against the gold of her skin—just as he'd remembered. Another blue vein, which began at her throat, ran down between her small breasts; that vein seemed to have a pulse in it, as if an animal lived under her skin. Maybe the animal affected her speech. At least he'd remembered her veins correctly.

"I used to think about which of us was the more damaged, but we're all right, aren't we?" Ingrid asked him; her poor voice sounded awful at that moment.

"Yes, I think so," Jack said, but he didn't really feel that he was all right—and he couldn't tell about Ingrid. She had the aura of an accepted sadness about her. Jack hated to think of her meeting people for the first time, and what that did to her. He was even angry at her son, who'd gone off to the university in Bergen. Couldn't the kid have stayed in Oslo and seen more of his mother?

Yet Ingrid's life, her seeming wholeness, impressed Jack as more likable than whatever life Andreas Breivik was living. Breivik's opinion—namely, that Ingrid had not had much success at anything—struck Jack as arrogant and wrong. But Andreas had known her better than Jack did. She was such a beautiful yet flawed woman; it hadn't been hard for Jack's mom to make the boy believe that Ingrid and William had been lovers. (Who *wouldn't* have been her lover?)

"It couldn't have been as bad for your father *anywhere* as it was in Copenhagen," Ingrid told Jack, "but I don't think that the problems with your mother ever got better. Not in Helsinki, anyway. Alice was perfectly awful to him there. But she didn't achieve her desired effect. I think your mom started running out of steam in Helsinki, Jack." (That had always been Jack's impression.)

"What happened in Helsinki?" he asked her.

"I don't know *everything,* Jack. I just know that Alice tried to break up a lesbian couple, but she couldn't manage it. They both slept with her—and had a good time, or not—but they went right on being a couple!"

"Who were they?" Jack asked.

"Music students—your dad's two best, like Andreas and me. Only one of them was an organist; the other one was a cellist."

"Ritva and Hannele were *gay*?" Jack asked.

"Their names sound familiar," Ingrid said. "The point is, Jack—your mother, once again, didn't get what she wanted. But neither did your father."

"You stayed in touch with him?" Jack asked.

"Till he left for Amsterdam," Ingrid told him. "Whatever happened there, he didn't write me about it. I lost touch with him when he left Helsinki."

The kissing had become more interesting; it was principally her speech that was damaged. There was something detectably but indefinably strange about her mouth—if not actual damage, a kind of involuntary tremor that felt like damage. Jack didn't know what it was, but it was very arousing.

It seemed the wrong time to ask her, but the thought had occurred to Jack—when she implied she'd had some limited correspondence with his father, if only when William was in Finland. Jack just had to ask her: "Was there anything romantic between you and my dad, Ingrid?"

"What a thing to ask me—you naughty boy!" she said, laughing. "He was a lovely man, but he wasn't my type. For one thing, he was too short."

"Shorter than I am?" Jack asked.

"A *little* shorter, maybe—not much. Of course I was never with him when I was lying down!" she added, laughing again. Ingrid grabbed Jack's penis, which in his experience implied an impatience with the particular conversation—whatever it was.

"So *I'm* not your type, either?" he asked.

She kept laughing; it was the most natural sound she was capable of making. (Except, perhaps, on the piano.) "I have other reasons for wanting to sleep with you, Jack," was all she told him.

"What other reasons, Ingrid?"

"When you've made love to me again and again, I'll tell you," she said. "I'll tell you later—I promise." There was an urgency about her speech impediment now, something more than impatience. He began by kissing her broken-heart tattoo, which seemed to make her happy.

In the morning, Jack woke her by kissing the tattoo again; it looked as if it were still bleeding. She smiled before she opened her eyes. "Yes, keep doing that," Ingrid said, with her eyes still closed. He kept kissing her wounded-heart tattoo. "If you keep doing that, I'll tell you what I believe about Hell." Her eyes were wide open now—Hell being an eye-opening subject. He kept kissing her, of course.

"If you hurt people, if you *know* you're hurting them, you go to Hell," Ingrid said. "In Hell you have to watch the people you hurt, the ones who are still alive. If *two* people you hurt ever get together, you have to watch everything they do very closely. But you can't hear them. Everyone in Hell is deaf. You just have to watch the people you hurt without knowing what they're talking about. Of course, Hell being Hell, you think they're talking about you—it's all you ever imagine, while you're just watching and watching. Kiss me everywhere, Jack—not just the tattoo." He kissed her everywhere; they made love again. "What a bad night's sleep your mother's had, Jack," Ingrid said. "She's been up all night, just *watching*."

Jack had fallen back to sleep when he heard the piano. There was the smell of coffee in the apartment. He got out of bed and went into the living room, where Ingrid was sitting naked at the piano, playing softly. "Nice way to wake up, isn't it?" she asked, with her back turned to him.

"Yes, it is," he told her.

"We both have to get dressed, and you have to go," she said. "My first pupil is coming."

"Okay," Jack said, turning to go back to her bedroom.

"But come kiss me first," she said, "while the bitch is watching."

There was a lot Jack didn't know about religion. His dad, apparently, was a *forgiver.* Ingrid Moe (now Amundsen) wasn't; she hadn't forgiven Andreas Breivik *or* Alice. As Jack kissed Ingrid on her damaged mouth, he was thinking that he wasn't much of a forgiver, either.

In Hell, where his mother was watching, Alice might have regretted giving Ingrid the wrong tattoo—or so Jack Burns was also thinking.

29

The Truth

Jack never saw what the rest of Finland looked like. It was dark all the way from the airport into Helsinki. Although it was April, it was almost snowing; one or two degrees colder, and the rain would have turned to snow.

He checked into the Hotel Torni, marveling at the large, round room on the first floor, which served the hotel as a lobby. Jack remembered it as the American Bar—a hangout for the young and wild, some brave girls among them. The old iron-grate elevator, which had been "temporarily out of service" for the duration of Jack's time in the Torni with his mom, was now working.

But although the American Bar was gone, the Torni was still a hangout for young people. On the ground floor was an Irish pub called O'Malley's; shamrocks all over the place, Guinness on draft. It was an unwise choice for the Jack Burnses of this world—it was packed with more moviegoers than Coconut Teaszer. But Jack wasn't hungry, and he'd slept on the plane. He didn't feel like eating or going to sleep.

A not-bad band of Irish folksingers was playing to the pub crowd—a fiddler, a guitarist, and a lead singer who said he loved Yeats. He'd left Ireland for Finland fifteen years ago.

Jack talked to the band members between sets. The young Finns in the pub were shy about speaking to Jack, although they did their share of staring. When the Irish folksingers went back to work, a couple of Finnish girls started talking to Jack. They didn't seem all that brave; in fact, they were very tentative. He couldn't tell what they expected, or what they wanted to happen. First one of them began to flirt with him; then she stopped flirting and the other one started.

"You can't dance to this music," the one who'd stopped flirting remarked.

"You look like you don't need music to dance," the one who'd started flirting said to Jack.

"That's right," he told her.

"I suppose you think I was suggesting something," she said.

Jack wasn't about to mess up his memory of Ingrid Moe by sleeping with either of the Finns, or with both of them. He thought he was hungry enough to eat a little something. But when he said good night to the Finnish girls, one of them remarked: "I guess we're not what you're looking for."

"Actually," Jack told them, "I'm looking for a couple of lesbians." What a waste of a good end line—in O'Malley's Irish pub in Helsinki, of all places!

He went to the lobby of the Torni and asked the concierge if there was still a restaurant called Salve. "It used to be popular with sailors," Jack said.

"Not anymore," the concierge told him. "And I'm not sure it's the right place for Jack Burns to walk into. It's a *local* place." (Given the moviegoing crowd in O'Malley's Irish pub, Jack was glad he'd registered at the Torni as Jimmy Stronach.)

Jack went up to his room and changed into what Leslie Oastler called his "tattoo-parlor clothes"—jeans and a black turtleneck. Mrs. Oastler had also packed Emma's bomber jacket; the sleeves were way too long on Jack, but he loved it.

It still felt cold enough to snow when he walked into Salve— an old-fashioned restaurant, the kind of place where you got fairly ordinary but home-cooked meals. If, as he'd once imagined, Helsinki was a tough town in which to be afflicted with self-doubts, Jack could see what the concierge had meant about a movie star showing up at Salve. Surely *some* of the locals were moviegoers; maybe they just hadn't liked Jack Burns's movies.

The waitresses were as he'd remembered them—hard-worked and fairly long-of-tooth. Jack was thinking about the tough waitress who'd been married to Sami Salo, the scratcher; she would have fit right in twenty-eight years later. She'd been tough enough to call Alice "dearie," Jack recalled—although he wondered if the bad feelings between them had really been about his mom putting Sami out of business.

Jack remembered Mrs. Sami Salo, if that's who she was, as a short, stout woman whose clothes were too tight. She'd squinted whenever she took a step, as though her feet hurt her; her fat arms had jiggled.

He was trying not to look at anybody too closely—certainly not to meet anyone's eye—when the waitress came up to his table, which needed wiping. She used a wet dishcloth. Jack tried not to look too hard at her, either. She was as thin as Mrs. Sami Salo had been fat, or maybe only Mrs. Salo's *arms* had been fat. He couldn't remember. The thin waitress had hunched shoulders and a coarse complexion, but there was a kind of tired prettiness in her long face and catlike eyes; when she stood facing Jack at his table, she cocked one hip to the side as if her legs were tired, too.

"I hope you're meeting someone," she said. "You didn't come here alone, did you?"

"Isn't it all right to come here alone?" he asked.

"It's not all right for *you* to come here alone," she told him. "It might be safer for you to come here as a *girl*."

"I was hoping you could tell me where to get a tattoo," Jack said. "This used to be the place to ask."

"*I'm* the one to ask," the waitress said. "Seriously—if you aren't meeting someone here, you better be sure you *leave* with someone."

"What about the tattoo?" he asked.

"Movie stars shouldn't get tattooed," she told him. "It ruins you for the nude scenes."

"There's makeup for that," Jack said.

"You probably shouldn't get tattooed alone, either," the waitress said. "Are you here making a movie?"

"Actually, I'm looking for a couple of lesbians. But I'll start with where to get a tattoo," he told her. She smiled for the first time; she was missing an eyetooth, which was probably why she was disinclined to smile.

"If you're alone, *I'll* go home with you," the waitress said. "You can't do much with a couple of lesbians." She could tell he was thinking about it—another close-up opportunity. But Jack was suddenly tired, and he wanted to hold on to the memory of Ingrid Moe a little longer. "I'm not *really* old enough to be your mother," the waitress added. "I just *look* it."

"It's not that. I'm just too tired," he told her. "I've been traveling."

"If you end up here, you've been traveling, all right," she said.

"I'll have the Arctic char, please," Jack said.

"What are you drinking?"

"I don't drink," he told her.

"I'll bring you a beer," the waitress said. "You can just pretend you're drinking it."

She was wise to do that, because the locals kept toasting him—all through his dinner. The toasts were somehow sinister, even hostile—more challenging than friendly. Jack would raise his beer glass and pretend to swallow. They didn't seem to notice that his glass stayed full, or they didn't care. If there were Jack Burns fans in Finland, they had a way of masking their affection.

Jack didn't go home with the waitress. She was nice about it. She made him wait at the table while she called him a taxi. Only when the cab was parked outside would she release him; she even walked him to the door, holding his arm the whole way.

"My name is Marianne. There are much more difficult names in Finland," she said.

"I'll bet there are, Marianne."

She gave him a black-and-white business card; it was a little scary. The place was called The Duck's Tattoo. There was an excellent drawing of Donald Duck, but he was smoking a blunt—a cigar filled with marijuana. His eyes were fried and he looked raving mad. Someone had wrapped a snake around the reefer-smoking duck, more in the manner of a straitjacket than a shawl.

There was a phone number written on the back of the business card. "That's *my* number," Marianne told Jack. "I've got a couple of tattoos I could show you, if you're ever not too tired."

"Thank you, Marianne."

"The tattooist you want to see is Diego," she said.

"Not a Finnish name, I guess."

"Diego's Italian, but he was born in Finland," Marianne said. "He's been in business here for fifteen years."

The Duck's Tattoo was on Kalevankatu—about a ten-minute walk from the Torni, the concierge said the next morning. The concierge also sent Jack to a gym near the hotel, Kuntokeskus Motivus. ("Call it Motivus for short," the concierge had recommended.) It was clean, with lots of free weights, but Jack was distracted during his workout by a pregnancy-aerobics class. The bouncing women were doing dangerous-looking things.

On his way to The Duck's Tattoo, Jack passed a porn shop. One of the magazines in the window was a German one called *Schwangere Girls*. All the women were pregnant; *more* bouncing women doing dangerous-looking things. Pregnancy seemed to have made itself the unwanted theme of Jack's day.

Helsinki struck him as a warren of construction sites. He found himself in a part of the city that had been built by the Russians a hundred years before. The Duck's Tattoo was opposite the former Russian Army Hospital. It had been a sailors' neighborhood, with lots of sailors' pubs and restaurants—like Salve used to be—but the neighborhood was growing trendier by the day, Diego later told Jack.

Diego was a small man with friendly eyes and a goatee; his forearms were completely covered with tattoos. One was a rather formal portrait of a woman, almost like a photograph. Another was an entirely less formal-looking woman, who was naked; in fact, she was naked with a duck. Diego had other tattoos, but the naked woman with the duck was the one Jack would remember best.

He liked Diego, who'd never met Daughter Alice but had heard of her. Diego had three children and was not a regular participant at the tattoo conventions. He'd studied with Verber in Berlin; he'd worked in Cape Town, South Africa. He was planning a trip to Thailand to get a handmade tattoo by a monk in a monastery. "A chest tattoo," he called it. He was inclined to "big works," Diego said—both getting them and doing them. He'd recently copied a whole movie poster onto someone's back.

Diego had two apprentices working with him. One of them was a muscleman in camouflage pants and a black Jack Daniel's T-shirt. The other was a blond woman named Taru. Evidently Taru did the piercing; she had a silver stud in her tongue. There was another guy in The Duck's Tattoo—a friend of Diego's named Nipa, who told Jack a fairly involved story about accidentally dropping a paperback novel in a toilet. It was his favorite novel, Nipa said, and he was trying to figure out a way to dry it.

Jack talked to Diego about the relationship between sailors and tattooing. Diego had his first boat when he was just fourteen. The flash in The Duck's Tattoo was impressive: Indian chiefs, dragons, skulls, birds, Harley engines, and many cartoon characters, like The Joker—and *ducks,* of course, lots of edgy ducks.

Diego admitted he wasn't much of a moviegoer—he mentioned his three children again—but Taru, the piercer, and the muscleman in the Jack Daniel's T-shirt had seen all of Jack's films. (Nipa told Jack he was more of a book person than a movie person, as one might surmise from the toilet accident.)

"I don't suppose you ever tattooed an organist named William Burns," Jack said to Diego. "Tattoo artists call him The Music Man. I guess most of his tattoos are music. He might be a full-body."

"*Might* be!" Diego said, laughing. "I never tattooed him— I never met the guy—but from what I hear, The Music Man hasn't got a whole lot of skin left!"

When Jack got back to his room at the Hotel Torni, he tried to write a letter to Michele Maher. As a dermatologist, maybe she would know why some people with full-body tattoos felt cold. It was a strange way to start a letter to someone he'd not written or spoken to for fifteen years, and quite possibly the full-body people only *thought* they felt cold. What if the part about feeling cold was all in their minds and had nothing to do with their skin?

Tattoo artists themselves didn't agree about the full-body types; Alice had believed that most full-bodies felt cold, but some of the tattooists Jack met at his mom's memorial service told him that many full-bodies felt normal.

"The ones who feel cold were either cold or crazy to begin with," North Dakota Dan had said.

But how else could Jack begin a letter to Michele Maher after fifteen years of silence?

Dear Michele,
    Here I am in Helsinki, looking for a couple of lesbians. What's up with you?

How was that for *too weird*? Jack crumpled up the piece of stationery. Perhaps a more general beginning would be better.

Dear Michele,
    Guess what? My mother died. It turns out she lied to me about my father—maybe about a lot of other things. I'm in Europe, where I once believed my dad had slept with just about everyone he met, but it turns out that my mom was the one who was sleeping with everybody—among them a twelve- or thirteen-year-old boy and a couple of lesbians. Interesting, huh? The things you think you know!

Jack crumpled up another page. He was beginning to believe that the only way he could communicate with Michele Maher was if he developed a skin problem. But wait! Hadn't she written to him to wish him luck on his adaptation of *The Slush-Pile Reader*? Michele was an Emma Oastler fan! Perhaps a more literary approach would impress her.

> *Dear Michele,*
>   *Thank you for your letter. Yes, I was close to Emma Oastler, although we never actually had sex. Emma just held my penis. And of course, as with any adaptation, I have had to take some liberties with her novel. The name of the porn star, for example—I don't exactly look like a Miguel Santiago, do I? And please don't think there will be any actual porn-film footage in* The Slush-Pile Reader; *it won't be that kind of movie. The pornography will be sort of* implied. *Besides, I have what I'm told is a rather small (or small*ish*) penis.*

Jack couldn't write a letter to Michele Maher. He *was* too weird for Michele, or for anyone else who wasn't desperately lonely or crazy or a kid or grief-stricken (or otherwise depressed) or cheating on her husband or tattooed (with an octopus on her ass) or an old lady!

Besides, he had used up what pathetically little stationery the Hotel Torni provided for guests. Jack blamed the day on the agitation the pregnancy-aerobics class had caused him—not to mention the added stress of seeing *Schwangere Girls.* He was even tempted to go buy the magazine, but what he really wanted—and this truly disturbed him—was to have sex with a *nice* pregnant woman. (Like a *wife,* Jack was thinking; like someone who was going to have *his* baby; like Michele Maher, he kept hoping.)

More realistically, because he wasn't hungry or too tired, Jack could try his luck with whomever he might pick up downstairs—in O'Malley's—or he could call the waitress at Salve. But by the time Marianne got off work, Jack probably *would* be too tired. And the very idea of looking for a brave girl in O'Malley's Irish pub was humiliating.

There was still some daylight left in the sky when Jack called

Sibelius Academy, the music college, and asked if there was anyone who might be able to tell him the whereabouts of two of their graduates in the early 1970s. The matter was complicated. Not only did it take the college a little time to connect him with someone who spoke English; Jack didn't even know the last names of the graduates. (Talk about taking a stab in the dark!)

"I know it sounds crazy," Jack said, "but Hannele was a cellist and Ritva was an organist, and I think they were a *couple*."

"A *couple*?" the woman who spoke English said on the phone. She had the doubting tone of voice of a knowledgeable bookseller who's convinced that the title of the book you're asking for is not the correct one.

"Yes, I mean a *lesbian* couple," he said.

The woman sighed. "I suppose you're a *journalist*," she said. Her tone of voice was worse than doubting now; she couldn't have made *journalist* sound any nastier if she'd said *rapist*.

"No, I'm Jack Burns—the actor," he told her. "I believe these women were students of my father, William Burns—the organist. I met them when I was a child. They also knew my mother."

"Well, well," the woman said. "Am I truly speaking with *the* Jack Burns—I mean *really*?"

"Yes, *really*."

"Well, well," she said again. "Hannele and Ritva aren't as famous as *you* are, Mr. Burns, but they're rather famous in *Finland*."

"Really?"

"Yes, *really*," the woman said. "It would be hard for them to hide in Helsinki. Practically anyone could tell you where to find them." Jack waited while the woman sighed again; she was taking the time to choose her next words very carefully. "It's an awful temptation, Jack Burns, but I'll refrain from asking you what you're *wearing*."

Later Jack called room service and ordered something to eat; he also called the front desk and requested more Hotel Torni stationery. He resisted both the faint impulse to explore O'Malley's and the slightly stronger desire to call Marianne the waitress and ask to see her tattoos.

The next morning he got up early again and went to the Motivus gym.

He wasn't at all sure how to approach Hannele and Ritva. The unpronounceable church where the two musicians practiced every midday was called Temppeliaukion kirkko. The Church in the Rock, as it was also called, was more famous in Helsinki than Hannele and Ritva. It was underground, buried under a dome of rock—an ultramodern design, presumably done for the acoustics. There were numerous concerts there—these in addition to the Sunday services, which were Lutheran. ("*Very* Lutheran," the woman from Sibelius Academy had told Jack—whatever that meant.)

Ritva was the regular organist at the principal Sunday service, but Hannele often accompanied her. Jack had inquired if much music had been written for organ and cello—he certainly hadn't heard any—but the woman from Sibelius Academy said that Ritva and Hannele were famous for being "improvisational." They were a most improvisational *couple,* Jack had already imagined. Indeed, if they'd both slept with Alice—yet they'd managed to stay a couple, as Ingrid Moe had told Jack—Hannele and Ritva were no strangers to successful experimentation.

Even their rehearsals were famous. People often went to the Church in the Rock during their lunch break just to hear Hannele and Ritva *practice.* Jack imagined that it wouldn't be easy to speak with them in such an atmosphere; in those surroundings, Hannele and Ritva and Jack were too well known to be afforded any privacy. Maybe he should just show up at the church in the early afternoon and invite them to dinner.

Jack was finishing his workout on the ab machine in the gym when his thoughts were interrupted. About half a dozen sweaty women from the pregnancy-aerobics class had surrounded him; Jack guessed that their workout, their dangerous-looking bouncing, was over. Given his Michele Maher state of mind—not to mention his disturbing memories of the *Schwangere Girls* magazine—these pregnant women were an intimidating presence.

"Hi," he said, from flat on his back.

"Hi," the aerobics instructor replied. She was a dark-haired young woman with an arresting oval face and almond-shaped eyes. Because her back had been turned to him during the aerobics class, Jack hadn't noticed that she was pregnant, too; he'd watched her lead the leaping women from behind.

"You look like Jack Burns, that *actor*," the most pregnant-looking of the women said. Jack wouldn't have been surprised to learn, later, that these were her last words before going into labor.

"But you can't be—not if you're here," another of the women said doubtfully. "You just *look* like him, right?"

"It's a curse," Jack told them bitterly. "I can't help it that I look like him. I *hate* the bastard." It was the last line that gave him away; it was one of Billy Rainbow's lines. In the movie, Jack said it three times—not once referring to the same person.

"It's *him*!" one of the women cried.

"I *knew* you were Jack Burns," the most pregnant-looking woman told him. "Jack Burns always gives me the creeps, and *you* gave me the creeps the second I saw you."

"Well, then—I guess that settles it," Jack said. He was still lying on his back; he hadn't moved since he'd noticed them surrounding him.

"What movie are you making here? Who else is in it?" one of them asked.

"There's no movie," he told them. "I'm just in town to do a little research."

One of the pregnant women grunted, as if the very thought of what *research* Jack Burns might be doing in Helsinki had given her her first contraction. Half the women walked away; now that the mystery was solved, they were no longer interested. But the aerobics instructor and two other women stayed, including the most pregnant-looking woman.

"What kind of research is it?" the aerobics instructor asked him.

"It's a story that takes place in the past—twenty-eight years ago, to be exact," Jack told them. "It's about a church organist who's addicted to being tattooed, and the woman whose father first tattooed him. They have a child. There's more than one version of what happened, but things didn't work out."

"Are you the organist?" the most pregnant-looking woman asked.

"No, I'm the child—all grown up, twenty-eight years later," he told them. "I'm trying to find out what really happened between my mother and father."

The pregnant woman who hadn't yet spoken said: "What a depressing story! I don't know why they make movies like that."

She turned and walked away—probably she was going to the women's locker room. The most pregnant-looking woman waddled after her. Jack was left alone with the aerobics instructor.

"You didn't say you were doing a little research for a *movie,* did you?" she asked him.

"No, I didn't," he admitted. "This research isn't for a movie."

"Maybe you need a *guide,*" she said. She was at least seven months pregnant, probably eight. Her belly button had popped; like an erect nipple, it poked out against the spandex fabric of her leotard. "I meant to say a *date.*"

"I've never had a pregnant date," Jack told her.

"I'm not married—I don't even have a boyfriend," she explained. "This baby is kind of an experiment."

"Something you managed all by yourself?" he asked.

"I went to a sperm bank," she answered. "I had an anonymous sperm donor. I kind of forget the insemination part."

From flat on his back on the ab machine, Jack made one of those too-hasty decisions that had characterized his sexually active life. Because he'd imagined that he wanted to be with *someone* who was pregnant, Jack chose to be with the pregnant aerobics instructor at the Motivus gym—this instead of even *trying* to make a dinner date with Hannele and Ritva, the lesbian couple who were the reason for his coming to Helsinki in the first place.

Jack rationalized that what he might learn from the organist and cellist, who were a couple when his mother and father knew them—and they were still a couple—was in all likelihood something he already knew or could guess. Jack's mother had somehow misrepresented them to him; they had slept with her, not his dad. Of course there would be other revelations of that kind, but nothing that couldn't be said over coffee or tea—nothing so complicated that it would require a dinner date to reveal.

Jack decided to go to the Church in the Rock about the time Hannele and Ritva would be finishing their rehearsal. He would suggest that they go somewhere for a little chat; surely that would suffice. Jack thought there was no reason *not* to spend his last night in Helsinki with a pregnant aerobics instructor. As it would turn out, there *was* a reason, but Jack was responding to an overriding instinct familiar to far too many men—namely, the desire to be with a certain *kind* of woman precluded any reasonable examination or in-depth consideration of the aerobics instructor herself, whose name was Marja-Liisa.

They made a date, which was awkward because they had to get a pen and some paper from the reception desk; other people were watching them. Marja-Liisa wrote out her name and cellphone number for him. She was clearly puzzled by what Jack wrote out for her—*Jimmy Stronach, Hotel Torni*—until he explained the business of always registering under the name of the character he plays in his next movie.

When Jack left the gym and returned to the Torni, he went first to that porn shop where he'd seen the unlikely but alluring *Schwangere Girls* in the window. He took the magazine back to his hotel room—just to look at the pictures, which were both disturbing and arousing.

When Jack left the hotel for the Church in the Rock, he threw the disgusting magazine away—not in his hotel room but in a wastebasket in the hall opposite the elevator. Not that you can really throw pictures like those away—not for years, maybe not *ever.* What those pregnant women were doing in those photographs would abide with Jack Burns in his grave—or in Hell, where, according to Ingrid, you were deaf but you could see everyone you ever knowingly hurt. You just couldn't hear what they were saying about you.

Since that afternoon in Helsinki, Jack could imagine what Hell might be like for him. For eternity, he would watch those pregnant women having uncomfortable-looking sex. They would be talking about him, but he couldn't hear them. For eternity, Jack could only guess what they were saying.

To Jack, the dome of Temppeliaukio Church looked like a giant overturned wok. The rocks, which covered all but the dome, had a pagan simplicity; it was as if the dome were a living egg, emerging from the crater of a meteorite. The apartment buildings surrounding the Church in the Rock had an austere sameness about them. (Middle-class housing from the 1930s.)

There were more rocks inside the church. The organist sat in view of those people on the left side of the congregation. The empty, rounded benches—for the choir—occupied a center-stage position. Choirs were important here. The copper organ pipes were very modern-looking against the darker and lighter woods. The pulpit was surrounded by stone; Jack thought it looked like a drinking fountain.

In the early afternoon, he sat and listened to Hannele and

Ritva—Ritva in profile to him, on the organ bench, Hannele facing him with her legs wide apart, straddling her cello. A small audience quietly came and went while the two women practiced. Jack could tell that Hannele had recognized him as soon as he sat down; she must have been expecting him, because she merely smiled and nodded in his direction. Ritva turned once to look at Jack; she smiled and nodded, too. (The lady he'd spoken to at Sibelius Academy must have forewarned Hannele and Ritva that Jack Burns was looking for them.)

It wasn't all church music—at least not the usual church music. As a former Canadian, Jack recognized Leonard Cohen's "If It Be Your Will"—not that he was used to hearing it played on organ and cello. As an American, Jack also recognized Van Morrison's "Whenever God Shines His Light on Me." Hannele and Ritva were very good; even Jack could tell that their playing together had become second nature. Of course he was predisposed to like them. Jack gave them a lot of credit in advance, just for surviving whatever assault his mom might have made on them as a couple.

Jack also listened to them rehearse two traditional pieces— "Come, Sing the Praise of Jesus" and "O Come, O Come, Emmanuel." The latter was an Advent hymn, and both hymns were better known in Scotland than in Finland, Hannele and Ritva told Jack later. But the hymns, they said, had been particular favorites of his father's.

"William taught us those two," Ritva said. "We don't care that it isn't the month before Christmas."

They were having tea in Hannele and Ritva's surprisingly beautiful and spacious apartment in one of those gray, somber buildings encircling the Church in the Rock. Hannele and Ritva had combined two apartments overlooking the dome of Temppeliaukio Church. Like the church, their apartment was very modern-looking—sparsely furnished, with nothing but steel-framed, black-and-white photographs on the walls. The two women, now in their late forties, were good-humored and very friendly. Naturally, they were not as physically intimidating as they'd seemed to Jack at four.

"You were the first woman I ever saw with unshaven armpits," he told Hannele. The astonishing hair in Hannele's armpits had been a darker blond than the hair on her head, although Jack didn't mention this detail—nor the birthmark over Hannele's navel, like a crumpled top hat the color of a wine stain, the shape of Florida.

Hannele laughed. "Most people remember my birthmark, not my armpits, Jack."

"I remember the birthmark, too," he told her.

Ritva was enduringly short and plump, with long hair and a pretty face. She still dressed all in black, like a drama student. "I remember how you fell asleep, Jack—how hard you were trying not to!" Ritva told him.

He explained that he'd thought, at the time, they had come for their half-a-heart tattoos because they'd both slept with his *father*.

"With *William*?" Hannele cried, spilling her tea. Ritva could not stop laughing.

They were the kind of gay women who were so comfortable with each other that they could flirt unselfconsciously with him, or with other young men, because they were confident that they wouldn't be misunderstood.

"I suppose I shouldn't be surprised," Hannele said. "William told us that your mom was capable of telling you *anything*, Jack. Ritva and I underestimated how far she would go."

Hannele explained that her relationship with Ritva was new and still uncommitted when Jack's mother had first hit on them; the young music students had even discussed sleeping with Alice as a kind of test of their relationship.

"It was 1970, Jack," Ritva said, "and Hannele and I were young enough to imagine that you could treat any relationship as an experiment."

William had warned them about Alice; he'd told Hannele and Ritva her history. Yet the girls had imagined that if they *both* were "unfaithful" with Jack's mother, they wouldn't hurt each other.

"It hurt us more than we expected," Hannele told Jack. "We decided to hurt your mother back. The tattoo we shared was a symbol of how we had hurt each other—a reminder to *not* be unfaithful to each other again, a reminder of what sleeping with your mom had cost us. And we let her know that we were *brave* enough to sleep with anybody—even with William."

"Of course we *wouldn't* have slept with William, Jack—not that your father would have slept with either of us," Ritva said. "But your mom was extremely sensitive about anyone your dad *might* sleep with, and it wasn't hard to convince her that Hannele and I were lawless."

"We even flirted with you, Jack—just to piss her off," Hannele said.

"Yes, I remember that part," Jack told them.

Their half-a-heart tattoos had been torn apart vertically; both women were tattooed on their heart-side breasts.

"You have eyelashes to die for, Jack," Hannele had told him. Under the covers, her long fingers had lifted his pajama top and stroked his stomach. When she was sleeping beside him, he'd almost kissed her.

"Go to sleep, Jack," his mom had told him.

"Tell me about the 'Sweet dreams' part," Jack asked Hannele and Ritva in their beautiful apartment. It was growing dark outside; the lights shone through the dome of the Church in the Rock like a fire burning windows in an eggshell. (Jack remembered that he'd thought "Sweet dreams" was something his dad probably said to all of his girlfriends.)

"He's not four anymore," Ritva said to Hannele, who was shaking her head. "Go on, *tell* him."

"It's what your mom whispered in our ears before she kissed us *down there,*" Hannele said, averting her eyes from Jack's.

"Oh."

Ritva had said, "Sweet dreams," to Jack, before she'd kissed him good night. "Isn't that what you say in English?" she'd asked Alice. "Sweet dreams."

"Sometimes," Alice had said, and Hannele's brave whistling had stopped for a second—as if the pain of the shading needles on her heart-side breast and that side of her rib cage had suddenly become unbearable. But Jack had been sure it was the "Sweet dreams" that had hurt her, not the tattoo. (Talk about a not-around-Jack subject!)

Jack told Hannele and Ritva about his mother's surprisingly long-lasting relationship with Leslie Oastler—not that Alice hadn't probably had other, lesser relationships in the same period of time, but her relationship with another woman was the only one that had endured. Were Hannele and Ritva surprised at that? he asked.

The two women looked at each other and shrugged. "There wasn't anything your mom wouldn't do, Jack," Ritva said, "not if she could have an effect—almost *any* effect—on your dad."

"After William, I don't think Alice cared who she slept with," Hannele told him. "Man, woman, or boy."

The black-and-white photographs on the walls of the apartment were mostly of Hannele and Ritva—many concert photographs among them. There was one of Ritva on the organ bench in the Johanneksen kirkko, where Jack had gone with his mother—this had been following a heavy snowfall, he remembered. Flanking Ritva on the organ bench were her two teachers—Kari Vaara, the organist with the wild-looking hair, and a handsome, thin-lipped young man whose long hair fell to his shoulders, framing a face as delicate as a girl's.

"My father?" Jack asked Ritva, pointing to the picture. William looked almost the same as he had that night in the restaurant of the Hotel Bristol.

"Yes, of course," Ritva told Jack. "You haven't seen his picture before?"

"What are you thinking, Ritva?" Hannele asked. "Do you imagine Alice kept a photo album for Jack?"

What Jack was unprepared for was how young his father looked. In 1970, in Helsinki, William Burns would have been thirty-one—a couple of years younger than Jack was now. (It is strange to see, for the first time, a photograph of your father when he is younger than you are.) Jack was also unprepared for the resemblance; William looked almost exactly like Jack.

Of course William seemed small beside Ritva and Kari Vaara. William was a small but strong-looking man, not slight but somehow feminine in his features, and with an organist's long-fingered hands. (Jack had his mom's small hands and short, square fingers.)

William was wearing a long-sleeved white dress shirt, open at the throat—the organ pipes of the Walcker from Württemberg rising above him. Jack asked Hannele and Ritva about his father's tattoos.

"Never saw them," Hannele said. Ritva agreed; she'd never seen them, either.

In the bedroom, Jack saw black-and-white photographs of Hannele's and Ritva's tattoos—just their naked torsos, the hearts cut in half on their left breasts. At least the tattoos were as he'd remembered them, but Hannele had shaved her armpit hair; her hands, folded flat above her navel, hid her birthmark from the photographer.

It was a mild surprise to see that they had other tattoos. There was some music on Hannele's hip, and more music—it looked like the same music—on Ritva's buttocks. Like the photos of their shared heart, these were close-ups—only partial views. But they were such different body types, Jack had no difficulty telling Hannele and Ritva apart.

"What's the music?" he asked them.

"We played it earlier—before you came to the church," Ritva said. "It's another piece William taught us, a hymn he used to play in Old St. Paul's."

" 'Sweet Sacrament Divine,' " Hannele told Jack. She began to hum it. "We only know the music, not the words, but it's a hymn."

It sounded familiar; perhaps he'd heard it, or had even sung it, at St. Hilda's. Jack knew he'd heard his mom sing it in Amsterdam, in the red-light district. If it was something his dad used to play at Old St. Paul's, it was probably Anglican or Scottish Episcopal.

The old scratcher's name almost didn't come up, but Hannele—pointing to the black-and-white photo of the tattoo on her hip—just happened to say it. "It's not bad for a Sami Salo."

Jack told Hannele and Ritva the story of the scary night at the Hotel Torni, when Sami Salo had banged on the door—not to mention how Sami's noticeably younger wife, that tough-talking waitress at Salve, had told Alice she was putting Sami out of business.

Hannele was shaking her head again—her short, curly blond hair not moving. "Sami's wife was long gone before you and your mom came to town, Jack," Ritva said. "That waitress at Salve was Sami's *daughter.*"

"Her name was Minna," Hannele told him. "She was William's friend, one of your dad's older women. I always thought it was a peculiar relationship, but Minna had gone through some hard times—like your dad. She had a child out of wedlock, and the child died as an infant—some upper-respiratory ailment."

"Your father wasn't looking for a girlfriend, Jack. He was probably still in love with the Dane," Ritva said. "Minna was just a comfort to him. I think that's all he thought he was good for, to be a comfort to someone. You know, it's that old Christian idea—you find someone down on their luck and you help them."

Certainly Agneta Nilsson, who'd taught William choral music

in Stockholm—and Jack how to skate on Lake Mälaren—was an older woman. Maybe Agneta had been down on her luck, too; after all, she'd had a bad heart.

"Look, we're musicians, Jack. Your dad was first and foremost a *musician,*" Hannele said. "I'm not claiming an artist's license for how I live—William wasn't, either. But what sort of license was your mom taking? There wasn't *anything* she didn't feel entitled to!"

"Hannele, the slut was his mother—no matter what you say about her," Ritva said.

"If somebody dumps you, you move on," Hannele told Jack. "Your mom made a feature-length film out of it!"

"Hannele!" Ritva said. "We've seen all *your* movies, Jack. We can't imagine how you turned out so *normal*!"

Jack didn't *feel* normal. He couldn't stop thinking about the waitress with the fat arms—Minna, Sami Salo's daughter. How her arms had jiggled; how she'd been a friend of his father's!

So Jack's mother had undermined even that—a *comfort* relationship. Hannele doubted that his dad and Minna had ever had sex; Ritva thought they probably had. But what did it matter? Alice had convinced Sami Salo that his unlucky daughter could expect nothing but betrayal and heartbreak from William Burns. Sami couldn't wait for Alice and Jack to go to Amsterdam, where William would be bound to follow.

It was true that Sami Salo was a scratcher; even so, he wasn't losing that much business to Daughter Alice. As Hannele and Ritva explained to Jack, his mom tattooed mostly students at the Hotel Torni; even well-to-do students weren't inclined to spend their money on tattoos. Most of the sailors still went to Sami; at that time, sailors spent more money on tattoos than students did.

Jack also learned that Kari Vaara traveled—Vaara was always giving concerts abroad. William was what amounted to the principal organist at the Johanneksen kirkko, where he loved the church and the organ. He loved his students at Sibelius Academy, too—Ritva and Hannele being two of the better ones.

William would have *no* students in Amsterdam, where his duties at the Oude Kerk were so demanding that he had no time for teaching, too. "You mean the organ-tuning?" Jack asked Hannele and Ritva.

"The *what*?"

Jack explained what he'd been told: namely, that his dad's only real job in Amsterdam was tuning the organ in the Oude Kerk, which was indeed *vast*, as Kari Vaara had described it, but the organ was always out of tune.

"William couldn't tune a *guitar*, much less an organ!" Ritva cried.

"He only agreed to play the organ at the Oude Kerk if the church hired an *additional* organ-tuner," Hannele told Jack.

"There was already someone who tuned the organ before every concert, but—at your dad's insistence—the new organ-tuner came almost every day," Ritva said.

"It was every *night*," Hannele corrected her.

That's when Jack knew who the *additional* organ-tuner had been—the dough-faced youngster who, Alice had said, was a "child prodigy." The young genius who'd put baby powder on the seat of his pants so that he could more easily slide on the organ bench, which was also *vast*—Frans Donker, who'd played for Jack and his mom, and whatever whores were on hand, one night when he, the "child prodigy," was supposed to be tuning the organ.

"They say that in the Oude Kerk, one plays to both tourists and prostitutes!" Kari Vaara had told Alice and Jack. Vaara was very proud of William, Hannele and Ritva said. Vaara had called William his best student ever.

Yet Alice had wanted Jack to see his father as a mere organ-*tuner;* she had purposely discredited William in his son's eyes.

"Something happened in Amsterdam," Jack said to Hannele and Ritva. "My dad stopped following us—something must have happened."

Hannele was shaking her head again, the blond curls holding fast to her head. "The lawyer made a deal with your mother, Jack," Ritva said. "It was a hard deal, but someone had to stop her."

"It was no *deal* for William!" Hannele said angrily.

"It was the best deal for *Jack*, Hannele," Ritva said.

"I don't remember any lawyer," Jack told them. "*What* lawyer?"

"*Femke* somebody. I don't remember her last name," Hannele said. "She was some super divorce lawyer—she'd been through some big-deal divorce herself."

Well, it was almost funny that Jack had thought Femke was a prostitute; there'd been some preposterous story about her becoming a prostitute to embarrass her ex-husband. (Femke was rich, as Jack recalled, yet she'd become a whore!) What *wouldn't* you believe when you were four, and your mom was the manager of your so-called memories?

"Begin with the cop, Jack," Ritva said. "There was a cop—he was your dad's best friend."

"He got you out of there—he was *your* best friend, too, Jack," Hannele said.

"Yes, I remember him," Jack said. He was a nice guy, Nico Oudejans. Nico's eyes were a robin's-egg blue, and high on one cheekbone he had a small scar shaped like the letter *L*. "Naturally, I thought he was my *mother's* friend," Jack told Hannele and Ritva. "And I thought Femke was a *prostitute*!"

They were sitting on the leather couch in the living room, with the darkness now fallen over the glowing dome of the Church in the Rock. The two women flanked Jack on the couch; they put their arms around him.

"Jack, your *mother* was a prostitute. Femke was just a lawyer," Hannele said.

"My mom was a prostitute for just one night!" Jack blurted out. "She took only one customer—a young boy. She said he was a virgin."

The two women went on hugging him. "Jack, no one's a prostitute for just one night," Ritva said.

"There's no such thing as a prostitute who takes only one customer, Jack," Hannele told Jack. "Not to mention one *virgin*!"

"We should all have dinner tonight!" Ritva cried suddenly.

"Unless Jack has a *date*," Hannele said, teasing him. "I refuse to share Jack with a *date*." Jack just sat on the leather couch, staring at the darkness out the window.

"From the look of him, he's got a date," Ritva said.

"Yes, he's got a date. I can see it in his eyes," Hannele said.

"I'm sorry," Jack told them. He just didn't know *how* sorry—not yet.

The aerobics instructor was thirty-one weeks pregnant and expecting her second child.

"Same anonymous sperm donor?" Jack asked as nonchalantly as the circumstances permitted. They were both naked and in bed, in his hotel room at the Torni, and Marja-Liisa was pressing

Jack's face against her big belly so that he could feel how a thirty-one-week-old fetus moved around in there.

"No, my husband died," she explained. "We were planning to have a second child, but it took me almost three years to get up the nerve to have the second one alone."

"Do you have a boy or a girl?"

"A four-year-old boy."

In the context of Jack's return trip to the North Sea and the Baltic, almost everything about a four-year-old boy was interesting to him; however, he sensed that this wasn't the time and place to tell Marja-Liisa how sorry he was to miss meeting her son. (Jack was leaving for Amsterdam very early in the morning.)

She said a friend was with the four-year-old, giving the boy his supper and putting him to bed. Marja-Liisa warned Jack that she couldn't stay late. It was unusual for her to stay out past her son's bedtime, and she was always back home, in her own bed, when the boy woke up in the morning.

The athleticism of the thirty-one-week-old fetus was a marvel to Jack—less so, the lovemaking of the aerobics instructor. He'd never been in bed with a pregnant woman; Jack had no idea what to expect. He probably shouldn't have been concerned by how *active* Marja-Liisa was—that is, for a woman in her condition. (After all, he'd watched her lead the leaping women in the aerobics class, and Jack knew that most of the uncomfortable-looking positions he'd seen in the *Schwangere Girls* magazine could not have been faked.)

Jack realized only later what he had wanted, which was not to have sex with her but just to hold her while he fell asleep. All he really desired was his hand on her big belly, his hand imagining that there were *two* people he loved—not just a woman but also the child she was about to have. It had been a great way to fall asleep.

The knock on the door was quiet at first, then more insistent. It was not a Sami Salo kind of knocking, but one Jack was able to incorporate into his dream—in the dream, Jack was a father.

"Marja-Liisa, are you there?" said a man's voice in the hall. Then he must have asked the same question in Finnish.

The pregnant aerobics instructor had gone. Jack woke up alone in the bed; he went into the bathroom and wrapped a towel around his waist. There was a Hotel Torni envelope stuck to the mirror with a dab of his toothpaste. It was a clever way for her to have left him a note. He realized now that he must have been talking in his sleep.

My name is Marja-Liisa, not Michele. Who's Michele?

Jack crumpled up the envelope and threw it in the bathroom wastebasket. Clutching the towel around his waist, he went to see who was at the door. Jack had a bad feeling that he already knew who it was. "Marja-Liisa—I know you're there," the man was saying, only a little more loudly.

Until Jack opened the door, he didn't know that the man had brought the four-year-old with him. But what else could the poor guy have done? If you were a responsible father, you didn't leave a four-year-old alone.

There was no question in Jack's mind that the young man with the dark-blond hair was Marja-Liisa's husband—not her *dead* husband, either. (Nor did the young man look like an *anonymous* sperm donor.) Any doubts Jack might have had were dispelled by the boy; the four-year-old had his dad's dark-blond hair, but the child's oval face and almond-shaped eyes were exactly like his mother's.

"I knew it," Marja-Liisa's husband said. "You're Jack Burns. Marja-Liisa said she saw you at the gym."

"She's not here," Jack told him.

The unhappy husband looked past Jack into the disheveled room. The little boy wanted his dad to pick him up; the child was wearing slipper-socks with reindeer on them, and a ski parka over his pajamas. Jack stepped back into the room and the father carried his son inside. The pillows and bedcovers were all in a heap; the young husband stared at the bed as if he could discern the imprint of his pregnant wife's body on the rumpled sheets.

Marja-Liisa had told her husband that she had a late-night aerobics class at the gym, but he found her gym bag in her closet after he'd put the four-year-old to bed; he had been tidying up the apartment and went to her closet to put some article of her clothing away, and there was the gym bag.

The young man showed Jack the piece of paper he'd found in the bag—*Jimmy Stronach, Hotel Torni*—but he'd guessed all along that Jimmy Stronach was Jack Burns.

"She kept telling me, 'There's a movie star in the gym, and I look like a whale!' You're not even her favorite movie star, but I suppose that doesn't matter," her husband said.

The four-year-old wanted to get down; his father looked distressed to see the boy climb onto the bed and burrow under the mound of pillows.

"She didn't want a second child," Marja-Liisa's husband told Jack. "The pregnancy was an accident, but she blames me for it because I wanted to have more children."

The four-year-old was sleepy-looking, but he had found a way to amuse himself with the feather quilt and all the pillows; the little boy moved in circles on all fours, like an animal trying to bury itself. Jack assumed that the child didn't speak English, and therefore couldn't understand them—not that the boy would have paid any closer attention to his dad and Jack if they'd been speaking in Finnish.

He's only four, Jack kept thinking. Jack hoped that the child wouldn't remember this adventure—being woken up and taken to a hotel in the middle of the night in his pajamas. Or perhaps the boy would remember no more than what he was told about this night, and why would his parents ever talk about it to him? (Maybe only if the night became a turning point in his family's history, which Jack hoped it wouldn't.)

"She's probably gone home, or she was on her way home and you just passed each other," Jack told Marja-Liisa's husband, who was looking more and more distraught. The four-year-old was completely hidden from view, under all the pillows and bedcovers. In a muffled voice, the little boy asked his father something.

"He wants to use the bathroom," the husband told Jack.

"Sure," Jack said.

There was more Finnish—both the language and the barrier of the bedcovers making the exchange incomprehensible. Jack could see that Marja-Liisa's husband didn't want to touch the bed, so Jack helped the little boy get untangled from the feather quilt and all the pillows.

The four-year-old left the bathroom door open while he was peeing; the boy was also talking to himself and singing. Thus Jack must have followed his mother through those Baltic and North Sea ports, peeing with the bathroom doors open, talking to himself and singing, remembering next to nothing—or only what his mom *told* him had happened, what she *wanted* him to remember.

"I'm sorry," Jack said to the unhappy husband and father. Jack wasn't going to make it worse for the poor man by telling him that his wife had told Jack her husband was dead, or that she was pregnant this time with the help of an anonymous sperm donor.

"Who is Jimmy Stronach?" the young man asked Jack.

Jack explained that it was the name of a character in the movie he hoped to make next; he didn't mention the porn-star part, or that he was not just an actor in this movie but also the screenwriter.

The little boy came out of the bathroom; Jack hadn't heard the toilet flush, and the four-year-old was disturbed about something. It appeared he had peed in the left-inside pocket of his ski parka. His father said some reassuring-sounding things to him in Finnish. ("Oh, we all pee in our parka pockets from time to time!" Jack imagined.)

Possibly Jack Burns had been a more *aware* four-year-old than Marja-Liisa's little boy, but Jack doubted it.

The little boy wanted his father to pick him up again, which his dad did; the child snuggled his face against his father's neck and closed his eyes, as if he were going to fall asleep right there. It was late; no doubt the boy could have fallen asleep almost anywhere.

Jack opened the hotel-room door for them—hoping the husband wouldn't give one last look at the landscape of the abused bed, but of course the betrayed man did.

As they were leaving, the husband said to Jack: "I guess Jimmy Stronach is the bad guy in *this* movie." Then they went down the hall, with the little boy singing a song in Finnish.

Jack went into the bathroom and flushed the toilet, noting that the four-year-old had peed all over the toilet seat; like a lot of four-year-olds, he'd not lifted the seat before he peed. Jack kept telling himself that if Marja-Liisa's son was a *normal* four-year-old, and he certainly had behaved normally, the boy would never remember this awful night—not a moment of it.

Jack had to look everywhere for the piece of paper with Marja-Liisa's name and cell-phone number on it. When he managed to find it, he called the number. Jack thought he should forewarn her that her husband and small son had paid him a visit. When Marja-Liisa answered the phone, she was at home and already knew that her husband and child were missing; she sounded frantic.

Jack told her that her husband had been visibly distressed but extremely well behaved. Jack also told her that her little boy had looked sleepy, but that the child had seemed to understand none of it.

"I wish you'd told me the truth," Jack said.

"The *truth*!" she cried. "What do *you* know about the truth?"

It was dark all the way from the Hotel Torni to the airport, which was some distance from Helsinki. It was very early in the morning, but it looked like the middle of the night; naturally, it was raining. A little after dawn, when the plane took off, Jack could see patches of what looked like snow in the woods.

He was thinking that there was nothing more he wanted to know; he'd already learned too much about what had happened. No more truth, Jack kept thinking—he'd had enough truth for a lifetime. He didn't really want to go to Amsterdam, but that's where the plane was going.

30

The Deal

Jack's second time in Amsterdam, he stayed at the Grand—
a good hotel on the Oudezijds Voorburgwal, about a two-minute
walk from the red-light district. The rain had followed him from
Finland. He walked through the district in the late-morning drizzle; the tourists appeared to be discouraged by the rain.

The blatancy of the prostitutes—in their underwear, in their
windows and doorways—made their business plain. Yet, despite
the obviousness of the undressed women, the four-year-old
whom Jack had recently met in Helsinki could have been persuaded that the women were *advice-givers*. (As Jack himself had
been persuaded.)

No one was singing a hymn or chanting a prayer; not one of
the women had the appearance of a first-timer, or of someone
who planned on being a prostitute for only one day.

The women would beckon to Jack, and smile, but if their
smiles weren't instantly returned—if he just kept walking or
wouldn't meet their gaze—they quickly looked away. He heard
his name a few times, only once as a question. "Jack Burns?"
one of the prostitutes asked, as he passed by. He didn't turn his
head or otherwise respond. Usually the *Jack Burns* seemed to be
part of a declarative sentence, but one he couldn't understand—
in Dutch, or in some other language that wasn't English. (Not
many of the women were Dutch.)

Jack walked as far north as the Zeedijk, just to see for himself
that Tattoo Theo's old shop, De Rode Draak—the departed Red
Dragon—was indeed gone. He easily found the small St. Olofssteeg, but Tattoo Peter's basement shop had moved many years
ago to the Nieuwebrugsteeg, a nearby street. Jack saw the new
tattoo parlor, but he didn't go in. When he asked one of the prostitutes what she knew about the shop, she said that someone

named Eddie was in charge—Tattoo Peter's second son, Jack thought she said.

"Oh, you mean Eddie Funk," someone else would later tell Jack, suggesting that the Eddie in the new shop wasn't actually related to Tattoo Peter. But what did it matter? Whoever Eddie was, he couldn't help Jack.

Tattoo Peter—Eddie's father or not—had died on St. Patrick's Day, 1984. Or so Jack had read in an old tattoo magazine when he and Leslie Oastler were cleaning out Daughter Alice in Toronto.

"Listen to this," he remembered saying to Mrs. Oastler. "Tattoo Peter was born in Denmark. I never knew he was a Dane! He actually worked for Tattoo Ole before moving to Amsterdam."

"So what?" Leslie had said.

"I never knew *any* of this!" Jack had cried. "He drove a Mercedes-Benz? I never saw it! He walked with a cane—I never saw the cane! I never saw him *walk*! His wife was French, a Parisian *singer*? People compared her to Edith Piaf!"

"I think Alice told me he stepped on a mine," Mrs. Oastler had said. "That's how he lost his leg."

"But she never told *me*!" he'd shouted.

"She never told you *fuck-all*, Jack," he remembered Leslie saying.

Jack walked around the Oude Kerk in the falling rain, but he didn't go inside. He didn't know why he was procrastinating. The kindergarten next to the Old Church looked fairly new. There were more prostitutes than he remembered on the Oudekerksplein, but the kindergarten children hadn't been there when Jack and his mom had traipsed through the district.

Jack had no difficulty finding the police station on the Warmoesstraat, but he didn't go inside the station, either. He wasn't ready to talk to Nico Oudejans, assuming Nico was still a policeman and Jack could find him.

Jack walked on the Warmoesstraat in the direction of the Dam Square, pausing at the corner of the Sint Annenstraat—exactly where he and his mom and Saskia and Els had encountered Jacob Bril, who had the Lord's Prayer tattooed on his chest. There was a tattoo of Lazarus leaving his grave on Bril's stomach. There were some things you didn't forget, no matter how young you were when you saw them.

"In the Lord's eyes, you are the company you keep!" Jacob Bril had told Alice.

"What would you know about the Lord's eyes?" Els had asked him. Or so Jack remembered—if *any* of it was true!

The Tattoo Museum on the Oudezijds Achterburgwal—maybe a minute's walk from Jack's hotel—was a warm and cozy place with more paraphernalia and memorabilia from the tattoo world than Jack had seen in any other tattoo parlor. He met Henk Schiffmacher at noon, when the museum opened, and Henk showed him around. Henk's tattoo shop was also there—Hanky Panky's House of Pain, as it was called. Whoever Eddie was, in the *new* Tattoo Peter, Henk Schiffmacher was the Tattoo Peter of his day; everyone in the ink-and-pain business knew Hanky Panky.

Henk was a big, heavy guy with a biker's beard and long hair. A female death's head, with what looked like a single breast on her forehead, was breathing fire on his left biceps. A spool of film was unwinding on his right forearm. Of course Hanky Panky had other tattoos; his body was a road map of his travels. But Jack would remember these two best.

He watched Henk give a Japanese guy an irezumi of a cockroach on his neck. (*Irezumi* means *tattoo* in Japanese.) Hanky Panky had traveled everywhere: Japan, the Philippines, Singapore, Bangkok, Sumatra, Nepal, Samoa.

While Henk tattooed the cockroach on the Japanese guy's neck, Jack listened to Johnny Cash sing "Rock of Ages" on the CD player. A good tattoo shop was a whole universe, he'd heard his mother say. "A place where every desire is forgiven," Henk Schiffmacher said. Why, then, couldn't Jack's mom forgive his dad? And how had William managed to forgive Alice, or *had* he? (Jack thought that *he* couldn't forgive her.)

"Is a guy named Nico Oudejans still a cop in the district?" Jack asked Hanky Panky.

"Nico? He's still the *best* cop in the district," Henk said. "Nico's a frigging *brigadier*."

On Jacob Bril's bony back was his favorite tattoo, the Ascension—Christ departing this world in the company of angels. As Jack walked through the red-light district to the Warmoesstraat police station, he remembered Bril's version of Heaven as a dark and cloudy place. It had stopped raining, but the cobblestones were greasy underfoot and the sky—like Jacob Bril's Heaven—remained dark and cloudy.

Jack Burns heard his name a few more times. Wherever they were from, some of the women in the windows and doorways were moviegoers—or they had been moviegoers in a previous life.

Jack crossed the bridge over the canal by the Old Church and came upon the small, foul-smelling pissoir—a one-man urinal—where he remembered peeing as a child. It had been dark; his mom had stood outside the barrier while he peed. She kept telling him to hurry up. She probably didn't want to be seen standing alone in the area of the Oudekerksplein at night. Jack could hear drunken young men singing as he peed; they must have been singing in English or he wouldn't have remembered some of the words in their song.

They were English football fans, his mother would tell him later. "They're the worst," she'd said. There'd been a football game, which the English team had either lost or won; it seemed to make no difference, in regard to how their fans behaved in the red-light district. They were "filthy louts," Jack remembered Saskia saying; *filthy louts* wasn't in his mom's vocabulary.

Jack walked around the Oude Kerk once more, on the side where the new kindergarten shared the street with the whores. Someone was following him; a man had fallen into step behind him at the corner of the Stoofsteeg, almost as soon as Jack had left the Tattoo Museum and the House of Pain. When Jack slowed down, the man slowed down, too—and when Jack sped up, the man picked up his pace again.

A fan, Jack thought. He hated it when they followed him. If they came up and said, "Hi, I like your movies," and then shook his hand, and went on their way—well, that was fine. But the *followers* really irritated Jack; they were usually women.

Not this one. He was a tough-looking guy with a dirty-blond beard, wearing running shoes and a windbreaker; his hands were shoved into the pockets of the windbreaker as he walked, his shoulders thrust forward as if it were still raining or he was cold. A guy in his fifties, maybe—late forties, anyway. The man didn't make the slightest effort to pretend he *wasn't* following Jack; it was as if he were daring Jack to turn around and face him.

Jack doubted that the bastard would have the balls to follow him into the police station, so he just kept walking.

Jack was one small street away from the Warmoesstraat when a brown-skinned prostitute stepped out of her doorway in her underwear and high heels; she almost touched him. "Hey, Jack—I've seen you in the *movies,*" she said. She had a Spanish-sounding accent; she might have been Dominican or Colombian.

When she saw the man who was trailing Jack, she immediately put up her hands as if the man were pointing a gun at her; she quickly stepped back inside her doorway. That was when Jack knew that the man following him was a cop. Clearly the Dominican or Colombian woman knew who the cop was; she didn't want any trouble with him.

Jack stopped walking and turned to face the policeman, whose eyes were still a robin's-egg blue, and high on one cheekbone was the small, identifying scar like the letter *L.* The beard had fooled Jack. When the cop had been in his late twenties or early thirties, when Jack had first met him, Nico Oudejans didn't have a beard. Jack had always thought that Nico was a nice guy; he'd been very nice to Jack when the boy was four. Now, in his fifties, Nico looked just plain tough.

"I've been expecting you, Jack. For a few years now, I've had my eye out for you. I keep telling the ladies," Nico said, with a nod to the Dominican or Colombian prostitute, who was smiling in her doorway, " 'One day Jack Burns, the actor, will show up. Give me a call when you see him,' I keep telling them. Well," Nico said, shaking Jack's hand, "I got half a dozen calls today. I knew at least one of the ladies had to be right."

When they turned onto the Warmoesstraat, the policeman put his hand on Jack's shoulder and steered him to the right—almost as if Nico didn't trust Jack to remember where the police station was. "Were you coming to see me, Jack?"

"Yes, I was," Jack said.

"So your mom's dead?" Nico asked.

Jack assumed that Nico had read about Alice's death; because she was Jack Burns's mother, her death had been reported in most of the movie magazines. But Nico Oudejans didn't read those magazines. The policeman had just guessed that Jack wouldn't have come back to Amsterdam if Alice were still alive.

"Why?" Jack asked him.

"I'll bet your mom would have talked you out of coming," Nico said. "She sure would have tried."

They went into the Warmoesstraat station and climbed the

stairs to a bare, virtually empty office on the second floor. There was just a table and three or four chairs, and Jack sat across the table from the policeman; it was as if Jack were going to be questioned about a crime. Jack thought it was funny that Nico left the office door open, as if they couldn't possibly have had anything *private* to discuss. Jack got the feeling that every cop in the building not only knew in advance everything he might ask Nico Oudejans—they had all the answers, too.

Maybe because he was with a cop, Jack just started talking. He told Nico everything. (As if all the deceits and deceptions of Jack's childhood were *his* crime, not his mother's; as if what he'd only recently learned was a story Jack had somehow concealed from himself.)

Jack didn't even pause, or interrupt himself, when another policeman came into the office and put some money on the table in front of Nico; after that cop left, a second and a third policeman came in and did the same thing. Maybe five or six cops did this—some in uniform, others in plainclothes like Nico—before Jack even got to the Amsterdam part of the story.

When Jack finally got to the Amsterdam part, he was pretty worked up. While Jack had talked, Nico had hand-rolled a few cigarettes. He had some dark-looking tobacco in a pouch, and he went on carefully rolling the cigarettes as if he were alone. Jack had the impression that putting a cigarette together mattered more to Nico than smoking it. But now Nico stopped making cigarettes. There were not more than three or four cigarettes on the table; the policeman hadn't lit one yet.

"I thought Mom did it for only one night," Jack said. "I thought there was just one kid, probably a virgin. He broke her pearl necklace."

"Nobody does it for only one night, Jack. When I told her to stop, or I'd have her deported, she just kept doing it. With Alice, they were always virgins. At least they *told* her they were virgins, or they looked like virgins."

"But why'd she do it?" Jack asked. "She had a job, didn't she? She was making money at Tattoo Peter's *and* at Tattoo Theo's."

Alice had two pretty good jobs, in fact, and William was giving her money for Jack's expenses—this in addition to whatever Mrs. Wicksteed was sending her. Alice didn't need money. However, the one way she hadn't tried to make William come back to her was that she hadn't exposed *Jack* to any risk; she hadn't yet done something to herself that a child of his age shouldn't see. But if she was a *prostitute,* Alice reasoned, and if Jack was exposed to *that*—well, how would it be for a boy growing up to remember his mother as a whore?

" 'What if Jack remembers that this is what you did to me?' she asked your dad," Nico Oudejans told Jack. " 'Since you like prostitutes so much that you play for them, William,' your mother said, 'what if Jack remembers how I became a whore because you stopped playing for me?' "

Nico told Jack that William played the organ for the prostitutes for strictly religious reasons. "He was a fanatical Christian, but the good kind of fanatic," Nico explained. William had insisted that there be an organ service for the prostitutes—at that early hour of the morning when many of them stopped working. William wanted them to know that the Oude Kerk was theirs at that time, and that he was playing for them. He wanted them to come to the Old Church and be soothed by the music; he wanted them to pray. (William wanted them to stop being prostitutes, of course, but the music was the only way he ever proselytized to them.)

Not everyone at the Oude Kerk was in favor of William's playing the organ for the prostitutes, but he silenced most of his critics by citing the zeal of St. Ignatius Loyola. William Burns said that he'd encountered a greater evil in Amsterdam than St. Ignatius had met on the streets of Rome. Ignatius had raised money among rich people; he'd founded an asylum for fallen women. It was in Rome where the saint announced that he would sacrifice his life if he could prevent the sins of a single prostitute on a single night.

"Naturally, some of the higher-ups at the Old Church expressed their doubts—after all, Loyola was a *Catholic,*" Nico Oudejans told Jack. "Among Protestants, your dad was sounding a little too close to Rome for comfort. But William said, 'Look, I'm not trying to prevent the sins of a single prostitute'— although, in his own way, he *was.* 'I'm just trying to make these women feel a little better. And if some of them hear Our Lord's noise in the music, what's the harm in that?' "

" 'Our Lord's *noise*'?" Jack asked.

"That's what William called it, Jack. He used to say that, if you could hear God's noise in the organ, you were at heart a believer."

"Did it work?" Jack asked. "Were any prostitutes *converted*?"

"He made believers out of some of those women," Nico said, "but I don't think any of them stopped working as prostitutes—at least not until long after your mother *started*. Some of the prostitutes didn't like your dad—they thought he was yet another Christian do-gooder who disapproved of them. William had just found an odd way in which to disapprove! But more of the ladies hated your mother. They wouldn't let their own children anywhere near the red-light district, but your mom dragged you through it every day and night—just to drive your dad crazy."

"You told her you'd have her *deported*?" Jack asked. Another policeman came into the office and put more Dutch guilders on the table.

"Prostitutes who weren't Dutch citizens used to get deported all the time," Nico said. "But your dad didn't want her deported. He didn't want to lose you, Jack. At the same time, he couldn't bear to see you in this environment."

Jack asked about Frans Donker, the organ-tuner. Nico said that Donker had imitated, or had tried to imitate, everything William did. Donker had spent half his time trying to play the organ instead of tuning it. "And when your dad needed a good night's sleep—when he was too tired to play for the ladies in the Oudekerksplein—Frans played for them. I think Frans Donker was a little simple; maybe someone had dropped him on his head when he was a baby," the policeman speculated. "But your dad treated Donker like a helpless pet. William indulged Donker, he pitied him, he was always charitable to him. Not that Donker deserved it—that boy didn't know what he was about."

"He put baby powder on his ass," Jack remembered out loud.

"Donker even imitated your dad's tattoos, but badly," Nico said. "Then he took a really stupid job—something only Donker would *dream* of doing—and we never saw him again in the district."

"I think I know what Donker did," Jack told the policeman. "He took a job on a cruise ship, playing the piano. He sailed to Australia, to be tattooed by Cindy Ray."

"Yes, that's it!" Nico Oudejans cried. "What a memory you have, Jack! That's a detail even a cop like me had forgotten."

Jack also remembered the dark-brown woman from Suriname; she was one of the first prostitutes to speak to him. He'd been surprised that she knew his name. She'd been in a window on either the Korsjespoortsteeg or the Bergstraat—not in the red-light district but in that same general area where Jack and his mom had met Femke. (And he'd thought that Femke was an unusual prostitute, when in fact she was a *lawyer*!)

The Surinamese prostitute had given him a chocolate the color of her skin. "I've been saving this for you, Jack," she'd said. And he'd believed, for years, that she must have been one of his dad's girlfriends—one of the prostitutes who'd taken William home with her, and had slept with him, as Jack's mother had led the boy to believe. But that wasn't true.

Jack's father had not had sex with a prostitute in Amsterdam; William had only played the organ for them, a sound both huge and holy, which had compelled them to just *listen*. As for some of them—those who'd managed to hear the Lord's noise in the music—William *may* have saved them from the sins of a single night, albeit later in their lives, when a few of them *did* stop being prostitutes.

"I called your dad the *Protestant* Loyola, which seemed to please him," Nico Oudejans told Jack.

Nico also told Jack that the Surinamese prostitute was one of William's earliest converts to Christianity; she'd heard God's noise in the organ and had become an overnight believer.

Jack had lost count of how many policemen had come into the office and put their guilders on the table in front of Nico, but when *another* cop had come and gone, Jack asked Nico if he had won a bet on a game or a horse.

"I won a bet on *you*, Jack," the policeman said. "I bet every cop in District Two that one day, before I retired, Jack Burns would walk into the Warmoesstraat station, and we'd have this little talk about his mom and dad."

The next evening, Wednesday, Jack went with Nico to the Oude Kerk to hear Willem Vogel, the organist, rehearse. Vogel had officially retired from teaching and conducting, but he still wrote music for organ and choir—a CD of his compositions had recently been released—and he still played in the Oude Kerk, the long service on Sunday and the Wednesday-evening rehearsal. Willem Vogel was in his late seventies but looked younger. He had long, hairless hands and was wearing a sweater with sagging elbows; in the unheated church, a wool scarf was tied around his neck.

Jack had correctly remembered the narrow, brick-lined stairs leading to the organist's hidden chamber above the congregation. The wooden handrail was on one side as you climbed; a waxed rope, the color of burned caramel, was on the other. There was a bare, bright, unshaded lightbulb behind the leather-covered organ bench; it cast the perfect, shadowless light upon the yellowed pages of the music. Vogel's well-worn shoes made a soft tapping on the foot pedals; his long fingers made an even softer clicking on the keys.

Jack could hear only the drone of the choir, in the distant background, when the organ was soft or not playing. When Vogel played hard, you could barely hear the accompanying voices from the organ chamber. At a moment when the choir sang without him, Vogel opened a small piece of hard candy—neatly putting the paper wrapper in his pocket before popping the candy in his mouth.

The names printed on the stops (the registers) were meaningless to Jack. It was a world beyond him.

BAARPIJP

8 VOET

OCTAAF

4 VOET

NACHTHOORN

2 VOET

TREMULANT POSITIEF

Jack struggled to hear the Lord's noise in the music. But even when Vogel played the *Sanctus* and the *Agnus Dei,* the Lord wasn't speaking to Jack.

Willem Vogel had never met Jack's dad. Once, in 1970, Vogel had been out to dinner rather late with some friends; one of the friends suggested that they go to the Oude Kerk and listen to William Burns's concert for the fallen ladies, but Vogel was tired and declined the invitation. "I regret I never heard him play," the organist told Jack. "Some say he was marvelous; others say that William Burns was too much of an *entertainer* to be taken seriously as a musician."

The next morning, Jack went with Nico Oudejans to a café where they were meeting Saskia for coffee. Saskia had stopped being a prostitute more than ten years before; her retirement hadn't improved her disposition, Nico forewarned Jack. She'd gone to a school for beauticians and had learned how to cut hair, maybe also how to do makeup and manicures; she worked in a beauty shop on the Rokin—a wide, busy street with many medium-expensive shops.

Saskia hadn't wanted Nico and Jack to come to the beauty shop. Given her former line of work, even a friendly visit from the police was unwelcome. And Saskia feared that—in a beauty shop, of all places—the ladies would make too much of a fuss over her knowing Jack Burns.

When Jack saw her coming, he thought she'd had more than a career change. She'd had a whole makeover. Gone was the winking armload of bracelets, hiding her burn scar. In her fifties now, she was still thin, but the gauntness had left her face. There wasn't a trace of the come-on of her former profession about her. Saskia's hair was cut as short as a boy's. Over a white turtleneck, she wore what looked like a man's tweed jacket. Her baggy jeans were unflattering; her ankle-high boots, with a low heel, gave her a mannish walk.

Jack got to his feet and kissed her, but Saskia was a little cool to him—not unfriendly but not warm, either. She was only marginally friendlier to Nico. She was carrying a Yorkshire terrier in her oversize handbag. The dog and Nico appeared to be old friends; the Yorkie hopped out of Saskia's handbag and sat contentedly in Nico's lap while the waiter took Saskia's order.

Jack half expected her to order a ham-and-cheese croissant, but she asked for a coffee instead. He wasn't surprised that she'd had her teeth fixed. Why wouldn't a new mouth have been included in her makeover?

"I know why you're here, Jack, and it doesn't interest me," Saskia began. "I don't go along with it." Jack didn't say anything. "Everyone took your dad's side. But I hate men, and I liked your mom. Besides, I wasn't working in the district to take time out to go to church and listen to him play his bleeding-heart organ."

"I remember bringing you ham-and-cheese croissants," Jack told her. (He was trying to calm her down, because she sounded angry.)

"Your father hung out there—that was where your mother let him see you, when she was buying a bloody ham-and-cheese croissant. I think I would die on the spot if I ever ate another one."

"You and Els took turns being my babysitter?" Jack asked her.

"Your mom helped Els and me pay the rent on our rooms," she answered. "Alice paid part of Els's rent and part of mine. The three of us shared two rooms. It made sense, *businesswise.*"

"And Mom admitted only virgins?" he asked.

"Some of those boys had been with half the ladies in the district! It only mattered to Alice that they *looked* like virgins," Saskia said.

"Did she honestly believe that my dad would get back together with her, just to stop her from being a prostitute?"

"She believed that your dad would do almost anything to protect *you*—to give you the life he thought you should have, which *wasn't* a life in the red-light district," Saskia said. "It was the fuckhead lawyer who worked out a way to make your mother stop being a prostitute."

"You didn't like the lawyer?" Jack asked. He remembered how Saskia and Els had screamed at Femke; how he'd thought that Els and Femke had come close to having a physical fight.

"Femke was as much of an asshole do-gooder as your fucking father, Jack. On the one hand, she was this outspoken advocate for prostitutes' rights; on the other hand, she wanted us all to go back to school or learn another profession!"

"What was the deal that she offered Mom?"

"Femke told your mother to get off the street and take you back to Canada. Your dad wouldn't follow you this time, Femke promised. *If* your mom would put you in a good school—if she *kept* you in school—your dad would pay for everything. But your mother was tough; she told Femke that your father had to promise he would never seek even *partial* custody of you. *And* he had to promise that he wouldn't look you up, not even when you were older—not even if Alice was *dead.*"

"But why would my dad promise *that*?"

"He opted to keep you *safe,* Jack—even if it meant he could never make contact with you," Nico Oudejans said.

"If your mom couldn't have your dad, then he couldn't have you," Saskia said. "It was that simple. Listen, Jack—your mother would have slashed her throat and bled to death in front of you, just to teach your fucking father a *lesson.*"

"What *lesson* was that?" Jack cried. "That he should never have left her?"

"Listen, Jack," Saskia said again. "I admired your mom because she put a *price tag* on his leaving her—a *high* one. Most women can never be paid enough for the terrible things men do to them."

"But what terrible thing did *he* do to *her*?" Jack asked Saskia. "He just *left* her! He didn't abandon me; he gave her money for my education, and for my other expenses—"

"You can't get a woman pregnant and then change your mind about her and *not* have it cost you, Jack," Saskia said. "Just ask your father."

Nico hadn't said anything since telling Jack that his dad had opted to keep him *safe.* Saskia, like Alice, had clearly chosen revenge over reason.

"Do you cut men's hair, too?" Jack asked her. "Or just women's?" (He was trying to calm himself down a little.)

Saskia smiled. She'd finished her coffee. She made a kissing sound with her lips, and the Yorkshire terrier sprang out of Nico's lap and into her arms. She put the tiny dog back in her handbag and stood up from the table. "Just women's," she told Jack, still smiling. "But now that you're all grown up, *Jackie boy,* if you ever want someone to cut your *balls* off, just ask me."

"I guess she didn't learn the castration part in beauty school," Nico Oudejans said, after they'd watched Saskia walk away. She didn't once turn to wave; she just kept going.

"What about Els?" Jack asked Nico. "I suppose you know what's happened to her, too."

"Fortunately for you," Nico said, "Els has a somewhat sweeter disposition."

"She's not cutting hair?" Jack asked.

"You'll see," the policeman said. "Everyone has a history, Jack."

* * *

Nico led Jack past the Damrak, away from the red-light district. They wound their way through streams of shoppers—across the Nieuwendijk to the tiny Sint Jacobsstraat, where Els occupied a second-floor apartment. Her window with the red light was a little uncommon for a prostitute's window, not solely for being outside the district but because her room was above street-level. Yet when Jack considered that Els had taken an overview of her life in prostitution—she'd grown up on a farm and took an *overview* of life on a farm as well—he thought that Els in her window *above* the street was where she belonged.

During the day, she greeted passersby with boisterous affection, but Nico told Jack that Els was more judgmental at night; if you were a drunk or a drug addict pissing in the street, she would turn her police-issue flashlight on you and loudly condemn your bad manners. On the Sint Jacobsstraat, Els was still a prostitute, but she was also a self-appointed sheriff. Drugs had changed the red-light district and driven her out of it; alcohol and drugs had killed her only children. (Two young men—they'd both died in their twenties.)

Jack had been wrong to think that Els was about his mother's age, or only a little older. Even from street-level, looking up at her, he could tell she was a woman in her seventies; when Jack had been a four-year-old, Els would have been in her forties.

"Jackie!" Els called, blowing him kisses. "My little boy has come back!" she announced to the Sint Jacobsstraat. "Jackie, Jackie—come give your old *nanny* a hug! You, too, Nico. You can give me a hug, if you want to."

They went up the staircase to her apartment. The window-room was only a small part of the place, which was spotlessly clean—the smell of all the rooms dominated by the coffee grinder in the kitchen. Els had a housekeeper, a much younger woman named Marieke, who immediately began grinding beans for coffee. As a former farm girl, Els hated cleaning chores, but she knew the importance of a tidy house. She shared the prostitute duties with another "girl," she explained to Jack; the women took turns using the window-room, although Petra, the other prostitute, didn't live in the apartment.

"Petra's the young one, I'm the old one!" Els exclaimed happily. (Jack didn't meet Petra, but Nico told him she was sixty-one.)

Els, who claimed to be "about seventy-five," said that most of her regular customers were morning visitors. "They take naps in the afternoon, and they're too old to go out at night." The only customers who visited her at night were the ones off the street— that is, if they happened to be passing by when Els was sitting in her upstairs window. For the most part, she let Petra sit in the window. "At night, I'm usually asleep," Els admitted, giving Jack's forearm a squeeze. "Or I go to the movies—especially if it's one of *your* movies, Jackie!"

Els had always been a big woman with an impressive bust. Her bosom preceded her with the authority of a great ship's prow; her hips rolled when she walked. She was massive but not fat, although Jack noticed how her forearms and the backs of her upper arms sagged—and she walked with a slight limp. She had a bad heart, she claimed—"and perhaps an embolism in the brain." Els pointed ominously to her head; she still wore a platinum-blond wig.

"Every day, Jackie," she said, kissing his cheek, "I take so many pills, I lose count!"

Els had landlord problems, too, she wanted Nico to know; maybe the police could do something about the building's new owner. "Like shoot him," she told Nico, with a smile, kissing him on the cheek—then kissing Jack again. There'd been a rent dispute and a tax issue; the new landlord was a prick, in her opinion.

Els was a longstanding spokesperson for the prostitutes' union; she regularly spoke to high school students about the lives of prostitutes. The students, many of them only sixteen, had questions for her about first-time sex. Years ago, she'd had a husband; she'd been married for three years before her husband found out she was a whore.

She had a bruise on her face. Nico asked her if she was getting over a black eye—perhaps something one of her off-the-street customers had given her.

"No, no," she said. "My customers wouldn't dare hit me." Els had gotten into a fistfight at a café on the Nes, just off the Dam Square. She'd run into a former prostitute who wouldn't speak to her. "Some holier-than-thou *cunt*," she said. "You should see *her* face, Nico."

Jack thought that the holier-than-thou subject might make a good starting point for a conversation about his father. Els had not only known him; unbeknownst to Alice, Els had often gone to the Oude Kerk in the wee hours of the morning to hear William play the organ. Jack gathered that Els had not heard any racket from the Lord—just the music. To his surprise, Els told Jack that she had taken him to the Old Church one night.

"I thought that even if you didn't remember hearing William play, some part of you might absorb the *sound,*" she said. "But I had to carry you there—you were asleep the whole way—and you never woke up or took your head off my breast the entire time. You slept through a two-hour concert, Jackie. You never heard a note! I don't know what you could possibly remember of any of it."

"Not much," he admitted.

Jack knew how hidden the organist's chamber in the Oude Kerk was. He knew that his father would never have seen him sleeping on the big prostitute's bosom—which was probably just as well, knowing his dad's opinion of what Nico had called "this environment."

Because Saskia and Alice were more popular—because they had more customers, Els informed Jack—Els was Jack's babysitter (what she called his "nanny") most of the time.

"And I was stronger than your mom or Saskia, so I got to carry you!" she exclaimed. She had lugged him from bed to bed. "I used to think you were like one of us—one of the prostitutes," she told Jack. "Because you never went to bed just once; because I was always taking you out of one bed and tucking you into another!"

"I remember that you and Femke almost came to blows," he said.

"I could have killed her. I *should* have killed her, Jackie!" Els cried. "But Femke was the deal-maker, and something had to be done. It's just that it was a bad deal—that's what made me so mad. Lawyers don't care about what's *fair.* What's a good deal to a lawyer is any deal that both parties will agree to."

"Something had to be done, Els—as you say," Nico said.

"Fuck you, Nico," Els told him. "Just drink your coffee."

It was good coffee; Marieke had made them some cookies, too.

"Did my dad see me leave Amsterdam?" Jack asked Els.

"He saw you leave *Rotterdam,* Jackie. He watched the ship sail out of the harbor. Femke had brought him to the docks; she'd driven him to Rotterdam in her car. Saskia would have none of it.

She accompanied your mom and me and you to the train station in Amsterdam, but that was as much *drama* as she would tolerate. That was Saskia's word for the good-bye business—*drama,* she called it."

"So you took the train to Rotterdam with us?"

"I went with you to the docks. I got you both on board, Jackie. Your mom wasn't in much better shape than your dad. It seemed to be just dawning on her that she wouldn't see William after that day, although the deal was what she said she wanted."

"You saw my dad at the docks?"

"Fucking Femke wouldn't get out of the car, but your dad did," Els said. "He just cried and cried; he fell apart. He lay down on the ground. I had to pick him up off the pavement; I had to carry him back to the fuckhead lawyer's Mercedes."

"Did Tattoo Peter really have a Mercedes?" Jack asked her.

"Femke had a better one, Jackie," Els said. "She drove William back to Amsterdam in her Mercedes. I took the train from Rotterdam. In my mind's eye, I kept seeing you wave from the ship. You thought you were waving to me—I was waving back, of course—but it was your father you were really waving good-bye to. Some *deal,* huh, Nico?" she asked the policeman sharply.

"Something had to be done, Els," he said again.

"Fuck you, Nico," the old prostitute once more told him.

When Jack got back to the Grand, two faxes were waiting for him; it didn't help that he read them in the wrong order. He began with a surprising suggestion from Richard Gladstein, a movie producer. Bob Bookman had sent Gladstein the script for *The Slush-Pile Reader.*

Dear Jack,

  Stay where you are, in Amsterdam! What do you say we have a meeting with William Vanvleck? I know you've worked with Wild Bill before. It strikes me that The Slush-Pile Reader *is a kind of remake, maybe right up The Remake Monster's alley. Think about it: the story is a remade porn film but* not *a porn film, right? We wouldn't* show *anything pornographic, but the very idea of James "Jimmy" Stronach's relationship with Michele Maher is a* little *pornographic, isn't it? (He's too big, she's too small. Brilliant!) We should discuss. But*

*first tell me your thoughts on The Mad Dutchman. As it
happens, he's in Amsterdam and you're in Amsterdam. If you
like the idea of Vanvleck as a director, I could meet you there.*

Richard

Everything became clearer when Jack read the second fax,
which he should have read first. It was from Bob Bookman at
C.A.A.

*Dear Jack,
    Richard Gladstein loved your script of* The Slush-Pile
Reader. *He wants to discuss possible directors with you.
Richard has the crazy—maybe not so crazy—idea of
using Wild Bill Vanvleck. Call me. Call Richard.*

Bob

Jack was so excited that he called Richard Gladstein at home,
waking him up. (It was very early in the morning in L.A.)
    Wild Bill Vanvleck was in his late sixties, maybe his early sev-
enties. He'd moved back to Amsterdam from Beverly Hills. No
one in Hollywood had asked him to direct a picture for a couple
of years. The Remake Monster had sold his ugly mansion on
Loma Vista Drive. Something had gone wrong with his whippets. Jack remembered the skinny little dogs running free in the
mansion, slipping and falling on the hardwood floors.
    Something bad had happened to Wild Bill's chef and gar-
dener, the Surinamese couple. Someone had drowned in Vanvleck's swimming pool, Richard Gladstein told Jack; Richard
couldn't remember if it was the child-size woman from Suriname or her miniature husband. (Possibly the drowning victim
had been one of the whippets!)
    So The Mad Dutchman was back in Amsterdam, where he
was living with a much younger woman. Vanvleck had a hit series on Dutch TV; from Richard Gladstein's description, Wild
Bill had remade *Miami Vice* in Amsterdam's red-light district.
    Richard talked about the difficulty of bringing Miramax
around to the idea of hiring William Vanvleck to direct *The
Slush-Pile Reader*—that is, assuming Richard and Jack had a
good meeting with The Mad Dutchman. But the idea, Gladstein

and Jack agreed, had possibilities. (Bob Bookman had already overnighted Jack's screenplay to Wild Bill.)

Richard and Jack also talked about the idea of Lucia Delvec-chio in the Michele Maher role. "She'd have to lose about twenty pounds," Jack told Richard.

"She'd *love* to!" Gladstein said. There was little doubt of that, Jack thought. There were a lot of women in Hollywood who wanted to lose twenty pounds—they just needed a reason.

The more he thought about Wild Bill Vanvleck, the better Jack liked the idea. What had always been wrong with The Remake Monster's material was the material itself—namely, Wild Bill's screenplays. Not only how he'd ripped them off from other, bet-ter material, but how he went too far; he always pushed the parody past reasonable limits. If you're irreverent about everything, the audience is left with nothing or no one to like. Conversely, there was sympathy in Emma's story—both for the too-small slush-pile reader *and* for the porn star and bad screenwriter with the big penis. Vanvleck had never directed a *sympathetic* script before.

Jack wished he could ask Emma what she thought of the idea, but he didn't think that his working with Wild Bill Vanvleck as a director would necessarily make Emma roll over in her grave.

Jack went back out in the rain. He passed the Casa Rosso, where they showed porn films and had live-sex shows—more advice-giving, Jack had once believed. He wasn't tempted to see a show, not even as research for *The Slush-Pile Reader.*

He walked once more to the Warmoesstraat police station, but Nico was out working in the red-light district. A couple of young cops, both in uniform, told Jack that they thought William Van-vleck's TV series about homicide policemen was reasonably au-thentic. Wild Bill had spent time in the Warmoesstraat station; he'd gone out in the district with real cops on the beat. It was a fa-vorable sign that real policemen actually liked a TV series about cops.

Jack worked out at a gym on the Rokin. It was a good gym, but the music was too loud and relentless; it made him feel he was rushing, though he was taking his time. His appointment with Femke, which Nico had arranged, wasn't until four o'clock that afternoon. He was in no hurry. When Jack returned to the Grand from the gym, Nico Oudejans had left a package at the re-ception desk—a videocassette of Vanvleck's homicide series.

Jack showered and shaved, put on some decent clothes, and went out again. The address of Marinus and Jacob Poortvliet's law firm was on the Singel. Femke, their mother, was retired. Jack saw at once how easy it had been for his mom to confuse him into thinking that Femke occupied a prostitute's room on the Bergstraat. The Poortvliets' law office was roughly halfway between the Bergstraat and the Korsjespoortsteeg—virtually around the corner from those streets where the more upscale prostitutes were in business.

Some small details about the office were familiar; both the cars on the Singel and the pedestrians on the sidewalk were visible from the leather reading chair and the big leather couch. On the walls of the office, a few of the landscapes were also familiar. Jack even remembered the rug, an Oriental.

Femke was late; Jack talked with her sons. Conservatively dressed gentlemen in their fifties, they'd been university students in 1970. But even people of their generation remembered the controversial organist, William Burns, who'd played for the prostitutes in the Oude Kerk in the early-morning hours. University students had made the organ concerts in the Old Church a favorite among their late-night outings.

"Some of us considered your father an activist, a social reformer. After all, he expressed a profound sympathy for the prostitutes' plight," Marinus told Jack.

"Others took a view that was common among some of the prostitutes—I'm referring to those women who were *not* in William's audience at the Old Church. William was a Holy Roller in their eyes; converting the prostitutes meant nothing less than steering them *away* from prostitution," Jacob explained.

"But he played great," Marinus said. "No matter what you thought of William, he was a terrific organist."

The Poortvliets had a family-law practice; they not only took divorce and child-custody cases, but they also settled inheritance disputes and were engaged in estate planning. What had made William Burns's case difficult was that he was still a citizen of Scotland, although he had a visa that permitted him to work in Holland for a limited period of time. Alice, who was a Canadian citizen, had no such visa—but in the case of foreigners who were apprenticed to Dutch tattoo artists, the police allowed them several months to earn a tax-free living. After that, they were pressured to leave or pay Dutch taxes.

There could be no child-custody case in the Dutch courts, because Jack's mom and dad weren't Dutch citizens. As outrageously as his mother was exposing Jack to her new life as a prostitute, his father had no means to claim custody of the boy. Alice, however, could be made to leave the country—chiefly on the grounds that, as a prostitute, she had repeatedly engaged in sex with underage boys. And she was a magnet for more widespread condemnation within the prostitute community. (As if the hymn-singing and prayer-chanting in her window and doorway weren't inflammatory enough, Alice had dragged her four-year-old through the district.)

"You were carried, day and night, in the arms of that *giantess* among the whores," Marinus Poortvliet told Jack.

"Half the time you were asleep, or as inert as *groceries*," his brother, Jacob, said.

"The prostitutes called you 'the whole week's shopping,' because in that woman's arms you looked like a bag of groceries that could feed a family for a week," Marinus explained.

"So Dutch law had the means to deport my mom, but not to gain custody of me for my dad," Jack said, just to be sure. The two sons nodded.

That was when Femke arrived, and Jack once again felt intimidated by her—not because she was a fearsome and different kind of prostitute, but because she struck him as a great *initiator*. (No matter what experience you thought you'd had, Femke could *initiate* you into something you'd never known or even imagined.)

"When I look at you in your movies," she said to Jack, without bothering to say hello, "I see someone as pretty and talented as your father, but not half so open—so utterly unguarded. You're very much *guarded*, aren't you, Jack Burns?" she asked, seating herself in the leather reading chair. And Jack had once thought she'd taken up that position in her sidewalk window to attract customers off the street!

"Thank you for seeing me," Jack said to her.

"Very much *guarded*, isn't he?" she asked her sons, not expecting so much as a nod or a shake of the head from either of them. It wasn't a real question; Femke had already decided upon the answer.

At seventy-eight, only a couple of years older than Els, Femke was still shapely without being fat. Her elegance of dress, which she had seemingly been born with, made it abundantly clear to Jack that only an idiot (or a four-year-old) could ever have mistaken her for a whore. Her skin was as unwrinkled as the skin of a well-cared-for woman in her fifties; her hair, which was her own, was a pure snow-white.

"If only you'd been Dutch, I would have got your dad custody of you in a heartbeat, Jack. I would have happily sent your mother back to Canada *childless,*" Femke said. "The problem was, your father forgave her. He would forgive her anything, if she just promised to do the right thing by you."

"Meaning good schools, a safe neighborhood, and some vestige of stability?" Jack asked.

"Those aren't bad things, are they?" Femke said. "You seem to be both educated and alive. I daresay, in the direction your mom was headed, that wouldn't have happened *here.* Besides, she was at least beginning to accept that William would never come back to her—that began to happen in Helsinki. But that William would accept the pain of losing all contact with you—*if* Alice would just take you back to Canada and look after you, as a mother should—well, what a surprise *that* was! To your mother *and* to me. We didn't expect him to *agree* to it! But we'd both underestimated what a good Christian William was." Femke did not say *Christian* in an approving way. "I was just the negotiator, Jack. I wanted to drive a harder bargain for your dad. But what can you do when the warring parties *agree*? Is a deal not a deal?"

"You drove him to the docks, in Rotterdam?" Jack asked her. "They both went along with it, right till the end?"

Femke looked out the window at the slowly passing traffic on the Singel. "Your little face on the ship's deck was the only smiling face I saw, Jack. Your mother had to hold you up, so you could see over the rail. You were waving to that giant whore. The way your dad dropped to the ground, I thought he'd had a heart attack. I thought I'd be taking a *body* back to Amsterdam—in all likelihood, in the backseat of my Mercedes. The big prostitute picked him up and carried him to my car; she carried him as easily as she used to carry *you*! Mind you, I still thought your dad was dead. I didn't want William in the front seat, but that's where the huge whore put him. I could see then that he was alive, but barely. 'What have I done? How could I? What *am* I, Femke?'

your father asked me. 'You're a flaming *Christian,* William. You forgive too much,' I told him. But the deal was done, and your dad was the only man on earth who would stick to his side of a bargain like that. From the look of you, Jack, your mom stuck to her side of the bargain, too—sort of."

At that moment, Jack hated them both—his mother *and* his father. In his mom's case, the reasons were pretty obvious. In his dad's case, Jack suddenly saw him as a *quitter.* William Burns had given up on his son! Jack was furious. Femke, a retired lawyer but a good one, could see the fury on Jack's face.

"Oh, get over it. Don't be a *baby!*" she told him. "What's a grown man in good health doing wallowing around in the past? Just move on, Jack. Get married, try being a good husband—and be a good father to your children. With any luck, you'll see how hard it is. Stop *judging* them—I mean William *and* your mother!"

From the way her two grown sons fussed over her, Jack could tell that they adored her. Femke once more looked out the window; there was something final about the way she turned her face in profile to Jack, as if their meeting were over and she had nothing more to say. Nico Oudejans had asked her to see Jack, and she probably had a fair amount of respect for Nico—more than she had for Jack. She'd done her duty, her face in profile said; Femke wasn't freely going to offer Jack more information.

"If I could just ask you if you know what happened to him—starting with where he went," Jack said to her. "I assume he didn't stay in Amsterdam."

"Of course William didn't *stay,*" she said. "Not when he could imagine *you* on every street corner—not when your mother's image was *engraved* in the lewd posture of every prostitute, in every gaudy window and dirty doorway in the district!"

Jack didn't say anything. By their imploring glances and gestures, Femke's sons were urging him to be patient. If he just waited the old woman out, Jack would get what he'd come for—or so Femke's sons seemed to be saying.

"Hamburg," Femke said. "What organist doesn't want to play in one of those *German* churches—maybe even somewhere Bach himself once played? It was inevitable that William would go to Germany, but there was something special about Hamburg. I can't remember now. He said he wanted to get his hands on a Herbert Hoffmann—a famous organ, probably."

Jack took some small pleasure in correcting her; she was that kind of woman. "A famous *tattooist,* not an organ," he told Femke.

"I never saw your dad's tattoos, thank God," Femke said dismissively. "I just liked to listen to him play."

Jack thanked Femke and her sons for taking the time to see him. He took a passing look at the prostitutes in their windows and doorways on the Bergstraat and the Korsjespoortsteeg before he walked back to the Grand, this time avoiding the red-light district. Jack was glad he had the videocassette of Wild Bill Vanvleck's homicide series to look at, because he didn't feel like leaving the hotel.

There was more than one episode from the television series on the videocassette. Jack's favorite one was about a former member of the homicide team, an older man who goes back to police school at fifty-three. His name is Christiaan Winter, and he's just been divorced. He's estranged from his only child—a daughter in university—and he's taking a training course for policemen on new methods of dealing with domestic violence. The police used to be too lenient with the perpetrators; now they arrested them.

Of course the dialogue was all in Dutch; Jack had to guess what they were saying. But it was a character-driven story—Jack knew Christiaan Winter from an earlier episode, when the policeman's marriage was deteriorating. In the episode about domestic violence, Winter becomes obsessed with how much of it children see. The statistics all point to the fact that children of wife-beaters end up beating *their* wives, and children who are beaten become child-beaters.

The social message wasn't new to Jack, but Vanvleck had connected it to the cop's personal life. While Winter never beat his wife, the verbal abuse—Winter's *and* his wife's—no doubt damaged the daughter. One of the first cases of domestic violence that Christiaan Winter becomes involved in ends in a homicide—his old business. In the end, he is reunited with his former team.

Vanvleck's homicide series was more in the vein of understated realism than anything on American television; there was less visible violence, and the sexual content was more frank. Nor did happy endings find their unlikely way into any of the episodes—Christiaan Winter is not reunited with his family. The best he can manage is a civil conversation with his daughter in a coffeehouse, where he is introduced to her new boyfriend. We can tell that the veteran policeman doesn't care for the boyfriend, but he keeps his thoughts to himself. In the last shot, after his daughter gives him a kiss on the cheek, Winter realizes that the boyfriend has left some money on the table for the coffee.

This was *noir warm,* which was Wild Bill at his best—at least this is what Jack said to Nico Oudejans when Nico called and asked Jack his opinion of Vanvleck's series. Nico liked the series, too. Nico didn't ask Jack how the meeting with Femke had gone. Nico knew Femke; as a good cop, he knew every detail of Daughter Alice's story, too. Jack told Nico about Herbert Hoffmann being a tattoo artist, not an organ. Naturally, Nico asked if Jack was going to Hamburg.

He wasn't. Jack knew actors may be more highly skilled at lying than other people, but they are no more adept at lying to themselves—and even actors should know better than to lie to cops.

"What more do I need to know?" Jack asked Nico, who didn't answer him. The policeman just kept looking at Jack's eyes—then at his hands, then at his eyes again. Jack began to speak more rapidly; to Nico, Jack's thoughts were more run-on than consecutive, but the cop didn't question him.

Jack said that he hoped, for his father's sake, that William had another family. Jack wouldn't invade his father's privacy; after all, William hadn't invaded Jack's. Besides, Jack knew that Herbert Hoffmann had retired. Alice had revered Hoffmann, but Jack would leave Herbert Hoffmann in peace, too. So what if Hoffmann had almost surely met William Burns?

"Now that you're getting close, maybe you're afraid to find him, Jack," Nico said.

It was Jack's turn not to say anything; he just tried to look unafraid.

"Maybe you're afraid that you'll cause your father pain, or that he won't want to see you," the policeman said.

"Don't you mean that I'll cause him *more* pain?" Jack asked.

"Now that you're getting close, maybe you don't want to get any closer—that's all I'm saying, Jack."

"Maybe," Jack said. He didn't feel like much of an actor anymore. Jack Burns was a boy who'd never known his father, a boy whose father had been kept from him; maybe what Jack was really afraid of was losing his missing father as an *excuse*. That's what Claudia would have told him, but Nico said nothing more.

If William had wanted a Herbert Hoffmann, Jack thought he knew which kind. He imagined it was one of Hoffmann's sailing ships—often seen sailing out of port, or in the open sea on a long voyage. Sometimes there was a dark lighthouse and the ship was headed for rocks. Herbert Hoffmann's Sailor's Grave was among his most famous; there were his Last Port and his Letzte Reise or Last Trip, too. In most cases, Hoffmann's ships were sailing into danger or unknown adventures; the feeling the tattoos gave you was one of farewell, although Herbert Hoffmann had done his share of homeward-bound tattoos as well.

A Homeward Bound would not have been his father's choice, Jack was thinking. On the ship that had carried Jack away from his dad, Jack sensed there would have been more of a Sailor's Grave or a farewell feeling—at least from William's point of view. A ship leaving harbor conveys an uncertain future.

Or else William Burns had stuck to music on his skin. Jack could imagine that, too.

There was a nonstop flight from Los Angeles to Amsterdam—a little more than ten hours in the air. Richard Gladstein was going to be tired. He would leave L.A. at 4:10 in the afternoon and land in Amsterdam at 11:40 in the morning, the next day. Jack assumed that Richard would want to take a nap before they met Vanvleck for dinner that evening.

For two days, Jack didn't leave his hotel room except to go to the gym on the Rokin. He lived on room service; he wrote pages and pages to Michele Maher. He came up with nothing he would send to her, but the stationery at the Grand was both more plentiful and more attractive than that at the Hotel Torni.

Jack did manage to come up with a clever way of asking Michele Maher the full-body tattoo question—that is, dermatologically speaking.

Dear Michele,
    As a dermatologist, can you think of any reason why a person with a full-body tattoo might feel cold?

Please return the stamped, self-addressed postcard—
checking the appropriate box.

> *Yours,*
> *Jack*

On a postcard of the Oudezijds Voorburgwal canal, he gave Michele the following options.

☐ *No.*
☐ *Yes. Let's talk about it!*

> *Love,*
> *Michele*

Of course he didn't send that letter or the postcard. For one thing, he didn't have a U.S. stamp for the return delivery; for another, the "*Love, Michele*" was taking a lot for granted after fifteen years.

His second day alone, Jack almost went to see Els again in her apartment on the Sint Jacobsstraat. He didn't want to sleep with a prostitute in her seventies—he just liked Els.

Mainly Jack would lie awake at night—imagining his little face on the ship's deck, where his mother had lifted him above the rail. Jack was just smiling, and waving to beat the band, while the damage was being done around him—especially to his dad.

In Hamburg, maybe William had met someone; that might have helped him to forget Jack, if he'd *ever* managed to forget his son. After all, he'd had a correspondence with Miss Wurtz when Jack was attending St. Hilda's. It wasn't as if William had stopped thinking about Jack, cold.

When Richard arrived, he went straight to bed and Jack went back to the gym. Jack was eating more carbs and had changed his weightlifting routine; he'd managed to put on a few pounds, but Jack was still no Jimmy Stronach. (Not that there was anything he could have done to acquire Jimmy's *penis*.)

In the gym on the Rokin, possibly in a failing effort to drown out the awful music in the weight room, Jack tried singing that ditty his mother had sung only when she was drunk or stoned—the one that seemed to resurrect her Scottish accent.

Oh, I'll never be a kittie
or a cookie
or a tail.
The one place worse than
Dock Place
is the Port o' Leith jail.
No, I'll never be a kittie,
of one true thing I'm sure—
I won't end up on Dock Place
and I'll never be a hure.

How funny that it had once been Alice's mantra to never be a whore.

Jack thought of their nightly prayer, which—when he was a child—they usually said together. He remembered one night in Amsterdam when she fell asleep before he did, and he said the prayer by himself. Jack had spoken a little louder than usual, because he had to pray for the two of them. "The day Thou gavest, Lord, is ended. Thank You for it." (Of course that had probably happened more than *once.*)

Jack took a footbridge across the canal on his way back to the Grand. He stood on the bridge and watched a sightseeing boat drift by. In the stern, a small boy sat looking up at the footbridge—his face pressed to the glass. Jack waved, but the boy didn't wave back.

It was already dark when Jack walked with Richard Gladstein to the Herengracht, to a restaurant called Zuid Zeeland, where they were meeting William Vanvleck. Jack was in no mood for the meeting. He kept thinking about the *other* William—the one he would have loved but was afraid to meet.

V

❧

Dr. García

31
Therapy

Five years later—as if striking the match that would set fire to Jack's life in Los Angeles, strip his character bare, and ultimately lead him to seek his father—a young woman (younger than he realized at the time) sat not quite fully clothed on Jack's living-room couch in that forlorn dump he still lived in on Entrada Drive. She was thumbing through his address book, which she'd picked up off his desk, and reading aloud the women's names. In an insinuating tone of voice, she would first say the name and then guess what relationship Jack might have had, or still had, with the woman.

This juvenile behavior should have alerted him to the fact that she was clearly younger than she'd told him she was—not that Jack shouldn't have guessed her real age for other reasons. But he *did* have difficulties with math.

She got into the *G*'s before Jack said, "That's enough," and took his address book away from her; that's when the trouble really started.

"Elena García," the girl had just said. "Your cleaning lady, or former cleaning lady? You definitely fucked her."

Elena García—*Dr.* García—was Jack's psychiatrist. He had never had sex with her. For five years, Dr. García had not once been a love interest—but Jack had never depended on anyone to the degree that he depended on her. Elena García knew more about Jack Burns than anyone had ever known—including Emma Oastler.

Jack had often called Dr. García in tears, not always but sometimes in the middle of the night. He'd called her from Cannes—once when he was at a party at the Hôtel du Cap. That same day Jack had pushed a female photographer, a stalker paparazzo, off a chartered yacht; he'd had to pay an outrageous fine.

Another time, he banged some bimbo on the beach of the Hotel Martinez. She said she was an actress, but she turned out to be one of those Croisette dog-walkers; she'd been arrested for fucking on the beach before. And Jack should have won the Palme d'Or for bad behavior for the fracas he got into in that glass-and-concrete eyesore, the Palais des Festivals. This happened after the evening's red-carpet promenade. Jack was on a narrow staircase leading to one of the Palais's upstairs rooms. Some journalist shoved him into one of those thugs who comprise the festival's security staff; the security guy thought that Jack had purposely shoved *him,* which led to Jack's impromptu lateral drop. Chenko would have been proud of Jack for the perfect execution of his move—Coaches Clum, Hudson, and Shapiro, too—but the incident was in all the papers. The security thug broke his collarbone, and Jack got another stiff fine. The weaselly French!

Lastly, from his ocean-front suite at the Carlton, Jack poured a whole bottle of Taittinger (chilled) onto that former agent Lawrence. The fink was giving Jack the finger from the terrace. Lawrence was just the kind of asshole you ran into at Cannes. Jack *hated* Cannes.

From Dr. García's point of view, Jack's behavior was only marginally better in Venice, Deauville, and Toronto—the three film festivals where Richard Gladstein, Wild Bill Vanvleck, Lucia Delvecchio, and Jack promoted *The Slush-Pile Reader.* (A recent headline in *Variety*—LOTS OF LIBIDO ON THE LIDO—could have been written about Jack Burns.)

They had a very good run with what Jack would usually call *Emma's* movie; careerwise, it may have been Jack's best year. They shot the film in the fall of '98 and took it to those festivals in August and September of '99—before the premieres in New York and London near the end of that year.

There was the unfortunate incident with Lucia Delvecchio in the Hotel des Bains in Venice; she'd had too much to drink, and bitterly regretted having slept with Jack. But no one knew—not even Richard or Wild Bill. And no one except Lucia's husband, who was not in Venice, would have cared. Bad things happened in that languid lagoon.

"Don't be so hard on yourself," Jack told Lucia. "The whole city is sinking. Visconti shot *Death in Venice* in the Hotel des Bains. I think he knew what he was doing."

But it was mostly Jack's fault. Lucia had been drunk; he knew she was married. That precipitated another call to Dr. García. He called her from the Hotel Normandie in Deauville, too. (It wasn't Lucia that time; worse, it was an older member of the jury.)

"The older-woman thing *again*?" Dr. García had asked Jack on the phone.

"I guess so," he'd told her.

Jack was with Mrs. Oastler at the Toronto film festival when they screened *The Slush-Pile Reader* in Roy Thomson Hall—a packed house, a triumphant night. It was gratifying to show the film in Emma's hometown. But Leslie had a new girlfriend, a blonde, who didn't like Jack. The blonde wanted him to remove all his clothes from Mrs. Oastler's house. Jack didn't think Leslie cared whether he left his clothes in her house or not, but the blonde wanted him (and his things) gone.

Jack was in Mrs. Oastler's familiar kitchen when the blonde handed him the two photographs of his mother's naked torso and the *Until I find you* tattoo. "Those are Leslie's," he explained. "I have two photos; she has the other two."

"Take them," the blonde told him. "Your mother's dead, Jack. Leslie doesn't want to look at her breasts anymore."

"I don't want to look at them anymore, either," Jack said, but he took the photos. Now he had all four—these in addition to that photograph of Emma naked at seventeen.

Mrs. Oastler's mansion, as Jack used to think of it, was different with the blonde there. Leslie's bedroom door was usually closed; it was hard to imagine Mrs. Oastler closing her bathroom door, too, but maybe the blonde had taught her how to do it.

That trip to Toronto, Jack resisted sleeping with Bonnie Hamilton. She wanted to sell him an apartment in a new condo being built in Rosedale. "For when you tire of Los Angeles," Bonnie told him. But Toronto wasn't his town, notwithstanding that he had long been tired of L.A.

When he was in Toronto, Jack had a less than heart-to-heart talk with Caroline Wurtz. She was disappointed in him; she thought he should be looking for his father. Jack couldn't tell her half of what he'd learned on his return trip to the North Sea and the Baltic. He was in no shape to talk about it. It was all he could do to tell the story to Dr. García, and too often he couldn't talk to her, either. He tried, but the words wouldn't come—or he would start to shout or cry.

It was Dr. García's opinion that Jack shouted and cried too much. "Especially the crying—it's simply indecent for a man," she said. "You really should work on that." To that end, she encouraged Jack to tell her what had happened to him in chronological order. "Begin with that awful trip you took with your mother," Dr. García instructed him. "*Don't* tell me what you *now* know about that trip. Tell me what you thought happened *at the time*. Begin with what you first *imagined* were your memories. And try not to jump ahead more than is absolutely necessary. In other words, go easy on the foreshadowing, Jack." Later, after he began—with Copenhagen, when he was four—Dr. García would frequently say: "Try not to *interject* so much. I know you're not a writer, but just try to stick to the story."

It hurt Jack's feelings to hear her say that he wasn't a writer; it felt especially unfair after his not-inconsiderable contributions to Emma's screenplay of *The Slush-Pile Reader*.

And to recite out loud the story of his life—that is, coherently *and* in chronological order—would take *years*! Dr. García knew that; she was in no hurry. She took one look at what a mess Jack was and knew only that she had to find a way to make him stop shouting and crying.

"It's woefully apparent that you can't tell me your life story without everyone in the waiting room hearing you," she said. "Believe me, it's only tolerable to listen to you if you calm down."

"Where does it *end*?" Jack asked Dr. García, when he'd been spilling his life story aloud for four, going on five, years.

"Well, it ends with looking for your father—or at least finding out what happened to him," Dr. García said. "But you're not ready for that part, not until you can spit out all the rest of it. The *end* of it, Jack, is where you find him—that's the last place you have to go. You're not through with traveling."

Jack too hastily concluded that if his retelling of his life were a book, for example, his finding his father would be the last chapter.

"I doubt it," Dr. García said. "Maybe your *penultimate* chapter, if you're lucky. When you find him, Jack, you're going to learn something you didn't know before, aren't you? I trust that the *learning* part will take an additional chapter."

And the whole thing had to have a name, too, didn't it? There had to be a *title* to the story of his life, which Jack was reciting— with such restraint *and* in chronological order—to his psychiatrist. But Jack knew the name of his life story before he started telling it; the first day he went to see Dr. García, when he'd been unable to tell her anything without shouting or crying, Jack knew that his mother's *Until I find you* tattoo had been her crowning deception. Certainly she'd been proudest of it; why else, if only after her death, had Alice wanted Leslie Oastler to show Jack the photographs?

"Why show me at all?" he'd asked his mom.

"I was beautiful once!" Alice had cried—meaning her breasts, when she was younger, he'd thought at the time, but the tattoo was what interested Jack.

She'd been so proud of keeping the tattoo from him that, even after everything, Alice had wanted him to see it! From the time he was four, that *Until I find you* tattoo said everything there was to say about Jack Burns.

As a psychiatrist, Dr. García was the opposite of an editor. Jack was not supposed to delete anything—he was instructed to leave nothing out. And not infrequently, Dr. García wanted *more*. She required "corroborating details." Instances of what Dr. García had identified, early on, as Jack's older-woman thing could not be overemphasized; in his boyhood, the seemingly unmotivated cruelty and aggressiveness he encountered in older girls was "an underlying problem." What was it about Jack that had provoked those older girls?

Ditto the penis-holding. Most surprising in Jack's case, in Dr. García's experience, was how this *didn't* necessarily lead to having sex. Then there was the closeness he'd felt to his mom as a child, but how swiftly and absolutely they had grown estranged; it was almost as if Jack knew that Alice's lies were lies before he actually found out.

Dr. García was further puzzled by the Emma relationship, which stood in contrast (but bore certain similarities) to Jack's relationship with Leslie Oastler. Did he still want to sleep with Leslie? Dr. García wanted to know. If so, why? If not, why not?

Dr. García was a stickler for *thoroughness*. "I think I'm done with the St. Hilda's part," Jack had told her on several occasions.

"Oh, no—you're not," Dr. García had said. "A boy with looks

like yours in an all-girls' school? Are you kidding? You're not only not done with St. Hilda's, Jack—you may *never* be done with it!"

Jack got tired of all the contradictions—his inglorious return to the North Sea and the Baltic, especially. But not Dr. García; there couldn't be too many contradictions for her. "How long's it been since you thought about dressing as a girl?" she asked him. "I don't mean in a *movie*!" (He must have hesitated.) "You see?" she said. "Give me *more* contradictions—give me all you've got, Jack."

Jack sometimes felt he wasn't seeing a psychiatrist—it was more like taking a creative writing class, but with nothing on paper to show for it. And when Dr. García gave him an *actual* writing assignment, he almost stopped the therapy altogether. She wanted him to write letters to Michele Maher—not to send to Michele, but to read out loud at their therapy sessions.

"There's no way I can explain myself to Michele," Jack told his psychiatrist. At the time, it had been more than a year—closer to *two* years—since Michele had written him. He *still* hadn't answered her letter.

"But explaining yourself to Michele is what you *want* to do, isn't it?" Dr. García asked him. He couldn't deny that.

It was further unnerving that Dr. García's office was on Montana Avenue in Santa Monica, within walking distance of that breakfast place where he'd first met Myra Ascheim—another older woman who had changed his life.

"Fascinating," Dr. García said. "But don't tell me about it *now*. Please keep everything *in chronological order,* Jack."

In 2000, when Jack won the Academy Award for Best Adapted Screenplay, Dr. García found it "illuminating" that he referred to the award (and the statuette itself) as *Emma's* Oscar. But Dr. García wouldn't allow him to tell her his feelings. Even the Oscar had to be rendered *in chronological order.*

And Dr. García disapproved of his first *actual* communication with Michele Maher, for several reasons. In the first place, Jack hadn't shown the doctor the letter he wrote Michele before he mailed it; in the second place, it was a ridiculous letter to have sent Michele after almost eighteen years of *nothing* between them.

But when Jack was nominated for *two* Academy Awards (one for Best Supporting Actor and the other for the screenplay), he felt he had a golden opportunity to make contact with Michele Maher—while at the same time sounding casual about getting together.

> *Dear Michele,*
>   *I don't know if you're married, or otherwise attached to someone, but—if you're not—would you be my date at the Academy Awards? This would mean coming to Los Angeles— Sunday, March 26. Naturally, I would take care of your travel expenses and hotel accommodations.*
>
> > *Yours truly,*
> > *Jack Burns*

What was wrong with *that*? Wasn't it polite, and to the point? (Michele's answer, which was prompt, was a little wishy-washy.)

> *Dear Jack,*
>   *Gosh, I would* love *to! But I have a boyfriend, sort of. I don't live with anyone, but I'm seeing someone—as they say. Of course I'm very flattered that you thought of me—after all these years! I'll make a point of actually staying up to watch the awards this year, and I'll keep my fingers crossed for you.*
>
> > *Best regards,*
> > *Michele*

"It's hard to tell if she really *wanted* to go, isn't it?" Jack asked Dr. García, which prompted his psychiatrist's third reason for disapproving of his letter to Michele.

"Jack, you are very fortunate that Michele turned you down," Dr. García said. "What a *wreck* you would have been if she'd said *yes*! If she'd been your date, you would have blown it."

Jack didn't think this was fair. He could have had a ball with the media—just telling them that his date for the Academy Awards was his *dermatologist*! But Dr. García was not amused; she considered his faux pas of inviting Michele Maher to the Oscars to be "in the denial category." Dr. García said that Jack was completely unaware of how far removed he was from the normal world, of normal people and normal relationships.

"But what about *her*?" he cried. (Jack meant Michele Maher.)

"What's she mean that she has a boyfriend, *sort of*? Is that *normal*?"

"You're not *ready* to make contact with Michele Maher, Jack," Dr. García said. "You have heaped so many unrealistic expectations upon a relationship that, as I understand it, never developed in the first place—well, I don't want to hear another word about this *now*! To me, you're still a four-year-old in the North Sea and the Baltic. Speaking strictly professionally, you've not recovered from your sea of girls—and I need to know much more about Emma and your older-woman thing. Keep it *in chronological order*. Is that understood?"

It was. He had a bitch psychiatrist, or so it seemed to Jack, but he had to admit that her therapy had noticeably cut down his tendency to shout and burst into tears—and his inclination to wake up weeping in the middle of the night, which became habitual after he came back from the North Sea and the Baltic the second time. So Jack stuck with her, and the unfinished telling of his life story went on and on. Jack had become what Emma said he could be—a *writer*, albeit one given to melancholic logorrhea. A storyteller, if only out loud. (Jack's actual writing was limited to those *un*mailed letters to Michele Maher.)

Dr. García was a heavyset but attractive Mexican-American. She appeared to be in her late forties. From the photographs in her office, she either came from a large family or had a large family of her own. Jack didn't ask her, and—from the photos— he couldn't tell.

Of the children in the many pictures, he couldn't recognize Dr. García as a child—so perhaps they were her children. Yet the older-looking man in the photographs seemed more like a father to her than a husband; he was always well dressed, to the point of fastidiousness, and his pencil-thin mustache and perfectly trimmed sideburns suggested a character actor of a bygone era. (A cross between Clifton Webb and Gilbert Roland, Jack thought.)

Dr. García didn't wear any rings; she wore no jewelry to speak of. Either she was married with more children than Jack could count in her office photos, or she'd come from such an overlarge family that this had persuaded her to never marry and have children of her own.

In a doomed effort to solve this mystery, Jack cleverly said:

"Maybe *you* should be my date for the Academy Awards, Dr. García. At a stressful event like that, a psychiatrist would probably come in handier than a dermatologist—don't you think?"

"You don't *date* your psychiatrist," Dr. García said.

"Oh."

"That's a word you overuse," Jack's psychiatrist said.

The distinguished-looking older man in Dr. García's family photographs had an air of detachment about him, as if he were withdrawing from a recurrent argument before it started. He seemed far removed from the clamor of the ever-present children in the photos; it was almost as if he couldn't hear them. Maybe Dr. García had married a *much* older man, or a deaf one. Jack's psychiatrist was such a strong woman, she was probably contemptuous of the convention of wedding rings.

Richard Gladstein had recommended Dr. García to Jack. "She knows actors," Richard had told him. "You wouldn't be her first movie star."

At the time, this had been a comforting thought. Yet Jack hadn't seen anyone famous in Dr. García's waiting room; it made him wonder if she made house calls to the *more* famous movie stars among her patients. But to judge Dr. García by the waiting room outside her office was confusing. There were many young married women, and some of them came with their small children; there were toys and children's books in a corner of the waiting room, which gave you the disquieting impression that you were seeing a pediatrician. The young married women who showed up with their children always brought friends or nannies with them; these other women looked after the kids when the young mothers went into Dr. García's office for their therapy sessions.

"Are you here to see the doctor or to watch someone's kid?" Jack asked one of the young women once; like Dr. García, she wasn't wearing a wedding ring.

"Are you trying to pick me up or something?" the young woman said.

Jack almost asked her if *she* would be his date at the Academy Awards, but he stopped himself when he considered what Dr. García might have to say about *that*.

"Who *should* I take to the Academy Awards?" he'd asked his psychiatrist.

"Please don't mistake me for a dating service, Jack."

Thus Jack was on his own for the Academy Awards. In addition to his two nominations, Lucia Delvecchio had a nomination for Best Actress, Wild Bill Vanvleck had one for Best Director, and Richard Gladstein got a Best Picture nomination, too.

No one thought Lucia had a shot. She was up against some very big guns—Meryl Streep and Julianne Moore and Annette Bening—and besides, it was Hilary Swank's year. (As an occasional cross-dresser, Jack was a big fan of Hilary in *Boys Don't Cry*.) And Richard Gladstein knew, going in, that *The Slush-Pile Reader* was a long shot for Best Picture. (It would go to *American Beauty*.)

William Vanvleck was just happy to be there. Not one review of *The Slush-Pile Reader* referred to Wild Bill as The Remake Monster; The Mad Dutchman had become almost acceptable. Not acceptable enough to win Best Director; there were some heavy hitters in the lineup that year. (Sam Mendes would win—*American Beauty* again.)

Nor did Jack realistically have a chance to win Best Supporting Actor—Michael Caine won. (Jack's role as a nice-guy porn star was sympathetic, but not *that* sympathetic.)

Jack knew long before the night of the awards that the film's best chance for an Oscar was in the Best Adapted Screenplay category—*Emma's* screenplay, as he thought of it. How could he *not* look at it as Emma's Oscar? It was *her* movie!

Yes, Jack had learned a little bit about screenwriting in the course of fine-tuning the script Emma had given him. But as a storyteller, he was learning more from his *therapy* with Dr. García. (Go easy on the foreshadowing; watch the interjections; keep it in chronological order.)

Miramax's promotion of *The Slush-Pile Reader* was exhausting, and the lion's share of it had fallen to Jack in February and March of 2000. Wild Bill Vanvleck was back in Amsterdam; his much younger girlfriend was an anchorwoman on Dutch television, and Wild Bill was completely taken with her. Besides, Vanvleck was a disaster at promoting his own picture—in this case. That pornography was such an issue in the United States offended The Mad Dutchman; nobody had a problem with pornography in the Netherlands. "It is only a problem in Puritan America, which is ruled by the Christian Right!" Vanvleck declared. (It was probably wise of Miramax to keep Wild Bill in Amsterdam, except for the film festivals.)

Following her tragic one-night error in Venice, Lucia Delvecchio had shunned Jack. She'd virtually turned her back on the film, too. Jack's old friend Erica Steinberg was the Miramax publicist. Jack had been on the road with Erica—in print and on television—for *The Slush-Pile Reader* almost nonstop.

It was the night after Jack did *Larry King Live* that he called Leslie Oastler and asked her if she would be his date at the Academy Awards. (*Fuck the blonde,* he thought.)

"I'm flattered you would think of me, Jack," Mrs. Oastler began. "But how would that make Dolores feel? And I don't know what I would *wear.*"

"It's *Emma's* night, Leslie," Jack said.

"No, it's gonna be *your* night, Jack. Emma's dead. Why don't you go with Miss Wurtz?" Mrs. Oastler asked him.

"The Wurtz! Are you kidding?"

"An Oscar would be wasted on me, Jack. What would I want with a gold, bald, naked man holding what is *alleged* to be his sword?" Leslie Oastler had always had a particularly pointed way of seeing things.

The next morning Jack called Caroline Wurtz and popped the question. Would she consider coming to Los Angeles to attend the Academy Awards with him?

"I've heard so many terrible things about the drive-by shootings," Miss Wurtz said. "But they don't shoot people at the Oscars, do they?"

"No," he told her. "They only wound you internally."

"Well, I suppose I should go see the movie, shouldn't I?" Caroline asked. "I've heard both wonderful and awful things from people who've seen it. As you know, your friend Emma was never one of my favorite writers."

"I think it's a pretty good film," Jack said. There was a lengthy pause, as if Caroline was considering the invitation—or perhaps The Wurtz had forgotten that he'd invited her to anything. Jack was a little miffed that she hadn't seen *The Slush-Pile Reader.* (The movie had five Oscar nominations! Everyone Jack knew had seen it.)

"Don't you have anyone else to ask, Jack? I can't be the best you can do," Caroline said.

"For a couple of years, I've been seeing a psychiatrist," he admitted to her. "I haven't been in the best shape."

"Goodness!" Miss Wurtz cried. "In that case, *of course* I'll go with you! I'm sure if Mrs. McQuat were alive, she'd want to go with us, too!"

Well, *there* was a concept! At Mrs. McQuat's urging, Jack had taken Miss Wurtz to that most memorable Toronto film festival—the one he went to with Claudia, when The Wurtz was convinced that the morons protesting the Godard film were outraged by the ritualistic suicide in the Mishima movie. Jack wondered what confusions awaited Miss Wurtz at the Shrine Civic Auditorium on the night of the Academy Awards. Whom might she mistake *Billy Crystal* for?

Jack explained to Caroline that he would arrange her air travel and all the rest of it. That Jack Burns was taking his third-grade teacher to the Oscars was a bonus bit of publicity; nor did it hurt that Emma Oastler had died and put him in charge of bringing her first and best novel to the screen. "The death connection," Jack had called it; that turned out to be a bonus bit of publicity for *both* Miramax and Jack Burns.

The issue of what Miss Wurtz would wear provided a down-to-earth return to the heart of the matter. Jack told her that Armani was dressing him for the Academy Awards. (They had called; he'd said okay. This was how it usually happened.)

"*Who* is dressing you?" The Wurtz asked.

"Armani—the *designer,* Caroline. Different fashion designers dress the nominees and their guests for the Oscars. If there's a particular designer you like, I'm sure I could arrange it. Or you could just wear something by Armani, too."

"I think I'll dress myself, if it's all the same to you," Miss Wurtz replied. "I have some perfectly lovely clothes your father bought for me. Naturally, William will be watching. He'll be so proud of you! I wouldn't want William to see me wearing a dress he didn't choose for me, Jack."

Well, there was a concept, too—namely, that Jack's father would be watching. The Wurtz would be dressing for *him*!

"You'll have to tell me who's nominated for what," Caroline was saying. "Then I'll go see *all* the movies."

Jack wondered how many Academy voters had the diligence of a third-grade teacher, but—when Jack would finally get to the

Oscar-winning part of his life story—Dr. García would call the "diligence" detail an example of his *interjecting* too much.

Jack doubted that every film nominated for an Oscar was still playing in a theater in Toronto; quite possibly, not every film had ever played there. But he knew this wouldn't deter Miss Wurtz from trying to see them all.

Jack almost called Leslie Oastler to thank her for suggesting The Wurtz as his date for the Academy Awards, but he didn't want to risk getting Leslie's blonde on the phone.

"Dolores," he would be tempted to say to the bitch, "I wanted to alert you to a large package that's coming your way—more of my clothes. If you or Leslie wouldn't mind hanging them in my closet as soon as they arrive, I'd appreciate it. I wouldn't want them to be wrinkled for my next visit." Or words to that effect; naturally, Jack didn't make the call. (Had she known, Dr. García would have been proud of him for exercising such restraint.)

The two-bedroom suite at the Beverly Hills Four Seasons, where Miramax put them up for the long Oscar weekend, was larger than Miss Wurtz's apartment—or so she told Jack. There was even a piano, which Miss Wurtz liked to play in her Four Seasons white terry-cloth bathrobe. She claimed to know only hymns and the St. Hilda's school songs, but her voice was pretty and she played well.

"Oh, I don't play well—nothing like your father, who used to tease me," she said. "William would say, 'If you want to be even a bit *more* tentative, Caroline, you might try *breathing* on the keys instead of using your fingers.' He could be funny, your father. I wish you'd tell me more about your *trip,* Jack. Why don't you begin with Copenhagen? I've never been there."

There were always a lot of parties prior to the Academy Awards. As a nondrinker escorting his third-grade teacher, a woman in her sixties, Jack didn't think that he and Caroline were in step with the bacchanalian behavior of many of his colleagues in the industry. But they went to those parties where Jack's absence would have been resented, even if they spent much of the time talking quietly to each other.

Having *calmly* described so many of the painful passages in his life to Dr. García, Jack found that he was in better control of himself while recounting to Miss Wurtz those discoveries he made in his return trip to the North Sea and the Baltic—beginning with the Ringhof family tragedy that Alice had engendered in Copenhagen, which Jack was able to relate in a deadpan narrative more closely resembling the written word than conversation. Not once did he raise his voice, nor did he shed a tear; Jack didn't even *blink*.

"Goodness!" was all Miss Wurtz had to say in reply.

They were at an outdoor luncheon at Bob Bookman's home. The screenwriters who were Jack's (or Emma's) principal competition in the Best Adapted Screenplay category that year were there—in addition to Jack, Bookman represented three of his fellow nominees. But there Jack was, in Bob Bookman's garden, with his third-grade teacher—his father's former lover—and Jack was back in those Baltic and North Sea ports of call, telling Miss Wurtz what he had learned.

"Don't downplay what happened in Stockholm, Jack— I mean just because it wasn't as bad as what happened in Copenhagen," Miss Wurtz would tell him later that same weekend. "And even if you had sex with someone in Oslo, please don't spare me any details."

He didn't. (Dr. García had taught him not to spare *her* any details.) Jack found that he could actually talk his way through it— at least to as sympathetic a soul as Caroline Wurtz. Jack doubted that he would have been able to tell the Baltic and North Sea story to Leslie Oastler and her unfriendly blonde—not without shedding a tear or two, or indulging in a little shouting. But he told Miss Wurtz everything about Copenhagen and Stockholm without batting an eye. He didn't even hesitate when he got to Oslo. He didn't want to be over-optimistic, but Jack thought that Dr. García's therapy was working.

32

Straining to See

The Weinstein brothers were backing more than one Oscar-nominated film that year. The night before the Academy Awards, Miramax had a party at the Regent Beverly Wilshire. The anti-pornography people were protesting *The Slush-Pile Reader* outside the hotel. The film had an R rating; it wasn't pornographic, but it was offensive to the anti-pornography people that Jack's character (Jimmy Stronach, the porn star) was sympathetically portrayed. Those other characters in the film who were part of the porn industry were also sympathetic—chiefly Hank Long and Muffy; and Mildred "Milly" Ascheim made a cameo appearance as herself. Worse, from the point of view of the anti-pornography people, all the porn stars were portrayed as having normal lives—to the degree that so-called L.A. dysfunctional is *normal,* and Emma believed it was.

There were fewer than a dozen protesters outside the hotel, but the media gave them undue attention. There were usually the same small number of zealots every year—some of them protesting what Jack's mother would have called "the deterioration of language" in movies in general. The anti-profanity people, the anti-pornography people—there would always be complainers with too much time on their hands. Jack thought that the best thing was to pay them no attention, but the media tended to inflate their importance and their numbers.

Miss Wurtz hadn't noticed the protesters. When Wild Bill Vanvleck was ranting at the Miramax party about the anti-pornography people, Caroline clutched Jack's arm and said anxiously: "There are *protesters*? What are they protesting?"

"Pornography," Jack said.

Miss Wurtz looked all around the room, as if there might be pornographic acts under way in their very midst and she had somehow mistaken them for more innocent forms of entertainment. Jack explained: "You know, Caroline—my character, Jimmy Stronach, is a porn star. I think that's what they're protesting."

"Nonsense!" Miss Wurtz shouted. "I did not see a single reproductive organ in the film—not one penis or one female *thingamajig*!"

"A *what*?" Wild Bill said, looking shocked.

"A *vagina,*" Jack whispered to him.

"You shouldn't say that word at a party," Caroline said.

It soon became clear that The Wurtz had seen too many films in too short a period of time—as many as three a day for the past several weeks, or so she'd told Jack. Miss Wurtz had never seen so many movies in her life; they were all a blur. And this year's films were mingled with movies she'd not seen since she was a child. To her, the recognizable celebrities at the party were not movie stars but the actual characters they'd played. Unfortunately, these movies had overlapped in her mind—to the extent that she'd merged the plots of several different films into one incomprehensible *epic,* in which virtually everyone she "recognized" at the Regent Beverly Wilshire had played a pivotal role.

"Oh, look—there's that envious young man who killed those people. One with an oar, I think," she said, indicating Matt Damon, who was Tom Ripley in *The Talented Mr. Ripley.* Not that The Wurtz made any distinction between Tom Ripley and the character Tom Cruise played in *Magnolia* that year. And she had convinced herself that Kevin Spacey was trapped in a bad marriage, which he periodically escaped by lusting after young girls. "Someone should be assigned to watch him," Miss Wurtz told Jack, who understood that by *watch,* she meant *control* him.

Seeking to change the subject, Jack said he admired how thin Gwyneth Paltrow was—to which The Wurtz replied: "She looks in need of intravenous feeding."

When you've seen too many movies, time stands still; no one grows old or dies. Miss Wurtz mistook Anthony Minghella for Peter Lorre. ("I thought Peter Lorre was dead," Caroline would tell Jack the next day. "He hasn't made a movie in years." To which Jack could only think to himself, *True!*)

Looking worriedly around, The Wurtz announced that a party of this size—and with so many celebrities—should have more than one bouncer; she thought that Ben Affleck was the sole bouncer.

Judi Dench was there, which prompted Caroline to confess to Jack that she'd always thought Judi Dench would be an inspired choice to play Mrs. McQuat—should anyone ever make a movie about The Gray Ghost.

"A movie about Mrs. McQuat?" Jack said, stunned.

"You know she was a combat nurse, Jack. The trouble with her breathing was because she'd been *gassed*—I'm not sure with what."

Thus Jack was doomed to think of Judi Dench as The Gray Ghost, *gassed* but come back to life—a troubling thought.

Jack kept giving Wild Bill Vanvleck the eye—the eye that meant, "Isn't it time to leave?"

But Wild Bill was nowhere near ready to go. He was back in Hollywood, reborn as the director of an Academy Award–nominated film. Jack didn't begrudge The Mad Dutchman his triumph; The Remake Monster had admirably restrained himself in directing *The Slush-Pile Reader.* Jack had always trusted Vanvleck as a craftsman, and Wild Bill had stuck to the craftsman-like part of his business; this time, he'd left the parody alone.

After they finally left the Miramax party, Jack and Miss Wurtz went out to dinner with Richard Gladstein and his wife and Vanvleck and his much younger anchorwoman, whose name was Anneke. Outside the Regent Beverly Wilshire, the protesters were still chanting and holding up posters of male and female reproductive organs—penises *and* thingamajigs galore. Miss Wurtz became incensed all over again.

"If you don't like pornography, stop *thinking* about it!" Caroline said sharply out the window of the limousine to a baffled-looking man in a lime-green short-sleeved shirt; he was holding a poster depicting a naked child, above whom the intimidating shadow of a grown-up loomed.

It was a good thing The Wurtz wasn't riding in the limo with Hank Long and Muffy and Milly Ascheim. Jack found out later that Milly had put down her window and shouted at the protesters: "Oh, go home and watch a movie and *beat off*! You'll feel better!"

"Goodness, it's already Sunday morning," Miss Wurtz declared, when she and Jack were having breakfast at the pool at the Four

Seasons in Beverly Hills. "And your story has bogged down in Oslo, as I recall. It's probably best not to try to imitate Ingrid Moe's speech impediment. Just tell me what she said the way you would normally say it, Jack. The speech impediment is too distracting."

Not surprisingly, Jack would elect to tell the story in this fashion when he told it to Dr. García, too. He made no effort to render an approximation of Ingrid's awful affliction. (Knowing Dr. García, she would have referred to any effort on Jack's part to recreate the speech impediment as an interjection.)

Thus Jack described Ingrid Moe's vision of Hell as if it were his personal account of an actual visit to the place. He paid particular attention to Ingrid's lack of forgiveness for his mother, which stood in such dramatic contrast to the fact that his father forgave his mother for everything—even the Amsterdam part of the story, which Jack was a long way from getting to on that Sunday morning in Beverly Hills. He felt certain that he and Miss Wurtz wouldn't get to Amsterdam—at least not before the Academy Awards, which would commence later that afternoon.

Having been to the Oscars once before, Jack knew they were in for a long night. Miss Wurtz, wearing a wide-brimmed straw hat and smeared from head to toe with more sunscreen than a naked newborn, was pressing Jack for details about Helsinki. She was clearly impatient with Oslo and Ingrid Moe, although William's appearance at the Hotel Bristol had thrilled her. The Wurtz was especially pleased to learn that William had not cut his hair.

"William had beautiful hair. You have his hair, Jack," Caroline said, taking his hand. "I'm so glad you haven't cut your hair short, the way everyone else does nowadays. Frankly, it doesn't matter whether long hair for men is *in* or *out*. If you have good hair, you should *grow* it."

The Helsinki part of the story took what remained of their private time that Sunday. Erica Steinberg had thoughtfully arranged for someone to come to the hotel to do Miss Wurtz's hair. "Whatever *do* means," The Wurtz whispered to Jack, before she went off with Erica after lunch. "I'm keeping it gray—that's all I know. It's too late for me to be a blonde—not that there aren't enough blondes already, especially out here."

Jack went to the gym, which was next to the pool. Sigourney

Weaver was there. (He came up to her collarbone.) "Good luck tonight, Jack," she said.

That was when he began to get nervous; that was when he realized that it meant everything to him to *win*.

"It's just possible, Jack," Dr. García would tell him later, "that winning the Oscar was some small consolation for what you've *lost*."

She didn't mean only his father. She didn't mean only Emma, either. She meant Michele Maher, notwithstanding Dr. García's assessment of the "unrealistic expectations" Jack had heaped upon Michele; she meant Jack's false memories, the childhood his mother had fabricated for him, which he'd lost, too. (Dr. García also meant his mom, of course.)

Erica rode in the stretch limo with Jack and Miss Wurtz to the Shrine Auditorium. They saw the protesters from the night before—the same righteous faces, the identical posters. The limo was moving so slowly that, this time, Jack could count them. There were nine anti-pornography people altogether—not that this would prevent *Entertainment Weekly,* in its post-Oscar issue, from describing the "scores" of protesters ringing the auditorium.

Miss Wurtz looked wonderful. She wore a long, slender gown with a Queen Anne neckline; it was the same silver color as her hair. Jack's all-black Armani, which included a black shirt as well as the black tuxedo and the black tie, made him resemble a shrunken gangster. He'd lost the twenty pounds he'd put on for the Jimmy Stronach role—he was looking lean and mean, as Michele Maher had once observed.

They weren't on the red carpet more than twenty minutes before Erica steered them in the direction of the obligatory Joan Rivers interview. Jack was dreading Miss Wurtz's answer to Joan's predictable question regarding "who" she was *wearing*. But rather than say, "Jack's father gave it to me when we were lovers," Caroline answered: "The dress is personal, a gift from a onetime admirer." That was perfect, Jack thought.

Joan Rivers knew all about the third-grade connection in advance; it seemed that everyone in the media knew. "What sort of a student was Jack?" she asked Miss Wurtz.

"Even as a child, Jack was as convincing as a woman as he was as a man," Caroline answered. "He just needed to know who his audience was."

"And who *is* your audience, Jack Burns?" Joan Rivers asked him.

"My father is my audience of one," he told her, "but I suppose I've picked up a few other fans along the way." Jack looked into the camera and said, for the first time in his life: "Hi, Dad." He noticed that Miss Wurtz was smiling shyly at the camera.

After that, Jack couldn't get off the red carpet fast enough. He was a wreck. (He almost called Dr. García.)

"Calm down," Caroline said. "It's not necessary for you to say anything to William. He just wants to see you—he wants, more than anyone, to see you win."

There was a lot of waiting at the Academy Awards. Erica took Jack and Miss Wurtz inside the auditorium, where they waited for an eternity. Jack drank too much Evian and had to pee—this was before Billy Crystal was carried onstage like a baby by a motorcycle cop in sunglasses and a white helmet, and the evening officially began.

Jack had a sixth-row aisle seat. All the nominees had aisle seats; Richard Gladstein sat in the aisle seat in front of Jack, and Wild Bill Vanvleck had the one behind him. Miss Wurtz was seated between Jack and Harvey Weinstein. Caroline didn't remember who Harvey was—Jack had introduced them *twice* at the party the previous night—but she knew he was someone important because there was a television camera pointed at him from start to finish. For reasons that would remain unclear to Jack, Miss Wurtz deduced that Harvey was a famous prizefighter—a former heavyweight champ. (Quite possibly she'd overheard someone saying how much Harvey enjoyed a good fight. Jack could think of no other explanation.)

The Best Supporting Actor award was announced fairly early in the program. When Michael Caine won, Jack knew it would be a long wait for the writing awards, which were near the end of the evening. Almost no one sat through the entire program—especially not if you'd had as much Evian as Jack. But you had to pick your pee-break pretty carefully; they would let you leave or go back to your seat only during the TV commercials.

Miss Wurtz became enraged at those award-winners who overspent their allotted forty-five seconds for their acceptance speeches. Pedro Almodóvar really pissed her off; in accepting the Oscar for Best Foreign Language Film for *All About My*

Mother, Pedro went on for so long that Antonio Banderas had to pull him offstage.

"*Buenas noches!*" Miss Wurtz called out to Almodóvar.

They took their pee-break—that is, they took *Jack's* pee-break, since he was the one in dire need of it—during the presentation of the Irving G. Thalberg Memorial Award. This year it went to Warren Beatty. Caroline was cross with Jack for causing her to miss it. Miss Wurtz had once had a crush on Warren Beatty. "Nothing compared to what I felt for your father, Jack, but it was a crush just the same."

By the time they were back in their seats, Jack had to pee again. He whispered to Miss Wurtz that if he *didn't* win, he would have to pee in his Evian bottle. (Jack was counting on there being a men's room backstage—if he could get there.)

Finally, the writing awards came; thankfully the Oscar for Best Adapted Screenplay preceded the award for Best Original Screenplay. Kevin Spacey was the lone presenter. Annette Bening was supposed to join him onstage, but she was arguably too pregnant to risk the short trip from her seat. Spacey made a joke about how she was "due to go into production herself." He said further: "I could not ask her to climb stairs, unless of course she wins the Oscar. Then she'll climb up here on all fours."

Jack took this as an unfavorable omen for his chances to win. Given his night in Helsinki with the pregnant aerobics instructor, the very idea of Annette Bening on all fours in her condition filled him with remorse. But it was only seconds after that bad moment when Kevin Spacey said, "And the Oscar goes to—" Jack didn't hear the rest because Miss Wurtz was shrieking.

"Think of how happy William is for you, Jack," she shouted in his ear, between kisses. Of course the camera was on them, and Jack was aware of The Wurtz looking past him to the camera; she knew exactly where the camera was because it had been pointed at Harvey Weinstein, the former prizefighter, all night. Jack was on his feet—Richard was kissing him, Wild Bill, too. Harvey crushed Miss Wurtz *and* Jack in one embrace. When Jack stepped into the aisle, he saw Caroline blow a kiss to the camera—her lips forming the name *William* as she did so.

Jack took the Oscar from Kevin Spacey and spoke for only thirty-five of his allotted forty-five seconds; in a small way, this made up for Pedro Almodóvar thanking the Virgin of Guadalupe, the Virgin of La Cabeza, the Sacred Heart of Mary, and all the rest of the living and the dead. Of course Jack thanked his third-grade teacher, Miss Caroline Wurtz, because he knew that the camera would go to her if he did. He thanked Mr. Ramsey, too, and naturally he thanked Richard, and Wild Bill, and everyone at Miramax. Most of all, Jack thanked Emma Oastler for everything she'd done for him, and—largely because he knew how angry it would make the blonde—he thanked Leslie Oastler for her contributions to the screenplay. Lastly, Jack thanked Michele Maher for staying up late to watch him. (In his heart, he hoped Michele's *sort-of* boyfriend was watching, too. Hearing Jack thank Michele might make the boyfriend jealous and lead to their breaking up.)

Jack might have used the full forty-five seconds if he hadn't had to pee so badly. When he left the stage with Kevin Spacey, they passed Mel Gibson coming on—Mel was the presenter for the Best Original Screenplay award, which would go to Alan Ball for *American Beauty*. Tom Cruise, a fellow former wrestler, tried to wrestle the Oscar away from Jack backstage; the way Jack had to pee, that bit of friendly fooling around could have ended badly. Clint Eastwood spoke to Jack. (He said: "Way to go, kid," or words to that effect. Jack knew he couldn't trust his memory of moments like that—the ones that mattered too much.)

Jack was still seeking the whereabouts of the men's room when Alan Ball came offstage with his Oscar, and Jack congratulated him. ("Good job, mate," Jack thought Mel Gibson said, but had Mel been speaking to Jack or to Alan?) After a night of waiting, everything seemed over so quickly.

At last Jack found the place he was looking for. His relief turned to awkwardness almost immediately, however, because he had never been to a men's room with an Academy Award before. Leslie Oastler had attempted to diminish Oscar by describing him as a "gold, bald, naked man holding what is *alleged* to be his sword," but in Jack's estimation, an Oscar was longer than a porn star's penis and a whole lot heavier. Jack wouldn't recommend peeing with one.

It was an experience in childlike clumsiness that reminded him of Marja-Liisa's four-year-old peeing in his parka pocket at the Hotel Torni. Jack couldn't quite get the hang of it, so to speak. He tried pinning the Oscar under one arm, but that didn't work very well. If you've just won your first Academy Award, fully understanding that you might never win another one, you're not inclined to put it down on the floor of a public men's room— nor would you attempt to balance it on the urinal by maintaining perilous little contact with Oscar's sleek head by means of your chin.

Jack was glad he was alone in the men's room; there was no one to observe his embarrassing struggle—or so he thought. Suddenly he saw, at the opposite end of the row of urinals, that there *was* someone else there. The fellow appeared to have finished with his business; no one could help but notice how Jack was failing to do his.

The man was broad-shouldered, with a weightlifter's crafted body and an unbreakable-looking jaw. Jack didn't recognize him right away, nor did he remember that the former bodybuilder had been a presenter; from Jack's perspective, the opposite end of the row of urinals seemed a football field away. But Jack had no trouble identifying the big man's inimitable Austrian accent.

"Would you like me to give you a hand with that?" Arnold Schwarzenegger asked.

"No, thank you—I can manage," Jack answered.

"Goodness, I hope he meant he would give you a hand with the *Oscar*!" Miss Wurtz said later, when Jack told her the story. Well, of *course* Arnold had meant the Oscar—he was just being nice! (That the future governor of California might have been offering to hold Jack's *penis* was unthinkable!)

It was bedlam backstage. At the next television commercial, Jack went back to his seat in the auditorium; he didn't want to leave Miss Wurtz unattended. She might ask Harvey Weinstein about his greatest fights, Jack was thinking. Or, God forbid, what if there were a power outage and Miss Wurtz suffered an uncontrollable flashback to her experience in the bat-cave exhibit at the Royal Ontario Museum? But by then the evening was winding down; *The Slush-Pile Reader* had won its only Oscar. It was *American Beauty*'s night, but it was Jack's night and Emma's night, too.

Miss Wurtz was perplexed that she could see no evidence of *dancing* at the Board of Governors Ball—the dinner party at the Shrine Auditorium after the Academy Awards. No amount of explaining could convince her that *ball* was an acceptable description of the occasion, but what did Jack care? He was happy.

They ate dinner at a table with Meryl Streep, who'd brought

her daughter. Jack could see the wheels of The Wurtz's mind spinning: here was that woman from *Sophie's Choice* with an actual, living child! Jack told Erica that he thought they should leave and go to another party before Caroline committed whatever she was imagining to words.

They went to the *Vanity Fair* party at Morton's next; Erica got them there somehow. Jack remembered how long he and Emma had waited to get into that party the night he'd been nominated but *didn't* win the Oscar. It makes a difference when you win. Their limo driver waved the gold, bald, naked man out the window and they were swiftly ushered through the traffic. Hugh Hefner (among others) appeared to have arrived before them; probably Hugh had come early because he hadn't been at the Shrine. The *Playboy* founding publisher had those twins with him—Sandy and Mandy.

Miss Wurtz was more incensed at Hef than she'd been at the anti-pornography people. "What does that dirty old man think he's doing with those young girls?" Caroline said to Erica and Jack.

Rob Lowe and Mike Myers and Dennis Miller were all talking about something, but they stopped the second Jack got near them. When that happened to him around men, Jack couldn't help but think that they'd been talking about him as a *girl*. As it happened, Jack was on his way to the men's room again—although this time he'd left his Academy Award with Erica and Miss Wurtz.

They went next to the Miramax party at the Polo Lounge in the Beverly Hills Hotel. Jack knew that Richard and Wild Bill would be there; he just wanted to be with friends. Miss Wurtz once more avoided making any prizefighter references to Harvey Weinstein.

Caroline had a little too much champagne. Jack had a beer—a green bottle of Heineken, which looked especially green alongside the gold of his Oscar. (He couldn't remember when he'd last had a whole beer—maybe when he was a college student.)

Then there was a breakfast party in another area of the Beverly Hills Hotel. They went to that, too. It must have started at three or four in the morning. Roger Ebert was there; he was eating his breakfast on a bed, which Jack found peculiar. Jack was nice to him, although Roger had savaged *The Slush-Pile Reader*. Roger's wife and daughter were very nice; they informed Miss

Wurtz that *they'd* liked the movie. It pleased Jack to think that he and Emma might have caused an argument in the Ebert family.

It was about 5:00 A.M. when Jack told Miss Wurtz that he was tired and wanted to go to bed. "We can go back to our hotel, Jack," she told him, "but you *can't* go to bed. Not until you tell me about the second time in Amsterdam." She'd had it on her mind the whole night, The Wurtz went on to say. She knew she couldn't sleep until she heard the story.

Jack told Erica that they had to leave, and she rode with them in the limo back to the Four Seasons. On a side street in Beverly Hills, they got stuck behind a garbage truck—the only traffic they encountered at that time on a Monday morning. The smell of the garbage wafted over them in their limousine, as if to remind Jack—even with his newly won Oscar in hand—that there are some things you can't escape, and they will find you.

Jack was okay telling Miss Wurtz about the Amsterdam business; only the end of the story was difficult. Dr. García would have been proud of him—no tears, no shouting. When Jack told Caroline how his heart wasn't in that first meeting with Richard Gladstein and William Vanvleck—that he kept thinking about the *other* William—the southern California sun was streaming in the open windows of the living room of the two-bedroom suite at the Four Seasons. Miss Wurtz and Jack were seated on the couch in their matching white terry-cloth bathrobes—their bare feet on the glass-topped coffee table, where the Oscar gleamed. Caroline's toenails were painted a rose-pink color. The sunlight seemed especially bright on her toenails, and on the Oscar—and on the lustrous black piano, which was shining like a pool of oil.

"Don't look at my feet, Jack," Miss Wurtz said. "My feet are the oldest part of me. I must have been born feet first."

But Jack Burns was miles away, in the dark of night—the streetlights reflecting in the Herengracht canal. Richard Gladstein and Wild Bill Vanvleck and Jack had been talking in the restaurant called Zuid Zeeland, and Wild Bill's much younger girlfriend—Anneke, the anchorwoman—was looking restless and bored. (How much fun is it to be young and green-eyed and beautiful, and have three men talking to one another and ignoring you—especially when they're talking about how to make a movie from a novel you haven't read?)

As little as Jack's heart was in it, he saw that he and Richard and Wild Bill were all on the same page; they seemed to agree about what needed tweaking in the script, and about the tone the film must have. Richard's eyes kept closing—he was falling asleep because of his jet lag. Wild Bill was teasing him, to the effect that Richard was not allowed to fall asleep before he signed the check. "Producers pay the bills!" Vanvleck was chanting; he was a man who loved his red wine.

Out on the Herengracht, Richard woke up a little in the damp night air. It seemed inevitable to Jack now that Wild Bill would suggest a stroll through the red-light district, but it took him by surprise at the time. When they walked past the first few girls in their windows and doorways, Jack could tell that Richard was wide awake. Anneke was still bored. Jack had the feeling that Wild Bill took all his out-of-town friends on a tour of the red-light district; after all, it was the homicide territory of his TV series and he knew the district well. (Almost as well as Jack knew it, but Jack didn't let on that he'd ever been there before.)

Anneke livened up a little, most noticeably when she observed how the prostitutes in their windows and doorways recognized Jack Burns as frequently as they recognized her. As an attractive anchorwoman, she was a famous fixture on Dutch television—but no more famous than Jack was. And not only was Jack a movie star; he had the added advantage of Nico Oudejans telling all the whores in the district to be on the lookout for him.

"You cocktease, Jack!" one of the transvestite prostitutes called out; she was Brazilian, probably. (Those chicks with dicks were out to get him.) This captured Anneke's attention, but Wild Bill had downed a couple of bottles of red wine; he didn't notice. The Mad Dutchman was lecturing Richard nonstop.

Suddenly Jack was irritated by it. Vanvleck was showing off the red-light district as if he'd invented it, as if he'd hired all the girls himself. Poor Richard was fighting off his jet lag and the overwhelming seediness of the place. By all counts, it had been a forgettable night for Anneke.

Well, Jack thought—*I'll show them something they'll all remember!* "This is nothing," Jack announced as they circled the Oudekerksplein. He began to lead them across the Warmoesstraat, out of the red-light district. "You haven't seen anything until you've seen Els."

"*Els?*" Vanvleck said.

"Where are we going?" Richard asked. (They were walking away from the hotel; that was all he knew.)

"Els is the oldest working prostitute in Amsterdam," Jack told them. "She's an old friend."

"She *is?*" Wild Bill said, stumbling along.

Jack led them across the Damrak. It was now late at night. He was sure that Els would have gone to bed. Petra, her colleague who was only sixty-one, might be sitting in the second-floor window. Or maybe Petra would have gone home and gone to bed, too. In either case, Jack would wake up Els—just to show Wild Bill and Richard and Anneke that he had a *history* in Amsterdam that ran a little deeper than a Dutch TV series.

When they came into the narrow Sint Jacobsstraat, Wild Bill was staggering. The street could seem a little menacing at night. Jack saw Richard look over his shoulder a couple of times, and Anneke took Jack's arm and walked close beside him.

To Jack's surprise, Els—not Petra—was in the window. ("Some drunk woke me up shouting," she would tell Jack later. "Petra had gone home, and I felt like staying up. Call it my *intuition, Jackie.*")

When Jack spotted her, he started waving. "Els is in her seventies," he said to Wild Bill, who was staring up at Els in her red-lit window as if he had seen one of Hell's own avenging spirits—a harpy from the netherworld, an infernal Fury.

"She's *how* old?" Richard asked.

"Think of your grandmother," Jack told him.

"Jackie!" Els shouted, blowing kisses. "My little boy has come back *again!*" she once more announced to the Sint Jacobsstraat.

Jack blew kisses to her; he waved and waved. That was when he lost it—when Els started waving back to him.

It is impossible that Jack could have "remembered" his mother lifting him above the ship's rail as they sailed from the dock in Rotterdam; *impossible* that he actually recalled waving to Els, twenty-eight years before, or that (when Jack was four) he truly saw his father fall to the ground with both hands holding his broken heart.

"Don't cry, Jackie—don't cry!" Els called to him from her second-floor window, but Jack had dropped to his knees on the

Sint Jacobsstraat. He was still waving good-bye, and Els kept waving back to him.

Richard and Wild Bill were struggling to get Jack to his feet, but Wild Bill was drunk. Richard, in addition to his jet lag, had been knocking back the red wine, too.

"You're her *little boy*?" Richard was asking, but Jack was waving good-bye to his dad and couldn't answer; Jack's heart was in his throat.

"You actually know this lady?" Wild Bill asked, losing his balance and sitting down in the street. Richard was holding Jack under one arm, but he let go. Jack just lay in the street beside Wild Bill; Jack was still waving.

"Jackie, Jackie—your mother loved you!" Els was calling. "As best she could!"

It was Wild Bill's pretty anchorwoman who finally helped Jack to his feet; she'd laid off the red wine, Jack had noticed. "For God's sake, stop waving to that old hooker!" Anneke said. "Stop *encouraging* her!"

"She was my *nanny*!" Jack blubbered.

"She was his *what*?" Wild Bill asked Richard.

"His babysitter," Richard explained.

"*Marvelous!*" Wild Bill exclaimed.

"Oh, shut up, Bill! Can't you see he's crying?" Anneke asked The Mad Dutchman.

"Jack, why are you crying?" Wild Bill asked.

"She looked after me while my mother was working," Jack told them.

"Working where? Working *here*?" Richard asked.

"My mom worked in a window, in one of those doorways— back there," Jack said, pointing in the general direction of the red-light district. "My mother was a prostitute," he told them.

"I thought his mom was a tattoo artist!" Wild Bill said to Richard.

"She was a tattoo artist, too," Jack said. "She wasn't a prostitute for very long, but she was one."

Jack began to wave good-bye to Els again, but Anneke wrapped her arms around him; she pinned his arms to his sides. "For God's sake, *stop*!" the anchorwoman said.

"Come back and see me before I die, Jackie!" Els was calling.

Wild Bill was still sitting in the street. He had begun to wave good-bye to Els, too, but Anneke kicked him. "What a great idea, Bill!" she said. "You give a tour of the red-light district to a guy whose mom was a whore!"

"Well, *I* didn't know!" Wild Bill shouted. Richard helped him to his feet; Anneke removed a candy-bar wrapper from Vanvleck's long, gray ponytail.

They were walking away from Els in her window, toward the red-light district; that was the most direct way back to the Grand. Richard, who was walking beside Jack, put his arm around him. "Are you all right, Jack?" Richard asked.

"I'll be fine," Jack told him.

But Richard was sober enough to be worried about Jack, and they were fast becoming friends. "When you get back to L.A., I know someone you could see," Richard said.

"Do you mean a psychiatrist?" Jack asked.

"Dr. García knows actors," Richard said. "You wouldn't be her first movie star."

The waving good-bye had stopped, but Jack could still see Els lifting his dad off the pavement and carrying him like a child to Femke's Mercedes. (In all probability, Alice had put Jack down on the deck and the boy could no longer see over the ship's rail.) The damp night air blew into Jack's face, like ocean air—like the air blowing all the way from Rotterdam to Montreal, which was where the ship was heading.

Jack heard the women and girls in their windows and doorways calling out his name, but he just kept walking. "Brilliant!" Jack heard Richard say once, for no apparent reason.

Anneke was holding Jack's arm again—this time as if to shield him from the greetings of the prostitutes. "When you get back to the hotel, just go straight to bed and try to forget about it," Anneke whispered to him.

"Good night, my dears!" Wild Bill was calling to the red-light women.

Jack would forever feel the movement of the ship pulling out of the harbor—the deck rolling under his four-year-old feet, Rotterdam receding. How he wanted to see his father's Herbert Hoffmann—the tattoo William got in Hamburg, if he got one. A sailing ship seen from the stern; the ship would be pulling away from shore. Hoffmann's Sailor's Grave or his Last Port—a tattoo like that was what William would have wanted. Jack felt pretty sure about it. That was when Jack knew he would have to find him.

* * *

In Beverly Hills, the sun was now high enough in the sky that the slanted rays of light no longer came in the open windows. Miss Wurtz's painted toenails were a less-bright shade of rose-pink. The black piano had taken on a more somber tone—less like a pool of oil, more like a coffin. But even without direct sunlight, the Oscar standing beside their bare feet on the glass-topped table was no less gold—no less dazzling.

"I know that William saw you last night, Jack," Miss Wurtz was saying. "I don't care what time of night or early morning it was in Europe, if that's where he is. I just know that he wouldn't have missed seeing you."

Caroline got up from the couch and kissed Jack on the forehead; holding her bathrobe tightly to her throat, she bent over and kissed Oscar on the top of his gleaming head. "I'm going to go to sleep, you two," she said.

Jack watched her walk across the living room, her hand trailing lightly for a moment on the keys of the black piano; there was just the tinkling of those soft notes before she went into her bedroom and closed the door behind her.

Jack got up and went into his bedroom and closed the door; he left the curtains closed, but he opened the windows. Some light came into the bedroom when the breeze stirred the curtains, and he could hear the sound of a hose; below him, in the garden, someone was watering the flowers. Oscar lay down beside Jack. The statuette had its own pillow. Jack looked at Oscar lying there, holding his alleged sword. In the dim light, Oscar looked like a dead soldier; maybe his comrades had found him on the battlefield and laid his body to rest in a dignified pose.

Jack slept until the phone woke him that Monday afternoon. It was Richard. Jack had forgotten that he and Vanvleck and Richard had agreed to go to a sound studio to record the commentary track for the DVD of their film. They had to screen the entire movie, pausing it occasionally, while they talked about the intention behind this shot or that scene—how a particular moment had come about, or how this line of dialogue or voice-over had actually been moved from somewhere else.

Jack took a shower and got dressed. He put the Oscar on the piano, on top of a note of explanation to Miss Wurtz; she was still sleeping. They would have dinner together—maybe with Richard and Wild Bill, Jack said in the note. So that no one would steal the Oscar or wake up Miss Wurtz, Jack left the DO NOT DISTURB card on the door to the suite; at the front desk, he told them not to put through any calls.

Then he walked out into the harsh sunlight, and joined Richard and Wild Bill in the limo for the ride to the sound studio. Wild Bill had a bad hangover, which had not been improved by Anneke getting sick in the middle of the night. "Something she ate," Wild Bill told them. "I wish I'd eaten it, too. I wish it had killed me."

Richard told Jack that no hangover was as bad as not winning the Oscar.

It seemed to take hours to record the DVD commentary. As when Jack first met with Richard and Wild Bill in Amsterdam, his heart wasn't in it. But Jack liked the movie they had made together, and when he watched the film, he remembered how it had all come about.

"Whose idea was this?" Wild Bill would say, from time to time.

"Yours, I think," Richard would tell him.

It went pretty well, all things considered. Wild Bill's hangover seemed to go away, or else he rose to the occasion. In a short while, Vanvleck was doing most of the talking. There was almost a half hour when Wild Bill just talked nonstop; it was amazing what he could remember. But hearing the Dutchman's voice like that was oddly dislocating. Jack could almost hear him asking, "You actually know this lady?"

Or when Jack had explained (that night in the Sint Jacobsstraat) that Els had been his *nanny,* how Wild Bill had asked Richard: "She was his *what*?"

"Jack, why are you crying?" The Mad Dutchman had also asked.

Here they were in Hollywood, in a sound studio, and Wild Bill Vanvleck was going on about how they'd made Emma's movie. But in the drone of the Dutchman's voice, his actual words were lost. Jack saw Wild Bill sitting drunk in the street, shouting to his girlfriend: "Well, *I* didn't know!" And later, as they made their way through the red-light district, Jack could still hear Vanvleck calling, "Good night, my dears!"

Well, they had a job to do—Richard, Wild Bill, and Jack— and they did it. Later that afternoon, when Jack got back to the Four Seasons, he found Miss Wurtz in the living room of their suite playing the piano. Jack sat on the couch for a while and just listened.

The Wurtz began to talk to him, but—at the same time—she kept playing. "I want to thank you, Jack—I had the *best* time! It was quite a night for an old lady!"

Jack's neck was stiff and his toes hurt—something he'd done in the gym, he was thinking.

"But I must enlighten you, Jack," Miss Wurtz went on. "Don't take this the wrong way, but not even a night like last night is as special to me as *every* night I spent with your father. If I never got to go to the Oscars, I would still have had *William* in my life—that's all that matters."

And that was when Jack knew why his neck was stiff and his toes hurt. In those few hours of that early Monday morning, following the Academy Awards—when he actually got to sleep— Jack knew what he'd been dreaming. He was standing on the deck of that ship, leaving Rotterdam, and he was straining to see over the rail. Jack was standing on his toes and stretching his neck; for the few hours he slept, Jack must have maintained this uncomfortable position. No matter how hard he tried, of course, he couldn't see the shore.

Jack Burns may not have been a big believer in so-called re-covered memory, but here is what Jack remembered, listening to Miss Wurtz play the piano, and he was sure it really happened— he knew it was true.

"Lift me up!" Jack had said to his mother on the deck of that ship. The docks were still in sight, but Jack couldn't see them. "Lift me up!" he'd begged his mom. "I want to see!" But she wouldn't do it.

"You've seen enough, Jack," his mom had said. She took his hand. "We're going below deck now," she'd told him.

"Lift me up! I want to *see*!" Jack had demanded.

But Alice was in no mood to be bossed around. "You've seen enough of Holland to last you a lifetime, *Jackie boy*," she'd said.

Under the circumstances, Jack had seen enough of Canada to last him a lifetime, too. Because the next country Jack saw was Canada, where his mother took him—where he would never see his dad.

33
Signs of Trouble

It had been Mrs. Machado's fondest hope, or so she'd said, that Mister Penis would never be taken advantage of. But by whom? By willful girls and venal women? Dr. García told Jack that many women who sexually molest children believe that they are protecting them—that what the rest of us might call abuse is for these women a form of mothering.

Dr. García further speculated that Mrs. Machado must have observed a certain absence of the mothering instinct in Alice. "Women like Mrs. Machado know which boys are vulnerable," Jack's psychiatrist said. "It helps, of course, if you know the boy's mother—if you see what's missing."

"*Principiis obsta!*" Mr. Ramsey had once warned him. "Beware the beginnings!"

If Jack had mother and father issues, one wonders what to make of Lucy. She was four, almost five, that early fall evening in 1987, when Jack discovered her in the backseat of her parents' silver Audi—his first and last night as a parking valet at Stan's in Venice.

When he saw Lucy again, in the waiting room of Dr. García's office in Santa Monica, it was more than a year after he'd won the Oscar—April or May 2001. Lucy would have been eighteen. Jack didn't recognize her, but she recognized him; everyone did. (A pretty girl—someone's nanny, Jack had assumed.)

He'd long ago learned to expect and tolerate the stares of girls Lucy's age, but Lucy's eyes were riveted to his face, his hands, his every glance and movement. Her keen interest in him went far beyond overt flirtation or the groupie thing. Jack almost asked the receptionist if he could wait in another room. He didn't know if there were other rooms—that is, other than a bathroom and a closet—but Lucy's wanton obsession with him was distressing.

Then the problem appeared to go away; they overlapped only that one time in Dr. García's waiting room. Jack completely forgot about the girl.

The reason Jack would remember the year and the season of his first reunion with Lucy, which (at the time) he didn't know was a reunion, is that he was getting ready for a trip to Halifax—his first trip there since he'd crossed the Atlantic and landed in Nova Scotia in his mother's womb. Dr. García had warned him against returning to his birthplace, which she viewed as a possible setback to his therapy. But Jack had other business in Halifax.

A not-very-good Canadian novelist and screenwriter, Doug McSwiney, and a venerable French director, Cornelia Lebrun, wanted him to play the lead in a movie about the Halifax Explosion in 1917. They probably couldn't get adequate financing for the film without a movie star attached, and—given the off-center nature of McSwiney's screenplay—not just any movie star would do. Because of the cross-dressing inclination of the main character, the movie star had to be Jack Burns.

The character Jack would play, a transvestite prostitute, loses his (or her) memory in the explosion, when all his clothes are blown off and he suffers second-degree burns over his entire body; then he falls in love with his nurse. At first, Jack's character doesn't remember that he's a transvestite prostitute, but it wouldn't be a movie if his memory didn't return.

Jack had some issues with the screenplay, but he'd always been interested in the Halifax Explosion—and in seeing the city of his birth. It appealed to him to work with Cornelia Lebrun as a director, too. She was by far the more accomplished element in this collaboration, and when she proposed a meeting in Halifax—where she was working with McSwiney, urging him to improve his tortured script—Jack seized the opportunity to see his birthplace. He would also have a chance to put in his two cents regarding Doug McSwiney's trivialization of the Halifax disaster.

After Jack had won the Oscar, he'd said no to an uncountable number of offers. Many of these were suggested adaptations. He'd read a lot of novels, looking for a possible adaptation that appealed to him. But ever since Jack had been telling the story of his life to Dr. García, the idea of writing *any* screenplay paled.

Jack Burns was back in the acting business, at least for the time being—or so he told Bob Bookman. But after the Oscar, Jack had been inclined to be picky about the acting opportunities, too. The thought of making a movie in Halifax, however, intrigued him. Who knows what so-called recovered memories he might unlock there? (Infant dreams and premonitions mainly, Jack imagined.)

That was his state of mind in June 2001, when he drove to Santa Monica for his appointment with Dr. García. It was a warm day; when he parked the Audi, he left all the windows open.

Jack had a number of reasons to be feeling positive. Three years after the fact, he had described his return trip to all but one of the Baltic and North Sea ports of call—and Jack had discovered that he could tell Dr. García what had happened while managing to hold himself together. (In a few instances, Dr. García had looked in danger of losing it.)

Furthermore, Jack was looking forward to his trip to Halifax—no small part of the reason being that his going there was *against* Dr. García's wishes. And last but not least, Jack had just heard from Michele Maher. This was all the more remarkable because he had *not* heard from her for well over a year—not even so much as a postcard congratulating him for the Academy Award.

Jack had concluded, of course, that the *sort-of* boyfriend had taken stronger possession of her; that the boyfriend had forbidden her to communicate with Jack Burns had also crossed Jack's mind. Now came her long, most informative—if not overaffectionate—letter. Naturally, Jack showed Michele's letter to Dr. García, but the doctor wasn't pleased.

In Jack's acceptance speech at the Academy Awards, his thanking Michele Maher for staying up late to watch him had backfired. It had prompted a heated discussion with her *sort-of* boyfriend—apparently on the subject of Michele's commitment to him, or lack thereof. Michele had never lived with anyone. To her old-fashioned thinking, cohabitation meant marriage and children; living with someone wasn't supposed to be an experiment. But because Jack mentioned her name—to an audience of millions—Michele's *sort-of* boyfriend insisted that they live together. Michele gave in, though she stopped short of marriage and children.

He was a fellow doctor, an internist—a friend of a friend she'd known in medical school. They were very much (perhaps too much) alike, she wrote.

"Everything in Dr. Maher's letter," Dr. García said, when she'd finished reading it, "suggests a pragmatism unlike your approach to anything in this world, Jack."

But Jack had come away with something a little different from Michele's letter—for starters, it hadn't worked out with the live-in boyfriend. (*"A year of commitment, in which I've never felt so uncommitted,"* as Michele put it.) She was living alone again; she had no boyfriend. She was finally free to congratulate Jack for winning the Oscar, and to suggest that—were he ever to find himself in the Boston area—they should meet for lunch.

"I realize that you don't get nominated for an Oscar every year," Michele wrote. *"Moreover, should you ever go back to the Academy Awards, I wouldn't expect you to consider asking me to go with you again. But, in retrospect, I might have spared myself an unhappy year by saying yes to you the first time."*

"There's more than a hint of a come-on in the 'in retrospect' part, isn't there?" Dr. García commented. (This was not phrased as a question she expected Jack to answer; this was simply Dr. García's way of presuming his agreement.)

"Später—vielleicht," Michele's letter concluded.

"You'll have to help me with the German," Dr. García said, almost as an afterthought.

" 'Later—perhaps,' " Jack translated.

"Hmm." (This was Dr. García's way of downplaying the importance of something.)

"I could come back from Halifax via Boston," he suggested.

"How old is Michele—thirty-five, thirty-six?" Dr. García asked, as if she didn't know.

"Yes, she's my age," Jack replied.

"Most doctors are workaholics," Dr. García said, "but, like any woman her age, Michele's clock is ticking."

He should have told Dr. García about Michele's letter *in chronological order,* Jack was thinking, but he didn't say anything.

"On the other hand, she doesn't exactly *sound* like a star-fucker, does she?" Dr. García said.

"She was just suggesting *lunch,*" Jack said.

"Hmm."

There were no new photographs in Dr. García's office; there

hadn't been any new photos in the three years he'd been her patient. But there wasn't any room for new ones, not unless she threw some of the old ones away.

"Call me from Halifax if you get in trouble, Jack."

"I won't get in any trouble," he told her.

Dr. García took a good look at the sky-blue, businesslike letterhead on Michele's stationery before handing the letter back to him. "Call me from *Cambridge, Massachusetts,* then," she said. "I can almost guarantee you, Jack—you're going to get in trouble there."

At the time, in the *chronological-order* part of his life story as told to Dr. García, he was up to what Miss Wurtz called "the second time in Amsterdam." Understandably, he was in no hurry to relate that part of his life story to the doctor. Jack thought that a little trip to Halifax, with a stopover in Boston on the way back, might do him a world of good.

When he came out into the waiting room, Jack was distracted by a woman—one of the young mothers who was a regular patient of Dr. García's. She commenced to scream the second she saw him. (Jack hated it when that happened.)

The receptionist quickly led him to the Montana Avenue exit. Jack saw that another young mother, or the screaming woman's friend or nanny, was trying to comfort the screamer, whose wailing had frightened the children; some of the kids were crying.

He got into his Audi and tucked Michele Maher's letter under the sun visor on the driver's side. He was approaching the intersection of Montana Avenue and Fourth Street when Lucy's face appeared in his rearview mirror. Jack almost had an accident when she said, "I'm not well enough behaved to eat in a grown-up restaurant."

He still didn't get it. Jack knew only that he'd last seen her in Dr. García's waiting room, but he didn't know who she was. (The nanny with groupie potential, as he'd thought of her.)

"I usually sleep on the floor, if I think anyone can see me sleeping on the backseat," the strange girl said. "I can't believe you keep buying *Audis,* and they're always *silver*!"

"Lucy?" Jack said.

"It took you long enough," she told him, "but I didn't have any tits when you met me. I guess it's understandable that you didn't recognize me."

An unfortunate coincidence, he realized. Lucy wasn't anyone's nanny; like Jack, she was one of Dr. García's *patients*. (One of the less stable ones, he would soon discover.)

It was hard to see what faint resemblance she still bore to the worried but courageous little four-year-old Jack had picked up in his arms at Stan's. Some of her courage had remained, or it had hardened into something else. Now in her late teens, Lucy wasn't worried about anything—not anymore.

She had dead-calm, unblinking eyes—suggesting the steely recklessness of a car thief. If you dared her to do it—or bet her five bucks that she couldn't—she would drive foot-to-the-floor through every red light on Wilshire Boulevard, all the way from Santa Monica into Beverly Hills. Unless she got broadsided in Brentwood, or shot by a cop in Westwood Village, there'd be no stopping her—her bare left arm would be lolling out the window, giving everyone the finger the whole way.

Jack turned right on Ocean Avenue and pulled the Audi to the curb. "I think you better get out of the car, Lucy," he said.

"I'll take off all my clothes before you can get me out of the backseat," the girl told him.

Jack held the steering wheel in both hands, looking at Lucy in his rearview mirror. She was wearing a pink tank top—barely more than a sports bra—and black Puma running shorts, like a jogger. Jack knew she could take off everything she was wearing in the time it would take him to get out of the driver's seat and open the back door.

"What do you want, Lucy?" he asked her.

"Let's go to your house," she said. "I know where you live, and I got a helluva story to tell you."

"You know where I live?" he asked the girl.

"My mom and I drive by your house all the time," she told him. "But we never see you. I guess you're not there much or something."

"Let's just talk in the car," Jack suggested.

"It's kind of a long story," the girl explained. In the rearview mirror, he could see that she was wriggling her running shorts down over her hips. Her thong was pink; it didn't look as if it would be comfortable to run in.

"Please pull your shorts up," he said. "We'll go to my house."

She was wearing dirty running shoes with those short socks that all the kids seemed to like—the kind that didn't even cover your ankles. She walked all over Jack's house on the balls of her feet, as if she were imitating Mr. Ramsey—or else she was too restless to sit down. Jack followed her around like a dog; it was as if they were in Lucy's house and she was in charge.

"When you head-butted my dad, that was a life-changing moment," Lucy told him. "That was when my mom decided she'd had enough of him. I remember she screamed at him all the way home. They would've been divorced before breakfast the next morning, if my mom could've arranged it."

"In my experience, you don't remember things with much accuracy when you're four years old," he cautioned her.

"You were my mother's fucking *hero,*" Lucy said. "You think I wouldn't remember that? When you got famous, we went to all your movies and my mom said, 'There's the guy who got me out of my miserable marriage.' Of course my dad *hated* you. When they were divorced, I had to listen to him talk about you, too. 'If I ever run into Jack Burns, he won't know what hit him!' my dad was always shouting."

"Your dad didn't handle himself too well the first time," Jack pointed out to her.

"Let me tell you—if my mom ever ran into you, she'd fuck your brains out and then tell my dad all about it," Lucy said. "All my life, you've been such a big fucking deal in my family."

"I was just appalled that your mom and dad would leave a four-year-old in the back of their car—in *Venice,*" he said.

Lucy was fingering the tattoo magnets Alice had given Jack for his fridge. Japanese flash—*irezumi,* Henk Schiffmacher had called them. There were half a dozen magnets the size of quarters. Jack had used them to hold the four photographs of his mom's naked torso against the refrigerator door—four slightly different views of her *Until I find you* tattoo, which he saw Lucy looking at very closely.

But Lucy wouldn't settle down. She went off to have a look at the stuff on Jack's desk. The flat glass paperweight, which slightly magnified the photo of Emma naked at seventeen, was an eye-catcher. (He'd always thought that one day he would regret keeping one of those photographs, which Claudia had asked him to get rid of.)

"I gotta use your bathroom," Lucy said. There were two other bathrooms in the house, but she waltzed right through Jack's bedroom and went into his bathroom and closed the door.

Jack had converted Emma's former bedroom into a small

gym—two kinds of stationary bikes, a treadmill, an ab machine, some benches, and a lot of free weights. There were no mirrors on the walls—just some of his favorite movie posters, including a couple from films he'd been in. There was a mat on the floor for stretching and rolling around—a long rectangle, about a third of a regulation-size wrestling mat.

Jack sat down on the mat and hugged his knees to his chest, wondering what he should do about Lucy. He heard the toilet flush and the water running in the sink; he heard the girl come out of the bathroom and pick up the telephone on the night table next to his bed. Jack could tell by her automatic tone of voice that she was talking to an answering machine.

"Hi, Mom—it's me," he heard Lucy say. "I'm in Jack Burns's house, I'm naked, I'm in his bed. Isn't this what you always wanted? Sorry I beat you to it, but what's it matter? The thought of you *or* me with Jack Burns is gonna drive Dad crazy. Love ya!"

Jack went into his bedroom and saw that Lucy hadn't been kidding. She'd pulled back the covers and was lying naked on his bed. "*Now* we're going to get in trouble," Lucy said.

"Maybe *you* are, Lucy, but I'm not," he told her.

He walked past her into the bathroom; he was intending to bring her clothes to her, but he couldn't see her clothes or imagine what she'd done with them. She'd put her dirty running shoes with the little socks on his bathroom scale, but the rest of her clothes were gone. (*How could they just disappear?* he was thinking.)

Jack went back into the bedroom. "You're leaving now, Lucy. Where are your clothes?"

She shrugged. Yes, she was a pretty eighteen-year-old. Even Jack could count the years from 1987, when he first came to L.A., and add them to four. (And after all, he'd been doing a lot of thinking about four-year-olds lately.) But Jack wasn't even *considering* having sex with Lucy, not even if it was legal—that wasn't the issue.

She was one of those willfully grimy girls with flecks of gold glitter in her hair; every toenail was painted a different color. The finger-shaped citron known as Buddha's Hand was tattooed on the inside of one thigh—high up, where her running shorts had covered it. Some young women were more arousing before they took their clothes off; besides, Jack had never liked being bullied.

"I'll give you a T-shirt and some running shorts of mine," he said. "I'll dress you myself, Lucy, if you don't get yourself dressed and get out of here."

"My mom's already called the cops," she told him. "She's home all day with nothing to do. She just screens all her calls, in case it's my dad. I'm telling you, she's already played my message twice—she's already given the cops your address, and everything."

Jack went into the kitchen and picked up the phone there. He called 911 and said he had an unwelcome eighteen-year-old girl in his house—she had hidden herself in his car. Now she'd undressed herself and called her mother. He hadn't touched her, Jack said—he didn't *want* to touch her. "If the girl won't dress herself, maybe one of the officers you send should be female," he said.

Jack was asked if this was a domestic dispute. Did he *know* the girl? "I haven't had any contact with her since she was a four-year-old!" he shouted.

Well, that meant he *did* know her, didn't it? Jack was asked. (He should have seen that coming.) "Look, she thinks I'm the reason her mother and father got divorced. She and her mother are *obsessed* with me. Her father *hates* me!"

"You know the whole family?" he was asked.

When Jack gave his address, he got a quick "Wait a minute" in response. A squad car had already been dispatched. Naturally, there'd been an earlier call—Lucy's mother. The first caller had said something about a rape-in-progress.

"That's not true!" Jack shouted.

"The toilet keeps flushing!" Lucy called from the bedroom. "Forget the cops. You better call a plumber!"

Jack hung up the phone and stomped back through his bedroom to the bathroom. Lucy had put her clothes in the water-tank part of the toilet. (They were soaked; Jack put them in the bathtub.) The rod that held the ball was bent out of shape; that was why the toilet kept flushing. At least he knew what to do about that.

When Jack went back into the bedroom, Lucy was writhing all around on his bed; the bedcovers were completely untucked, and one of the pillows had been flung on the floor. The bed looked as if he'd just had sex with *several* eighteen-year-olds—all of them gymnasts.

"This is nothing but a big nuisance," he told the little bitch. "Believe me, you're not going to think this is so funny when they check you for *bodily fluids*."

"I'm just so sick of hearing how you fucked up my entire family!" the girl shouted.

Jack walked out of the bedroom, closing the door behind him. He went outside and stood leaning against his Audi in the driveway. He was still waiting for the police to arrive when he noticed the photographer, an overfamiliar paparazzo—best known for his photos of a young actress barfing in a swimming pool at a wedding in Westwood. Jack saw the paparazzo looking at him through the long telephoto lens from the far side of the street.

When the cops came, Jack was glad that one of the two was a female officer. Jack told her where Lucy was, and the policewoman went into the house to find her while he told his story to the other officer.

"Are you sure she's eighteen?" the policeman interrupted Jack once; otherwise, he just listened. The paparazzo had crossed the street and was photographing them from the foot of Jack's driveway.

"She can't wear her own clothes—they're all wet," Jack was explaining to the officer, just before Lucy ran naked out the front door and threw her arms around Jack's neck. The policeman tried to shield her from the photographer.

The female officer came out of the house carrying a bath towel. She tried to wrap the towel around Lucy, but Lucy kept wriggling out of the towel. It took both officers to disengage the girl from around Jack's neck. Jack just stood there, doing his best not to touch Lucy, while the paparazzo kept snapping away. If the photographer had taken one step up the driveway, Jack might have broken all the fingers on the guy's hands—one finger at a time, even with the police officers there.

"I suppose stuff like this happens to you on a regular basis," the male cop was saying to Jack.

"Whatever he's been telling you, I'll bet it's true," the female officer told her partner. "If this girl were my daughter, I'd be tempted to drown her in a toilet."

She was a tall, lean black woman with a despairing expression that was accented by a scar; the scar had dug a groove through one of her eyebrows. Her partner was a husky white guy with a crew cut and pale-blue eyes; his eyes were as calm and unblinking as Lucy's.

"Be sure to check her for evidence of *bodily fluids,*" Jack told the officers, "in case I'm lying."

The black woman smiled. "Don't *you* get in trouble, too," she told him. "Behave yourself."

"We'd like to have a look inside your house, just to corroborate a few things," the husky policeman said.

"Sure," Jack told him.

It was a long day. Jack kept looking out the window. He was hoping the paparazzo would come onto his property, but the photographer maintained his vigil at the foot of the driveway. After the police took Lucy away—Jack insisted on *giving* Lucy the bath towel—the photographer went away, too.

Jack was surprised that both police officers never once appeared to doubt his story, but the female officer had cautioned him about the photos of Alice's breasts and her tattoo on the refrigerator. When Jack explained the history of the photographs, the policewoman said: "That doesn't matter. If there's ever any trouble here, you don't want pictures like those on your *fridge.*"

He showed her the photo of Emma naked at seventeen—the one under the paperweight on his desk. "Ditto?" he asked her.

"You're learning," the female officer said. "I sense that you have real potential."

After everyone had gone, Jack found Lucy's thong in his bathtub; it was so small that the police must have missed it. He put it in the trash, together with the four photos of his mom and the old one of Emma.

If he hadn't been leaving for Halifax in the morning, Jack might have been more careful about the trash. It would make sense to him later—how the magazine that bought the paparazzo's photographs had sent someone to the house on Entrada Drive to sort through Jack's trash. It made sense that the magazine would talk to Lucy, too—and that she would dismiss the incident as a "prank."

All Jack said, when the magazine later asked him for a comment—allegedly for a follow-up story—was that the police had behaved properly. First of all, they'd believed Jack. Wasn't Lucy the one they'd taken away? "You figure it out," Jack said to the woman from the magazine, who called herself a "diligent fact-checker." (He meant that the police hadn't taken *him* away, had they?)

But Jack knew nothing about any of this when he left in the morning for Halifax. Given all the things that had happened to him—the bad choices he'd made, those years he would regret—the Lucy episode struck him as a virtual nonevent. He didn't even call Dr. García and tell her about it. (*Let her wait; let her hear about it in chronological order,* Jack thought.)

But sometimes even a nonevent will be registered in the public consciousness. Jack had done nothing to Lucy—except try to look after her, when she was four. But in a scandal-mongering movie magazine, complete with photos, the girl's irritating "prank" would carry with it a whiff of something truly scandalous; it would appear as if Jack Burns had gotten away with something.

This would be hard to say to Dr. García, when the time came, but—although it didn't yet exist—a trap had been set for Jack. Lucy wasn't the trap, but she was a contributing factor to a trap that waited in his future. That nice female officer had tried to tell him. Jack had thrown away the photographs, but the photos hadn't been all she was warning him about.

"If there's ever any trouble here—" Wasn't that how she'd put it?

34

Halifax

Jack called Michele Maher's office on his cell phone en route to the airport. It was very early in the morning in L.A., but Dr. Maher's nurse answered the phone in the doctor's Cambridge office; it was three hours later in Massachusetts. The nurse was a friendly soul named Amanda, who informed him that Dr. Maher was with a patient.

Jack told Amanda who he was and where he was going. He said he'd gone to school with Michele—that was as far as he got with their history.

"I know all about it," Amanda said. "Everyone in the office wanted to *kill* her for not going to the Oscars with you."

"Oh."

"Are you going to have lunch with her?" Amanda asked. Jack guessed that *everyone in the office* knew about the letter Michele had written him; possibly Amanda had typed it.

Jack explained that he was hoping to see Dr. Maher on his return trip from Halifax. He'd booked a stopover in Boston. If Michele was free for dinner that night, or lunch the next day—that was as far as he got.

"So now it's *dinner*!" Amanda said eagerly. "Maybe lunch *and* dinner. Maybe *breakfast*!"

Jack told Amanda that he would call later in the week from Halifax—just to be sure Dr. Maher had the time to see him.

"You should stay at the Charles Hotel in Cambridge. You can walk to the hospital and our office. I can reserve a room for you, if you want," Amanda told him. "The hotel has a gym and a pool, and everything."

"Thank you, Amanda," he said. "That would be very nice—if Dr. Maher has the time to see me."

"What's with the *Dr. Maher*?" Amanda exclaimed.

Jack didn't bother to tell Amanda to reserve a room for him at the Charles under a different name, although not only Michele but *everyone in the office* would know that Jack Burns was in town and where he was staying. As interested as Jack was in the Halifax Explosion, or the idea of making a movie in his birthplace, he was by no means committed to the role of the amnesiac transvestite prostitute in Doug McSwiney's screenplay; in fact, the more Jack thought about the issues he had with McSwiney's script, the less he felt like registering in *any* hotel as an amnesiac transvestite prostitute. (At the hotel in Halifax, he'd made the reservation in his own name.)

Jack thanked Amanda for her friendliness and help and gave her the phone number of his hotel in Halifax, and his cell-phone number—just in case Michele wanted to call him.

Jack had sufficient airplane reading for the trip, beginning with Doug McSwiney's screenplay, which he read two more times. Called *The Halifax Explosion,* McSwiney's script was purportedly based on Michael J. Bird's *The Town That Died*— a chronicle of the Halifax disaster first published in 1967. Bird's book, which was by far the best of Jack's airplane reading, had been rendered a disservice.

On December 6, 1917, two ships collided in the Narrows— a mile-long channel, only five hundred yards wide, that connects Bedford Basin with Halifax Harbor and the open sea. A French freighter, the *Mont Blanc,* was bound for Bordeaux, loaded with munitions for the war effort. A Norwegian vessel, the *Imo,* had arrived in Halifax from Rotterdam and was sailing to New York. The *Mont Blanc*'s cargo included more than two thousand tons of picric acid and two hundred tons of TNT.

Upon impact, the *Mont Blanc* caught fire; less than an hour later, the ship's lethal cargo blew up. People were watching the burning ship from almost everywhere in town; they didn't know they were about to be blown up, too. Almost two thousand people were killed, nine thousand injured, and two hundred blinded.

The explosion leveled the North End of the city, which Bird describes as "a wilderness, a vast burning scrap yard." Hundreds of children were killed. There was incalculable damage to other ships in the harbor, and to the piers and dockyards and the Naval College—in addition to the Wellington Barracks and the Dartmouth side of the Narrows, where the captain and crew of the *Mont Blanc* had swum ashore.

Jack thought that the character of the French captain, Aimé Le Medec, was the most challenging for an actor. Bird describes him as "not more than 5 feet 4 inches in height but well built, with a neatly trimmed black beard to add authority to his somewhat youthful face." A contemporary of Le Medec called the captain "a likeable but moody man, at times inclined to be truculent," and "a competent, rather than a brilliant, sailor."

Jack Burns wasn't *that* short, but—as an actor—even Le Medec's physique appealed to him, and Jack was good at accents.

In the inquiry following the disaster, much was made of the fact that the *Mont Blanc*'s pilot, Frank Mackey, didn't speak French. Le Medec, who spoke English, was disinclined to speak the language because he didn't like it when people misunderstood him. Mackey and Le Medec had communicated with hand signals.

Jack liked everything he read about this "truculent" French captain. In Jack's view, that was the role he should have been offered. (And the screenplay should have stuck to the facts, which were interesting enough without creating fictional characters to coexist with the historical figures.)

The Canadian authorities in Halifax found Captain Le Medec and his pilot, Frank Mackey, responsible for the collision in the Narrows. The Supreme Court of Canada later found that both ships were to blame—they were equally liable. But Le Medec and his crew were French; in the eyes of many English-speaking Canadians, not just Nova Scotians, the French were to blame for everything.

The French director Cornelia Lebrun took the view that Le Medec deserved only half the blame. (The French government would take no action against Le Medec, who didn't retire from the sea until 1931—whereafter he was made a Chevalier de la Légion d'Honneur.) But this didn't explain Madame Lebrun's attachment to Doug McSwiney's script, in which Le Medec is a minor character and the Halifax Explosion itself is given merely a supporting role.

McSwiney had an eye for the periphery. Following the disaster, Bird comments in passing, many Halifax prostitutes moved to Toronto or Montreal—"to return later when conditions had improved." As for those prostitutes who never left town, "business was brisk."

Perhaps it was from this small mention of the life of prostitutes in Halifax that Doug McSwiney invented his peripheral story. At some Water Street location (this is given scant mention in Bird's book), a prostitute watches a customer—"a merchant seaman"—leaving her door and going off in the direction of the waterfront. It's early morning; the *Mont Blanc* is about to explode.

In McSwiney's screenplay, this prostitute (or someone based on her) breathes in the cold morning air a little too long. The blast rips the whore's clothes off, detaches her wig, and hurls her into the air—revealing to the audience that the prostitute, now naked and burning, is a *man*! Jack Burns, of course—who else?

While devastation reigns, the amnesiac transvestite prostitute is taken to a hospital. Pitiful sights abound. As Bird writes: "Two hundred children, the matron and every other member of the staff, died under the fallen roof and walls of the Protestant Orphanage on Campbell Road. Those who were not killed outright were slowly burned to death."

Yet the audience is supposed to feel sympathy for Jack's character, an amnesiac transvestite prostitute? Despite the many burned women and children in the hospital, an attractive nurse feels especially sympathetic toward Jack's character. The historical background of the film, which is given short shrift, is intercut with the amnesia victim's slow recovery and the evolving love affair with his nurse.

The transvestite prostitute can't remember who he is—not to mention what he was doing naked, flying, and burning in the air above Water Street at a little after 9:00 A.M. on that fateful Thursday. When he is well enough to leave the hospital, the nurse takes him home with her.

There then comes the inevitable scene in which the amnesia victim recovers his memory. (Knowing Jack Burns, you can see this coming.) The nurse has gone off to work at the hospital, and Jack's character wakes up in her bedroom. He spots one of her uniforms on a chair—her clothes from the day before. He puts them on, and when he sees himself in the mirror—well, you can imagine. Flashbacks galore! Unseemly behavior in female attire!

Thus the audience is treated to a *second* version of the Halifax Explosion. We get to see the disastrous life of a transvestite prostitute, leading up to that *other* disaster—the *real* one. As Bird observes: "In this moment of agony a greater number had been killed or injured in Halifax than ever were to be in any single air raid on London during the whole of World War II." But what was Doug McSwiney *thinking*?

Jack hated those movie meetings where he went in knowing that he detested the script, but he liked the director and the idea behind the film. He knew he would be perceived as the interfering movie star who was trying to distort the material to better serve *himself.* Or in this case—in Doug McSwiney's eyes, without a doubt—the Academy Award–winning screenwriter (talk about beginner's luck!) who was trying to tell a writer of McSwiney's vastly greater experience how to *write.*

Aside from Halifax being his birthplace, Jack was beginning to wonder why he had come—this being well before he touched down in Nova Scotia, where he had last landed in utero thirty-six years before. Maybe this *would* set back his therapy, as Dr. García had warned.

Jack checked into The Prince George; he made a dinner reservation at a nearby restaurant called the Press Gang. The restaurant was virtually across the street from the corner of Prince and Barrington, where William Burns had once played the organ in St. Paul's. Close by, on Argyle and Prince, was the St. Paul's Parish House, where the Anglicans had put up Jack's pregnant mother; it might even have been the building where Jack was born, no C-section required.

St. Paul's was built with white wooden clapboards and shingles in 1750. In memory of the Halifax Explosion, the church had preserved an unfrosted second-story window—a broken window, facing Argyle Street. When the *Mont Blanc* exploded, a hole had been blown in the window in the shape of a human head. The face in profile, especially the nose and chin, reminded Jack of his mother's.

The organ in St. Paul's had been erected in memory of an organist who'd died in 1920. The organ pipes were blue and white, and there was a second commemoration of another organist.

TO THE GLORY OF GOD
AND IN GRATEFUL MEMORY
OF NATALIE LITTLER
1898–1963
ORGANIST 1935–62

They must have needed a new organist in '62. There was no commemoration of William Burns, who Jack hoped was still among the living. He'd come to Halifax to play the organ in St. Paul's in 1964. (God knows how long William had stayed; there was no mention of his ever being there.)

Jack went outside the church and stood in the Old Burying Ground on Barrington Street, looking in the direction of Halifax Harbor. He was wondering what would have happened if he and his mother had stayed in Halifax—if they might have been happy there.

Jack knew that what was called "the explosion window" in St. Paul's Church—that perfectly preserved head, in profile, which memorialized the 1917 disaster—was better material for a movie about the Halifax Explosion than that piece-of-crap screenplay Doug McSwiney had written. Jack was embarrassed to have come all this way for a meeting about a film he knew would never be made—not with Jack Burns as the amnesiac transvestite prostitute, anyway.

Furthermore, Jack didn't *ever* want to meet Doug McSwiney. He decided he should just tell Cornelia Lebrun how he felt about the project, and leave it at that. (Jack knew there were a lot of movie meetings that could be avoided if people just told one another how they felt before they met.)

Jack knew that Cornelia Lebrun was staying at The Prince George, too, but he'd learned from Emma that it was better to express yourself *in writing*—especially if you're pissed off about something. Before dinner, Jack had just enough time to go back to the hotel and write out what he should have told the French director in a simple phone call from Los Angeles.

He had a personal interest in spending a little time in Halifax, Jack explained to her, but he would not be associated with a film about the Halifax Explosion that trivialized the disaster. Jack wrote that he was attracted to the character of Le Medec, and wanted to know more about him. Jack pointed out to Cornelia Lebrun that his physique was suitable for the role of Le Medec, and that the sea captain's reported moodiness and truculence were well within Jack's range as an actor. (He mentioned his gift for accents, too.)

Another good role, among the *real* people involved in the historical disaster, was that of Frank Mackey, the pilot who didn't speak French. And there was a third role of interest to any actor—that of C. J. Burchell, the counsel for the Norwegian shipping company. At that time, Burchell was the best-known maritime lawyer on the Eastern Seaboard. Representing the *Imo*'s owners, Burchell was—in Bird's words—"capable of the most ruthless court-room tactics." Given the judge's bias in favor of the *Imo*, and how local opinion was stacked against the *Mont Blanc* (and the French), Burchell must have been further encouraged "to attack and browbeat witnesses."

What need was there for a *fictional* story? Jack asked Cornelia Lebrun in his letter. With almost two thousand people killed and nine thousand injured—with nearly two hundred *blinded*—who *cared* about an amnesiac transvestite prostitute who gets burned a little and loses his (or her) clothes and his memory and his *wig*? Jack told the French director that McSwiney's screenplay, in a word, *sucked*. (Dr. García would have cautioned Jack against this particular *interjection*, and—as things turned out— she would have been right. But that's what he wrote in the heat of the moment.)

He apologized for wasting Madame Lebrun's *and* Mr. McSwiney's time by agreeing to a meeting in Halifax, which he now believed was pointless. Jack added that his one look at the so-called explosion window in St. Paul's Church drove home to him how McSwiney had managed to write a disaster movie both *prurient* and *banal;* he'd made a sordid love story out of the Halifax Explosion.

Jack forgot to tell Cornelia Lebrun that he remained interested in working with her as a director, which of course had initially persuaded him that the meeting in Halifax was a good idea. He also forgot to tell her that he'd been involved in enough cross-dressing to satisfy whatever *slight* yearning he might have felt for transvestite roles; as an actor, Jack didn't feel it was asking too much to be allowed to be a man.

Notwithstanding these omissions, he left a great mess of pages at the front desk of the hotel—a virtual ream of Prince George stationery, to be delivered to Madame Lebrun's room. Then Jack went off to the Press Gang restaurant for a solitary dinner. When Jack returned to the hotel, he inquired at the front desk if Cornelia Lebrun had left a message for him; he was told she was in the bar.

Jack had only a dim idea of what the French director looked like. (A small woman in her sixties—about the same age as Miss

Wurtz, he thought.) He spotted her easily. How many women in Halifax were likely to wear a suede pantsuit in lily-pad green?

"Cornelia?" Jack said to the little Frenchwoman, whose lipstick was a bold orange.

"Zzzhhhack Burns!" she cried, but before he could kiss her offered cheek, a large, hirsute man forced his way between them.

The man was bigger than any of his book-jacket photographs, and more hairy than a lumberjack. Jack had been unable to read the fur-faced author's novels due to the persistence of the rugged outdoors on every page—a characteristic relentlessness in the prose. (Fir trees bent by the wind, the gray rock of the Canadian Shield, the pitiless sea—harsh weather and hard drinking.) Even the whisky on the author's breath was bracing—Doug McSwiney, of course. Jack was reaching to shake his hand when McSwiney's left hook caught him on the right temple. Jack never saw it coming.

"*Suck* on that!" McSwiney said, but Jack heard only the *suck;* he was out on his feet before he fell. He should have had the brains to expect a cheap shot from a writer insensitive enough to turn the Halifax Explosion into an unwholesome love story.

Jack came to in his hotel room. He was lying on his back on his bed with his clothes on but his shoes off; his head was pounding. Cornelia Lebrun was sitting on the bed beside him. She had wrapped a wet washcloth around some ice cubes, which she held against the swollen bruise on Jack's right temple. *The drunken, bearded bastard could have killed me,* Jack was thinking.

"Eet's my fauld," Madame Lebrun was saying. "I can't read English when eet's in *writing-by-hand.*"

"*Longhand,*" Jack corrected her.

"I asked Dougie to read your notes out *lout* to me. Beeeg faux pas, *oui*? I theenk the word *sucked* was what deed eet to heem."

"Or *banal*—or *prurient,* maybe."

"*Oui.* Alzo hee's dreenking."

"I've had bad reviews myself," Jack told her. "I didn't try to club Roger Ebert to death with my Oscar."

"Clup *who* to dead?" the little Frenchwoman asked.

"It doesn't matter. I don't want to be in the movie," he told her.

"I would cast a Frenchman to play Le Medec, Zzzhhhack—no matter how goot your axzent ees."

She would never get the movie made, anyway. Later that year, after the terrorist attacks on September 11, it would be too diffi-

cult to find financing for a film about the Halifax Explosion—
even with a movie star in it. Suddenly, disaster movies weren't
all that appealing. (This feeling would persist for a whole year or
more.)

Something about the Halifax Explosion appeared on Canadian television, but that happened a couple of years later and
Jack never saw it. He didn't even know if it was a documentary
or what Miss Wurtz would have called a *dramatization*. Jack
only knew that Doug McSwiney had had nothing to do with it.
And after that introduction in the bar of The Prince George, Jack
doubted that he would ever work with Cornelia Lebrun.

The hotel sent a female doctor to Jack's room while Madame
Lebrun was still attending to his head injury. The doctor told
Jack that he had a mild concussion; from the beat of his pulse in
his right temple, he might have disputed the word *mild* with her.
She also told him that he shouldn't sleep for more than two hours
at a time. The doctor left instructions at the front desk to give
Jack Burns a wake-up call every two hours; if he didn't answer
his phone, someone had to go into his room and wake him up.
And he shouldn't travel for another day, the doctor said.

That night, between the wake-up calls, he had dreams of being on a movie set. "Hold the talking, please," someone on the
set would say, for what seemed like the hundredth time.

"Picture's up."

"Stand by."

It made Jack realize that he missed the process. Maybe it had
been too long since he'd made a movie.

In the morning, Jack walked along Barrington Street, looking
for something to read. He found a bookstore called The Book
Room. The owner recognized him and invited him to have a coffee with him. Jack volunteered to sign some books—just what
they had on hand of the screenplay of *The Slush-Pile Reader*.
(Emma's paperback publisher had published the script; in most
bookstores, the screenplay was on the shelf alongside the movie
tie-in edition of Emma's novel.)

The bookseller's name was Charles Burchell; he turned out to
be the grandson of C. J. Burchell, the legendary maritime lawyer
who'd led the court-room attack on the *Mont Blanc*'s captain and
pilot. When Jack told Charles that he thought he'd been born in
the St. Paul's Parish House, Charles told Jack that the vestry of
the church had been used as an emergency hospital in the days

following the Halifax Explosion; the bodies of hundreds of victims had been laid in tiers around the walls.

Charles was kind enough to take Jack on a tour of the harbor. Jack wanted to see the ocean terminals, particularly the pier where the immigrants landed. Charles also drove Jack to the Fairview Lawn Cemetery. Jack was curious to see the *Titanic* grave site. Halifax had seen its share of disasters.

Jack walked with Charles among the gravestones.

> ERECTED TO THE MEMORY
> OF AN
> UNKNOWN CHILD
> WHOSE REMAINS
> WERE RECOVERED
> AFTER THE
> DISASTER TO
> THE "TITANIC"
> APRIL 15, 1912

There were many more.

> ALMA PAULSON
> AGED 29 YEARS
> LOST WITH FOUR CHILDREN

Some were just names with their ages.

> TOBURG DANDRIA AGED 8
> PAUL FOLKE AGED 6
> STINA VIOLA AGED 4
> GOSTA LEONARD AGED 2

Others were just numbers.

> DIED
> APRIL 15, 1912
> 227

A small headstone marked J. DAWSON had the largest number of flowers—bouquets of flowers dwarfed the headstone, almost obscuring the oddly familiar name. Charles told Jack why the name was familiar. The character Leonardo DiCaprio played in the *Titanic* movie was named Jack Dawson.

"You don't mean he was *real*," Jack said.

"I have no idea," Charles said.

The J. DAWSON on the headstone could have been a different Dawson. *Jack* Dawson, DiCaprio's character, might have been invented. But since the movie had been released, visitors to the *Titanic* grave site put flowers on J. DAWSON's headstone because they believed he was that character. Worse—whether or not Jack Dawson in the movie was related to J. DAWSON on the headstone, the young girls bringing flowers thought there was someone in that grave who had once looked like Leonardo DiCaprio.

"*Movies*," Jack said with disgust. Charles laughed.

But Jack saw it then—*this* was where that hair-faced novelist and screenwriter had gotten the idea to make a love story out of the Halifax Explosion. It was a bad idea to begin with, but it hadn't even been McSwiney's idea. He'd stolen it from the *Titanic* movie; he'd ripped it off from a graveyard full of children!

"Does Doug McSwiney come from Halifax?" Jack asked Charles Burchell. Since Charles was a bookseller, Jack knew that Charles would know.

"Born and raised," Charles said. "He's an awful man—he's always punching people."

The *Titanic* grave site gave Jack additional grounds for wanting to kick the crap out of McSwiney, and Jack still had a headache. (As cheap shots go, a blow to someone's temple is asking for trouble.)

Jack went back to the hotel and took a short nap. He probably did have a concussion, mild or not, because he wasn't feeling well. He was wondering why Michele Maher hadn't called him—just to say she was looking forward to lunch or dinner, or whatever. Maybe she was shy; probably she was busy. Jack didn't sleep very soundly, or for long. At the first ring of the wake-up call, he sat up too suddenly and saw stars. The stars continued to twinkle while he brushed his teeth.

A separated shoulder would be a justifiable injury to inflict on Doug McSwiney, Jack was thinking. Given that McSwiney had hit Jack with a left hook, he was probably right-handed; if so, a separated *right* shoulder would be a good idea.

Jack called Dr. Maher's office and once again got Michele's

nurse, Amanda, on the phone. "Hi, Amanda—it's Jack Burns. I'm calling to confirm breakfast, lunch, *and* dinner."

He could tell right away that something was wrong; the formerly friendly Amanda was ice-cold to him. "Dr. Maher is with a patient," the nurse said.

"What's with the *Dr. Maher*, Amanda?"

"No breakfast, no lunch, no dinner," Amanda said. "Dr. Maher doesn't want to see you—she won't even *talk* to you. I canceled your reservation at the Charles."

"Maybe I've misunderstood you," Jack said. "I have a concussion."

"That girl gave you a *concussion*?" Amanda asked.

"*What* girl?"

"I'm talking about the *Lucy* business—the photographs, the whole story. Don't they have *news* in Canada?"

Jack could see that flaming paparazzo as if the photographer were still standing at the foot of the driveway, snapping away. One of the sleazier movie magazines had bought the photographs. The story, and the tamer of the photos, had also been on television.

"You don't come off very well," Amanda explained.

"I did not have sex with that young woman!" he told her.

"I'm sure you didn't," Amanda said. "The girl just knew that you *wanted* to, and that you definitely *would* have had sex if she hadn't called her mother."

"That's not true! I called the cops and asked them to come get her! I waited outside my own house until the police came!"

"You had a naked eighteen-year-old in your bed—you even have the same psychiatrist," Amanda pointed out. "You knew Lucy when she was a child—you beat up her father! And why did you keep her *thong*, and those terrible pictures? There was a photo of what looked like *another* naked eighteen-year-old on your desk! There were photographs of a naked woman's tattooed breast on your *refrigerator*!"

"I threw all that away!" Jack shouted.

"Where? On your front lawn?" the nurse asked.

"Please let me speak to Michele," he begged her.

"Michele said, 'If Jack calls, tell him he's just *too weird* for me.' That's what the doctor said," Amanda told him, hanging up the phone.

Jack turned on the television in his hotel room. It took him a while to find an American network among the Canadian TV channels, although (as Leslie Oastler would soon inform him) the Lucy story had already been picked up by the Canadian media. When he found *Headline News,* Jack discovered that he was the lead item in the entertainment segment.

When Lucy was told that her pink thong had been recovered from Jack's trash—together with those incriminating photographs, which Lucy had earlier described to reporters—she speculated that Jack must have wanted to have some *keepsake* of her visit and had therefore hidden her thong from the police. Apparently, he'd had second thoughts and had thrown out the thong with the other "evidence." (The thong looked really small on TV; it appeared that Jack had stolen it from a *child.*)

Jack needed to see the sleazy magazine itself before he could understand everything that was incriminating about the photographs—that is, the ones not fit for television. He left the hotel and walked over to The Book Room. Charles Burchell was a bookseller; Charles would know where every newsstand in Halifax was. Naturally, Charles already had a copy of the movie magazine.

"I called you at the hotel, Jack, but they said you were napping." None of the saleswomen in The Book Room would look at Jack; they'd all seen the photos and had read the insinuating story.

The magazine's cover photo was of Lucy hanging naked from around Jack's neck, resembling a pornographic ornament. Both police officers appeared to be struggling as much with Jack as with Lucy. The photographs inside the magazine—particularly the ones that had been rescued from his trash—were no less condemning. The pink thong was not only very small; it was still wet. Emma naked at seventeen had been doctored for magazine propriety. Jack thought that the black slash across Emma's eyes made her unrecognizable, even to anyone who knew her at that age. And who but Jack had really known her *naked* at that age? (He'd forgotten that Mrs. Oastler was familiar with that photograph.)

In the case of those photos of his mother, the movie magazine had selected only one; there were two black slashes, across Alice's nipples. The photo of Emma had been so badly mangled in the trash that you couldn't see her nipples very distinctly; the magazine hadn't bothered to conceal them, although they'd had the decency to crop the photograph above Emma's waist.

Dr. García was mentioned in the article. Jack was sure that she would have refused to comment. But a former patient, whose name was withheld and who described the therapist's methods as "unorthodox, to say the least," said that Dr. García strongly discouraged her patients from dating one another. Jack knew perfectly well that Dr. García didn't believe for a moment that he was *dating* Lucy, but everyone knows what kind of magazine would do this; the story is implied, and nothing is stated. Even the headline, the very *name* of the article, was deliberately misleading; in the case of the Lucy story, the headline was a real winner.

JACK BURNS DENIES ANY HANKY PANKY, BUT WHAT'S HE HIDING IN HIS TRASH?

Jack hadn't done anything, but he looked guilty. It was *too weird,* as Michele would say.

Charles Burchell was a good guy; he gave Jack his heartfelt condolences. Jack had a pounding headache by the time he got back to The Prince George. He took a couple of Tylenol, or maybe it was Advil—he wouldn't remember taking anything.

Jack had fun calling his number in L.A. and listening to all the messages on his answering machine. Commiserations from Richard Gladstein, Bob Bookman, and Alan Hergott; Wild Bill Vanvleck had called from Amsterdam. (Jack found out later that The Mad Dutchman's anchorwoman girlfriend had been the first to report the scandal in the Netherlands.) Someone with a St. Hilda's connection had alerted Leslie Oastler to the story; Mrs. Oastler was hopping mad. "I can't believe you kept that photograph of Emma, *and* those pictures of your mother. You idiot, Jack!"

"I'm surprised you haven't called me," he heard Dr. García's voice say on his answering machine. "I trust you've changed your mind about the stopover in Boston, or that Michele has changed *her* mind about it. And I wouldn't recommend any further contact with Lucy, Jack. We might want to reconsider how much time you spend in the waiting room. You might run into Lucy's *mother.*"

Jack wondered how the sleazy movie magazine had missed that little tidbit—namely, that Lucy's mom was *also* Dr. García's patient. (It made perfect sense that she would be *somebody's* patient.)

Once, in the waiting room, one of the young mothers had explained to Jack that Dr. García was unique among all the psychiatrists she'd ever seen. You didn't have to make an appointment. Apparently, this young mother tended to feel the need to see her psychiatrist on the spur of the moment. Many of the young mothers in Dr. García's waiting room said that they found the presence of *other* young mothers comforting. It was such a loose arrangement, no therapist in New York or Vienna would have allowed it. (No psychiatrist's *patient* in New York or Vienna would have accepted the situation, either.) But loose arrangements were what Jack appreciated about living in Santa Monica.

He gave his plane tickets to the concierge at The Prince George and asked her to do what she could to change his flights. "Just get me back to Los Angeles tomorrow—the most direct way you can," he told her. "No stopover in Boston, please."

Then Jack went off to the Press Gang, where he had made another dinner reservation; he hadn't eaten all day and was hungry.

Jack sat alone at his small table and ordered one of the appetizers. Except for his table for one, the restaurant was crowded and noisy. Maybe the Press Gang seemed noisier than it was because Jack was alone and had a concussion. He sat facing a window, with his back to the other tables. He'd brought a book with him—something Charles had recommended—but when he tried to read, his headache came back and the noise in the restaurant was amplified. The table nearest him was the loudest, but Jack couldn't see the people at that table; if they were looking at him, all they could see was his back.

One loudmouth in particular was the dominant storyteller. He was braying about an altercation in a hotel bar—according to him, it had been a fair fight. "Fucking *wrestlers*!" he shouted. "They can't take a punch." That certainly got Jack's attention, concussion and all. "Jack Burns landed like a dead fish," the man was telling his friends.

As someone engaged in telling the story of his life in chronological order, Jack had discovered that what many people lazily referred to as *coincidences* weren't necessarily coincidental. One might think, for example, that it was *coincidental* for Jack

to find himself in the same restaurant with Doug McSwiney—
only one night after the fat, fur-faced author had coldcocked
Jack with a sucker punch. But Halifax was not a big city, and the
Press Gang was a popular place.

Jack tried to get a look at him, but McSwiney's broad back
was all there was to see. The way one of the writer's friends suddenly recognized Jack, Jack could tell that none of them had
known he was there—McSwiney hadn't been telling his tale for
Jack's benefit. Jack got up from his table and walked over to
McSwiney. The big man's friends let McSwiney know that Jack
was there, but the bastard didn't stop his story. "The little light-
weight just lay there," McSwiney was saying.

Jack stood beside McSwiney but a little behind him. There
were three couples at the table; Jack couldn't tell which of the
women was with McSwiney. The two men were smiling at
Jack—they were almost smirking—but the women were expressionless as they observed the unfolding drama.

"I want to apologize," Jack said to Doug McSwiney. "Those
notes I wrote about your screenplay weren't meant for you. I
would never have expressed myself that frankly, that personally—
not to you directly. It was only because Cornelia couldn't read
my handwriting that she showed those notes to you. She can't
read English if it's in longhand. I hope you know it was an accident. I wouldn't have said anything to intentionally hurt your
feelings."

Now McSwiney's two male friends were *definitely* smirking,
but the women were smarter; women had always known how to
read Jack Burns.

Jack wasn't really apologizing—he was just being nice twice,
as Mrs. Wicksteed had taught him. (Back in the bar at The Prince
George, when he'd offered to shake Doug McSwiney's hand,
that had been being nice the first time.) Of course Jack knew that
McSwiney was too drunk and too belligerent to understand this.
The author just went on with his story.

"That little Frenchwoman called the bellman and together
they loaded Jack Burns on a luggage cart—they wheeled him off
to his room like a baby in a stroller!" McSwiney was saying. The
two men laughed but the women didn't; the women were tense
and watchful.

When Jack put his hand on the back of McSwiney's neck and
gently pushed the big, shaggy head in the direction of the fat

man's dinner plate, he already knew that McSwiney was the stronger of the two. Jack was prepared for the big man to place both hands on the table and push himself to his feet. Jack never expected to hold McSwiney down with one hand; Jack just wanted McSwiney to spread his arms and brace himself against the table, because that made it easier for Jack to slap the full nelson on him before McSwiney could stand up.

Jack overlapped one hand with the other on the back of McSwiney's neck and drove the writer's face into his paella, up to his ears; Jack could feel the warm food on his wrists. An errant shrimp, coated with saffron-colored rice, flew off the plate—also a sausage. McSwiney rooted around in the paella, trying to clear some space to breathe.

In wrestling, there's more than one reason why a full nelson is illegal. Yes, you can break someone's neck with the hold, but—from a wrestling point of view—that's not the only thing wrong with it. It's nearly impossible to pin someone with a full nelson—unless you break your opponent's neck in the process. And the hold is very hard to get out of; in addition to a full nelson being dangerous, it's also a stalling tactic.

McSwiney wasn't going anywhere; he had no leverage, especially sitting in a chair. Jack kept pushing McSwiney into the paella. The fur-faced writer's forehead was pressed against the bottom of the plate; from the sound of him, he must have gotten some rice up his nose. McSwiney's two male friends weren't smirking now; Jack never took his eyes off them. If one of them had stood up, Jack would have changed the full nelson to a chicken-wing, with which he would have driven McSwiney's right elbow past his right ear—in all likelihood breaking the collarbone but almost certainly separating McSwiney's right shoulder. Then Jack would have gone after one of the other two guys, starting with the tougher-looking one.

But Jack could see that there wasn't going to be any trouble; the two men just sat there. McSwiney was bigger than both of them together, and they could observe for themselves that their friend wasn't doing too well. The women were more fidgety than the men. They exchanged glances with one another, and they kept looking at Jack's face—not at McSwiney's head in the paella.

McSwiney sounded as if he were still eating, but there was something more nasal than eating involved. If the big man had started to choke, Jack would have tipped him out of his chair and put a gut-wrench on him until McSwiney threw up on the floor. But that wasn't necessary; the writer was breathing okay, just noisily. A fat man doesn't breathe too comfortably with his chin on his chest, even without the paella factor.

"*Writers!*" Jack said, more to McSwiney's friends than to McSwiney. "They can't even eat without saying too much."

One of the women smiled, which may or may not have eliminated her as the woman who was with McSwiney.

Jack ground his chin into the top of McSwiney's head; he wanted to be sure that McSwiney could hear him. "There's another thing about your screenplay," Jack told him. "Just what do you think would have happened to a transvestite prostitute in a town full of sailors in 1917? Some sailor would have killed him—long before the Halifax Explosion could have done the job. The story isn't only *prurient* and *banal*—it's also *unbelievable.*"

Jack could tell that McSwiney was trying to say something, but Jack wasn't about to let the overweight author wriggle out of his paella. The woman who'd smiled at Jack spoke for McSwiney.

"I think Dougie is trying to say that we're all *dying* to hear about *Lucy,*" the woman said. Jack guessed that she probably *was* the woman with McSwiney, if not his wife. She was about the writer's age, which Jack estimated to be late forties—maybe early fifties.

"Well, Lucy is a lot younger than anyone at this table—better tits, and everything," Jack told them—the way Billy Rainbow would have said it. No one was smiling now.

"Please don't hurt him," the woman said.

"That's all anyone ever had to say," Jack told them. He lightened up on the full nelson. "I hope you know that I *could* have hurt you," Jack said to McSwiney, who tried to nod.

Jack let him go and stepped away from their table. He half expected McSwiney to stagger to his feet and come at him, swinging. But the fat man just sat there, looking more subdued than combative.

The woman who'd spoken to Jack wet her napkin in her water glass and began to fuss over McSwiney. She picked the rice out of his hair and beard, finding a shrimp or two and some sausage—also a piece of chicken. She cleaned him up as best she could, but there was nothing she could do about the saffron; the writer's beard and forehead were stained a pumpkin-orange color.

A waiter who'd been watching the whole time kept his eye on Jack, who returned to his table but sat with his back to the window, facing McSwiney's party. Jack didn't look at any of them directly, but he wanted to see McSwiney coming if the big man came at him. The woman who'd asked him not to hurt McSwiney looked at Jack from time to time, with no discernible expression.

Jack waved the waiter over and told him: "If they're staying, please offer Mr. McSwiney another paella. I'll pay for it."

"They're not staying," the waiter said. "Mr. McSwiney is experiencing chest pains—that's why they're leaving."

It would be bad luck to have contributed to the death of the drunken lout—the overweight writer was a blustering god of Canadian letters. The autopsy might reveal that McSwiney had rice in his lungs. He'd been murdered with food; the murder weapon had been the paella! Eulogies would abound, nationwide; a voice blowing over the Canadian landscape like a gale-force wind had been silenced. Worst of all would be the lengthy quotations from McSwiney's prose, gargantuan descriptions of rocks and trees and seagulls in *Quill & Quire*.

"Would you know if Mr. McSwiney has experienced chest pains *before*?" Jack asked the troubled-looking waiter.

"Oh, all the time," the waiter said. "He has terrible heartburn."

Jack ordered a beer. He hadn't had one since the Heineken he'd had at that party in the Polo Lounge after the Academy Awards. He noticed that a large gob of McSwiney's paella had landed on his pants; he'd been busy and had somehow missed seeing it. The shrimp coated with saffron-colored rice, the sticky sausage—Jack wiped off the mess with a napkin, but (like McSwiney) there was nothing he could do about the saffron stain.

Whenever he saw the troubled-looking waiter, Jack was distracted by his thoughts of McSwiney's chest pains. He sincerely hoped it was just heartburn. McSwiney was an asshole, but he was too young to die. Jack had restrained himself from hurting the bastard; it would have been too cruel for it to turn out that Jack had had even an inadvertent hand in *killing* Doug McSwiney!

And that was Halifax. Jack would beg Dr. García to allow him to tell her a little bit about what happened there. (After all, it might be a year or more before Jack got around to that part of his life story in chronological order.) Because his psychiatrist could see that Jack was agitated, and because she'd already talked to Lucy *and* Lucy's mother about the Lucy business, Dr. García indulged him. She at least let him tell her the part about Doug McSwiney.

Jack was fortunate, he admitted to Dr. García, that McSwiney's chest pains hadn't amounted to anything. Mrs. Oastler found a small account in the newspaper of a "drunken brawl" in the Press Gang restaurant in Halifax—a case of "two feuding writers who'd earlier come to blows in the bar of The Prince George Hotel," one Canadian journalist had reported. Because Leslie knew that Jack didn't drink, she was all the more perplexed by the reporter noting that Jack had calmly sipped a beer while McSwiney was attended to by his friends.

"Jack," Dr. García said, "it seems to me that you should hire a bodyguard."

"I don't need a bodyguard," he told her. "I just need to watch out for a left hook."

"I meant that you need a bodyguard to keep you from hurting someone else," she said.

"Oh."

"Well, we've got our work cut out for us—let's leave it at that," his psychiatrist said.

"What should I do?" Jack asked her sincerely.

"You better find a movie to be in soon," Dr. García told him. "I think you should take a break from being Jack Burns, don't you?"

35

Forgettable

The following year, Jack was in three movies; the year after
that, he did two more. His handicapped math notwithstanding,
even Jack could count that he'd been in five films in two years.
He'd taken a *big* break from being Jack Burns.

In two years' time, he'd not heard from Michele Maher; she
made no response to his letter of explanation about the Lucy
episode. Dr. García had urged Jack to recognize that the Michele
Maher chapter of his life was behind him, or *should* be. It was a
good thing that he hadn't heard from Michele, the doctor said.

In those two years, Jack made a lot of money and spent very
little. About the only expensive thing he bought was a new Audi;
naturally, it was another silver one. He could not motivate himself to sell the place on Entrada Drive and buy something more
suitable. This was because what he really wanted was to get out
of L.A.—although no other city beckoned, and Jack held fast to
Emma's idea that it was somehow good to be an outsider. Besides, as long as his life story was a work-in-progress, he
couldn't imagine cutting his ties to Dr. García. She was the closest Jack had come to a good marriage, or even a possible one. He
saw her twice a week. Putting his life in chronological order for
Dr. García had become a more regular and restorative activity in
Jack's life than having sex.

As for sex, in the last two years—since adamantly *not* having
sex with Lucy—Jack had briefly comforted Lucia Delvecchio,
who was in the throes of a nasty divorce. Lucia's divorce was obdurately ongoing—one of those drawn-out battles involving
children and credit cards and summer homes and motor vehicles
and dogs—and because her irate husband viewed *Jack* as the
root cause of their marital difficulties, Jack's presence in Lucia's
*un*married life was of little comfort to her and not long-lasting.

He was romantically linked with three of his co-stars—in three out of his last five films—but these rumors were false in two out of three cases. The one co-star Jack did sleep with, Margaret Becker, was a single mom in her forties. She had a twelve-year-old son named Julian and a house on the ocean in Malibu. Both Margaret and Julian were very sweet, but fragile. The boy had no relationship with his father, and he'd had unrealistic expectations of every boyfriend his mother had had—they'd all left her.

As a result, Julian's expectations of Jack were aimed a little lower. The boy kept anxiously looking for signs that Jack was preparing to leave him and his mom. Jack liked the boy—he *loved* having a kid in his life—but Julian was very needy. Margaret, Julian's mom, was a full-fledged *clinger*.

Whenever Jack had to go away, she stuffed his suitcase with photographs of herself; in the photos, which were pointedly taken for the occasion of Jack's trip, Margaret looked stricken with the fear that he would never come back to her. And Jack would often wake up at night and find Margaret staring at him; it was as if she were attempting to penetrate his consciousness, in his sleep, and brainwash him into never leaving.

Julian's sorrowful eyes followed Jack as if the boy were a dog Jack had neglected to feed. And Margaret said to Jack, at least once a day: "I know you're going to leave me, Jack. Just try not to walk away when I'm feeling too vulnerable to handle it, or when it would be especially harmful to poor Julian."

Jack was with her six months; it felt like six years, and leaving Julian hurt Jack more than leaving Margaret. The boy watched him go as if Jack were his absconding father.

"We take terrible risks with the natural affection of children," Jack would one day say to Dr. García, but she complained that he had told her about these relationships in a sketchy fashion. Or was it that he'd had nothing but sketchy relationships?

Months later, although the dominant sound in Jack's house on Entrada Drive was the traffic on the Pacific Coast Highway, he would lie in bed hearing the ocean—the way he had listened to it in Margaret's house in Malibu, while waiting for Julian to come into the bedroom and wake him and Margaret. Jack sincerely missed them, but they had driven him away—almost from the first moment Jack entered their lives. It was Dr. García's assessment that they were "even needier" than *Jack* was.

"I'm not *needy*!" Jack replied indignantly.

"Hmm," Dr. García said. "Have you considered, Jack, that what you crave most of all is a real relationship and a normal life, but you don't know anyone who's normal or real?"

"Yes, I have considered that," he answered.

"I've been seeing you for five years, yet I can't recall hearing you express a political opinion—not one," Dr. García said. "What are your politics, Jack?"

"Generally more liberal than conservative," he said.

"You're a Democrat?"

"I don't vote," Jack admitted. "I've never voted."

"Well, *there's* a statement!" Dr. García said.

"Maybe it's because I started my life as a Canadian, and then I became an American—but I'm really not either," he said.

"Hmm."

"I just like my work," Jack told her.

"You take no vacations?" she asked. "The last vacation I remember hearing about was a *school* vacation."

"When an actor isn't making a movie, he's on vacation," Jack said.

"But that's not exactly true, is it?" Dr. García asked. "You're always reading scripts, aren't you? You must spend a lot of time considering new roles, even if you eventually turn them down. And you've been reading a lot of novels lately. Since you've been *credited* with writing a screenplay, aren't you at least thinking about another adaptation? Or an original screenplay, perhaps?"

Jack didn't say anything; it seemed to him that he was *always* working, even when he wasn't.

"You go to the gym, you watch what you eat, you don't drink," Dr. García was saying. "But what do you do when you're just *relaxing*? Or are you never relaxed?"

"I have sex," he said.

"The kind of sex you have is not relaxing," Dr. García told him.

"I hang out with my friends," Jack said.

"*What* friends? Emma's dead, Jack."

"I have other friends!" he protested.

"You have no friends," Dr. García said. "You have professional acquaintances; you're on friendly terms with some of them. But who are your *friends*?"

Jack pathetically mentioned Herman Castro—the Exeter heavyweight, now a doctor in El Paso. Herman always wrote, "*Hey, amigo,*" on his Christmas cards.

"The word *amigo* doesn't make him your friend," Dr. García pointed out. "Do you remember his wife's name, or the names of his children? Have you ever visited him in El Paso?"

"You're depressing me," Jack told her.

"I ask my patients to tell me about their life's most emotional moments—the ups and downs, Jack," Dr. García said. "In your case, this means what has made you laugh, what has made you cry, and what has made you feel angry."

"I'm doing it, aren't I?" he asked her.

"But the *purpose* for doing this, Jack, is that when you tell me your life story, you reveal yourself—at least that's what usually happens, that's what's *supposed* to happen," Dr. García said. "I regret that, in your case, you've been a very faithful storyteller—and a very *thorough* one, I believe—yet I don't feel that I know you. I know what's *happened* to you. Do I ever know it—ad nauseam! But you haven't *revealed* yourself, Jack. I still don't know who you *are*. Please tell me who you are."

"According to my mother," Jack began in a small voice, which both he and Dr. García recognized as Jack's voice as a child, "I was an actor before I was an actor, but my most vivid memories of childhood are those moments when I felt compelled to hold my mother's hand. I wasn't acting then."

"Then I guess you better find a way to forgive her," Dr. García told him gently. "You might learn a lesson from your father. I'm just guessing, but when *he* forgave your mom, maybe it enabled him to move on with his life. You're thirty-eight, Jack—you're rich, you're famous, but you don't have a life."

"My dad shouldn't have moved on with his life without me!" Jack cried. "He shouldn't have left me!"

"You better find a way to forgive him, too, Jack." Dr. García sighed. (Jack hated it when she sighed.) "Now you're crying again," she observed. "It doesn't do you any good to cry. You have to stop crying."

What a *bitch* Dr. García could be! That's why Jack didn't tell her when he heard from Michele Maher. He went to the national convention of dermatologists without letting Dr. García know that he was going, because he knew that she would do everything in her power to persuade him not to go; because Jack was afraid of what the doctor would say; because he knew she was always right.

As for Michele—as if there'd been no hard feelings between them, as if the twenty years they'd not been in each other's company were shorter than those fleeting summer vacations when they'd been at Exeter—Michele Maher wrote Jack that she was coming to Los Angeles, where she very much looked forward to seeing him.

She didn't attend the dermatology convention every year, she wanted him to know—usually only when it was in the Northeast. But she'd never been to L.A. (*"Can you imagine?"* she wrote.) And because the convention this year provided Michele with an opportunity to see Jack—well, she made it sound as if he were the reason she'd decided to blow a long weekend in a glitzy Hollywood hotel with a bunch of skin doctors.

The dermatologists had chosen one of those annoying Universal City hotels. Rising out of a landscape of soundstages that resembled bomb shelters, the Sheraton Universal overlooked the Hollywood Hills and was across the street from Universal Studios—the theme park. The hotel had the feeling of a resort, the look of a place where conventioneers not infrequently brought their families.

While the dermatologists talked about skin, their children could go on the rides at the theme park. In the southern California climate, Jack imagined that the children of dermatologists would be sticky with sunscreen and wrapped up to their eyes; in fact, he was surprised that dermatologists would hold a convention in such a *sunny* place.

Michele Maher's letter was positively perky; she wrote to Jack with the flippancy of a prep-school girl, her former self. Her letter caused him to remember her old *Richard III* joke. "Where's your hump, Dick?" she had asked him.

"It's in the costume closet, and it's just a football," Jack had answered, for maybe the hundredth time.

But she'd been a good sport when he'd beaten her out for the part of Lady Macbeth, and of course Jack also remembered that Michele was over five-ten—a slim honey-blonde with a model's glowing skin, and (in Ed McCarthy's vulgar estimation) "a couple of high, hard ones."

"Why don't you have a girlfriend, Jack?" Michele had asked

him—when they were seventeen. She was just kidding around, or so he'd thought.

But he had to go and give her a line—Jack was just acting. "Because I get the feeling you're not available," he'd said.

"I had no idea you were interested in me, Jack. I didn't think you were interested in *anyone*," she'd told him.

"How can anyone not be interested in you, Michele?" he'd asked her, thus setting in motion a disaster.

What had drawn them together in the first place was *acting*. The one honest thing Jack had done was not sleep with her— only because he thought he'd caught the clap from Mrs. Stackpole, the dishwasher, and he didn't want Michele to catch it. But this was hardly *honest*, as Dr. García had already pointed out to him. Jack didn't tell Michele *why* he wouldn't sleep with her, did he?

Of course he'd thought at the time that almost no one would have believed he was banging Mrs. Stackpole—especially not Michele, who was so beautiful, while Mrs. Stackpole was so *unfortunate-looking*. (Even in the world of *much* older women.)

Why, then, didn't the flirtatious chirpiness of Michele's letter warn Jack away from her? How desperate was he to connect with someone, to have a so-called real or normal relationship outside the world of acting, that he failed to see the crystal-clear indications? Michele and Jack had never had a real relationship; they hadn't even *almost* had a relationship. If he *had* slept with her— and not given her the clap, which Jack hadn't caught from Mrs. Stackpole—how soon after that would they have broken up? When Michele went off to Columbia, in New York City, and Jack went off to the University of New Hampshire? Probably. When he met Claudia? *Definitely!*

In short, Michele Maher had always been Jack's illusion. The concept of the two of them together had been more the fantasy of other students at Exeter than it had ever been a reality between them. They were the most beautiful girl and the most handsome boy in the school; maybe that's all they *ever* were.

"*I have meetings all day, and there are lectures every night,*" Michele wrote to him about the dermatologists' convention at the Sheraton Universal. "*But I can skip a lecture or two. Just tell me which night, or nights, you're free. I'm dying to see where you hang out. What I mean, Jack, is that you must own that town!*"

But Hollywood wasn't that kind of town. It was a perpetual, glittering, ongoing award; for the most part, Hollywood kept escaping you. There *was* one night when you owned the town—the night you won the Oscar. But then there came the night (and the next night) after that. How quickly it happened that Hollywood was *not* your town anymore, and it *wouldn't* be—not unless or until you won *another* Academy Award, and then another one.

The studios once owned Hollywood, but they didn't own it anymore. There were agents who *behaved* as if they owned it; there were actors and actresses who *thought* they owned it, but they were wrong. The only people who truly owned Hollywood had more than one Oscar; they just kept winning Oscars, one after the other, and Jack Burns was *not* one of those people and never would be. But to Michele Maher, he was a movie star. She believed that was all that mattered.

According to Dr. García, Jack had come closest to having a *real* or *normal* relationship with Claudia—it was, at least, an *actual* relationship, before they went their separate ways. But Michele Maher was both more dangerous and more unforgettable to Jack, because she'd only ever existed as a *possible* relationship. "They're the most damaging kind, aren't they?" Dr. García had asked him. (Of course she also meant the relationship that Jack could only imagine having with his father.)

Thus warned, Jack drove out to Universal City to pick up Michele Maher—*Dr.* Maher, a thirty-eight-year-old unmarried dermatologist. What was he thinking? He already suspected that he might have a better time with an amnesiac transvestite prostitute. That was Jack's state of mind when he walked into the lobby of the Sheraton Universal, which was overrun with hyperactive-looking children returning from their day of theme-park rides. Michele had said she would meet him in the bar, where he found her drinking margaritas with three or four of her fellow dermatologists. They were all sloshed, but Jack was heartened to see that Michele could manage to stand; at least she was the only one who stood to greet him.

She must have forgotten how short Jack was, because she was wearing *very* high heels; at five-ten, even barefoot she towered over him. "You see?" she said to the other doctors. "Aren't movie stars always smaller than you expect them to be?" (The unkind thought occurred to Jack that, if Penis McCarthy had been there, he would have observed that Jack came up to her high, hard ones.)

He took Michele out to dinner at Jones—a trendy Hollywood hangout. It was not Jack's favorite place—crowded, irritatingly thriving—but he figured that Michele would be disappointed if he didn't provide her with an opportunity for a little sightseeing. (The food wasn't all that interesting, but the clientele was hip—models, starlets, lots of fake boobs with the pizzas and pasta.)

Of course Jack saw Lawrence with one of the models; Jack and Lawrence automatically gave each other the finger. Michele was instantly impressed, if a little unsteady on her feet. "I haven't eaten all day," she confessed. "I should have skipped that second margarita."

"Have some pasta," Jack said. "That'll help." But she downed a glass of white wine while he was still squeezing the lemon into his iced tea.

He kept looking all around for Lawrence, who probably wanted to pay Jack back for the bottle of Taittinger Jack had poured on him in Cannes.

"My *Gawd*," Michele was saying—a conflation of the worst of Boston and New York in her accent. "This place is cool."

Alas, she wasn't. Her skin, which he'd remembered as glowing, was dry and a trifle raw-looking—as if she'd just emerged from a hot bath and had stood outside for too long on a New England winter day. Her honey-blond hair was dull and lank. She was too thin and sinewy, in the manner of women who work out to excess or diet too rigorously—or both. She hadn't had all that much to drink, but her stomach was empty—Michele was one of those people who looked like her stomach was empty most of the time—and even a moderate amount of alcohol would have *looped* her.

She was wearing a streamlined gray pantsuit with a slinky silver camisole showing under the jacket. New York clothes—Jack was pretty sure you couldn't buy a suit like that in Boston or Cambridge, and she probably didn't get those *very* high heels anywhere but New York, either. Even so, she looked like a *doctor.* She held her shoulders in an overerect way, the way someone with a neck injury does—or as if she'd been born in a starched lab coat.

"I don't know how you do what you do," she was telling Jack. "I mean how you're so natural doing such *un*natural things—

a cross-dressing ski bum, for example. A dead rock star—a *female* one! A limo driver who's married to a hooker."

"I've known a lot of limo drivers," he told her.

"How many homophobic veterinarians have you known, Jack?" Michele asked him. (She had even seen that unfortunate film.)

"I'm *weird,* you mean," he said to her.

"But you bring it off. You're a *natural* at being weird," Michele told him.

Jack didn't say anything. She was fishing for something that had fallen to the bottom of her second glass of white wine, which was half empty. It was a ring that had slipped off her finger.

"I've lost so much weight for this date," she said. "I'm two sizes smaller than I was a month ago. I keep moving my rings to bigger fingers."

Jack used a spoon to scoop her ring out of her wineglass. The ring had slipped off the middle finger of her right hand; the middle finger of her left hand was even smaller, Michele explained, but the ring was too small to fit either index finger.

It was a somewhat old-fashioned-looking ring for a woman her age to wear. A little clunky—a big sapphire, wreathed by diamonds. "It has some sentimental value, this ring?" Jack asked her.

Michele Maher knocked over her wineglass and burst into tears. Against Jack's advice, she'd ordered a pizza—not pasta. The pizza at Jones had a pretty thin crust; Jack didn't think the pizza had a rat's ass of a chance of absorbing the alcohol in her.

It had been her mother's ring—hence the bursting into tears. Her mother had died of skin cancer when Michele was still in medical school. Michele had instantly developed a skin ailment of her own; she called it stress-related eczema. She'd specialized in dermatology for personal reasons.

Her father was remarried, to a *much* younger woman. "The gold digger is *my* age," Michele said. She'd ordered a third glass of white wine, and she hadn't touched her pizza.

"You remember my parents' apartment in New York, don't you, Jack?" she asked. She had placed her dead mother's unwearable ring on the edge of her plate, where it seemed poised to eat the pizza. (The ring honestly looked more interested in eating the pizza than Michele did.)

"Of course," Jack answered. How could he forget that Park

Avenue apartment? The beautiful rooms, the beautiful parents, the beautiful *dog*! And the Picasso, toilet-seat-high in the guest-room bathroom, where it virtually *dared* you to pee on it.

"That apartment was supposed to be my inheritance," Michele said. "Now the *gold digger* is going to get it."

"Oh."

"Why didn't you sleep with me, Jack?" she asked. "How could you have proposed that we *masturbate* together? Mutual masturbation is much more intimate than having conventional sex, isn't it?"

"I thought I had the clap," he admitted. "I didn't want you to get it."

"The clap from *whom*? You weren't seeing anyone else, were you?"

"I was sleeping with Mrs. Stackpole, the dishwasher. You probably don't remember her, Michele."

"Those women who worked in the kitchen were all old and fat!" she cried.

"Yes, they were," Jack said. "Well—Mrs. Stackpole was, anyway."

"You could have slept with *me,* but you slept with an old, fat *dishwasher*?" she asked, in a ringing voice. (She said *dishwasher* the way she'd said *gold digger.*)

"I was sleeping with Mrs. Stackpole before I knew I *could* sleep with you," Jack reminded her.

"And your relationship with Emma Oastler—what was that, exactly?" Michele asked.

Here we go, Jack thought; *here comes "too weird," and all the rest of it.* "Emma and I were just roommates—we lived together, but we never had sex."

"That's so hard to imagine," Michele said, toying with the ring on the edge of her plate. "You mean you just *masturbated* together?"

"Not even that," he told her.

"What did you *do*? You must have done *something*," Michele said.

"We kissed, I touched her breasts, she held my penis."

In reaching for her wineglass, Michele's elbow came down on the edge of her plate; her mother's ring went flying. The ring landed on an adjacent table, startling two models who were on a red-wine diet.

One of the models picked up the ring and looked at Jack. "Oh, you shouldn't have," she said, slipping the ring onto one of her pretty fingers.

"I'm sorry—it's her mother's ring," Jack told the model; she pouted at him while Michele looked mortified.

"You don't remember me, do you, Jack?" the other model asked.

Jack got up and went over to their table, holding his hand out to the model who was still wearing Michele's ring. He was trying to buy a little time, struggling to remember who the other model was.

"I was afraid you'd forgotten me," he told her. (It was one of Billy Rainbow's lines—Jack had always liked it.)

It was not the answer the model had been expecting. Jack still couldn't place her, or else he'd never met her before in his life and she was just playing a game with him.

The model who had Michele's ring was playing another kind of game with Jack; she was trying to put the ring on one of his fingers. "Who would have thought Jack Burns had such little hands?" she was saying. (The ring was a loose fit on his left pinkie; Jack went back to his table wearing it.)

"Jack Burns has a little *penis*," the other model said.

Jack guessed that she *did* know him, but he still didn't remember her. Michele just sat there looking glassy-eyed. "I don't feel very well," she told Jack. "I think I'm drunk, if you want to know the truth."

"You should try to eat something," he said.

"Don't you know that you can't tell a doctor what to do, Jack?"

"Come on. I'll take you back to the hotel," he said.

"I want to see where you live!" Michele said plaintively. "It must be fabulous."

"It's a hole in the wall," the model who knew Jack said. "Don't tell me you've actually moved out of that nookie house on Entrada, Jack."

"We're much closer to your hotel than we are to where I live," he told Michele.

"Did you sleep with that girl?" Michele asked him, when they were back in the Audi. "You didn't look like you knew her."

"I don't remember sleeping with her," Jack said.

"What's a *nookie house*?" she asked him.

"It's slang for *brothel*," Jack explained.

"Do you really live in a hole in the wall on La Strada?" Michele asked.

"Yes, I do," he admitted. "It's on *Entrada*."

"But why do you live in a *hole in the wall*? Why wouldn't Jack Burns live in a *mansion*?"

"I don't really know where I want to live, Michele."

"My *Gawd*," she said again.

Michele fell sound asleep on the Hollywood Freeway. Jack had to carry her into the lobby of the Sheraton Universal. He didn't know her room number; he couldn't find her room key in her purse. He carried her into the bar, where he was sure he would find a few of her drunken colleagues. Jack hoped that one of them would be sober enough to recognize Michele.

Another woman dermatologist came to Jack's assistance; she was a homely, caustic person, but at least she hadn't been drinking. Together they got Michele to her room. The other doctor's name was Sandra; she was from somewhere in Michigan. Sandra must have assumed that Jack was sleeping with Michele, because she proceeded to undress Michele in front of him.

"Run a bath for her," Sandra said. "We can't let her pass out like this. If she vomits, she might choke. People who are dead-drunk often aspirate their vomit. It's better to wake her up, and let her be sick when she's awake."

Jack did what the doctor said. Then he carried Michele to the bath and, with Sandra's assistance, slid her into it. Naked, she was much too thin—emaciated. Like a woman who'd been recently pregnant, Michele had stretch marks on her small breasts; the skin there looked wrinkled. (It was the weight loss; she hadn't been pregnant.)

"Christ, how much weight has she lost?" Sandra asked Jack, as if he were the one who'd put Michele up to it.

"I don't know what she weighed before," Jack said. "I haven't seen Michele in twenty years."

"Well, this is a wonderful way to see her," Sandra said.

Michele had told him more about the stress-related eczema; it occurred on her elbows and knees. When it was bad, the eczema was the color and nubbly texture of a rooster's wattle. Jack kept staring at Michele's elbows and knees while she lolled in the bath; he half expected her mysterious skin ailment to suddenly appear.

"What are you *looking* at?" Sandra asked him. (Michele, even in the bathwater, was still out cold; Jack held her under her armpits so her head wouldn't slip underwater.)

He explained about the stress-related eczema, but Sandra assured him that it wasn't about to blossom before his eyes. "It's not like time-lapse photography," she said. Sandra looked at his hands. "Nice *ring*," she commented. (Michele's mother's ring was still on Jack's left pinkie.)

When Michele started coming around, she was unaware that Sandra was with them. "I'll leave you two lovebirds alone. Just don't let her throw up in her sleep," Sandra said. "You seem to enjoy staring at her, anyway."

"Did we do it yet?" Michele asked him. He heard Sandra letting herself out of the hotel room, the door closing on her harsh laugh.

"No," Jack said. "We didn't do it."

"When are we going to do it, Jack? Or do you think you have the clap again?"

"I didn't have it the first time. I just thought I *might* have it," he explained to her.

"But you can't even remember who you've slept with," Michele reminded him. "And it's not as if you drink or anything. You must sleep with an awful lot of women, Jack."

"Not really," Jack said.

He felt nothing for her but the kind of pity and contempt you feel for people who aren't in control of themselves. (As a nondrinker, Jack would have admitted to feeling superior to people who drank too much—whatever the circumstances.) And the pity he felt for Michele was all caught up in those expectations she'd had—for their big night out on the town together; for her parents' New York apartment, which the gold digger had stolen from her; even for her dead mother's ring, which didn't fit any of her fingers. (Jack took the ring off his left pinkie and put it in the soap dish above the bathroom sink.)

He helped Michele dry herself off; she was a little shaky. She wanted to be alone in the bathroom for a moment.

The hotel maid had already turned down the bed and closed the curtains, but Jack opened the curtains to get a look at the view of the Hollywood Hills. The room had floor-to-ceiling windows; it was a spectacular view, but not even the Hollywood Hills could divert him from the sound of Michele retching in the toilet. Jack went and stood next to the bathroom door, to be sure she wasn't choking. Later, when he heard the toilet flush and the water in the sink running, Jack went back and stood at the giant windows.

It was 2003. He'd been in Los Angeles for sixteen years. He was trying to remember sleeping with that model at Jones—the one who'd said that his penis was small—but he couldn't remember anything about her. When he closed the curtains, Jack was thinking that he'd seen enough of the Hollywood Hills.

When Michele came out of the bathroom, she was wearing one of the hotel's terry-cloth robes; she seemed shy, and relatively sober, and she smelled like a whole tube of toothpaste. Jack was sorry that she wanted to sleep with him—he'd been hoping that she wouldn't want to. But he couldn't turn her down a second time, not when he knew she was still thinking about the first time he'd rejected her.

It was only later that it occurred to Jack that Michele probably felt as resigned to the act as he did. And there was nothing remarkable about their sexual performance, nothing that would override the longer-lasting impression—namely, that they hadn't really wanted to sleep with each other. (They had simply expected it would happen.)

"Just what is so terribly *universal* about this place, anyway?" Michele asked him, after they'd had sex and Jack was touching her breasts. She was lying on her back with her long arms held straight against her sides, like a soldier.

Jack guessed that she meant the name of the hotel, the Sheraton Universal—or where the hotel was located, which was Universal City—but before he could say something, Michele said: "I can tell you one thing that's universal about tonight, and that is it's a *universal* disappointment—like loneliness, or illness, or death. Or like knowing you'll never have children. It's just one big *universal* letdown, isn't it?"

"Actually, it's the name of a *studio*," Jack said. "Universal Studios."

"Your penis isn't *too* small, Jack," Michele Maher said. "That model was simply being cruel."

"Maybe she had a nose job since I last saw her," he speculated. "I mean, she's a model—she could have had her chin done, or her eyes done. I'll bet she had some kind of face-lift. There's got to be a reason why I don't remember her."

"Oh, I don't know," Michele said. "What about *us*? In a few years, *this* isn't going to be memorable, is it?"

So much for *that* expectation, as he would one day tell Dr. García. It would come as no surprise to Dr. García, but one can appreciate what a blow it was to Jack to discover how quickly Michele Maher could become *forgettable*.

36

Claudia's Ghost

Bad things happened after that. Jack's psychiatrist tried to shed a positive light on his failure to connect with Michele Maher. Maybe this would disabuse Jack of what Dr. García called his "if-only romanticism about the past"—meaning *if only* it had worked out with Michele Maher the first time, he might have been spared the ensuing years of incomplete relationships.

"You always attached too much importance to your botched opportunity with Michele, Jack," Dr. García said. "You never attached enough importance to what worked with Claudia. At least that relationship lasted."

"Only four years," Jack reminded her.

"Who else lasted an eighth as long, Jack? And don't say Emma! The penis-holding doesn't count as *complete,* does it?"

But Jack resisted his psychiatrist's efforts to shed a positive light on *anything*. He was down. He embraced the movie-magazine version of himself, his bad-boy image. Jack didn't care how many models he wouldn't remember a month later. He had ceased caring about what kind of "nookie house" he lived in, too. (His "Entrada Drive state of mind," Dr. García called it.)

Jack was in that state of mind in May 2003 when he went to New York to make a movie. He had accepted the Harry Mocco role in *The Love Poet*—a film by Gillian Scott, the Australian director. Gillian had also written the screenplay.

Harry Mocco is a crippled male model—"*half* a model," Harry calls himself. His legs were crushed in a New York elevator accident. He has always wanted to be an actor; he has a great voice. But there aren't a lot of roles for a guy in a wheelchair.

Even as a model, Harry's career is marginal. He is often seen sitting up in bed in the morning—just his top half, naked. (The rest of him is under the sheets.) These are advertisements for *women's* clothes; the female model, usually in the foreground of the photograph, is already dressed or half dressed. Her clothes are what's being sold; the top half of Harry, in the background, is depicted as one of her accessories.

Or, if he's the one modeling the clothes, you see Jack-as-Harry sitting at a desk or in the driver's seat of an expensive car. He does a lot of ads for wristwatches, usually in a tuxedo—but the naked, half-a-male *accessory* in those advertisements for women's clothing are his specialty.

Harry Mocco doesn't really need the money. He made a fortune suing the building with the elevator that crushed his legs; in and around New York, where the film is set, Jack-as-Harry is quite a famous and photogenic cripple. The modeling is more for what little remains of his dignity than it is a financial necessity. He actually lives pretty well—in one of those New York buildings with a doorman. Naturally, Harry's gym is wheelchair-accessible. He lifts weights half the day and plays wheelchair basketball—even wheelchair tennis.

Jack-as-Harry also memorizes and recites love poems, or parts of love poems—not always a welcome activity, especially since he's not *with* anyone. He's always urging his friends—gym friends, male-model friends—to woo their girlfriends with love poetry. No one seems interested. Harry knows a lot of supermodels—some of the hottest female models in New York. But they're just friends; the supermodels are unmoved by the love poetry.

Jack-as-Harry has sex only once in the first hour and fifteen minutes of the film; to no one's surprise, it's a disaster. His partner is a young woman who frequently dresses him for the photo shoots—she's very plain and nervous, an unglamorous girl with a pierced lower lip. The love poetry works on her, but his being crippled doesn't. Jack had to give Gillian Scott credit for capturing a sex scene of award-winning awkwardness.

The voice-over, which is Harry Mocco's, is all love poetry. Everything from the grimmest of the grim, Thomas Hardy, to Philip Larkin; everything from George Wither to Robert Graves. (There was too much Graves, in Jack's opinion.)

Harry Mocco usually doesn't get to recite more than a couplet, rarely a complete stanza. Nobody he knows wants to hear a whole poem.

"I'm not sure about the suitability of this role for you," Dr. García had forewarned Jack. "A crippled male model who hasn't found his audience. Isn't that coming a little close to home?" Nor, in Dr. García's opinion, was the length of his separation from her advisable. "I don't do house calls as far away as New York, Jack—although I could stand to do a little shopping."

Why don't your children, if that's who they are, grow older? he'd wanted to ask her. The photographs in Dr. García's office were an irreplaceable, seemingly permanent collection. The older husband—or her father, if that's who he was—was fixed in time. *All* of them seemed fixed in time, like bugs preserved in amber. But Jack didn't ask her about it.

He just went to New York and made the movie. "Work is work, Dr. García," he'd said defensively. "A part is just a part. I'm not Harry Mocco, nor am I in danger of becoming him. I'm not anybody."

"That's part of your problem, Jack," she had reminded him.

The whole movie had a fifty-two-day shooting schedule. For the Harry Mocco part, including rehearsals, Jack had to be in New York a couple of months.

He was in the habit of seeing Dr. García twice a week—two months without seeing her would necessitate a certain number of phone calls. He couldn't tell her his life story over the phone; in an emergency, he could *talk* to her, but the chronological-order part would have to wait.

In Dr. García's view, the chronological-order part was what determined how Jack was doing. It was one thing to babble out loud about an emotionally or psychologically disturbing moment; it was quite another obstacle to organize the story and tell it (exactly as it had happened) to an actual person. In this respect, the chronological-order part was like acting; in Dr. García's view, if Jack couldn't tell the story in an orderly fashion, that meant that he couldn't handle it psychologically and emotionally.

Jack Burns put everything he had into Harry Mocco. He remembered how Mrs. Malcolm had tyrannized the classroom, her head-on crashing into desks—her racing up and down the aisles in the St. Hilda's chapel, skinning her knuckles on the pews. He remembered how Bonnie Hamilton could climb into her wheelchair, or extricate herself from it, the second his head was turned. He never saw her slip or fall, but he noticed the bruises—the evidence that she wasn't perfect.

Jack not only did wheelchair tricks on the set of *The Love Poet;* he insisted on using the wheelchair when he was off the set, too. He pretended he was crippled. Jack wheeled around the hotel like a psycho invalid; he made them load him into limos, and unload him. He practiced falling, too. He did a fantastic, head-over-heels *wheelie* in the lobby of the Trump International on Central Park West—the startled bellman and concierge running to assist him.

They had a great gym at the Trump. Jack went there in his wheelchair; he would get on the treadmill and run for half an hour with the wheelchair parked alongside, as if it were for another person.

When Harry Mocco has wheelchair accidents in *The Love Poet,* the voice-over is heavy on Robert Graves. (A little of Graves goes a long way. "Love is a universal migraine," for example.)

Or:

> Why have such scores of lovely, gifted girls
>   Married impossible men?
> Simple self-sacrifice may be ruled out,
>   And missionary endeavour, nine times out of ten.

When Jack-as-Harry is crawling on all fours from the bed to the bathroom, the girl who's just slept with him is watching him—repulsed. The voice-over is Harry's, reciting e. e. cummings.

> i like my body when it is with your
> body.

Jack-as-Harry tries to win over the pierced-lip girl with a love poem by Ted Hughes, but a little of Hughes goes a long way, too. The girl is out the door before he can finish the first stanza.

> We sit late, watching the dark slowly unfold:
> No clock counts this.

Harry's more self-pitying moments—repeatedly banging his head on a bathtub drain, unable to climb out of the slippery tub—are pure pathos. (The voice-over to the bathtub scene is Harry's recitation of George Wither.)

> Shall I, wasting in despair,
> Die because a woman's fair?

The Love Poet is a *noir* love story—more *noir* than love story for three quarters of the film, more love story than *noir* at the end. Jack-as-Harry meets a recently crippled young woman in his gym. She is wheelchair-bound, too. Harry can tell it's her first public outing in her new but permanent condition; she's tentative. She's being introduced to various weight machines and exercises by a blowhard personal trainer whom Harry despises. The girl is what wheelchair veterans like Harry call a "newborn."

"Leave the newborn to me," Jack-as-Harry tells the trainer.

Harry then proceeds to demonstrate every weight machine and exercise *in slapstick;* he drops things, he stages spectacular falls.

"See? This is *easy!*" he tells the newborn, imitating the hearty bullshit of the personal trainer. Jack-as-Harry hurls himself out of his wheelchair as awkwardly as possible, demonstrating to the recently crippled young woman that *nothing* is going to be easy for her.

When they fall in love, the voice-over is Harry's; he's reciting A. E. Housman. (In a gym, of all places.)

> Oh, when I was in love with you,
> Then I was clean and brave,
> And miles around the wonder grew
> How well did I behave.

Shame on Jack Burns—those two months in New York, he was not as well behaved as Harry Mocco. He met a transvestite dancer at a downtown club. Jack was distracted by her strong-looking hands and her prominent Adam's apple. He knew she was a man. Still, he went along with the seduction-in-progress—up to a point. Jack let her wheel him through the lobby of the Trump, and into the hotel's bar. She sat in his lap in the wheelchair and they sang a Beatles song together, the bar crowd joining in.

> *When I get older losing my hair,*
> *Many years from now.*
> *Will you still be sending me a Valentine,*
> *Birthday greetings bottle of wine?*

Jack tried to say good night to the transvestite dancer at the elevator, but she insisted on coming to his room with him. All the way up on the elevator, they kept singing. (She sat in his lap in the elevator, too.)

> *If I'd been out till quarter to three*
> *Would you lock the door,*
> *Will you still need me, will you still feed me,*
> *When I'm sixty-four?*

The transvestite wheeled him down the hall to his hotel room. At the door, Jack tried again to say good night to her.

"Don't be silly, Jack," she said, wheeling him inside the room.

"I'm not going to have sex with you," Jack told her.

"Yes, you are," the pretty dancer said.

Jack soon had a fight on his hands. When a transvestite wants to have sex, she feels as strongly about it as a guy—because she *is* a guy! Jack had a *battle* on his hands. The room got trashed a little—one lamp, especially. Yes, Jack *was* aroused—but even he knew the difference between wanting to have sex and actually having it. Not even he would submit to *every* desire.

"Look, it's obvious you want me," the dancer said. "Stop fighting it." She'd taken off all her clothes and had managed to destroy most of Jack's. "You have a *hard-on*," she kept pointing out, as if Jack didn't know.

"I get a hard-on in my sleep," he told her.

"*Look* at me!" she screamed. "*I* have a hard-on!"

"I can see that you do," Jack said. "*And* you have breasts." (They were as hard as apples; Jack knew, because he was trying to push them out of his face.)

This time, he saw the left hook coming—and the right uppercut, and the head-butt, too. She may have been a dancer, but she was not without some other training; this wasn't her first fight.

Naturally, the phone was ringing—the front-desk clerk, Jack assumed. There had probably been calls to the front desk from those rooms adjacent to Jack's, within hearing distance of the destroyed lamp and all the rest. *Well, wouldn't Donald Trump love this!* Jack was thinking. (The Trump's fabulous view of Central Park—for the time being, utterly ignored.)

He heard the security guys picking at the lock on his hotel-room door, but Jack had a Russian front headlock on the dancer and he wasn't letting go—not even to open the door. Her finger-nails were like claws, and he had to give up the front headlock when she bit him in the forearm.

"You fight like a girl," Jack told her.

He knew that would *really* piss her off. When she came at him, Jack hit a pretty good duck-under and got behind her. He held her chest-down on the rug with a double-armbar, where she couldn't bite him. The security guys finally got the door open; there were two of them, plus the night manager.

"We're here to help you, Mr. Burns—I mean Mr. *Mocco,*" the night manager said.

"I have a distraught dancer on my hands," Jack told them.

"He had a hard-on. I saw it," the transvestite said.

One of the security guys had thought that Jack really *was* a cripple. He'd never seen Jack out of the wheelchair—not even in the movies. (He wasn't a moviegoer, clearly.) From the other se-curity guy's reaction when the three of them were forcibly dress-ing the dancer, chicks with dicks were new to him.

Jack never went to bed; he stayed up, rehearsing how he would tell this part of the story of his life to Dr. García. He knew this episode wouldn't wait for chronological order. Jack kept a cold washcloth on his forearm, where the transvestite dancer had bitten him. She hadn't broken the skin, but the bite marks were sore and ugly-looking.

In the late morning, when Jack talked to Dr. García from the set of *The Love Poet,* he told her that the unfortunate incident was out of character for Harry Mocco but sadly typical of Jack Burns. (Jack thought he might preempt her criticism by criticiz-ing himself.)

"You acquiesce too much, Jack," Dr. García said. "You should never have let the transvestite into the elevator—you should have had the fight in the lobby, where it would have been a shorter fight. For that matter, you should never have let her sit in your lap in the bar."

"It wouldn't have been a good idea to have had that fight in the bar," he assured Dr. García.

"But why did you leave the nightclub with her in the first place?" Dr. García asked him.

"She turned me on. I was aroused," he admitted.

"I'm sure you were, Jack. That's what transvestites *do,* isn't it? They go to great lengths to turn men on. But what does that lead to, Jack? Every time, where does that go?"

He couldn't think of what to say.

"You keep getting in trouble," Dr. García was saying. "It's always just a *little* trouble, but you know what that leads to—don't you, Jack? Don't you know where that goes?"

It was July 2003 when they had the wrap party for *The Love Poet* in New York, and Jack flew back to L.A. He'd succumbed to Harry Mocco's habit of reciting fragments of love poems to total strangers, but in the case of the attractive stewardess on his flight from New York to Los Angeles, this wasn't entirely Jack's fault. She'd asked him to tell her about his next movie, and Jack began by explaining to her that Harry Mocco compulsively memorizes love poems and recites them at the drop of a hat.

"For example, do you know the poem 'Talking in Bed' by Philip Larkin?" he asked her. (She was probably Jack's age.)

"Do I *want* to know it?" she asked him warily. "I'm *married.*"

But he kept trying. (Jack hadn't slept with a stewardess in years.) "Or 'In Bertram's Garden' by Donald Justice," he went on, as if the flight attendant were encouraging him. " 'Jane looks down at her organdy skirt/As if *it* somehow were the thing disgraced—' "

"Whoa!" the stewardess said, cutting him off. "I don't want to hear about it."

That's what happens when you ask an actor to tell you about his next movie.

When Jack walked into his place on Entrada Drive, he immediately called a real estate agent and asked to have the house put on the market. (*Sell the fucker!* Jack was thinking; *maybe that would force me to live a little differently.*)

He headed off for his appointment with Dr. García—his first in two months—feeling like a new man.

"But you haven't really made a decision about where you want to live, Jack," Dr. García pointed out. "Aren't you pulling the rug out from under your feet, so to speak?"

But if Jack couldn't make up his mind about his life, he had at least decided to make something happen.

"Is it the house itself that let Lucy come inside?" Dr. García asked him. "Is it *because of* your mother's lies to you, *or* your missing father, that you are an unanchored ship—in danger of drifting wherever the wind or the currents, or the next sexual encounter, will take you?"

Jack didn't say anything.

"Think about Claudia," Dr. García said. "If you want to make something meaningful happen—if you *really* want to live differently—think about finding a woman like that. Think about committing yourself to a relationship; it doesn't even have to last four years. Think about being with a woman you could live with for *one* year! Start small, but start *something*."

"You asked me not to mistake you for a dating service," Jack reminded her.

"I'm recommending that you *stop* dating, Jack. I'm suggesting that, if you tried to live with someone, you would have to live a lot differently. You don't need a new house. You need to find someone you can live with," Dr. García said.

"Someone like Claudia? She wanted *children,* Dr. García."

"I don't mean someone like Claudia in that respect, but a relationship like that—one that has a chance of lasting, Jack."

"Claudia is probably very fat now," he told Dr. García. "She had an epic battle with her weight ahead of her."

"I don't necessarily mean someone like Claudia in that respect, either, Jack."

"Claudia wanted children so badly—she's probably a *grandmother* now!" he said to Dr. García.

"You never could count, Jack," she told him.

Jack didn't blame Dr. García. He would take full responsibility for what happened. But the very idea of Claudia—the *reason* she was recently on his mind—surely came from the Claudia conversation in his therapy session with Dr. García. Jack was thinking about her—that's all he would say in his own defense—when he drove back home to Santa Monica from a dinner party one warm night that summer.

Jack was remembering the first time Claudia let him borrow her Volvo—the incredible feeling of independence that comes from being young and alone and driving a car.

He pulled into his driveway on Entrada—his headlights illuminating the arrestingly beautiful, incontestably Slavic-looking young woman who sat on her battered but familiar suitcase on Jack's absurdly small lawn. She sat so serenely still, as if she were placidly posing for a photograph beside the FOR SALE sign, that for a moment Jack forgot what was for sale. He thought *she* was for sale, before he remembered he was selling his house—and that thought would come back to haunt him, because she was more for sale than Jack could possibly have imagined.

He knew who she was—Claudia, or her ghost. It was a wonder he didn't lose control of the Audi and drive over her—either killing Claudia on the spot, or killing her ghost again. *But how can it be Claudia?* Jack was thinking. The young woman on his lawn was as young as Claudia had been when he'd known her, or younger. (Besides, Claudia had always looked older than she was, *and* she had the habit of lying about her age.)

"God damn you, Jack," Claudia had said. "After I die, I'm going to haunt you—I promise you I will—I might even haunt you *before* I die."

Since Claudia had promised that she would haunt him, wasn't it forgivable that Jack assumed the apparition sitting beside his FOR SALE sign was Claudia's *ghost*? A ghost doesn't usually travel with a suitcase, but maybe Heaven or Hell had kicked her out—or her mission to haunt Jack had required her to have several changes of clothes. After all, Claudia was (or had been) an actress—and she'd loved the theater, more than Jack had. In the case of Claudia's ghost, the suitcase could have been a *prop*.

Jack somehow managed to get out of the Audi and walk up to her, although his legs had turned to stone. He knew that driving away, or running away, wasn't an option—you can't get away from a ghost. But he left the Audi's headlights on. When approaching a ghost, you at least want to see her clearly. Who wants to walk up to a ghost in the dark?

"Claudia?" Jack said, his voice trembling.

"Oh, Jack, it's been too long," she said. "It's been *forever* since I've seen you!"

She was the same old Claudia, only younger. The same stage presence, the same projection of her voice—as if, even one-on-

one, she was making sure that those poor souls in the worst seats in the uppermost balcony could hear her perfectly.

"But you're so *young*," he said.

"I died young, Jack."

"*How* young, Claudia? You look even younger than you *were*! How is that possible?"

"Death becomes me, I guess," she said. "Aren't you going to ask me inside? I've been *dying* to see you, Jack. I've been sitting on this freakin' lawn for an *eternity*."

The word *freakin'* was new, and not at all like Claudia. But who knew where she'd been—and, among the dead, with whom? She held out her hands and Jack helped her to her feet. He was surprised that he could feel her not-inconsiderable weight. Who would have guessed that ghosts weighed anything at all? But from the look of her—even in Heaven, or that other place— Claudia still had to watch her weight.

She was still self-conscious about her hips, too. She wore the same type of long, full skirt that she'd always liked to wear— even in the summer. She was as heavy-breasted as Jack remembered her; in fact, given what people who believed in ghosts were generally inclined to believe, she was disarmingly full-figured for a spirit.

Jack ran to the car and turned off the Audi's headlights, half expecting Claudia's ghost to disappear. But she waited for him, smiling; she let him carry her old leather suitcase inside. She went straight to Jack's bedroom, as if they were still a couple and she'd been living with him all these years—even though Claudia had never been in that house. He waited in shock while she used his bathroom. (The things ghosts had to do!)

Jack was deeply conflicted. He both believed her *and* suspected her. She had the same creamy-smooth skin, the same prominent jaw and cheekbones—a face made for close-ups, he'd always said. Claudia should have been in the movies, despite the problem with her weight; she had a face that was wasted in the theater, Jack had always told her.

When Claudia's ghost emerged from the bathroom, she came up to Jack and nuzzled his neck. "I've even missed your smell," she said.

"Ghosts have a sense of smell?" he asked.

Jack held her by the shoulders, at arm's length, and looked into her eyes; they were the same yellowish brown they'd always been, like polished wood, like a lioness's eyes. But there was something about her that wasn't quite the same; the resemblance was striking but inexact. It wasn't only that she seemed too young to be the Claudia he'd known—even if she'd died the day after they parted company, even if death (as the ghost had said) *did* become her.

"A thought occurs to me, Claudia," he said. Holding her, even at arm's length, Jack could feel her body's heat. And all this time, he'd thought that ghosts (if you could feel them at all) would feel *cold*. "Since my mother died, I've been wondering about this," he told her. "If ghosts get to keep the tattoos they had in life—I mean in the hereafter."

Again, the smile—but even her smile wasn't exactly as Jack remembered it. He didn't think that Claudia's teeth had ever been quite this white. She slowly lifted the long, full skirt. The seductiveness in her eyes was unchanged, and there, high up on her inner thigh, which was even a little plumper than he remembered it, was the tattoo of the Chinese scepter—the short sword symbolizing *everything as you wish*.

"It took long enough, but it finally healed," she told him.

It was a pretty good Chinese scepter, Jack thought, but it was not as perfect as the one his mom had learned from Paul Harper.

"It's real," the young woman said. "It won't rub off on your hand. See for yourself, Jack—go on and touch it."

The voice, her *projection,* may have been the same, but the language lacked Claudia's exactness—her correctness of speech, her good education. The "go on and touch it"—the casual use of the word *and*—was no more like Claudia than the word *freakin'* that had caught Jack's attention earlier.

He touched the young woman's tattoo, high up on her inner thigh—her *imitation* Chinese scepter, as Jack thought of it.

"Who *are* you?" he asked her.

She took his hand and made him touch her, higher up. She wasn't wearing any panties, not even a thong. "Doesn't it feel familiar, Jack? Don't you want to be back there—to be young again?"

"You're not Claudia," Jack told her. "Claudia was never crude." And ghosts, he could have said, not only don't have body heat; *female* ghosts don't get wet. (Or do they?)

"You have a hard-on, Jack," the girl said, touching him.

"I get a hard-on in my sleep," he told her, as if the episode with that transvestite dancer at the Trump had been a dress rehearsal. "It's no big deal."

"It's big enough," the young woman said, kissing him on the mouth; she didn't come close to kissing like Claudia. But it took no small amount of willpower on Jack's part to stop touching her. To make *her* stop, he had to let her know that he knew who she was.

"What would your mother say about this?" Jack asked Claudia's daughter. "The very idea of you having sex with me! That wouldn't make your mom happy, would it?"

"My mom's dead," the girl told him. "I'm here to haunt you—it's what she would have wanted."

"I'm sorry your mother's dead," he replied. "But *what* would she have wanted?"

"I don't believe in ghosts," Claudia's daughter said. "I'm here to haunt you because I don't believe that Mom can do it."

"What's your name?" Jack asked her.

"Sally," the girl said. "After Sally Bowles, the part in *Cabaret* Mom always wanted—the part she told me *you* wanted, too. Only you probably would have been better at it, Mom said."

"What did your mom die of, Sally? When did she die?"

"Cancer, a couple of years ago," Sally said. "I had to wait till I was eighteen—so it would be *legal* to haunt you."

She looked like a woman in her early twenties, but then her mother had always looked older than she was, too.

"Are you really eighteen, Sally?"

"Just like Lucy. Wasn't Lucy eighteen?" Sally asked him.

"I guess everyone knows about Lucy," Jack said.

"The Lucy business was the last thing my mom knew about you—it happened just before she died. Maybe it made it easier for her to die without you," Sally said.

Like Lucy, Sally was walking around in Jack's house as if she owned it. He noticed she had kicked off her shoes; she walked barefoot on the wrestling mat in his gym. Her beige, sleeveless blouse was a gauzy fabric; her bra, which Jack could see through the blouse, was the same beige or light-tan color. Sally's skirt made a swishing sound as she walked. She paused at his desk, reading the title page of a screenplay lying there. (That was when she picked up Jack's address book.)

"My mom never stopped loving you," Sally said. "She always wondered what might have happened if she'd stayed with you—

if you ever would have given her a child, or children. She regretted breaking up with you, but she had to have *children*."

The way Sally said *children*, Jack got the feeling that she didn't like kids—or that the need to have them wasn't as urgent an issue to her as it had been to Claudia.

Sally plopped herself down on Jack's living-room couch and opened his address book. He sat down beside her.

"Do you have siblings, Sally?"

"Are you kidding? Mom popped out four kids, one right after the other. Lucky me—I was the first. I got to be the babysitter."

"And your dad?" Jack asked her.

"He means no harm," Sally said. "Mom would have married the first guy she met after she split up with you. He just had to promise to give her children. My dad was the first guy she met, the pathetic loser."

"Why is he a pathetic loser, Sally?"

"He got to go to all your movies with Mom. What a kick that had to be for him, if you know what I mean," Sally said. "Of course, when I was old enough, I got to watch all your movies, too—with Mom *and* Dad. There wasn't anything she didn't tell Dad about you. There wasn't anything she didn't tell *me* about you, too. That trip you took to the Toronto film festival; how your mother tattooed her. How you made Mom show her tattoo to the customs agent—that was a good one. How she gave you the clap she caught from Captain Phoebus, when you were a gay Esmeralda in *The Hunchback of Notre Dame;* how you were such a prick about it, as if you'd never fooled around yourself."

"But your dad loved her?" Jack asked Sally.

"Oh, he *worshiped* her!" Sally said. "Mom got as big as a cow—she completely let herself go—and it was painfully evident that she never got over you. But Dad *adored* her."

"You're very beautiful, Sally," he told the girl. "You look so much like your mom, I almost believed you. For a moment, I thought you *were* Claudia's ghost."

"I can haunt you as good as any ghost—believe me, Jack." She wasn't looking at him; she just kept thumbing through the pages of his address book, as if she were searching for someone. Suddenly she flipped to the front of the book; she began with the *A*'s. In her mother's stage voice, she read aloud the first woman's name.

"Mildred ('Milly') Ascheim," Sally said; then her tone of

voice became insinuating. "Did you screw her, Jack? Are you still screwing her?"

"No, never," he replied.

"Uh-oh. Here's another Ascheim—*Myra*. You crossed her name out. That's a pretty clear indication that you fucked her. Then you dumped her, I suppose."

"I never had sex with her. I crossed out her name because she died. Sally, let's not play this game," Jack said.

But she kept reading; she became very excited when she got to Lucia Delvecchio's name. "Even Mom said you *must* have slept with her," Sally said. "Mom said she could tell you were going to sleep with her when she saw you with her in the movie."

Jack let it go on too long. Sally was into the *G*'s when the trouble really started. (Jack knew what Dr. García would say— namely, that he shouldn't have been sitting next to Sally on the couch in the first place.)

"Elena García," Sally said. This must have registered on Jack's face; he clearly found this disrespectful to Dr. García, whom he never called by her first name. Dr. García was the most important person in this stage of Jack's life, and Sally saw it. "Your cleaning lady, or former cleaning lady?" Sally asked, *more* disrespectfully. "You definitely fucked her."

"She's my doctor—my psychiatrist," Jack said. "I don't even call her by her first name."

"Oh, yes—she's *Lucy's* shrink, too, isn't she? How could I forget that!" Sally said. "I'll bet Lucy's *mom* is stalking you now."

The girl was good; she had her mother's talent, if not half her training. And at that moment, when she was teasing him, she reminded Jack more of Claudia than at any time when he'd imagined she was Claudia's ghost.

"Please don't be angry with me, Jack," Sally said, very much the way her mother would have said it. "I just miss my mom, and I thought that being with you might bring her back to me."

Jack couldn't move; he just sat there. In his experience, women, even young women, knew when they had frozen you. Claudia had known those moments when Jack couldn't resist her. Sally knew, too. She pressed herself against him on the couch; she started unbuttoning his shirt. He didn't stop her. "Remember when you were John the Baptist?" Sally asked him.

"I was just his head—a small part," he answered her. "His severed head—that's all I was."

"His decapitated head, on a table," Sally reminded him, slipping off his shirt. Jack didn't know when she'd unbuttoned her blouse; he noticed only that it was unbuttoned. "Mom was Salomé, wasn't she?" Claudia's daughter asked him.

"Yes," Jack answered; he could barely talk. The girl had undressed him *and* herself. Naked, she was more like Claudia than Claudia—Chinese scepter and all.

"Mom said that was the best kiss she ever gave you."

That was some kiss, he remembered. Yet the damage to Claudia and Jack's relationship had already been done; not even that kiss could undo their drifting apart.

Jack recognized the blue foil wrapper of his favorite brand of Japanese condom. Sally was tearing the wrapper with her teeth. It seemed entirely too strange that Claudia's daughter would know, in advance, his preference for Kimono MicroThins. Then he remembered that the girl had used his bathroom, where she'd no doubt discovered his condoms in the medicine cabinet.

Jack looked into her dark-gold eyes and saw Claudia, as if she were alive and young again. The same wide mouth, but whiter teeth; the same full breasts and broad hips of a girl who would wage her own war with her weight one day. Like her mother, Sally was the kind of woman you sank into.

There would be no need to explain the problem to Dr. García—anyone but Jack could have done the math. If he'd last seen Claudia in June 1987, even if she'd met Sally's dad *immediately*—and married him, *and* gotten pregnant, all in that same month—Sally *couldn't* have been born before March 1988. In that case, in July 2003, Sally was *fifteen*. In order for her to be eighteen, she would (in all likelihood) have to have been *Jack's* daughter! As Dr. García had reminded him, he never could count.

As it happened, as Sally explained to him—this was *after* they had sex, unfortunately—in June 1987, Claudia went off to some Shakespeare festival in New Jersey, where she met a young director and Shakespearean scholar. They were married that August, and Claudia got pregnant in September; Sally was born in June 1988. When she and Jack had sex in his house on Entrada Drive, Sally had been fifteen for all of one month. But she looked a lot older!

Sally quickly ran a bath and sat in it, with the bathroom door open. She hated to have sex and run, she said, but she was in a hurry. She had a curfew; she had to get back to The Georgian

Hotel in Santa Monica, where she was staying with her mom and dad and the rest of her family.

"Your mom is *alive*?"

"She's as big as a barn, but she's very healthy," Sally said. "You wouldn't have slept with me if you thought Mom was alive, would you?"

Jack didn't say anything; he just sat on the bathroom floor with his back against a towel rack, watching Claudia's near-perfect likeness in the tub.

"My parents are the happiest couple I know," Sally was saying. "My mother gets embarrassed when we tease her about being your ex-girlfriend. But my sisters and I, *and* my dad, think it's the funniest thing in the world. We order a pizza and watch one of your movies—we all just *howl*! Mom sometimes has to leave the room. We make her laugh so hard she has to pee! 'Pause it—I'll be right back,' Mom says. When you won the Oscar, I thought we were all going to wet our pants."

"You're *how* old?" he asked her.

"Your math is *ridiculous*—Mom wasn't kidding," Sally said. "For your self-protection, Jack, you ought to look up the California Penal Code—the part about unlawful sexual intercourse with a minor. You're over twenty-one, I'm under sixteen—that's really all that matters. You're guilty of either a misdemeanor or a felony. You could go to jail for one, two, three, or four years—and you're liable for a civil penalty, not to exceed twenty-five thousand dollars. That is, if I tell anybody."

She stood up in the tub and hastily dried herself off, throwing the towel on the bathroom floor. He followed her through his bedroom and into the living room, where her clothes were scattered everywhere; while Sally got dressed, Jack searched for her shoes.

"This is kind of my summer job," she was explaining to him.

"*What* is?" (Seducing Jack Burns? Extortion?)

Sally further explained that her dad—who was hardly a pathetic loser, in Sally's fond opinion—managed a small, community-operated theater in Vermont. It was called The Nuts & Bolts Playhouse. They did summer-stock productions; they ran workshops in acting, directing, and playwriting during the school months. A nonprofit foundation funded everything. When Claudia and her Shakespearean husband weren't engaged in their theater productions and workshops, they were full-time fund-raisers.

"We're a big family—four girls," Sally elaborated. "We all have to go to college one day. My parents' whole life is by example. We love the theater, we learn to be independent, we don't *care* about money, but we always *need* money. Do you get it?"

"How much do you want?" Jack asked Claudia's daughter.

"It would *kill* my mom to know that I slept with you," she said.

"How much, Sally?"

She grabbed his wrist and looked at his watch. "Shit! You have to drop me off at The Georgian, or near it. I supposedly went to a movie screening, where I had an opportunity to meet you. Damn curfew!"

"Your mom and dad *knew* you were meeting me?" he asked her.

"Yes, but not to have *sex*!" Sally cried, laughing. "They're really terrific parents—I *told* you."

She gave him a brochure of The Nuts & Bolts Playhouse— there were pictures of Claudia and her husband, and the other daughters. The check was to be made payable to The Nuts & Bolts Foundation; it being a nonprofit meant that Jack's "donation" was tax-deductible, Sally told him.

For years, the children had asked their mother why she didn't ask Jack Burns for money for their theater enterprise. Jack was a movie star and Claudia knew him; surely he would give *something*.

"Why didn't *you* just ask me for a donation?" he asked Sally.

"Would you have given me this much?" Sally asked. (He'd written out a check to The Nuts & Bolts Foundation for $100,000. Compared to what the California Penal Code could cost him, it was a bargain.)

Jack drove the girl and Claudia's old suitcase back to Ocean Avenue. At least he'd been right about the suitcase; it had been a prop.

Sally's parents were night people. After they put the younger daughters to bed, Claudia and her husband went downstairs to have a drink in the bar; that's where they would be waiting for Sally to come back from the "screening." They'd agreed to let her go out and meet Jack Burns, solely for the purpose of asking Jack to make a donation to their efforts on behalf of Claudia's first and most enduring love—the theater. (This must have been what Sally meant by learning to be *independent*.) As for Claudia's old suitcase, Sally had stuffed it full of brochures of The Nuts & Bolts Playhouse—just in case she met *other* rich and famous movie stars at the alleged screening.

Sally and Jack discussed whether it was a good idea or not for him to come into the lobby of The Georgian with her. Meet her dad—say hello to Claudia, for old times' sake. Sally could announce the extraordinary generosity of Jack's donation. Gifts of $100,000 were rare; gifts of that size constituted "naming opportunities," Sally told him. A fellowship for a young student-actor, director, or playwright in Jack Burns's name; there was a capital campaign for a new six-hundred-seat theater, too. (*Lots* of naming opportunities, apparently.)

"Or you could choose to remain anonymous," Sally said.

Jack opted to remain anonymous. He told Sally that he thought he *wouldn't* go meet her dad and renew his acquaintance with her mom in the bar of The Georgian Hotel.

"That's probably best," Sally said. "Frankly, *I* could pull it off. I've rehearsed this for freakin' *forever.* But I honestly don't know if you're a good enough actor to just walk in there and pretend that you *haven't* fucked my brains out."

"I'm probably not that good," he admitted.

"Jack, I think you're very sweet," Claudia's daughter said, kissing his cheek. "Mom and Dad are going to write you— I know they will. A big thank-you letter, at the very least. For the rest of your life, you'll be on their mailing list; they'll probably ask you for money every year. I don't mean another hundred-thou or anything, but they'll ask you for *something.* I always thought they *should* ask you."

In the Nuts & Bolts Playhouse brochure, Claudia was wearing a tent-shaped dress and looked bigger than Kathy Bates climbing into that hot tub with Jack Nicholson in whatever that movie was. Her husband was a tall, bearded man who looked as if he were always cast as a betrayed king. The younger daughters were as big-boned and pretty as Sally.

When Jack pulled up to the curb at The Georgian Hotel on Ocean Avenue, Sally kissed him on his forehead. "You seem like a good guy, Jack—just a sad one," she said.

"Please give your mother my fondest regards," he told the fifteen-year-old.

"Thanks for the money, Jack. It means a lot—I'm not kidding."

"How does this constitute *haunting* me?" he asked her. "I mean, it was a sting. A pretty good one—I'll give you that, Sally. But how have you *haunted* me, exactly?"

"Oh, you'll see," Sally said. "This *will* haunt you, Jack—and I don't mean the money."

He went back to Entrada Drive—the scene of the crime, so to speak. It *was* a crime, not only according to the California Penal Code; it felt very much like a crime to Jack Burns. He'd had sex with a fifteen-year-old girl, and it had cost him only $100,000.

Jack stayed up late reading every word of the brochure Sally had left with him; he looked at all the pictures, over and over again. The Nuts & Bolts Playhouse was dedicated to that noble idea of theater as a public service. A neighbor who was an electrician had installed the new stage lights for free; a couple of local carpenters had built the sets for three Shakespearean productions, also at no charge. In a small southern Vermont town, virtually everyone had contributed something to the community playhouse.

The area schoolchildren performed their school plays in the theater; a women's book club staged dramatizations of scenes from their favorite novels. A New York City opera company rehearsed there for the month of January, before going on tour; some local children with good voices were taught to sing by professional opera singers. Poets gave readings; there were concerts, too. The summer-stock productions, while pandering to tourists' fondness for popular entertainment, included at least two "serious" plays every summer. Jack recognized a few of the guest performers in the summer casts—actors and actresses from New York.

There were two pictures of Claudia; in both she looked radiant and joyful, and fat. Her daughters were most photogenic—self-confident girls who'd been taught to perform. Certainly Claudia could be proud of Sally for possessing both poise and determination beyond her years. Did Claudia and her husband know that Sally was a model of self-assurance and independent thinking? Probably. Did her parents also know that Sally was as sexually active (on her family's behalf) as she was? Probably not.

Claudia had made the theater her family's business—perhaps more successfully than she knew. But no matter how hard Jack tried to understand the financing, he couldn't grasp how a so-called nonprofit foundation worked. (His math let him down again.) All Jack knew was that he would be writing out checks to The Nuts & Bolts Foundation for the rest of his life; *regular* donations of $100,000, or more, seemed a small price to pay for what he had done.

He wanted to call Dr. García, but it was by now two or three in the morning and he knew what she would say. "Tell me *in chronological order,* Jack. I'm not a priest. I don't hear confessions." What she meant was that she didn't give absolution, not that there was any forgiveness for his having had sex with Claudia's daughter—not even if Jack could have convinced himself that Sally really *was* Claudia's ghost.

Jack was turning out the lights in the kitchen, before he finally went to bed, when he saw the rudimentary grocery list he had fastened to the refrigerator with one of his mom's Japanese-tattoo magnets.

COFFEE BEANS

MILK

CRANBERRY JUICE

It didn't add up to much of a life. He was already beginning to see how Claudia had kept her promise to haunt him.

Jack discovered that when you're ashamed, your life becomes a *what-if* world. Claudia's daughter Sally was fifteen; it wasn't hard to imagine a girl of that age having some sort of falling-out with her mom. Teenage girls didn't need legitimate provocation to hate their mothers. What if, for some stupid reason, Sally wanted to *hurt* her mom? What if Sally *told* Claudia that she'd slept with Jack?

Or what if, later in her life, Sally came to the illogical conclusion that Jack had taken advantage of her? What if—for a host of reasons, possibly having nothing to do with what had inspired Sally to seduce Jack in the first place—the wayward girl simply decided that he deserved to pay for his crime, or that Jack Burns should at least be publicly exposed?

"Well, Jack, I'm sure your shame is even greater than your

fear of the California Penal Code," Dr. García would later tell him. "But in our past, don't many of us have someone who could destroy us with a letter or a phone call?"

"*You* don't have someone like that, do you, Dr. García?"

"I'm not the patient, Jack. I don't have to answer that kind of question. Let's just say, we all have to learn to live with *something*."

It was August 2003. Jack's house on Entrada Drive was still for sale, but he felt that Claudia's ghost had moved in to stay; it was as if she were living with him. Wherever else he might go, before or after that wretched house was sold, Jack had no doubt that Claudia's ghost would come with him.

Krung, the Thai kickboxer from that long-ago gym on Bathurst Street, had told him once: "Gym rats always gotta find a new ship, Jackie." Well, Jack was a gym rat who would soon have to find a new ship, but now he was a gym rat with a ghost.

Jack found that you don't sleep well when you're living with a ghost. He had meaningless but disturbing dreams, from which he would awaken with the conviction that his hand was touching Emma's tattoo. (That perfect vagina, the *not*-a-Rose-of-Jericho, which his mom had tattooed on Emma's right hip—just below the panty line.)

Jack took his real estate agent's advice and moved out; this allowed her to empty the house of all the old and ugly furniture, most of which Emma had acquired for their first apartment in Venice, as well as the rugs and Jack's gym equipment; the floors were sanded and the walls were painted white. The house became a clean and spare-looking dump, at least—and Jack moved into a modest set of rooms at the Oceana in Santa Monica.

It was a third-floor suite with four rooms, including a kitchen, overlooking the courtyard and the swimming pool. He could have chosen a view of Ocean Avenue, but the Oceana was a moderately priced residential hotel that appealed to families; Jack liked the sound of the children playing in the pool. Some of the families were Asian or European; Jack liked listening to the foreign languages, too. He accepted the transience of staying there, because Jack Burns was transient—impermanent, almost ceasing to exist.

He kept next to nothing from Entrada Drive. He gave three quarters of his clothes to Goodwill and his Oscar to his lawyer for safekeeping.

Jack kept his most recent Audi, of course. The gym at the Oceana was a joke, but there were two gyms in Venice that he liked—and, from the Oceana, Jack was even closer to Dr. García's office on Montana Avenue than he'd been on Entrada Drive.

Jack registered at the Oceana as Harry Mocco; as usual, the few important people in his life knew where to find him. Somehow it seemed fitting (to a man in limbo) that Jack would hear from Leslie Oastler shortly after his move. Mrs. Oastler called because she hadn't heard from him in a while—which was all right with her, she added quickly. And just fine with Dolores, no doubt.

Dolores had made such a fuss about the ongoing presence of Jack's clothes that Mrs. Oastler had donated them to St. Hilda's, where Mr. Ramsey had happily accepted the clothes as costumes for the school's dramatic productions. Mr. Ramsey *and* Miss Wurtz had called to thank Leslie for the unusual gift. ("We never have enough men's clothes for the dramatizations," Caroline had explained.)

Jack's *former* bedroom, Mrs. Oastler told him, had been converted to a studio for Dolores. (Leslie's blonde must have been a poet or a painter—some kind of artist, surely—but Jack didn't ask.) As for Emma's old bedroom, it was now the *official* guest room. The wallpaper was different—"more feminine," Leslie said. The furniture and curtains were "more feminine," too. All this was Dolores's doing, Jack guessed, but again he didn't ask.

"When you're back in town, you'll probably prefer to stay in a hotel," Mrs. Oastler said.

"Probably," Jack replied. He couldn't tell why she had called.

"Any *new* news from or about your dad, Jack?" Leslie asked.

"No. But I'm not looking for him," Jack explained.

"I wonder why not," Leslie said. "He would be a man in his sixties, wouldn't he? Things happen to men at that age. You might lose him before you find him, if you know what I mean."

"He might die, you mean?"

"He might be dead already," Mrs. Oastler said. "You were so curious about him. What happened to your curiosity, Jack?" (This was what Dr. García was always asking him.)

"I've been seeing a psychiatrist," he half explained.

"I'm glad you're seeing *somebody*!" Leslie exclaimed. "But you used to be able to do more than one thing at a time."

"What Mrs. Oastler may mean, Jack," Dr. García would soon

tell him, "is that seeing a psychiatrist is not something you necessarily do *in lieu of* having a little natural curiosity."

But Jack was guilty of an indefensible crime. He'd not only
had sex with a fifteen-year-old girl—he had *acquiesced* to it. He
carried an awful secret, and—provided Claudia's daughter let
him—Jack would bear its burden to his grave. *Shame* had
robbed him of his curiosity. When you're ashamed, you don't
feel inclined to undertake another adventure—at least not right
away.

The thank-you letter from Claudia and her husband (whom Jack
would forever imagine as a bearded, betrayed king) came with
family photographs—among them one of Sally as a little girl
and one of Claudia when she was noticeably thinner. There was
also a photo of the husband and father of four when he was
clean-shaven; Jack could understand why the king had grown a
beard.

"*Should you ever be inclined to return to the theater,*" Claudia
wrote, "*just say the word!*" A month or six weeks in Vermont in
midsummer, a stage so small it would seem his very own, his
pick of the play and the part. Under the circumstances, Jack was
both touched and repelled by the offer.

"*We're all so grateful to you, Jack,*" Claudia went on.

"*And we're so proud of Sally for having the temerity to approach you!*" Claudia's husband (Sally's father) wrote.

Jack would write back to Claudia and her husband that he was
glad to have helped, in what modest way he could. But he lacked
Sally's *temerity;* Jack wrote that he no longer had the nerve to
stand alone on a stage. "*The out-of-context moments of film-
making, which I've grown used to, allow the actor room to hide.*"
(Whatever *that* meant!) But Jack would think of their little theater often, he wrote—and every summer he would regret the
missed opportunity of an idyllic month or six weeks in Vermont.
(In truth, he would rather *die*!)

Jack felt Claudia's ghost watching over him; she was all
smiles when he mailed that letter.

Immediately following this insincere correspondence, Jack
experienced contact of another kind. There was nothing insincere about Caroline Wurtz's phone call, which woke him early
one August morning from his umpteenth dream of touching
Emma's vagina tattoo. A family from Düsseldorf, with whom

he'd been testing the limits of his Exeter German, were already up and swimming in the Oceana pool.

"Jack Burns, as Mr. Ramsey might say," Miss Wurtz began. "Rise and shine!" The Wurtz, of course, had no idea of what a shameful thing Jack had done. (That he would rise, and go on rising, seemed likely; that he might ever *shine* again seemed unthinkable.)

"How nice to hear your voice, Caroline," he told her truthfully.

"You sound awful," Miss Wurtz said. "Don't pretend I didn't wake you. But I have news worth waking you for, Jack."

"You've heard from him?" Jack asked, wide awake if not exactly *shining*.

"I've heard *of* him, not from him. You have a *sister,* Jack!"

Biologically speaking, if his father had remarried—as it appeared that William had—it was conceivable that Jack had a *half* sister, which was indeed news to him *and* Miss Wurtz.

Her name was Heather Burns, and she was a junior lecturer on the Faculty of Music at the University of Edinburgh, where (some years earlier) she'd also completed her undergraduate studies in the Department of Music. Heather was a pianist and an organist, and she played a wooden flute. She'd done her Ph.D. in Belfast.

"On Brahms," Caroline informed him. "Something about Brahms and the nineteenth century."

"My dad is back in Edinburgh?" he asked The Wurtz.

"William isn't well, Jack—he's in a sanatorium. He was playing the organ again at Old St. Paul's, and teaching in Edinburgh, but he has osteoarthritis. His arthritic hands have put an end to his playing, at least professionally."

"He's in a sanatorium for *arthritis*?" Jack asked her.

"No, no—it's a *mental* place," Miss Wurtz said.

"He's in an insane asylum, Caroline?"

"Heather says it's very nice. William *loves* it there. It's just that it's very expensive," Miss Wurtz said.

"My sister was calling for money?" Jack asked.

"She was calling for *you,* Jack. She wanted to know how to reach you. I told her I would call you. As you know, I give your phone number to *no one*—although in this case I was tempted. Yes, Heather needs money—to keep William happy and safe in the sanatorium."

Jack's sister was twenty-eight. A junior lecturer at the University of Edinburgh didn't make enough money to afford to have children, The Wurtz explained. Heather couldn't be expected to pay for William's confinement.

"Heather is married?" Jack asked Miss Wurtz.

"Certainly not!"

"You mentioned children, Caroline."

"I was being hypothetical—about the poor girl's meager salary," Miss Wurtz elaborated. "Heather has a boyfriend. He's Irish. But she's not going to marry him. Heather merely said that her income didn't permit her to even *think* about starting a family, and that she needs your help with William."

I have a sister! Jack was thinking; that she needed his help (that *anyone* needed him) was the most wonderful news!

Better still, Jack's sister loved their father. According to Miss Wurtz, Heather adored William. But she'd not had an easy time of it; nor had he. After talking with Jack's sister, The Wurtz had quite a story to tell.

If not surpassing or even equaling his feelings for the commandant's daughter, the next love of William Burns's life was a young woman he'd met and married in Germany. Barbara Steiner was a singer; she introduced William to Schubert's songs. The singing of German lieder, accompanied by the pianoforte—"the ancestor of the modern piano," as Miss Wurtz described it to Jack—was new and exciting to William. It was no minor art to him, nor was Barbara Steiner a passing infatuation; they performed and taught together.

"I have a son, but I may never see him again," William told Barbara, from the beginning.

Jack Burns was an emotional and psychological presence in her childhood, Heather told Miss Wurtz—even before Jack became a movie star and his dad began to watch him obsessively on the big screen, and on videotape and DVD. (According to The Wurtz, William had Jack's dialogue—in *all* the movies—"down pat.")

William Burns and Barbara Steiner had lived in Munich, in Cologne, in Stuttgart; they were together in Germany for about five years. When Barbara was pregnant with Heather, William was offered an opportunity to return "home" to Edinburgh; he seized it. Heather was born in Scotland, where both her parents taught in the Department of Music at the University of Edinburgh before her.

William was once again playing the Father Willis at Old St. Paul's—not that the organ hadn't been altered and enlarged since he'd last played it. Given the church's fabled reverberation time, this hardly mattered; it was Old St. Paul's Scottish Episcopal Church, which William loved, and Edinburgh was his city.

Miss Wurtz, bless her heart, too quickly jumped to the conclusion that William's life had come full circle. Wasn't it wonderful that, for all his wanderlust and the upheavals of his younger days, William Burns had at last "settled down"? He'd found the right woman; their daughter would give Jack's father some measure of peace, a sense of replacement for losing his son.

But it was not to be. Barbara Steiner was homesick for Germany. In her view, Edinburgh was not a great city for classical music; there was a lot of music, but much of it was mediocre. The climate was damp and dreary. Barbara believed that the weather exacerbated her chronic bronchitis; she half joked that she had become a singer with a permanent cough, but the cough was persistent and more serious than she knew.

What Heather, Jack's sister, imparted to Miss Wurtz—in one phone call—was a portrait of her mother as a complainer. According to Barbara, Scottish men (excluding William) were unattractive and dressed badly; the women were even less attractive and didn't know how to dress at all. Whisky was a curse, not only for the drunkenness it caused (William didn't drink); it also killed the taste buds and made the Scots incapable of recognizing how bad their food was. Kilts, like lederhosen, should be worn only by children—or so Barbara believed. (William wouldn't have been caught dead in a kilt.) In the summer, when the weather finally improved, there were too many tourists—especially Americans. Barbara was allergic to wool; no tartan would ever please her.

Her mother, Heather told Miss Wurtz, found one child such an overwhelming burden that she resisted William's wishes to have one or two more. Barbara was not a natural mother, yet she reduced her teaching duties (by half) in order to spend more time with Heather, although time spent with an infant was torture to her.

Barbara Steiner was a child of divorced parents; she had such a dread of separation and divorce that she periodically suspected

William of planning to divorce her. He wasn't; in fact, William was (in Heather's words) "slavishly devoted" to his griping wife. He held himself accountable for her unhappiness, for taking her away from her beloved homeland; he offered to move back to Germany, but Barbara believed that such a move would make her husband so unhappy that he would be driven to divorce her all the more quickly.

Before Barbara Steiner's parents had separated, she had cherished the family ski holidays they would take—every winter and spring—to the Swiss and Austrian Alps. After the divorce, the ski trips, which Barbara took alone with her mother, or alone with her father, became a form of enforced exercise—athletic stoicism and silent dinners, where one or the other of her parents drank too much wine. Yet the names of these ski resorts in Austria and Switzerland were reverentially repeated to Heather by her unhappy mother; it was as if they were saints' names, and Barbara had converted to Catholicism.

St. Anton, Klosters, Lech, Wengen, Zermatt, St. Christoph. When they'd lived in Germany, Barbara Steiner had actually taught William Burns how to ski—albeit badly. (Jack had trouble envisioning his dad, a tattooed organist, on skis.) But the Swiss and Austrian Alps were a long way from Scotland.

"We'll take you skiing *when you're old enough*," Heather's mom had told her.

One can imagine how The Wurtz's account of this had echoes of Alice's litany to Jack.

But the so-called chronic bronchitis turned out to be lung cancer, which Barbara believed she had "caught" (like the flu) in Edinburgh. "I wouldn't be surprised if lung cancer *originated* in Scotland," she half joked between coughs. It was the death of her singing, but not of her.

Heather was too young at the time to remember anything positive about her mother's recovery from the cancer. Heather recalled nothing about the radiation, Caroline told Jack—and only "the vomiting part" and "the wig part" of her mother's chemotherapy. Heather would have been five, Miss Wurtz speculated. The child could barely remember the first ski trip of her life, to Klosters—except that her mother, Barbara, had been depressed because she was too tired to ski.

Jack suggested to Caroline that, when Heather was five, her memory of *anything* was unreliable. Miss Wurtz countered this argument; although she was only five at the time, his sister's most enduring memory of her mother had prevailed. Barbara Steiner had *hated* how the Scots drove on the wrong side of the road. She cited the numerous deaths of foreign tourists in Edinburgh every summer. (They stepped off the curb, looking left instead of right.)

"If the cancer doesn't come back and kill me," Barbara used to say to William, *and* to their five-year-old daughter, "I swear I shall be struck down by a car going the wrong way on the street." She was.

She stepped off the curb, where it was written—as plain as day—LOOK RIGHT. She looked left instead, although she'd lived in Edinburgh for almost six years, and a taxi killed her.

"I believe Heather said it was in the vicinity of Charlotte Square," Miss Wurtz informed Jack. "A children's book author was reading at some sort of writers' festival. Her mother had taken Heather to the reading, which was in a tent. When they were leaving, and about to cross the street, Heather reached for her mother's hand. Heather looked the right way and saw the taxi coming; her mother looked the wrong way and stepped off the curb. The taxi killed Barbara instantly. Heather remembers that her fingers only slightly grazed her mother's hand."

Whether Jack's sister had freely divulged these painful details to Miss Wurtz, or whether Caroline had coaxed the details out of her, Jack didn't know. He knew only that The Wurtz was a tireless believer in *dramatizing* important information—hence the detail that Barbara Steiner's wig flew off on impact was conveyed to Jack, and the fact that Heather and her mom (at her mother's insistence) spoke only German when they were alone together.

That Jack's five-year-old sister was crying for her dead mother *in German* confused the witnesses to the accident. (There were many parents with children among the witnesses; they'd also attended the reading by the children's book author at the writers' festival.) The police reconstructed the accident incorrectly: a German tourist had been struck down by a car in the unexpected lane; the astonishingly bald woman was carrying no identification, and her five-year-old daughter, who was hysterical, spoke only German.

Actually, Barbara had been carrying a purse. It must have been flung far away from her when the taxi hit her—lost forever, like the wig. Heather, when she calmed down, told a policeman, in English, that she wanted to go "home"; she took the cop by the hand and showed him the way. Heather had walked everywhere in Edinburgh with her mother and father; no one in the family (including Heather, when she grew up) drove a car.

Thus William Burns became a single parent to a five-year-old girl. "Knowing William," Miss Wurtz said, "he would have held himself accountable for the death of the poor child's mother, too."

"Did Heather say that?" Jack asked.

"Of course she didn't *say* it, Jack! But I know William. He forgave your mother for *everything,* but he never forgave himself."

"And now he's crazy?" Jack asked.

"You should talk to your sister, Jack. You should meet Heather before it's too late."

But did Heather want to meet him? he inquired of The Wurtz. (Jack wondered if he should send his sister a check first.)

"You have to call her and talk to her yourself," Miss Wurtz said. "I'm sure you have some things in common."

"Name one, Caroline."

"Your mothers weren't your favorite people," Miss Wurtz said.

"I *loved* my mom when I was a little boy," Jack pointed out.

"Goodness, Jack, I'm sure your sister loved *her* mom when she was a little girl. But, with hindsight, Heather has at least considered what a difficult woman her mother could be. Doesn't that sound familiar?"

It was The Wurtz's view that Jack's father had *not* abandoned him; on the contrary, William had provided for Jack. William's deal with Alice at least made her responsible for doing all the outwardly correct things. Jack had gone to good schools, he'd worn clean clothes, he wasn't beaten or abused—that is, not to Alice's knowledge.

It was also Miss Wurtz's view—and Caroline was no fan of Jack's mother—that Alice had, to some degree, shielded Jack from what The Wurtz called the "adult choices" in Alice's own dark life. (Notwithstanding Leslie Oastler and some of Alice's friends in the tattoo world.)

"You must tell me how William is when you find him," Miss Wurtz said. "Meanwhile, be thankful you have a sister."

"I have a sister," Jack repeated.

That was the message he would leave on the answering machine in Dr. García's office, because it was too early in the morning to make an appointment to see her. Merely discovering that he had a sister was in the category of what Dr. García called "incomplete information"—by which she meant that Jack's news didn't merit calling her at home.

Jack called his sister, Heather Burns, instead. It was only 7:00 A.M. in Santa Monica—10:00 A.M. in Toronto, where Miss Wurtz had been calling from. But it was already midafternoon in Edinburgh. There was music playing when Heather answered the phone—voices and an organ, maybe trumpets.

"Give me a moment," his sister said, turning down the volume on the CD player.

"It's Jack Burns, your brother," he told her.

"It's Heather—your *half* sister, actually," she said. "But I feel I know you. It was almost as if I grew up with you. 'If your brother knew you, he would love you,' Daddy said every night, when he put me to bed. And there was always this refrain: 'I have a son!' he would shout. 'I have a son *and* a daughter!' Daddy would say. It could be tiresome, but I got the point."

"I wish I'd grown up with you," Jack told her.

"You don't know that yet," she said. Her voice was crisp and even, with less of a Scottish accent than he'd expected. (There was some Irish in her accent, Jack thought—the effect of those years in Belfast, perhaps, or the Irish boyfriend.) Above all, she sounded very practical.

"I want to meet you," he told her.

"You don't know that, either, Jack Burns," Heather said. "I'm not comfortable asking you for money, but I need it. Our father needs it, I should say—not that he knows he needs it."

"He took care of me; I'll take care of him," Jack told her.

"Don't *act* with me, Mr. Movie Star," Heather said. "Say only what you mean."

"I mean it," he told her.

"Then you better come meet me. Let's see how that goes," she said.

"I should have been there, when you had your first date," Jack told his sister. "I could have warned you about the guy."

"Don't go there, as Billy Rainbow would say," Heather said. "I could have warned you about some of your dates, too."

"No doubt about it," he told her. It was another Billy Rainbow line. (That character never said anything that hadn't been said a million times before, but Billy said the most mundane things sincerely.)

"You sound just like him," Heather said. "Like Billy Rainbow, I mean."

"But I'm not like him—I'm really someone else," Jack said, hoping it was true. His sister made no response. Jack could hear the music playing; it sounded like a hymn. "I have a sister," he said. (It seemed to go with the hymn.)

"Yes, you do, Jack Burns. You have a father, too. But I'll tell you how it is," his sister said. "You have to go through me to get to him. Not for all your money, Mr. Movie Star, do you see him without seeing me first—not for all the money in the world!"

"You can trust me, Heather."

"You have to go through me to get to him," she said again. "I have to trust you with *him*."

"I swear to God—you can trust me," he told her.

"You *swear to God*? Are you religious, Jack Burns?"

"No, not really," Jack admitted.

"Well, *he* is. You better prepare yourself for that, too," his sister said.

"Are *you* religious, Heather?"

"Not so religious that I can ever forgive your mother," she told him. "Not *that* religious. But *he* is."

After Barbara Steiner's death, William Burns and his daughter *really* learned to ski. They went only once a year, for a week or ten days, to one of those sacred-sounding places; they eventually added Davos and Pontresina to the list. Skiing, like music—like everything they did together—became a ritual. (According to Jack's sister, she and her father became halfway-decent skiers.)

Heather told Jack that she'd started practicing the piano a year after her mother died, when she was six years old. William Burns encouraged his daughter to practice for five hours a day, alone. As a teenager, Heather took up the wooden flute. "The flute is more sociable," she explained to Jack; that there was a lot of Irish music for the flute led her to do her doctorate in Belfast.

The Irish boyfriend was still in Ireland. Heather held out little hope for the future of any long-distance relationship. But they'd played together in a band in Belfast, and they'd traveled together—

a trip to Portugal the previous Easter. ("I like him, in small doses," was all Heather would say about him.)

As a junior lecturer, she made £22,000 a year. In Belfast, she'd paid £380 a month for a two-bedroom flat; in Edinburgh, she paid £300 for a single room in an apartment she shared with five roommates. However, Heather's one-year contract had been extended; she would get a raise and be making £23,000 next year. For the time being, Heather liked Edinburgh and her job; if she stayed another five or six years, and if she was successful in getting published, she'd be doing well enough to start a family. But Heather doubted she would stay in Scotland. (All she would tell Jack was that she had "other plans.")

Her last year in Belfast, she'd played the organ in a church. One of her senior colleagues at the University of Edinburgh, John Kitchen, had been the organist at Old St. Paul's since 1988, when William Burns's arthritis had forced him to retire as principal organist. For almost fifteen years, William had continued to play the organ at Old St. Paul's—officially, he'd been John Kitchen's assistant. Heather was the backup organist to John Kitchen at Old St. Paul's now. Kitchen had long been their father's friend, Heather told Jack. (He was "like an uncle" to her, she said.)

She played Irish music on her wooden flute one night a week at the Central Bar, a pub at the bottom of Leith Walk. "I'll show you the Central when you're here," Heather told him.

"I want to know everything about you," Jack said.

"You don't know that yet," his sister reminded him.

Jack parked the Audi at the curb on Montana Avenue; he was waiting for Elizabeth, Dr. García's receptionist, to arrive and unlock the office. Elizabeth would be the first to play Jack's *I-have-a-sister* message. Jack would give her time to play all the messages on the answering machine before he asked her if he could be Dr. García's first appointment.

Jack never waited in the waiting room anymore. He waited in his car for his therapy sessions with Dr. García. When it was Jack's turn, Elizabeth would call him on his cell phone; then Jack would put some money in the parking meter and go inside. His presence in the waiting room made the young mothers—and, occasionally, their friends or nannies—"borderline hysterical," Dr. García had said.

Jack was listening to an Emmylou Harris CD, his fingers keeping time on the steering wheel to "Tougher than the Rest," when Elizabeth came into view on the sidewalk. She shook her key ring at him, but Jack couldn't hear the keys jingle—not over Emmylou.

"I'll show you *tougher than the rest*," Elizabeth said, letting him into the office. She was a tall, hawk-faced woman in her fifties; her gunmetal gray hair was always in a ponytail. There was something of Mrs. McQuat's severity in the tensed muscles of her neck.

"I left a message on Dr. García's machine," Jack said.

"I heard it. Nice message. I always access the messages from my car," she explained. "I suppose you want the first appointment."

"I would appreciate it, Elizabeth."

He sat in Dr. García's office, not in the waiting room, while Elizabeth made a pot of coffee. Jack had never been alone in that office; he took the time to look more closely at the family photographs, noting that Dr. García was much younger in the photos than he'd first assumed. If those children were hers, they were grown now—probably with children of their own.

"How old is Dr. García?" he asked Elizabeth, when she brought him a cup of coffee.

"Sixty-one," Elizabeth said.

Jack was amazed. Dr. García looked much younger. "And the gentleman in the pictures?" he asked Elizabeth. "Is he her husband or her father?"

"He *was* her husband," Elizabeth said. "He's been dead for almost twenty years—he died before I met her."

Perhaps this explained the older-looking man's spectral presence in the photographs; he was a spirit who haunted the family, no longer a participant.

"She didn't remarry?" Jack asked.

"No. She lives with one of her daughters, and her daughter's family. Dr. García has too many grandchildren to count."

It turned out that Elizabeth had been Dr. García's patient before becoming the doctor's receptionist. Elizabeth had been divorced; she was a former alcoholic who'd lost custody of her only child, a little boy. When she stopped drinking and got a job, the boy—who was then a teenager—chose to come live with her. Elizabeth credited Dr. García with saving her life.

Jack sat alone with his coffee in Dr. García's office; he felt in-consequential in the company of her family, who were frozen in time. It was instructive to Jack that his therapist had chosen to decorate her office with those photographs of herself and her children that predated her husband's death, as if she needed to be reminded that self-pity was not allowed. (Feeling sorry for yourself was not part of the healing process, or so Dr. García told her patients.)

Live with it, the photos said. *Don't forget, but forgive the past.*

In her daughter's house, where Dr. García lived as a grandmother—a somewhat stern one, Jack imagined—there were probably newer photographs. (Of her children as grown-ups, of her countless grandchildren—possibly of family pets.) But in her place of business, where she counseled those who felt terminally sorry for themselves, Dr. García had assembled an austere reminder of her earlier joy and abiding sorrow. She'd once told Elizabeth that she'd always known, when she married an older man, that her husband would predecease her. "I just never guessed by how many years!" she'd said, with a laugh.

"*With a laugh?*" Jack asked Elizabeth. "Did Dr. García really *laugh* when she said that?"

"That's the trick, isn't it?" Elizabeth said.

Here was another loose arrangement that would never have been tolerated in Vienna or New York, where Elizabeth's candor to Jack would have been considered unprofessional—where, Jack suspected, Dr. García's insistence on chronological order as therapy probably would have been considered "unprofessional," too. But it was working, wasn't it?

There was a prescription pad on Dr. García's desk. Jack thought about what he wanted to say to her, and if it would fit on one page of the prescription paper. He decided he could make it fit, if he kept his handwriting small.

Dear Dr. García,
    I'm going to Edinburgh to meet my sister—maybe my father, too! I'll put it all in chronological order for you, when I get back.

                                            I'm sorry about your husband.
                                            Jack

Then he went into the waiting room, where a nanny was reading a children's book to a four- or five-year-old. (In a world of loose arrangements, Jack had learned not to question why the young mothers didn't just leave their kids at home with their nannies.) The nanny looked up at Jack when he came out of Dr. García's office, but the child didn't bother to look. On a small couch, one of the young mothers lay curled in a fetal position with her back to the waiting room. Jack couldn't hear her crying, but her shoulders were shaking.

"I left Dr. García a note—it's on her desk," he told Elizabeth.

"Is there anything else you want me to tell her? I mean in addition to the note," Elizabeth said.

"Tell her I don't need to see her today," he said. "Tell her I looked happy."

"Well, that's a stretch. How about I say 'happier than usual'?" Elizabeth suggested.

"That's okay," he said.

"Be safe, Jack. Don't go crazy, or anything like that."

37
Edinburgh

Jack was thirty-eight; his sister, Heather, was twenty-eight. How do you meet someone you should have known most of your life? In Jack's case, he stalled. He arrived in Edinburgh a day before he'd told Heather he was coming. He had his mother's business to attend to. It was his father who had brought Jack and Heather together. Jack wanted to keep Heather separate from his mom's history in Edinburgh.

The hotel doorman at the Balmoral, a strapping young man in a kilt, was the first to ask Jack if he was in town for "the Festival"— a question he would repeatedly be asked.

Jack had a corner suite overlooking Princes Street. (He had a view of a chaotic-looking trampoline park.) Princes Street was clogged with pedestrian traffic: people carrying shopping bags, tourists folding and unfolding maps. With the concierge's assistance, Jack hired a car and driver to take him to Leith—Alice's old turf. It was less crowded there—not everybody's favorite part of town, apparently.

The driver's false teeth were too loose. His name was Rory, and his teeth clicked when he talked.

Jack wanted to see St. Thomas's, where Alice had sung in the choir—innocently, *before* she met William in South Leith Parish Church. St. Thomas's no longer existed, but Rory, who'd been born in Leith, remembered its location and knew what it had become. For more than twenty years, St. Thomas's had been a Sikh temple. The view of what was once Leith Hospital, which had so depressed Alice that she'd left St. Thomas's for another church, was depressing still. The former hospital, Rory told Jack, was only an outpatient clinic now. The unused parts looked neglected and broken; half the ground-floor windows were smashed.

Jack knew what Dr. García would have said if she'd been with him and Rory at that moment. "If St. Thomas's is gone, if an entire church can let go of the past, why can't you let go, too, Jack?"

South Leith Parish Church, where Alice first sang for William, made a more complex impression on Jack. The high walls along Constitution Street, which were meant to keep people out of the popular graveyard, stood in juxtaposition to a toppled gravestone. It read: HERE LYE THE REMAINS OF ROBERT CALDCLEUGH. The date, which was hard to read, was 1482. Among the gravestones, Jack saw that the most recent burial was in 1972.

Jack wouldn't have wanted to be buried there. If you were lying in that graveyard, facing south, you would be looking at an ugly seventeen-story high-rise for the rest of your death.

As for that area of Leith Walk where a rail bridge once joined Manderston Street to Jane Street—Aberdeen Bill's tattoo parlor, Persevere, had been situated under the rumble of the trains—there was little or no evidence of the "old tenements" Alice had described to Jack. (In her childhood, these were mostly small shops with flats above them, "meeting the minimum standards of comfort and safety"—or so she'd said.) But only the railway arches remained, and these were used as car garages; a Volkswagen repair place was prominent among them.

The apartments were newer here than the shabby late-nineteenth-century buildings along much of Leith Walk—not the "old tenements" Alice had deplored, but sheltered housing for the elderly. Built in the late seventies—according to Rory, "for widows and widowers."

Jack couldn't find the cinema house, which his mom had maintained was "within a stone's throw of Persevere." But Rory remembered where the local cinema had been—it was now a bingo parlor called The Mecca.

Elsewhere on Leith Walk, there were convenience stores, which Rory called "corner shops." While Leith Walk appeared largely residential, there were pubs, and places serving carry-out food, and the ever-present video stores. Young people seemed to live here, many Asians among them.

Alice had once spoken of her excitement upon first seeing the Leith Central Station, when she was a child, but the former station was now the Central Bar, where Jack's sister played her wooden flute. Rory said that strippers had performed there as recently as the late seventies or early eighties. It was midafternoon when Jack looked inside the Central; there were no strippers. The jukebox was playing Frank Sinatra's "My Way." Smoke blurred the tiled walls and the long mirrors and half concealed the high Victorian ceiling, which was heavily patterned.

At the intersection of Constitution Street and Bernard Street, there was a bank on the corner and what looked like a shipping agency. Jack and Rory crossed a bridge over the Water of Leith and ran into Dock Place. Jack remembered the song his mom sang, if only when she was drunk or stoned—the song he'd first heard her sing in Amsterdam. It was his mom's mantra, he'd thought at the time—to never be a whore.

> Oh, I'll never be a kittie
> or a cookie
> or a tail.
> The one place worse than
> Dock Place
> is the Port o' Leith jail.
> No, I'll never be a kittie,
> of one true thing I'm sure—
> I won't end up on Dock Place
> and I'll never be a hure.

Jack's Scottish accent needed practice, but he sang the song to Rory, who said he'd never heard it before. As for Dock Place, it didn't look like such a bad place to end up—not to Jack, not anymore. (The "hures," if they'd ever been there, had moved on.)

Rory drove Jack back to the Balmoral, where he had a late-afternoon nap. He slept for only two or three hours, but it was enough to shake the jet lag. After dinner at the hotel, he walked out on Princes Street and asked the doorman to recommend a good pub in Leith. Jack didn't want to drink, but he felt like sipping a beer in the unnameable atmosphere of his mother's birthplace. (Maybe he was pretending to be his grandfather Aberdeen Bill.)

The doorman recommended two places; they were both on Constitution Street, very near each other. Jack took a taxi and asked the driver to wait—he was sure he wouldn't be long. The Port o' Leith, where he went first, was small and crowded; it was a very mixed bar. There were the obvious regulars—locals, old standbys—and sailors off the docks, and young students having their first glass. (The legal age was eighteen, which appeared to Jack to mean sixteen.)

The ceiling was a mosaic of flags; on the walls, there were ribbons from sailors' hats and life preservers from ships. There was a KEEP LEITH sign on the mirror. The barmaid explained to Jack that this was a political issue—in response to an unpopular plan to rename Leith "North Edinburgh."

Jack declined the offered bar snacks—something called "pork scratchings" among them—and sipped a Scottish oatmeal stout.

Farther down Constitution Street was a cavernous Victorian pub called Nobles Bar; it was as empty as The Port o' Leith had been crowded, but even with the mob from The Port o' Leith, Nobles would have seemed empty by comparison. There were no women in the bar, and fewer than half a dozen unfortunate-looking men—squinty eyes, pasty complexions, noses of all sorts. Jack deliberated between ordering a Newcastle Brown Ale and something called Black Douglas; it didn't really matter, since he knew he would finish neither. Jack Burns couldn't remember the last time he'd been in a bar and no one had recognized him; now, on the same night, he'd been in *two*.

Back at the Balmoral, Jack had a mineral water at the bar, where they were playing Bob Dylan's "Lay, Lady, Lay." The old song, which he'd once liked, took Jack by surprise. He'd been saying good-bye to his mother, never suspecting that nothing in Edinburgh, the city of her birth, would resurrect her—not the way Bob Dylan could bring her back to him every time.

"Are you here for the Festival, Mr. Burns?" the bartender asked.

"Actually, my mother was born here," he told the man. "I just spent a little time in her old neighborhood, in Leith. And my sister lives here. I'm meeting her tomorrow." Jack *didn't* say, "For the first time!"

He had arranged to meet Heather the next morning in a coffee shop called Elephants and Bagels on Nicolson Square. This was less than a ten-minute walk from his hotel, and very near her office at the university. The music department offices and practice rooms were in Alison House on Nicolson Square.

Jack walked along North Bridge, over the train yards for British Rail. He passed the big glass building on Nicolson Street, the Festival Theatre, and turned right into Nicolson

Square. He was early, as usual. In Elephants and Bagels, Jack sat at a table near the door and ordered a mug of coffee. An advertisement for the coffee shop said: THE BEST HANGOVER CURE IN EDINBURGH.

The walls were painted a bright yellow. There were plants in the windows, and a glass case filled with elephant figurines—carved stone, painted wood, ceramic, and porcelain elephants. A large, round support column was covered with children's drawings—birds, trees, *more* elephants. The coffee shop had the educational yet whimsical atmosphere of a kindergarten classroom.

When Heather came in the shop, Jack didn't at first see how she resembled him. She had short blond hair, like her German mother, but her brown eyes and sharp facial features were Jack's, or William's, and she was both lean and compact—as small and fit as a jockey. Her tortoiseshell eyeglasses were almond-shaped; she was as nearsighted as her mother had been, she explained, but she refused to wear contacts. She hated the feeling of something in her eyes. She was waiting to be a little older before trying the new laser surgery. (She told Jack all this before she sat down.)

They had shaken hands, not kissed. She ordered tea, not coffee. "You look just like him," she said. "I mean you look less like Jack Burns than I thought you would, and more like our dad."

"I can't wait to see him," he told her.

"You *have* to wait," she said.

"It's just an expression," Jack explained. They were both nervous.

She talked about her five roommates. She was moving out soon, with one other girl. Two of her flatmates directed a non-smoking clinic; they were vegans who believed that everything with a spiky shape attracted bad energy. Heather had started a small cactus garden in the kitchen area, but this had to go—"too many spikes." The vegans had also beseeched the landlord to remove the weather vane from the top of the apartment building. *My sister is living with lunatics!* Jack was thinking.

Jack explained that he was selling his house in Santa Monica, but that he had no idea where he wanted to live.

Heather knew he was registered at the Balmoral as Harry Mocco; she wondered why. Jack wanted to know what she taught at the university. (She taught five courses—historical and theoretical music classes, mostly to beginners, and keyboard skills.)

"Our department is all old men!" Heather said good-naturedly.

Jack thought that his sister was a pretty girl with glasses; she had an air of academic aloofness or detachment about her. She wore little or no makeup, but an attractive linen skirt with a fitted T-shirt and sensible-looking walking shoes.

Jack asked to see where she worked and where she lived. Heather moved her fingers all the while they were walking, as if she were unconsciously playing a piano or an organ.

The music practice rooms in the basement of Alison House were like prison cells. They were small cubicles, poorly ventilated; the walls were a dirty, pea-soup green, and the floors were a hideous orange linoleum. The lighting, which was adequate, was of a fluorescent variety that Heather said was bad for your sanity.

Jack thought that the word *sanity* might lead them into a conversation about their dad, but Jack and Heather were experiencing the equivalent of a first date. (They needed to get through an unbearable amount of trivia before the more serious subjects could emerge.)

The lecture room in Alison House was more pleasant than the practice rooms. The large windows let in lots of natural light, although the view was a limited one—of an old stone building. There were two pianos and a small organ in the room, but when Jack asked Heather to play something for him, she just shook her head and directed him to a narrow, twisting staircase, which led to her office. Jack got the feeling that she wanted him to go ahead of her, up the stairs.

"Can we talk about him?" he asked her. "Maybe we could begin with the arthritis, if that's an easy part to talk about."

She stared at the blue carpet on her office floor, her fingers seemingly searching for the right keys on a keyboard only she could see; she plucked at her skirt. The cream-colored walls had a spackled, unsmooth finish. There were two desks—the larger one with a computer on it, the smaller with a German dictionary. The stereo equipment was probably worth more than everything else in the office, including the small piano; there were more CDs than books on the bookshelves, and a bulletin board with a sepia photograph of Brahms tacked to it. There was also a postcard pinned to the bulletin board—a color photo of a very old-looking pianoforte, the kind of thing you'd find in a museum of musical history. A friend might have sent her the postcard—her Irish boyfriend, perhaps—or maybe William had sent it to her, if William was capable of sending a postcard.

"I want to get to know you a little at a time," Heather said, still staring at the rug. She had Jack's thin lips; her upper lip was a small, straight line.

"It's a tight space, but nice," Jack said, meaning her office.

"I don't need more space—I need more time," she told him. "The summer is good—no teaching, and I can get a lot of research done. In the school year, Easter is about the only time I have to do my writing."

Jack nodded, glancing at the photo of Brahms—as if Brahms had understood what Heather meant. (Jack hadn't a clue.)

Heather turned out the lights in her office. "You go first," she said, before they started down the stairs. Maybe she found it easier to talk when he couldn't look at her. "Daddy hides his hands, or he wears gloves, because of the deformities. The disfiguration of osteoarthritic joints is quite noticeable—not just a gnarling of the knuckles but actual bumps. They're called Heberden's nodes."

"Where are the bumps?" Jack asked, descending the stairs ahead of her.

"At the far knuckles of his fingers—that junction between the middle bone of the finger and the little bone at the tip. But his hands don't look as deformed as he imagines they do; it's mainly how his hands hurt when he plays."

"Can't he stop playing?" Jack asked.

"He goes completely insane if he doesn't play," Heather said. "Of course he also wears gloves because he feels cold."

"Some people with full-body tattoos feel cold," Jack told her.

"No kidding," his sister said. (He assumed that she got the sarcasm from her German mother.)

They walked through a parking lot, past more university buildings, down Charles Street to George Square. Heather was a fast walker; even when they were side by side, she wouldn't look at Jack when she talked. "The arthritis has affected his playing for more than fifteen years," she said. "The disease involves degeneration of cartilage and what they call hypertrophy—overgrowth of the bones of the joint. For a pianist or an organist, there's a wear-

and-tear factor. The pain of osteoarthritis is increased by activity, relieved by rest. The more he plays, the more it hurts. But the pain makes him feel warm." She smiled at this. "He likes that about it."

"There must be medication for it," Jack said.

"He's tried all the nonsteroidal anti-inflammatory drugs—they upset his stomach. He's like you—he doesn't eat. You don't eat, do you?"

"He's thin, you mean?"

"To put it mildly," Heather said. They had passed some tents for the Festival and were walking through the Meadows—a large park, the paths lined with cherry trees. A woman with a tennis racquet was hitting a ball for her dog to fetch.

"Where are we going?" Jack asked his sister.

"You said you wanted to see where I lived."

They passed Bruntsfield Links, a small golf course where a young man (without a golf ball) was practicing his swing; the fields, Heather told Jack matter-of-factly, had been an open mass grave during the plague.

"Daddy takes glucosamine sulfate, a supplement—it comes mixed with chondroitin, which is shark cartilage. He thinks this helps," she said, in a way that implied she didn't believe it did anything at all. "And he puts his hands in melted paraffin, which he mixes with olive oil. The hot wax dries on his hands. He makes quite a mess when he picks the wax off, but he seems to enjoy doing that. It fits right in with his obsessive-compulsive disorder."

"His what?"

"We're not talking about the mental part, not yet," his sister told him. "He puts his hands in ice water, too—for as long as he can stand it. This is a bit masochistic for someone who feels cold most of the time, but the hot wax and the ice water work—at least they give him some temporary relief."

It was a warm, windy day, but the way Heather walked—with her head down, her arms swinging, and her shoulders rolling forward—you would have thought that they were marching into a gale.

"All the years I was growing up, Daddy told me every day that he loved you as much as he loved me," Heather said, still not looking at Jack. "Because he never got to be with you, he said that every minute he was with me, he loved me twice as much. He said he had to love me enough for two people."

Her fingers were playing on an imaginary keyboard of air; there was no way for Jack to follow the music in his sister's head. "Naturally, I hated you," Heather said. "If he had to love me enough for two people, because of how much he missed you, I interpreted this to mean that he loved you *more*. But that's what kids do, isn't it?" She stopped suddenly, looking at Jack. Without waiting for an answer, she said: "We're here—my street, my building." She folded her arms across her small breasts, as if they'd been arguing.

"You don't *still* hate me, do you?" he asked her.

"That's a work-in-progress, Jack."

The street was busy—lots of small shops, a fair amount of traffic. Her apartment building was five or six stories tall— a wrought-iron fence surrounding it, a bright-red door. There were tiled walls in the foyer, a wood-and-iron banister, a stone staircase.

"You go first," Heather said, pointing up the stairs.

Jack wondered if she was superstitious about stairs. He went up three flights before he turned to look at her. "Keep going," she told him. "No woman in her right mind would want Jack Burns watching her go up or down stairs. I would be so self-conscious, I would probably trip and fall."

"Why?" he asked her.

"I would be wondering how I compare to all the beautiful women you've seen—from behind and otherwise," Heather said.

"Is the elevator broken?" Jack asked.

"There's no lift," she said. "It's a fifth-floor walk-up. Lots of high ceilings in Edinburgh—high ceilings mean long flights of stairs."

The colors in the hallway were warm but basic—mauve, cream, mahogany. The flat itself had the high ceilings Heather had mentioned, and brightly painted walls; the living room was red, the kitchen yellow. The only indication of the five roommates was the two stoves and two refrigerators in the kitchen. Everything was clean and neat—as it would have to be, to make living with five roommates tolerable. Jack didn't ask how many bathrooms were in the flat. (There couldn't have been enough for *five* roommates.)

Heather's room—with a desk and a lot of bookshelves and a queen-size bed—had mulberry-colored walls and giant windows overlooking Bruntsfield Gardens. The books were mostly fiction, and—as at her office at the university—there were more CDs than books, and some serious-looking stereo equipment. There was a VCR and a DVD player, and a television facing the bed. Jack saw some of his films among the DVDs and videotapes on her bedside table.

"I watch you when I can't fall asleep," his sister said. "Sometimes without the sound."

"Because of the roommates?" he asked.

She shrugged. "It doesn't matter to them if the sound is on or off," she said. "It's because I know all your lines by heart, and sometimes I feel like saying them."

There was nowhere to sit—only the one desk chair or the bed. It was basically a dormitory room, only larger and prettier.

"You can sit on the bed," Heather said. "I'll make some tea."

On her desk was a framed photograph of a young-looking William Burns playing the organ with Heather-as-a-little-girl in his lap. When Jack sat down on the bed, Heather handed him a leather photo album. "The pictures are reasonably self-explanatory," she said, leaving him alone in her room.

She was kind to have left him alone; she must have known he'd not seen many photographs of their father and would prefer seeing so much of him, so suddenly, by himself.

The album was chronological. Barbara Steiner was small and blond, but fuller in the face than her daughter—not nearly as pretty. Heather's good looks came from William. He had kept his long hair—Miss Wurtz would have been pleased—and he got thinner as he grew older. There were many more pictures of him with Heather—as a little girl, and as a teenager—than there were of Heather with her mother, or of William Burns with Barbara Steiner. Of course it was Heather's album, and she must have selected which photos to put in it.

She seemed to be most fond of the photographs from those father-and-daughter ski trips; postcards from Wengen and Lech and Zermatt were intermingled with photos of Heather and William on skis. (A cold sport for someone who was inclined to feel cold, Jack thought, but William Burns looked comfortable in ski clothes—or else he was so happy to be skiing with his daughter that the feeling warmed him.)

There was nothing complaining about Heather's mother's expressions in any of the photographs, nor could you tell that she'd once had a wonderful singing voice. There *was* something overposed about her—especially in the photos when she was wearing a wig—and then she simply disappeared without a trace. Jack turned a page in the album and Barbara Steiner was gone. He knew exactly when he had passed the moment of her death; all the photographs from that point forward were of Heather and her dad, just the two of them, or one or the other alone.

There had been concert brochures attached to the earlier pages, but from the time Heather appeared to be twelve or thirteen, there had been no more concerts for William Burns.

Jack recognized the interior of the Central Bar, where—in addition to Heather playing her wooden flute—there were photos of William playing a piano-type instrument, both alone and with his daughter accompanying him on her flute. It was some kind of electric keyboard—a synthesizer, Jack thought it was called—and from the look on William's and Heather's faces, Jack doubted they were playing anything classical.

Jack knew why his father appeared to be overdressed in many of the photos—that is, too warmly dressed for the season. (William often felt cold, except when he was skiing.) But even in those summer-vacation snapshots, when William was on a beach in a bathing suit, his tattoos were not very clear or distinguishable from one another. Music, when it's too small to see in detail, looks like handwriting—especially to someone like Jack, who couldn't read music.

Jack was ashamed he'd told Claudia that he *never* wanted children—"not till the day I discover that my dad has been a loving father to a child, or children, he *didn't* leave," was how he'd put it to her.

Well, Jack held the evidence of that in his lap—Heather's photo album was a record of her love for their dad and William's love for her. Jack had finished the album, and had composed himself sufficiently to be making his way through the pictures a second time, when Heather came back to her room with the tea. She sat down beside him on the bed.

"There are some places where you removed photos, or they fell out of the album by themselves," he said to her.

"Old boyfriends. I removed them," she said.

Jack hadn't seen anyone who could have been the Irish

boyfriend; he got the impression that the boyfriend was clearly less than the love of her life, but he didn't ask.

He turned to the photos of Heather and William Burns playing their instruments at the Central. "I went there yesterday, to have a look at where you play your flute," he said.

"I know. A friend saw you. How come you didn't ask me to go with you?"

"I was looking around Leith, mostly at places I remembered hearing about from my mother," Jack explained.

He turned to the end pages of the album, where their father was wearing gloves. "What's *wrong* with him?" Jack asked. "I mean the mental part, not the arthritis."

Heather tilted her head; it rested on Jack's shoulder. He held her hand in one hand, his teacup in the other. The album lay open on his lap, with the man who looked so much like Heather and Jack looking up at them. "I want you to hear the Father Willis in Old St. Paul's," Heather said. "I want to play something for you, just to prepare you."

They went on sitting together; Jack sipped his tea. With her head on his shoulder, it would have been awkward for Heather to sip hers. "Don't you want to drink your tea?" he asked.

"I want to do exactly what I'm doing," Heather told him. "I want to never take my head off your shoulder. I want to hug you and kiss you—and beat you with both fists, in your face. I want to tell you every bad thing that ever happened to me—especially those things I wish I could have talked to you about, when they happened. I want to describe every boyfriend you might have saved me from."

"You can do all of that," Jack told her.

"I'll just do this, for now," she said. "You want everything to happen too fast."

"What is he obsessive-compulsive *about*?" Jack asked.

She squeezed his hand and shook her head against his shoulder. She'd had to sell the flat William had lived in—where she'd grown up, in Marchmont. "It's a big student area, but some lecturers live there, too," Heather said. It would have been perfect if she could have stayed there, but she'd had to sell the flat and find a less expensive place.

"To pay for the sanatorium?" he asked. Heather nodded her head against him. Most of her things, and all of William's, were in storage. "Why don't I buy you a flat of your own?" Jack said.

She took her head off his shoulder and looked at him. "You can't *buy* me," she said. "Well, actually, I suppose you *can*. But it wouldn't be right. I don't want you to do *everything* for me—just help me with *him*."

"I *will*, but you haven't told me what to do," he said.

She sipped her tea. She'd not let go of his hand, which she pulled into her lap and examined more closely. "You have his small hands, but his fingers are longer. You don't have an organist's hands," she said. She held up her fingers to Jack's, palm to palm; hers were longer. "Every inch of his body is tattooed," she began, still looking at their hands pressed together. "Even the tops of his feet, even his toes."

"Even his *hands*?" Jack asked.

"No, not his hands, not his face or neck, and not his penis," she said.

"You've seen his penis, or did he *tell* you it wasn't tattooed?" Jack asked her.

"You'd be surprised how many people have seen Daddy's penis," Heather said, smiling. "I'm sure you'll get to see it, too—it's bound to happen."

She had put together a smaller photo album for Jack; it was about the size of a paperback novel, with some of the same photos from the larger album or slightly different angles of those moments in time. The smaller album had no pictures of her mother—only of Heather and William. Jack and Heather sat looking at the pictures, drinking their tea.

"I could learn to ski," Jack said. "Then we could all ski together."

"Then you could ski with *me*, Jack. Daddy's skiing days are over."

"He can't ski anymore?"

"The first thing you'll think when you see him is that there's nothing wrong with him—that he's just a little eccentric, or something," his sister said. She took off her glasses and put her face so close to Jack's that their noses touched. "Without my glasses, I have to be this close to you to see you clearly," Heather said. She pulled slowly back from him, but only about six or eight inches. "I lose you about here," she said, putting her glasses back on. "Well, when you meet him, he'll make you believe that you could take him to Los Angeles—where you would have a great time together. You'll think I'm cruel or stupid for sending him away, but he needs to be taken care of and they know how to do it. Don't think *you* can take care of him. If I can't take care of him—and I *can't*—you can't take care of him, either. You may not think so at first, but he's where he belongs."

"Okay," Jack said. He took her glasses off and put his face close to hers, their noses touching. "Keep looking at me," he told her. "I believe you."

"I've seen close-ups of you half my life," she said, smiling.

"I can't look at you enough, Heather."

She ran her hand through her hair, wiping her lips with the back of her other hand. Jack recognized the gesture. It was the way he'd removed his wig and wiped the mauve lip gloss off his lips with the back of his ski glove in *My Last Hitchhiker*. In a near-perfect imitation of Jack's voice, Heather said: "You probably thought I was a girl, right?"

"That's pretty good," he told her, looking into her brown eyes.

"This isn't a very safe place to stop," Heather said, just the way he'd said it in *My Last Hitchhiker*. "I'm sorry for the trouble, but I catch more rides as a girl," she went on. "I try not to buy my own dinner," Heather said, with a shrug; she had Jack's shrug down pat, too.

"How about Melody in *The Tour Guide*?" he asked her.

Heather cleared her throat. "It's a good job to lose," she said perfectly.

"How about Johnny-as-a-hooker in *Normal and Nice*?" (*No girl can get that right,* Jack was thinking.)

"There's something you should know," his sister said, in that hooker's husky voice. "Lester Billings has checked out. I'm afraid he's really left his room a *mess*."

"Put your glasses back on," Jack told her, getting up from the bed. He went to her closet and opened the door. Jack picked out a salmon-pink camisole and held it up by the hanger, against his chest.

"Boy, I'll bet this looks great on you," Heather said, just the way Jack-as-a-thief had said it to Jessica Lee.

He hung up the camisole in her closet, and they went into the kitchen and washed and dried their teacups and put them away in the cupboard. To someone like Jack, the five-roommates idea was unthinkable.

"It must be like living on a ship," he said to Heather.

"I'm moving out soon," she told him, laughing.

They walked back the way they had come, through the Meadows. Jack carried the small photo album in one hand, although Heather had volunteered to carry it in her backpack.

Just before they got to George Square, they saw an old man with snow-white hair playing a guitar and whistling. He was always there, every day, Heather told Jack—even in the winter. The old man was often there at eight o'clock in the morning and would stay the whole day.

"Is he *crazy*?" Jack asked her.

"*Crazy* is a relative word," his sister said.

She talked about playing squash, which she seemed to take very seriously. (The music department had a squash team, and she was one of the better players on it.) She also spoke of "a plague of urban seagulls."

"*Urban* seagulls?" Jack said.

"They're all over Edinburgh—they attacked one man so badly, he had to go to hospital!" Heather told him.

They came along South Bridge to where it intersected with the Royal Mile. Jack was not aware that he had looked the wrong way, but as they started to cross the street, Heather took his hand and spoke sharply to him: "Look *right,* Jack. I don't want to lose you."

"I don't want to lose *you*," he told her.

"I mean crossing the street," she said.

Jack doubted that he could have found Old St. Paul's without a map and some detailed directions. The church was built into a steep hill between the Royal Mile and Jeffrey Street, where the main entrance was. There was a side entrance off Carruber's Close, a narrow alley—and an even narrower alley called North Gray's Close, where there was no entrance to the church.

Jack began to tell Heather the story his mom had told him. One night, shortly before midnight, William was playing the organ in Old St. Paul's—a so-called organ marathon, a twenty-four-hour concert, with a different organist playing every hour or half hour—and their dad's playing had roused a drunk sleeping in one of the narrow alleys alongside the church. The foul-mouthed down-and-out had complained about the sound of the organ.

That was as far as Jack got before Heather said: "I know the story. The drunk said something like 'that fucking racket—that fucking bloody fuck of a fucking organ making a sound that would wake the fucking dead.' Isn't that the story?"

"Yes, something like that," Jack said.

"I'll play that piece for you," Heather told him. "You can't hear much outside the walls of this church. Either the story is exaggerated, or that drunk was asleep in a *pew*. Not even Boellmann's Toccata could wake a drunk in Carruber's or North Gray's Close."

While the side door to Old St. Paul's, on Carruber's Close, was locked, the front entrance on Jeffrey Street was open. The church was empty, but the oil lamps by the altar were lit. They were always lit, Heather told Jack—even when she played the organ very late at night. "It's a bit spooky here at night," she confessed. "But you have to practice playing in the dark."

"Why?" he asked her.

"Lots of interesting things begin in darkness," his sister told him. "The Easter vigil service, for example. You can learn to play in the dark, provided you've memorized the music."

From the nave of the church, looking toward the high altar, the organ pipes stood nearly as tall as the stained-glass windows. The church was not vast, but dark and contained. One had no sense of the season outside, and—except for the muted light that made its way through the stained-glass windows and portals— no real sense of day or night, either.

Heather saw Jack looking at the Latin inscription on the altar. As Mr. Ramsey had observed, Jack struggled with Latin.

VENITE

EXULTEMUS

DOMINO

" 'Come let us praise the Lord,' " his sister said.

"Oh, right," he said.

"You'll get used to it," she told him.

Heather crossed herself at the altar and took off her backpack. Jack sat on one end of the bench beside her.

"I'll play something softer for you later," Heather said, "but Boellmann's Toccata isn't supposed to be quiet. And when you hear *him* play it, it'll be louder. A different church," she said softly, shaking her head.

Jack wasn't prepared for the way her hands pounced on the

keyboard, transforming her. It was the loudest, most strident piece of music he'd ever heard inside a church. As the new chords marched forth, the old chords kept reverberating; the organ bench trembled under them. It was the soundtrack to a vampire movie—a Gothic chase scene.

"Jesus!" Jack said, forgetting he was in a church.

"That's the idea," Heather said; she had stopped playing, but Old St. Paul's was still reverberating. "Now go outside and tell me if you can hear it." She began the Boellmann again; it made his heart race to hear it.

Jack went out the Jeffrey Street door to the church and walked up North Gray's Close, toward the Royal Mile. The alley was dirty and smelled of urine and beer; there were broken pieces of glass where bottles had been smashed against the church, and empty cigarette packages and chewing-gum wrappers were littered everywhere. Halfway up the alley, Jack pressed his ear to the stone wall of the church; he could barely hear the Boellmann, just enough to follow the tune.

On the Royal Mile, you couldn't hear the organ at all—probably because of the traffic, or the other street sounds—and in Carruber's Close, either a restaurant's air conditioner or a kitchen's exhaust fan made too much noise in the alley for the toccata to be followable. The organ was a distant, intermittent murmur. But when Jack went back inside Old St. Paul's, the sound of the Father Willis was deafening. His sister was really putting herself into it.

As Heather said, the story about the drunk had been exaggerated—or the down-and-out must have been sleeping in a pew when the Boellmann came crashing down on him. The more important part of the story, Heather decided, was that William Burns had played the toccata so loudly that *everyone* inside the church—including Alice and the organist who was waiting his turn to play—had been forced to flee from the nave and stand outside in the rain.

"It was one of Daddy's bipolar moments," Jack's sister said. "I think that's what the story is really about. He drove your mother out in the rain, so to speak—didn't he?"

"He's bipolar?" Jack asked.

"No, he's obsessive-compulsive," Heather said, "but he has his bipolar moments. Don't *you,* Jack?"

"I suppose so," he said.

Heather was playing more softly now—she had moved on from the Boellmann. "This is from an aria in Handel's *Solomon*," she said, as softly as she was playing.

"Do you have bipolar moments, too?" Jack asked her.

"The desire to never leave your side, the desire to never see you again," his sister said. "The desire to see your face asleep on the pillow beside my face, and to see your eyes open in the morning when I lie next to you—just watching you, waiting for you to wake up. I'm not talking about *sex*."

"I know," he told her.

"The desire to live with you, to never be separated from you again," Heather went on.

"I get it," he said.

"The constant wish that I never knew of your existence, and that our father had never said a word to me about my having a brother—this in tandem with the desire to never see another Jack Burns movie, and that every scene in every film you were ever in, which I have committed to memory, would vanish from my mind as if those movies had never been made."

She had not stopped playing, but her pace had quickened. The organ's volume was increasing, too; Heather was almost shouting to be heard over the reverberations.

"We just need to spend more time together," Jack told her.

She brought both hands down on the keyboard, which made a harsh, discordant sound. She slid toward her brother on the organ bench and threw her arms around his neck, hugging him to her.

"If you see him once, you have to keep seeing him, Jack. You can't suddenly appear in his life and then go away again. He loves you," Heather said. "If you love him back, I'll love you, too. If you can't bear to be with him, I'll despise you forever."

"That's pretty clear," he told her.

She pushed herself away from him so violently that Jack thought she was going to hit him. "If you're *not* Billy Rainbow, don't give me his lines," she snapped.

"Okay," he said, holding his arms out to her. When she let him take her in his arms, he kissed her cheek.

"No, not like that—that's not how you kiss your sister," Heather said. "You should kiss me on the lips, but not the way you kiss a girl—not with your lips parted. Like *this*," she said, kissing him—her dry lips brushing Jack's, their lips tightly closed.

Who would have thought that Jack Burns could ever love kissing someone as chastely as that? But he was thirty-eight and had never kissed a sister.

They spent the night together in Jack's suite at the Balmoral. They ordered dinner from room service and watched a bad movie on television. In the backpack, Heather had brought her toothbrush and an extra-large T-shirt, which she wore as a nightgown, and a change of clothes for the morning. They would be getting up early, she'd warned Jack.

She had planned everything, including the reenactment of what she'd told Jack in Old St. Paul's: that desire to see his face asleep on the pillow beside her face, and to see his eyes open in the morning when she was lying next to him—just watching him, waiting for him to wake up.

Heather told Jack that the Irish boyfriend was no one special; the love of her life, so far, had been one of her professors in Belfast. She'd known he was married, but he told her he was leaving his wife; he left Heather instead.

Jack told his sister about Mrs. Machado—and Mrs. Adkins, and Leah Rosen, and Mrs. Stackpole. (They were the early casualties; they were among the first to mark him and disappoint him in himself.) He told Heather about Emma and Mrs. Oastler, and Claudia and her daughter—and all the rest. Even that crazy woman in Benedict Canyon—the one who was driven mad by the screams and moans of the Manson murder victims whenever the Santa Anas were blowing.

Heather told Jack that she'd lost her virginity to one of William's music students, someone who was in university when she was still in secondary school. As she put it: "We had comparable keyboard skills at the time, but I'm much better than he is now."

Jack told Heather that, for the past five years, Dr. García had been the most important woman in his life.

Heather said that she was spending almost as much time improving her German as she was playing the organ—or the piano, or her wooden flute. She'd spoken a child's German with her mother, and had originally studied German because of her interest in Brahms; now she had an additional reason to learn the language. If she taught in Edinburgh for another two or three years, her teaching credentials would greatly enhance her résumé. By apprenticing herself to John Kitchen at Old St. Paul's, she was already a better organist. In two or three years' time, if her German was good enough, she could move to Zurich and get a job there.

"Why Zurich?" Jack asked.

"Well, there's a university, and a music conservatory, and a disproportionate number of churches for such a small city—in other words, *lots* of organs. And then I could visit Daddy every day, instead of only once a month or every six weeks."

"He's in *Zurich*?"

"I never said he was in Edinburgh, Jack. I just said you had to see me first."

Jack propped himself up in bed on his elbows and looked down at his sister's face on the pillow; she was smiling up at him, her golden hair pushed back from her forehead and tucked behind her small ears. She cupped the back of Jack's neck and pulled his face closer to hers. He'd forgotten that she couldn't be more than a few inches away from his face—not if she wanted to see him clearly without her glasses.

"So we're going to Zurich?" he asked her.

"You're going alone, this trip," Heather told him. "You should see him alone, the first time."

"How can you afford to go to Zurich once a month, or every six weeks?" he asked her. "You should let me pay for that."

"The sanatorium costs three hundred and fifty thousand Swiss francs a year—that's two hundred and twelve thousand U.S. dollars—to keep him in the private section of the clinic. If you pay for that, I can pay for my own travel." She pulled his head down to the pillow beside her. "If you want to buy me a flat, why don't you buy something big enough for both of us—in Zurich," she suggested. "I was born in Edinburgh. I don't need your help here."

"I'll buy a whole house in Zurich!" Jack said.

"You want everything to happen too fast," she reminded him.

He didn't know when or if she slept. When Jack woke up, Heather was staring at him—her large brown eyes close to Jack's, her small nose almost touching his face. "You have four gray hairs," she told him.

"Let me see if you have any," he said, but Heather's hair was golden to its roots. "No, not yet, you don't."

"It's because I'm pretty happy, all things considered," she

said. "Look at me. I just slept with a movie star, and it was no big deal—'no biggie,' as Billy Rainbow would say."

"It was a big deal to me," Jack told her.

Heather gave him a hug. "Well, *actually,* it was a big deal to me, too—a *very* big deal."

While Jack was in the shower, Heather took his plane tickets down to the concierge's desk in the lobby; she booked his flight to Zurich, with a connection out of Amsterdam, and his return trip to L.A. from Zurich.

She also arranged for his first meeting, later that afternoon, with a team of doctors at the Sanatorium Kilchberg; there were five doctors and one professor, in all. Heather gave Jack a brochure of the buildings and grounds of the clinic, which overlooked Lake Zurich. Kilchberg was on the western shore of the lake—in Zurich, they called it the *left* shore—about fifteen minutes by car from the center of the city.

So Jack was leaving for Switzerland as soon as they finished their breakfast; Heather had reserved a room for him at the Hotel zum Storchen in Zurich.

"You might like the Baur au Lac better," she told him, "but the Storchen is nice, and it's on the river."

"I'm sure it will be fine," he said.

"The doctors are excellent—I think you'll like them," Heather said. She had stopped looking at him. They were in the breakfast café at the Balmoral—a few tired tourists, families with small children. Jack could tell that Heather was nervous again, as they both had been when they'd first met. Jack tried to hold her hand, but she wouldn't let him.

"People will think we're sleeping together—I mean *really* sleeping together," she told him. "Being with you in public takes a little getting used to, you know."

"You'll get used to it," he said.

"Just don't let anything happen to you—don't do anything *stupid,*" Heather blurted out.

"Can you read lips?" Jack asked her.

"Jack, *please* don't do anything stupid," Heather said. She looked cross, in no mood to play games.

Jack moved his lips without making a sound, forming the words as slowly and clearly as he could. "I have a sister, and I love her," he told her, without actually saying it out loud.

"You want everything to happen too fast," Heather said again, but Jack could tell that she'd understood him. "We should go to the airport now," she announced, looking at her watch.

In the taxi, she seemed distracted—lost in thought. She was once again not looking at him when she said: "When you've seen him, I mean *after* you've spent a little time together, please call me."

"Of course," Jack said.

"All you have to say is, 'I love him.' You don't have to say anything more, but don't you dare say anything less," his sister said. Her fingers were playing Boellmann's Toccata, or something equally strident, on her tensed thighs.

"You can relax about me, Heather," he told her.

"Can *you* read lips?" she asked, still not looking at him.

"All actors can read lips," Jack said. But Heather just stared out the window, not saying anything—her lips as tightly closed as when she'd given him his first kiss as a brother.

It was still early in the morning when they got to the airport. Jack hadn't expected Heather to come to the airport with him, much less accompany him inside; now she led him to the check-in counter. Obviously, it was a trip she was familiar with.

"I hope you like Switzerland," Heather said, scuffing her feet.

She was wearing blue jeans and a darker-colored T-shirt than she'd worn the day before; with the backpack and her cropped hair, she looked more like a university student than a junior lecturer. If you didn't notice her constantly moving fingers, you could discern nothing musical about her. She was simply a small, pretty girl—made more serious-looking by her glasses and the determined way in which she walked.

Near the metal-detection equipment, where a security guard had a look at Jack's passport and examined his carry-on bag, there was a Plexiglas barrier that kept Heather from accompanying her brother to his gate. Jack wanted to kiss her, but she kept her face turned away from him.

"I'm not saying good-bye to you, Jack. Don't you dare say good-bye to me," she said, still scuffing her feet.

"Okay," he said.

With the Plexiglas barrier between them, Jack could still see her as he started walking toward his gate. He kept turning to look at her; Jack stopped walking away from her when he saw she was finally looking at him. Heather was pointing to her heart, and her lips were moving—slowly, without uttering a word.

"I have a brother, and I love him," Jack's sister was saying, although he couldn't hear a syllable.

"I have a sister, and I love her," he said back to her, not making a sound.

Other people were getting between them. Jack had momentarily lost sight of Heather when two young women stepped up close to him, and the black girl with the diamond nose-stud said, "You aren't Jack Burns, are you? You simply *can't* be, right?"

"I'll bet you anything he isn't," her companion said. She was a white girl with sunburned shoulders in a tank top; her nose was peeling a little.

They were Americans, college kids on their way home from a summer trip to Europe—or so Jack guessed. When he looked for his sister, she was gone.

"Yes, I'm Jack Burns," he said to the girls. (Jack couldn't have explained it, but he felt that—for the first time in his life—he really *was* Jack Burns!) "You're right—it's me. I actually am Jack Burns."

For some reason, he was delighted that they'd recognized him. But the young women's expressions radiated disbelief; they were as suddenly indifferent to Jack as they had at first seemed curious about him.

"Good try," the white girl told him sarcastically. "You're not going to fool anyone into thinking you're Jack Burns—not that way."

"Not *what* way?" he asked her.

"Not by being so *normal*," the young white woman said.

"Not by looking like you're *happy* or something," the young black woman said.

"But I *am* Jack Burns," he told them unconvincingly.

"Let me tell you—you're awful at this," the white girl said. "And you're too old to get away with it."

"Since when was Jack Burns so *sincere* or something?" the black girl asked him.

"Let me hear you do *noir*," the white girl said.

"Let me hear you say *one* thing Jack Burns ever said," the black girl challenged him.

Where was Heather when he needed her? Jack was thinking. Where was his dad, who allegedly had Jack Burns down pat?

The girls were walking away. Jack untucked his T-shirt and held the bottom hem up to his chest, as if he were holding up a dress on a hanger. "Boy, I'll bet this looks great on you," he said, in no way resembling the thief whom Jessica Lee caught messing around in her closet.

"Give it up!" the young white woman called to him.

"You know what?" the black girl asked Jack, her diamond nose-stud winking in the bright airport light. "If the *real* Jack Burns ever saw you, he wouldn't look twice!"

"It's a good job to lose!" Jack called after them, but they kept walking. He was so bad as Melody, even Wild Bill Vanvleck would have made him repeat the line.

The point was—he wasn't *acting*. It was as if he'd forgotten how! Jack still knew his lines, but he was out of character. He had a sister, and he loved her; she'd said she loved him, too. Jack had *stopped* acting. He was just Jack Burns—the *real* Jack Burns at last.

38

Zurich

When that last unmarked area of skin has been tattooed and their bodies become a completed notebook, full-body types don't all react the same way.

Alice had maintained that some full-bodies simply started tattooing over their old tattoos. But if you keep doing that, the skin eventually turns as dark as night—the designs become indiscernible. Jack once saw a client of his mother's whose arms, from his wrists to his armpits, were an unvarying black; it was as if he'd been burned. In less radical instances, twice-tattooed skin appears to be covered with curved, abstract figures—the body wrapped in a skin-tight paisley shawl.

But for other full-bodies, the completed notebook amounts to a sacred text; it is unthinkable to tattoo over a single tattoo, or even part of one. Most of William's tattoos had been done by accomplished tattoo artists, but even his bad or clumsy tattoos were of music that mattered to him. Both the music and the words had marked more than his skin for life.

Heather had told Jack that their father had no gaps of bare skin between his tattoos. The toccatas and hymns, the preludes and fugues, overlapped one another like loose pages of music on a cluttered desk; every inch of the desk itself was covered.

On William's back, Heather said, where he would have had to make a considerable effort to see it, was a sailing ship—a distant view of the stern. The ship was pulling away from shore, parting the waves of music that all but engulfed it. The full sails were also marked with music, but the ship was so far from shore that the notes were unreadable. It was their father's Herbert Hoffmann, but Heather said it was "almost lost on a vast horizon of music"—a Sailor's Grave or a Last Port tattoo, but smaller than Jack had imagined and completely surrounded by *sound*.

The piece from his dad's favorite Easter hymn, "Christ the Lord Is Risen Today," was partially covered by Walther's "Wachet auf, ruft uns die Stimme"—the top two staffs beginning where the alleluia chorus to "Christ the Lord" *should* have been. Elsewhere, Bach's mystical adoration for Christmas ("Jesu, meine Freude") was overlapped by Balbastre's "Joseph est bien marié"; the word *Largo,* above the top staff of the Bach, was half hidden.

Both the familiar words and music in the chorus ("For Unto Us a Child Is Born") from Handel's *Messiah* ran into Widor's Toccata—from the Fifth Symphony, Op. 42—with even the *Op. 42* being part of the tattoo, which included the composer's full name. It surprised Jack to hear that the composers' names were always tattooed in full—not *Bach* and *Widor,* but *Johann Sebastian Bach* and *Charles-Marie Widor*—and the names were tattooed not in cursive but in an italic font, which (over time, and subject to fading) was increasingly hard to read.

Time and fading had taken their toll on some of William's other tattoos as well—among them John Stanley's Trumpet Voluntary, his Trumpet Tune in D, which marked Jack's father's chest in the area of his right lung, where the bottom or pedal staff (indicating the notes you played with your feet) had faded almost entirely from view, as had the word *Vivo* above the first staff of Alain's "Litanies," but not the quotation from Alain on William's buttocks. The French was tattooed in cursive on the left cheek of his bum, the English translation on the right; they would fade from Jack's father's skin more slowly than youth itself.

Reason has reached its limit.
Only belief keeps rising.

Reason had reached its limit in William Burns, too. Evidently that was what Jack's sister had been saying. Every inch of their dad's body was a statement; each of his tattoos existed for a reason. But now there was no room left, except for belief.

"You'll know what I mean when you see him naked, and you will," Heather had told Jack.

"I *will*?"

His sister wouldn't elaborate. To say that Jack was apprehensive when his plane landed in Zurich would be an understatement.

The Swiss, Heather had forewarned him, made a point of remembering your name; they expected you to remember theirs. As an actor, Jack had confidence in his memorization skills—but his abilities, not only as an actor, were severely tested by the task at hand. The cast of characters he would be meeting at the Sanatorium Kilchberg had daunting names, and their specific roles (like his father's tattoos) were interconnected—at times overlapping.

With Heather's help, Jack had studied these five doctors and one professor; he'd tried to imagine them, as best he could, before their first meeting. But he was not acting in this performance—*they* were. They were in charge of his dad; it was Jack's job to learn from them.

The head of the clinic, Professor Lionel Ritter, was German. His English was good, Heather had told Jack, and the professor took such pains to be diplomatic that one forgave him for being a bit repetitious. He was always neatly but casually dressed—a trim, fit-looking man who took pride in the Sanatorium Kilchberg's 136-year history as a private psychiatric clinic. (Jack had envisioned Professor Ritter as looking a little like David Niven dressed for tennis.)

The deputy medical director, Dr. Klaus Horvath, was Austrian. Heather had described him as a handsome, hearty-looking man—an athlete, most notably a skier. William enjoyed talking about skiing with Dr. Horvath, who had great faith in the psychological benefits of the Sanatorium Kilchberg's *jogging* program—in which William Burns, at sixty-four, was an enthusiastic participant. Jack had some difficulty seeing his dad as a fully tattooed *jogger,* and he could imagine Dr. Horvath only with Arnold Schwarzenegger's accent—possibly in combination with Arnold's cheerful, optimistic disposition, which was best on display in that comedy where the former bodybuilder is supposed to be Danny DeVito's twin.

The second German, Dr. Manfred Berger, was a neurologist and psychiatrist; he was head of gerontopsychiatry at the clinic. According to Jack's sister, their dad was a *youthful*-looking sixty-four-year-old—not yet a candidate for Dr. Berger's principal area of expertise. Dr. Berger, in Heather's view, was "a fact man"—little was given to speculation.

Upon his arrival in Kilchberg, William Burns had exhibited the kind of mood swings common to a bipolar disorder. (Euphoric moments, which crashed in anger; he would be high for a whole week, with no apparent need of sleep, but this would end in a stuporous depression.) As it turned out, William was *not* bipolar. But before this diagnosis could be made, Dr. Berger had insisted on a neurological examination.

Dr. Berger, Heather had informed Jack, was a man who liked to rule things out. Did William have a brain tumor? Dr. Berger doubted that William did, but what was most dire simply had to be ruled out. Something called temporal lobe epilepsy could also present itself with mood swings not unlike William's—in particular, his flights of euphoria and his clamorous episodes of anger. But William Burns was not afflicted with temporal lobe epilepsy, nor was he bipolar.

There was no aura of discouragement about Dr. Berger; it was as if he expected to be proved wrong, but he was not one to be deterred by failure.

Jack refrained from jumping to the conclusion that the most interesting psychiatric ailments were not easily diagnosed or cured. After all, upon seeing his dad's full-body tattoos, who *wouldn't* have guessed that William Burns was obsessive-compulsive? And that it physically hurt him to play the organ, yet it drove him completely insane *not* to play—well, who wouldn't have been depressed and subject to mood swings about that?

But Dr. Berger was "a fact man"; his role was ruling things out, not zeroing in. He was an essential member of the team, Jack's sister said—if not the easiest of the doctors to like. Although a German, he had adopted the Swiss habit of shaking hands zealously for prolonged periods of time, which Dr. Berger did with what Heather called "a competitive vengeance."

This guy confused Jack in advance; someone vaguely resembling Gene Hackman or Tommy Lee Jones came to mind. (As it would turn out, Jack couldn't have been more wrong.)

The rest of the team members were women. In Heather's view, they were the most formidable. Dr. Regula Huber, for example— she was head of internal medicine. She was a Swiss woman in her forties, blond and tireless. There were many elderly patients at the Sanatorium Kilchberg; an internist was kept busy there.

Most of the older patients had been committed by family members; these patients were not free to leave.

Heather told Jack that she'd had many meetings with Professor Ritter and the team of doctors looking after William; on every occasion, Dr. Huber's pager had gone off and she'd left to attend to an emergency. In the case of William Burns, who'd been committed to the psychiatric clinic by his daughter but had stayed of his own volition—happily, without protest—Dr. Huber, like Dr. Berger, first wanted to *rule out* a few things.

Did their father have an underfunctioning thyroid gland? (This could make you feel cold.) No, he did not. Did he have Curschmann-Steinert disease? Thankfully, no! And why was William Burns so *thin*? Because he didn't drink, and he thought that overeating was a sin; their dad kept to a strict diet, as if he were a fashion model or a jockey or an *actor*. (Like father, like son!)

It was Dr. Huber who treated, or attempted to treat, their dad's arthritis. She'd recently tried a new class of nonsteroidal anti-inflammatory drugs that were supposed to be more stomach-friendly than the older anti-inflammatories, but they gave William so much gastric irritation that Dr. Huber instead applied a conventional drug topically.

And it was Dr. Huber who took the view that some so-called placebos *worked*—that is, if the patients thought they did. She raised no objection to William's fondness for hot wax and ice water, or his taking glucosamine with the extract of shark cartilage. William Burns also wore copper bracelets, except when he was playing the piano or the organ.

Heather liked Dr. Huber, whom she called a pragmatist. (Jack thought inexplicably of Frances McDormand, one of his favorite actresses.)

The third German, Dr. Ruth von Rohr, had a curiously incomplete title—she was some sort of department head. Of *what* department was unclear, or perhaps deliberately not stated. She was a tall, striking woman with a wild mane of tawny hair that had a silver streak, which Heather said looked natural but couldn't have been. Dr. von Rohr had a regal, head-of-department demeanor. She usually let others speak first, although her impatience was demonstrable and calculated. She knew when to sigh, and she had considerable dexterity in her long fingers—in which she frequently twirled a pencil, almost never dropping it. When she spoke—usually last, and often dismissively—she turned her prominent jaw and angular face in profile to her audience, as if her head were about to be embossed on a coin.

"On the other hand," she liked to begin, as if she were head of the *doubt* department—as if the silver streak in her hair were a banner to that gray area of every argument. It was Dr. von Rohr's job to make the others feel less sure of themselves; she liked opening the door to those things that could *never* be ruled out.

Everyone at the Sanatorium Kilchberg thought that William Burns was a model patient. He *had* to be happy there; after all, he'd not once attempted to run away. He rarely complained about the place, or his treatment. Yes, he occasionally gave in to his demons; he had his rages and irrational moments, but he had far fewer of these episodes in Kilchberg than he'd experienced in the outside world. Jack's sister maintained that their father was where he belonged; remarkably, William seemed to accept this. (Hadn't he positively *embraced* the idea? Dr. Horvath had enthusiastically asked.)

Yet it was Dr. von Rohr's department to raise the *un*asked question. "Isn't hospitalism a second disease for some of our patients?" she would inquire, just when everything seemed fine. "What if we're *too* successful with William? In a sense, if he's happy here, haven't we made him *dependent* on us and this place? I'm just asking," she was fond of saying, once a seed of doubt had been sown.

It was Dr. von Rohr who would not stop asking *why* William often felt cold. "But what *triggers* this?" she frequently inquired. (At the Sanatorium Kilchberg, Jack's sister had told him, the word *triggers* was hugely popular.)

It was Dr. von Rohr who suggested that William Burns might have a narcissistic personality, or even a narcissistic personality disorder. He shampooed his gray-white, hippie-length hair daily; he was very particular about which conditioner and gel he used. (He'd had a fit—a running-naked-and-screaming episode—because his hair dryer had blown a fuse!) And then there was the meticulousness of his tattoos, not to mention how protective he was of them. For the most part, he concealed them. He wore long-sleeved shirts, buttoned at the throat, and long pants, and shoes with socks—even in the summer. (Yet when William Burns *wanted* you to see his tattoos, he showed you *all* of them.)

It was not uncommon among schizophrenics to wear long

pants and long-sleeved shirts; they felt so unprotected. But Jack and Heather's dad wasn't diagnosed with schizophrenia. The issue Dr. von Rohr had raised was William's fastidiousness, his vanity—the way he watched his weight, for example. "Isn't William an impossible perfectionist?" Dr. von Rohr would say. "I'm just asking."

The osteoarthritis was the reason William Burns could no longer play the organ professionally—hence his early retirement, which had precipitated his mental decline. But he could have kept teaching—even keyboard skills, albeit to a limited degree, Heather had said. William certainly could have continued to teach musical theory and musical history; yet he had retired totally, and perhaps unnecessarily.

"A failure to live up to previous standards or expectations, which can also lead to someone's early retirement, is a signature feature of a narcissistic personality, isn't it?" Dr. von Rohr had said to the team. (The "I'm-just-asking" part was always implied, if not stated.)

"A piece of work," Jack's sister had called her. "A head-of-department type, if I ever met one."

Trying to envision Dr. Ruth von Rohr, Jack thought of Dr. García, who was a good listener, and who raised a lot of unasked questions. Boy, was Dr. García ever a head-of-department type!

Last, but not least, was the sixth member of the team—an attractive young woman, authoritative but self-contained—Dr. Anna-Elisabeth Krauer-Poppe. She always wore a long, starched, hospital-white lab coat—seemingly *not* to assert her medical credentials but to protect her fashionable clothes. (She was Swiss but her clothes weren't, Heather had claimed.)

Like the two unambiguous hyphens in her name, Dr. Anna-Elisabeth Krauer-Poppe was as perfectly assembled as a *Vogue* model in Paris or Milan; she seemed too chic to be Swiss, although she'd been born in Zurich and her knowledge of the city was as irreproachable as her command of her field. Dr. Krauer-Poppe was head of medication at the Sanatorium Kilchberg, where it was everyone's opinion that she knew her prescriptions as well as she knew her clothes.

It had frustrated her that William was not treatable with those new (and so-called stomach-friendly) nonsteroidal anti-inflammatory drugs and that he could tolerate only the topical solution. His hot-wax routine made Dr. Krauer-Poppe cringe, not least for what a mess William made of what he was wearing when he picked the dried wax off. And to see him with his hands plunged in ice water must have made Dr. Krauer-Poppe want to change her entire ensemble. (As for the copper bracelets, she couldn't even look at them; the glucosamine, particularly the extract of shark cartilage, she dismissed as "a folk remedy.")

But when it came to William Burns's obsessive-compulsive disorder, Dr. Krauer-Poppe had prescribed an antidepressant; the medication had had a calming effect. She'd tried two drugs, in fact, Zoloft and Seropram. Each one had its merits, both being selective serotonin reuptake inhibitors used to treat depression.

As for the side effects, Heather had said, their father had tolerated the dizziness, the dry mouth, the drowsiness, and the loss of appetite; the latter was the most persistent problem. (But William was so devoted to being thin that his loss of appetite probably thrilled him.) He'd complained about occasionally painful and prolonged erections, and there were certain "changes"—which Heather had not specified to Jack—in William's sexual interest and ability. But over time, William Burns appeared to have tolerated—or at least accepted—these side effects, too.

The drugs did not impair William's motor functions. His keyboard skills were unaffected by the antidepressants. The music he'd committed to memory remained intact, and he could sight-read music as quickly as ever.

Dr. Krauer-Poppe had worried that William's ability to concentrate might suffer, and he admitted to being more easily distracted; it took him longer to memorize new pieces, and he occasionally complained of fatigue, which was unusual for him. He was used to having more energy, he said; on the other hand, he was sleeping better.

Dr. Krauer-Poppe had also watched William closely for signs that prolonged administration of the drugs might make him feel indifferent or less emotional; this was sometimes referred to as "the poop-out syndrome," Dr. Krauer-Poppe said, but William had shown no such signs. According to Heather, their father was indifferent to nothing or no one—and he was, "regrettably," as emotional as ever.

Dr. Krauer-Poppe thought that, in William's case, the antidepressants had been successful. She noted that his sexual "changes" did not include impotence, another possible side effect; she called the drugs "an acceptable trade-off." (Dr. Krauer-

Poppe was a woman at ease with hyphens, apparently. No one like her came to Jack's mind.)

Jack couldn't wait to meet these people, and he was relieved that he was meeting them first—that is, before he would see his father.

William Burns had been twenty-five when he met Jack's mom; he'd been twenty-six when Jack was born. At that age, how long would Jack have stayed married to anyone? And what if he'd fathered a child at twenty-six, when he and Emma were burning the candle at both ends in L.A.? What kind of dad would he have been?

Jack knew what Dr. García's answer would be—her less-than-one-word response: "Hmm."

Jack checked into the Hotel zum Storchen on the Weinplatz. His room overlooked the Limmat, where he watched a tour boat drifting past the hotel's riverfront café. He was staying in the Old Town—cobblestoned streets, many of them for pedestrians only. The church bells seemed to ring every quarter hour, as if Zurich were obsessed with the passage of time. He shaved and dressed for dinner, although it was still only midafternoon.

In the taxi—at the airport, in Kloten—Jack had considered going directly to the Sanatorium Kilchberg, but his appointment with Professor Ritter and the others wasn't until late afternoon. He didn't want to risk running into his father before he'd met with the doctors. Although he wasn't expecting Jack, William would surely have recognized him.

Jack had questioned the clinic's decision not to tell his father that he was coming, but both Heather and the psychiatric team had thought it best if Jack's dad didn't know; if he knew, he would be too anxious.

Nor had Dr. Krauer-Poppe recommended upping William's dosage of the Zoloft or the Seropram, whether they told him about Jack or not. Even Dr. von Rohr had refrained from making her usual, on-the-other-hand argument; in fact, she said that giving William more antidepressants might make him near-catatonic or completely out of it for his son's first visit.

Dr. Horvath, the hearty Austrian and deputy medical director who often jogged with William, had told his patient to expect "a special visitor." Since it was too soon for more visiting time with his daughter, William was probably expecting someone from the world of music—a musician from out of town, a fellow organist making a guest appearance at a concert or playing in a church in Zurich. (Such distinguished visitors occasionally came to Kilchberg to pay William Burns their respects.)

Jack had asked the concierge at the Storchen to recommend a restaurant within walking distance of the hotel. William would be allowed to have dinner with his son, although Professor Ritter or one (or more) of the doctors at the clinic would accompany him.

"Better make the reservation for three or four people," Heather had told Jack. "They won't want you to take him away from the sanatorium alone. And believe me, Jack, you wouldn't *want* to do that—not the first time, anyway."

The concierge—a laconic man with a hoe-shaped scar on his forehead, probably from hitting a car's windshield with his head—had booked a table for four at the Kronenhalle. It was an excellent restaurant and a pleasant walk, the concierge had assured Jack. "And because you're Jack Burns, I actually managed to get you a table—even on such short notice."

Jack went outside the hotel and watched the swans and ducks swimming in the Limmat. He checked the time on his watch against the clock towers of the two most imposing churches he could see from the Weinplatz, where he could also see a taxi stand. It was only a ten- or fifteen-minute drive to Kilchberg from the Storchen, and he didn't want to be early *or* late.

Jack felt guilty about how much he had blamed his mother for everything. If she'd been alive and Jack were waiting to meet *her* for the first time, he believed he would have felt as nervous and excited about that as he felt about meeting his dad. It suddenly seemed ridiculous that he couldn't forgive her; in fact, Jack missed her. He wished he could call her, but what would he have said?

It was Miss Wurtz who was waiting to hear from him; it was Caroline Jack *should* have called. But all he could think about was talking to his mother.

"Hi, Mom—it's me," he wanted to tell her. "I'm not doing this to hurt you, but I'm on my way to meet my dad—after all these years! Got any advice?"

Jack took a taxi out of town, along the shore of Lake Zurich—a nice drive, the road passing close to the lake the whole way. A theater festival had set up tents along the waterfront. It was sunny and warm, but the air was dry—mountain air, not nearly as humid as it had been in Edinburgh. There were these sudden, dramatic moments when Jack could see the Alps beyond the lake. Everything was clean, almost sparkling. (Even the taxi.)

Kilchberg was a community of about seven thousand. Because of all the sailboats on the lake—and the stately homes, many with gardens—the town somewhat resembled a resort. Jack's taxi driver told him that the right shore of the lake was slightly more prosperous. "Europeans prefer to face west," he said. Kilchberg, on the left shore of Lake Zurich, faced east.

But Jack thought Kilchberg was charming. There was even a small vineyard, or at least what looked like a working farm, and the sanatorium was high on a hill overlooking the lake, with a spectacular view of Zurich to the north; to the south were the Alps.

"Most of the patients take the bus from the Bürkliplatz—there's a sanatorium stop in Kilchberg," his taxi driver told him. "I mean the patients who are free to come and go," he added—looking warily at Jack in the rearview mirror, as if he were certain that Jack had *escaped*. "You might want to consider taking the bus next time—the number *one-sixty-one* bus, if you can remember that."

The driver was Middle Eastern, or possibly Turkish. (He'd mentioned "Europeans" with evident distaste.) His English was much better than his German, which was as clumsy and halting as Jack's. When they'd first tried to speak German together, Jack's driver had quickly switched to English instead. Jack wondered why he'd been mistaken for a patient at the clinic; the taxi driver was not much of a moviegoer, maybe.

Not so the preternaturally thin young woman in running shoes and a jogging suit who greeted Jack in what he thought was the main entrance to the hospital part of the clinic. There was a waiting room and a reception desk, where the young woman was pacing back and forth when Jack came in. A fitness expert, he assumed—perhaps she was the nurse in charge of physical therapy, or a kind of personal trainer to the patients. *She should put on a little weight,* Jack was thinking; *one can take the athletic-looking thing too far.*

"Stop!" she said, in English—pointing to him. (There was

no one else in the entranceway or the waiting room; there was no one behind the reception desk, either.) Jack stopped.

A nurse appeared, emerging hurriedly from a corridor. "Pamela, *er ist harmlos,*" the nurse said.

"Of course he's harmless—he's not real," Pamela said. "The medication is working. You don't have to worry about that. I *know* he's harmless—I *know* he's not real."

She sounded American, yet the nurse had spoken to her in German and she'd understood the nurse. Maybe the thin young woman had been a patient in the clinic for a long time—long enough to learn German, Jack speculated.

"*Es tut mir leid,*" the nurse said to Jack, leading the young American woman away. ("I'm sorry," she said.)

"You should speak English to him," Pamela said. "If he were real, he would speak English—like in his movies."

"I have an appointment with Professor Ritter!" Jack called after the nurse.

"*Ich bin gleich wieder da!*" the nurse called back to him. ("I'm coming right back!")

They had disappeared down the corridor, but Jack could still hear the too-thin patient—her voice rising. It registered as a kind of insanity on his part that he'd mistaken her for someone who worked at the place.

"They don't usually *say* anything," Pamela was telling the nurse. "Normally they just *appear*—they don't talk, too. God, maybe the medication *isn't* working!"

"*Das macht nichts,*" the nurse told her, gently. ("It doesn't matter," she said.)

Jack Burns was a movie star in a psychiatric clinic; not surprisingly, the first patient who saw him thought he was a talking hallucination. (Not a bad definition for an actor, Dr. García might have said.)

When the nurse came back, she was shaking her head and talking to herself—almost inaudibly and in German. Were it not for her uniform, and if he hadn't seen her before, Jack would have believed that her self-absorbed muttering marked *her* as a patient. She was a short woman in her fifties, stout and brusque with curly gray hair—a former blonde, Jack guessed.

"It's funny that the first person *you,* of all people, should meet here is our *only* American," the nurse said. "Bleibel," she added, vigorously shaking Jack's hand.

"Excuse me?"

"Waltraut Bleibel—I'm telling you my *name*!"

"Oh. Jack Burns."

"I know. Professor Ritter is expecting you. We've *all* been expecting you, except for poor Pamela."

They went outside the building and walked across a patio; there was a sculpture garden and a shallow pond with lily pads. (*Nothing anyone can drown in,* Jack was thinking.) Most of the buildings had big windows, some of them with those black silhouettes of birds painted on the glass. "Our anti-bird birds," Nurse Bleibel said, with a wave of her hand. "You must have them in America."

"I guess I went to the wrong building," Jack told her.

"A women's ward wouldn't be *my* first choice for you," Nurse Bleibel said.

The grounds were beautifully maintained. There were a dozen or more people walking on the paths; others sat on benches, facing the lake. (No one *looked* insane.) There must have been a hundred sailboats on the lake.

"I take William shopping for clothes, on occasion," the nurse informed Jack. "I've never known a man who likes shopping for clothes as much as your father does. When he has to try things on, he can be difficult. Mirrors are a challenge—*triggers,* Dr. von Rohr would call them. But William is very well behaved with me. No fooling around, generally speaking."

They went into what appeared to be an office building, although there were cooking smells; maybe a cafeteria, or the clinic's dining hall, was in the building. Jack followed the nurse upstairs, noting that she took two steps at a time; for a short woman in a skirt, this required robust determination. (He could easily imagine his dad not being inclined to *fool around* with Waltraut Bleibel.)

They found Professor Ritter in a conference room; he was sitting all alone, at the head of a long table, making notes on a pad of paper. He jumped to his feet when Nurse Bleibel brought Jack into the room. A wiry man with a strong handshake, he looked a little like David Niven, but he wasn't dressed for tennis. His pleated khaki trousers had sharply pressed pant legs; his tan loafers looked newly shined; he wore a dark-green short-sleeved shirt.

"Ah, you found us!" the professor cried.

"*Er hat zuerst* Pamela *gefunden*," Nurse Bleibel said. ("He found Pamela first," she told him.)

"Poor Pamela," Professor Ritter replied.

"*Das macht nichts.* Pamela just thinks it's her medication again," the nurse said as she was leaving.

"*Merci vielmal,* Waltraut!" Professor Ritter called after her— a bilingual "Many thanks!" in French and Swiss German.

"*Bitte, bitte,*" Nurse Bleibel said, waving her hand as she had at the anti-bird birds on the big windows.

"Waltraut has a brother, Hugo, who takes your father to town—on occasion," Professor Ritter told Jack. "But Hugo doesn't take William shopping for *clothes.* Waltraut does a better job of that."

"She mentioned something about mirrors," Jack said. "She called them *triggers,* or she said one of the doctors did."

"Ah, yes—we'll get to that!" Professor Ritter said. He was a man used to running a meeting. He was friendly but precise; he left no doubt about who was in charge.

When the others filed into the conference room, Jack wondered where they'd been waiting. On what signal, which he hadn't detected, had they been summoned forth? They even seemed to know where to sit—as if there were place cards on the bare table, where they put their almost identical pads of paper. They'd come prepared; they looked positively *poised* to take notes. But first Jack had to endure the obligatory handshakes— which, in each case, went on a shake or two too long. And each doctor, as if their meeting had been rehearsed, had a characteristic little something to say.

"*Grüss Gott!*" Dr. Horvath, the hearty Austrian, cried— pumping Jack's hand up and down.

"Your on-screen persona may precede you, Mr. Burns," Dr. Berger (the neurologist and fact man) said, "but when I look at you, I see a young William first of all!"

"On the other hand," Dr. von Rohr said, in her head-of-department way, "should we presume that we know Jack Burns because of our familiarity with William? I'm just asking."

Dr. Huber had a look at her pager while shaking Jack's hand. "I'm just an internist," she was telling him. "You know, a *normal* doctor." Then her pager beeped and she dropped Jack's hand as suddenly as she might have if he had died. She went to the telephone in the room, which was just inside the door. "Huber *hier,*" she said into the phone. There was a pause before she added: "*Ja, aber nicht jetzt.*" ("Yes, but not now.")

Jack was sure that he recognized Dr. Anna-Elisabeth Krauer-Poppe—the fashion model who protected her clothes in a long, starched, hospital-white lab coat. She looked knowingly into his eyes, as if trying to discern what medication he was on—or what she thought he *should* be taking. "You have your father's good hair," she observed, "if not—I *hope* not—his obsessions."

"I'm not tattooed," Jack told her, shaking her hand.

"There are other ways to be marked for life," Dr. on-the-other-hand von Rohr remarked.

"Not all obsessions are unhealthy, Ruth," Dr. Huber, the internist, said. "It would appear that Mr. Burns adheres to his father's diet. Don't we all approve of how William watches his weight?"

"His *narcissism,* do you mean?" Dr. von Rohr asked, in her head-of-department way.

"Are *you* seeing a psychiatrist, Mr. Burns?" Dr. Berger, the fact man, asked. "Or can we rule that out?"

"Actually, I *have* been seeing someone," Jack told them.

"Ah, well . . ." Professor Ritter said.

"It's nothing to be ashamed of!" the deputy medical director, Dr. Horvath, shouted.

"I don't suppose you have any indication of osteoarthritis," Dr. Huber said. "You're too young," she added. "Mind you, I'm not saying that William's arthritic hands are anything *you* need to worry about. You don't play the piano or the organ, do you?"

"No. And I don't have any symptoms of arthritis," Jack said.

"Any *medications* we should know about?" Dr. Krauer-Poppe asked. "I don't mean for arthritis."

"No, nothing," he told her. She looked somewhat surprised, or disappointed—Jack couldn't be sure.

"Now, now!" Professor Ritter called out, clapping his hands. "We should let Jack ask *us* some questions!"

The doctors cheerfully tolerated Professor Ritter, Jack could tell. The professor was head of the clinic, after all—and he doubtless bore lots of responsibilities of a public-relations kind, which the doctors probably wanted nothing to do with.

"Yes, please—ask us *anything*!" Dr. Horvath, the skier, said.

"In what way are mirrors *triggers*?" Jack asked.

The doctors seemed surprised that he knew about the mirrors—not to mention *triggers*.

"Jack had a conversation with Waltraut, about taking William shopping for clothes," Professor Ritter explained to the others.

"Sometimes, when William sees himself in a mirror, he just looks away—or he hides his face in his hands," Dr. Berger said, sticking to the facts.

"But *other* times," Dr. von Rohr began, "when he catches a glimpse of himself, he wants to see his tattoos."

"*All* of them!" Dr. Horvath cried.

"It might not be the appropriate time and place for such a *detailed* self-examination," Professor Ritter explained, "but William seems not to notice such things. Occasionally, when he starts taking off his clothes, he has already begun a *recitation*."

"A what?" Jack asked.

"His body is a tapestry, which he can recite—both a history of music and a *personal* history," Dr. Huber said. Her pager beeped, and she went back to the phone by the door. "Huber *hier. Noch nicht!*" she said, annoyed. ("Not yet!")

"The problem for someone with your father's meticulousness is that he can never be meticulous *enough*," Professor Ritter told Jack.

"He's proud of his tattoos, but he's very critical of them, too," Dr. Berger said.

"William thinks that some of his tattoos are in the wrong place. He blames himself for a lack of foresight—he has *regrets*," Dr. Horvath elaborated.

"*Other* times," Dr. von Rohr chimed in, "it's a matter of which tattoo should have been closest to his heart."

"But you can have only a limited number of things that are *truly* close to your heart," Dr. Krauer-Poppe interjected. "He has marked his body with what he loves, but he has also recorded his grief. The antidepressants have calmed him, have made him less anxious, have helped him sleep—"

"But they don't do much for the grief," Dr. von Rohr said, bluntly—turning her head-on-a-coin profile to Jack.

"Not enough, anyway," Dr. Krauer-Poppe admitted.

"It might be overwhelming to discuss specific diagnoses right away. For now, let's just say that your father has suffered *losses*," Professor Ritter told Jack. "The Ringhof woman, the German wife, but first of all *you*."

"He is an absurdly *emotional* man," Dr. Berger said, shaking his head—wishing that William Burns were more of a *fact* man, apparently.

"The antidepressants have *helped*—that's all I'm saying," Dr Krauer-Poppe said.

"Keeping him away from mirrors *helps*," Dr. von Rohr remarked in her silver-streaked, head-of-department way.

"Are there other triggers?" Jack asked the team.

"Ah, well . . ." Professor Ritter said. "Maybe Jack should meet his father first?" (The team, Jack could tell, didn't think so.)

"Bach!" Dr. Horvath roared. "Anything by Bach."

"Bach, Buxtehude, Stanley, Widor, Vierne, Dubois, Alain, Dupré—" Dr. Berger recited.

"Handel, Balbastre, Messiaen, Pachelbel, Scheidt—" Dr. von Rohr interrupted.

"And anything to do with Christmas, or Easter—any *hymn*," Dr. Huber added; she was glaring at her pager, as if daring it to go off.

"*Music* is a trigger? Or even the names of certain composers?" Jack asked.

"Music *and* the names of certain composers," Dr. Krauer-Poppe answered.

"And when he plays the piano, or the organ?" Jack asked.

"Ah, well . . ." Professor Ritter said.

"When the pain starts—" Dr. Krauer-Poppe began.

"When his fingers *cramp*—" Dr. Huber interjected.

"When he makes *mistakes*," Dr. von Rohr said, with what sounded like finality—at least in her mind. With almost everything she said, Dr. von Rohr spoke with the emphasis and certainty of a concluding remark—this in tandem with the way, as a tall person, she was always looking down at others. Dr. von Rohr seemed no less tall sitting down. (When he'd shaken her hand, Jack had observed that he came up to her shoulder.)

"Yes, mistakes are triggers," Professor Ritter worriedly agreed.

"William's *meticulousness,* once again," Dr. Berger pointed out.

"*And,* albeit only occasionally, when he sees your *movies,*" Dr. von Rohr said, looking at Jack.

"Particular lines of dialogue, mainly," Professor Ritter said.

"But for the most part, the movies *help* him!" Dr. Krauer-Poppe insisted.

"But *other* times—" Dr. von Rohr started to say.

"Ah, well . . ." Professor Ritter said. "I think Jack should *see* his father, *hear* him play, *talk* to him—"

"In what order?" Dr. Berger asked, perhaps sarcastically; Jack couldn't tell.

Dr. Huber's pager beeped again; she got up from the table and went to the phone by the door. Dr. Krauer-Poppe covered her face with her hands.

"Maybe we should tell Jack a little bit about William's *schedule*?" Professor Ritter asked.

"Talk about *meticulousness*!" Dr. Horvath cried.

"Your father likes to know in advance what he's doing every day," Dr. von Rohr explained.

"Every *hour*!" Dr. Horvath shouted.

"Just tell him the schedule," Dr. Krauer-Poppe said. "Maybe it will help."

"Huber *hier*," Dr. Huber was saying into the phone by the door. "*Ich komme sofort.*" ("I'm coming right away.") She came back to the table. "An emergency," she told Jack, shaking his hand. "*Noch ein Notfall.*" ("Another emergency.") Jack had stood up to shake her hand; all the others stood up, too.

The team and Jack, minus Dr. Huber, prepared to leave the conference room. (Dr. Huber had left in a flash.)

"Wake up, hot wax, ice water, breakfast—" Dr. Horvath was saying as they marched down the stairs. Jack realized that the *recitation* of his dad's schedule had begun.

"Finger exercises in the exercise hall, immediately after breakfast," Dr. Berger explained.

"Finger exercises?" Jack asked.

"What William calls playing the piano for the dance class, because he is blindfolded and plays only the pieces he has memorized," Dr. von Rohr told him.

"Why is he blindfolded?" Jack asked.

"There are mirrors in the exercise hall," Professor Ritter said. "Lots of mirrors. William always wears the blindfold there, or— sometimes, at night—he plays in the dark."

"*Jogging,* after the finger exercises—depending on the weather," Dr. Horvath carried on. "Or sometimes a trip to town, with Hugo."

"We haven't really talked about Hugo," Professor Ritter told the others.

"*Must* we talk about him?" Dr. von Rohr asked. "Maybe not *now*? I'm just asking."

"Sometimes—I mean after the finger exercises—William needs more ice water, doesn't he?" Dr. Berger asked.

"It seems to help," Dr. Krauer-Poppe said with resignation.

"Lunch—I mean *after* the jogging," Dr. Horvath continued.

"Or after the *Hugo* business," Dr. Berger said, shaking his head.

"Not *now,* Manfred!" Dr. von Rohr said.

"More hot wax, after lunch," Dr. Krauer-Poppe noted. "More ice water, too. William often does this while he watches a movie."

"One of *yours,* actually," Dr. Berger told Jack. "A different Jack Burns film every afternoon."

"And another one in the evening!" Dr. Horvath cried. "Always a movie before bed!"

"You're jumping ahead, Klaus," Dr. von Rohr said.

They entered the building with the exercise hall, which was outfitted like a dance studio; barres and mirrors ran the length of the interior walls. A piano, a C. Bechstein, shone a glossy black in the late-afternoon light—like the coat of a well-groomed animal.

"For the finger exercises, both the morning and the afternoon sessions," Dr. Krauer-Poppe said, pointing to the piano. "He plays again after the movie, in the afternoon. This time, not for dancers—it's a yoga class. The music he plays is more atmospheric, softer—like *background* music, you might say. But he's always blindfolded if there's any daylight in the room."

"The finger-cramping can be disturbing to the yoga class," Dr. Berger interjected. "Less so to the dancers, even if William is in obvious pain."

"He *hates* to have to stop playing," Dr. Krauer-Poppe said. "He pushes himself."

"Ah, well . . ." Professor Ritter said. "After the yoga class, we have the ice water ready—and the hot wax, too, if he wants it."

"And the ice water *again,*" Dr. Berger stated; he was making sure that Jack had all the facts, in proper order.

"Calisthenics!" Dr. Horvath continued, waving his arms. "Especially if there's been no jogging. Just some abdominal *crunches,* some *lunges,* some *jumping*!" (Dr. Horvath was demonstrating the *lunges* and the *jumping,* his big feet thudding on the hardwood floor of the exercise hall.)

"We have group therapy three times a week—the patients discuss dealing with their disorders. Your father's German is quite good," Professor Ritter told Jack. "And his concentration is improving."

"Just so long as no one starts humming a tune," Dr. Berger interjected. "William *hates* humming."

"Another trigger?" Jack asked.

"Ah, well . . ." Professor Ritter said.

"We have a movie night, every other Wednesday—in this case, usually *not* a Jack Burns movie," Dr. Berger stated. "Once a week, we have an evening of lotto, which William doesn't like, but he loves the storytelling café—this is when we read stories out loud, or the patients do. And we have a night when our *younger* patients visit the gerontopsychiatric ward. William is very sympathetic to our patients who are growing old."

"Some nights we bring the older patients to the exercise hall, where they like to hear William play the piano in the dark," Dr. von Rohr said.

"I like it, too!" Dr. Horvath cried.

"We have patients with schizophrenic or schizo-affective manifestations," Dr. Krauer-Poppe told Jack. "I mean those who are in a relatively stable remission phase, the ones who have sufficient ability to concentrate. Well, you'd be surprised—the schizophrenics like listening to your father play the piano in the dark, too."

"And the piano-playing seems to soothe our patients who suffer from panic attacks," Dr. Berger said.

"Except for those who suffer from panic attacks in the *dark,*" Dr. von Rohr pointed out. (Jack saw that she was conscious of the light from the windows catching the silver streak in her hair.)

"Are there other patients in Kilchberg who have been committed by a family member—I mean *for life*?" Jack asked.

"Ah, well . . ." Professor Ritter sighed.

"It's highly unusual for a private patient to stay here for a number of years," Dr. Berger said.

"We are expensive," Dr. von Rohr cut in.

"But *worth* it!" Dr. Horvath bellowed. "And William *loves* it here!"

"I'm not concerned about the cost," Jack said. "I was wondering about the long-term effect."

"*Hospitalism,* do you mean?" Dr. von Rohr asked in her just-asking way.

"What exactly is hospitalism?" Jack asked.

"The disease of being in a hospital—a condition *in addition to* your reason for being here, a second disease," Dr. Berger stated, but in such a way that he didn't seem to believe it—as if hospitalism were a speculative illness of the kind Dr. von Rohr was *just asking* about, an almost dreamy disease, which a fact man, like Dr. Berger, generally *ruled out.*

"There's no medication for hospitalism," Dr. Krauer-Poppe said—as if the disease didn't really exist for her, either.

"But William is *happy* here!" Dr. Horvath insisted.

"He's *happier* in St. Peter," Dr. von Rohr corrected Dr. Horvath. "*Die Kirche* St. Peter—the church," she explained to Jack. "Your father plays the organ there—Monday, Wednesday, and Friday morning, at eight o'clock."

"Jack can hear him play tomorrow morning!" Dr. Horvath cried.

"That should be worth the trip—even all the way from Los Angeles," Dr. Berger told Jack.

"One of us should go with Jack—he shouldn't go with William alone," Professor Ritter said.

"William never goes to St. Peter *alone*!" Dr. von Rohr exclaimed.

"They shouldn't go with Hugo, either," Dr. Krauer-Poppe suggested. "One of *us* should go with Jack and William."

"That's what I *meant*!" Professor Ritter said in an exasperated voice.

"I can take them!" Dr. Horvath shouted. "Your father will be excited to play for you!" he told Jack.

"*Too* excited, maybe," Dr. Krauer-Poppe said. "I should go, too—just in case there's a need for medication. A sedative might be in order."

"*Too excited* can be a trigger," Dr. Berger explained.

"*Can* be, usually *isn't*," Dr. von Rohr told Jack.

"Anna-Elisabeth and I will *both* go to St. Peter with them. Nothing can happen that we're not prepared for!" Dr. Horvath said assertively.

"Your father is special to us, Jack. It's a privilege to take care of him," Professor Ritter said.

"It is an *honor* to protect him," Dr. von Rohr countered—in her hairsplitting way.

"And what does he do with Hugo, when they go to town?" Jack asked the team.

Dr. Horvath *jumped* on the floor of the exercise hall. Professor Ritter restrained himself from saying "Ah, well . . ." for once. Dr. Krauer-Poppe emphatically folded her arms across the chest of her lab coat, as if to say there was no medication for what William and Hugo did in town. Dr. von Rohr uncharacteristically covered her face with her hands, as if she momentarily thought she were Dr. Krauer-Poppe.

"Sometimes they just go to a coffeehouse—" Professor Ritter started to say.

"They go to look at women, but they just *look,*" Dr. Horvath maintained.

"Is my father seeing someone?" Jack asked.

"He's not oblivious to women," Dr. Krauer-Poppe said. "And he's very attractive to women; that hasn't changed. Not a few of our patients here are attracted to him, but we discourage relationships of that kind in the clinic—of course."

"Is he still sexually interested or active?" Jack asked.

"Not *here,* we hope!" Dr. Horvath cried.

"I meant in town," Jack said.

"On occasion," Dr. Berger began, in his *factual* way, "Hugo takes your father to see a prostitute."

"Is that safe?" Jack asked Dr. Krauer-Poppe, who (he imagined) might have prescribed some *medication* for it.

"Not if he has sex with the prostitute, but he doesn't," Dr. Krauer-Poppe said.

"These visits are unofficial—that is, we don't *officially* approve of them," Professor Ritter told Jack.

"We just *un*officially approve of them," Dr. von Rohr said; she was back to her head-of-department self, sarcastic and on-the-other-hand to her core.

"He's a physically healthy man!" Dr. Horvath cried. "He *needs* to have sex! Naturally, he shouldn't have sex with anyone here—certainly not with another patient *or* with someone on the staff."

"But you said he *doesn't* have sex," Jack said to Dr. Krauer-Poppe.

"He masturbates when he's with the prostitute," she told Jack. "There's no medication required for that."

"Like a picture of a woman in a magazine, I suppose—only she's a real woman instead of a photograph," Dr. Berger said.

"Like pornography?" Jack asked.

"Ah, well . . ." Professor Ritter said *again*.

"William has those magazines, too," Dr. von Rohr announced disapprovingly.

"The magazines are safe sex, aren't they?" Dr. Krauer-Poppe asked. "And the prostitute is safe, too—the way he sees her."

"I get the picture," Jack told them. "I'm okay about it."

"We believe your sister is okay about it, too," Professor Ritter said. "We're just not *officially* okay about it."

"Is there a logic I'm missing in being *un*officially okay about it?" Dr. von Rohr asked.

Dr. Horvath was doing lunges across the exercise hall, the floor creaking. "*Bitte,* Klaus," Professor Ritter said.

"Does my dad always see the same prostitute, or is it a different woman every time?" Jack asked.

"For those details, perhaps you should ask Hugo," Dr. Berger told him.

"*Must* he meet Hugo? I'm just asking," Dr. von Rohr said. (Dr. Berger was shaking his head.)

"Whether here, in Kilchberg, or in the outside world, we all eventually must meet a *Hugo,*" Professor Ritter said.

"There's no medication for a *Hugo,*" Dr. Krauer-Poppe said.

"*Leider nicht,*" Dr. von Rohr remarked. ("Unfortunately not.")

"Well, unless it's a bad time, I think I'd like to meet my father now," Jack told the team.

"It's a *good* time, actually!" Dr. Horvath cried.

"It's our reading hour. William is a good reader," Dr. Berger said.

"It's our quiet time," Dr. von Rohr said.

"I believe he's reading a biography of Brahms," Dr. Krauer-Poppe said.

"Brahms isn't a trigger?" Jack asked.

"*Reading* about him isn't," Dr. Berger said matter-of-factly.

"Your father has two rooms, plus a bath, in the private section," Professor Ritter told Jack.

"Hence expensive," Dr. von Rohr said.

"I made a dinner reservation for tonight," Jack told them. "I don't know who else wants to come along, but I booked a table for four at the Kronenhalle."

"The *Kronenhalle*!" Dr. Horvath boomed. "You must have the Wiener schnitzel or the bratwurst!"

"There are *mirrors* at the Kronenhalle," Dr. Krauer-Poppe said. "One by each entrance, and another one over the sideboard."

"Surely they are *avoidable*," Professor Ritter said to her.

"The one in the men's room isn't!" Dr. Horvath said.

"Who's going to go with them?" Dr. Berger asked. "I can't—not this evening."

"I can go," Dr. Krauer-Poppe said. "I had a date, but I can break it."

"That would be best, Anna-Elisabeth—in case William needs some medication," Professor Ritter said.

"I'm sure that Hugo is also available," Dr. von Rohr suggested.

"I'd rather not go with Hugo, Ruth," Dr. Krauer-Poppe said. "The Kronenhalle isn't exactly Hugo's sort of place."

"I can't go to the Kronenhalle tonight *and* to St. Peter tomorrow morning!" Dr. Horvath exclaimed.

"Maybe I can go—I'll check my schedule," Professor Ritter said. "Or perhaps Dr. Huber can go."

"It makes sense to go to a restaurant with an *internist*," Dr. Berger remarked. "In case anyone gets sick."

"No one gets sick at the *Kronenhalle*!" Dr. Horvath cried.

"Dr. Huber has too many emergencies," Dr. Krauer-Poppe said. "If she gets called away, I'm alone with William and Jack—*and* the mirrors. Besides, there should be another man—in case William wants to go to the men's room."

"But *I'll* be there," Jack reminded her.

"I mean another man who knows your father," Dr. Krauer-Poppe said.

"I'll check my schedule," Professor Ritter said again.

Dr. von Rohr had a head-of-department look on her face, but she was smiling. The smile was something new to Jack, but the others seemed familiar with it.

"What is it, Ruth?" Dr. Krauer-Poppe asked her colleague.

"You couldn't keep me away from a trip to the Kronenhalle with William and Jack Burns—not in a million years!" she said. "You couldn't keep me *out* of the men's room, not if William went there—not if you tried!"

Dr. Krauer-Poppe covered her face with her hands; there was no medication that could keep Dr. von Rohr away from the Kronenhalle, apparently. (Dr. Berger was shaking his head again.)

"Okay, that settles it," Professor Ritter said uncertainly.

"Anyone but Hugo, I guess," Dr. Krauer-Poppe, who had recovered herself, said philosophically. "Ruth and I will go with them, then."

"I can't tell you how I'm looking forward to it, Anna-Elisabeth," Dr. von Rohr said.

"I think I'd like to go home and get ready for dinner," Dr. Krauer-Poppe announced to Professor Ritter.

"Of course!" the professor said. They all watched Dr. Krauer-Poppe leave the room. She was so beautifully dressed; not even her lab coat looked out of place.

"I can't wait to see what Anna-Elisabeth will *wear* tonight," Dr. von Rohr said, after her colleague had gone. "She's going home to get *dressed,* and I don't mean to change her lab coat!"

"She had a date with her *husband* tonight," Dr. Berger told everyone. "She's probably going home to break her date, in a nice way."

Jack felt sorry that he'd caused Dr. Krauer-Poppe to change her plans. (Dr. von Rohr, on the other hand, seemed pleased to have changed hers.)

"Don't worry!" Dr. Horvath told Jack, pounding his shoulder. "Whatever else happens tonight, you're going to the *Kronenhalle*!"

"I just want to see my father. That's why I came," Jack reminded them.

"We just want to *prepare* you for seeing him," Dr. Berger stated.

Dr. Horvath had stopped pounding Jack's shoulder, but he was massaging the back of Jack's neck with his big, strong hand. "I have a favor to ask you, if you'll indulge me," the Austrian said.

"Of course. What is it?" Jack asked him.

"If you could *say* something—I mean the way Billy Rainbow says it. I know you can do it!" Dr. Horvath urged him.

"No doubt about it," Jack-as-Billy said. (After the episode in the Edinburgh airport, he was relieved he could still *act*.)

"*Wunderschön!*" Dr. Horvath cried. ("Beautiful!")

"How embarrassing, Klaus," Dr. von Rohr said. "I hope you'll forgive me," she said to Jack, "but Billy Rainbow gives me the creeps."

"He's supposed to," Jack told her.

"I must tell you, Jack," Professor Ritter said, "William says that line the exact same way you say it!"

"Your father has made quite a *study* of you," Dr. Berger told him.

"You should prepare yourself, Jack—William knows more about you than you may think," Dr. von Rohr said. (Dr. Horvath had stopped massaging Jack's neck, but Dr. von Rohr had put her arm around Jack's shoulders in a comradely way.)

"Yes, Heather told me—he's memorized all my lines," Jack said.

"I didn't mean only your *movies*, Jack," Dr. von Rohr cautioned him.

"I think that's enough preparation, Ruth," Dr. Berger stated.

"*Ja, der Musiker!*" Dr. Horvath shouted to Jack. ("Yes, the musician!") "It's time for you to meet the musician!"

39

The Musician

There was a serenity to the private section of the Sanatorium Kilchberg, which Jack may have underappreciated on his first visit. (He was not in a serene state of mind.) The building itself, which was white stucco with shutters the same gray-blue color as the lake, looked more like a small hotel than a hospital. His father's third-floor, corner rooms—overlooking the rooftops of Kilchberg—faced the eastern shore of Lake Zurich. The Alps rose in the hazy distance to the south of the lake.

The hospital bed where Jack's father lay reading was cranked to a semireclined position. The bed and the fact that there were no carpets on the noiseless, rubberized floors were the only indications that this private suite was part of an institution—and that the man reading on the bed was in need of care. While the windows were open, and a warm breeze blew off the lake, William was dressed as if it were a brisk fall day—a thick flannel shirt over a white T-shirt, corduroy trousers, and white athletic socks. (If Jack had been dressed that way, he would have been sweating—although it instantly made him feel cold to look at his father.)

The bedroom, which opened into another room—with a couch, and a card table with a couple of straight-backed chairs—was not cluttered with furniture or mementoes. Jack saw only photographs—massive bulletin boards crammed with overlapping snapshots. There were also movie posters hung on the peach-colored walls of both rooms. They were posters of Jack Burns's movies; at a glance, Jack thought that his dad had framed and hung all of them. Jack could see that the surrounding bookshelves displayed a more balanced collection of CDs and DVDs and videocassettes *and* actual books than he'd seen in his sister's office, or in her bedroom.

The team of doctors, together with Professor Ritter and Jack, had entered his father's attractive but modest quarters in the utmost silence. Jack first thought that his dad didn't know they were there. (William had not looked up from his book.) But—as indicated by the door from the corridor, which had been ajar—living in a psychiatric clinic had made Jack's father familiar with intrusions. William was accustomed to doctors and nurses who didn't necessarily knock.

Jack's dad was aware of their presence in his bedroom; he had *deliberately* not looked up from his book. Jack understood that his father was making a point about privacy. William Burns did indeed love the Sanatorium Kilchberg, as the hearty Dr. Horvath had maintained, but that didn't mean he loved everything about it.

"Don't tell me—let me guess," Jack's father said, staring stubbornly into his book. "You've had a meeting; remarkably, you've come to a decision. Oh, what joy—you've sent a *committee* to tell me your most interesting thoughts!" (William was still refusing to look at them—his copper bracelets glowing in the dull late-afternoon light.)

William Burns had spoken with no discernible accent, as if those years in foreign cities and their churches had replaced whatever was once Scottish about him. He certainly didn't sound American, but he didn't sound British, either. It was a European English, spoken in Stockholm and Stuttgart, in Helsinki and Hamburg. It was the unaccented English of hymns, of all voices put to music—from the Citadel Church, the Kastelskirken in Frederikshavn, to the Oude Kerk in Amsterdam.

As for William's sarcasm, Jack realized that his sister, Heather, might not have inherited hers from her German mother, as he'd first thought.

"Don't be childish, William," Dr. von Rohr said.

"You have a special visitor, William," Dr. Berger said.

Jack's father froze; he wasn't reading, but he wouldn't look up from his book.

"Your son, Jack, has come all this way to take you out to dinner!" Professor Ritter cried.

"To the *Kronenhalle*!" Dr. Horvath thundered.

William closed the book and his eyes; it was as if he could see or imagine his son better with his eyes shut. Jack couldn't look at him that way; he looked instead at the photographs on the nearest bulletin board, waiting for his father to open his eyes or speak.

"We'll leave you two alone," Professor Ritter said reluctantly.

Jack had expected to see photographs of himself—chiefly the ones snipped from movie magazines, all the film premieres, the red-carpet crap, and the Academy Awards. But not the personal snapshots, of which there were many. (There were more of Jack than of Heather!)

There he was in one of Miss Wurtz's many *dramatizations* at St. Hilda's. Naturally, he recognized himself as a mail-order bride—that pivotal and blood-soaked performance in Mr. Ramsey's histrionic production. Miss Wurtz and Mr. Ramsey must have taken the pictures. (Jack was pretty sure it was Caroline who had sent his dad the photographs.)

But that didn't explain the photos of Jack with Emma—though Lottie must have taken the ones in Mrs. Wicksteed's kitchen, there were more pictures of Jack with Emma in Mrs. Oastler's house—or the ones of Jack with Chenko in the Bathurst Street gym, or the ones of Jack wrestling at Redding! Had Leslie Oastler sent William photographs? Had Jack's mother relented, if only a little?

But Mrs. Oastler and Jack's mom had never been to *Redding*. Had Coach Clum sent those wrestling pictures to William? There were Exeter wrestling photographs, too; maybe Coach Hudson and Coach Shapiro had also been messengers.

Jack heard the door to the corridor close softly. When he looked at his father on the hospital bed, William's eyes were open and he was smiling. Jack had no idea how long his father had been watching him. Jack had barely glanced at one of the dozen or more bulletin boards; he'd seen only a fraction of the photographs, but enough to know that his dad had surrounded himself with images of Jack's childhood and his school years. (It explained something about Heather's anger toward Jack—namely, that *Jack's* past was more of a visual presence in their father's confined quarters than *hers*.)

"I was afraid you'd forgotten me," his dad said. It was one of Billy Rainbow's lines. Jack had always liked that line, and his father delivered it perfectly.

Jack made a feeble gesture to all the photographs. "I was afraid you'd forgotten *me*!" he blurted out—in his own voice, not Billy Rainbow's.

"My dear boy," his dad said; he patted the bed and Jack sat beside him. "You don't have children of your own; when you do, you'll understand that it's *impossible* to forget them!"

Jack only now noticed his father's gloves. They must have been women's gloves—close-fitting and of such thin material that William could turn the pages of his book as well as if he were bare-handed. The gloves were a light tan, almost skin-colored.

"My hands are so ugly," Jack's father whispered. "They got old before the rest of me."

"Let me see them," Jack said.

William winced once or twice, pulling the gloves off his fingers, but he wouldn't allow Jack to help him. He put his hands in his son's hands; Jack could feel his father trembling a little, as if he were cold. (The room now felt hot to Jack.) The gnarling of his dad's knuckles was so extreme that Jack doubted his father could slide a ring on or off his fingers—William wore no rings. And the bony bumps, Heberden's nodes, which had formed on the far-knuckle joints, disfigured his father's hands more than Jack had anticipated.

"The rest of me is okay, Jack," his dad said. He held one hand on his heart. "Except *here,* on occasion." He put the index finger of his other hand to his temple, as if he were pointing a gun at his head. "And *in here,*" he added, giving Jack a mischievous little smile. "How about you?"

"I'm okay," Jack told him.

It was like looking at himself on a hospital bed, in clothes he would never wear—as if Jack had fallen asleep one night when he was thirty-eight, and had woken up the next day when he was sixty-four.

William Burns was thin in the way that many musicians were. With his long hair and the small-boned, feminine prettiness of his face, he looked more like a rock musician than an organist— more like a lead singer (or one of those skinny, androgynous men with an electric guitar) than "a keyboard man," as Heather had called him.

"Are we really going to the Kronenhalle?" Jack's father asked.

"Yes. What's so special about it?" Jack asked him.

"They have real art on the walls—Picasso, and people like that. James Joyce had his own table there. And the food's good,"

William said. "We're not going with Dr. Horvath, I hope. I like Klaus, but he eats like a farmer!"

"We're going with Dr. von Rohr and Dr. Krauer-Poppe," Jack told him.

"Oh, what joy," William said, as he had before—sarcastically. "They're two of the best-looking shrinks you'll ever see—I'll give them that—but a little of Ruth goes a long way, and Anna-Elisabeth never takes me anywhere without bringing some *medication* along."

Jack was struggling against the feeling that his sister had warned him he would have: his father seemed almost normal to him, or not half as eccentric as he'd expected. William certainly wasn't as wound up as Professor Ritter, or as obstreperous as Dr. Horvath—nor was he a third as intense as Dr. Berger, or Dr. von Rohr, or Dr. Krauer-Poppe. In fact, among the team attending to William Burns, only Dr. Huber had struck Jack as *normal*—and she was an internist, not a psychiatrist. (A *pragmatist,* Heather had called her.)

"You have so many photographs," Jack said to his dad. "Of *me,* I mean."

"Well, yes—of *course*!" William cried. "You should have a look at them. You never knew that some of them were being taken, I'm sure!"

Jack got up from the bed and looked at the bulletin boards, his father following him in his socks—as closely and silently as Jack's shadow.

There were more wrestling photos—too many, Jack thought. Who could have taken them all? There were as many as *ten* of the same match! This was true of one of his matches at Redding and two at Exeter. Jack wasn't aware that he'd had such a devoted admirer at either school. Of course Jack knew that his father had paid the tuition, both at Exeter and at Redding; perhaps William had felt entitled to ask someone to take pictures of Jack wrestling, but *who*?

Jack felt his father's arms around his chest, under his own arms; the long, knobby fingers of William's small hands were interlocked on his son's heart. Jack felt his father kiss the back of his head. "My dear boy!" his dad said. "It was so hard to imagine my son as a *wrestler*! I simply had to see it for myself."

"You saw me wrestle?"

"I promised your mother that I wouldn't make contact with

you. I didn't say I'd never *see* you!" he cried. "Your wrestling matches were public; even if she'd known, and she didn't, she couldn't have kept me away!"

"You *took* some of these photographs?" Jack asked him.

"*Some* of them, of course! Coach Clum was a nice man, if not a very gifted photographer, and Coach Hudson *and* Coach Shapiro—what wonderful people! Your friend Herman Castro is a great kid! You should keep in touch with Herman. I mean, more than you do, Jack. But I took many of the wrestling pictures myself. Yes, I did!" William seemed suddenly irritated that Jack looked so stunned. "Well, I wasn't going to go all that way and *not* take a few pictures!" his father said, with a measure of indignation in his voice. "What a pain in the ass it is, to go to *Maine*—and it's not a whole lot easier to get to New Hampshire."

Jack was thinking that Heather had just been born when he was first wrestling at Redding; William might have traveled to Maine when Barbara was pregnant, or when Heather was an infant. And when William had come to New Hampshire, when Jack was wrestling at Exeter, Heather would have been a little girl—too young to remember those times when her father was away. But had those wrestling trips been difficult for Barbara? Jack wondered. First she'd had cancer; then she was killed by a taxi, and there'd been no more trips.

On one of William's bulletin boards, there was a snapshot of Jack at Hama Sushi—the way he was smiling at the camera, only Emma could have taken the photograph. And another of Jack with Emma in his lap; he remembered Emma taking that one. They were in their first apartment, their half of that rat-eaten duplex in Venice. There was also a photo of Jack dressed for his waiter's job at American Pacific; only Emma could have taken that one, too.

"Emma sent you these?" Jack asked his father.

"I know that Emma could be difficult, at times," his dad replied, "but she was a good friend to you, Jack—loyal and true. I never met her in person—we just talked on the telephone from time to time. Look here!" his dad suddenly cried, pulling Jack to another bulletin board. "Your friend Claudia sent me pictures, too!"

There they were, Claudia and Jack—that summer they did Shakespeare in the Berkshires. He'd wanted to be Romeo but had played Tybalt instead. And there were photos from the theater in Connecticut where both Claudia and Jack were women in that Lorca play—*The House of Bernarda Alba.* (No pictures of the food-poisoning episode, thankfully.)

"Did you ever meet Claudia?" Jack asked his dad.

"Only on the telephone, alas," William said. "A nice girl, very serious. But she wanted babies, didn't she?"

"Yes, she did," Jack said.

"You meet some people at the wrong time, don't you?" his dad asked. "I met your mother at the wrong time—the wrong time for her *and* for me, as it turned out."

"She had no right to keep you away from me!" Jack said angrily.

"Don't be such an *American*!" his father said. "You Americans believe you have so many *rights*! I met a young woman and told her I would love her forever, but I didn't. In fact, I didn't love her very long at all. To tell you the truth, I changed my mind in a hurry about her—but not before I had changed her *life*! If you change someone's life, Jack, what rights *should* you have? Didn't your mom have a *right* to be angry?"

His father seemed as sane as anyone Jack had ever met. *Why is my dad here?* Jack kept thinking, although Heather had warned him against thinking any such thing.

There were photographs of Jack as a Kit Kat Girl, the summer both he and Claudia wanted to be Sally Bowles in *Cabaret,* and a bunch of pictures from the summer of '86, when Jack had met Bruno Litkins, the gay heron, who'd cast him as a transvestite Esmeralda in *The Hunchback of Notre Dame*—thus sending Jack down a questionable career slope, but one he had survived with his heterosexual orientation mostly intact.

"You were good as a girl," his dad was telling him, "but—quite understandably, as your father—I preferred seeing you in male roles."

There were pictures of Jack with his mother and Leslie Oastler, and one of him and his mom in Daughter Alice. Had Mrs. Oastler or a tattoo client taken that photograph?

"Emma thought I should see what her mother looked like," his dad explained, "because she worried about what *hold* her mother might have on you. I don't mean a *wrestling* hold!"

"Did Mrs. Oastler send you photographs, too?" Jack asked. "Did you ever talk to *her* on the telephone?"

"I got the feeling that Leslie sent me pictures or called me only when she was angry at your mother," Jack's father explained.

"Probably when Mom was unfaithful to her," Jack said.

"I never inquired about your mother, Jack. I only asked about you."

There was a photograph of Jack with Miss Wurtz that time he and Claudia took her to the Toronto film festival. Miss Wurtz looked radiant, in her former-film-star attire. Claudia must have taken the picture, but there was no mistaking the way The Wurtz was smiling seductively at the camera; Caroline clearly knew that either she or Claudia would be sending the photo to William.

And there was one of Jack and Claudia, which Miss Wurtz had to have taken. Jack couldn't remember if it was the night before the Mishima misunderstanding or the night after it. They'd successfully crashed a private party, because the bouncers had mistaken Miss Wurtz for a celebrity. In the snapshot, Claudia is looking fondly at Jack, but his eyes are elsewhere; he's not looking at her or the camera. (Knowing Jack, he was scanning the party to see if he could spot Sonia Braga.)

"How did you find me, dear boy?" his dad asked.

"*Heather* found *me*. She called Miss Wurtz. Caroline always knows where to find me."

"Dear Caroline," William said, as if he'd been meaning to write her a letter. "Talk about meeting someone at the wrong time!"

"I was just in Edinburgh with Heather," Jack told him.

"She's a *bossy* little thing, isn't she?" his dad asked.

"I love her," Jack said.

"So do I, dear boy—so do I!"

There were more photos of Jack with Emma—for so much of his life, Emma had been there. In the Bar Marmont, around the pool at the Skybar at the Mondrian Hotel on Sunset Boulevard, and in one of those private villas on the grounds of the Sunset Marquis in West Hollywood. There were shots of Jack holding the steering wheel of his Audi, of one Audi after another. (He knew now that Emma had snapped all of these, but he'd never paid much attention to anyone taking his picture, because it was always happening.)

There were photographs of Heather and *her* mother, too—some were duplicates of those photos Heather had shown Jack—and there were more skiing pictures, but most surprising was the number of times that *Alice* appeared in the photographs of Jack. (He wondered why his father hadn't cut her out of the pictures; *Jack* would have.) And some of these photos were from Jack's first trip to those Baltic and North Sea ports, when he'd been four and was still inclined to hold his mother's hand.

There they were on the Nyhavn, in front of Tattoo Ole's; either Ladies' Man Madsen or Ole himself had to have taken the picture. And in Stockholm, posing by a ship from the archipelago—it was docked at the Grand. Had Torsten Lindberg taken that one? Jack would never forget that he'd met his father, but he hadn't known it, in the restaurant of the Hotel Bristol—in Oslo, where William had never slept with Ingrid Moe. But who had taken the photograph of Jack holding his mom's hand in front of the Domkirke, the Oslo Cathedral?

From his grave, Jack would not fail to recognize the American Bar in what was now the lobby of the Hotel Torni, but which of those lesbian music students in Helsinki had snapped that shot of Jack and his mom going up the stairs? (They were always climbing the stairs, because the elevator was never working, and they were always—as they were in the snapshot—holding hands.)

Why hadn't William Burns removed every trace of Jack's mother from his sight?

Jack was staring so intently at the pictures from Amsterdam that he hadn't noticed how close to him his father was standing, or that William was staring intently at his son. There was a photograph of Jack with his mother and Tattoo Theo, and another of Jack with Tattoo Peter—the great Peter de Haan, with his left leg missing below the knee. Tattoo Peter had the same slicked-back hair that Jack remembered, but in the photo he seemed more blond; Tattoo Peter had the same Woody Woodpecker tattoo on his right biceps, too.

"Tattoo Peter was only fifteen when he stepped on that mine," William was saying, but Jack had moved on. He was looking at himself as a four-year-old, walking with his mom in the red-light district. Cameras were not welcome there; the prostitutes didn't want their pictures taken. Yet someone—Els or Saskia, probably—must have had a camera. Alice was smiling at the photographer as if nothing were the matter, as if nothing had *ever* been the matter.

"How dare you look at your mother like that?" his father asked him sharply.

"What?"

"My dear boy! She's been dead how many years? And you still haven't forgiven her! How *dare* you not forgive her? Did she blame *you*?"

"She shouldn't have blamed you, either!" Jack cried.

"*De mortuis nihil nisi bonum.* How's your Latin, Jack?" (William clearly knew that Jack's Latin wasn't strong.) "Speak nothing but good of the dead."

"That's a tough one," Jack said.

"If you don't forgive her, Jack, you'll never have a worthwhile relationship with a woman in your life. Or have you had a worthwhile relationship that I'm unaware of? Dr. García doesn't count! Emma *almost* doesn't count." (He even knew about Dr. García!)

Jack hadn't noticed when his father had started to shiver, but William was shivering now. He paced back and forth, from the bedroom to the sitting room—and into the bedroom again, with his arms hugging his chest.

"Are you cold, Pop?" Jack asked him. He didn't know where the "Pop" came from. (Not Billy Rainbow, thankfully—not this time.)

"What did you call me?" his dad asked.

" 'Pop.' "

"I *love* that!" William cried. "It's so *American*! Heather calls me 'Dad' or 'Daddy'—you can't call me that, too. It's *perfect* that you call me 'Pop'!"

"Okay, Pop." Jack was thinking that his father might let him off the hook about his mom, but no such luck.

"It's time to close the windows—it's that time of the evening," William was saying, his teeth chattering. Jack helped him close the windows. Although the sun hadn't set, the lake was a darker color than before; only a few sailboats still dotted the water. His father was shaking so violently that Jack put his arms around him.

"If you can't forgive your mother, Jack, you'll never be free of her. It's for your own sake, you know—for your *soul*. When you forgive someone who's hurt you, it's like escaping your *skin*— you're that free, outside yourself, where you can see everything." William suddenly stopped shivering. Jack stepped a little away from him, so that he could see him better; William's mischievous little smile was back, once more transforming him. "Uh-oh," Jack's father said. "Did I say *skin*? I didn't say *skin*, did I?"

"Yes, you did," Jack told him.

"Uh-oh," his dad said again. He was beginning to unbutton his flannel shirt, but he unbuttoned it only halfway before pulling the shirt off—over his head.

"What's wrong, Pop?"

"Oh, it's nothing," William said impatiently; he was busy taking off his socks. " 'Skin' is one of those triggers. I'm surprised they didn't tell you. They can't give me antidepressants and expect me to remember all the stupid *triggers*!"

On the tops of both feet, where it is painful to be tattooed, were Jack's name and Heather's—*Jack* on his father's right foot, *Heather* on his left. (Since Jack couldn't read music, he didn't know what the notes were, but their names had been put to music.)

By now, Jack's father had taken off his T-shirt and his corduroy trousers, too. In a pair of striped boxer shorts, which were too big for him—and which Jack could not imagine his father buying on one of the shopping trips with Waltraut Bleibel—his dad appeared to have the body of a former bantamweight. At most, William weighed one-thirty or one-thirty-five—Jack's old weight class. The tattoos covered his father's sinewy body with the patina of wet newspaper.

Doc Forest's tattoo stood out against all the music as vividly as a burn. The words, which were not as near to his heart as William would have liked them, marked the left side of his rib cage like a whiplash.

The commandant's daughter; her little brother

"It's not the tattoos, my dear boy," Jack's father said, standing naked before him—the shocking white of William's hands and face and neck and penis being the only parts of him that weren't an almost uniform blue-black, some of which had faded to gray. "It's everything I truly heard and felt—it's everything I ever *loved*! It's not the *tattoos* that marked me." For a small man, he had overlong arms—like a gibbon.

"Perhaps you should put your clothes on, Pop—so we can go out to dinner."

Jack saw that messy music, a wrinkled scrap of a page on his dad's left hip, where Jack's mom was once convinced that Beachcomber Bill had marked him—the tattoo that had failed in the planning phase, according to Tattoo Ole. Jack got only a glimpse of those notes that curled around the underarm side of his father's right biceps; most of that tattoo was lost from view, either the Chinaman's mistake or the Beachcomber's. And that fragment of a hymn on his left calf—the *"Breathe on me, breath of God,"* both the words and the music—was every bit as good as Tattoo Ole had said. (It had to be Charlie Snow's work, or Sailor Jerry's.)

As for his dad's favorite Easter hymn, "Christ the Lord Is Risen Today," it was upside down to Jack—but when his father sat on the toilet, William could read the music. Since this tattoo was strictly notes, without the words, Jack knew it was "Christ the Lord" only because of where it was, and it was upside down—and of course Jack remembered that Aberdeen Bill had given it to William. As Heather had told Jack, this long-ago tattoo had been overlapped by a newer one, Walther's "Wachet auf, ruft uns die Stimme"—the top two staffs beginning where the alleluia chorus to "Christ the Lord" *should* have been.

His father was leaping up and down like a monkey on the bed; with a remote, which William held in one hand, he had lowered the hospital bed to a flat position. It was hard to get a definitive look at all his tattoos—for example, to ascertain exactly *which* lengthy and complicated phrase by Handel was in the area of William's kidneys. Jack knew only that Tattoo Ole had done that one. ("More Christmas music," Ole had said dismissively.) But Jack got a good enough look to guess that this was the chorus ("For Unto Us a Child Is Born") from Handel's *Messiah*—and, in that case, Widor's Toccata was right next to it.

All but lost in an ocean of music, Herbert Hoffmann's disappearing ship was even more difficult to see because of William's monkey business on the bed. And there, on his father's right shoulder, Jack recognized another Tattoo Ole—it lay unfurled like a piece ripped from a flag. It was more Bach, but not the Christmas music Jack's mother had thought it was—neither Bach's *Weihnachtsoratorium* nor his *Kanonische Veränderungen über das Weihnachtslied*. It was tough to see his dad's shoulder clearly, with all the bouncing up and down, but Jack's Exeter German was getting better by the minute—"Der Tag, der ist so freudenreich."

Jack also caught Pachelbel's name, if not the particular piece of music, and—in a crescent shape on his father's coccyx— Theo Rademaker's cramped fragment, "Wir glauben all' an einen Gott." (The composer was Samuel Scheidt.)

Bach's "Jesu, meine Freude" ("Jesus, My Joy"), which Tattoo Peter had given Jack's dad in Amsterdam, was indeed missing part of the word *Largo*—as his sister had said. The Balbastre tattoo ("Joseph est bien marié"), which was newer and only slightly overlapped the Bach, was not by a tattoo artist Jack could identify.

Jack's French, which was nonexistent, gave him fits with Dupré's *Trois préludes et fugues pour orgue*—not to mention Messiaen's "Dieu parmi nous," which followed the Roman numeral IX.

Did that mean "God is among us"? Jack was wondering.

"I have a son!" his father was shouting, as he bounced up and down on the bed. "Thank you, God—I have a son!"

"Dad, don't hurt yourself."

" '*Pop*,' " his father corrected him.

"Better be careful, Pop."

You can give yourself a headache trying to decipher the tattoos on a naked man who's leaping up and down on a bed. Jack was trying to identify the Bach tattoo Sami Salo was alleged to have given William on his backside—and the notes that Trond Halvorsen (the *scratcher*) gave him in Oslo, where Halvorsen also gave William an infection—but Jack was making himself dizzy with the effort.

"Do you know what *toccata* means, Jack?"

"No, Pop."

"It means *touch*, basically—almost a *hammered* kind of touch," his father explained; he wasn't even out of breath. Jack saw no evidence that Dr. Horvath had been right about the *psychological* benefits of the Sanatorium Kilchberg's jogging program, but the *aerobic* benefits were obvious.

Stanley's Trumpet Tune in D, which marked William's chest in the area of his right lung, seemed to make a visual proclamation. (Didn't you need good lungs to play the trumpet?) And there was that fabulous Alain quotation, in French and English, on his

dad's bare ass—not that William was standing still enough for
Jack to be able to read it.

"Pop, maybe you should get dressed for dinner."

"If I stop, I'll get a chill, dear boy. I don't want to feel cold!"
his father shouted.

For Professor Ritter and the doctors—they were listening outside, in the corridor—this must have been a familiar enough utterance to give them a signal. There was a loud, rapid knocking
on the door—Dr. Horvath, probably.

"Perhaps we should come in, William!" Professor Ritter
called; it wasn't really a question.

"*Vielleicht!*" Jack's father shouted. ("Perhaps!")

William bounded off the bed; he put his hands on the rubberized floor and bent over, facing Jack while he lifted his bare bottom to the opening door. When Professor Ritter and the doctors
entered, William was *mooning* them.

Reason has reached its limit.
Only belief keeps rising.

"I must say, William—this is a little disappointing," Professor
Ritter said.

"Only a *little*?" Jack's father asked; he'd straightened up and
had turned to face them, naked.

"William, this is not what you should wear to the Kronenhalle!" Dr. Horvath admonished him.

"I won't have dinner with a naked man—at least not in public,"
Dr. von Rohr announced, but Jack could see that she instantly regretted her choice of words. "*Es tut mir leid,*" she added. ("I'm
sorry," she said to Jack's father.) The other doctors and Professor
Ritter all looked at her with dismay. "I *said* I was sorry!" she told
them in her head-of-department way.

"I think I heard the word *naked,*" William said to his son,
smiling. "Talk about *triggers!*"

"I said I was sorry, William," Dr. von Rohr told him.

"Oh, it's nothing," Jack's father said irritably. But Jack saw the
first sign that his dad felt cold again—a single tremor. "It's just
that I've *told* you I'm *not* naked. You *know* that's not how I *feel!*"

"We know, William," Dr. Berger said. "You've told us."

"But Jack hasn't heard this," Professor Ritter joined in.

Dr. von Rohr sighed; if she'd been holding a pencil in her long fingers, she would have twirled it. "These tattoos are your father's *real* clothes, Jack," Dr. von Rohr said. She put her hands on William's shoulders—running her hands down the length of his arms, which she then held at the wrists. "He feels cold because so many of his favorite composers have died. Most of them are dead, in fact. Aren't they, William?"

"Cold as the grave," Jack's father said, nodding his head; he was shivering.

"And what is here, and here, and here, and *everywhere*?" Dr. von Rohr asked, pointing to William's tattoos repeatedly. "Nothing but praise for the Lord—hymns of praise—and prayers of lamentation. With you, everything is either adulation or mourning. You thank God, William, but you mourn almost everyone or everything else. How am I doing so far?" she asked him. Jack could tell that she had calmed his father down, but nothing could stop the shivering. (Dr. Horvath was trying, rubbing William's shoulders while attempting to pull a T-shirt over his shaking head—more or less at the same time.)

"You're doing a very good job," Jack's father told Dr. von Rohr sincerely. He was too cold for sarcasm; his teeth were chattering again.

"Your body is *not* naked, William. It is gloriously covered with hymns of jubilation, and with the passion of an abiding love of God—but also an abiding *loss,*" Dr. von Rohr continued.

Dr. Horvath went on dressing Jack's father as if William were a child. Jack could see that his dad had completely succumbed, not only to Dr. Horvath dressing him but to Dr. von Rohr's litany—which William had doubtless delivered to her on more than one occasion.

"You are wearing your grief, William," Dr. von Rohr went on, "and your broken heart is thankful—it just can't keep you warm, not anymore. And the *music*—well, some of it is triumphant. *Jubilant,* you would say. But so much of it is sad, isn't it, William? Sad like a dirge, sad like a *lamentation,* as I've heard you say repeatedly."

"The *repeatedly* was sarcastic, Ruth," Jack's father said. "You were doing fine till then."

Dr. von Rohr sighed again. "I'm just trying to get us to dinner on time, William. Forgive me if I'm giving Jack the *abridged* version."

"I think I get it," Jack told Dr. von Rohr. (He thought she'd done a good job, under the circumstances.) "I get the idea, Pop—I really do."

"Pop? *Was heisst* 'Pop'?" Dr. Horvath asked. ("What is 'Pop'?")

"*Amerikanische Umgangssprache für 'Vater,'*" Professor Ritter told him. ("American colloquial speech for 'Father.'")

"He doesn't need to wear a tie, Klaus," Dr. von Rohr said to Dr. Horvath, who was struggling to knot a necktie at William's throat. "Jack's not wearing a tie, and he looks fine."

"But it's the *Kronenhalle*!" Jack was certain Dr. Horvath was going to yell; however, Dr. Horvath put the tie away and was silent.

"There's more to life than grieving and singing praise to God, William," Dr. Berger intoned. "I mean, factually speaking."

"I won't use that word I used *again*, William," Dr. von Rohr said carefully, "but allow me to say that you can't go to the Kronenhalle wearing *only* your tattoos, because—as I know you know, William—they're not socially acceptable."

"Not socially acceptable," Jack's father repeated, smiling. Jack could see that being socially *un*acceptable pleased William Burns, and that Dr. von Rohr knew this about him.

"I want to say that I can see what good care you're taking of my dad," Jack told them all. "I want you to know that my sister and I appreciate it—and that my father appreciates it." Everyone seemed embarrassed—except William, who looked irritated.

"You don't need to make a *speech,* Jack. You're not a *Canadian* anymore," his dad told him. "We all can be socially acceptable, when we have to. Well, maybe not *Hugo,*" his father added, with that mischievous little smile Jack was getting used to. "Have you met Hugo yet, Jack?"

"*Noch nicht,*" Jack said. ("Not yet.")

"But I suppose they've told you about the nature of the little excursions I take with Hugo, on occasion," his father said, the mischief *and* the smile disappearing from his face, as if one word—not necessarily *Hugo,* but the *wrong* word—could instantly make him another person. "They've told you, haven't they?" He wasn't kidding.

"I know a little about it," Jack answered him evasively. But his father had already turned to Professor Ritter and the others.

"Don't you think a father and his son should have those awkward but necessary conversations about sex *together*?" William asked his doctors.

"*Bitte,* William—" Professor Ritter started to say.

"Isn't that what any *responsible* father would do?" Jack's dad went on. "Isn't that my *job*? To talk about sex with my son—isn't that *my* job? Why is that *your* job?"

"We thought that Jack should be informed about the Hugo business, William," Dr. Berger said. "We didn't know you would bring the matter up with him."

"Factually speaking," William said, calming down a little.

"We can talk about it later, Pop."

"Perhaps over dinner," his father said, smiling at Dr. von Rohr, who sighed.

"Speaking of which, you should be *leaving*!" Dr. Horvath cried. But when they started for the corridor—his father bowing to Dr. von Rohr, who preceded him—Dr. Horvath grabbed Jack by both shoulders, holding him back.

"Which of the *triggers* was it?" the doctor whispered in Jack's ear; even Dr. Horvath's whisper was loud. "*Das Wort,*" he whispered. ("The word.") "What was it?"

"*Skin,*" Jack whispered. "It was the word *skin.*"

"*Gott!*" Dr. Horvath shouted. "That's one of the *worst* ones— that one is *unstoppable*!"

"I'm glad *some* of the triggers are stoppable," Jack told him. "*Naked,* for example. Dr. von Rohr seemed to stop that one."

"*Ja, naked*'s not so bad," Dr. Horvath said dismissively. "But you better not bring up the word *skin* at the Kronenhalle. And the *mirrors*!" he remembered, with a gasp. "Keep William away from the mirrors."

"Is a mirror one of the *unstoppable* triggers?" Jack asked.

"A mirror is more than a trigger," Dr. Horvath said gravely. "A mirror is *das ganze Pulver*!"

"What?" Jack asked him; he didn't know the phrase.

"*Das ganze Pulver!*" Dr. Horvath cried. "All the ammunition!"

Their evening at the Kronenhalle began with William complimenting Dr. von Rohr on the silver streak in her tawny hair— how it had always impressed him that she must have been struck by lightning one morning on her way to work. By the time she met with her first patient, he imagined, she was acutely aware of that part of her head where the lightning bolt had hit her—

mainly because the lightning had done such extensive dam~~age~~
her roots that her hair had already died and turned gray.

"Is this actually a *compliment,* William?" Dr. von Rohr asked.

They had not yet been seated at their table, which was in a
room with a frosted-glass wall. They'd entered the Kronenhalle
from Rämistrasse. Dr. von Rohr, who was much taller than
Jack's father, purposely blocked any view he might have had of
the mirror by the bar. They passed both the women's and the
men's washrooms, which harbored more mirrors, but these mirrors were not within sight of the corridor they followed to their
glassed-in room. (The mirror over the sideboard was in another
part of the restaurant.)

William was looking all around, but he couldn't see past Dr.
von Rohr—he came up to her breasts—and Dr. Krauer-Poppe
held his other arm. Jack followed them. His father was constantly turning his head and smiling at him. Jack could tell that
his dad thought it was great fun to be escorted into a fancy
restaurant like the Kronenhalle by two very good-looking women.

"If you weren't so tall, Ruth," William was saying to Dr. von
Rohr, "I could get a look at the top of your head and see if that
silver streak is dyed all the way down to your roots."

"There's just no end to your *compliments,* William," she said,
smiling down at him.

Jack's dad patted the little purse Dr. Krauer-Poppe carried on
her arm. "Got the sedatives, Anna-Elisabeth?" he asked.

"Behave yourself, William," Dr. Krauer-Poppe said.

William turned and winked at Jack. Dr. Horvath had dressed
Jack's father in a long-sleeved black silk shirt; because William's
arms were long, but his body was small, every shirt looked too
big on him. His silver shoulder-length hair, which was the same
glinting shade of gray as Dr. von Rohr's electric streak, added to
the feminine aspect of his handsomeness—as did the copper
bracelets and his gloves. His "evening" gloves, as William called
them, were a thin black calfskin. The way his father bounced on
the balls of his feet reminded Jack of Mr. Ramsey. As Heather
had put it, William Burns was a *youthful*-looking sixty-four.

"Ruth, alas, is no fan of Billy Rainbow, Jack," William said, as
they were being seated.

"Alas, she *told* me," Jack said, smiling at Dr. von Rohr, who
smiled back at him.

"Even so," Jack's father said, clearing his throat, "I gotta say we're with the two best-looking broads in the place." (He really did have Billy Rainbow down pat.)

"You're such a flatterer, William," Dr. von Rohr told him.

"Have you had a look at Ruth's purse?" Jack's dad asked him, indicating Dr. von Rohr's rather large handbag; it was too big to fit under her chair. "More like a suitcase, if you ask me—more like an *overnight* bag," William said, winking at Jack. His father was outrageously suggesting that Dr. von Rohr had prepared herself for the possibility of spending the night at the Hotel zum Storchen with Jack!

"It's not every day you meet a man who compliments a woman's *accessories,*" Dr. von Rohr told Jack, smiling.

Dr. Krauer-Poppe didn't look so sure, nor was she smiling; despite her supermodel attire, Dr. Krauer-Poppe's dominant personality trait radiated medication.

Jack also knew that Dr. Krauer-Poppe was married, and she had young children, which was why his father had focused his embarrassing zeal for matchmaking on Jack and Dr. von Rohr. (She was no longer married but *had* been, Heather had said; she was a divorced woman with no children.)

"Jack's been seeing a psychiatrist—for longer than I've known you two ladies," William announced. "How's that been going, Jack?"

"I don't know if there's a professional name for the kind of therapy I've been receiving," Jack told them. "A psychiatric term, I mean."

"It doesn't need to have a psychiatric term," Dr. Krauer-Poppe said. "Just describe it."

"Well, Dr. García—she's this truly wonderful woman in her early sixties, with all these children and grandchildren. She lost her husband some years ago—"

"Aren't most of her patients women, Jack?" his dad interrupted. "I had that impression from one of those articles I read about the Lucy business—you remember that episode, the girl in the backseat of Jack's car?" William asked his doctors. "Both she and her mother were seeing the same psychiatrist Jack was seeing! From the sound of it, you'd think there was a shortage of psychiatrists in southern California!"

"William, let Jack describe his therapy for us," Dr. von Rohr said.

"Oh," his father responded; it gave Jack a chill that his dad said, "Oh," exactly the way Jack did.

"Well, Dr. García makes me tell her everything in chronological order," Jack explained. Both doctors were nodding their heads, but William suddenly looked anxious.

"*What* things?" Jack's father asked.

"Everything that ever made me laugh, or made me cry, or made me feel angry—just those things," Jack told him.

Dr. Krauer-Poppe and Dr. von Rohr weren't nodding their heads anymore; they were both observing William closely. The idea of what might have made his son laugh, or cry, or feel angry seemed to be affecting him.

His dad had moved his right hand to his heart, but his hand hadn't come to rest there. He appeared to be inching his fingers over the upper-left side of his rib cage—as if feeling for something under his shirt, or under his skin. He knew exactly where to find it, without looking. As for what might have made William Burns laugh or cry, her name was Karin Ringhof—the commandant's daughter. As for what might have made him cry *and* made him feel angry, that would have been what happened to her little brother.

"It sounds as if this therapy could be quite a *lengthy* endeavor," Dr. Krauer-Poppe said to Jack, but she'd not taken her eyes from William's gloved hand—black-on-black against his shirt, touching the tattoo she knew as well as Jack did.

The commandant's daughter; her little brother

From the pained expression on his father's face, Jack could tell that William had his index finger perfectly in place on the semicolon—the first (and probably the last) semicolon Doc Forest had tattooed on anyone.

"Your therapy sounds positively *book-length,*" Dr. von Rohr said to Jack, but her eyes—like those of her colleague—had never strayed from his father.

"You're putting *in chronological order* everything that ever made you laugh, or made you cry, or made you feel angry," his dad said, grimacing in pain—as if every word he spoke were a tattoo on his rib cage, or in the area of his kidneys, or on the tops of his feet, where Jack had seen his own name and his sister's. All those places where Jack knew it hurt like Hell to be tattooed, yet William Burns had been tattooed there—he'd been marked for life everywhere it hurt, except for his penis.

"And has this therapy helped?" Dr. von Rohr asked Jack doubtfully.

"Yes, I think it has—at least I feel better than when I first went to see Dr. García," he told them.

"And you think it's the *chronological-order* part that has helped?" Dr. Krauer-Poppe asked. (In her view, Jack could tell, putting the highs and lows of your life in chronological order was not as reliable as taking medication.)

"Yes, I think so . . ." Jack started to say, but his father interrupted him.

"It's *barbaric*!" William shouted. "It sounds like *torture* to me! The very idea of *imposing* chronological order on everything that ever made you laugh or cry or feel angry—why, that's the most *masochistic* thing I've ever heard of! You must be *crazy*!"

"I think it's working, Pop. The chronological-order part keeps me calm."

"My son is obviously deluded," William said to his doctors.

"Jack's not the one in an institution, William," Dr. von Rohr reminded him.

Dr. Krauer-Poppe covered her pretty face with her hands; for a moment, Jack was afraid that the word *institution* might have been a trigger. The Doc Forest tattoo on the upper-left side of his father's rib cage was clearly a trigger, but a *stoppable* one—or so it appeared. Jack's dad had returned both his hands to the table.

Just then their waiter materialized—a short man bouncing on the balls of his feet, as vigorously as William or Mr. Ramsey ever had, although the waiter was fat. He had a small mouth and an overlarge mustache, which seemed to tickle his nose when he spoke. "*Was darf ich Ihnen zu Trinken bringen?*" he inquired. (It sounded as if "What may I bring you to drink?" were all one word.)

"Fortuitous," Jack's father said, meaning the timely appearance of the waiter, but the waiter thought that William had ordered something.

"*Bitte?*" the waiter asked.

"*Ein Bier,*" Jack said—pointing to himself, to avoid further confusion. ("A beer.")

"I didn't know you *drank*!" his dad said with sudden concern.

"I don't. You can watch me. I won't finish one beer," Jack told him.

"*Noch ein Bier!*" his father told the waiter, pointing to himself. ("Another beer!")

"William, you don't drink—not even half a beer," Dr. von Rohr reminded him.

"I can have what Jack has," William said, acting like a child.

"Not with the antidepressants. You shouldn't," Dr. Krauer-Poppe said.

"I can *un*order the beer," Jack suggested. *"Das macht nichts."*

"Jack's German will improve over time," William said to his doctors.

"Jack's German is *fine,* William," Dr. von Rohr told him.

"You see? She likes you, Jack," his father said. "I told you that was an *overnight* bag!"

The doctors, choosing to ignore him, ordered a bottle of red wine. William ordered a mineral water. Jack told the waiter that he'd changed his mind. Would the waiter bring them a *large* bottle of mineral water, please—and no beer?

"No, no! Have the beer!" William said, taking Jack's hand in his gloved fingers.

"*Kein Bier,*" Jack said to the waiter, *"nur Mineralwasser."* ("No beer, only mineral water.")

Jack's dad sat sulking at the table, making an unsteady tower of his knife and spoon and fork. "Fucking *Americans,*" William said. He looked up to see if that would get a rise out of his son. It didn't. Dr. von Rohr and Dr. Krauer-Poppe gave each other a look, but they said nothing. "Don't have the Wiener schnitzel, Jack," his father continued, as if the menu, which he'd just that second picked up, had been all that was on his mind from the beginning.

"Why not, Pop?"

"They butcher a whole calf and put half of it on your plate," William said. "And don't have the *Bauernschmaus,*" he added. (A *Bauernschmaus* was a farmer's platter of meats and sausages; it was very popular with Austrians and sounded like something Dr. Horvath would have ordered, but Jack could see that it wasn't even on the Kronenhalle's menu.) "And, above all, don't have the bratwurst. It's a veal sausage the size of a horse's penis."

"I'll stay away from it, then," Jack told him.

Dr. von Rohr and Dr. Krauer-Poppe were talking rapid-fire

Swiss German. It was not the High German Jack had studied in school—*Schriftdeutsch,* the Swiss call it, meaning "written German."

"*Schwyzerdütsch,*" Jack's father said contemptuously. "They speak in Swiss German when they don't want me to understand them."

"If you didn't talk about horses' penises, maybe they wouldn't have to talk about you, Pop."

"I think you should find a new psychiatrist, Jack. Someone you can talk to about things as they come up—not necessarily in chronological order, for Christ's sake."

Jack was surprised by the *for Christ's sake,* and not because it was exactly the way Jack always said it—he only occasionally said it—but because Jack had *never* said it in any of his films. (As Dr. Berger had told him, William had made quite a study of his son; as Dr. von Rohr had warned Jack, she didn't mean only his *movies.*)

"Interesting what he knows, isn't it?" Dr. von Rohr asked Jack.

The waiter—that timely, bouncing fat man—was back to take their orders. Jack's father unhesitatingly ordered the Wiener schnitzel.

"William, I know how you eat—you can't possibly eat half of it," Dr. Krauer-Poppe said to him.

"I'm just like Jack with his one beer," William said. "I don't have to finish it. And I didn't order the *pommes frites* that come with it—just the green salad. *Und noch ein Mineralwasser, bitte,*" he told the waiter. Jack was surprised to see that the liter bottle was empty.

"Slow down, William," Dr. Krauer-Poppe said, touching the back of his black-gloved hand. William pulled his hand away from her.

The restaurant was lively, but not too crowded; their reservation was on the early side of when things get really busy at the Kronenhalle, or so the concierge had told Jack. But everyone in the restaurant had recognized Jack Burns. "Look around you, William," said Dr. von Rohr—her voice as commanding as the silver-gray, lightning-bolt streak in her hair. "Be proud of your famous son." But William wouldn't look.

"And all these strangers who recognize Jack can't help but see that you are his father—they are recognizing you, too, William," Dr. Krauer-Poppe said.

"And what must they be thinking?" William asked. " 'There is Jack Burns's old man with what must be his second or third wife'—that would be *you,* Ruth," William said to Dr. von Rohr, "because you're obviously the older of the two lovely ladies at this table, but you're clearly not old enough to be Jack's mother."

"William, don't—" Dr. Krauer-Poppe began.

"And what must they be thinking about *you,* Anna-Elisabeth?" William asked. " 'Who is that pretty young woman with the wedding ring? She must be Jack Burns's *date*!' They haven't figured out the part about Ruth's overnight bag."

"Dad—"

" '*Pop*'!" his father corrected him.

"Let's just have a normal conversation, Pop."

"Would that be the sex-with-prostitutes or the *Hugo* conversation?" William asked. Dr. Krauer-Poppe opened her purse with a snap. "Okay, I'll stop. I'm sorry, Anna-Elisabeth," Jack's dad said.

"I was looking for a *tissue,* William. I have something in my eye," Dr. Krauer-Poppe said. "I wasn't even *thinking* about your medication; not yet." She opened a small compact—it held a tiny mirror, no doubt, although Jack's father couldn't see it—and dabbed at the corner of her eye with a tissue.

"Perhaps we could talk about the time we all woke up at two in the morning and watched Jack win the Oscar!" Dr. von Rohr said, taking William's gloved hand. He looked at her hand holding his as if she were a leper.

"You mean *Emma's* Oscar, Ruth?" William asked her. "That screenplay had *Emma* written all over it. Didn't it, Jack?"

Jack didn't respond; he just watched Dr. von Rohr let go of his father's hand. "When the food comes, William, I'll help you take those gloves off," she told him. "It's better not to eat with them."

"*Ich muss bald pinkeln,*" Jack's dad announced. ("I have to pee soon.")

"I'll take him," Jack told the two doctors.

"I think I should come with you," Dr. von Rohr said.

"*Nein,*" William told her. "We're boys. We're going to the boys' room."

"Just behave yourself, William," Dr. Krauer-Poppe warned

him. Jack's dad stuck his tongue out at her as he stood up from the table.

"If you're not back in a few minutes, I'll come check on you," Dr. von Rohr said, touching Jack's hand.

"Jack, your father cried when you won the Oscar—he cried and he cheered," Dr. Krauer-Poppe said. "He was so proud of you—he *is* so proud of you."

"I just meant that Emma must have *helped* him," William said; he was indignant.

"You cried and cheered, William—we *all* did," Dr. von Rohr replied.

It slowly registered with Jack, when he was walking with his father to the men's room—that if they'd watched Jack Burns at the Academy Awards in 2000, his father had been in the Sanatorium Kilchberg for more than three years. No one, not even Heather, had told Jack how long William had been there.

"Of course Emma helped me, Pop," Jack admitted. "She helped me a *lot.*"

"I didn't mean I wasn't proud of you, Jack. Of *course* I'm proud of you!"

"I know you are, Pop."

In the men's room, Jack tried to block his father's view of the mirror, but William planted himself in front of the sink, not the urinal. They did a little dance. William tried to look over Jack's shoulder at the mirror; when Jack stood on his toes to block his dad's view, William ducked his head and peered around his son. They danced from side to side. It was impossible to prevent William from seeing himself in the mirror.

If mirrors were triggers, they didn't affect Jack's father in quite the same way as the word *skin* had. This time, he didn't try to take off his clothes. But with every glimpse he caught of himself, his expression changed.

"Do you see that man?" Jack's dad asked, when he saw himself. It was as if a third man were in the men's room with them. "Things have happened to him," his father said. "Some terrible things."

Jack gave up trying to shield his dad and looked in the mirror, too. The third man's face kept changing. Jack saw his father as William might have looked when he first caught sight of Jack as an infant, before the boy's mother had whisked him away—a kind of expectancy giving way to wonder on William's suddenly boyish-looking face. Jack saw what his father must have seen in a mirror that day in Copenhagen, when they pulled Niels Ringhof's body from the Kastelsgraven—or when William learned that Alice had slept with the boy, and then abandoned him.

His dad was slumping in Jack's arms, as if William wanted to kneel on the men's room floor—the way he'd dropped to his knees at the waterfront in Rotterdam, when Els had to carry him to Femke's car. Or when the policeman had brought Heather home—and the cop told William the story of how they'd mistaken Barbara, his dead wife, for a German tourist who looked the wrong way crossing the street at Charlotte Square.

"That man's body is a map," William said, pointing at the slumping man in the mirror. "Should we look at the map together, Jack?"

"Maybe later, Pop. Not now."

"*Nicht jetzt,*" his father agreed.

"You said you had to pee, Pop," Jack reminded him.

"Oh," Jack's father said, stepping away from his son. "I think I have."

They both looked at his pants. William was wearing khaki trousers with the same pleats and sharply pressed pant legs that Professor Ritter favored, but William's were stained dark; his feet were standing in a puddle of urine on the floor.

"I hate it when this happens," his dad said. Jack didn't know what to do. "Don't worry, Jack. Dr. von Rohr will be coming to the rescue. What did you think her *overnight* bag was really for?" William turned abruptly away from the mirror—as if the third man in the mirror had insulted him, or made him feel ashamed.

Seemingly part of his father's daily schedule, there came a head-of-department knock on the men's room door. "*Herein!*" William called. ("Come in!")

Dr. von Rohr's long arm reached into the men's room; she was offering Jack her oversize handbag without showing them her face. "*Danke,*" Jack said, taking the bag from her hand.

"It's different when he sees himself in the mirror *without* his clothes," she warned Jack, letting the door close.

Jack undressed his father and wiped his body down with paper towels, which he soaked in warm water; then he dried his dad off with more paper towels. William was as accepting of this treatment as a well-behaved child.

Jack was able to guide him out of sight of the mirror. But when William was standing there, naked—while Jack searched for the change of clothes in Dr. von Rohr's big bag—a well-dressed gentleman entered the men's room, and he and Jack's father exchanged stares. To the gentleman, who looked like a middle-aged banker, Jack's dad was a naked, tattooed man. To William Burns, if Jack could read his father's indignant expression, the well-dressed banker was an intruder; moreover, he was intruding on a tender father-and-son moment. Furthermore, to the gentleman, William Burns was a naked, tattooed man with *gloves* on—and there was no telling what the gentleman might have made of the copper bracelets.

The banker gave Jack an overfamiliar, I-know-who-you-are look. (He had come to pee, but he'd walked into some twisted *movie*!)

"*Er ist harmlos,*" Jack said to the man, remembering what Nurse Bleibel had told poor Pamela. ("He's harmless.")

The banker clearly doubted this. Jack's dad had filled his lungs and proceeded to puff out his chest like a rooster; he made two fists and held out his gloved hands.

Jack reached back for his Exeter German, hoping for the best. "*Keine Angst. Er ist mein Vater,*" he told the banker. ("Don't be afraid. He's my father.") And this was the hard part: "*Ich passe auf ihn auf.*" ("I'm looking after him.") The banker retreated, not believing a word of it.

Then the man was gone—the only *actual* third man to have momentarily shared the men's room with Jack and his dad—and Jack dressed his father, trying to remember how efficiently and gently Dr. Horvath had dressed William in the clinic.

It seemed to soothe his dad to explain musical notes to Jack; William must have known that his son knew nothing about music. "Quarter notes are colored in, with stems," his father told him. "Eighth notes are also colored in, with either flags or beams joining two or more together. Sixteenth notes are colored in, and they have a double beam joining them together."

"What about half notes?" Jack asked.

"Half notes, which are white-faced—well, in my case, you could say *flesh*-colored," his dad said; he abruptly stopped.

Flesh: they'd both heard it. But was it a trigger? (As unstoppable as *skin,* maybe, Dr. Horvath might have said.)

"Half notes, which are white-faced," Jack prompted his father, to make him move on. "White-faced and *what*?"

"White-faced *with stems*," Jack's dad replied, haltingly—*flesh* perhaps flickering in the half-light, half-dark of his mind, where all the triggers lay half asleep or half awake. "Whole notes are white-faced and have *no* stems."

"Stop! Hold everything," Jack suddenly said, pointing to his father's right side. "What's *that* one?"

The tattoo was neither words nor music; it more closely resembled a wound in William's side. Worse, at the edges of the gash, there was a blood-red rim—like a ring of blood. (As for the blood, Jack should have known, but he'd been only four at the time.)

"That is where Our Lord was wounded," Jack's father told him. "They put the nails in His hands," he said, holding his black-gloved hands together, as if in prayer, "and in His feet, and *here*—in His side," William said, touching the tattoo on the right side of his rib cage. "One of the soldiers pierced His side with a spear."

"Who did the tattoo?" Jack asked his dad. Some *scratcher,* Jack expected him to say, but Jack should have known.

"There was a time, Jack, when every religious person in Amsterdam was at least *tempted* to be tattooed by a man named Jacob Bril. Maybe you were too young to remember him."

"No, I remember Bril," Jack said, touching the blood-edged gash in his dad's side—then drawing his father's shirt over the wound.

It was a great restaurant, the Kronenhalle. Jack had been foolish to order only a salad, but he ate two thirds of his father's Wiener schnitzel. William Burns was a finicky eater.

"At least Jack brought his appetite to dinner, William," Dr. Krauer-Poppe scolded him, but both William and Jack were in a fairly upbeat mood.

They had weathered the word *flesh,* which turned out to be in the stoppable category of triggers—not in the *skin* category—and while Jack had seen a third man's sorrow on his father's face, he knew that they had also escaped the men's room without confronting the worst of what mirrors could do to his dad. It was different when William was *naked* in front of one, or so Dr. von Rohr had said. Jack guessed that was *das ganze Pulver*—all the ammunition, which Dr. Horvath had spoken of. Jack would get to see it one day, and that day would come soon enough. Tonight in the Kronenhalle, Jack was quite content to wait.

They talked briefly about the younger nurses at the Sanatorium Kilchberg. How they virtually stood in line, or took turns, to shave his dad every morning; how William was such a flirt.

"You don't shave yourself?" Jack asked him.

"*You* try it, without a mirror," his father said. "You should try it with the younger nurses, too, Jack."

"If you don't behave yourself, William, I'm going to put *Waltraut* in charge of shaving you," Dr. von Rohr told him.

"Just so you don't put *Hugo* in charge of it, Ruth," Jack's dad said.

That was how William managed to steer their conversation back to Hugo, and the sex-with-prostitutes subject. Dr. von Rohr, in her head-of-department way, was smart enough to see it coming, but she couldn't prevent it.

"It is chiefly Hugo whom these lovely ladies object to, Jack," his dad began, "not the prostitutes." (Sighing from Dr. von Rohr, of course; the head-in-her-hands thing from Dr. Krauer-Poppe.)

"You said *prostitutes*—plural. You see more than one?" Jack asked his father.

"Not at the same time," William said with that mischievous little smile of his. (Fork-twirling, spoon-spinning, knife-tapping from Dr. von Rohr's part of the table—and Dr. Krauer-Poppe had something in her eye again.)

"I'm just curious to know, Pop, if you see the same two or three women—I mean one at a time—or a different prostitute each visit."

"I have my favorites," his father said. "There are three or four ladies I keep going back to."

"You're faithful in your fashion—is that what you mean, William?" Dr. Krauer-Poppe asked. "Isn't there a song that goes like that?" (She'd had more red wine than Dr. von Rohr.) "Or have I got the translation all *upfucked*?"

"All *fucked up*, Anna-Elisabeth," Dr. von Rohr corrected her.

"And it's *safe*?" Jack asked his father.

"I don't have sex with them, if that's what you mean," William answered, with that now-familiar tone of indignation in his voice.

"I know. I meant is it safe in *every* way?" Jack asked. "The place, for example. Is it dangerous?"

"I have *Hugo* with me!" his dad cried. "I don't mean in the same room with me, of course."

"Of course," Jack said.

The silverware, which Dr. von Rohr had set in motion, came crashing down.

"Wait till you meet Hugo," Dr. Krauer-Poppe told Jack. "Your father is safe with Hugo."

"Then what is it you object to about him?" Jack asked both doctors.

"Wait till you meet him," was all Dr. von Rohr would say.

"Don't pity me, Jack," his dad said. "Don't think of me as *resigning* myself to masturbation with a prostitute. It isn't an act of resignation."

"I guess I don't understand what it is," Jack admitted.

They all saw William's right hand reaching for his heart again; once more the fingers of his black-gloved hand inched their way toward that tattoo with the semicolon in it. (He had, with Dr. von Rohr's assistance, removed the gloves to eat. But now that he'd finished his meal, the gloves were back on.)

"I have had women in my life that I wanted to have—if not for as *long* as I wish I'd had them," William began sadly. "I couldn't do that again. I can't go through losing someone else."

The doctors and Jack knew everything about the tattoo William Burns had for Karin Ringhof, and where it was. But Jack didn't know if his father had a tattoo for Barbara, his German wife—or where it was, if he had it. Maybe that one was in the music; Jack would ask Heather about it.

"I get it, Pop. I understand," Jack told him.

He wondered if William ever touched his rib cage on the other side, where Jacob Bril had pierced him and made him bleed. Jack wanted to know if *that* tattoo was ever as tender or sensitive to his father's touch as the tattoo of the commandant's daughter and her little brother. He hoped not. Of all his dad's tattoos, Jacob Bril's rendition of Christ's blood was the only one with any color.

"It's time for us to be going along, William," Dr. Krauer-Poppe told him gently. "What are you going to play for us tomorrow— for Jack and me, and Dr. Horvath?"

It was a good trick, and Jack's father seemed to be unaware of it. His right hand drifted away from the area of his heart and the upper-left side of his rib cage. He spread the fingers of his black-gloved hands on the white tablecloth—his feet shuffling under his chair, as if he were familiarizing himself with the foot pedals. You could see it in his eyes—there was a keyboard in his mind. There was an organ the size of the Oude Kerk in his heart; when Jack's dad shut his eyes, he could almost hear it.

"You don't expect me to *hum* it for you, do you, Anna-Elisabeth?" William asked Dr. Krauer-Poppe. She hadn't fooled him, after all. In fact, she held her breath—as Jack and Dr. von Rohr did—because they all knew that *hum* was a possible trigger. As Dr. Berger had warned Jack, his father *hated* humming. (Although maybe it was the humming itself and not the word he hated.)

"Why not wait and surprise them in the morning, William?" Dr. von Rohr suggested. "I'm just asking."

"Why not?" Jack's dad said; he was looking tired.

"I have a little something to make you drowsy in the car," Dr. Krauer-Poppe told William.

Jack's dad was shaking his head; he was already drowsy. "I'm not going to be happy to say good-bye to Jack," William said testily. "I've said good-bye to you before—too many times, dear boy. I've said good-bye to you *here*," his father said, the gloved hand touching his heart again, "and *here*," he said, pointing to his eyes, "and *in here*!" William was weeping now, holding his index finger to his temple.

"You're going to see me in the morning, Pop." Jack held his father's face in his hands. "You're going to see me again and again," Jack promised him. "I intend to keep coming here. Heather and I are buying a house in Zurich."

William instantly stopped crying and said: "You must be *crazy*! It's one of the most expensive cities in the world! Ask Ruth, ask Anna-Elisabeth! *Tell* him!" he shouted at the women. "I don't want my children to *bankrupt* themselves," he moaned, wrapping both arms around his chest and hugging himself as if he were cold.

"*Sehr bald wird ihm kalt werden,*" Dr. von Rohr said to her colleague. ("Very soon he'll feel cold.")

"*Mir ist nicht immer kalt,*" Jack's father argued. ("I don't always feel cold.")

Dr. Krauer-Poppe had stood up and put her hand on William's

shoulder; he sat shaking in his chair. "Open up, William," she said. "If you take this, you won't feel cold—you'll just feel sleepy."

Jack's father turned his head and stuck his tongue out at her. (Jack realized that he might have misunderstood when his dad had done this before.) Dr. Krauer-Poppe put a pill on the tip of William's tongue; she raised the water glass to his lips and he swallowed.

"I'll just see if Hugo has the car here. He was supposed to," Dr. von Rohr said, leaving the table.

"Professor Ritter has a home in one of those overpriced monstrosities across the lake from the sanatorium," Jack's father started up again, as soon as he'd swallowed the pill Dr. Krauer-Poppe had given him. "It's in Zollikon or Küsnacht—one of those precious places."

"It's in Küsnacht, William—it's very beautiful," Dr. Krauer-Poppe assured Jack. "That side of the lake gets more sun."

"My taxi driver told me," Jack said.

"But do you know what it *costs*?" Jack's father asked him. "Four million Swiss francs, and for *what*? A house of three hundred or four hundred square meters, and you pay more than three million dollars? That's *crazy*!"

"The house has a view of the lake; it has a garden, too," Dr. Krauer-Poppe explained. "The garden must be a thousand square meters, William."

"It's still crazy," Jack's dad said stubbornly; at least he wasn't shivering. Dr. Krauer-Poppe stood behind William's chair, massaging his shoulders. She was just waiting for the pill to kick in.

"William, Jack could buy a small house in town—something not that expensive," Dr. Krauer-Poppe said. "I'm sure he doesn't care if he can see the lake."

"*Everything* in Zurich is expensive!" Jack's father declared.

"William, you go shopping for clothes and prostitutes. What else do you go shopping for in Zurich?" Dr. Krauer-Poppe asked him.

"You see what I'm up against, Jack? It's like being *married*!" his dad told him. William saw that Dr. von Rohr was back. "To *both* of them!"

"Believe it or not, Hugo's here with the car," Dr. von Rohr announced. "He actually remembered."

"You're too hard on poor Hugo," William said to Dr. von

Rohr. "Wait till you meet him, Jack. He's a Herman Castro kind of fellow."

A heavyweight, in other words—Jack could tell at first glance, when he saw Hugo hulking over the black Mercedes. Hugo was shining the hood ornament with the sleeve of his white dress shirt. He was attired more in the manner of a waiter than of either a limo driver or a male nurse, which he was. But—even in a long-sleeved white dress shirt—Jack could see that Hugo had the sculpted bulk of a bodybuilder.

Whereas his older sister, Waltraut—the *other* Nurse Bleibel—was short and stout, Hugo was unambiguously huge. He had *made* himself huge. He'd developed those powerful shoulders, and his bulging upper arms; he'd worked to make his neck nearly as big around as William's waist. And Hugo had shaved his head, unfortunately—though it was not unthinkable that this might have been an improvement. His face had the flat, blunt purposefulness of a shovel. The one gold earring, signifying nothing, drew your attention to the fact that the *other* ear was missing a lobe. (An encounter with a dog in a nightclub, Jack's dad had told him on their trip into Zurich from Kilchberg.)

"But don't feel sorry for Hugo," his father had said. "The dog got the worst of it." (Hugo had killed the dog for eating his earlobe, Dr. Horvath would later tell Jack.)

It was easy to see what Dr. von Rohr and Dr. Krauer-Poppe held against Hugo. He was not the sort of young man women of education and sophistication liked, nor was he a man most women would feel attracted to. Alas, Hugo had not only the appearance of a bodyguard; he had the personality of one as well.

At Kilchberg, those younger nurses—the ones who stood in line to shave Jack's father—wouldn't have given Hugo the time of day. The older women there—Hugo's sister and the doctors included—probably bossed him around. Hugo was a thug; he knew no other way to behave. But at least Jack had met someone who could tell him where a good gym was in Zurich, and Jack saw in their first meeting that Hugo *doted* on William.

For a young man who consorted with prostitutes, Hugo, by his association with a handsome older gentleman like William Burns, had doubtless upped his standing in *that* community of ladies.

"Hugo!" Jack's father hailed the big brute, like an old friend. "I want you to meet my son, Jack—*den Schauspieler.*" ("The ac-

or," William called his son—exactly as he'd introduced Jack to everyone on the number one-sixty-one bus.)

William had insisted that Jack and Dr. von Rohr ride with him from Kilchberg into Zurich on the bus. Jack's dad was proud of his knowledge of the public-transportation system, and he wanted Jack to see how he usually rode to and from the city—on his shopping trips with Waltraut, and his *other* shopping trips with Hugo. (The black Mercedes was for nighttime travel only.)

Most of the passengers on the bus seemed to know Jack's father, and to all of them William had said: "I want you to meet my son, Jack—*den Schauspieler.*"

"I've seen all your movies," Hugo said, introducing himself to Jack. "William and I have watched them together. They never get old!" he cried, shaking (and shaking) Jack's hand.

Jack saw the look that passed between Dr. von Rohr and Dr. Krauer-Poppe—as if *old* were a trigger, maybe, or in certain contexts perhaps could be. But not this time. Jack's dad was smiling—possibly swaying on his feet more than he was bouncing on them. (Either *old* was not a trigger or the pill that Dr. Krauer-Poppe had given William was taking effect.)

"I'm *not* saying good-bye to you, Jack," his father told him. William put his arms around Jack's neck; his head fell on Jack's chest as lightly as a baby's.

"You don't have to say good-bye to Jack, William," Dr. von Rohr said. "Just say '*bis morgen*' to him." ("Just say 'until tomorrow' to him.") "You're seeing him in the morning."

"*Bis morgen,* Pop."

"*Bis morgen,*" his dad whispered. "I am already imagining that I'm tucking you into bed, dear boy, or maybe you're tucking *me* in."

"I'm afraid it's time for *Hugo* to tuck you in, William," Dr. Krauer-Poppe told him.

"Oh, what joy," Jack's father said, releasing his son.

Jack kissed his father on the mouth—a dry kiss, just brushing his dad's lips with his own lips tightly closed—the way Heather had taught him. William kissed Jack the same way.

"I know what you've been up to, dear boy. I can tell you've been kissing your sister!"

Jack took a chance, but he felt it was the right time. After all, Hugo and the two doctors were with them—in case anything went wrong.

"I love you, Pop," Jack told his father, heedless of whether or not *love* was a trigger. "I love every inch of your skin. I really mean it."

Hugo looked as if he might punch Jack. Dr. von Rohr and Dr. Krauer-Poppe closely watched William. How was *skin* going to affect him? they all wondered. Were they in unstoppable territory, or—in this context—was *skin* suddenly acceptable?

"Say that again, Jack," his dad said. "I dare you."

"I love you and every inch of your skin," Jack told him.

William Burns put his black-gloved hands on his heart and smiled at Hugo and the doctors, not looking at Jack. "He's got balls, hasn't he?" his father asked them.

"That's not an area of my expertise," Dr. von Rohr answered.

"I just do *medication*, William," Dr. Krauer-Poppe said.

But Jack's father was fine. He was holding his heart because he wanted to feel it beating. "I love you and every inch of *your* skin, dear boy! Please don't forget to call your sister."

Suddenly William seemed exhausted. Hugo helped him into the backseat of the Mercedes, where William Burns looked as small as a child on his way to his first day of school. The body builder had to buckle the seat belt for him, and—before he got into the driver's seat—Hugo came up to Jack and shook (and shook) his hand again. Jack thought that Hugo might pull his arm off.

"You've got balls as big as *der Mond*," Hugo told Jack ("You've got balls as big as the moon.") Then Hugo got in the car and they drove away.

"*Bis morgen!*" Dr. Krauer-Poppe called after them.

"Now I'm taking a taxi home," Dr. von Rohr said. "I live in another part of the city," she explained to Jack.

There was a taxi stand in the vicinity of the Bellevueplatz, where Dr. Krauer-Poppe and Jack waited with Dr. von Rohr until she found an available taxi. The two women kissed each other on both cheeks and said good night.

"I assure you, Jack, I was never struck by lightning," Dr. von Rohr said, when they shook hands. "Not on my head, anyway. I think your father has hit me with a lightning bolt, not on my head but in my heart."

Jack walked with Dr. Krauer-Poppe over the Quaibrücke; they walked back to the Hotel zum Storchen together. "Are you sure I can't walk you home?" he asked her.

"I live near your hotel," she said, "but you'd never find your way back. The streets are small and go every which way."

"Your children are how old?" he asked her. It was a beautiful night, with the lights from the city winking up at them from the Limmat.

"They are ten and twelve, both boys," Dr. Krauer-Poppe told him. "If I ever had to say good-bye to them, the way your father had to say good-bye to you, I would kill myself. Or, if I were lucky, I would be in a place like the Sanatorium Kilchberg. I don't mean as a *doctor.*"

"I understand," Jack said to her.

"I love your father *and* every inch of his skin," she said, smiling.

"Will he ever get better?" Jack asked her.

"He can be much worse than he was with you tonight. He was on his best behavior for you," she told him. "But he will neither get worse *nor* get better. William is what he is."

"He's very lucky to be with all of you, in Kilchberg," Jack said to her.

"You have to thank your sister for that, Jack. She has made her share of sacrifices," Dr. Krauer-Poppe told him. "Are you serious about buying a house here?"

"Yes, *very* serious," he answered.

"My husband knows something about real estate—he can probably be of some help to you. I'm just in the *medication* business."

They were back in the Weinplatz, in front of the Storchen.

"Are you sure—" Jack started to ask her again, about walking her home.

"Yes, I'm sure," she interrupted him. "I'll be home in bed while you're still talking on the phone to Heather. Don't forget to call her."

But Dr. Krauer-Poppe stood there, not leaving. Jack could tell there was something more she wanted to say, but perhaps she felt that she didn't know him well enough to say it.

"You're *not* going home, Anna-Elisabeth?" he asked.

She covered her face with her hands again; for such a serious (and such a beautiful) woman, it was a curiously girlish gesture.

"What is it?" he asked her.

"It's not my business—you have a psychiatrist," she said.

"Please tell me what you're thinking," Jack said to her.

"I'm thinking that you should finish this chronological-order therapy," she told him, "and when you *do* finish, you should ask your doctor about a little something she might give you. You just wouldn't want to take this while you were still trying to put everything in chronological order."

"You mean a pill?" he asked her.

"Yes, a pill," Dr. Krauer-Poppe said. "It's not unlike what we give your father, but it's newer and a little different from Zoloft or Seropram. It's Cipralex; it's *like* the Seropram we give William, but this one has a new agent in it, escitalopram. You get a more rapid onset of action—a week compared to two or three weeks— and because of the higher potency, a normal dosage would be ten milligrams instead of twenty."

"It's an antidepressant?" Jack asked.

"Of course it is," she said. "I think the brand name is Lexapro in the States, but Dr. García would know. With escitalopram, there were supposed to be fewer side effects. But not all studies have shown that this is true. You might not like the loss of libido, possible impotence, or prolonged ejaculation." Dr. Krauer-Poppe paused to smile at him. "You *definitely* wouldn't like what it might do to your ability to tell the story of your life in chronological order, Jack. So first finish what you're telling Dr. García. Then try it."

"Do you think I'm depressed, Anna-Elisabeth?"

"What a question!" she said, laughing. "If you're putting in chronological order everything that ever made you laugh, or made you cry, or made you feel angry—and if you are truly leaving nothing out—then *of course* you're depressed! I'm surprised you're not in a place like the Sanatorium Kilchberg yourself, Jack. I don't mean as a *visitor*."

"But how will I know when I'm finished? It just goes on and on," he said to her.

"You'll know when you're finished, Jack," Dr. Krauer-Poppe said. "It ends when you feel like thanking Dr. García for listening to you. It ends when there's someone else you feel like telling everything to—someone who *isn't* a psychiatrist."

"Oh."

"*Gott!*" she said. "Who would have thought the way someone said, 'Oh,' could be genetic?"

Dr. Krauer-Poppe shook Jack's hand; walking away, with her high heels somewhat unsteadily navigating the cobblestones, she called over her shoulder. "I'll meet you right where you're standing in the morning, Jack. I'll take you to the church. William will come with Dr. Horvath."

"*Bis morgen!*" he called to her. Then he went into the hotel and called his sister.

On the little pad of paper for messages—on the night table, next to the telephone—Jack recognized his handwriting in the morning.

> *Cipralex, 10 mg*
> *(Lexapro in the States?)*
> *Ask Dr. García*

What had Professor Ritter said? "Your father has suffered *losses*." The losses alone were enough to make anyone feel cold; maybe William's tattoos had nothing to do with it.

The conversation with Heather had gone well; even though Jack woke her up, she was happy that he called.

"Well, I *finally* met him. It took long enough! I've been with him for several hours," Jack began. "Dr. von Rohr and Dr. Krauer-Poppe and I took him out to dinner at the Kronenhalle. I met Hugo, of course—and all the others."

"Just *say* it!" his sister yelled.

"I love him," he told her quickly.

"That's all you have to say, Jack," she said; she started to cry.

"I love him and every inch of his skin," Jack told her.

"My God—you didn't say the word *skin*, did you?" she asked him.

"In the context of telling him I loved him, I got away with it," Jack said. "He thought I had balls for saying it."

"*I'll* say you have balls!" Heather cried.

"There were just a few episodes—nothing too terrible," he explained.

"There will always be episodes, Jack. I don't need to hear about them."

"Are you okay about the prostitutes?" he asked her.

"Are *you* okay about them, Jack?"

Jack told her that he was, all things considered. "He can't get in trouble if Hugo's with him," was how he put it.

They talked about whether or not Jack should tell Miss Wurtz about the prostitutes. Jack was eager to call Caroline and tell her everything. ("Maybe not *everything,* Jack," Heather had cautioned him. "Maybe save the prostitutes for a later conversation?")

They asked themselves if Hugo—having lost part of one ear to a dog in a nightclub—could have conceivably done anything more preposterous than dangle a gold earring from his remaining earlobe. "Do you think Hugo wants to draw attention to the earlobe the dog bit off?" Heather asked Jack.

"He could have put the earring in the *top* part of the damaged ear, and not worn anything in the good one," Jack suggested.

Heather wondered if Jack might meet the particular prostitutes their dad was in the habit of visiting—that is, if Hugo would introduce him. "Just to see if they're nice, and to ask them to be nice to him," Jack's sister said.

"He has very little privacy as it is," Jack said. They agreed that you have to give the people you love a little privacy, even if you're afraid for their lives.

"Don't you love them all?" she asked him. "I mean his doctors—even Professor Ritter."

"Ah, well . . ." Jack started to say. "Of *course* I do!" he told her.

"Will you call me every day?" his sister asked.

"Of *course* I will! If I forget, you can call me collect," he said.

She was crying again. "I think you've bought me, Jack. I've completely *sold myself* to you!" she cried.

"I love you, Heather."

"I love you and every inch of your skin," she said.

Jack told Heather how their dad had thrown a tantrum over how expensive Zurich was, and that the issue of his children buying a house there had struck him as *crazy.* (This objection from a man who had no idea how expensive the Sanatorium Kilchberg was—or that the money had run out to pay for his care, which was why Heather had contacted Jack in the first place!)

Jack and his sister also talked about mundane things—those things Jack had imagined he would *never* talk to anyone about. The specific details of the house they were going to share in Zurich, for example: the number of rooms they needed; how many *bathrooms,* for Christ's sake. (Exactly as William would have said it.)

It seemed too obvious to put into words, but Jack realized that when you're happy—especially when it's the first time in your life—you think of things that would never have occurred to you when you were *un*happy.

What a morning it was! First the light streaming into his room at the Storchen, then having coffee and a little breakfast in the café on the Limmat. Simple things had never seemed so complex, or was it the other way around? Jack was as powerless to stop what would happen next as he had been that fateful day William Burns impregnated Alice Stronach.

And standing in front of the Hotel zum Storchen—on the same cobblestones where Jack had stood when he'd called, "*Bis morgen!*" to her, in the Weinplatz—was that supermodel of medication, Dr. Anna-Elisabeth Krauer-Poppe. Once again, she was wearing something smashing; Jack could understand why she wore the lab coat in Kilchberg, just to tone herself down.

They walked uphill on the tiny streets to St. Peter; one day he would know the names of these streets by heart, Jack was thinking. Schlüsselgasse, opposite the Veltliner Keller, and Weggengasse—he would hear them in his head, like music.

"It's a beautiful morning, isn't it?" Dr. Krauer-Poppe asked him. She was nice about it, when she saw that he couldn't speak. "St. Peter has the largest clock in Europe—a four-sided clock on its tower," she told him, making small talk as they walked. "Would you like a *tissue*?" she asked, reaching into her purse. Jack shook his head.

The sun would dry the tears on his face, he wanted to tell her, but the words wouldn't come. Jack kept clearing his throat.

By the blue-gray church, there was a small, paved square with lots of trees; there were plants in the window boxes of the surrounding shops and houses. Some construction workers were renovating what looked like an apartment building. The building was across the square from the church, and the workers were standing on the scaffolding—working away. A hammer was banging; two men were doing something complicated with a flexible saw. A fourth man was fitting pipes—to build more scaffolding, probably.

It was the pipefitter who first spotted Dr. Krauer-Poppe and waved to her. The three other workers turned to look at her; two of them applauded, one whistled.

"I guess they know you," Jack said to Anna-Elisabeth, relieved that he had found his voice. "Or are they just like construction workers everywhere?"

"You'll see," she told him. "These workers are a little different."

It seemed strange that there were people going into the church and it was not yet eight on a weekday morning. Was there some kind of mass? Jack asked Dr. Krauer-Poppe. No, the Kirche St. Peter was a Protestant church, she assured him. There was no mass—only a service every Sunday.

"We can't keep them away," Dr. Krauer-Poppe said. "St. Peter is open to the public."

More people were walking up the broad, flat stairs to the church; they looked like locals, not tourists. Jack saw men in business suits, like the banker his dad had surprised in the men's room at the Kronenhalle; he saw women with young children, and whole families. There were even teenagers.

"They all come to hear him play?" Jack asked Anna-Elisabeth.

"How can we stop them?" she asked. "Isn't it what sells books and movies? What you call *word of mouth,* I think."

The Kirche St. Peter was packed; there was standing room only. "You're not going to sit down, anyway," Dr. Krauer-Poppe told Jack. "And you're going to leave, just before your father finishes. William doesn't want you to see the end of it—not the first time."

"The end of *what*?" Jack asked her. "Why would I leave before he finishes?"

"Please trust me," Anna-Elisabeth said. "Klaus—Dr. Horvath—will take you outside. He knows the right moment." She covered her face with her hands again. "We *all* know it," she said, with her face hidden.

The stone floor of the church was polished gray marble. There were blond wooden chairs instead of pews, but the chairs stood in lines as straight as pews. The congregation faced front, with their backs to the organ—as if there were going to be an actual service, with a sermon and everything. Jack wondered why the audience didn't turn their chairs around, so they could at least *see* the organist they had come to hear—so faithfully, as he now understood it.

The organ was on the second floor, to the rear of the church—

above the congregation. The organ bench—what little Jack could see of it—appeared to face away from the altar. The organist looked only at the silver organ pipes, framed in wood, which towered above him.

How austere, Jack was thinking. *The organist turns his back to the congregation, and vice versa!*

A black urn of flowers stood beneath the elevated wooden pulpit. Above the altar was an inscription.

> *Matth. IV. 10.*
> *Du solt anbätten*
> *Den Herren deinen Gott*
> *Und Ihm allein*
> *dienen.*

It was a kind of old-fashioned German. Jack had to ask Dr. Krauer-Poppe for a translation. " 'You shall worship the Lord your God and Him only you shall serve,' " she told him.

"I guess my dad is what you'd call a true believer," Jack said.

"William never proselytizes," Anna-Elisabeth said. "He can believe what he wants. He never tells me or anyone else what to believe."

"Except for the forgiveness part," Jack pointed out to her. "He's pretty clear on the subject of my forgiving my mother."

"That's not necessarily religious, Jack," Dr. Krauer-Poppe said. "That's just common sense, isn't it?"

She led Jack outside the church again, and they went in a door and up some stairs to the second floor—where the organ was. It was a smaller organ than Jack was used to seeing—very pretty, with light-colored wood. It had fifty-three stops and was built by a firm called Muhleisen in Strasbourg.

Jack looked down at the congregation and saw that even the people who were standing were facing the altar, not the organ. "Nobody wants to *see,* I guess," he said to Anna-Elisabeth.

"Just leave with Dr. Horvath when he tells you," Dr. Krauer-Poppe told him. "After William plays, he will need some ice water, and then the hot wax, and then *more* ice water. If you come out to Kilchberg in the late morning, maybe you can go jogging with him—and with Dr. Horvath. Later this afternoon, you can hear him play blindfolded—for the yoga class. Or you can watch one of your own movies with him!" she said excitedly. "Just *leave* when it's time—okay? I'm not kidding."

"Okay," Jack said to her.

When Dr. Horvath and Jack's father came up the stairs to the second floor, many people in the congregation turned their heads to look at William Burns. William was all business; he acknowledged no one, not even Jack. His dad just nodded at the organ. Jack felt Dr. Krauer-Poppe brush against his arm. Anna-Elisabeth wanted Jack to know that this was how William was before he played. (How had she put it the night before? "William is what he is.")

There was no applause from the congregation to acknowledge him; there wasn't a murmur, but Jack had never heard such a respectful silence.

Dr. Horvath was carrying the music. (There was what looked like a lot of music.) "Normally he plays for one hour," Dr. Horvath whispered loudly in Jack's ear. "But today, because you're here, he's playing a half hour longer!"

Naturally, Dr. Krauer-Poppe overheard him; perhaps everyone in the congregation could hear Dr. Horvath *whisper.* "Do you think that's a good idea, Klaus?" Anna-Elisabeth asked Dr. Horvath.

"Is there a pill to make me stop?" Jack's father asked Dr. Krauer-Poppe, but Jack could tell that his dad was just teasing her; his mischievous smile was intact. When William sat down on the organ bench, he looked into Jack's eyes—as if Jack had told him, at that very moment, how much he loved him and every inch of his skin. "Did you remember to call your sister, Jack?" his dad asked him.

"Of course I called her. We talked and talked."

"Dear boy," was all William said. His eyes had drifted to the keyboard; Jack could hear his father's feet softly brushing the pedals.

Anna-Elisabeth had taken the music from Dr. Horvath and was looking through it. "I see finger-cramping possibilities, William—*lots* of them," she told him.

"I see *music,*" William said, winking at her. "*Lots* of it."

Jack was nervous and counted the chandeliers. (They were glass and silver; he counted twenty-eight of them.)

"Later we'll go *jogging!*" Dr. Horvath told Jack. "I'm going to dinner with you and William tonight. We'll give the girls the night off!"

"Great—I'm looking forward to it," Jack told him.

"Unfortunately, it's not the Kronenhalle," Dr. Horvath said. "But it's a special little place. The owner knows me, and he loves your father. They always cover the mirrors when they know William's coming!" Dr. Horvath whispered—for everyone to hear. "How brilliant is that?"

"*Bitte,* Klaus!" Dr. Krauer-Poppe said.

Jack could see that she was going to turn the music for his dad, who appeared ready to play. No one in the congregation was looking in their direction now. The congregation faced that stern command from the Gospel According to Saint Matthew: "You shall worship the Lord your God and Him only you shall serve."

William held his hands at shoulder level, above the keyboard. Jack heard him take a deep breath. By the way the congregation straightened their backs, Jack could tell that they'd heard his father, too—it was a signal.

"Here comes!" said Dr. Horvath; he bowed his head and closed his eyes.

William's hands appeared to be floating on a body of warm, rising air—like a hawk, suspended on a thermal. Then he let his hands fall. It was a piece by Bach, a choral prelude—"Liebster Jesu, wir sind hier." ("Blessed Jesus, We Are Here.")

"*Tranquillo,*" Dr. Horvath said with surprising softness, in Italian.

After that, Jack just listened to his father play. Jack couldn't believe how William kept playing, or how no one in the congregation left—how they never moved a muscle. They were standing, Dr. Horvath and Jack—Dr. Krauer-Poppe stood the whole time, too. Jack couldn't speak for the others, but his legs didn't get tired; he just stood there, absorbing the sound. William Burns played on and on—all his favorites. (What Heather had called "the old standards.")

William played for over an hour. They heard Handel, and everyone else. When his dad began Bach's Toccata and Fugue in D Minor—the famous piece that had been such a crowd-pleaser among the prostitutes in the Oude Kerk in Amsterdam—Dr. Horvath nudged Jack.

"We are *almost* leaving," Dr. Horvath said.

Naturally, Jack didn't want to go, but he saw that Anna-

Elisabeth was watching him. Jack trusted her; he trusted them all. It was a hard piece of music to go down the stairs to, but Dr. Horvath and Jack quietly descended. His father was too busy playing to see them go.

It was warm in the church; all the doors were open, and the windows that would open were open, too. The sound of the Bach poured into the little square; it came outdoors with them. The Bach was not as loud outside—in the trees, or on the stone stairs leading away from the church—but you could hear every note of it, almost as clearly as you could hear it in St. Peter.

That was when Jack saw all the people in the open windows and doorways of the surrounding buildings. Everywhere he looked, there were people—just listening.

"Of course it's not quite like this in the *winter*!" Dr. Horvath was saying. "But still they come to hear him play."

Jack stood at the bottom of the church stairs, in the middle of the little square—just listening and looking at all the people. There wasn't a sound from the construction workers, who had long ago stopped working. They were standing at attention on the scaffolding, their tools at rest—*just listening*. The man who'd been wielding the hammer had his shirt off; the two men who'd been working with the flexible saw were smoking. The fourth worker, the pipefitter, held a small piece of pipe in one hand—like a baton. He was pretending to be a conductor, conducting the music.

"Those clowns!" Dr. Horvath said. He looked at his watch. "No finger-cramping episodes so far!"

The Bach sounded like it was winding up, or down. "There's more?" Jack asked. "Another piece after this?"

"*One* more," Dr. Horvath said, nodding.

Jack realized, from the way they were standing, that the construction workers on the scaffolding knew the program as well as Dr. Horvath knew it; they looked as if they were getting ready for something.

Suddenly the Bach was over. It happened simultaneously with a puzzling exodus—families with children were leaving the church. Some of the mothers with younger children were running; only the adults and the teenagers stayed.

"Cowards!" Dr. Horvath said contemptuously; he kicked a stone. "Get ready, Jack. I'll see you later—for some *jogging*!" Jack realized that Dr. Horvath was preparing to leave him.

Jack also realized that he knew the last piece. In his case, he'd just heard Heather play it in Old St. Paul's. How could he ever forget it? It was Boellmann's horror-movie Toccata. The construction workers knew the Boellmann, too—perhaps William Burns always played it last. The construction workers clearly knew everything that was coming.

It wasn't at all like not being able to hear it, when Jack had stood outside Old St. Paul's. What poured out of the Kirche St. Peter was deafening. Jack was not familiar enough with the Boellmann to detect his father's first mistake, the first finger-cramping episode, but Dr. Horvath obviously heard it; he winced and made a fist of one hand, as if he'd just shut his fingers in a car door. "Time for me to go back inside!" Dr. Horvath cried.

There came a second mistake, and a third; now Jack could hear the errors.

"His fingers?" he asked Dr. Horvath.

"You can't believe how the Boellmann hurts him, Jack," Dr. Horvath said, "but he can't stop playing."

Jack thought of those prostitutes within hearing distance of the Oude Kerk, no matter how late at night or how early in the morning; now he knew why they couldn't go home if William Burns was playing.

At the fourth mistake, Dr. Horvath was off running. "I like to be there when he starts *undressing*!" he called to Jack, taking the stairs three at a time.

The music raged on—the soundtrack for a chase scene to end all chase scenes, Jack imagined. In his next movie, there might be such a scene. Maybe he could get his dad to play the Boellmann—mistakes and all.

The errors, even Jack could tell, were mounting. The construction workers were poised on the scaffolding.

"I have a son!" Jack heard his father yell, over the deteriorating toccata. "I have a daughter *and* a son!" his dad shouted. Then William's fingers locked—his fists came crashing down on the keyboard. A flock of pigeons exploded from the clock tower of the Kirche St. Peter, and the construction workers started singing.

"I have a son!" they sang; they had even learned English, listening to William Burns. "I have a daughter *and* a son!" they sang out. They had more enthusiasm than talent, but Jack had to love them.

"*Venite exultemus Domino!*" his father sang, the way you would sing or chant a psalm.

One might assume that ordinary construction workers in Zurich wouldn't necessarily know Latin, but this wasn't the first time these men had listened to William Burns, and—as Anna-Elisabeth had told Jack—these workers were a little different.

"*Venite exultemus Domino!*" the four workers sang back to Jack's father.

The man who'd earlier been hammering now held his hammer in one hand, his arm high above his head; the two workers with the flexible saw held it aloft, as if they were offering a sacrifice. The pipefitter had seized a long length of pipe, which he held straight up—like a flagpole.

"*Venite exultemus Domino!*" Jack's dad and the workers sang out, together.

Jack knew the Latin only because he'd just been at Old St. Paul's with his sister. "Come let us praise the Lord!" their father was singing. "I have a son. I have a daughter *and* a son! Come let us praise the Lord!"

The construction workers went on singing with William.

People were coming out of the church—now that the Boellmann no longer thundered on, now that there was no impending collision. Jack knew that his dad had taken off all his clothes, or he was in a partly undressed phase of the process. Back at the Sanatorium Kilchberg, Nurse Bleibel—either Waltraut or Hugo—would be getting the ice water ready. And then the hot wax, and then *more* ice water—as Anna-Elisabeth had explained.

Soon William Burns would be standing naked in the Kirche St. Peter, if he wasn't naked already—his full-body tattoos his only choir. And then, both gently and efficiently, Dr. Horvath would begin to dress him—or both Dr. Horvath and Dr. Krauer-Poppe would dress him. After that, they would be on their way—back to the clinic.

The concert was over, but the construction workers were still applauding. That was when Jack knew that he and his father had always been playing to an audience of more than one—although it had helped Jack, as a child, to believe that he was performing only for his father. (Jack and his dad would have to have a conversation about William's dispute with The Wurtz over the word *audience*—that and many other conversations.)

Jack walked away from the square, down those narrow streets.

Some of his father's congregation were in the streets; they walked along with him. It was quite a wonderful feeling to know that Zurich was where Jack belonged, at least until William Burns was sleeping in the needles.

Jack was thinking that he would go back to the Hotel zum Storchen and change into something more suitable for jogging.

It was after midnight in Los Angeles—too late to call Dr. García at home. But Jack didn't need to have a conversation with his psychiatrist. He would call her office and leave a message on her answering machine. "Thank you for listening to me, Dr. García," Jack would tell her.

It was four-thirty in the morning in Toronto, or some ungodly hour like that. Caroline would still be sleeping, but she wouldn't mind a wake-up call from Jack—not if it was about his father, her dear William. In fact, Jack couldn't wait to tell Miss Wurtz that he had found him.

Acknowledgments

In Toronto: Helga Stephenson, Bruce Smuck, Dr. Martin Schwartz, Detective Ray Zarb, Debbie Piotrowski.

In Edinburgh: Mary Haggart, Bishop Richard Holloway, Florence Ingleby, Alan Taylor, Kerstie Howell, Aly Barr, Bill Stronach, David Valentine, John Kitchen, Elaine Kelly, Euan Ferguson.

In Halifax and New Glasgow, Nova Scotia: Charles Burchell; Jerry Swallow, a.k.a. Sailor Jerry; Dave Schwarz.

In Copenhagen: Susanne Bent Andersen, Kirstin Ringhof, Merete Borre, Trine Licht, Morten Hesseldahl, Lisbeth Møller-Madsen, Lasse Ewerlöf, Bimbo.

In Stockholm: Charlotte Aquilonius, Doc Forest, Torvald Torén, Unn Palm, Anna Andersson.

In Oslo: Mai Gaardsted, Janneken Øverland, Kåre Nordstoga.

In Helsinki: Olli Arrakoski, Päivi Haarala, Jaakko Tapaninen, Tapio Tittu, Diego, Nipa, Taru.

In Amsterdam: Robbert Ammerlaan; Joep de Groot; Henk Schiffmacher, a.k.a. Hanky Panky; Louise van Teylingen; Willem Vogel.

In Los Angeles: Robert Bookman, Richard Gladstein, Alan Hergott.

In Zurich: Ruth Geiger, Anna von Planta, Professor Waldemar Greil, Dr. Andreas Horváth, Dr. Oliver Hartmann, Dr. Stephanie Krebs, Dr. Alice Walder, Dr. Christine Huwig-Poppe.

Special thanks to: Kelly Harper Berkson, David Calicchio, Kate Medina, Harvey Ginsberg, Craig Nova, Alyssa Barrett, Amy Edelman, Janet Turnbull Irving.

Permission Acknowledgments

Grateful acknowledgment is made to the following for permission to reprint previously published material:

Carcanet Press Limited: Excerpt from "A Slice of Wedding Cake" from *Complete Poems in One Volume* by Robert Graves, published by Carcanet Press Limited. Reprinted by permission.

Hope Publishing Company and Stainer & Bell Ltd.: Excerpt from "Lord of the Dance" by Sydney Carter (1915–2004), copyright © 1963 by Stainer & Bell Ltd. Rights in the United States and Canada administered by Hope Publishing Company, Carol Stream, IL 60188. Rights throughout the rest of the world administered by Stainer & Bell Ltd., 23 Gruneisen Road, London, N3 1DZ, England. Reprinted by permission of Hope Publishing Company and Stainer & Bell Ltd.

Sony/ATV Music Publishing LLC: Excerpt from "When I'm 64" by John Lennon and Paul McCartney, copyright © 1967 (renewed) by Sony/ATV Tunes LLC. All rights administered by Sony/ATV Music Publishing, 8 Music Square West, Nashville, TN 37203. All rights reserved. Used by permission.

Special Rider Music: Excerpt from "Don't Think Twice, It's All Right" by Bob Dylan, copyright © 1963 by Warner Bros. Inc. and copyright renewed 1991 by Special Rider Music; excerpt from "Mama, You Been on My Mind" by Bob Dylan, copyright © 1964 by Warner Bros. Inc. and copyright renewed 1992 by Special Rider Music; excerpt from "Mr. Tambourine Man" by Bob Dylan, copyright © 1964 by Warner Bros. Inc. and copyright renewed 1992 by Special Rider Music; excerpt from "Just Like a Woman" by Bob Dylan, copyright © 1966 by Dwarf Music; excerpt from "It's All Over Now Baby Blue" by Bob

Dylan, copyright © 1964 by Warner Bros. Inc. and copyright renewed 1992 by Special Rider Music; excerpt from "Idiot Wind" by Bob Dylan, copyright © 1974 by Ram's Horn Music; excerpt from "I Want You" by Bob Dylan, copyright © 1966 by Dwarf Music. All rights reserved. International copyright secured. Reprinted by permission.

The Society of Authors: Excerpt from "Oh When I Was in Love with You" by A. E. Housman. Reprinted by permission of The Society of Authors as the Literary Representative of the Estate of A. E. Housman.